Welcome to Morganville.

MORGANVILLE VAMPIRES OMNIBUS

a&b

MORGANVILLE VAMPIRES OMNIBUS

GLASS HOUSES

THE DEAD GIRLS' DANCE

MIDNIGHT ALLEY

RACHEL CAINE

This omnibus first published in Great Britain in 2010 by
Allison & Busby Limited
13 Charlotte Mews
London W1T 4EJ
www.allisonandbusby.com

A CIP catalogue record for this book is available from the British Library.

10 9 8 7 6 5 4 3 2 1

ISBN 978-0-7490-0920-5

Typeset in 11/17pt Century Schoolbook by
Allison & Busby Ltd.

Paper used in this publication is from sustainably managed sources.
All of the wood used is procured from legal sources and is fully traceable.
The producing mill uses schemes such as ISO 14001
to monitor environmental impact.

Printed and bound in the UK by
CPI Mackays, Chatham ME5 8TD

Available from Allison & Busby

The Morganville Vampires series

Glass Houses
The Dead Girls' Dance
Midnight Alley
Feast of Fools
Lord of Misrule
Carpe Corpus
Fade Out
Kiss of Death
Ghost Town

The Weather Warden series

Ill Wind
Heat Stroke
Chill Factor
Windfall
Firestorm
Thin Air

Glass Houses

To Liz, who asked.

To my dad, Robert V Longstreet, who dared to dream – and to be a dreamer – when it wasn't cool.

To my mom, Hazel Longstreet, who took on the tough job of being practical in a family of impractical people, and did it brilliantly and with love. I love you both. Miss you, Dad.

Chapter One

On the day Claire became a member of the Glass House, somebody stole her laundry.

When she reached into the crappy, beat-up washing machine, she found nothing but the wet slick sides of the drum, and – like a bad joke – the worst pair of underwear she owned, plus one sock. She was in a hurry, of course – there were only a couple of machines on this top floor of Howard Hall, the least valued and most run-down rooms in the least valued, most run-down dorm. Two washing machines, two dryers, and you were lucky if one of them was working on any given day and didn't eat your quarters. Forget about the dollar-bill slot. She'd never seen it work, not in the last six weeks since she'd arrived at school.

'No,' she said out loud, and balanced herself on the edge of the washer to look down into the dark, partly rusted interior. It smelt like mould and cheap detergent. Getting a closer look didn't help.

One crappy pair of underwear, fraying at the seams. One sock.

She was missing every piece of clothing that she'd worn in the last two weeks. Every piece that she actually *wanted* to wear.

'No!' She yelled it into the washer, where it echoed back at her, and slumped back down, then kicked the washer violently in the dent made by all the other disappointed students before her. She couldn't breathe. She had some other clothes – a few – but they were *last-choice* clothes, oh-my-God-wouldn't-be-caught-dead clothes. Pants that were too short and made her look like a hick, shirts that were too big and too stupid, and made her look like her mom had picked them out. And she had.

Claire had about three hundred dollars left to last her for, well, months, after the latest round of calling out for pizza and buying yet *another* book for Professor Clueless Euliss, who didn't seem to have figured out yet what subject he was teaching.

She supposed she could find some clothes, if she looked around, that wouldn't totally blow her entire budget. After all, downtown Morganville, Texas, was the thrift shop capital of the world. Assuming she could find *anything* she could stand to wear.

Mom said this would happen, she thought. *I just have to think. Keep my cool.*

Claire threw herself into an orange plastic chair, dumped her backpack on the scratched linoleum, and put her head in her hands. Her face felt hot, and she was shaking, and she knew, just *knew*, that she was going to cry. Cry like the baby they all said she was, too young to be here, too young to be away from Mommy.

It sucked to be smart, because this was where it got you.

She gulped deep, damp breaths and sat back, willing herself not to bawl (because they'd hear), and wondered if she could call Mom and Dad for an extension on her allowance, or use the credit card that was 'just for emergencies'.

Then she saw the note. Not so much 'note' as graffiti, but it was addressed to her, on the painted cinderblock wall above the machines.

Dear Dork, it read, *We found trash in the machines and threw it down the chute. If you want it, dive for it.*

'Shit,' she breathed, and had to blink back tears again, for an entirely different reason. Blind, stupid rage. *Monica.* Well, Monica and the Monickettes, anyway. Why was it the hot mean girls always ran in packs, like hyenas? And why, with all the shimmery hair and long tanned legs and more of Daddy's money than Daddy's accountants, did they have to focus on *her?*

No, she knew the answer to that.

She'd made Monica look stupid in front of her friends, and some hot upperclassmen. Not that it had been all that hard; she'd just been walking by, heard Monica saying that World War II had been 'that dumbass Chinese war thing'.

And by simple reflex, she'd said, 'It wasn't.' The whole lot of them, slouched all over the couches in the dorm lobby, looked at her with as much blank surprise as if the Coke machine had just spoken up. Monica, her friends, three of the cool older frat boys.

'World War II,' Claire had plunged on, panicked and not quite sure how to get out of what she'd got herself into. 'I just meant – well, it wasn't the Korean War. That was later. World War II was with the Germans and the Japanese. You know, Pearl Harbor?'

And the guys had looked at Monica and laughed, and Monica had flushed – not much, but enough to ruin the cool perfection of her make-up. 'Remind me not to buy any history papers off of you,' the cutest of the guys had said. 'What kind of dumbass doesn't know that?' Though Claire had been sure none of them had, really. 'Chinese. Riiiiight.'

Claire had seen the fury in Monica's eyes, quickly covered over with smiles and laughter and flirting. Claire had ceased to exist again, for the guys.

For the girls, she was brand-new, and unwelcome as hell. She'd been dealing with it all her life. Smart and small and average-looking wasn't exactly winning the life lottery; you had to fight for it, whatever *it* was. Somebody was always laughing at, or hitting, or ignoring you, or a combination of the first two. She'd thought when she was a kid that getting laughed at was the worst thing, and then – after the first couple of school-yard showdowns – getting hit jumped up to number one. But for most of her (brief, two-year) high school experience, being ignored was worse by far. She'd got there a year earlier than everybody else, and left a year ahead of them. Nobody liked that.

Nobody but teachers, anyway.

The problem was that Claire really *loved* school. Loved books, and reading, and learning things – OK, not calculus, but pretty much everything else. Physics.

What normal girl loved *physics*? Abnormal ones. Ones who were not ever going to be hot.

And face it, being hot? That was what life was all about. As Monica had proved, when the world had wobbled off its axis for a few seconds to notice Claire, and then wobbled right back to revolve around the pretty ones.

It wasn't fair. She'd dived in and worked her ass off through high school. Graduated with a perfect 4.0, scored high enough on the tests to qualify for admission to the great schools, the legendary schools, the ones where being a brainiac mutant girl-freak wasn't necessarily a downside. (Except that, of course, at those schools, there were probably *hot tall leggy* brainiac mutant girl-freaks.)

Didn't matter. Mom and Dad had taken one look at the stack of enthusiastic thumbs-up replies from universities like MIT and Caltech and Yale, and clamped down hard. No way was their sixteen-year-old daughter (nearly seventeen, she kept insisting, although it wasn't really true) going to run off three thousand miles to go to school.

At least not at first. (Claire had tried, unsuccessfully, to get across the concept that if anything would kill her budding academic career worse than being a transfer student at one of those places, it was being a transfer student from *Texas Prairie University*. Otherwise known as TPEwwwwwww.)

So here she was, stuck on the crappy top floor of a crappy dorm in a crappy school where eighty per cent of the students transferred after the first two years – or dropped out – and the Monickettes were stealing her wet laundry and dumping it down the trash chute, all because Monica couldn't be bothered to know anything about one of the world wars big enough to rate a Roman numeral.

But it isn't fair! something in her howled. *I had a plan! An actual plan!* Monica slept late, and Claire had got up early just to do laundry while all the party crowd was comatose and the studious crowd was off to classes. She'd thought she could leave it for a couple of minutes to grab her shower – another scary experience – and she'd never even thought about anybody doing something so incredibly *low*.

As she bit back her sobs, she noticed – again – how quiet it was up here. Creepy and deserted, with half the girls deep asleep and the other half gone. Even when it was crowded and buzzing, the dorm was creepy, though. Old, decrepit, full of shadows and corners and places mean girls could lurk. In fact, that summed up the whole town. Morganville was small and old and dusty, full of creepy little oddities. Like the fact that the streetlights worked only half the time, and they were too far apart when they did. Like the way the people in the local campus stores seemed *too* happy. Desperately happy. Like the fact that the whole town, despite the dust, was *clean* – no trash, no graffiti; nobody begging for spare change in alleyways.

Weird.

She could almost hear her mother saying, *Honey, it's just that you're in a strange place. It'll get better. You'll just have to try harder.*

Mom always said things like that, and Claire had always done her best to hide how hard it was to follow that advice.

Well. Nothing to do but try to get her stuff back.

Claire gulped a couple more times, wiped her eyes, and hauled the arm-twisting weight of her backpack up and over her shoulder. She stared for a few seconds at the wet pair of panties and one sock clutched in her right hand, then hastily unzipped the front pocket of the backpack and stuffed them in. Man, that would kill whatever cool she had left, if she walked around carrying those.

'Well,' said a low, satisfied voice from the open door opposite the stairs, 'look who it is. The dumpster diver.'

Claire stopped, one hand on the rusted iron railing. Something was telling her to run, but something always told her that: fight-or-flight – she'd read the textbooks. And she was tired of flighting. She turned around slowly, as Monica Morrell stepped out of the dorm room – not hers, so she'd busted Erica's lock again. Monica's running buddies Jennifer and Gina filed out and took up flanking positions. Soldiers in flip-flops and low-rise jeans and French manicures.

Monica struck a pose. It was something she was good at, Claire had to admit. Nearly six feet tall, Monica had flowing, shiny black hair, and big blue eyes accented with just the right amount of liner and mascara. Perfect skin. One of those model-shaped faces, all cheekbones and pouty lips. And if she had a model's body, it was a Victoria's Secret model, all curves, not angles.

She was rich, she was pretty, and as far as Claire could tell, it didn't make her a bit happy. What did, though – what made those big blue eyes glow right now – was the idea of tormenting Claire just a little more.

'Shouldn't you be in first period at the junior high by now?' Monica asked. 'Or at least *getting* your first period?'

'Maybe she's looking for the clothes she left lying around,' Gina piled on, and laughed. Jennifer laughed with her. Claire swore their eyes, their pretty jewel-coloured eyes, just glowed with the joy of making her feel like shit. 'Litterbug!'

'Clothes?' Monica folded her arms and pretended to think. 'You mean, like those rags we threw away? The ones she left cluttering up the washer?'

'Yeah, those.'

'I wouldn't wear those to sweat in.'

'I wouldn't wear them to scrub out the boys' toilet,' Jennifer blurted.

Monica, annoyed, turned and shoved her. 'Yeah, you know all about the boys' toilet, don't you? Didn't you do Steve Gillespie in ninth grade in there?' She made sucking sounds, and they all laughed again, though Jennifer looked uncomfortable. Claire felt her cheeks flare red, even though it wasn't – for a change – a dis against her. 'Jeez, Jen, Steve Gillespie? Keep your mouth shut if you can't think of something that won't embarrass yourself.'

Jennifer – of course – turned her anger on a safer target. Claire. She lunged forward and shoved Claire back a step, towards the stairs. 'Go get your stupid clothes already! I'm sick of looking at you, with your pasty skin—'

'Yeah, Junior High, ever heard of sunshine?' Gina rolled her eyes.

'Watch it,' Monica snapped, which was odd, because all three of them had the best tans money could buy.

Claire scrambled to steady herself. The heavy backpack pulled her off-balance, and she grabbed on to the banister. Jen lunged at her again and slammed the heel of her hand painfully hard into Claire's collar-bone. 'Don't!' Claire yelped, and batted Jen's hand away. Hard.

There was a second of breathless silence, and then Monica said, very quietly, 'Did you just hit my friend, you stupid little bitch? Where do you think you get off, doing things like that around here?'

And she stepped forward and slapped Claire across the face, hard enough to draw blood, hard enough to make flares and comets streak across Claire's vision, hard enough to make everything turn red and boiling hot.

Claire let go of the banister and slapped Monica right back, full across her pouty mouth, and for just a tight, white-hot second she actually felt *good* about it, but then Monica hissed like a scorched cat, and Claire had time to think, *Oh crap, I really shouldn't have done that.*

She never saw the punch coming. Didn't even really feel the impact, except as a blank sensation and confusion, but then the weight of her backpack on her shoulder was pulling her to one side and she staggered.

She almost caught herself, and then Gina, grinning spitefully, reached over and shoved her backward, down the stairs, and there was nothing but air behind her.

She hit the edge of every stair, all the way to the bottom. Her backpack broke open and spilt books as she tumbled, and at the top of the stairs Monica and the Monickettes laughed and hooted and high-fived, but she saw it only in disconnected little jerks of motion, freeze-frames.

It seemed to take forever before she skidded to a stop at the bottom, and then her head hit the wall with a nasty, meaty sound, and everything went black.

She later remembered only one more thing, in the darkness: Monica's voice, a low and vicious whisper. 'Tonight. You'll get what's coming to you, you freak. I'm going to make sure.'

It seemed like seconds, but when she woke up again there was somebody kneeling next to her, and it wasn't Monica or her nail-polish mafia; it was Erica, who had the room at the top of the stairs, four doors down from Claire's. Erica looked pale and strained and scared, and Claire tried to smile, because that was what you did when somebody was scared. She didn't hurt until she moved, and then her head started to throb. There was a red-hot ache near the top, and when she reached up to touch it she felt a hard raised knot. No blood, though. It hurt worse when she probed the spot, but not in an oh-my-God-skull-fracture kind of way, or at least that was what she hoped.

'Are you OK?' Erica asked, waving her hands kind of helplessly in mid-air as Claire wiggled her way up to a sitting position against the wall. Claire risked a quick look past her up the stairs, then down. The coast looked Monica-clear. Nobody else had come out to see what was up, either – most of them were afraid of getting in trouble, and the rest just flat didn't care.

'Yeah,' she said, and managed a shaky laugh. 'Guess I tripped.'

'You need to go to the quack shack?' Which was college code for the university clinic. 'Or, God, an ambulance or whatever?'

'No. No, I'm OK.' Wishful thinking, but although basically everything in her body hurt like hell, nothing felt like it had broken into pieces. Claire got to her feet, winced at a sore ankle, and picked up her backpack.

Notebooks tumbled out. Erica grabbed a couple and jammed them back in, then ran lightly up a few steps to gather the scattered textbooks. 'Damn, Claire, do you really need all this crap? How many classes do you have in a day?'

'Six.'

'You're nuts.' Erica, good deed done, reverted to the neutrality that all the non-cool girls in the dorm had shown her so far. 'Better get to the quack shack, seriously. You look like crap.'

Claire pasted on a smile and kept it there until Erica got to the top of the stairs and started complaining about the broken lock on her dorm room.

Tonight, Monica had leant over and whispered. *You'll get what's coming to you, you freak.* She hadn't called anybody, or tried to find out if Claire had a broken neck. She didn't care if Claire died.

No, that was wrong. The problem was, she *did* care.

Claire tasted blood. Her lip was split, and it was bleeding. She wiped at the mess with the back of her hand, then the hem of her T-shirt before realising that it was literally the only thing she had to wear. *I need to go down to the basement and get my clothes out of the trash.* The idea of going down there – going anywhere alone in this dorm – suddenly terrified her. Monica was waiting. And the other girls wouldn't do anything. Even Erica, who was probably the nicest one in the whole place, was scared to come right out on her side. Hell, Erica got hassled, too, but she was probably just as glad that Claire was there to get the worst of it. This wasn't just as bad as high school, where she'd been treated with contempt and casual cruelty – this was worse, a lot worse. And she didn't even have any friends here. Erica was about the best she'd been able to come up with, and Erica was more concerned about her broken door than Claire's broken head.

She was alone. And if she hadn't been before, she was scared now. Really, really scared. What she'd seen in the Monica Mafia's eyes today wasn't just the usual lazy menace of cool girls versus the geeks; this was worse. She'd got casual shoves or pinches before, trips, mean laughter, but this was more like lions coming in for the kill.

They're going to kill me.

She started shakily down the flights of stairs, every step a wincing pain through her body, and remembered that she'd slapped Monica hard enough to leave a mark.

Yeah. They're going to kill me.

If Monica ended up with a bruise on that perfect face, there wasn't any question about it.

CHAPTER TWO

Erica was right about the quack shack being the logical first stop; Claire got her ankle wrapped, an ice pack, and some frowns over the forming bruises. Nothing broken, but she was going to be black-and-blue for days. The doctor asked some pro forma questions about boyfriends and stuff, but since she could truthfully say that no, her boyfriend hadn't beaten her up, he just shrugged and told her to watch her step.

He wrote her an excuse note, too, and gave her some painkillers and told her to go home.

No way was she going back to the dorm. Truth was, she didn't have much in the room – some books, a few photos of home, some posters... She hadn't even had a chance to call it home, and for whatever reason, she'd never really felt safe there. It had always felt like...a warehouse. A warehouse for kids who were, one way or another, going to leave.

She limped over to the Quad, which was a big empty concrete space with some rickety old benches and picnic tables, cornered on all sides by squat, unappealing buildings that mostly just looked like boxes with windows. Architecture-student projects, probably. She heard a rumour that one of them had fallen down a few years back, but then, she'd also heard rumours about a janitor getting beheaded in the chem lab and haunting the building, and zombies roaming the grounds after dark, so she wasn't putting too much stock in it.

It was mid-afternoon already, and not a lot of students were hanging around the Quad, with its lack of shade – great design, considering that the weather was still hovering up in the high nineties in September. Claire picked up a campus paper from the stand, carefully took a seat on the blazing-hot bench, and opened it to the 'Housing' section. Dorm rooms were out of the question; Howard Hall and Lansdale Hall were the only two that took in girls under twenty. She wasn't old enough to qualify for the co-ed dorms. *Stupid rules were probably written when girls wore hoop-skirts*, she thought, and skipped the dorm listings until she got to OFF CAMPUS. Not that she was really allowed to be living off campus; Mom and Dad would have a total freak-out over it, no question. But...if it was between Monica and parental freakage, she'd take the latter. After all, the important thing was to get herself someplace where she felt safe, where she could study.

Right?

She dug in her backpack, found her cell phone, and checked for coverage. It was kind of lame in Morganville, truthfully, out in the middle of the prairie, in the middle of Texas, which was about as middle of nowhere as it was possible to get unless you wanted to go to Mongolia or something. Two bars. Not great, but it'd do.

Claire started dialling numbers. The first person told her that they'd already found somebody, and hung up before she could even say, 'Thanks.' The second one sounded like a weird old guy. The third one was a weird old lady. The fourth one...well, the fourth one was just plain weird.

The fifth listing down read,

THREE ROOMMATES SEEKING FOURTH, *huge old house, privacy assured, reasonable rent and utilities.*

Which... OK, she wasn't sure that she could afford 'reasonable' – she was more looking for 'dirt cheap' – but at least it sounded less weird than the others. Three roommates. That meant three more people who'd maybe take up for her if Monica and company came sniffing around...or at least take up for the house. Hmmmmm.

She called, and got an answering machine with a mellow-sounding, *young*-sounding male voice. 'Hello, you've reached the Glass House. If you're looking for Michael, he sleeps days. If you're looking for Shane, good luck with that, 'cause we never know where the hell he is' – distant laughter from at least two people – 'and if you're looking for Eve, you'll probably get her on her cell phone or at the shop. But hey. Leave a message. And if you're looking to audition for the room, come on by. It's 716 West Lot Street.' A totally different voice, a female one lightened by giggles like bubbles in soda, said, 'Yeah, just look for the mansion.' And then a third voice, male again. '*Gone with the Wind* meets *The Munsters*.' More laughter, and a beep.

Claire blinked, coughed, and finally said, 'Um...hi. My name is Claire? Claire Danvers? And I was, um, calling about the, um, room thing. Sorry.' And hung up in a panic. Those three people sounded...normal. But they sounded pretty close, too. And in her experience, groups of friends like that just didn't open up to include underage, undersized geeks like her. They hadn't sounded mean; they just sounded – self-confident. Something she wasn't.

She checked the rest of the listings, and felt her heart actually sink a little. Maybe an inch and a half, with a slight sideways twist. God, I'm dead. She couldn't sleep out here on a bench like some homeless loser, and she couldn't go back to the dorm; she had to do something.

Fine, she thought, and snapped her phone shut, then open again to dial a cab.

Seven sixteen Lot Street. *Gone with the Wind* meets *The Munsters*. Right.

Maybe they'd at least feel sorry enough for her to put her up for one lousy night.

* * *

The cabbie – she figured he was just about the only cabdriver in Morganville, which apart from the campus at TPU on the edge of town had only about ten thousand people in it – took an hour to show up. Claire hadn't been in a car in six weeks, since her parents had driven her into town. She hadn't been much beyond a block off the campus, either, and then just to buy used books for class.

'You meeting someone?' the cabbie asked. She was staring out the window at the storefronts: used-clothing shops, used-book shops, computer stores, stores that sold nothing but wooden Greek letters. All catering to the college.

'No,' she said. 'Why?'

The cabbie shrugged. 'Usually you kids are meeting up with friends. If you're looking for a good time—'

She shivered. 'I'm not. I'm – yes, I'm meeting some people. If you could hurry, please...?'

He grunted and took a right turn, and the cab went from Collegetown to Creepytown in one block flat. She couldn't define how it happened exactly – the buildings were pretty much the same, but they looked dim and old, and the few people moving on the streets had their heads down and were walking fast. Even when people were walking in twos or threes, they weren't chatting. When the cab passed, people looked up, then down again, as if they'd been looking for another kind of car.

A little girl was walking with her hand in her mother's, and as the cab stopped for a light, the girl waved, just a little. Claire waved back.

The girl's mother looked up, alarmed, and hustled her kid away into the black mouth of a store that sold used electronics. *Wow*, Claire thought. *Do I look that scary?* Maybe she did. Or maybe Morganville was just ultra-careful of its kids.

Funny, now that she thought about it, there was something missing in this town. Signs. She'd seen them all her life stapled to telephone poles... advertisements for lost dogs, missing kids or adults.

Nothing here. Nothing.

'Lot Street,' the cabbie announced, and squealed to a stop. 'Ten fifty.'

For a five-minute ride? Claire thought, amazed, but she paid up. She thought about shooting him the finger as he drove away, but he looked kind of dangerous, and besides, she really wasn't the kind of girl who did that sort of thing. Usually. It was a bad day, though.

She hoisted her backpack again, hit a bruise on her shoulder, and nearly dropped the weight on her foot. Tears stung at her eyes. All of a sudden she felt tired and shaky again, scared... At least on campus she'd kind of been on relatively familiar ground, but out here in town it was like being a stranger, all over again.

Morganville was brown. Burnt brown by the sun, beaten down by wind and weather. Hot summer was starting to give way to hot autumn, and the leaves on the trees – what trees there were – looked grey-edged and dry, and they rattled like paper in the wind. West Lot

Street was near what passed for the downtown district in town, probably an old residential neighbourhood. Nothing special about the homes that she could see... ranch houses, most of them with peeling, faded paint.

She counted house numbers, and realised she was standing in front of 716. She turned and looked behind her, and gasped, because whoever the guy had been on the phone, he'd been dead-on in his description. Seven sixteen looked like a movie set, something straight out of the Civil War. Big greying columns. A wide front porch. Two stories of windows.

The place was huge. Well, not *huge* – but bigger than Claire had imagined. Like, big enough to be a frat house, and probably perfectly suited to it. She could just imagine Greek letters over the door.

It looked deserted, but to be fair every house on the block looked deserted. Late afternoon, nobody home from work yet. A few cars glittered in the white-hot sunshine, finish softened by a layer of dirt. No cars in front of 716, though.

This was such a bad idea, she thought, and there were those tears again, bubbling up along with panic. What was she going to do? Walk up to the door and beg to be a roommate? How lame-ass was that? They'd think she was pathetic at best, a head case at worst. No, it had been a dumb idea to even blow the money on cab fare.

It was hot, and she was tired and she hurt and she had homework due, and no place to sleep, and all of a sudden, it was just too much.

Claire dropped her backpack, buried her bruised face in both hands, and just started sobbing like a baby. *Crybaby freak*, she imagined Monica saying, but that just made her sob harder, and all of a sudden the idea of going home, going home to Mom and Dad and the room she knew they'd kept open for her, seemed better, better than anything out here in the scary, crazy world...

'Hey,' a girl's voice said, and someone touched her on the elbow. 'Hey, are you OK?'

Claire yelped and jumped, landed hard on her strained ankle, and nearly toppled over. The girl who'd scared her reached out and grabbed her arm to steady her, looking genuinely scared herself. 'I'm sorry! God, I'm such a klutz. Look, are you OK?'

The girl wasn't Monica, or Jen, or Gina, or anybody else she'd seen around the campus at TPU; this girl was way Goth. Not in a bad way – she didn't have the sulky I'm-so-not-cool-I'm-cool attitude of most of the Goths Claire had known in school – but the dyed-black, shag-cut hair, the pale make-up, the heavy eye-liner and mascara, the red-and-black-striped tights and clunky black shoes and black pleated miniskirt...very definitely a fan of the dark side.

'My name's Eve,' the girl said, and smiled. It was a sweet, funny kind of smile, something that invited Claire to share in a private joke. 'Yeah, my parents really named me that, go figure. It's like they knew how I'd turn out.' Her smile faded, and she took a good look at Claire's face. 'Wow. Jeez, nice black eye. Who hit you?'

'Nobody.' Claire said it instantly, without even thinking why, although she knew in her bones that Goth Eve was in no way bestest friends with preppy Monica. 'I had an accident.'

'Yeah,' Eve agreed softly. 'I used to have those kinds of accidents, falling into fists and stuff. Like I said, I'm a klutz. You OK? You need a doctor or something? I can drive you if you want.'

She gestured to the street next to them, and Claire realised that while she'd been sobbing her eyes out, an ancient beater of a black Cadillac – complete with tail fins – had been docked at the kerb. There was a cheery-looking skull dangling from the rearview mirror, and Claire had no doubt that the back bumper would be plastered with stickers for emo bands nobody had ever heard of.

She liked Eve already. 'No,' she said, and swiped at her eyes angrily with the back of her hand. 'I, uh – look, I'm sorry. It's been a really awful day. I was coming to ask about the room, but—'

'Right, the room!' Eve snapped her fingers, as if she'd forgotten all about it, and jumped up and down two or three times in excitement. 'Great! I'm just home for break – I work over at Common Grounds, you know, the coffee shop? – and Michael won't be up for a while yet, but you can come in and see the house if you want. I don't know if Shane's around, but—'

'I don't know if I should—'

'You should. You totally should.' Eve rolled her eyes.

'You wouldn't believe the losers we see trying to get in the door. I mean, seriously. Freaks. You're the first normal one I've seen so far. Michael would kick my ass if I let you get away without at least trying a sales pitch.'

Claire blinked. Somehow, she'd been thinking that she'd be the one begging for them to consider *her*...and normal? Eve thought she was normal?

'Sure,' she heard herself say. 'Yeah. I'd like that.'

Eve grabbed her backpack and slung it over her own shoulder, on top of her black silver-studded purse in the shape of a coffin. 'Follow me.' And she bounced away, up the walk to the gracious Southern Gothic front porch to unlock the door.

Up close, the house looked old, but not really run-down as such; weathered, Claire decided. Could have used some paint here and there, and the cast-iron chairs needed a coat, too. The front door was actually double-sized, with a big stained-glass panel at the top.

'Yo!' Eve yelled, and dumped Claire's backpack on a table in the hallway, her purse next to it, her keys in an antique-looking ashtray with a cast-iron monkey on the handle. 'Roomies! We've got a live one!'

It occurred to Claire, as the door boomed shut behind her, that there were a couple of ways to interpret that, and one of them – the *Texas Chainsaw Massacre* way – wasn't good. She stopped moving, frozen, and just looked around.

Nothing overtly creepy about the inside of the house, at least. Lots of wood, clean and simple. Chips of paint knocked off of corners, like it had seen a lot of life. It smelt like lemon polish and – chilli?

'Yo!' Eve yelled again, and clumped on down the hall. It opened up to a bigger room; from what Claire could see, there were big leather couches and bookshelves, like a real home. Maybe this was what off-campus housing looked like. If so, it was a big step up from dorm life. 'Shane, I smell the chilli. I know you're here! Get your headphones out of your ears!'

She couldn't quite imagine *Texas Chainsaw Massacre* taking place in a room like that, either. That was a plus. Or, for that matter, serial-killing roommates doing something as homey as making chilli. Good chilli, from the way it smelt. With…garlic?

She took a couple of hesitant steps down the hallway. Eve's footsteps were clunking off into another room, maybe the kitchen. The house seemed very quiet. Nothing jumped out to scare her, so Claire proceeded, one careful foot after another, all the way into the big central room.

And a guy lying sprawled on the couch – the way only guys could sprawl – yawned and sat up rubbing his head. When Claire opened her mouth – whether to say hello or to yell for help, she didn't know – he surprised her into silence by grinning at her and putting his finger over his mouth to shush her. 'Hey,' he whispered. 'I'm Shane. What's up?' He blinked a couple of times, and without any change in his expression, said, 'Dude, that is a badass shiner. Hurts, huh?'

She nodded slightly. Shane swung his legs off the couch and sat there, watching her, elbows on his knees and hands dangling loosely. He had brown hair, cut in uneven layers that didn't quite manage to look punk. He was an older boy, older than her, anyway. Eighteen? A big guy, and tall to match it. Big enough to make her feel more miniature than usual. She thought his eyes looked brown, but she didn't dare meet them for more than a flicker at a time.

'So I guess you're gonna say that the other chick looks worse,' Shane said.

She shook her head, then winced when motion made it hurt even more. 'No, I – um – how did you know it was—?'

'A chick? Easy. Size you are, a guy would have put you in the hospital with a punch hard enough to leave a mark like that. So what's up with that? You don't look like you go looking for trouble.'

She felt like she ought to take offence about that, but honestly, this whole thing was starting to feel like some strange dream anyway. Maybe she'd never woken up at all. Maybe she was lying in a coma in a hospital bed, and Shane was just her lame-ass equivalent of the Cheshire cat. 'I'm Claire,' she said, and waved awkwardly. 'Hi.'

He nodded towards a leather wing chair. She slid into it, feet dangling, and felt a weird sense of relief wash over her. It felt like home, although of course it wasn't, and she was starting to think that it really couldn't be. She didn't fit here. She couldn't actually imagine who would.

'You want something?' Shane asked suddenly. 'Coke, maybe? Chilli? Bus ticket back home?'

'Coke,' she said, and, surprisingly, 'and chilli.'

'Good choice. I made it myself.' He slid off the couch, weirdly boneless for his size, and padded barefoot into the kitchen where Eve had gone. Claire listened to a blur of voices as the two of them talked, and relaxed, one muscle at a time, into the soft embrace of the chair. She hadn't noticed until now, but the house was kept cool, and the lazy circle of the ceiling fan overhead swept chilly air over her hot, aching face. It felt nice.

She opened her eyes at the sound of Eve's shoes clomping back into the room. Eve was carrying a tray with a red and white can, a bowl, a spoon, and an ice pack. She set the tray on a coffee table and nudged the table towards Claire with her knee. 'Ice pack first,' she said. 'You can never tell what Shane puts in the chilli. Be afraid.'

Shane padded back to the couch and flopped, sucking on his own can of soda. Eve shot him an exasperated look. 'Yeah, man, thanks for bringing me one, too.' The raccoon eye make-up exaggerated her eye roll. 'Dork.'

'Didn't know if you wanted zombie dirt sprinkled on it or anything. If you're eating this week.'

'*Dork!*' Eve turned towards Claire. 'Don't worry, you go on and eat. I'll go get my own drink.'

Claire picked up the spoon and tried a tentative bite of the chilli, which was thick and meaty and spicy, heavy on the garlic. Delicious, in fact. She'd got used to cafeteria food, and this was just...wow. *Not.* Shane watched her, eyebrows up, as she started to shovel it in. ''Sgood,' she mumbled. He gave her a lazy salute. By the time she was halfway through the bowl, Eve was back with her own tray, which she plunked down on the other half of the coffee table. Eve sat on the floor, crossed her legs, and dug in.

'Not bad,' she finally said. 'At least you left out the oh-my-God sauce this time.'

'Made myself a batch with it,' Shane said. 'It's got the biohazard sticker on it in the fridge, so don't bitch if you get flamed. Where'd you pick up the stray?'

'Outside. She came to see the room.'

'You beat her up first, just to make sure she's tough enough?'

'Bite me, chilli boy.'

'Don't mind Eve,' he told Claire. 'She hates working days. She's afraid she'll tan.'

'Yeah, and Shane just hates working. So what's your name?'

Claire opened her mouth, but Shane beat her to it, clearly happy to one-up his roomie. 'Claire. What, you didn't even ask? A chick beat her up, too. Probably some skank in the dorms. You know how that place is.'

They exchanged a look. A long one. Eve turned back to Claire. 'Is that true? You got beat up in the dorm?' She nodded, hastily shovelling more food in her mouth to keep from having to say much. 'Well, that totally blows. No wonder you're looking for the room.' Another nod. 'You didn't bring much with you.'

'I don't have much,' she said. 'Just the books, and maybe a couple of things back at my room. But – I don't want to go back there to get stuff. Not tonight.'

'Why not?' Shane had grabbed a ratty-looking old baseball from the floor and tossed it up towards the tall ceiling, narrowly missing the spinning blades of the fan. He caught it without effort. 'Somebody still looking to pound you?'

'Yeah,' Claire said, and looked down into her fast-diminishing chilli. 'Guess so. It's not just her, it's – she's got friends. And...I don't. That place just – well, it's creepy.'

'Been there,' Eve said. 'Oh, wait, still there.'

Shane mimed throwing the baseball at her. She mimed ducking.

'What time is Michael getting up?'

Shane gave her another mock throw. 'Hell, Eve, I don't know. I love the guy, but I don't *love* the guy. Go bang on his door and ask. Me, I'm gonna go get ready.'

'Ready for what?' Eve asked. 'You're not seriously going out again, are you?'

'Seriously, yeah. Bowling. Her name's Laura. If you want more details, you're gonna have to download the video like everybody else.' Shane rolled off the couch, stood up, and padded off towards the wide stairs leading up to the second floor. 'See you later, Claire.'

Eve made a frustrated sound. 'Wait a minute! So what do you say? You think she'd do OK here, or what?'

Shane waved a hand. 'Whatever, man. Far as I'm concerned, she's OK.' He gave Claire one quick look and a crooked and oddly sweet smile, and bounded up the stairs. He moved like an athlete, but without the swagger she was used to. Kind of hot, actually.

'Guys,' Eve sighed. 'Damn, it'd be good to have another girl in here. They're all like, *Yeah, whatever,* and then when it comes to tidying up the place or washing dishes, they turn into ghosts. Not that you have to, like, be a maid or anything, I mean...you just got to yell at 'em until they do their part or they walk all over you.'

Claire smiled, or tried to, but her split lip throbbed, and she felt the scab break open again. Blood dribbled down her chin, and she grabbed the napkin Eve had put on the tray and applied pressure to her lip. Eve watched in silence, frowning, and then got up from the floor, picked up the ice pack, and settled it gently against the bump on Claire's head. 'How's that?' she asked.

'Better.' It was. The ice began to numb the ache almost immediately, and the food was setting up a nice warm fire in her stomach. 'Um, I guess I should ask... about the room...'

'Well, you have to meet Michael, and he has to say yes, but Michael's a sweetie, really. Oh, and he owns this place. His family does, anyway. I think they moved away and left him the house a couple of years ago. He's about six months older than I am. We're all about eighteen. Michael's sort of the oldest.'

'He sleeps days?'

'Yeah. I mean, I like to sleep days, but he's got a thing about it. I called him a vampire once, 'cause he really doesn't like being up in the daytime. Like, ever. He didn't think it was real funny.'

'You're sure he's not a vampire?' Claire said. 'I've seen movies. They're sneaky.' She was kidding. Eve didn't smile.

'Oh, pretty sure. For one thing, he eats Shane's chilli, which, God knows, has enough garlic to explode a dozen high-quality Dracs. And I made him touch a cross once.' Eve took a big swallow of her Coke.

'You – what? *Made him*?'

'Well, sure, yeah. I mean, a girl can't be too careful, especially around here.' Claire must have looked blank, because Eve did the eye-roll thing again. It was her favourite expression, Claire was sure. 'In Morganville? You know?'

'What about it?'

'You mean you don't *know?* How can you not know?' Eve set her can down and got up to her knees, leaning elbows on the coffee table. She looked earnest under the thick make-up. Her eyes were dark brown, edged with gold. 'Morganville's full of vampires.'

Claire laughed.

Eve didn't. She just kept staring.

'Um...you're kidding?'

'How many kids graduate TPU every year?'

'I don't know... It's a crappy college, almost everybody transfers out...'

'Everybody *leaves.* Or at least, they stop showing up, right? I can't believe you don't know this. Didn't anybody tell you the score before you moved in? Look, the vamps run the town. They're in charge. And either you're in, or you're out. If you work for them, if you pretend like they're not here and they don't exist, and you look the other way when things happen, then you and your family get a free pass. You get *Protection.* Otherwise...' Eve pulled a finger across her throat and bugged out her eyes.

Right, Claire thought, and put down her spoon. *No wonder nobody rented a room with these people. They're nuts.* It was too bad. Except for the crazy part, she really liked them.

'You think I'm wacko,' Eve said, and sighed. 'Yeah, I get that. I'd think I was, too, except I grew up in a Protected house. My dad works for the water company. My mom is a teacher. But we all wear these.' She extended her wrist. On it was a black leather bracelet, with a symbol on it in red, nothing Claire recognised. It looked kind of like a Chinese character. 'See how mine's red? Expired. It's like health insurance. Kids are only covered until they're eighteen. Mine was up six months ago.' She looked at it mournfully, then shrugged and unsnapped it to drop it on her tray. 'Might as well stop wearing it, I guess. It sure wouldn't fool anybody.'

Claire just looked at her, helpless, wondering if she was the victim of a practical joke, and if any second Eve was going to laugh and call her an idiot for buying it, and Shane would go from kind of lazy-sweet to cruel and shove her out the door, mocking all the way. Because this wasn't the way the world worked. You didn't like people, and then have them turn all crazy, right? Couldn't you *tell*?

The alternative – that Eve wasn't crazy at all – just wasn't anything Claire wanted to think about. She remembered the people on the street, walking fast, heads down. The way the mother had yanked her little girl off the street at a friendly wave.

'Fine. Go ahead, think I'm nuts,' Eve said, and sat back on her heels. 'I mean, why wouldn't I be? And I won't try to convince you or anything. Just – don't go out after dark unless you're with somebody. Somebody Protected, if you can find them. Look for the bracelet.' She nudged hers with one finger. 'The symbol's white when it's active.'

'But I—' Claire coughed, trying to find something to say. *If you can't say anything nice...* 'OK. Thanks. Um, is Shane—?'

'Shane? Protected?' Eve snorted. 'As if! Even if he was, which I doubt, he'd never admit it, and he doesn't wear the bracelet or anything. Michael – Michael isn't, either, but there's sort of a standard Protection on houses. We're sort of outcasts here. There's safety in numbers, too.'

It was a very weird conversation to be having over chilli and Coke, with an ice pack perched on the top of her head. Claire, without even knowing she was going to do it, yawned. Eve laughed.

'Call it a bedtime story,' she said. 'Listen, let me show you the room. Worst case, you lie down for a while, let the ice pack work, then bug out. Or hey, you wake up and decide you want to talk to Michael before you leave. Your choice.'

Another cold chill swept over her, and she shivered. Probably had to do with the bang on the head, she figured, and how tired she was. She dug in her pocket, found the package of pills the doc had prescribed for her, and swallowed one with the last gulp of Coke. Then she helped Eve carry the trays into the kitchen, which was huge, with stone sinks and ancient polished counters and two modern conveniences – the stove and the refrigerator – stuck awkwardly in the corners.

The chilli had come from a Crock-Pot, which was still simmering away.

When the dishes had been washed, trays stacked, trash discarded, Eve retrieved Claire's backpack from the floor and led her through the living room, up the stairs. On the third riser, Eve turned, alarmed, and said, 'Hey, can you make it up the stairs? Because, you know—'

'I'm OK,' Claire lied. Her ankle hurt like hell, but she wanted to see the room. And if they were likely to throw her out later, she at least wanted to sleep one more time in a bed, however lumpy and old. There were thirteen steps to the top. She made every one of them, even though she left sweaty fingerprints on a banister Shane hadn't even bothered to touch on his way up earlier.

Eve's steps were muffled here by a rich old-looking rug, all swirls and colours, that ran down the centre of the polished wood floor. There were six doors up here on the landing. As they passed them, Eve pointed and named. 'Shane's.' The first door. 'Michael's.' The second door. 'He's got that one, too – it's a double-sized room.' Third door. 'Main bathroom.' Fourth. 'The second bathroom's downstairs – that's kind of the emergency back-up bathroom when Shane's in there moussing his hair for like an hour or something...'

'*Bite me!*' Shane yelled from behind the closed door. Eve pounded a fist on the door and led Claire to the last two in the row. 'This one's mine. Yours is on the end.'

When she swung it open, Claire – prepared for disappointment – actually gasped. For one thing, it was huge. Three times the size of her dorm room. For another, it was on a corner, with three – *three!* – windows, all currently shaded by blinds and curtains. The bed wasn't some dorm-sized miniature; it was a full-sized mattress and box spring with massive wooden columns at the corners, dark and solid. There was a dresser along one wall big enough to hold, well, four or five times the clothes that Claire had ever owned. Plus a closet. Plus...

'Is that a TV?' she asked in a faint voice.

'Yeah. Satellite cable. You'd pitch in, though, unless you want to take it out of the room. Oh, and there's Internet, too. Broadband, over there. I should probably warn you, they monitor Internet traffic around here, though. You have to be careful what you say in messages and stuff.' Eve put the backpack on top of the dresser. 'You don't have to decide right now. You probably ought to rest first. Here, here's your ice pack.' She followed Claire to the bed and helped her pull back the covers, and once Claire had pulled off her shoes and settled, she tucked her in, like a mother, and put the ice pack on her head. 'When you get up, Michael'll probably be awake. I have to get back to work, but it'll be OK. Really.'

Claire smiled at her, a little fuzzily; the painkillers were starting to take effect. She got another chill. 'Thank you, Eve,' she said. 'This is – wow.'

'Yeah, well, you look like you could use a little wow today.' Eve shrugged, and gave her a stunning smile back. 'Sleep well. And don't worry, the vampires won't come in here. This house has Protection, even if we don't.'

Claire turned that over in her mind for a few seconds as Eve left the room and shut the door, and then her mind wandered off in happy clouds of noticing the softness of the pillow and how good the bed felt, and how crisp the sheets were...

She dreamt about the strangest thing: a silent room, with someone pale and quiet sitting on a velvet sofa, turning pages in a book and weeping. It didn't scare her, exactly, but she felt cold, on and off, and the house...the house seemed like it was full of whispers.

Eventually, she fell into a deeper, darker place, and didn't dream at all.

Not even about Monica.

Not even about vampires.

CHAPTER THREE

She woke up in the dark with a panicked flinch that sent the ice pack – water sloshing in a bag now – thumping off her pillow and onto the floor. The house was quiet, except for the creaky, creepy noises houses made at night. Outside, wind rattled the dry leaves on the trees, and she heard music coming from the other side of the bedroom door.

Claire slid out of bed, fumbled for a lamp, and found one next to the bed – Tiffany-style glass, really nice – and the colourful glow chased away any nightmare fears she'd been trying to have. The music was slow and warm and contemplative, kind of guitar alternative. She got her shoes on, took a look in the dresser mirror, and got a nasty shock. Her face still hurt, and it was obvious why – her right eye was swollen, the skin around it purple. Her split lip looked shiny and unpleasantly thick, too. Her face – always pale – looked even paler than normal. Her short pixie-cut black hair had a serious case of bed-head, but she fluffed it out into something like order. She'd never really been much for make-up, even when she'd been stealing Mom's to try on, but today maybe a little foundation and concealer couldn't hurt... She looked ragged, and beaten, and homeless.

Well. It was nothing but the truth, after all.

Claire took a deep breath and opened her bedroom door. Lights were on in the hall, warm and glowing gold; the music was coming from downstairs, in the living room. She checked a clock hanging on the wall at the far end; it was after midnight – she'd slept for more than twelve hours.

And missed all her classes. Not that she'd have wanted to show up looking like this, even if she hadn't been so paranoid about Monica following her around... but she'd need to hit the books later. At least the books didn't hit back.

Her bruises felt better, and in fact her head hurt only a little. Her ankle was still the worst of it, sending sharp glassy jabs of pain up her leg with every step down the stairs.

She was halfway down when she saw the boy sitting on the couch, where Shane had been sprawled before. He had a guitar in his hands.

Oh. The music. She'd thought it was a recording, but no, this was real, this was live, and he was playing it. She'd never heard live music before – not really *playing*, not like this. He was...wow. He was wonderful.

She watched him, frozen, because he clearly didn't even know she existed yet; it was just him and the guitar and the music, and if she had to put a name to what she could see on his face, it would be something poetic, like *longing.* He was blond, his hair cut kind of like Shane's, in a careless mop. Not as big as Shane, and not as muscled, though he was maybe as tall. He was wearing a T-shirt, too, black, with a beer logo. Blue jeans. No shoes.

He stopped playing, head down, and reached for the open beer on the table in front of him. He toasted empty air. 'Happy birthday to you, man.' He tossed back three swallows, sighed, and put the bottle down. 'And here's to house arrest. What the hell. Own it or get owned.'

Claire coughed. He turned, startled, and saw her standing there on the stairs; his frown cleared after a second or two. 'Oh. You're the one Shane said wanted to talk about the room. Hey. Come on down.'

She did, trying not to limp, and when she got into the full light she saw his quick, intelligent blue eyes catalogue the bruises.

He didn't say a word about them. 'I'm Michael,' he said. 'And you're not eighteen, so this is going to be a real short conversation.'

She sat, fast, heart pounding. 'I'm in college,' she said. 'I'm a freshman. My name is—'

'Don't bullshit me, and I don't care what your name

is. You're not eighteen. It's a good bet you're not even seventeen. We don't take anybody in this house who isn't legal.' He had a deep voice, warm but – at least right now – hard. 'Not that you'd be signing on to Orgy Central, but sorry, me and Shane have to worry about things like that. All it takes is you living here and somebody even hinting there's something going on—'

'Wait,' she blurted. 'I wouldn't do that. Or say that. I'm not looking to get you guys in trouble. I just need—'

'No,' he said. He put the guitar aside, in its case, and latched it shut. 'I'm sorry, but you can't stay here. House rules.'

She'd known it was coming, of course, but she'd let herself think – Eve had been nice, and Shane hadn't been horrible, and the room was so nice – but the look in Michael's eyes was as final as it got. Complete and utter rejection.

She felt her lips trembling, and hated herself for it. Why couldn't she be a badass, stone-cold bitch? Why couldn't she stand up for herself when she needed to, without breaking down into tears like a baby? *Monica* wouldn't be crying. Monica would be snapping some comeback at him, telling him that her stuff was already in the room. Monica would slap money down on the table and dare him to turn it down.

Claire reached in her back pocket and pulled out her wallet. 'How much?' she asked, and started counting out bills. She had twenties, so it looked like a lot. 'Three hundred enough? I can get more if I have to.'

Michael sat back, surprised, a little frown bracketing his forehead. He reached for his beer and took another sip while he thought about it. 'How?' he asked.

'What?'

'How would you get more?'

'Get a job. Sell stuff.' Not that she had much to sell, but in an emergency there was always the panicked call to Mom. 'I want to stay here, Michael. I really do.' She was surprised at the conviction in her voice. 'Yeah, I'm under eighteen, but I swear, you won't have any trouble from me. I'll stay out of your way. I go to school, and I study. That's all I do. I'm not a partyer, I'm not a slacker. I'm useful. I'll – I'll help clean and cook.'

He thought about it, staring at her; he was the kind of person you could actually see thinking. It was a little scary, although he probably didn't mean it to be. There was just something so...*adult* about him. So sure of himself.

'No,' he said. 'I'm sorry, kid. But it's just too much risk.'

'Eve's only a little bit older than I am!'

'Eve's eighteen. You're what, sixteen?'

'Almost seventeen!' If you were a little fluid on the definition of *almost*. 'I really am in college. I'm a freshman – look, here's my student ID...'

He ignored it. 'Come back in a year. We'll talk about it,' he said. 'Look, I'm sorry. What about the dorm?'

'They'll kill me if I stay there,' she said, and looked down at her clasped hands. 'They tried to kill me today.'

'What?'

'The other girls. They punched me and shoved me down the stairs.'

Silence. A really long one. She heard the creak of leather, and then Michael was on one knee next to the chair. Before she could stop him, he was probing the bump on her head, tilting it back so he could get a good, impersonal look at the bruises and cuts.

'What else?' he asked.

'What?'

'Besides what I can see? You're not going to drop dead on me, are you?'

Wow, sensitive. 'I'm OK. I saw the doctor and everything. It's just – bruises. And a strained ankle. But they pushed me down the stairs, and they meant it, and she told me—' Suddenly, Eve's words about *vampires* came back to her and made her trip over her tongue. 'The girl in charge, she told me that tonight, I'd get what was coming to me. I *can't* go back to the dorm, Michael. If you send me out that door, they'll kill me, *because I don't have any friends and I don't have anyplace to go!*'

He stayed there for a few more seconds, looking her right in the eyes, and then retreated to the couch. He unlatched the guitar case again and cradled the instrument; she thought that was his comfort zone, right there, with the guitar in his arms. 'These girls. Do they go out in daylight?'

She blinked. 'You mean, outside? Sure. They go to classes. Well, sometimes.'

'Do they wear bracelets?'

She blinked. 'You mean, like—' Eve had left hers behind on the table, so she picked up the leather band with its red symbol. 'Like this? I never noticed. They wear a lot of stuff.' She thought hard, and maybe she did remember something after all. The bracelets didn't look like this, though. They were gold, and Monica and the Monickettes all had them on their right wrists. She'd never paid much attention. 'Maybe.'

'Bracelets with white symbols?' Michael made the question casual; in fact, he bent his head and concentrated on tuning his guitar, not that it needed it. Every note sounded perfect as it whispered out of the strings. 'Do you remember?'

'No.' She felt a pure burst of something that wasn't quite panic, wasn't quite excitement. 'Does that mean they have Protection?'

He hesitated for about a second, just long enough for her to know he was surprised. 'You mean condoms?' he asked. 'Doesn't everybody?'

'You know what I mean.' Her cheeks were burning. She hoped it wasn't as obvious as it felt.

'Don't think I do.'

'Eve said—'

He looked up sharply, and those blue eyes were suddenly angry. 'Eve needs to keep her mouth shut. She's in enough danger as it is, trolling around out there in Goth gear. They already think she's mocking them. If they hear she's talking...'

'They, who?' Claire asked. It was his turn to look away.

'People,' he said flatly. 'Look, I don't want your blood on my hands. You can stay for a couple of days. But only until you find a place, right? And make it fast – I'm not running a halfway house for battered girls. I've got enough to worry about trying to keep Eve and Shane out of trouble.'

For a guy who made such beautiful music, he was bitter, and a little scary. Claire put the money hesitantly on the table in front of him. He stared at it, jaw tense.

'The rent's a hundred a month,' he said. 'You buy groceries once a month, too. First month in advance. But you're not staying past that, so keep the rest.'

She swallowed and picked up two hundred of the three hundred she'd counted out. 'Thanks,' she said.

'Don't thank me,' he said. 'Just don't get us into trouble. I mean it.'

She got up, went into the kitchen, and spooned chilli into two bowls, added the bowls to trays along with spoons and Cokes, and brought it all back to set it on the coffee table. Michael stared at it, then her. She sat down on the floor – painfully – and began eating. After a pause, Michael took his bowl and tasted it.

'Shane made it,' Claire said. 'It's pretty good.'

'Yeah. Chilli and spaghetti, that's pretty much all Shane can cook. You know how to make anything?'

'Sure.'

'Like?'

'Lasagna,' she said. 'And, um, sort of a hamburger hash thing, with noodles. And tacos.'

Michael looked thoughtful. 'Could you make tacos tomorrow?'

'Sure,' she said. 'I have classes from eleven to five, but I'll stop and pick up the stuff.'

He nodded, eating steadily, glancing up at her once in a while. 'I'm sorry,' he finally said.

'About what?'

'Being an asshole. Look, it's just that I can't – I have to be careful. Really careful.'

'You weren't being an asshole,' she said. 'You're trying to protect yourself and your friends. That's OK. That's what you're supposed to do.'

Michael smiled, and it transformed his face, made it suddenly angelic and wonderful. *Dude*, she thought in amazement. *He's totally gorgeous.* No wonder he'd been worried about her being underage. A smile like that, he'd be peeling girls off of him right and left.

'If you're in this house, you're my friend,' he said. 'What's your name, by the way?'

'Claire. Claire Danvers.'

'Welcome to the Glass House, Claire Danvers.'

'But only temporarily.'

'Yeah, temporarily.'

They shared a smile, uneasily, and Michael cleared up the plates this time, while Claire went back up to her room, where she spread her books out on the built-in desk and started the day's studying.

She listened to him playing downstairs, the soft and heartfelt accompaniment to the night, as she fell into the world she loved.

CHAPTER FOUR

Morning dawned bright and early, and Claire woke up to the smell of frying bacon. She stumbled to the bathroom down the hall, yawning, barely aware that she was scantily dressed in her extra-long T-shirt until she remembered, *Oh my God, boys live here, too.* Luckily, nobody saw, and the bathroom was free. Somebody had already been in it this morning; the mirrors were still frosted with steam, and the big black-and-white room glistened with drops of water. It smelt clean, though. And kind of fruity.

The fruity smell was the shampoo, she found, as she lathered and rinsed. When she wiped the mirror down and stared at herself, she saw the patterns of bruises up and down both sides of her pale skin. *I could have died.* She'd been lucky.

She tossed the T-shirt back on, then dashed back to her room to dig out the panties she'd rescued yesterday from the washer. They were still damp, but she put them on anyway, then dragged on her blue jeans.

On impulse, she opened the closet, and found some old stuff pushed to the back. T-shirts, mostly, from bands she'd never heard of, and a few she remembered as ancient. A couple of sweaters, too. She stripped off her bloodstained shirt and dragged on a faded black one, and, after thinking about it, left her shoes on the floor.

Downstairs, Eve and Shane were arguing in the kitchen about the right way to make scrambled eggs. Eve said they needed milk. Shane said milk was for pussies. Claire padded silently past them, over to the refrigerator, and pulled out a carton of orange juice. She splashed some into a glass, then silently held the carton up for the other two. Eve took it and poured herself a glass, then handed it to Shane.

'So,' Shane asked, 'Michael didn't pitch you out.'

'No.'

Shane nodded slowly. He was even bigger and taller than she remembered, and his skin was a golden brown colour, like he'd spent a lot of time in the sun over the summer. His hair had that bronzy sheen, too. Sun-bleached where Michael was naturally blond. *OK, truthfully? They're both hotties.* She wished she hadn't really thought that, but at least she hadn't said it out loud.

'Something you should know about Michael,' he said. 'He doesn't like taking chances. I wasn't sure he'd let you stay. If he did, then he got a good vibe off of you. Don't disrespect that, because if you do – I won't be happy, either. Got it?'

Eve was silently watching the two of them, which Claire figured was a new experience for Eve, at least the not-talking part. 'He's your friend, right?'

'He saved my life,' Shane said. 'I'd die for him, but it'd be a dumbass thing to do to thank him for it. So yeah. He's been my friend all my life, and he's more like a brother. So don't get him in trouble.'

'I won't,' she said. 'No milk in the eggs.'

'See?' Shane turned back to the counter and started cracking eggs into a bowl. 'Told ya.'

'Traitor,' Eve sighed, and poked at the frying bacon with a fork. 'Fine. So. How was Linda last night?'

'Laura.'

'Whatever. Not like I have to remember a name for more than one date, anyway.'

'She bowled a one fifty.'

'God, you're *such* a disappointment. Share, already!'

Shane smiled tightly down at the eggs. 'Hey, not in front of the kid. You got the note.'

'Kid?' That hurt. Claire dropped plates on the counter with a little too much force. '*Note?*'

Shane handed over a folded piece of paper. It was short and sweet, and signed 'Michael'...and it told them that Claire was underage, and that the two of them were supposed to look out for her while she was in the house.

Cute. Claire didn't know whether to be pissed or flattered. On reflection...pissed. 'I'm not a kid!' she told

Shane hotly. 'I'm only, like, a year younger than Eve!'

'And girls are much more mature.' Eve nodded wisely. 'So you're about ten years older than Shane, then.'

'Seriously,' Claire insisted. 'I'm not a kid!'

'Whatever you say, kid,' Shane said blandly. 'Cheer up. Just means you don't have to put up with me telling you how much sex I didn't get.'

'I'm telling Michael,' Eve warned.

'About how much sex I didn't get? Go ahead.'

'No bacon for you.'

'Then no eggs for you. Either of you.'

Eve glowered at him. 'Prisoner exchange?'

They glared at each other, then swapped pans and started scooping.

Claire was just about to join in when the front doorbell rang, a lilting silvery sound. It wasn't a scary sound, but Eve and Shane froze and looked at each other, and that was scary, somehow. Shane put his plate down on the granite countertop, licked bacon grease from his fingers, and said, 'Get her out of sight.'

Eve nodded. She dropped her own plate onto the counter, grabbed Claire's wrist, and hustled her to the pantry – a door half hidden in the shadow of the awkwardly placed refrigerator. It was big, dark, and dusty, shelves crowded with old cans of yams and asparagus and glass jars of ancient jellies. There was a light with a string pull above, but Eve didn't turn it on. She reached behind a row of murky-looking cans of fruit and hit some kind of a switch. There was a grating rumble, then a click, and part of the back wall swung open.

Eve pushed it back, reached in, and grabbed a flashlight that she handed to Claire. 'Inside,' she said. 'I'm going to turn the light on out here, but try to keep that flashlight off if you hear voices. It could show through the cracks.' Claire nodded, a little dazed, and crouched down to crawl through the small opening into...a big empty room, stone floored, no windows. A few spiderwebs in the corners, and loads of dust, but otherwise it didn't look too bad.

Until Eve shut the door, and then the darkness slammed down, and Claire hastily flicked on the flashlight, moved to the nearest corner, and knelt down there, breathing fast and hard.

Just one minute ago, they'd been laughing about bacon and eggs, and all of a sudden...what the hell had just happened? And why was there a secret compartment in this house? One with – so far as she could tell – no other entrances or exits?

She heard distant voices, and hastily thumbed off the flashlight. That was bad. She'd never really been afraid of the dark, but dark wasn't really *dark* most of the time... There were stars, moonlight, distant streetlights.

This was pitch-black, take-no-prisoners dark, and she had the ice-cold thought that anything could be right next to her, reaching out for her, and she'd never see it coming.

Claire bit down hard on her lip, gripped the flashlight

tightly, and slid down the wall until her searching hand found the rough wood of the door she'd come in through. A little light was leaking in around it, barely a glimmer but enough to ease the pounding in her chest.

Voices. Shane's, and someone else's. A man's voice, deeper than Shane's. '...standard inventory.'

'Sir, there's nobody living here but what's on the roster. Just the three of us.' Shane sounded subdued and respectful, which didn't seem like him. Not that she knew him that well, but he was kind of a smart-ass.

'Which one are you?' the voice asked.

'Shane Collins, sir.'

'Get your third in here,' the voice said.

'Well, I would, but – Michael's not here. He's out until tonight. You want to check back then...?'

'Never mind.' Claire, straining her ears, heard paper rustling. 'You're Eve Rosser?'

'Yes, sir.' Eve sounded respectful, but brisk.

'Moved out of your parents' house – eight months ago?'

'Yes, sir.'

'Employed?'

'At Common Grounds, you know, the coffee—'

The man, whoever he was, interrupted her. 'You. Collins. Any employment?' Clearly talking to Shane.

'I'm between jobs, sir. You know how it is.'

'Keep looking. We don't like slackers in Morganville. Everybody contributes.'

'Yes, sir. I'll keep it in mind, sir.'

A brief pause. Maybe there had been a little bit more smart-ass in Shane's response than there should have been. Claire deliberately slowed her breathing, trying to hear more.

'You left town for a couple of years, boy. What brings you back?'

'Homesick, sir.' Yes, it was definitely back in his voice, and even *Claire* knew that was a bad thing. 'Missed all my old friends.'

She heard Eve clear her throat. 'Sir, I'm sorry, but I've got work in a half hour...?'

More paper shuffling. 'One other thing. Here's a picture of a girl that disappeared from her dorm last night. You haven't seen her?'

They both chorused a 'No.'

He must not have believed them, because he didn't sound convinced. 'What's in here?' He didn't wait to hear a response; he just opened the outer door of the pantry. Claire flinched and held her breath. 'You always leave the light on?'

'I was getting some jam when you rang, sir. I probably forgot to turn it off,' Eve said. She sounded nervous. 'Sorry.'

Click. The light in the pantry went out, taking what little there was seeping through the door with it. Claire barely controlled a gasp. *Don't move. Don't move.* She just knew he – whoever he was – was standing there in the dark, looking and listening.

And then, finally, she heard him say, 'You ring the

station if you see that girl. She's got herself in some trouble. We're supposed to help her get straightened out.'

'Yes, sir,' Eve said, and the pantry door shut. The conversation moved away, became softer and softer until it faded into nothing.

Claire switched on the flashlight, covered it with her hand, and pointed it at the corner – only a little light escaped, just enough to convince her that no evil zombie was sneaking up on her in the dark. And then she waited. It seemed like a long time before there were two sharp raps on the door, and it swung open in a blaze of electric light. Eve's stark white make-up and black eyeliner looked even scarier than before.

'It's OK,' she said, and helped Claire out of the hidden room. 'He's gone.'

'Oh, the hell it's OK,' Shane said behind her. He had his arms folded across his chest, and rocked back and forth, frowning. 'Those assholes have her picture. They're *looking* for her. What'd you do, Claire? Knife the mayor or something?'

'Nothing!' she blurted. 'I – I don't know why – maybe it's that they're just worried because I didn't show up last night?'

'Worried?' Shane laughed bitterly. 'Yeah, that's it. They're *worried* about you. Right. I'm going to have to talk this over with Michael. If they're going to turn the town upside down looking for you, either you're too hot to stay in Morganville, or we need to get you under some kind of Protection, fast.'

He said it the same way Eve had. 'But – maybe the police—?'

'That was the police,' Eve said. 'Told you. They run the town. These guys work for the vamps – they're not vamps themselves, but they're scary enough without the fangs. Look, can you call your parents? Get them to pull you out of school and take you home or something?'

Sure. That would be the easiest thing in the world, only it would mean failure, and they'd never believe a word of this stuff, ever, and if she tried to explain it, she'd end up drugged and in therapy for the rest of her life. And any chance – *any* chance – of making it to Yale or MIT or Caltech would be blown completely. She supposed it was kind of dumb to be thinking of it that way, but those things were *real* to her.

Vampires? Not so much.

'But – I haven't done anything!' she said, and looked from Shane to Eve, and back again. 'How can they be after me if I didn't do anything?'

'Life ain't fair,' Shane said, with all the certainty of two more years of experience at it. 'You must have pissed off the wrong people, is all I know. What's the girl's name? The one who smacked you around?'

'M-Monica.'

They both stared at her.

'Oh, crap,' Eve said, horrified. 'Monica *Morrell*?'

Shane's face went...blank. Completely blank, except for his eyes, and there was something pretty scary going on behind them. 'Monica,' he repeated. 'How come nobody told me?'

Eve was watching him, biting her lip. 'Sorry, Shane. We would have – I swear, I thought she left town. Went off to college somewhere else.'

Shane shook it off, whatever it was, and shrugged, trying to look like he didn't care. It was obvious to Claire that he did, though. 'She probably couldn't stand not being the queen bee, and had to come begging back to Daddy to buy her some grades.'

'Shane—'

'I'm fine. Don't worry about me.'

'She probably doesn't even remember you,' Eve blurted, and then looked as if she wished she hadn't said it. 'I – that's not what I meant. I'm sorry.'

He laughed, and it sounded wrong and a little bit shaky. There was a short, odd silence, and then Eve changed the subject by resolutely picking up her plate of cooling bacon and eggs.

And then went still and round-eyed. 'Oh, shit,' she said, and then covered her mouth.

'What?'

She pointed at the plates on the counter. Shane's, hers...and Claire's. 'Three plates. He knew something was up. We told him Michael wasn't around. No wonder he kept poking.'

Shane said nothing, but Claire could see he was – if possible – even more upset. He didn't show it much, but he picked up his plate and walked away, out into the living room, then up the steps two at a time.

His upstairs door slammed.

Eve bit her lip, watching after him.

'So... Shane and Monica...?' Claire guessed.

Eve kept staring at the doorway. 'Not like you're thinking,' she said. 'He wouldn't touch that skank in a million years. But they were in high school together, and Shane – got on her bad side. Just like you did.'

Claire's appetite for breakfast was suddenly gone. 'What happened?'

'He stood up to her, and his house burnt. He nearly died,' she said. 'His – his sister wasn't so lucky. Michael got him out of town, off on his own, before he did something crazy. He's been gone a couple of years. Just came back right before I moved in here.' Eve forced a bright smile. 'Let's eat, yeah? I'm starving.'

They sat out in the living room, chatting about nothing, not talking about the thing that was most important: what to do.

Because, Claire sensed, neither one of them had a clue.

CHAPTER FIVE

Claire watched the clock – some old-style wall clock, with hands – crawl slowly up to, and past, eleven o'clock. Professor Hamms is starting the lecture, she thought, and felt a nauseating twist in her stomach. This was the second day in a row she'd missed school. In her whole life she'd never missed two days of school back-to-back. Sure, she'd read the textbook already – twice – but lectures were important. That was how you found out the good stuff, especially in classes like physics, where they did practical demonstrations. Lectures were the fun part.

It was Thursday. That meant she had a lab class later, too. You couldn't make up lab class, no matter how good your excuse.

She sighed, forced herself to look away from the time, and opened up her Calc II book – she'd tested out of Calc I, could have tested out of Calc II, but she'd thought maybe she might learn something new about solving linear inequalities, which had always been a problem for her.

'What the hell are you doing?' Shane. He was on the stairs, staring at her. She hadn't heard him coming, but that was probably because he was barefoot. His hair was a mess, too. Maybe he'd been asleep.

'Studying,' she said.

'Huh,' he said, like he'd never actually seen it done before. 'Interesting.' He vaulted over the railing three steps from the bottom and flopped down on the leather couch next to her, flicking the TV on with the remote next to him, then changing inputs. 'This going to bother you?'

'No,' she said politely. It was a lie, but she wasn't quite ready to be, you know, blunt. It was her first day.

'Great. Want to take a break?'

'A break?'

'That's when you stop studying' – he tilted his head to the side to look at the book – 'OK, whatever the hell that is, and actually do something fun. It's a custom where I come from.' He dumped something in the centre of her open book with a plastic *thump*. She flinched and picked up the wireless game controller with two fingers. 'Oh, come on. You can't tell me you've never played a video game.'

Truthfully, she had. Once. She hadn't liked it very much. He must have read that in her expression, because he shook his head. 'This is just sad. Now you *have* to take a break. OK, you've got a choice: horror, action, driving, or war.'

She blurted, 'Those are my *choices?*'

He looked offended. 'What, you want *girl games?* Not in my house. Never mind, I'll pick for you. Here. First-person shooter.' He yanked a box from a stack next to the couch and loaded a disc into the machine. 'Easy. All you have to do is pull the trigger. Trust me. Nothing like a little virtual violence to make you feel better.'

'You're crazy.'

'Hey, prove me wrong. Unless you think you can't.' He didn't look at her as he said it, but she felt it sting, anyway. 'Maybe you're just not up to it.'

She shut her Calc II book, picked up the controller, and watched the colourful graphics load up on the screen. 'Show me what to do.'

He smiled slowly. 'Point. Shoot. Try not to get in my way.'

He was right. She'd always thought it was kind of creepy, hanging out in front of a TV and killing virtual monsters, but damn if it wasn't...*fun.* Before too long, she was flinching when things lunged out of the corners of the screen, and whooping just like Shane when some monster got put down for the count.

When it ended for her, and the screen suddenly showed a snarling zombie face and splashes of red, she felt it like an ice cube down her back.

'Oops,' Shane said, and kept on firing. 'Sorry. Some days you're the zombie, some days you're the meal. Good try, kiddo.'

She put the controller on the couch cushions, and watched him play for a while. 'Shane?' she finally asked.

'Hang on – damn, that was close. What?'

'How did you get on Monica's—'

'Shit list?' he supplied, and drilled a few dozen bullets into a lunging zombie in a prom dress. 'You don't have to do much, just not crawl on your belly every time she walks in a room.' Which, she noticed, wasn't exactly an answer. Exactly. 'What'd you do?'

'I, uh… I made her look stupid.'

He hit some control and froze the game in mid-scream, and turned to look at her. 'You what?'

'Well, she said this thing about World War II being about the Chinese, and—'

Shane laughed. He had a good laugh, loud and full of raw energy, and she smiled nervously in return. 'You're feistier than you look, C. Good one.' He held up a hand. She awkwardly smacked it. 'Oh, man, that's sadder than the video game thing. Again.'

Five hand smacks later, she had mastered the high five to his satisfaction, and he unfroze the video game.

'Shane?' she asked.

This time, he sighed. 'Yeah?'

'Sorry, but – about your sister—'

Silence. He didn't look at her, didn't give any indication he'd heard a word. He just kept on killing things.

He was good at it.

Claire's nerve failed. She went back to her textbook. It didn't seem quite as exciting, somehow. After half an hour, she bagged it, stood, stretched, and asked, 'When does Michael get up?'

'When he wants to.' Shane shrugged. 'Why?' He made a face and narrowly avoided getting his arm clawed off on-screen.

'I – I figured I might go back to the dorm and get my things.'

He hit a button, and the screen paused in mid-shot again. 'What?' He gave her his full attention, which made her heart stutter, then pound harder. Guys like Shane did not give mousy little bookworms like her their full attention. Not like that.

'My stuff. From my dorm room.'

'Yeah, that's what I thought you said. Did you miss the part where the cops are looking for you?'

'Well, if I check in,' she said reasonably, 'I won't be missing anymore. I can say I slept over somewhere. Then they'll stop looking for me.'

'That's the dumbest thing I've ever heard.'

'No, it isn't. If they think I'm back in the dorm, they'll leave me to Monica, right? It could be a few days before she figures out I'm not coming back. She could forget about me by then.'

'Claire—' He frowned at her for a second or two, then shook his head. 'No way are you going over there by yourself.'

'But – they don't know where I am. If you go with me, they'll know.'

'And if you don't come back from the dorm, I'm the one

who has to explain to Michael how I let you go off and get yourself killed like a dumbass. First rule of horror movies, C. – never split up.'

'I can't just hide here. I have classes!'

'Drop 'em.'

'No way!' The whole thought horrified her. Nearly as much as *failing* them.

'Claire! Maybe you're not getting this, but *you're in trouble!* Monica wasn't kidding when she pushed you down the stairs. That was light exercise for her. Next time, she might actually get mad.'

She stood up and hoisted her backpack. 'I'm going.'

'Then you're stupid. Can't save an idiot,' Shane said flatly, and turned back to his game. He didn't look at her again as he started working the controls, firing with a vengeance. 'Don't tell them where you were last night. We don't need the hassle.'

Claire set her jaw angrily, chewed up some words, and swallowed them. Then she went into the kitchen to grab some trash bags. As she was stuffing them into her backpack, she heard the front door open and close.

'A plague upon all our houses!' Eve yelled, and Claire heard the silver jingle of her keys hitting the hall table. 'Anybody alive in here?'

'Yes!' Shane snapped. He sounded as mad as Claire felt.

'Damn,' Eve replied cheerfully. 'I was so hoping.'

Claire came out of the kitchen and met Eve on her

way up the hall. She was in plaid today – a red and black tartan skirt, black fishnet hose, clunky patent leather shoes with skulls on the toes, a white men's shirt, suspenders. And a floor-length black leather coat. Her hair was up in two pigtails, fastened with skull-themed bands. She smelt like...coffee. Fresh ground. There were some brown splatters on her shirtfront.

'Oh, hey, Claire,' she said, and blinked. 'Where are you going?'

'Funeral,' Shane said. On-screen, a zombie shrieked and died gruesomely.

'Yeah? Cool! Whose?'

'Hers.' Shane said.

Eve's eyes widened. 'Claire – you're going back?'

'Just for some of my stuff. I figure if I show up every couple of days, let people see me, they'll think I still live there...'

'Whoa, whoa, whoa, bad idea. *Bad.* No cookie. You can't go back. Not by yourself.'

'Why not?'

'They're looking for you!'

Shane put the game on pause again. 'You think I didn't already tell her that? She's not listening.'

'And you were going to let her just *go?*'

'I'm not her mom.'

'How about just her *friend!*'

He gave her a look that pretty clearly said, *Shut up.* Eve glared back, then looked at Claire. 'Seriously. You can't just... It's dangerous. You have no idea. If Monica's really gone to her Patron and tagged you, you can't just, you know, wander around.'

'I'm not wandering,' Claire pointed out. 'I'm going to my dorm, picking up some clothes, going to class, and coming home.'

'Going to *class!*' Eve made helpless little flapping motions with her black-fingernailed hands. 'No no no! No class, are you kidding?'

Shane raised his arm. 'Hello? Pointed it out already.'

'Whatever,' Claire said, and stepped around Eve to walk down the hall to the front door. She heard Shane and Eve whispering fiercely behind her, but didn't wait.

If she waited, she was going to lose her nerve.

It was only a little after noon. Plenty of time to get to school, do the rest of her classes, stuff some clothes in a garbage bag, say enough hellos to make everything OK, and get home before dark. And it was after dark that was dangerous, right? If they were serious about the vampire thing.

Which she was starting to believe, just a teeny little bit.

She opened the front door, stepped out, closed it, and walked out onto the porch. The air smelt sharp and crisp with heat. Eve must have been cooking in that coat; there were ripples of hot air rising up from the concrete sidewalk, and the sun was a pale white dot in a washed-denim sky.

She was halfway to the sidewalk, where Eve's big car lurked, when the door slammed behind her. 'Wait!' Eve blurted, and came hurrying after with the leather coat flapping in the hot wind. 'I can't let you do this.'

Claire kept walking. The sun burnt on the sore spot on her head, and on her bruises. Her ankle was still sore, but not enough to bother her that much. She'd just have to be careful.

Eve darted around her to face her, then danced backward when Claire kept walking. 'Seriously. This is dumb, Claire, and you don't strike me as somebody with a death wish. I mean, *I* have a death wish – it takes one to know one – OK, *stop*! Just *stop*!' She put out a hand, palm out, and Claire stopped short just a few inches away. 'You're going. I get that. At least let me drive you. You shouldn't be walking. This way I can call Shane if – if anything happens. And at least you'll have somebody standing by.'

'I don't want to get you guys into any trouble.' Michael had been pretty specific about that.

'That's why Shane's not coming. He's – well, he attracts trouble like TV screens attract dust. Besides, it's better not to put him anywhere near Monica. Bad things happen.' Eve unlocked the car doors. 'You have to call shotgun.'

'What?'

'You have to call shotgun to get the passenger seat.'

'But nobody else is—'

'I'm just telling you, get used to the idea, because if Shane was here? He'd already have it and you'd be in the back.'

'Um...' Claire felt stupid even trying to say it. 'Shotgun?'

'Keep practicing. Got to be fast on the trigger around here.'

The car had slick vinyl seats, cracked and peeling, and aftermarket seat belts that didn't feel any too safe. Claire tried not to slide around on the upholstery too much as the big car jolted down the narrow, bumpy road. The shops looked as dim and uninviting as Claire remembered, and the pedestrians just as hunched in on themselves.

'Eve?' she asked. 'Why do people stay here? Why don't they leave? If, you know...vampires.'

'Good question,' Eve said. 'People are funny that way. Adults, anyway. Kids pick up and leave all the time, but adults get all bogged down. Houses. Cars. Jobs. Kids. Once you have stuff, it's easy enough for the vamps to keep you on a leash. It takes a lot to make people just leave everything behind and run. Especially when they know they might not live long if they do. *Oh crap, get down!*'

Claire unhooked her seat belt and slithered down into the dark space under the dash. She didn't hesitate, because Eve hadn't been kidding – that had been pure panic in her voice. 'What is it?' She barely dared to whisper.

'Cop car,' Eve said, and didn't move her lips. 'Coming right towards us. Stay down.'

She did. Eve nervously tapped fingernails on the

hard plastic steering wheel, and then let out a sigh. 'OK, he went past. Just stay down, though. He might come back.'

Claire did, bracing herself against the bumps in the road as Eve turned towards the campus. Another minute or two passed before Eve gave her the all clear, and she flopped back into the seat and strapped in.

'That was close,' Eve said.

'What if they'd seen me?'

'Well, for starters, they'd have hauled me in to the station for interfering, confiscated my car...' Eve patted the steering wheel apologetically. 'And you'd have just... disappeared.'

'But—'

'Trust me. They're not exactly amateurs around here at making that happen. So let's just get this done and hope like hell your plan works, OK?'

Eve steered slowly through crowds of lunchtime students walking across the streets, hit the turnaround, and followed Claire's pointed directions towards the dorm.

Howard Hall didn't look any prettier today than it had yesterday. The parking lot was only half-full, and Eve cruised the big Caddy into a parking space near the back. She clicked off the ignition and squinted at the sunlight glaring off the hood. 'Right,' she said.

'You go in, get your stuff, be back here in fifteen minutes, or I start launching Operation Get Claire.'

Claire nodded. She wasn't feeling so good about this

idea, now that she was staring at the door's entrance.

'Here.' Eve was holding something out. A cell phone, thin and sleek. 'Shane's on speed dial – just hit star two. And remember, fifteen minutes, and then I freak out and start acting like your mom. OK?'

Claire took the phone and slipped it in her pocket. 'Be right back.'

She hoped she didn't sound scared. Not too scared, anyway. There was something about having friends – even brand-new ones – that helped keep the tremors out of her voice, and shakes out of her hands. *I'm not alone. I have back-up.* It was kind of a new sensation. Kind of nice, too.

She got out of the car, waved awkwardly to Eve, who waved in reply, and turned to walk back into hell.

Chapter Six

The cold air of the lobby felt dry and lifeless, after the heat outside; Claire shivered and blinked fast to adjust her eyes to the relative dimness. A few girls were in the lobby with books propped up on tables; the TV was running, but nobody was watching it.

Nobody looked at her as she walked by. She went to the glassed-in attendant booth, and the student assistant sitting inside looked up from her magazine, saw her bruises, and made a silent O with her mouth.

'Hi,' Claire said. Her voice sounded thin and dry, and she had to swallow twice. 'I'm Claire, up on four? Um, I had an accident yesterday. But I'm OK. Everything's fine.'

'You're the – they were looking for you, right?'

'Yeah. Just tell everybody I'm OK. I've got to get to class.'

'But—'

'Sorry, I'm late!' Claire hurried to the stairs and went up as fast as her sore ankle would allow. She passed a couple of girls, who gave her wide-eyed looks, but nobody said anything.

She didn't see Monica. Not on the stairs, not at the top. The hallway was empty, and all the doors were shut. Music pounded from three or four different rooms. She hurried down to the end, where her own room was, and started to unlock it.

The knob turned limply in her fingers. *Great.* That, more than any graffiti, said *Monica wuz here.*

Sure enough, the room was a wreck. What wasn't broken was dumped in piles. Books were defaced, which really hurt. Her meagre clothes had been dragged out of the closet and scattered over the floor. Some of the blouses had been ripped, but she seriously didn't care that much; she sorted through, found two or three that were intact, and stuffed them in the garbage bag. One pair of sweatpants was fine, and she added that, too. She had a lucky find of a couple of ratty old pairs of underwear that hadn't been discovered, shoved in the corner of the drawer, and added those to the sack.

The rest was another pair of shoes, what books she could salvage, and the little bag of make-up and toiletries she kept on the shelf next to the bed. Her iPod was gone. So were her CDs. No telling if that had been Monica's doing, or the work of some other dorm rat who'd scavenged later.

She looked around, swept the worst of the mess into a

corner, and grabbed the photo of her mom and dad off of the dresser to take with her.

And then she left, not bothering to try to lock the door.

Well, she thought shakily. That went OK, after all.

She was halfway down the steps when she heard voices on the second-floor landing. '—swear, it's her! You should see the black eye. Unbelievable. You really clocked her one.'

'Where the hell is she?' Monica's voice, hard-edged. 'And how come nobody came to get me?'

'We – we did!' someone protested. Someone who sounded as scared as Claire suddenly felt. She reached in her pocket, grabbed the phone, and held on to it for security. *Star two. Just press star two – Shane's not far away, and Eve's right downstairs...* 'She was up in her room. Maybe she's still there?'

Crap. There was nobody in the dorm she could trust, not now. Nobody who'd hide her, or who'd stand up for her. Claire retreated back up the steps to the third-floor landing and went to the fire stairs, flung open the door, and hurried down the concrete steps as fast as she dared, ducking to avoid the glass window at the second-floor exit. She made it to the lobby exit door sweating and trembling from the effort, with her backpack and the garbage bag dragging painfully on her sore muscles, and risked a quick look out the window to the lobby itself.

Monica-groupie Jennifer was on guard, watching the stairs. She looked tense and focused, and – Claire thought – a little bit scared, too. She kept fooling with the bracelet around her right wrist, turning it over and over. One thing was certain: Jennifer would see her the second she opened the door. And sure, maybe that wouldn't matter; maybe she could get by Jen and out the door and they wouldn't be attacking her in *public*, would they?

Watching Jennifer's face, she wasn't so sure. Not so sure at all.

The fire door a couple of floors up boomed open, and Claire flinched and looked for a place to hide. The only possible spot was under the concrete stairs. There was some kind of storage closet crammed under there, but when she tried the knob it was locked, and she didn't have Monica's lock-smashing superpowers.

And she didn't have time, anyway. There were footsteps coming down. Either she could hope the person didn't look back in the corner, or she could make a break for the door. Once again, Claire touched the phone in her pocket. *One phone call away. It's OK.* And once again, she left the phone where it was, took a deep breath, and waited.

It wasn't Monica; it was Kim Valdez, a freshman like Claire. A band geek, which put her only a tiny step higher than Claire's status as resident freak of nature. Kim kept to herself, and she didn't seem to be all that afraid of Monica or her girls; Kim didn't seem afraid of much. Not friendly, though. Just...solitary.

Kim looked back at her, blinked once or twice, then

stopped before putting her hand on the door to exit. 'Hey,' she said. She pushed back the hood of her knit shirt, revealing short, shiny black hair. 'They're looking for you.'

'Yeah, I know.'

Kim was holding her instrument case. Claire wasn't exactly clear on which instrument it was, but it was big and bulky in its scuffed black case. Kim set it down. 'Monica do that?' She gestured at Claire's bruises. Claire nodded wordlessly. 'I always knew she was a bitch. So. You need to get out of here?'

Claire nodded again, and swallowed hard. 'Will you help me?'

'Nope.' Kim flashed her a sudden, vivid grin. 'Not officially. Wouldn't be too smart.'

They had it worked out in a matter of frantic seconds: Claire zipped up in the shirt, pulled the hood down around her face, and held the instrument case by the handle.

'Higher,' Kim advised. 'Tilt it so it covers your face. Yeah, like that. Keep your head down.'

'What about my bags?'

'I'll wait a couple of minutes, then come out with 'em. Wait outside. And don't go nowhere with my cello, and I mean it. I'll kick your ass.'

'I won't,' she swore. Kim opened the door for her, and she took a gasping breath and barged out, head down, trying to look like she was late for a rehearsal.

As she passed Jennifer, the girl gave her a reflexive

glance, then dismissed her to focus back on the stairs. Claire felt a hot rush of adrenaline that felt like it might set her face on fire, and resisted the urge to run the rest of the way for the door. It seemed to take forever, her crossing the lobby to the glass doors.

She was swinging the door open when she heard Monica say, 'That freak couldn't get out of here! Check the basement. Maybe she went down the trash chute, like her stupid laundry.'

'But—' Jen's feeble protest. 'I don't want to go down to the—'

She would, though. Claire suppressed a wild grin – mostly because it still hurt too much to do that – and made it out of the dorm.

The sunlight felt amazing. It felt like...safety.

Claire took a deep breath of hot afternoon air, and walked around the corner to wait for Kim. The heat was brutal out against the sunbaked walls – suffocating. She squinted against the sun and saw the distant glitter of Eve's car, parked all the way at the back. Even hotter in there, she guessed, and wondered if Eve had got out of that Goth-required leather coat yet.

And just as she was thinking that, she saw a shadow fall across hers from behind, and half turned, but it was too late. Something soft and dark muffled her vision and clogged her mouth and nose, and pressure around her head yanked her off-balance. She screamed, or tried to, but somebody punched her in the stomach, which took care of the screaming and most of the breathing, and Claire saw a weak, watery sunshine through the weave of the cloth over her face, and shadows, and then everything got dark. Not that she fainted, or anything like that, although she was wanting to, badly.

The hot pressure of the sun went away, and then she was being dragged and carried into someplace dark and quiet.

Then down a flight of stairs.

When the moving stopped, she heard breathing and whispers, sounds of more than a few people, and then she was shoved backward, hard, and fell off-balance onto a cold concrete floor. The impact stunned her, and by the time she clawed her way out of the bag that had been jammed onto her head – a black backpack, apparently – she found there was a whole circle of girls standing around her.

She had no idea where this room was. Some kind of storage room, maybe, in the basement. It was crammed with stuff – suitcases, boxes labelled with names, all kinds of things. Some of the boxes had collapsed and spilt out pale guts of old clothes. It smelt like moulding paper, and she sneezed helplessly when her frantic gasps filled her mouth and nose with dust.

A couple of girls giggled. Most didn't do anything, and didn't look very happy to be there, either. Resigned, Claire guessed. Glad it wasn't them lying on the floor.

Monica stepped out of the corner.

'Well,' she said, and put her hands on her hips. 'Look what the cats dragged in.' She flashed Claire a cold toothpaste-ad smile, as if the rest of them weren't even here. 'You ran away, little mouse. And just when we were starting to have *fun*.'

Claire faked more sneezing, lots of it, and Monica backed away in distaste. Faking sneezing, Claire discovered, wasn't as easy as she'd thought. It hurt. But it provided time and cover for her to pull the phone out of her pocket, cover it with her body, and frantically punch 2.

She pressed SEND and shoved it between two boxes, hoping the blue glow of the buttons wouldn't attract Monica's attention. Hoping Shane wouldn't be iPoding or Xboxing and ignoring the phone. Hoping…

Just hoping.

'Oh, for God's sake. Get her up!' Monica ordered. Her Monickettes sprang forward, Jen taking one of Claire's arms, Gina the other. They hauled her up to her feet and held her there.

Monica pulled the hood back from Claire's bruised face and smiled again, taking in the damage. 'Damn, freak, you look like hell. Does it hurt?'

'What did I ever do to you?' Claire blurted. She was scared, but she was angry, too. Furious. There were seven girls standing around doing *nothing* because they were scared, and of what? *Monica*? What the hell gave the Monicas the right to run the world?

'You know exactly what you did. You tried to make me look stupid,' Monica said.

'*Tried?*' Claire shot back, which was dumb, but she

couldn't stop the impulse. It got her hit in the face. Hard. Right on top of the first bruise, which took away her breath in slow throbs of white-hot agony. Everything felt funny, rattled by the impact of Monica's jab. Claire felt pressure on her arms, and realised that the Monickettes were holding her up. She put some stiffness back into her legs, opened her eyes, and glared at Monica.

'How come you live in Howard?' she asked.

Monica, inspecting her knuckles for signs of bruising, looked up in honest surprise.

'What?'

'Your family's rich, right? You could be living in an apartment. Or in a sorority house. How come you live in Howard Hall with the rest of us freaks?' She caught her breath at the sudden cold blaze in Monica's eyes. 'Unless you're a freak, too. A freak who gets off on hurting somebody weaker than you. A freak your family's ashamed of. Somebody they hide here where they don't have to look at you.'

'Shut up,' Jennifer hissed, low in her ear. 'Don't be stupid! She'll kill you – don't you get it?'

She jerked her head away. 'I heard you went away to college,' Claire continued. Her stomach was rolling, she felt like she was going to puke and die, but all she had to do was stall for time. Shane would come. Eve would come. Maybe Michael. She could imagine Michael standing in the doorway, with those ice-cold eyes and that angel's face, staring holes through Monica. Yeah, that would *rock*. Monica wouldn't look so big then. 'What's the matter? Couldn't you cut it? I'm not surprised – anybody who thinks World War Two was in China isn't exactly going to impress—'

She saw the punch coming this time, and ducked as best she could. Monica's fist smashed into her forehead, which hurt, but it must have hurt Monica a whole lot more, because she let out a shrill little scream and backed off, clutching her right hand in her left. That made the horrible throbbing in Claire's head almost OK.

'Careful,' Claire gasped, nearly giggling. The scab on her lip had broken open, and she licked blood from her lips. 'Don't break a nail! I'm not worth it, remember?'

'Got *that* right!' Monica snarled. 'Let that bitch go. What are you waiting for? Go on, do it! Do you think that wimp's going to *hurt* me?'

The Monickettes looked at each other, clearly wondering if their queen bee had lost her mind, then let go of Claire's arms and stepped back. Jennifer bumped into the towering column of boxes, spilling an avalanche of dust and old papers, but when Claire looked at her, Jennifer was staring at a spot between the boxes.

The spot where Claire had hidden the phone. Jen had to have seen it, and Claire gasped out loud, suddenly a whole lot more afraid than she'd thought she was.

'What the hell are *you* looking at?' Monica snarled at Jen, and Jen very deliberately turned her back on the incriminating phone, folded her arms, and stood there blocking it from view. Not looking at Claire at all. *Wow. That's*...what? Not lucky, exactly. Jennifer had shown some cracks already. And maybe she wasn't a complete convert to the First Church of Monica.

Maybe Monica had just pissed her off one too many times. Not that she would be stepping in on Claire's side anytime soon.

Claire wiped the blood from her lip and looked at the other girls. The ones who were standing, uneasy and indecisive. Monica had been challenged and, so far, hadn't exactly delivered the smackdown everybody – Claire included – had expected. Kind of weird, really. Unless Claire really struck some nerve besides the ones running through Monica's knuckles.

Monica was rubbing her hand, looking at Claire as if she'd never seen her before. Assessing her. She said, 'Nobody's told you the facts of life, *Claire*. The fact is, if you suddenly just up and disappear…?' She jerked her pretty, pointed chin at the dusty towers of boxes. 'Nobody but the janitor's ever going to know or care. You think Mommy and Daddy are going to get all upset? Maybe they would, but by the time they spend their last dime putting your picture on milk cartons and chasing down rumours of how you ran off with somebody else's boyfriend? They're going to hate to even think about you. Morganville's got it down to a science, making people disappear. They never disappear *here*. Always somewhere else.'

Monica wasn't taunting her. That was the scary part. She was talking evenly, quietly, as if they were two equals having a friendly conversation.

'You want to know why I live in Howard?' she continued. 'Because in this town, I can live anywhere I want. Any way I want. And you – you're just a walking organ donor. So take my advice, Claire. Don't get in my face, because if you do, you won't have one for long. Are we clear?'

Claire nodded slowly. She didn't dare look away. Monica reminded her of a feral dog, one that would jump for your throat the second you showed weakness. 'We're clear,' she said. 'You're kind of a psycho. I get that.'

'I might be,' Monica agreed, and gave her a slow, strange smile. 'You're one smart little freak. Now run away, smart little freak, before I change my mind and stick you in one of these old suitcases for some architect to find a hundred years from now.'

Claire blinked. 'Archaeologist.'

Monica's eyes turned winter cold. 'Oh, you'd *better* start running away now.'

Claire went back to where Jennifer was standing, and reached behind her to drag the phone out from between the boxes. She held it up to Monica. 'Speak clearly for the microphone. I want to make sure my friends get every word.'

For a second, nobody moved, and then Monica laughed. 'Damn, freak. You're going to be fun.' She glanced away from Claire, behind her. 'Not until I say so.'

Claire looked over her shoulder. Gina was standing there, *right there*, and she had some kind of metal bar in her hand.

Oh my God. There was something awful and cold in Gina's eyes.

'She'll get hers,' Monica said. 'And we'll get to watch. But hey, why hurry? I haven't had this much fun in years.'

Claire's legs felt like they'd suddenly turned into overcooked spaghetti. She wanted to throw up, wanted to cry, and didn't dare do anything but pretend to be brave. They'd kill her down here if they thought she was bluffing.

She walked past Gina, between two girls who wouldn't meet her eyes at all, and put her hand on the doorknob. As she did, she glanced down at the phone's display.

No signal.

She opened the door, walked outside, and found her bags dumped on the grass where she'd been abducted. She pocketed the phone, picked up the bags, and walked across the parking lot to Eve's car. Eve was still sitting in the driver's seat, looking clown-pale and scared.

Claire tossed her bag in the back as Eve asked, 'What happened? Did they see you?'

'No,' Claire said. 'No problems. I've got class. I'll see you later. Thanks, Eve. Um – here's your phone.' She passed it over. Eve took it, still frowning. 'I'll be home before dark.'

'Better be,' Eve said. 'Seriously, Claire. You look – weird.'

Claire laughed. 'Me? Check the mirror.'

Eve flipped her off, but the same way she'd have

flipped off Shane. Claire grabbed her backpack, closed the door, and watched Eve's big black car cruise away. Heading back to work, she guessed.

She got halfway to her chem lab when her reaction hit her, and she sat down on a bench and cried silently into her hands.

Oh my God. Oh my God, I want to go home! She wasn't sure if that meant back to Michael's house, or all the way home, back in her room with her parents watching over her.

I can't quit. She really couldn't. She never in her life had been able to, even when it might have been the smart thing to do.

She wiped her swollen eyes and went to class.

Nobody killed her that afternoon.

After the first couple of hours, she quit expecting it to happen, and focused on class. Her back-to-back labs weren't too much of a disaster, and she actually knew the answers in history. *Bet Monica wouldn't*, she thought, and looked guiltily around the classroom to see if Monica was there, or one of her crew. It wasn't a big class. She didn't see anybody who'd been in the basement.

She made it to the grocery store after class without getting killed, too. Nobody jumped her while she was picking out lettuce and tomatoes, or while she was in line for checkout. She thought the guy at the meat counter had looked suspicious, though.

She walked back to the Glass House, watching for vampires in the fading afternoon and feeling pretty stupid for even thinking about it. She didn't see anybody except other college students, strolling along with bulging backpacks. Most of them travelled in bunches. Once she got past the area that catered to students, the stores were closed, lights off, and what few people were walking were hurrying.

At the corner of *Gone with the Wind* and *The Munsters*, the front gate was open. She closed it behind her, unlocked the door with the shiny new key that she'd found on her dresser that morning, and slammed the door behind her.

There was a shadow standing at the end of the hallway. A tall, broad shadow in a grungy yellow T-shirt and low-slung, faded jeans frayed at the bottom. A shadow in bare feet.

Shane.

He just looked at her for a few seconds, then said, 'Eve put your crap up in your room.'

'Thanks.'

'What's that?'

'Stuff for dinner.'

He cocked his head slightly, still staring at her. 'For a smart girl, you do some stupid things. You know that?'

'I know.' She walked towards him. He didn't move.

'Eve says you never saw Monica.'

'That's what I said.'

'You know what? I'm not buying it.'

'You know what?' she shot back. 'I don't care. Excuse me.' She ducked past him, into the kitchen, and set her bags down. Her hands were shaking. She balled them into fists and started setting out things on the counter. Ground beef. Lettuce. Tomatoes. Onions. Refried beans. Hot sauce, the kind she liked, anyway. Cheese. Sour cream. Taco shells.

'Let me guess,' Shane said from the doorway. 'You're making Chinese.'

She didn't answer. She was still too pissed and – all of a sudden – too scared. Scared of what, she didn't know. Everything. Nothing. Herself.

'Anything I can do?' His voice sounded different. Quieter, gentler, almost kind.

'Chop onions,' she said, although she knew that wasn't exactly what he meant. Still, he came over, picked up the onions, and grabbed a huge scary-looking knife from a drawer. 'You have to peel it first.'

He shot her a dirty look, just like he would have Eve, and got to work.

'Um – I should probably call my mom,' Claire said. 'Can I use the phone?'

'You pay for long distance.'

'Sure.'

He shrugged, reached over, and grabbed the cordless phone, then pitched it underhanded to her. She nearly dropped it, but was kind of proud she didn't. She got out a big iron skillet from under the cabinet and put it on the counter, heated up the burner, and found some oil. As it was warming, she read over the thin little recipe book she'd bought at the store one more time, then dialled the phone.

Her mom answered on the second ring. 'Yes?' It was never *hello* with her mother.

'Mom, it's Claire.'

'Claire! Baby, where have you been? I've been trying to call you for days!'

'Classes,' she said. 'Sorry. I'm not home that much.'

'Are you sleeping enough? If you don't get enough rest, you'll get sick – you know how you are—'

'Mom, I'm fine.' Claire frowned down at the recipe on the counter in front of her. What did *sauté* mean, exactly? Was it like frying? *Diced*, she understood. That was just cutting things into cubes, and Shane was doing that already. 'Really. It's all OK now.'

'Claire, I know it's hard. We really didn't want you to go even just the few hundred miles to TPU, honey. If you want to come back home, your dad and I would be so glad to have you back!'

'Honestly, Mom, I don't – I'm fine. It's OK. Classes are really good' – that was stretching the truth – 'and I've made friends here. They're looking out for me.'

'You're sure.'

'Yes, Mom.'

'Because I worry. I know you're very mature for your age but—'

Shane opened his mouth to say something. Claire made frantic *NO NO NO* motions at him, pointing at the phone. *Mom!* she mouthed. Shane held up both hands in surrender and kept chopping. Mom was still talking. Claire had missed some of it, but she didn't think it really mattered exactly. '—boys, right?'

Wow. Mom radar worked even at this distance. 'What, Mom?'

'Your dorm doesn't allow boys to come up to the rooms, does it? There's someone on duty at the desk to make sure?'

'Yes, Mom. Howard Hall has somebody on duty twenty-four/seven to keep the nasty evil boys out of our rooms.' She hadn't actually lied, Claire decided. That was completely true. The fact that she wasn't actually *living* in Howard Hall...well, that wasn't really something she needed to throw in, right?

'It's not a laughing matter. You've been very sheltered, Claire, and I don't want you to—'

'Mom, I have to go. I need to eat dinner and I have a ton of studying to do. How's Dad?'

'Dad's just fine, honey. He says hello. Oh, come on, Les, get up and say hello to your very smart daughter. It won't break your back.'

Shane handed her a bowl full of diced onions. Claire cradled the phone against her ear and dropped a handful of them into the pan. They started sizzling immediately, much to her panic; she lifted the pan off the burner and almost dropped the phone.

'Hi, kiddo. How are classes?' That was Dad. Not *How was your day?* or *Have you made any friends?* No, his philosophy had always been, *Eyes on the prize; the other stuff just gets in your way.*

And she loved him anyway. 'Classes are great, Daddy.'

'Are you frying something? Do they let you have hot plates in the dorm? Didn't in my day, I can tell you...'

'Um...no, I just opened a Coke.' OK, that was a straight-up lie. She hastily put the pan down, walked to the fridge, and pulled out a cold Coke so she could open it. There. Retroactively truthful. 'How are you feeling?'

'Feel fine. Wish everybody would stop worrying about me, not like I'm the first man in history to have a little surgery.'

'I know, Daddy.'

'Doctors say I'm fine.'

'That's great.'

'Gonna have to go, Claire, the game's on. You're OK down there, aren't you?'

'Yes. I'm just fine. Daddy—'

'What is it, honey?'

Claire bit her lip and sipped Coke, indecisive. 'Um... do you know anything about Morganville? History, that kind of thing?'

'Doing research, eh? Some kind of report? No, I don't know much. The university's been there for nearly a hundred years – that's all I know about it. I know you're on fire to get to the bigger schools, but I think you need to spend a couple of years close to home. We talked about all that.'

'I know. I was just wondering... It's an interesting town, that's all.'

'OK, then. You let us know what you find out. Your mother wants to say goodbye.' Dad never did. By the time Claire got out 'Bye, Dad!' he was already gone, and Mom was back on the line. 'Honey, you call us if you get worried about anything, OK? Oh, call us whatever happens. We love you!'

'Love you, too, Mom. Bye.'

She put the phone down and stared at the sizzling onions, then the recipe. When the onions turned transparent, she dumped in the ground beef.

'So, finished lying to the folks?' Shane asked, and reached around Claire to snag a bite of grated cheese from the bowl on the counter. 'Tacos. Brilliant. Damn, I'm glad I voted somebody in with skills.'

'I heard that, Shane!' Eve yelled from the living room, just as the door slammed. Shane winced. 'Do your own bathroom cleaning this weekend!'

Shane winced. 'Truce!'

'Thought so.'

Eve came in, still flushed from the heat outside. She'd sweated off most of her make-up, and underneath it, she looked surprisingly young and sweet. 'Oh my God, that looks like real food!'

'Tacos,' Shane said proudly, as if it were his idea. Claire elbowed him in the ribs, or tried to. His ribs were a lot more solid than her elbow. 'Ow,' he said. Not as if it hurt.

Claire glanced out the window. Night was falling fast, the way it did in Texas at the end of the day – furious burning sun all of a sudden giving way to a warm, sticky twilight. 'Is Michael here?' she asked.

'Guess so.' Shane shrugged. 'He's always here for dinner.'

The three of them got everything ready, and sometime midway through the assembly-line process they'd developed – Claire putting meat in taco shells, Eve adding toppings, Shane spooning beans onto the plates – a fourth pair of hands added itself to the line. Michael looked as if he'd just got up and showered – wet hair, sleepy eyes, beads of water still sliding down to soak the collar of his black knit shirt. Like Shane, he was wearing jeans, but he'd gone formal, with actual shoes.

'Hey,' he greeted them. 'This looks good.'

'Claire did it,' Eve jumped in as Shane opened his mouth. 'Don't *even* let Shane take credit.'

'Wasn't going to!' Shane looked offended.

'Riiiiiight.'

'I chopped. What did you do?'

'Cleaned up after you, like always.'

Michael looked over at Claire and made a face. She laughed and picked up her plate; Michael picked up his, and followed her out into the living room.

Someone – Michael, she guessed – had cleared the big wood table next to the bookcases, and set up four chairs around it. The stuff that had been piled there – video game cases, books, sheet music – had been dumped in other places, with a cheerful disregard for order. (Maybe, she amended, that had been Shane's idea.) She set her plate down, and Eve promptly slapped her own down next to Claire's and slid a cold Coke across to her, along with a fork and napkin. Michael and Shane strolled back in, took seats, and began shovelling in food like – well, like boys. Eve nibbled. Claire, who was surprisingly hungry, found herself on her second taco before Eve had got through her first one.

Shane was already headed back for more.

'Hey, dude,' he said as he returned with a reloaded plate, 'when are you going to get a gig again?'

Michael stopped chewing, flashed a look at Eve, then Claire, and then finished the bite before saying, 'When I'm ready.'

'Pussy. You had a bad night, Mike. Get back on the horse, or whatever.' Eve frowned at Shane, and shook her head. Shane ignored her. 'Seriously, man. You can't let them get you down.'

'I'm not,' Michael said. 'Not everything is about beating your head against the wall until it breaks.'

'Just most things.' Shane sighed. 'Whatever. You let me know when you want to stop hermitting.'

'I'm not hermitting. I'm practising.'

'Like you don't play good enough. Please.'

'I get no respect,' Michael said. Shane, busy taking another crunchy bite, rubbed his thumb and forefinger together. 'Yeah, I know, world's smallest violin playing just for me. Change the subject. How was that hot date with Lisa, anyway? Rented shoes turn her on or what?'

'It's Laura,' Shane said. 'Yeah, she was hot, all right,

but I think she had the hots for you – kept saying how she saw you over at the Waterhouse last year and you were all, like, wow, amazing. It was like a *ménage a trois*, only you weren't there, thank God.'

Michael looked smug. 'Shut up and eat.'

Shane shot him the finger.

All in all, it was a pretty good time.

Michael and Eve washed dishes, having lost out on the coin toss, and Claire hovered in the living room, not sure what she wanted to do. Studying sounded ...boring, which surprised her. Shane was concentrating on the video game selection, bare feet propped up on the coffee table. Without looking directly at Claire, he asked, 'You want to see something cool?'

'Sure,' she said. She expected him to put a game in, but he dumped it back in the pile, got up off the couch, and padded up the stairs. She stood at the bottom, staring up, wondering what to do. Shane appeared at the top of the stairs again and gestured, and she followed.

The second floor was quiet, of course, and dimly lit; she blinked and saw Shane already halfway down the hall. Was he heading for her room? Not that she didn't have a crazy hot picture in her head of sitting on the bed with him, making out...and she had no idea why that popped into her head, except that, well, he was just... yeah.

Shane moved aside a picture hanging on the wall

between her room and Eve's, and pressed a button underneath.

And a door opened on the other side of the wall. It was built into the panelling, and she'd never have even known it was there. She gasped, and Shane beamed like he'd invented the wheel. 'Cool, huh? This damn house is full of crap like that. Trust me, in Morganville it pays to be up on the hiding places.' He pushed open the door, revealed another set of stairs, and padded up them. She expected them to be dusty, but they weren't; the wood was clean and polished. Shane's feet left prints of the ball of his foot and his toes.

It was a narrow pitch of just eight steps, half a story, really, and there was another door at the top. Shane opened it and flipped on a switch just inside. 'First time I saw this, and the room back of the pantry, I figured, yep. Vampire house. What do you think?'

If she believed in vampires, he might have been right. It was a small room, no windows, and it was...old. It wasn't just the stuff in it, which was antique and dark; it had this sense of...something ancient, something not quite right. And it was cold. Cold, in the middle of a Texas heat wave.

She shivered. 'Does everybody know about this room?'

'Oh yeah. Eve says it's haunted. Can't really blame her. It creeps me the hell out, too. Cool, though. We'd have stuck you in here when the cops came, only they'd have seen you through the windows coming out of the kitchen. They're nosy bastards.' Shane wandered across the thick

Persian carpet to flop on the dark red Victorian couch. Dust rose in a cloud, and he waved it off, coughing. 'So what do you think? Think Michael sleeps off his evil-undead days in here, or what?'

She blinked. 'What?'

'Oh, come on. You think he's one of them, right? 'Cause he doesn't show up during the day?'

'I – I don't think anything!'

Shane nodded, eyes downcast. 'Right. You weren't sent here.'

'Sent – sent here by *who*?'

'I got to thinking... The cops were looking for you, but maybe they were looking for you to make us want to keep you here, instead of pitch you out. So which is it? Are you working for them?'

'Them?' she echoed thinly. 'Them, who?' Shane suddenly looked at her, and she shivered again. He wasn't like Monica, not at all, but he wasn't playing around, either. 'Shane, I don't know what you mean. I came to Morganville to go to school, and got beaten up, and I came here because I was scared. If you don't believe me – well, then I guess I'll go. Hope you liked the tacos.'

She went to the door, and stopped, confused.

There wasn't a doorknob.

Behind her, Shane said quietly, 'The reason I think this is a vampire's room? You can't get out of it unless you know the secret. That's real convenient, if you like to bring victims up here for a little munch session.'

She whirled around, expecting to see him standing

there with that huge knife he'd used on the onions, and she'd broken the first rule of horror movies, hadn't she, or was it the second one? She'd trusted someone she shouldn't have...

But he was still sitting on the couch, slumped at ease, arms flung over the back on both sides.

Not even looking at her.

'Let me out,' she said. Her heart was hammering.

'In a minute. First, you tell me the truth.'

'I *have!*' And, to her fury and humiliation, she started to cry. Again. 'Dammit! You think I'm trying to hurt you? Hurt Michael? How could I? *I'm the one everybody hurts!*'

He looked at her then, and she saw the hardness melt away. His voice was a lot gentler when he spoke. 'And if I was somebody who wanted to kill Michael, I'd put somebody like you in to do it. Be real easy for you to kill somebody, Claire. Poison some food, slip a knife in his back...and I have to look out for Michael.'

'I thought he looked out for you.' She swiped angrily at her eyes. 'Why do you think somebody wants to kill him?'

Shane raised his eyebrows. 'Always somebody wanting to kill a vampire.'

'But – he's not. Eve said—'

'Yeah, I know he's not a vampire, but he doesn't get up during the day, he doesn't go out of the house, and I can't get him to tell me what happened, so he might as well be. And somebody's going to think so, sooner or later. Most people in Morganville are either Protected or clueless – kind of like you can raise rabbits for either pets or meat. But some of them fight back.'

She blinked the last of the brief storm of tears away. 'Like you?'

He cocked his head to one side. 'Maybe. How about you? You a fighter, Claire?'

'I'm not working for anybody. And I wouldn't kill Michael even if he was a vampire.'

Shane laughed. 'Why not? Besides the fact that he'd snap you in two like a twig if he was.'

'Because – because—' She couldn't put it into words, exactly. 'Because I like him.'

Shane watched her for another few, long seconds, and then pressed a raised spot on the head of the lion-carving armrest of the couch.

The door clicked and popped open half an inch.

'Good enough for me,' he said. 'So. Dessert?'

Chapter Seven

She couldn't sleep.

Maybe it was the memory of that creepy little Gothic room – which she suspected Eve really, deeply loved – but all of a sudden, her lovely cosy room seemed full of shadows, and the creaks of old wood in the wind sounded...stealthy. *Maybe the house eats people*, Claire thought, lying there alone in the dark, watching the bone-thin shadows of branches shudder on the far wall. The wind made twigs tap her window, like something trying to get in. Eve had said vampires couldn't get in, but what if they could? What if they were already inside? What if Michael...?

She heard a soft, silvery note, and knew that Michael was playing downstairs. Something about that helped – pushed the shadows back, turned the sounds into something normal and soothing. It was just a house, and they were just kids sharing it, and if there was anything wrong, well, it was outside.

She must have slept then, but it didn't feel like it; some noise startled her awake, and when Claire checked the clock next to her bed it was close to five thirty. The sky wasn't light outside, but it wasn't totally dark, either; the stars were faded, soft sparkles in a sky gradually turning dark blue.

Michael's guitar was still going, very quietly. Didn't he ever sleep? Claire slid out of bed, tossed a blanket over her shoulders over the T-shirt she wore to bed, and shuffled out and into the still-dark hallway. As she passed the hidden door she glanced at it and shivered, then continued on to the bathroom. Once she'd got that out of the way – and brushed her hair – she crept quietly down the steps and sat down, blanket around her, listening to Michael play.

His head was down, and he was deep into it; she watched his fingers move light and quick on the strings, his body rock slowly with the rhythm, and felt a deep sense of…safety. Nothing bad could happen around Michael. She just knew it.

Next to him, a clock beeped an alarm. He looked up, startled, and slapped it off, then got up and put his guitar away. She watched, puzzled… Did he have someplace to be? Or did he actually have to set an alarm to go to bed? Wow, that was obsession…

Michael stood, watching the clock as if it were his personal enemy, and then he turned and walked over to the window.

The sky was the colour of dark turquoise now, all but the strongest stars faded. Michael, holding a beer in his hand, drank the rest of the bottle and put it down on the table, crossed his arms, and waited.

Claire was about to ask him what he was waiting for when the first ray of sun crept up in a blinding orange knife, and Michael gasped and hunched over, pressing on his stomach.

Claire lunged to her feet, startled and afraid for the look of sheer agony on his face. The movement caught his attention, and he jerked his head towards her, blue eyes wide.

'No,' he moaned, and pitched forward to his hands and knees, gasping. 'Don't.'

She ignored that and jumped down the stairs to run to his side, but once she was there she didn't know what to do, didn't have any idea how to help him. Michael was breathing in deep, aching gasps, in terrible pain.

She put her hand on his back, felt his fever-hot skin burning through the thin cloth, and heard him make a sound like nothing she'd ever heard in her life.

Like someone dying, she thought in panic, and opened her mouth to scream for Shane, Eve, *anybody.*

Her hand suddenly went right through him. The scream, for whatever reason, locked tight in her throat as Michael – *transparent* Michael – looked up at her with despair and desperation in his eyes.

'Oh, God, don't tell them.' His voice came from a

long, long way off, a whisper that faded on the shafts of morning sun.

And so did he.

Claire, mouth still open, utterly unable to speak, waved her hand slowly through the thin air where Michael Glass had been standing. Slowly, then faster. The air felt cold around her, like she was standing in a blast from an air conditioner, and the chill slowly faded.

Like Michael.

'Oh my God,' she whispered, and clapped both hands over her mouth.

And muffled the scream that she had to let out or explode.

She might have blacked out a little, because next thing she knew, she was sitting on the couch, next to Michael's guitar case, and she felt kind of funny. Bad funny, as if her brain had turned liquid and sloshed around in her head.

Weirdly calm, though. She reached over and touched the leather cover of his guitar case. It felt real. When she flipped up the latches and pulled her shaking fingers across the strings, they made a wistful sort of whisper.

He's a ghost. Michael's a ghost.

He wasn't a ghost. How could he be a ghost, if he sat here – right here! – at the table and ate dinner? Tacos! What kind of ghost ate tacos? What kind of...?

Her hand went right through him. *Right through him.*

But he was real. She'd touched him. She'd—

Her hand went right through him.

'Don't panic,' she said numbly, out loud. 'Just...don't panic. There's some explanation...' Yeah, right. She'd stumble over to Professor Wu's physics class and ask. She could just imagine how *that* would go over. They'd toss a net over her and pump her full of Prozac or whatever.

He'd said, *Oh, God, don't tell them.* Tell who? Tell...? Was he gone? Was he *dead?*

She was about carried away by panic again, and then something stopped it cold. Something silly, really.

The alarm clock sitting on the table next to the sofa. The one that had gone off just a few minutes ago.

The one that had warned Michael that sunrise was coming.

This happens...every day. He hadn't acted like it was odd, just painful.

Shane and Eve had both said that Michael slept days. They were both night owls; they were sound asleep right now, and wouldn't be up for hours yet. Michael could have...disappeared...daily like this with nobody paying attention.

Until she came along, and got nosy.

Don't tell them. Why not? What was so secret?

She was crazy. That was the only rational explanation. But if she was crazy, she wasn't rational...

Claire curled up on the sofa, shivering, and felt cold air brush over her again. Ice-cold. She sat up. 'Michael?' she blurted, and sat very still. The chill went away, then brushed over her again. 'I – I think I can feel you.

Are you still here?' Another second or two without the icy draft, and then it drifted across her skin. 'So – you can see us?' Yes, she figured, since the warm-cold cycle repeated. 'You don't go away during the day? Oh – um, stay where you are if it's no, OK?' The chill stayed steady. 'Wow. That's – harsh.' A yes, and weirdly, she felt a little cheered. OK, she was having a conversation with a *breeze*, but at least she didn't feel alone. 'You don't want me to tell Shane and Eve?' Clearly, a no. If anything, it got colder. 'Is there anything – anything I can do?' Also a no. 'Michael – will you come back?' Yes. 'Tonight?' Yes, again. 'We are *so* going to talk.'

The chill withdrew completely. *Yes.*

She collapsed back on the sofa, feeling giddy and strange and exhausted. There was a ratty old blanket piled near the guitar case; she carefully moved the instrument over to the table (and imagined an invisible Michael following her anxiously the whole way), then wrapped herself in the blanket and let herself drift off into sleep, with the ticking of the grandfather clock and memories of Michael's guitar as a soundtrack.

That day, Claire went to class. Eve argued with her; Shane didn't. Nothing much happened, although Claire spotted Monica twice on campus. Monica was surrounded by admirers, both male and female, and didn't have time for grudges. Claire kept her head down and stayed out of any deserted areas. It was an early afternoon for her – no labs – and although she wanted to get home and wait around for Michael to show up (and boy, she wanted to see how that happened!) she knew she'd drive herself crazy, and make Shane suspicious.

As she walked in that general direction, she spotted the small coffee shop, wedged in between the skateboard shop and a used-book store. Common Grounds. That was where Eve worked, and she'd said to stop by...

The bell rang with a silvery tinkle as Claire pushed open the door, and it was like walking into the living room of the Glass House, only a little more Gothic. Black leather sofas and chairs, thick colourful rugs, accent walls in beige and blood red, lots of nooks and crannies. There were five or six students scattered at café tables and built-in desks. None looked up from their books or computers. The whole place smelt like coffee, a constant simmering warmth.

Claire stood for a second, indecisive, and then walked over to an empty desk and dumped her backpack before going to the counter. There were two people behind the waist-high barrier. One was Eve, of course, looking perky and doll-like with her dye-dark hair in two pigtails, eyes rimmed with liner, and lipstick a dramatic Goth black. She was wearing a black mesh shirt over a red camisole, and she grinned when she spotted Claire.

The other was an older man, tall, thin, with greying curly hair that fell nearly to his shoulders. He had a nice, square face, wide dark eyes, and a ruby earring in his left ear. Hippie to the core, Claire guessed. He smiled, too.

'Hey, it's Claire!' Eve said, and hurried around the counter to slip her arm around Claire's shoulders.

'Claire, this is Oliver. My boss.'

Claire nodded hesitantly. He looked nice, but hey, a boss. Bosses made her nervous, like parents. 'Hello, sir.'

'Sir?' Oliver had a deep voice, and an even deeper laugh. 'Claire, you've got to learn about me. I'm not a *sir*. Believe me.'

'That's true.' Eve nodded wisely. 'He's a *dude*. You'll like him. Hey, want a coffee? My treat?'

'I – uh—'

'Don't touch the stuff, right?' Eve rolled her eyes. 'One non-coffee drink, coming up. How about hot cocoa? Chai? Tea?'

'Tea, I guess.'

Eve went back behind the counter and did some stuff, and within a couple of minutes, a big white cup and saucer appeared in front of Claire, with a tea bag steeping in the steaming water. 'On the house. Well, actually, on me, because, yikes, boss is right here.'

Oliver, who was working on some complicated machine that Claire guessed was something that made cappuccino, shook his head and grinned to himself. Claire watched him curiously. He looked a little bit like a distant cousin she'd met from France; the same kind of hook nose, anyway. She wondered if he'd been a professor at the university, or just a perpetual student. Either looked possible.

'I heard you had some trouble,' Oliver said, still

concentrating on unscrewing parts on the machine. 'Girls in the dorm.'

'Yeah,' she admitted, and felt her cheeks burn. 'Everything's OK, though.'

'I'm sure it is. Listen, though: if you have trouble like that, you come here and tell me about it. I'll make sure it stops.' He said it with absolute assurance. She blinked, and his dark eyes moved to rest on hers for a few seconds. 'I'm not without influence around here. Eve tells me that you're very gifted. We can't have some bad apples driving you off.'

'Um...thanks?' She didn't mean to make it a question; it just came out that way. 'Thanks. I will.'

Oliver nodded and went back to his work dissecting the coffeemaker. Claire found a seat not far away. Eve slipped out from behind the counter and pulled up a chair next to her, leaning forward, all restless energy. 'Isn't he *great*?' she asked. 'He means it, you know. He's got some kind of pipeline to—' She made a V sign with her fingers. V, for *vampires*. 'They listen to him. He's good to have on your side.'

Claire nodded, dunking the tea bag and watching the dark stains spread through the water. 'You talk about me to everybody?'

Eve looked stricken. 'No! Of course I don't! I just – well, I was worried. I thought maybe Oliver knew something that... Claire, you said it yourself – they tried to kill you. Somebody ought to be doing something about that.'

'Him?'

'Why not him?' Eve jittered her leg, tapping the thick heel on her black Mary Janes. Her hose had green and black horizontal stripes. 'I mean, I get that you're all about being self-sufficient, but come on. A little help never hurts.'

She wasn't wrong. Claire sighed, took the tea bag out, and sipped the hot drink. Not bad, even on a blazing-hot day.

'Stay,' Eve said. 'Study. It's a really good place for that. I'll drive you home, OK?'

Claire nodded, suddenly grateful; there were too many places to get lost on the way home, if Monica had noticed her after all. She didn't like the idea of walking three blocks between the student streets, where things were bright and busy, and the colourless hush of the rest of the town, where the Glass House lived. She put the tea to one side and unpacked books. Eve went back to take orders from three chattering girls wearing sorority T-shirts. They were rude to her, and giggled behind her back. Eve didn't seem to notice – or if she did, she didn't care.

Oliver did. He put down the tools he was using, as Eve bustled around getting drinks, and stared steadily at the girls. One by one, they went quiet. It wasn't anything he did, exactly, just the steadiness of the way he watched them.

When Eve took their money, each one of the girls meekly thanked her and took her change.

They didn't stay.

Oliver smiled slightly, picked up a piece of the disassembled machine, and polished it before reattaching it. He must have known Claire was watching, because he said, in a very low voice, 'I don't tolerate rudeness. Not in my place.'

She wasn't sure if he was talking about the girls, or her staring at him, so she hurriedly went back to her books.

Quadratic equations were a great way to pass the afternoon.

Eve's shift ended at nine, just as the nightlife at Common Grounds picked up; Claire, not used to the babble, chatter, and music, couldn't keep her mind on her books anyway. She was glad of an excuse to go when Eve's replacement – a surly-looking pimpled boy about Shane's age – took her place behind the counter. Eve went in the back to get her stuff, and Claire packed up her backpack.

'Claire.' She looked up, startled that somebody remembered her name other than, well, people who wanted to kill her, and saw Kim Valdez, from the dorm.

'Hey, Kim,' she said. 'Thanks for helping me out—'

Kim looked mad. Really mad. 'Don't even start! You left my cello just laying around out there! Do you have any idea how hard I worked for that thing? Way to be an asshole!'

'But – I didn't—'

'Don't lie. You bugged out somewhere. Hope you got

your bags and crap. I left them out there just like you left my stuff.' Kim jammed her hands in her pockets and glared at her. '*Don't* ask me for any favours again. Right?'

She didn't wait for an answer, just moved off towards the counter. Claire sighed. 'I won't,' she said, and zipped the backpack. She waited for a few minutes, but the crowd was getting thicker, and Eve was nowhere in sight. She stood up, stepped out of the way of a group of boys, and backed into a table in the shadowy corner.

'Hey,' a voice said softly. She looked back and saw a coffee cup tipping over, and a pale, long-fingered hand catching it before it did. The hand belonged to a young man – she couldn't really call him a boy – with thick dark hair and light-coloured eyes, who'd claimed the table when she wasn't looking.

'Sorry,' she said. He smiled at her and licked a couple of drops of coffee from the back of his hand with a pale tongue.

She felt something streak hot down her backbone, and shivered. He smiled wider.

'Sit,' he said. 'I'm Brandon. You?'

'Claire,' she heard herself say, and even though she didn't intend to, she sat, backpack thumping on the floor beside her. 'Um, hi.'

'Hello.' His eyes weren't just light; they were – pale, a shade of blue so faint it was almost silver. Scary-cool. 'Are you here alone, Claire?'

'I – no, I – ah—' She was babbling like an idiot, and

didn't know what was wrong with her. The way he was looking at her made her feel naked. Not in a secretly cool, wow-I-think-he-likes-me way, but in a way that made her want to hide and cover herself. 'I'm here with a friend.'

'A friend,' he said, and reached across to take her hand. She wanted to pull it back – she *did* – but somehow she couldn't get control of herself. All she could do was watch as he turned her hand palm down, and brought it to his mouth to kiss. The warm, damp pressure of his lips on her fingers made her shiver all over.

Then he brushed his thumb across her wrist. 'Where is your bracelet, little Claire? Good girls wear their bracelets. Don't you have one?'

'I—' There was something sick and terrible happening in her head, something that made her tell the truth. 'No. I don't have one.' Because she knew now what Brandon was, and she was sorry she'd laughed at Eve, sorry she'd ever doubted any of it.

You'll get yours, Monica had promised.

Well, here it was.

'I see.' Brandon's eyes seemed to get even paler, until they were pure white with tiny black dots for pupils. She couldn't breathe. Couldn't scream. 'The only question is who will have you, then. And since I'm here first—'

He let go of her, both her hand and her mind, and she fell backward with a breathless little gasp. Somebody was standing behind her chair, a solid warmth, and Brandon was frowning and staring past her.

'You offend my hospitality,' Oliver said, and put his

hand on Claire's shoulder. 'You ever bother my friend Claire in here again, Brandon, and I'll have to revoke the privileges for everyone. Understand? I don't think you want to be explaining that.'

Brandon looked furious. His eyes were blue again, but as Claire watched, he snarled at Oliver, and revealed fangs. Real, genuine fangs, like a snake's, that snapped down into place from some hidden spot inside of his mouth, and then back up again, quick as a scorpion's sting.

'None of that,' Oliver said calmly. 'I'm not impressed. Off with you. Don't make me have a conversation with Amelie about you.'

Brandon slid out of his chair and slouched away through the crowd, towards the exit. It was dark outside now, Claire noticed. He went out into the night and disappeared from sight.

Oliver still had his hand on her shoulder, and now he squeezed it gently. 'That was unfortunate,' he said. 'You need to be careful, Claire. Stay with Eve. Watch out for each other. I'd hate to see anything happen to you.'

She nodded, gulping. Eve came hurrying out of the back, leather coat flapping around her ankles. Her smile died at the sight of Claire's face. 'What happened?'

'Brandon came in,' Oliver said. 'Trolling. Claire happened to run into him.'

'Oh,' Eve said in a small voice. 'Are you OK?'

'She's fine. I spotted him before any permanent

damage was done. Take her home, Eve. And keep a sharp eye out for that one; he doesn't take being ordered off very well.'

Eve nodded and helped Claire to her feet, picked up the backpack, and got her outside. The big black Caddy was parked at the kerb, and Eve unlocked it and thoroughly checked it over, backseat and trunk, before putting Claire inside of it. When Claire was fastening the seat belt, she noticed two things: first, Oliver was standing in the doorway of Common Grounds, watching them.

Second, Brandon was standing at the corner, in the very edge of the glow of the streetlamp. And he was watching them, too.

Eve saw, too. 'Son of a bitch,' she said furiously, and shot him the finger. Which might not have been too smart, but it made Claire feel better. Eve cranked the engine and squealed out of her parking space, driving like she was breaking the record at a NASCAR race, and screeched to a halt in front of the house just a couple of minutes later. 'OK, you go first,' she said. 'Run for the door, bang on it while you're opening it. *Go, Claire!*'

Claire bailed out breathlessly and slammed the gate back, pounded up the paved walk and up the stairs as she was digging her key out of her pocket. Her hands were shaking, and she missed the keyhole on the first try. She kicked the door and yelled, 'Shane! Michael!' as she tried again.

Behind her, she heard the car door slam, and Eve's shoes clatter on the sidewalk…and stop.

'Now,' said Brandon's low, cold voice, 'let's not be rude, Eve.'

Claire whirled, and saw Eve standing absolutely still ten steps from the porch, her back to the house. Hot wind whipped her leather coat behind her with a dry snapping sound.

Brandon was facing her, his eyes completely white in the pale starlight.

'Who's your sweet little friend?' he asked.

'Leave her alone.' Eve's voice was faint and shaking. 'She's just a kid.'

'You're all just kids.' He shrugged. 'Nobody asks the age of the cow that gave you hamburger.'

Claire, purely terrified now, concentrated, turned back to the door, and rammed the key into the lock…

…just as Shane whipped it open.

'Eve!' she gasped, and Shane pushed her out of the way, jumped down the steps, and got between Eve and Brandon.

'Inside,' Michael said. Claire hadn't heard him, hadn't seen him coming, but he was in the doorway, gesturing her in. As soon as she was over the threshold he grabbed her arm and pushed her out of sight behind him. She peeked around him to see what was happening.

Shane was talking, but whatever he was saying, she couldn't hear it. Eve was backing up, slowly, and when the back of her heels touched the porch steps she whirled and ran up, diving into the doorway and Michael's arms.

'Shane!' Michael shouted.

Brandon lunged at Shane. Shane dodged, yelled, and kicked the vampire with all his weight. Brandon flew backward into the fence, broke through, and rolled into the street.

Shane fell flat on the ground, scrambled up, and ran for the door. It was impossible for Brandon to move that fast, but the vampire seemed to *flash* from lying in the street to reaching for Shane's back...

...and grabbed hold of Shane's T-shirt, yanking him to a sudden stop. But Shane was reaching, too, for Michael's hand, and Michael pulled him forward.

The shirt ripped, Shane stumbled in over the threshold, and Brandon tried to follow. He bounced off an invisible barrier, and for the second time Claire saw his fangs snap down, deadly sharp.

Michael didn't even flinch. 'Try it again, and we'll come stake you in your sleep,' he said. 'Count on it. Tell your friends.'

He slammed the door. Eve collapsed against the wall, panting and trembling; Claire couldn't stop shaking, either. Shane looked flushed and more worried about the damage to his T-shirt than anything else.

Michael grabbed Eve by the shoulders. 'You OK?'

'Yeah. Yeah, he never – wow. That was close.'

'No kidding. Claire?'

She waved, unable to summon up a word.

'Where the hell did he come from?' Shane asked.

'He picked up Claire's scent at the coffee shop,' Eve said. 'I couldn't shake him. Sorry.'

'Damn. That's not good.'

'I know.'

Michael clicked the locks on the front door. 'Check the back. Make sure we're secure, Shane. Upstairs, too.'

'Check.' Shane moved off. 'Dammit, this was my last Killers T-shirt. Somebody's paying for this...'

'Sorry, Michael,' Eve said. 'I tried, I really did.'

'I know. Had to happen sooner or later, with four of us here. You did OK. Don't worry about it.'

'I'm glad you and Shane were here.'

Michael started to say something, then stopped, looking at Claire. Eve didn't seem to notice. She stripped off her leather coat and hung it on a peg by the door, and clumped off in the direction of the living room.

'We were just *attacked*,' Claire finally managed to say. 'By a *vampire*.'

'Yeah, I saw,' Michael said.

'No, you don't understand. We were *attacked*. By a *vampire*. Do you know how impossible that is?'

Michael sighed. 'Truthfully? No. I grew up here, and so did Eve and Shane. We're just kind of used to it.'

'That's crazy!'

'Absolutely.'

It hit her then that there was another impossible thing she'd nearly forgotten about, in the press of panic, and she started to blurt it out, then looked around to be sure Shane and Eve were nowhere in sight. 'What about, you know? You?' She pointed at him.

'Me?' He raised his eyebrows. 'Oh. Right. Upstairs.'

She expected him to take her to the secret room Shane had shown her, but he didn't; instead, he took her to his own room, the big one on the corner. It was about twice the size of her own room, but didn't have much more furniture; it did have a fireplace – empty this time of year – and a couple of chairs and a reading lamp. Michael settled in one. Claire took the other, feeling small and cold in the heavy leather seat. The wing chair was about twice her size.

'Right,' Michael said, and leant forward, resting his elbows on his knees. 'Let's talk about this morning.' But having said that, he didn't seem to know how to start. He fidgeted, staring at the carpet.

'You died,' Claire said. 'You vanished.'

He seemed glad to have something to respond to.

'Not exactly, but – yeah. Close enough. You know I used to be a musician?'

'You still are!'

'Musicians play someplace besides their own houses. You heard Shane at dinner. He's pushing to find out why I'm not playing gigs. Truth is, I can't. I can't go outside of this house.'

She remembered him standing in the doorway, white-faced, watching Shane face off with Brandon. That hadn't been caution; he wanted to be out there, fighting next to his friend. But he couldn't.

'What happened?' she asked softly. She could tell it wasn't going to be an easy story.

'Vampire,' he said. 'Mostly they just feed, and eventually they kill you if they feed hard enough. Some of them like that kind of thing, not all of them. But – this one was different. He followed me back from a gig and tried – tried to make me—'

She felt her face burn, and dropped her gaze. 'Oh. Oh God.'

'Not that,' he said. 'Not exactly. He tried to make me a vampire. But he couldn't. I guess he – killed me. Or nearly, anyway. But he couldn't make me into what he was, and he was trying. It nearly killed us both. When I woke up later, it was daylight, he was gone, and I was a ghost. Wasn't until night came that I realised I could make myself real again. But only at night.' He shook his head slowly, rubbing his hands together as if trying to wash off a stain. 'I think the house keeps me alive.'

'The house?' she echoed.

'It's old. And it has a kind of—' He shrugged. 'A kind of power. I don't know what it is, exactly. When my parents traded up to this house, they only lived here for a couple of months, then moved away to New York. Didn't like the vibes. I liked it fine. I think it liked me, too. But anyway, I can't leave it. I've tried.'

'Even during the day? When you're not, you know, here?'

'Doesn't matter,' he said. 'Can't go out any door, window, or crack. I'm trapped here.'

He looked oddly relieved to be telling her. If he hadn't told Shane or Eve, he probably hadn't told anybody. That felt odd, being the keeper of that secret, because it was a big one. Attacked by a vampire, left for dead, turned into a ghost, trapped in the house? How many secrets *was* that, anyway?

Something occurred to her. 'You said the vampire, did he...drink your blood?'

Michael nodded. He didn't meet her eyes.

'And you – died?'

Another silent nod.

'What happened to your – you know – body?'

'I'm still kind of using it.' He gestured at himself. Claire, unable to stop herself, reached out and touched him. He felt real and warm and alive. 'I don't know how it works, Claire, I really don't. Except I do think it's the house, not me.'

She took a deep breath. 'Do you drink blood?'

He looked up this time, surprised, lips parted. 'No. Of course I don't. I told you, he couldn't – make me what he was.'

'You're sure.'

'I eat Shane's garlic chilli. Does that sound like a vampire to you?'

She shrugged thoughtfully. 'Until today, I thought I knew what a vampire was, all capes and fake Romanian accents and stuff. What about crosses? Do crosses work?'

'Sometimes. Don't rely on them, though. The older

ones aren't stopped by things like that.'

'How about Brandon?' Since he was her main concern right now.

Michael's lip curled. 'Brandon's a punk. You could melt him with a Super Soaker full of tap water, so long as you told him it was blessed. He's dangerous, but so far as vampires go, he's at the bottom of the food chain. It's the ones who *don't* go around flashing fangs and trying to grab you off the street you need to worry about. And yeah, wear a cross – but keep it under your clothes. You'll have to make one if you don't already have one – they don't sell them anywhere in town. And if you can find things like holy water and Eucharist, keep them on hand, but the vampires in this town closed down most of the churches fifty years ago. There's still a few operating underground. Be careful, though. Don't believe everything you hear, and never, ever go by yourself.'

That was the longest speech she'd ever heard from Michael. It tumbled out in a flood, driven with intensity and frustration. *He can't do anything. He can't do anything to help us when we go outside the door.*

'Why did you let us move in?' she asked. 'After – what happened to you?'

He smiled. It didn't look quite right somehow. 'I got lonely,' he said. 'And since I can't leave the house, there's too much I can't do. I needed somebody to help with groceries and stuff. And...being a ghost doesn't exactly pay the bills. Shane – Shane was looking for a place to stay, and he said he'd pitch in for rent. It was perfect. Then Eve...we were friends back in high school. I couldn't just let her wander around out there after her parents threw her out.'

Claire tried to remember what Eve had said. Nothing, really. 'Why did they do that?'

'She wouldn't take Protection from their Patron when she turned eighteen. Plus, she started dressing Goth when she was about your age. Said she was never going to kiss any vampire ass, no matter what.' Michael made a helpless gesture with his hands. 'At eighteen, they threw her out. Had to, or it would have cost the whole family their Protection. So she's on her own. She's done OK – she's safe here, and she's safe at the coffee shop. It's only the rest of the time she has to be careful.'

Claire couldn't think of anything to say. She looked away from Michael, around the room. His bed was made. *Oh my God, that's his bed.* She tried to imagine Michael sleeping there, and couldn't. Although she could imagine some other things, and shouldn't have because it made her feel hot and embarrassed.

'Claire,' he said quietly. She looked back at him. 'Brandon's too young to be out before dark, so you're safe in the daytime, but *don't* stay out after dark. Got it?'

She nodded.

'About the other thing...'

'I won't tell,' she said. 'I won't, Michael. Not if you don't want me to.'

He let out his breath in a long, slow sigh. 'Thanks. I know it sounds stupid, but...I just don't want them to know yet. I need to figure out how to tell them.'

'It's your business,' Claire said. 'And Michael? If you start, you know, getting this craving for red stuff...?'

'You'll be the first to know,' he said. His eyes were steady and cool. 'And I expect you to do whatever you have to do to stop me.'

She shivered and said yes, OK, she'd stake him if she had to, but she didn't mean it.

She hoped she didn't, anyway.

CHAPTER EIGHT

Shane's turn for cooking dinner, and he came up with chilli dogs – more chilli, but at least he did a good job with it. Claire had two, watching in amazement as Michael and Shane downed four each, and Eve nibbled one. She smiled at Shane, and shot back barbs whenever he sent one sailing her way, but Claire noticed something else.

Eve couldn't keep her eyes off of Michael. At first, Claire thought, *She knows something*, but then she saw the flush in Eve's cheeks showing through the pale make-up, and the glitter in her eyes.

Oh. Well, she guessed Michael had looked pretty hot, grabbing her out of danger like that and dragging her out of harm's way. And now that she thought about it, Eve had been making little glances his direction every time they'd been together.

Eve finally shoved her plate away and claimed dibs on

the bathroom for a long, hot, soaking bubble bath. Which Claire wished she'd thought of first. She and Michael did the dishes while Shane practiced his zombie-fighting skills on Xbox.

'Eve likes you, you know,' she said casually as she was rinsing off the last plate. He nearly dropped the one he was drying.

'What?'

'She does.'

'Did she tell you that?'

'No.'

'I don't think you understand Eve, then.'

'Don't you like her?'

'Of course I like her!'

'Enough to...?'

'I am *not* talking about this.' He put the plate into the drainer. 'Jesus, Claire!'

'Oh, come on. You like her, don't you?'

'Even if I did—' He stopped short, glancing towards the doorway and lowering his voice. 'Even if I did, there are a few *problems*, don't you think?'

'Everybody's got problems,' she said. 'Especially in this town. I've only been here six weeks, and I already know that.'

Whatever he thought about that, he dried his hands and walked out. She heard him talking to Shane, and when she went out the two of them were deep into the video game, elbowing each other and fighting for every point.

Boys. Sheesh.

She was on her way to her room, passing the bathroom, when she heard Eve crying. She knocked quietly, and looked in when Eve muffled her sobs. The door wasn't locked.

Eve was dressed in a black fluffy robe, sitting on the toilet; she'd stripped off her make-up and let her hair down, and she looked like a little girl in a too-large adult outfit. Fragile. She gave Claire a shaky grin and wiped tear tracks from her face. 'Sorry,' she said, and cleared her throat. 'Kind of a suck-ass day, you know?'

'That guy. That vampire. He acted like he knew you,' Claire said.

'Yeah. He – he's the one who gives my family Protection. I turned him down. He's not too happy.' She gave a hollow little laugh. 'Guess nobody likes rejection.'

Claire studied her. 'You OK, though?'

'Sure. Peachy.' Eve waved her out. 'Go study. Get smart enough to blow this town. I'm just a little bit down. Don't worry about it.'

Later, when Michael started playing, Claire heard Eve crying through the wall again.

She didn't go investigate, and she didn't watch Michael vanish. She didn't think she had the courage.

Shane went with her the next day to buy some clothes. It was only three blocks to the colourless retail section of town, with all its dingy-looking thrift stores; she didn't want his company, but he wasn't letting her go alone.

'You let Eve go alone,' she pointed out as he sat on the couch putting on his shoes.

'Yeah, well, Eve has a car,' he said. 'Besides, I wasn't up. You get escorted. Live with it.'

She felt secretly pleased about it. A little. It was another typically sunny day, the sidewalks almost vibrating with heat. Not a lot of pedestrians, but then, there rarely were. Shane walked with a long, loping stride, hands in his pockets; she had to hurry to keep up. She kept waiting for him to say something, but he didn't. After a while, she just started talking. 'Did you have a lot of friends, growing up here?'

'Friends? Yeah, I guess. A few. Michael. I kind of knew Eve back then, but we hung with different crowds. Couple of other kids.'

'What – what happened to them?'

'Nothing,' Shane said. 'They grew up, got jobs, claimed Protection, kept right on going. That's how it works in Morganville. You either stay in, or you run.'

'Do you ever see them?' Because she'd been amazed how much she'd missed her friends back home, especially Elizabeth. She'd always thought she was a loner, but... maybe she wasn't. Maybe nobody really was.

'No,' he said. 'Nothing in common these days. They don't want to hang with somebody like me.'

'Somebody who doesn't want to fit in.' Shane glanced at her and nodded. 'Sorry.'

He shrugged. 'Nobody's fault. So what about you? Any friends back home?'

'Yeah. Elizabeth, she's my best friend. We talked all the time, you know? But...when she found out I was going away to school, she just...' Claire decided a shrug was about the best opinion she could offer about it.

'Ever call her?'

'Yeah,' she said. 'But it's like we don't know each other anymore. You know? We have to think about what to say. It's weird.'

'God, I know what you mean.' Shane suddenly stopped and took his hands out of his pockets. They were in the middle of the block, in between two stores, and at first she thought he was going to look in a window, but then he said tensely, 'Turn around and walk away. Just go into the first store you see, and hide.'

'But—'

'Do it, Claire. Now.'

She backed away and turned, walked as fast as she dared to the store they'd already passed. It was a skanky-looking used-clothing store, nowhere she'd willingly shop, but she pushed open the door and looked back over her shoulder as she did.

A cop car was gliding to the kerb next to Shane. He was standing there, hands at his sides, looking bland and respectful, and the cop who was driving leant out of the window to say something to him.

Claire nearly fell forward as the door was jerked open, and stumbled over the threshold into a darkened, musty-smelling interior.

'Hey there,' the uniformed cop who'd opened the door

said to her. He was an older man, blond, with thinning hair and a thick moustache. Cold blue eyes and crooked teeth. 'Claire, right?'

'I—' She couldn't think what to say to that. All her life she'd been told not to lie to the police, but... 'Yes, sir.' She could tell he already knew, anyway.

'My name's Gerald. Gerald Bradfield. Pleased to meet you.' He held out his hand. She swallowed hard, wiped her sweaty palm, and shook. She half expected that he'd click handcuffs around her wrists, but he just half crushed her hand as he pumped it twice, up and down, and let go. 'People been looking for you, you know.'

'I – didn't know that, sir.'

'Didn't you?' Cold, cold eyes, no matter what the smile said. 'Can't imagine that, little girl. Fact is, the mayor's daughter was worried about where you might have got off to. Asked us to find you. Make sure you were all right.'

'I'm fine, sir.' She could barely talk. Her mouth had gone dry. 'I'm not in trouble, am I?'

He laughed. 'Why would you be in trouble, Claire? No, you don't have to worry about that. Fact is, we already know where you are. And who you're running with. You should be more careful, honey. You're brand-new here, but you already know a hell of a lot more than you ought. And your friends aren't exactly the kind that guarantee a peaceful life in this town. Troublemakers. You don't look like a troublemaker to me. Tell you what, you move back into the dorm, be a good girl, go to classes, I'll personally make sure nothing happens to you.'

Claire wanted to nod, wanted to agree, wanted to do *anything* to get away from this man. She looked around the store. There were other people in there, but she couldn't get any of them to look at her. It was like she didn't even exist.

'You don't think I can do it,' he said. 'I can. Count on it.'

She looked back at him, and his eyes had gone white, with little dots of pupils in the middle. When he smiled, she saw a flash of fangs.

She gasped, backed away, and grabbed for the door handle. She lunged out into the street, running, and saw Shane standing right where he'd been, watching the police car pull away from the kerb. He turned and grabbed her as she practically crashed into him.

'Vampire!' she gasped. 'V-vampire cop. In the store!'

'Must have been Bradfield,' Shane said. 'Tall guy? Kind of bald, with a moustache?'

She nodded, shaking all over. Shane didn't even look surprised, much less alarmed. 'Bradfield's OK,' he said. 'Not the worst guy in town, that's for sure. He hurt you?'

'He – he just shook my hand. But he said he knew! He knew where I was living!'

Again, Shane didn't look surprised. 'Yeah, well, that was just a matter of time. They pulled over to ask me your full name. They added it to inventory.'

'*Inventory?*'

'That's what they call it. It's like a census. They always know how many are living in a place. Look, just walk, OK? And don't look so scared. They aren't going to jump us in broad daylight.'

Shane had a lot more confidence in that than she did, but she got control of her shaking and nodded, and followed him up another block to a thrift shop that looked brighter, friendlier, and less likely to have vampires lurking inside. 'This is Mrs Lawson's place. She used to be a friend of my mom's. It's OK.' Shane held open the door for her, like a gentleman. She supposed his mom had taught him that. Inside, the place smelt nice – incense, Claire thought – and there were lots of lights burning. No dark corners here, and a bell rang with a pleasant little tinkling sound when Shane let the door shut behind them.

'Shane!' A large woman in a brightly coloured tie-dyed shirt and big, swirly skirt hustled over from behind the counter at the back, gathered Shane up in a hug, and beamed at him when she stepped back. 'Boy, what the hell are you doing back here? Up to no good?'

'Up to no good, ma'am. Just like always.'

'Thought so. Good for you.' The woman's dark eyes landed on Claire. 'Who's your little friend?'

'This is Claire. Claire Danvers. She's – she's a student at the college.'

'Nice to meet you, Claire. Now. I'll bet you didn't come in here just to say "hey", boy, so what can I do for you?'

'Clothes,' Claire said. 'I'm looking for some clothes.'

'Those we got. You're about a size four, right? Come with me, honey. I've got some really nice things just your size. Shane, you look like you could use some new clothes, too. Those jeans are raggedy.'

'Supposed to be.'

'Lord. Fashion. I just don't understand it anymore.'

Maybe she didn't, but Mrs Lawson had all kinds of cute tops and jeans and things, and cheap, too. Claire picked an armload and followed her to the counter, where she counted out a grand total of twenty-two dollars, including tax. As Mrs Lawson was ringing it up, Claire looked behind her to the things on the wall. There was some kind of official-looking certificate hanging there, framed, with an embossed seal... No, that wasn't a seal. That was a symbol. The same symbol as the one on the bracelet Mrs Lawson wore.

'You take care,' Mrs Lawson said as she handed over the bag with the clothes. 'Both of you. Tell Shane he needs to get himself right, and he needs to do it quick. They've been cutting him some slack, given what he went through, but that won't last. He needs to be thinking about his future.'

Claire looked over her shoulder to where Shane was staring out the window, looking bored. Eyes half-closed.

'I'll tell him,' she said doubtfully.

She couldn't imagine Shane was thinking about anything else.

Days slipped away, and Claire just let them go. She was worried about class, but she was tired and her bruises had turned Technicolor, and the last thing she wanted to do was be the centre of attention. It was better – Shane had convinced her – to do some home study and get back to class when she was better, and Monica had had some time to let things blow over.

The week slipped away. She fell into a regular routine – up late with Michael and Shane and Eve, sleep until noon, argue over bathroom rights, cook, clean, study, do it all again. It felt…good. Real, somehow, in a way that dorm life didn't, exactly.

The following Monday, when she got up and made breakfast, she had to make it for two: Shane was awake, looking grumpy and groggy. He silently grabbed the bacon and fried some up while she did the eggs; there wasn't any banter, as there had been between him and Eve a couple of mornings back. She tried a little conversation, but he wasn't in the mood. He just grunted replies. She waited until he was done with his breakfast – which included a cup of coffee, brewed in the tiny little coffeemaker on the corner of the counter – before she asked, 'What are you doing up so early?'

Shane leant his chair back on two legs, balancing as he chewed. 'Ask Michael.'

Can't exactly do that… 'You doing something for him?'

'Yeah.' He thumped his chair back down and brushed his hand over his hair, which still looked like a mess. 'Don't expect me to dress up or anything.'

'What?'

'What you see is what you get.' She just looked at him, frowning, trying to figure out what he was saying. 'I'm taking you to class. You were going back today, right?'

'You're kidding,' she said flatly. He shrugged. 'You're *kidding*. I'm not some six-year-old who needs her big brother to walk her to school! No way, Shane!'

'Michael thinks you should have an escort. Brandon was pretty pissed. He could find a way to take it out on you, even if he can't do it himself. He's got plenty of people who'd kick your ass on his say-so.' Shane's eyes slid away from hers. 'Like Monica.'

Oh, crap. 'Monica belongs to Brandon?'

'The whole Morrell family does, far as I know. He's their own personal badass. So.' He rubbed his hands together. 'What exciting classes do we have today?'

'You can't go to *class* with me!'

'Hey, you're welcome to knock me out and stop me, but until you do, I'm your date for the day. So. What classes?'

'Calculus II, Physics of Sound, Chemistry III, chem lab, and Biochemistry.'

'Holy crap. You really *are* smart. Right, I'll take some comics or something. Maybe my iPod.'

She kept glaring at him. It didn't seem to do any good – if anything, it just made him more cheerful.

'I always wanted to be a big man on campus,' Shane said. 'Guess this is my chance.'

'I'm dead,' she moaned, and rested her forehead on her hands.

'Not yet. And that's kind of the point.'

* * *

She was afraid Shane would make a big deal out of it, but he didn't. He even combed his hair, which turned out to make him look totally hot in ways that she was afraid to notice. Especially if she had to spend the whole day with him. He'd picked a plain white shirt and his best pair of blue jeans, which were still out at the knees and frayed at the hems. And plain running shoes. 'In case we have to do any retreating,' he said. 'Plus, kicking somebody when you're wearing flip-flops hurts.'

'But you're not kicking anybody,' she said quickly. 'Right?'

'Nobody who doesn't deserve it,' he said. 'What else do I need to fit in?'

'Backpack.' She found her spare – she'd brought two – and tossed it to him. He stuck in some paperbacks, a PSP, and his iPod and headphones, then raided the cabinets for Twinkies and bottled water. 'We're not exactly going to the wilderness, Shane. You don't have to take *everything*. There are vending machines.'

'Yeah? I didn't see any lunch in that schedule. You'll thank me later.'

In fact, she did feel better with Shane loping along beside her; he was watching the shadows, the dark alleys, the empty buildings. Watching everything. Even though he'd packed the iPod, he wasn't listening to it. She missed hers, all of a sudden, and wondered if Monica had it.

They made it to campus without incident, and they were halfway across it, heading for her first class, when

Claire suddenly thought of something and came to a full stop. Shane kept going for a couple of paces, then looked back.

'Monica,' she said. 'Monica's going to be hanging around. She usually is. She'll see you.'

'I know.' Shane hitched his backpack to a more comfortable spot. 'Let's go.'

'But – *Monica*!'

He just looked at her, and started walking. She stayed where she was. 'Hey! You're supposed to be *with* me, not leaving me!'

'Monica's my business,' he said. 'Drop it.' He waited for her, and she reluctantly caught up. 'She doesn't mess with us, I won't mess with her. How's that?'

Wishful thinking, to Claire's mind. If Monica really had got it in for Shane, even a year or two ago, and gone far enough to *kill his sister*, she couldn't imagine any situation where Shane just walked away. Shane wasn't a walking-away kind of guy.

The square concrete courtyard between the Architecture Building and the Math Sciences Building was packed with students crossing between classes. Now that Claire knew what to look for, she couldn't help but notice how many of them had bracelets – leather, metal, even braided cloth – with symbols on them.

And how many students *didn't*.

The ones who wore the symbols were the shiny, confident ones. Sorority girls. Frat guys. Athletes. Popular kids. The loners, the sideliners, the dull and average and strange...they were the ones who weren't Protected.

They were the cattle.

Shane was scanning the crowd. Claire kept walking quickly towards the Math Building; she knew for a fact that Monica wouldn't be caught dead – or killing anybody – in a place that geeky. The only problem was that the third building on the Quad was the Business Administration Building, and that was, of course, where Monica liked to spend her time hanging out, looking for rich boys.

Almost there...

She was actually on the steps leading up to the Math Building when she heard Shane stop behind her. He was staring off into the Quad, and as Claire turned, she saw Monica, surrounded by a clique of admirers, staring right back at him. The two of them might as well have been alone. It was the kind of look that people in love exchanged, or people who were about to kill each other.

'Son of a bitch,' Shane breathed. He sounded shaken.

'Come on,' Claire said, and grabbed his elbow. She was afraid he wouldn't let her pull him on, but he did, as if his mind was somewhere else. When he finally glanced at her, his eyes were dark and hard.

'Not here,' she said. 'She won't come in.'

'Why not?'

'It would embarrass her.'

He nodded slowly, as if that made sense to him, and followed her to class.

Claire had a hard time keeping her mind on the droning lecture, which was familiar anyway, and she'd read far ahead of where the professor was teaching...but mostly, she kept thinking about Shane, sitting motionless next to her, hands on the desk, staring blankly into space. He wasn't even listening to his iPod. She could sense the tenseness in his body, like he was just waiting for the chance to hit something.

I knew this was a bad idea.

It was an hour-and-a-half lecture with a fifteen-minute break in the middle; when Shane got up and walked out, she hastily followed him. He went up to the glass doors and looked out over the Quad.

'She's gone,' he said, without looking at Claire. 'Quit worrying about me. I'm OK.'

'She – Eve said she burnt your house.' No reply. 'And – your sister—?'

'I couldn't get her out,' Shane said. 'She was twelve, and I couldn't get her out of the house. That was my job. Watch out for her.'

He still didn't look at her. She couldn't think of anything to say. After a while, he walked away, into the boys' bathroom; she dashed into the girls', waiting impatiently for the line to clear, and came back out to find him nowhere in sight.

Oh, crap.

But when she went back to the lecture hall he was

sitting right where he'd been, this time with his iPod earbuds in place.

She didn't say anything. Neither did he.

It was the longest lecture, and the least enjoyable, that Claire could remember.

Physics was in the same building; if Monica was waiting out in the wilting sun on the Quad, she'd be getting a really good tan. Shane sat like a statue, if a statue wore headphones and radiated angry coiled tension that made hair stand up on a person's arms. She felt like she was sitting next to an unexploded bomb, and given all of the physics she'd had, she understood exactly what that meant. Talk about potential energy...

Physics crawled slowly by. Shane broke out water and Twinkies, and shared. Chemistry was in the next building, but Claire made sure that they went out the side entrance, not through the Quad. No sign of Monica. She suffered through another hour and a half of chemistry and tension. Shane gradually unwound to the point that her nerves didn't jangle like sleigh bells every time he moved, and ended up playing on his PSP through most of the class. Killing zombies, she hoped. That seemed to put him in a good mood.

In fact, he was positively cheerful during chem lab, interested in the experiment and asking so many questions that the teaching assistant, who'd never had to come to Claire's table before, wandered over and stared at Shane as if trying to figure out what he was doing there.

'Hey, man,' Shane said, and stuck out his hand. 'Shane Collins. I'm – what's the word I'm looking for? Auditing. Auditing the class. With my friend here. Claire.'

'Oh,' said the TA, whose name Claire had never learnt. 'Right. OK, then. Just – follow along.'

Shane gave him a thumbs-up and a goofy grin. 'Hey,' he said in an undertone, leaning close to Claire. 'Any of this stuff blow up?'

'What? Um...yeah, if you do it wrong, I guess.'

'I'm thinking about practical applications. Bombs. Things like that.'

'Shane!' He really was distracting. And he smelt good. Guy good, which was different from girl good – darker, spicier, a smell that made her go all fluttery inside. *Oh, come on, it's* Shane*!* she told herself. That didn't help, especially when he shot her that crooked smile and a look that probably would kill most girls at ten feet. *He's a slacker. And he's – not that smart.*

Maybe he was, though. Just in different places than she was. It was a new idea to her, but she kind of liked it.

She slapped his hand when he reached for the re-agents, and concentrated on the details of the experiment.

She was concentrating so hard, in fact, and Shane had got so engrossed in watching what she was doing, that neither of them heard footsteps behind them. The first

Claire knew about it was a searing, burning sensation down the right side of her back. She dropped the beaker she was holding and screamed – couldn't help it, because *God*, that hurt – and Shane whirled around and grabbed somebody by the collar who was backing away.

Gina, the Monickette. She snarled and slapped at him, but he didn't let go; Claire, gasping in pain and trying to twist to see what was happening on her back, could see that it was taking everything Shane had not to deck his prisoner then and there. The TA came rushing over and other students started realising there was something wrong, or at least more interesting than lab work; Claire slipped off the stool at the table and tried to look at what was happening to her back, because it *hurt*. She smelt something terrible.

'Oh my God!' the TA blurted. He grabbed the bottled water out of Shane's backpack, opened it, and dumped the contents over Claire's back, then dashed to a cupboard on the side and came back with a box of baking soda. She heard it sizzle when it hit her back, and nearly passed out. 'Here. Sit. Sit down. You, call an ambulance. Go!' As Claire sank down breathlessly again on another, lower stool, the TA grabbed a pair of scissors and cut her shirt up the back, and folded it aside. He cut her bra strap, too, and she just barely had the presence of mind to grab hold before the whole thing slid down her arms. *God, it hurts, it hurts...* She tried not to cry. The burn was easing up a little as the baking soda did its work. *Acid has a low pH; baking soda has a high one...* Well, at least she'd retained some grasp of chemistry, even now.

She looked up and saw that Shane still had hold of Gina. He'd twisted her arm behind her back and made her let go of the beaker; what remained of the acid she'd splashed on Claire was still in the glass, looking as innocent as water.

'It was an accident!' she yelped, and stood on her tiptoes as Shane twisted harder. 'I tripped! I'm sorry! Look, I didn't mean it...'

'We're not working with H2SO4 today,' the TA said grimly. 'You've got no reason to be walking around with it. Claire? Claire, how bad is the pain?'

'I – it's OK. I'm OK,' she said, though truthfully she had no idea if she was or not. She felt light-headed, sick, and cold. Shock, probably. And embarrassment, because *God*, she was half naked in front of the entire chem lab, and... Shane... 'Can I put something on?'

'No, you can't let anything touch that. The burn's through several layers of skin. It'll need treatment, and antibiotics. You just sit still.' The TA turned to Shane and Gina, and levelled a finger at her. '*You*, you're talking to the campus police. I will not tolerate this kind of attack in my classroom. I don't care *who* your friends are!'

So he knew her. Or at least he knew enough. Shane was whispering something in Gina's ear, something too low for Claire to hear, but it couldn't be good, by the expression on the girl's face.

'Sir?' Claire asked faintly. 'Sir, can I have a make-up on the lab work and—'

And she passed out before she finished saying, *and I'm sorry for the mess.*

Chapter Nine

When she woke up, she was on her side, and she felt warm all over. Sleepy. There was someone sitting next to her, a boy, and she blinked twice and realised that it was Shane. Shane was in her bedroom. No, wait, this wasn't her bedroom; it was somewhere else...

'Emergency room,' he said. She must have looked confused. 'Damn, Claire. Warn a guy before you do a face-plant on the floor next time. I could have looked all heroic and caught you or something.'

She smiled. Her voice came out sounding lazy and slow. 'You caught Gina.' That was funny, so she said it again. 'You caught Geeeeeeeeeena.'

'Yeah, ha-ha, you're high as a kite, you know? And they called your parents.'

It took her a little while to realise what he'd just said. 'Parents?' she repeated, and tried to lift her head. 'Oh. Ow. Not good.'

'Not so much. Mom and Dad were pretty freaked to hear you became a lab accident. The campus cops forgot to mention the part where Gina deliberately threw acid on your back. They seem to think it was just one of those funky accidents.'

'Was it?' she asked. 'Accident?'

'No way. She meant to hurt you.'

Claire plucked at the ugly blue hospital gown she was wearing. 'Killed my shirt.'

'Yeah, pretty much.' Shane looked pale and tense. 'I've been trying to call Michael. I don't know where he is. I don't want to leave you alone here, but—'

'He's OK,' she said softly, and closed her eyes. 'I'm OK, too.'

She thought she felt his hand on her hair, a second of light, sweet pressure. 'Yeah,' Shane said. 'You're OK. I'll be here when you wake up.'

She nodded sleepily, and then everything faded into a lemon yellow haze, like she was lying in the sunlight.

Ouch.

Waking up was *not fun*. No hazy druggy lemon sunlight; this was more like a blowtorch burning on her back right on the shoulder blade. Claire whimpered and burrowed into her pillow, trying to get away from the pain, but it followed close behind.

The drugs had worn off.

She blinked and whimpered and slowly sat up; a passing nurse stopped and came in to check her over.

'Congratulations,' she said. 'You're doing well. That burn is going to hurt for a while, but if you take the antibiotics and keep the wound clean, you'll be fine. You're lucky somebody was there to wash it off and neutralise the reaction. I've seen battery acid burns down to the bone.'

Claire nodded, not sure she could actually speak without throwing up. Her whole side felt hot and bruised.

'Do you want to get down?'

She nodded again. The nurse helped her down, and gave her what was left of her clothes when she asked. The bra, cut through, was a total loss. The shirt – not much left of that, either. The nurse came up with a loose black T-shirt from lost and found and got her presentable, and the doctor came around to give her a quick once-over. From the brisk way they dispensed with her, a little sulphuric acid burn was barely worth working up a sweat about, at least in Morganville.

'How bad is it?' she asked Shane as he wheeled her through the halls to the exit. 'I mean, is it, like, really gross?'

'Unbelievably gross,' he said. 'Horror movie gruesome.'

'Oh God.'

He relented. 'It's not so bad. It's about the size of a quarter. Your teacher guy did a good job chopping up your clothes and getting it away from your skin. I know it hurt like hell, but it could have been a lot worse.'

There had been a lot more in the beaker in Gina's hand. 'Do you – do you think she was going to—?'

'Pour it all on you? Hell yeah. She just didn't have time.'

Wow. That was...unpleasant. She felt hot and cold and a little sick, and it had nothing to do with shock this time. 'I guess that was Monica's payback.'

'Some of it, anyway. She'll be really pissed now that it didn't go over the way she thought it would.'

The idea of Monica being really pissed wasn't the best way to end the day – and it *was* the end of the day, she realised as Shane rolled her up to the automatic glass double doors.

It was dark.

'Oh,' she said, and covered her mouth. 'Oh no.'

'Yeah, well, we've got transpo covered, at least. Ready?'

She nodded, and Shane suddenly accelerated her chair into a flat-out run. Claire yelped and grabbed for the handles, feeling utterly out of control as the chair bounced its way down the ramp and skidded to a halt just inches from the shiny black side of Eve's car. Eve threw open the passenger door, and Claire tried to get up on her own, but Shane grabbed her around the waist and lifted her straight into the seat. It took seconds, and then he was kicking the wheelchair back towards the ramp, where it bumped into the railing and sat there, looking lost.

Shane dived into the back. 'Punch it!' he said. Eve did, as Claire struggled to find some kind of seat belt setting that wouldn't reduce her to gasps and tears of pain. She settled for hunching forward, bracing herself on the massive dashboard, as Eve peeled out of the parking lot and raced down the dark street. The street-lights looked eerie and too far apart – was that deliberate? Did the vampires control even how far apart they built the lights? Or was she just freaked beyond belief?

'Is he there?' Shane asked, leaning over the seat back. Eve shot him a look.

'Yeah,' she said. 'He's there. But don't put me in the middle of it. I have to work there, you know.'

'I promise, I won't tick off your boss.'

She didn't believe him – that much was clear – but Eve turned right instead of left at the next light, and in about two minutes pulled up at the kerb in front of Common Grounds, which was ablaze with light. Crowded, too. Claire frowned, but before she could even ask, Shane was out of the car and heading inside the coffee shop.

'What's he doing?' she asked.

'Something stupid,' Eve said. 'How's the burn? Hurts, huh?'

Claire would have shrugged, but when she even *thought* about it the imagined pain made her flinch.

'Not so bad,' she said bravely, and tried a smile. 'Could have been a lot worse, I guess.'

'I guess,' Eve agreed. 'Told you classes were dangerous. We need to get this under control. You can't go back if this kind of thing happens.'

'I can't *quit*!'

'Sure you can,' Eve said cheerfully. 'People do it all

the time. Just not people like you – oh, damn.'

Eve bit her black-painted lip, eyes wide and worried as she stared through the window at the brightly lit interior of the shop. And after a few seconds, Claire saw what she was worried about: the hippie manager, Oliver, was standing at the window watching them right back, and behind him, Shane was pulling up a chair to the far-corner table, where a dark shape was sitting.

'Tell me he's not talking to Brandon,' Claire said.

'Um… OK. He's not talking to Brandon.'

'You're lying.'

'Yeah. He's talking to Brandon. Look, let Shane do his thing, OK? He's not as stupid as he looks, mostly.'

'But he's not – Protected, right?'

'That's why he's talking in Common Grounds. It's sort of a truce spot. Vampires don't hunt there, or they're not supposed to, anyway. And it's where all kinds of deals and treaties and stuff get made. So Shane's safe enough in there.'

But she was still biting her lip and looking worried. 'Unless?' Claire guessed.

'Unless Shane attacks first. Self-defence doesn't count.'

Shane was being good, as far as Claire could see… His hands were on the table, and although he was bent over saying something, he wasn't slugging anybody. That was good, right? Although she had no idea what he could be saying to Brandon, anyway. Brandon wasn't the one who had poured acid on her back.

Whatever Shane said, it didn't seem to go down too hard; eventually, Shane just shoved his chair back and walked out, nodding to Oliver on the way out. Brandon slid out from behind the table, dark and sleek, to follow Shane to the doorway, close enough to reach out and grab him. But that was just a mind game, Claire realised as she started to yell a warning. Brandon wanted to freak him out, not hurt him.

Shane just looked over his shoulder, shrugged, and exited the coffee shop. When Brandon started to follow, Oliver reached across and put his arm in the way. By the time Brandon had snarled something at him, Shane was in the car, and Eve was already gunning it away from the kerb.

'Do we need to be afraid now?' she asked. 'Because I'd like a head start before the official terror alert goes up.'

'Nope. We're clear,' Shane said. He sounded tired, and a little strange. 'Claire's got a free pass. Nobody's going to come after her. Including Monica and her sock puppets.'

'But – what? Why?' Claire asked. Eve evidently didn't have to ask. She just looked grim and angry.

'We did a trade,' Shane said. 'Vampires are all about the one-up.'

'You're such an *idiot*!' Eve hissed.

'I did what I had to do! I couldn't ask Michael. He wasn't—' Shane bit off whatever he was about to say, violently, and got the anger in his voice under tight control. 'He wasn't around. Again. I had to do something.

Claire wasn't kidding. They'll kill her, or at least, they'll hurt her so bad she'll wish they'd finish it up. I can't let that happen.'

There was, Claire thought, a silent *not again* at the end of that. She wanted to turn and look at him, but it hurt too much to try. She tried to meet his eyes in the mirror instead.

'Shane,' she said. 'What did you promise?'

'Nothing I can't afford to lose.'

'Shane!'

But Shane didn't answer. Neither did Eve, although she parted her lips a couple of times, then shut them without making a sound. The rest of the drive was done in silence, and once they'd pulled in at the kerb, Eve got out and hurried up the walk to unlock the door. Claire opened the passenger door and started to get out, but again, Shane was there ahead of her, helping her up. Man, he was...strong. And he had big, warm hands. She shivered, and he immediately asked, 'Cold?' but it wasn't that. Not that at all.

'Shane, what did you promise?' she blurted, and grabbed his forearm. Not that he couldn't have pulled free, but...he didn't. He just looked down at her. They were standing really close together, close enough she felt every nerve in her body fizz like a shaken can of Coke. 'You didn't – do something—'

'Stupid?' he asked. He looked down at her hand, and after a second, he touched it with his own. Just for a second, and then yanked away from her like she'd burnt him. She'd been right; he could break free without even thinking about it. 'Yeah. That's what I'm good at. The stupid stuff. Probably for the best; having two big brains in the house might get kinda crowded.' When she tried to say something, he motioned her towards the house. 'Unless you want to hang a This Vein for Rent sign around your neck, *move* already!'

She moved. The front door was open, and Shane followed behind her, close behind, until she was going up the steps.

She didn't hear his footsteps anymore, and turned to look. He was standing at the bottom of the stairs, watching the street.

There was a vampire standing at the corner, under the glow of a streetlight. Brandon. Just standing there, arms folded, he was leaning against the lamppost like he had all the time in the world.

He blew them a kiss, turned, and walked away.

Shane shot him the finger and practically shoved Claire across the threshold. 'Don't you ever stop out there!'

'You said I got a free pass!'

'It doesn't come with a written guarantee!'

'What did you promise him?' she yelled.

Shane slammed the door, hard, and started to push past her to go down the hall, but just as he got there, Michael stepped into his path. And Michael looked pissed.

'Answer her,' he said. 'What the hell did you do, Shane?'

'Oh, *now* you care? Where the hell were you, man? I called! I came and looked for you. Hell, I even picked the lock to your room!'

Michael's blue eyes flickered from Shane to Claire and back. 'I had things to do.'

'Dude, today you had things to do? Whatever, man. You weren't around, and I had to make the call. So I made it.'

'Shane.' Michael reached out and grabbed him by the arm, dragging him to a stop. 'It sounds like she deserves an answer. We all do.' Behind him, Eve stepped around the corner, arms folded.

Shane let out a short, harsh laugh. 'Ganging up on me with the girls? Low blow, man. Low blow. What happened to male bonding?'

'Eve says you talked to Brandon.'

Claire watched the fight go out of Shane's shoulders. 'Yeah. I did. I had to. I mean – look, they *threw acid on her* and the damn cops wouldn't even... I had to go to the source. You taught me that.'

'You made a deal with Brandon,' Michael said, and Claire heard the sick tremor in his voice. 'Oh, dammit to hell, Shane. You didn't.'

Shane shrugged. He wasn't meeting Michael's eyes. 'Dude, it's done. Don't make a thing out of it. It's only twice. And he can't drain me or anything.'

'Shit!' Michael turned and slammed his hand hard into the wooden doorframe. 'You don't even know her, man! You can't make a crusade out of this!'

'I'm not!'

'She's not Alyssa!' Michael yelled, and that was the loudest shout she'd ever heard in her life. Claire flinched and stepped back, and saw Eve do the same behind him.

Shane didn't move. It was like he couldn't. He just stood there, head down.

And then he took a deep breath, raised his head, and met Michael's furious eyes.

'I know she's not Alyssa,' he said, and his tone was still, quiet, and completely cold. 'You need to back the hell off, Michael, and you need to stop thinking I'm the screwed-up kid you knew back then. I know what I'm doing, and you're not my dad.'

'I'm the closest thing you have to family around here!' Michael had stopped yelling, but Claire could hear the anger bubbling in his voice. 'And I'm *not* letting you play the hero. Not now.'

'I wouldn't have to if you'd step up and watch my back!'

Shane shoved past him this time, pounded up the stairs, and slammed the door to his room. Michael stood there, staring after him until Claire took a step forward. She froze when he looked at her, afraid he'd be angrier at her than he had been at Shane. After all, it had been her fault...

'Come sit down,' Michael said. 'I'll get you something to eat.'

'I don't—'

'Yes, you do. Sit. Eve, hold her down if you have to.'

He took her hand for a second, squeezed it, and stood aside for her to move to the couch. She sank onto it with a sigh of relief and rested her forehead on her hands. God, what a miserable day. It had started out so – and Shane – but—

'You understand what Shane did, right?' Eve asked, plopping next to her. 'How he, you know, made the deal?'

'No.' She felt hot, and miserable, and she definitely didn't want food. But Michael wasn't exactly in the mood to take no for an answer. 'I have no idea what's going on.'

'Shane traded two sessions to Brandon in exchange for him leaving you alone.'

'He – what?' Claire looked up, mortally confused. Was Shane gay? She hadn't even thought about the possibility…

'Sessions. You know, bites.' Eve mimed fangs. 'The agreement is that Brandon can fang him twice. He just can't, you know, kill him. It's not about food, it's pleasure. And power.' Eve smoothed her pleated skirt and frowned down at her short, black fingernails. 'Michael's right to be angry about it. Not killing somebody is a hell of a long way from not hurting them. And Brandon's got a lot of experience at making deals. Shane doesn't.'

Somehow, she'd known that – from the way Shane had acted, the way Brandon had been watching them, the way Michael had been so angry. It wasn't just that Shane had told Brandon to back off, or made some dumbass promise. Shane had traded his life for hers – or at least, he was risking it.

Claire gasped, and fear prickled her skin so hard it was like rolling in needles. 'But if he gets bitten, is he – won't he—?'

'Turn into a vampire?' Eve shook her head. 'It can't work that way, or Morganville'd be the Undead Metroplex by now for sure. All my life, I've never seen or heard of anybody turned into a vampire from a bite. The suckers around here are really old. Not that Shane wouldn't look completely hot with a nice set of fangs, but…' She fiddled with the pleats on her skirt. 'Shit. This is stupid. Why not me? I mean, not that I exactly *want* to – not anymore but…it's worse for guys.'

'Worse? Why?'

Eve shrugged, but Claire could see she was avoiding the question. 'Shane's *definitely* not going to be able to handle it. Boy can't even let somebody else have the last corn dog, and he doesn't even like corn dogs. He's a total control freak.' She fidgeted for a few more seconds, then added, softly, 'And I'm afraid for him.'

As Michael came back into the room, Eve jumped up and ran around moving things, stacking things, until Michael gave her a none-too-subtle signal to leave. Which she did, making some excuse Claire didn't hear, and clattered upstairs to her room.

Michael handed Claire a bowl. 'Chilli. Sorry. It's what we've got.'

She nodded and took a spoonful, because she'd always

pretty much done what she was told…and the second the chilli hit her tongue, she realised that she was starving. She swallowed it almost without chewing, and was scooping up the next bite before she knew what she was doing. Shane needed to go into the chilli business.

Michael slipped into the leather armchair to the left and picked up the guitar he'd laid aside. He started tuning it as if the whole scene with Shane hadn't even happened. She ate, stealing glances at him as he bent over the instrument, drawing soft, resonant notes.

'You're not mad?' she finally asked, or mumbled.

'Mad?' He didn't raise his curly blond head. 'Mad is what you get when somebody flips you the finger on the freeway, Claire. No. I'm scared. And I'm trying to think what to do about it.'

She stopped chewing for a few seconds, then realised that choking on her food wasn't likely to make things any better.

'Shane's hotheaded,' Michael said. 'He's a good guy, but he doesn't think. I should have thought for him, before I brought you in here.'

Claire swallowed. The food had suddenly gone a little sour in her mouth, so she put the spoon down. 'Me?'

Michael's fingers stilled on the guitar strings. 'You know about his sister, right?'

Alyssa. That was the name Michael had thrown out. The one that had hurt Shane. 'She's dead.'

'Shane's not a complicated guy. If he cares about somebody, he fights for them. Simple. Lyssa – Lyssa was a sweet kid. And he had that whole big-brother thing working. He'd have died for her.' Michael slowly shook his head. 'Nearly did. Anyway, the point is that Lyssa would have been your age by now, and here you are getting hurt by the same bitches who killed his sister, trying to get him. So yeah. He'd do anything – *anything* – not to have to live through that again. You may not be Lyssa, but he likes you, and more than that, he *hates* Monica Morrell. So much he—' Michael couldn't seem to say it. He stared off into space for a few seconds, then went on. 'Making deals with the vampires in this town will keep you alive on the outside, but it eats you on the inside. I watched it happen to my folks, before they got out of here. Eve's parents, too. Her sisters. If Shane goes through with this, it'll kill him.'

Claire stood up. 'He's not going through with it,' she said. 'I'm not letting him.'

'How exactly are you going to stop him? Hell, I can't stop him, and he listens to me. Mostly.'

'Look, Eve said – Eve said vampires own this town. Is that true? Really?'

'Yes. They've been here as long as anybody can remember. If you live here, you learn to live with them. If you can't, then you go.'

'They don't just run around biting people, though.'

'That would be rude,' he said gravely. 'They don't need to. Everybody in town – everybody who's a resident – pays taxes. Blood tax. Two pints a month, down at the hospital.'

She stared. 'I didn't have to!'

'College kids don't. They get taxed a different way.' He looked grim, and with a sick, twisting sense of horror she realised what he was going to say right before he made it real. 'Vamps have a deal with the school. They get to take two per cent a year, right off the top. Used to be more, but I think they got worried. Couple of close calls with the media. There's nothing TV stations like more than a pretty young college girl gone missing. Claire, what are you thinking?'

She took a deep breath. 'If the vamps have this all planned out, then they've got, you know, structure. Right? They can't all just be running their own shows. Not if there are a lot of them. There's got to be somebody in charge.'

'True. Brandon's got a boss. And his boss probably has a boss.'

'So all we have to do is make a deal with his boss,' she said. 'For something other than Shane getting bit.'

'All?'

'They have to want something. Something more than what they already have. We just need to find out what it is.'

There was a creak on the stairs. Michael turned to look, and so did Claire. Eve was standing there.

'Didn't hear you coming,' Michael said. She shrugged and padded down the steps; she'd taken off her shoes. Even her black-and-white hose had little skulls on the toes.

'I know what they want,' she said. 'Not that we're going to be able to find it.'

Michael looked at her for a long time. Eve didn't look away; she walked right up to him, and Claire suddenly felt like she was in the middle of something personal. Maybe it was the way he was looking at her, or how she was smiling at him, but it made Claire fidget and closely examine a stack of books on the end table.

'I don't want you in this,' Michael said. Out of the corner of her eye, she saw him reach out and take Eve's hand.

'Shane's in it. Claire's in it. Hey, even *you're* in it.' Eve shrugged. 'You know how much I hate being left out. Besides, if there's a way to stick it to Brandon, I'm all for it. That guy needs a poke in the eye with a nice, sharp stake.'

They were still holding hands. Claire cleared her throat, and Michael let go first. 'What is it? What do they want?'

Evc grinned. 'Oh, you're gonna *love* this,' she said. 'They want a book. And I can't think of anybody who'd have a better shot at finding it than you, book girl.'

There were a lot of rules to Morganville Claire hadn't even thought about. The blood donation, that was one – and she was starting to wonder how Michael was getting away with not paying his taxes. He couldn't, right? If he couldn't leave the house?

She sat down cross-legged on the floor with a ledger

notebook, turned to a fresh sheet of paper, and made a heading that read *Pluses for Vampires.* Under that column, she wrote down *blood donation, Protection, favours, deals.*

'Oh, put down *curfew*,' Eve said.

'There's a curfew?'

'Well, yeah, of course. Except for the school. They don't care if the students roam around all night, because, you know—' Eve mimed fangs in the neck. Claire swallowed and nodded. 'But for locals? Oh yeah.'

'How is that a plus for them?'

'They don't have to worry about who's safe to bite and who's not. If you're out running around, you're lunch.'

She wrote down *curfew.* Then she turned the page and wrote down *Minuses for Vampires.*

'What are they afraid of?' she asked.

'I don't think we were done with the pluses,' Michael said. He sat down on the floor next to the two girls – well, closer to Eve, Claire noticed. 'Probably a lot you didn't write down.'

'Oh, let the girl feel better about it,' Eve said. 'It's not all gloomy. Obviously, they don't like daytime—'

Claire wrote it down.

'And garlic...silver...um, holy water—'

'You sure about those?' Michael asked. 'I always thought they pretended on a lot of that, just in case.'

'Why would they do that?'

Claire answered without looking up. 'Because it

makes it easier to hide what really can hurt them. I'm writing it down anyway, but it may not be right.'

'Fire is for real,' Michael said. 'I saw a vampire die once, when I was just a kid. One of those revenge deals.'

Eve pulled in a deep breath. 'Oh, yeah. I remember hearing about it. Tom Sullivan.'

Claire asked, wide-eyed, 'The vampire was named—?'

'Not the vampire,' Michael said. 'The guy who killed him. Tommy Sullivan. He was kind of a screw-up, drank a lot, which isn't too unusual around here. He had a kid. She died. He blamed the vampires, so he doused one with gas and set him on fire, sitting right in the middle of the restaurant.'

'You saw that?' Claire asked. 'How old were you?'

'You grow up fast in Morganville. The point is, there was a trial the next night. Not much chance for Tommy. He was dead before morning. But...fire works. Just don't get caught.'

Claire wrote down *fire*. 'What about stakes?'

'You've seen Brandon,' Eve said. 'You want to try to get close enough to stake him? Yeah, me neither.'

'But do they *work*?'

'Guess so. You have to fill out a form when you buy wood.'

Claire wrote it down. 'Crosses?'

'Definitely.'

'Why?'

'Because they're evil, soulless, bloodsucking fiends?'

'So was my sixth-grade gym teacher, but *he* wasn't afraid of a cross.'

'Funny,' Eve said, in the way that meant *not*. 'Because there are hardly any churches, and so far as I know, crosses are impossible to come by unless you make 'em yourself. Also, all these guys grew up – isn't that weird, thinking of them growing up? – when religion wasn't just something you did on Sundays. It was something you *were*, every minute, every day, and God was always up for a little recreational smiting of the wicked.'

'Don't,' Michael murmured. 'God's scarce enough around here.'

'No offence to the Big Guy, Michael, but he made himself scarce,' Eve shot back. 'You know how many nights I spent in bed praying, *Dear God, please take away all the bad people?* Yeah, that really worked.' Michael opened his mouth to say something. 'And please don't tell me God loves me. If God loved me, he'd drop a bus ticket to Austin in my lap so I could blow this town once and for all.'

Eve sounded – well, *angry*. Claire tapped her pencil against the pad, not making eye contact.

'How do they keep people from leaving?' she asked.

'They don't. Some people leave. I mean, Shane did,' Michael said. 'I think the question you're looking for is, how do they keep them from *talking*? And that's where it gets weird.'

'*That's* where?' Claire murmured. Eve laughed.

'I don't know myself, because I never got out of town,

but Shane says that once you get about ten miles outside of Morganville, you get this terrible headache, and then you just...start to forget. First you can't remember what the name of the town was, and then you can't remember how to get there, and then you don't remember that the town had vampires. Or the rules. It just – doesn't exist anymore for you. It comes back if you return to town, but when you're out, you can't run around telling all about Morganville because you just don't remember.'

'I heard rumours,' Eve said. 'Some people start remembering, but they get—' She made a graphic throat-cutting gesture. 'Hit squads.'

Claire tried to think of things that would cause that kind of memory loss. Drugs, maybe? Or...some kind of local energy field? Or... OK, she had no idea. But it sounded like magic, and magic made her nervous. She supposed vampires were magic, too, when you got right down to it, and that made her even more nervous. Magic didn't exist. Shouldn't exist. It was just...*wrong*. It offended her scientific training.

'So where does all that leave us?' Michael asked. It was a reasonable question.

Claire flipped another page, wrote down *memory loss aft. depart*, and said, 'I'm not sure. I mean, if we're going to put together any kind of a plan, we have to basically know as much as we can to make sure it's a good enough approach. So keep talking. What else?'

It went on for hours. The grandfather clock solemnly announced the arrival and departure of nine o'clock, then ten, then eleven. It was nearly midnight, and Claire had scribbled up most of the ledger pages, when she looked at Michael and Eve and asked, 'Anything else?' and got negative shakes of their heads in reply. 'OK, then. Tell me about the book.'

'I don't know a lot,' Eve said. 'They just put out a notice about ten years ago that they were looking for it. I heard they have people all over town going through libraries, bookstores, anyplace it could be hidden. But the weird thing is that vamps can't actually read it.'

'You mean it's in some other language?'

Michael raised his eyebrows. 'I don't think it's that easy. I mean, every one of these suckers has got to speak a dozen languages, at least.'

'*Dead* languages,' Eve said. When they looked at her, she grinned. 'What? Come on. Funny!'

'Maybe they can't read it for the same reason people can't remember anything outside of town,' Claire said slowly. 'Because something doesn't want them to.'

'That's kind of a leap, but the Russian judge gave you a nine point five for style, so OK,' Eve said. 'The important thing is that *we* know what it looks like.'

'Which is?' Claire put her pencil to paper.

'A book with a brown leather cover. Some kind of symbol on the front.'

'What kind?' Because *brown leather cover* didn't exactly narrow things down when it came to books.

Eve pushed up the sleeve of her skin-tight black mesh top, and held out her forearm. There, tattooed in plain blue, was a symbol that looked kind of like an omega, only with some extra waves in it. Simple, but definitely nothing Claire could remember seeing before. 'They've been searching for it. They gave everybody growing up in a Protected family the tattoo so that we remember what to look for.'

Claire stared for a couple of seconds, wanting to ask how old Eve was when she got the tattoo, but she didn't quite dare. She dutifully marked the symbol down in her notebook. 'And nobody's found it. Are they sure it's here?'

'They seem to think so. But I'll bet they've got their sources searching all over the world for it. Seems pretty important to them.'

'Any idea why?'

'Nobody knows,' Michael said. 'I grew up asking, believe me. Nobody has a clue. Not even the vampires.'

'How can they be looking for something and not even know why?'

'I'm not saying *somebody* doesn't know why. But the vampires have ranks, and the only ones I've ever really talked to aren't exactly in charge. Point is, we can't find out, so we shouldn't waste time worrying about it.'

'Good to know.' Claire put *contents unknown* next to the symbol of the book, then *valuable!!!!!* underneath, underscored with three dark lines. 'So if we can find this book, we can trade it to get Monica off my back, and make sure Shane's deal is called off.'

Michael and Eve looked at each other. 'Did you miss

the part where the vamps have been turning Morganville upside down trying to find it?' Eve asked.

Claire sighed, flipped back a page, and pointed at a note she'd made. Eve and Michael both craned over to read it.

Vampires can't read it.

They looked blank.

'I'm going to need to spend some time at the library,' Claire said. 'And we're going to need some supplies.'

'To do what?' Eve still wasn't catching on, but Michael was.

'Fake the book?' he asked. 'You really think that'll work? What do you think happens when they figure out we cheated?'

'Bad idea,' Eve said. 'Very bad idea. Honest.'

'Guys,' Claire said patiently. 'If we're careful, they'll never suspect we're smart enough to do something like that. Not to mention brave enough. So we give them a fake – it's still more than anybody else has. They may be pissed, but they'll be pissed that *somebody* faked it. We just found it.'

They were both looking at her now like they'd never seen her before. Michael shook his head.

'Bad idea,' he said.

Maybe so. But she was going to try it anyway.

Chapter Ten

She was too wired to sleep, and besides, her back hurt, and she couldn't stand the thought of waiting even one more night to get started. Brandon hadn't seemed like the kind of guy to wait for his revenge, and Shane – Shane wasn't the kind of guy to not hold up his end of a deal, either.

If he's stupid enough to want to get bitten, fine, but he's not using me for an excuse.

Shane hadn't come out of his room all night. She hadn't heard a thing when she'd listened – carefully – at his door. Eve had mimed headphones and turning up an invisible stereo. Claire could understand that; she'd spent lots of hours trying to blow out her own eardrums to avoid the world.

Eve lent her a laptop – a retro thing, big and black and clunky, with a biohazard-symbol sticker on the front. When Claire plugged it into the broadband connection and booted it up, the desktop graphic was a cartoon Grim Reaper holding a road sign instead of a scythe – a road sign that read MORGANVILLE, with an arrow pointing down.

Claire clicked on a couple of folders – guiltily, but she was curious – and found they were full of poetry. Eve liked death, or at least, she liked to write about it. Florid romantic stuff, all angst and blood and moonlit marble... and then Claire noticed the dates. The last of the poetry had been done three years ago. Eve would have been, what, fifteen? She'd been starry-eyed about vampires back then, but something had changed. No poetry at all for the past three years...

Eve walked in the open door. 'Working OK?' she asked. Claire jumped, guilty, and gave her the thumbs-up as she clicked open the Internet connection. 'OK, I called my cousin in Illinois. She's going to let us use her PayPal account, but I have to send her cash, like, tomorrow. Here's the account.' She handed over a slip of paper. 'We're not going to get her killed, right?'

'Nope. I'm not buying much from any one place. A lot of people buy leather and tools and stuff. And paper – how old is this book supposed to be?'

'Old.'

'Was it on vellum?'

'Is that paper?'

'Vellum is the oldest kind of paper they used in books,' Claire said. 'It's sheepskin.'

'Oh. I guess that, then. It's really old.'

Vellum would be hard. You could get it, but it was easy to trace. But it wasn't any good being freak smart if you couldn't get around things like that... Oh, yeah, she needed to think about using somebody else to do the research, too. Too dangerous having tracks that led right back here to the Glass House...

Claire went to work. She didn't even notice Eve going and shutting the door behind her.

For four days, Claire studied. Four *solid* days. Eve brought her up soup and bread and sandwiches, and Shane dropped by once or twice to tell her she was crazy and he wanted her to stay the hell out of his business; Claire didn't pay any attention. She got like that when she was completely inside of something. She heard him, and she said something back, but no way was she listening. Like her parents, Shane eventually gave up and went away.

Michael came to her room just a little before dawn. That one surprised her long enough to drag her out of her trance for a while. 'How's it going?' he asked.

'Mission Save Shane? Yeah, it's going,' she said. 'I have to work the long way around. No traces. Don't worry – even if the vamps get angry, they won't be able to prove we did anything but bring them what we thought they were looking for.'

Michael looked pleased, but worried. He worried a lot. She supposed that being trapped the way he was, that was really all he could do – fight anything that got inside to hurt them, and worry about everything else. Frustrating, she guessed.

'Hey,' she said, 'when does Eve go to work?'

'Four o'clock.'

'But that's—'

'The night shift. I know. She's safe enough there, though, and I don't think any vamp is stupid enough to try to get in the way of that damn car. It's like being run over by a Hummer. I made her promise that Oliver would walk her to the car, and Shane's going to get her from the sidewalk inside.'

Claire nodded. 'I'm going with her.'

'To the coffee shop? Why?'

'Because it's anonymous,' she said. 'Every college student in there has a laptop, and the place has free wireless. If I'm careful, they won't be able to trace who's looking up how to fake-age a book.'

He gave her an exasperated look. On him, it looked cute. *God.* She was still noticing. She really needed to stop that, but hey. Sweet sixteen and never been kissed...

'I don't like *Eve* out there at night. You're *definitely* not going.'

'If I do it here, everybody could be in danger. Including Eve.'

Oh, low blow – she saw his eyes shift, but he toughed it out. 'So your answer is that I let you go out there, risk your life, sit in a coffee shop with *Brandon*, and pretend like that's safer? Claire. In no way does that equal safer.'

'Safer than the vampires deciding that everybody in this house deliberately set out to cheat them out of the thing they want most,' Claire said. 'We're not playing, are we? I mean, I can stop if you want, but we don't have anything else we can trade for Shane's deal. Nothing big enough. I'd let Brandon – you know – but somehow I don't think—'

'Over my—' Michael stopped and laughed. 'I was going to say, "Over my dead body" but—'

Claire winced.

'No,' he said.

'You're not my dad,' she pointed out, and all of a sudden…*remembered.*

Shane, at the hospital, when she'd been drugged up, had said, *They called your parents.* Also, she distinctly remembered the words *freaked out.*

Oh, *crap*!

'Dad,' she said aloud. 'Oh no…um, I need to use the phone. Can I?'

'Calling your parents? Sure. Long distance—'

'Yeah, I know. I pay for it. Thanks.'

She picked up the cordless phone and dialled her home number. It rang five times, then flipped over to the machine. 'Hello, you've reached Les and Katharine Danvers and their daughter, Claire. Leave us a message!' It was her mom's bright, businesslike voice.

When the beep sounded, Claire had a second of blind panic. Maybe they were just out shopping. Or…

'Hi, Mom and Dad, it's Claire. I just wanted to –

um – say hi. I should have called you, I guess. That lab accident thing, that was nothing, really. I don't want you to be worried about me – everything's just fine. Really.'

Michael, leaning against the doorframe, was making funny faces at her. That seemed like Shane's job, somehow. She stuck her tongue out at him.

'I just – I just wanted to say that. Love you. Bye.'

She hung up. Michael said, 'You ought to get them to come and take you home.'

'And leave you guys in this mess? You're in it because of me. *Shane's* in it because of me. Now that Monica knows he's back...'

'Oh, believe me, I'm not underestimating how much trouble we're in, but you can still go. And you should. I'm going to try to convince Shane to get out, too. Eve – Eve won't go, but she should.'

'But—' *That leaves you alone*, she thought. *Really alone*. There was no getting out for Michael. Not ever.

Michael looked up and out the window, where the sky was gradually washing from midnight blue to a paler dawn. 'My time's up,' he said. 'Promise me you won't go with Eve tonight.'

'I can't.'

'Claire.'

'I can't,' she said. 'I'm sorry.'

He didn't have time to argue, though she could see he wanted to. He walked down the hall; she heard his bedroom door close, and thought about what she'd seen downstairs in the living room. She wasn't sure how she'd handle that if she had to face it every day – it looked really painful. She supposed the worst of it, though, was his knowing that if he'd been alive, been able to walk around in the daylight, he'd have been able to stop Shane from doing what he'd done.

I wouldn't have to if you'd step up and watch my back! Shane had yelled at him, and yeah, that must have hurt just about worse than dying.

Claire went back to work. Her eyes burnt, her muscles ached, but in some strange and secret place, she was *happy* to finally be doing something that wasn't just protecting herself, but protecting other people, too.

If it worked.

The strange thing was, she just knew it would. She knew.

She really was a freak, she decided.

Claire woke up at three thirty, bleary-eyed and aching, and struggled into a fresh T-shirt and a pair of jeans that badly needed washing. One more day, she decided, and then she'd brave the washing machine in the basement. She had monster bed-head, even though she'd barely slept for three hours, and had to stick her head under the faucet and finger fluff her hair back to something that wasn't too puke-worthy.

She stuck the laptop into the messenger-bag case and dashed downstairs; she could hear Eve's shoes clumping through the house, heading for the door.

'Wait up!' she yelled, and pelted down the stairs and

through the living room just as the front door slammed. 'Crap...'

She opened it just before Eve succeeded in locking it. Eve looked guilty. 'You were going to leave me,' Claire said. 'I told you I wanted to go!'

'Yeah, well...you shouldn't.'

'Michael talked to you last night.'

Eve sighed and fidgeted one black patent leather shoe. 'Little bit, yeah. Before he went to bed.'

'I don't need everybody protecting me. I'm trying to help!'

'I get it,' Eve said. 'If I say no and drive off, what are you going to do?'

'Walk.'

'That's what I was afraid of.' Eve shrugged. 'Get in the car.'

Common Grounds was packed with students reading, chatting, drinking chai and mochas and lattes. And, Claire was gratified to see, working on laptops. There must have been a dozen going at once. She gave Eve a thumbs-up, ordered a cup of tea, and went in search of a decent spot to work. Something with her back to the wall.

Oliver brought her tea himself. She smiled uncertainly at him and minimised the browser window; she was reading up on famous forgeries and techniques. Dead giveaway, with emphasis on *dead*. Not that she disliked Oliver, but any guy who seemed to be able to enforce rules on the vampires was somebody she couldn't trust real far.

'Hello, Claire,' he said. 'May I sit?'

'Sure,' she said, surprised. Also, uncomfortable. He was old enough to be her dad, not to mention kind of hippie-dippie. Though, being a fringer herself, she didn't mind that part so much. 'Um, how's it going?'

'Busy today,' he said, and settled into the chair with a sigh of what sounded like gratitude. 'I wanted to talk to you about Eve.'

'OK,' she said slowly.

'I'm concerned about her,' Oliver said. He leant forward, elbows on the table; she hastily closed the cover of the laptop and rested her hands protectively on top of it. 'Eve seems distracted. That's very dangerous, and I'm quite sure that by now you understand why.'

'It's—'

'Shane?' he asked. 'Yes. I thought that was probably the case. The boy's got himself into a great deal of trouble. But he did it with a pure heart, I believe.'

Her pulse was hammering faster, and her mouth felt dry. Boy, she really didn't like talking to authority figures. Michael was one thing – Michael was like a big brother. But Oliver was...different.

'I might be able to help,' Oliver said, 'if I had something to trade. The problem is, what does Brandon want that you, or Shane, can give? Other than the obvious.' Oliver looked thoughtful, and tapped his lips with a fingertip. 'You are a very bright girl, Claire, or so Eve tells me. Morganville can use bright girls. We might be able to bypass Brandon altogether, perhaps, and find a way to make a deal with someone...else.'

Which was pretty much exactly what they'd already talked about, only without the Oliver part. Claire tried not to look horribly guilty and transparent. 'Who?' she asked. It was a reasonable question. Oliver smiled, and his dark eyes looked sharp and cool.

'Claire. Do you really expect me to tell you? The more you know about this town, the less safety there is for you. Do you understand that? I've had to create my own peace here, and it only works because I know exactly what I'm doing, and how far I can go. You – I'm afraid your first mistake might be your last.'

Her mouth wasn't dry anymore; it was mummified. She tried to swallow, but got nothing but a dry click at the back of her throat. She hastily picked up her tea and sipped it, tasting nothing but glad of the moisture.

'I wasn't going to—'

'Don't,' he cut her off, and his voice wasn't so kind this time. 'Why else would you be here today, when you know Brandon is likely to show up any time after dark? You want to make a deal with him to save Shane. That much is obvious.'

Well, it wasn't why she was here, but still, she tried to look guilty about that, too. Just in case. It must have worked, because Oliver sat back in his chair, looking more relaxed.

'You're clever,' he said. 'So is Shane. But don't let it go to your heads. Let me help.'

She nodded, not trusting her voice not to quiver or

break or – worse – betray how relieved she was.

'That's settled, then,' Oliver said. 'Let me talk to Brandon and a few others, and see what I can do to make this problem go away.'

'Thanks,' she said faintly. Oliver got up and left, looking like any skinny ex-hippie who hadn't quite let go of the good old days. Inoffensive. Ineffective, maybe.

She couldn't rely on adults. Not for this. Not in Morganville.

She opened up the laptop, maximised the browser window, and went back to work.

Like always, time slipped away; when she looked up next, it was night outside the windows, and the crowd in the coffee shop had switched over from studious to chatty. Eve was busy at the bar, talking and smiling and generally being about as cheerful as a Goth chick could be.

She went quiet, though, when Brandon slouched in from the back room and took his accustomed seat at the table in the darkest corner. Oliver brought him some kind of drink – *God*, she hoped it wasn't blood or anything! – and sat down to have some intense and quiet conversation. Claire tried to look like she wasn't there. She and Eve exchanged a few glances between customers at the bar.

Putting together the book, Claire had learnt during the long research marathon, was work for experts, not sixteen-year-old (nearly seventeen) wannabes. She could put *something* together, but – to her vast disappointment – anybody with an eye for rare books could spot a fake pretty easily, unless it was expertly done. She suspected that her leatherworking and bookbinding skills needed work.

All of which brought her back to square one, Shane Gets Bitten. Not acceptable.

A line in one of the dozens of windows she'd opened caught her eye. *Nearly anything can be created for the movies, including reproductions of ancient books, because the reproduction only has to fool one of the senses: vision...*

She didn't have time – or cash – to get some Hollywood prop house to make a book for her, but it gave her an idea.

A really good idea.

Or a really bad one, if it didn't work.

Nearly anything can be created for the movies.

She didn't need the book. She just needed a picture.

By the time midnight rolled around – and Common Grounds ushered the last caffeine addict out into the night – Claire was reasonably sure she could pull it off, and she was too tired to care if she couldn't. She packed up the laptop and leant her head on her hand, watching while Eve cleaned up cups and glasses, loaded the dishwasher, chatted with Oliver, and deliberately ignored the dark shadow sitting in the corner.

Brandon hadn't taken off after his walking snacks.

Instead, he kept sitting there, nursing a fresh cup of whatever it was he was drinking, smiling that cruel, weird little smile at Eve, then Claire, then Eve.

Oliver, drying ceramic cups, had been watching the watcher. 'Brandon,' he said, and tossed the towel across his shoulder as he began slotting cups into their pull racks. 'Closing time.'

'You didn't even call last round, old man,' Brandon said, and turned that smile on Oliver.

Where it died, fast. After a moment of silence, Brandon stood up to stalk away.

'Wait,' Oliver said, very quietly. 'Cup.'

Brandon looked at him in utter disbelief, then picked up the cup – disposable paper – and dumped it in the trash can. First time he'd bused his own table in a few dozen years, Claire guessed. If ever. She hid a nervous grin, because he didn't seem like the kind of guy – much less vamp – who'd appreciate her sense of humour.

'Anything else?' Brandon asked acidly. Not as if he actually cared.

'Actually, yes. If you wouldn't mind, I'd like the ladies to leave first.'

Even in the shadows, Claire saw the gleam of sharp teeth when Brandon silently opened his mouth – flashing his fangs. Showing off. Oliver didn't seem impressed.

'If you wouldn't mind,' he repeated. Brandon shrugged and leant against the wall, arms folded. He was wearing a black leather jacket that drank in light, a black knit shirt, dark jeans. Dressed to kill, Claire thought, and wished she hadn't.

'I'll wait,' he said. 'But they don't need to worry about me, old man. The boy made a deal. I'll stick to it.'

'That's what I'm worried about,' Oliver said. 'Eve, Claire, get home safe. Go.'

Eve slammed the door on the dishwasher and turned it on; she grabbed her purse from behind the counter and ducked out to take Claire's hand and pull her towards the door. She flipped the front sign from OPEN to CLOSED and unlocked the door to let Claire out. She locked it back behind them with a set of keys, then hustled Claire quickly to the car, which sat in the warm glow of the streetlight. The street looked deserted; wind whipped trash and dust into clattering ghosts, and the blinking red stoplights danced and swayed along. Eve unlocked the car in record time, and both of them slammed down the locks once they were inside. Eve started up the Caddy and motored away from the kerb; only then did she sigh a little in relief.

And then she gasped, because another car turned the corner and whipped past them in a black blur, stopping at the kerb where they'd been parked. 'What the hell?' Eve blurted, and slowed down. Claire turned to look back.

'It's a limo,' she said. She didn't even think Morganville *had* a limo, but then she thought about funeral homes and funerals, and got chills. For all she knew, maybe Morganville had more limos than any city in Texas...

This one wasn't part of a procession, though. It was big and black and gleamed like the finish on a cockroach, and as the Caddy inched along, Claire saw a uniformed driver get out and walk around to the back.

'Who is it?' Eve asked. 'Can you see?'

The driver handed out a woman. Small – not much taller than Claire herself, she guessed. Pale, with hair that glowed white or blond in the streetlights. They were too far for Claire to get a really good look, but she thought the woman looked...sad. Sad, and cold.

'She's not very tall – white hair? And kind of elegant?'

Eve shrugged. 'Nobody I've met, but most of the vamps don't mingle with the little people. Kind of like the Hiltons don't shop at Wal-Mart.'

Claire snorted. As Eve turned the corner, she saw the woman standing in front of the door of Common Grounds, and saw Oliver opening it for her. No sign of Brandon. She wondered if Oliver had already sent him out, or if he was making the vamp give them a head start. 'How does Oliver do this?' she asked. 'I mean, why don't they just...?'

'Kill him? I wish I knew. He's got balls of platinum, for one thing,' Eve said. Passing streetlights strobed across her face. 'You saw how he did Brandon back there? Dissing him? Unbelievable. Anybody else would be dead by dawn. Oliver...just gets away with it.'

Which made Claire even more curious about the why. Or at least the how. If Oliver could get away with it, maybe other people could, too. Then again, maybe other people had already tried, and ended up as organ donors.

Claire turned back face forward, lost in thought, as Eve sped through the silent, watching streets for home. A police car prowled a side street, but somehow in Morganville she thought they weren't looking so much for criminals as potential victims.

At first, she thought she was so tired she was imagining things – that happened when you didn't sleep; you saw ghosts in mirrors and spooky faces at the window – but then she saw something moving fast through the glow of a streetlight. Something pale.

'They're following,' Eve said grimly. 'Damn.'

'Brandon?' Claire tried to scan the sides of the street, but Eve pressed the gas and went faster.

'Not Brandon. Then again, he doesn't have to get his fangs dirty personally—'

Fifty feet ahead, someone stepped in front of the car.

Claire and Eve screamed, and Eve stamped on the brakes. Claire pitched forward against the seat belt, which snapped tight and grabbed so hard she just knew she was going to pass out from pain as the acid burn on her back rubbed against the seat. But the pain flashed away, buried by fear, because the car was fishtailing to a stop on the dark street, and there was a vampire standing there, resting its hands on the hood.

Grinning with way, way too many teeth.

'Claire!' Eve yelled. 'Don't look at him! Don't look!'

Too late. Claire had, and she felt something going

soft in her head. The fear went away. So did all her good sense. She reached for the lock on the door, but Eve lunged across and grabbed her arm. 'No!' she screamed, and held on as she slammed the car into reverse and burnt rubber backward. She didn't get far. Another vampire stepped out, blocking the street. This one was tall, ugly, and old. Same number of gleaming teeth. 'Oh, God...'

Claire kept fumbling for the lock on the door. Eve muttered something that would have definitely got Claire grounded at home, hit the brakes again, and said, 'Claire, honey, this is going to hurt,' and then she pushed Claire forward and slapped her on the burn. Hard.

Claire screeched loud enough to deafen dogs three counties away, nearly fainted, and quit trying to get out of the car. Even the two vampires outside the car – who were all of a sudden *right there at the doors* – flinched and stepped back.

Eve gunned the engine. Claire, half fainting from the red-hot throbbing agony in her back, heard noise like iron nails on a chalkboard, but then it stopped and they were moving, driving, flying through the night.

'Claire? Claire?' Eve was shaking her by the other shoulder, the one that didn't feel like she'd taken another acid bath. 'Oh, God, I'm sorry! It was just – he was going to get you to open the door, and I couldn't – I'm sorry!'

Panic was still a hot wire through her nerves, but Claire managed a nod and a weak, sick smile. She understood. She'd always wondered how in the hell anybody could be stupid enough to open up a door to the scary bad thing in the movies, but now she knew. She absolutely knew.

Sometimes, you just didn't have a choice.

Eve was gasping for breath and crying furiously in between. 'I hate this,' she said, and slammed her hand into the hard plastic steering wheel, over and over. 'I hate this town! I hate them!'

Claire got that. She was starting to really hate them, too.

Chapter Eleven

Shane was in the doorway, ready for action, when Eve screeched the car to a stop; if he was still mad, at least he wasn't letting it get in the way of a good fight. Eve frantically signalled for him to stay where he was, on safe ground, and checked the street on all sides.

'Do you see anything?' she asked Claire anxiously. Claire shook her head, still sick. 'Damn. *Damn!* OK... but you know the drill, right? Asses and elbows. Bail!'

Claire fumbled open the lock, bolted out of the car, and hit the sidewalk running. She heard Eve's door slam and running footsteps. Déja vu, she thought. Now all they needed was for Brandon to show up and act like a total asshole...

She nearly ran into Shane as she pelted across the threshold; he stepped out of the way in time, just far enough to let her pass, and grabbed Eve to pull her inside as he slammed the door and locked it.

'You have *got* to get a better job,' he said. Eve wiped at her ruined make-up with the back of one hand and threw him a filthy look.

'At least I *have* a job!'

'What, professional blood donor? Because that's all you're going to be if you—'

Claire turned, ran into a vampire, and screamed her lungs out.

OK, so she wasn't a vampire. That was established in about thirty more seconds by a combination of Shane doubling over with laughter, the vampire screaming in fright and cowering, and – last of all – Eve saying, in blank surprise, 'Miranda! Honey, what the hell are you doing here?'

The vamp – she *looked* like a vamp, Claire amended, but now that her heart rate was going down below race-car speeds she saw that it was make-up and drama, not nature – slowly lowered her arms, peered at Claire uncertainly through thick black mascaraed eyelashes, and made a little O with her ruby red lips. 'I had to come,' she said. She had a breathy, floaty voice, full of drama. 'Oh, Eve! I had such a terrible vision! There was blood and death, and it was all about *you*!'

Eve didn't seem impressed. She sighed, turned to Shane, and said, 'You let her in? I thought you hated her!'

'Couldn't leave her out there, could I? I mean, she's got a pulse. Besides, she's your friend.'

From the look Eve gave him, *friend* might have been stretching things.

Miranda gave Shane a loopy smile. *Great*, Claire thought, annoyed and disgusted and still trying to contain the aftermath of a nuclear terror explosion. The girl was tall and most of her was thin, storklike legs revealed by a black leather miniskirt. She had lots of make-up, the standard dyed-black hair, shag cut around a long white face. Ragged Magic Marker crosses drawn on her wrists and around her neck.

Miranda suddenly swung around and looked up at the ceiling. She raised her hands to her mouth in dread, but, Claire noticed, didn't smudge her lipstick. 'This house,' she said. 'Oh my. It's so…strange. Don't you feel it?'

'Mir, if you wanted to warn me about something, you could have called,' Eve said, and steered her into the living room. 'Now we've got to figure out how to get you home. Honestly, don't you have any sense? You know better than this!'

As Miranda sat down on the couch, Claire caught sight of something else on her neck…bruises. And in the centre of thc bruises, two raw, red holes. Eve saw it, too, and blinked, looked at Shane, and then at Claire. 'Mir?' she asked gently, and turned the girl's chin to one side. 'What happened to you?'

'Nothing,' Miranda said. 'Everything. You've really got to try it. It's everything I dreamt it would be, and for a second I could see, I could really see—'

Eve let go of her like she'd caught on fire. 'You *let* somebody bite you?'

'Just Charles,' Miranda said. 'He loves me. But Eve,

you have to listen – this is serious! I tried to call, but I couldn't get anyone, and I had this terrible dream—'

'Thought you said it was a vision,' Shane said. He'd followed Claire into the room and was standing near her, arms folded. She felt a little bit of the tight knot of anger and tension unravel at his closeness, even if he wasn't looking at her. *Yeah, Claire, way to go. He treats you like the furniture. Maybe you need some hooker lipstick and Kleenex in your bra, too.*

'Don't, Shane, she's been through hell—' Eve evidently remembered, too late, that whatever Miranda had been through, it waited for Shane, too, unless they could somehow negate his deal with Brandon. 'Um, right. Vision. What did you see, Mir?'

'Death.' Miranda said it with hushed relish, leaning forward and rocking gently back and forth. 'Oh, he fought, he didn't want it, didn't want the gift, but...and there was blood. Lots of blood. And he died...right... here.' She put out a hand and pointed to a spot on the floor covered by a throw rug.

Claire realised, with a sinking sense of horror, that she was probably talking about *Michael*.

'Is it – is it Shane? Are you seeing Shane's future?' Eve asked. She sounded spooked, but then, they'd had a spooky night all around. And worrying about Shane made sense.

'She can't see the future,' Shane said flatly. 'She makes crap up. Right, Mir?'

Miranda didn't answer. She craned her neck up

and looked at the ceiling again. Claire realised, with a strange creepy sensation, that she was looking exactly at where the secret room would be. Did Miranda know? How?

'This house,' she said again. 'This house is so strange. It doesn't make sense, you know.'

There was a creak on the stairs, and Claire looked over to see Michael padding down to join them, barefoot as usual. 'Yeah,' he said. 'It's not the only one. Eve, what the hell is *she* doing here?'

'Don't ask me! Shane let her in!'

'Hello, Michael,' Miranda said absently. She was still staring at the ceiling. 'This one's new.' She waved at Claire.

'Yeah. That's Claire.' He hadn't exactly come bounding to the rescue when Claire had screamed, and she wondered why. Maybe he'd been trying to stay away from Miranda; she understood why he'd want to. Talk about freaky weird...even Eve seemed not quite sure what to do with her.

She realised he hadn't heard Miranda's eerie description of his death. Maybe that was for the best.

'Claire,' Miranda whispered, and suddenly looked directly at her. She had pale blue eyes, really strange. They seemed to look right through her. 'No, it's not her, not her. Something else. Something strange in this house. Something not right. I need to read the cards.'

'The hell?' Shane asked. Miranda grabbed Eve's hand and jumped up, and practically dragged her to the stairs. 'OK, now this is just too much. Eve?'

'Um...right, it's OK!' Eve called back, as Miranda practically yanked her arm out of its socket. 'She just wants to do some tarot or something. It's OK! I'll bring her back down! Just a sec!'

Shane, Michael, and Claire just looked at one another for a few seconds, and then Shane made a loopy gesture at his temple and whistled.

Michael nodded. 'She didn't use to be that bad,' he said.

'I guess it's this Charles guy she was talking about,' Shane said grimly. 'Should have known that if anybody would hook up with a bloodsucker for troo wuv' – Shane made it sound ridiculous – 'it'd be some ditz like Miranda. I should have made her walk home. She'd probably get off on another bite.'

'She's a kid, Shane,' Michael said. 'But the sooner we get her out of here, the better I'll feel. She gets Eve a little – nervous.'

Eve? But Eve didn't really believe all that crap, did she? Claire had become convinced that it was just costuming, that underneath, Eve was just a normal girl after all, all the Goth stuff just posturing. But did she really believe in visions and crystals and tarot cards? Magic was just science misunderstood, she reminded herself. Or, on the other hand, just crazy talk.

The two boys looked at Claire. 'What?' she asked. 'Oh, by the way, I'm fine, thanks for asking. Got chased by some vampires. Business as usual.'

'Told you not to go,' Shane said, and shrugged. 'So, who's going to get Miranda to leave?'

They kept looking at her, and Claire finally understood that somehow, it had become her job. Probably because she was new, and didn't know Miranda, and she was a girl. Michael was too polite to ask her to go. Shane – she couldn't tell what Shane felt about Miranda, except that he wanted her the hell out of the house.

'Fine,' Claire said. 'I'll go.'

'That girl's smart,' Shane said without smiling, to Michael, as she started up the steps.

'Yep,' Michael agreed. 'I like that about her.'

The bedroom doors were all closed except for Eve's, which was casting a flickering light out onto the polished wood floor. Claire smelt the bright flare of matches. They were lighting candles.

Oh, she *really* didn't want to do this. Maybe if she just kept walking, went to her room, and locked the door...?

She took a deep breath and looked around the doorway with a smile that felt totally forced. Eve was lighting the candles – and boy, she had a lot of them, sitting basically everywhere. Big tall black ones, purple ones, blue ones. Nothing in the pastel family. Her bed was black satin, and there was a pirate flag – skull and crossbones – hanging above it like a billowing headboard. Little Christmas lights strung everywhere – no, not Christmas lights after all. Halloween pumpkins and ghosts and skulls. Cheery and strange.

'Hey,' Eve said, not looking up from the black pillar candle she was lighting. 'Come on in, Claire. I guess you haven't really met Miranda exactly.'

Not unless screaming and fleeing counted. 'Hi,' she said awkwardly. She didn't know what to do with her hands. Miranda didn't seem to notice or care, and *her* hands were up and in the air, petting some invisible cat or something. Weird. The longer that Claire was around the girl, the younger she looked – younger than Eve, for sure. Maybe even younger than Claire herself. Maybe it was all make-believe for her...except the bite. That was deadly serious stuff.

'Um... Eve? Can I talk to you for a sec?' Claire asked. Eve nodded, opened a black-painted dresser, and took out a black lacquer box. When opened, it had a blood-red interior. There was a black silk package inside, which, as Eve unwrapped it, proved to be a deck of cards.

Tarot cards.

Eve held them between her two palms for a few seconds, then cut the deck several times and handed it to Miranda. 'I'll be right back,' she said, and went out into the hall with Claire, closing the door behind her. Before Claire could say anything, Eve held up her hand. She wouldn't meet Claire's eyes. 'The guys sent you up?' At Claire's nod, she muttered, 'Pansies, both of them. Fine. They want her out, right?'

'Um...yeah. I guess.' Claire rocked uncomfortably back and forth. 'She is a little...weird.'

'Miranda's – yeah, she's weird. But she's also kind of

gifted,' Eve said. 'She sees things. Knows things. Shane ought to get that. She told him about the fire before—' Eve shook her head. 'Doesn't matter. If she came all the way over here in the dark, something's wrong. I should try to find out what.'

'Well...can't you just, you know, ask her?'

'Miranda's a psychic,' she said. 'It's not that simple – she can't just blurt it out. You have to *work* with her.'

'But she can't really see the future, right? You don't believe that?' *Because if you do*, Claire thought, *you're crazier than I thought you were when I first met you.*

Eve finally met her eyes. Angry. 'Yes. Yes, I do believe that, and for a smart kid you're pretty dumb if you don't understand that science isn't perfect. Things happen. Things that physics and math and crap that gets measured in a lab can't explain. People aren't just laws and rules, Claire. They're...sparks. Sparks of something beautiful and huge. And some of the sparks glow brighter, like Miranda.' Eve looked away again, obviously uncomfortable now. But not half as uncomfortable as Claire felt, because this was...wow. Space cadet city. 'You guys just leave us alone for a little while. It'll be fine.'

She went back into the room and shut the door. It wasn't quite a slam. Claire swallowed hard, feeling hot all over and wishing she hadn't let the boys push her into that, and slowly went back down the stairs. Michael and Shane were sitting on the couch and playing a video game with open beers on the table in front of them. Elbowing each other as their on-screen cars raced around turns.

'Not exactly legal,' she said, and sat down on the steps. 'The beer. Nobody here's twenty-one.'

Michael and Shane clicked bottles. Honestly, it was *juvenile.* 'Here's to crime,' Shane said, and tipped his up. 'Hey, it was a birthday present. Two six-packs. We're only one down, so give us a break. Morganville's got the highest alcoholics per capita of any place in the world, I'll bet.'

Michael put the game on pause. 'Is she leaving yet?'

'No.'

'If she starts trying to tell me I'm going to meet a tall dark stranger, I'm leaving,' Shane said. 'I mean, the kid's a head case, and I don't want to be mean, but jeez. She really believes this stuff. And she's got Eve half-convinced, too.'

There was no *half* about it, but Claire wasn't going to say that. She just sat there, trying not to think too hard about anything…about her plans to get Shane free of his agreement, which had seemed really good back in the coffee shop and not so solid now. About the dull-knife scrape of pain in her back. About the desperation in Eve's eyes. Eve was *scared.* And Claire didn't know how to help that, because she was scared half to death herself.

'She was looking at the secret room,' Claire said. 'When she was standing down here. She was staring right at it.'

Michael and Shane looked at her. Two sets of eyes, both guilty and startled. And one by one, they shrugged and went for the beer. 'Coincidence,' Michael said.

'Total coincidence,' Shane agreed.

'Eve said that Miranda had some kind of vision about you, Shane, when—'

'Not that again! Look, she said she had a vision of the house on fire, but she didn't say that until later, and even if she did, fat lot of good it did.' Shane's jaw was tight. A muscle fluttered in it. He punched a button to release the game from pause, and road noise poured out of the television speakers, closing out any chance of conversation on the subject.

Claire sighed. 'I'm going to bed.'

But she didn't. She was tired, and aching, and jittery... but her brain was way too busy picking over things. She finally nudged Shane over on the couch and sat next to him as he and Michael played, and played, and played...

'Claire. Wake up.' She blinked and realised that her head was on Shane's shoulder, and Michael was nowhere to be seen. Her first thought was, *Oh my God, am I drooling?* Her second was that she hadn't realised she was so close to him, snuggled in.

Her third was that although Michael's part of the couch was empty, Shane hadn't moved away. And he was watching her with warm, friendly eyes.

Oh. Oh, wow, that was nice.

Embarrassment flooded in a second later and made her pull away. Shane cleared his throat and scooted over.

'You should probably get some sleep,' he said. 'You're beat.'

'Yeah,' she said. 'What time is it?'

'Three a.m. Michael's making a snack. You want anything?'

'Um…no. Thanks.' She slid off the couch and then stood there like an idiot, unwilling to leave because he was still smiling and…she liked it. 'Who won?'

'Which game?'

'Oh. I guess I was asleep for a while.'

'Don't worry. We didn't let the zombies get you.' This time, his smile was positively wicked. Claire felt it like a hot blanket all over her skin. 'If you want to stay up, you can help me kick his ass.'

There were not one but three empty beer bottles on the table in front of Shane. And three where Michael had been, too. No wonder Shane was still smiling at her, looking so friendly. 'That depends,' she said. 'Can I have a beer?'

'Hell no.'

'Because I'm sixteen? Come on, Shane.'

'Drinking kills brain cells, dumbass. And besides. If I give you one, that's one less for me.' Shane tapped his forehead. 'I can do the math.'

She needed a beer, to stay down here next to him, because she was afraid she was going to do or say something stupid, and at least if there was alcohol involved, it wouldn't be her fault, would it? But just as she opened her mouth to try to convince him, Michael came out of the kitchen with a bag of neon-coloured cheese puffs. Shane grabbed a handful and stuffed his mouth. 'Claire wants a beer,' he mumbled through orange goo.

'Claire needs to go to bed,' Michael said, and flopped down. 'Scoot over, man. I don't like you that much.'

'Dick. That's not what you said last night.'

'Bite me.'

'I want another beer.'

'You're cut off. It was my birthday present, not yours.'

'Oh, that's low. You really are a dick, and just for that, I'm totally thrashing you.'

'Promises, promises.' Michael glanced at Claire. 'You're still here. No beer. I'm not corrupting a minor.'

'But *you're* a minor,' she pointed out. 'At least for beer.'

'Yeah, and by the way, how much does it suck that I'm an adult if I kill somebody, and not if I want a beer?' Shane jumped in. 'They're all dicks.'

'Man, seriously, you are one cheap drunk. Three beers? My junior high girlfriend could hold her liquor better.'

'Your junior high girlfriend—' Shane brought himself up short without finishing that sentence, and flushed bright red. Must have been good, whatever it was. 'Claire, get the hell out of here. You're making me nervous.'

'Dick!' she flung at him, and went up the stairs before he could nail her with the pillow he grabbed. It plunked into the wall behind her and slithered down to the bottom of the stairs. She was laughing, but she stopped when a shadow suddenly blocked access to the hallway at the top.

Eve. And Miranda, looking weirder than ever.

'Miranda's leaving!' Claire called down. Which wasn't such a great idea, because Eve looked upset, and Shane was drunk, and letting some vampire-crazy maybe-psychic kid walk home by herself was…bad, at best.

'Miranda's not leaving,' Eve said, and clunked down the stairs, with Miranda drifting like a black-and-white ghost behind her. 'Miranda's going to do a séance.'

Below, in the living room, she heard Michael say, in outright horror, 'Oh, shit.'

Chapter Twelve

Eve was so intense about it that not even Shane, three beers down, was able to exactly say no. Michael didn't say anything, just watched Miranda with eyes that were way too clear for somebody who'd had the same amount to drink as Shane. As Eve cleared stuff off the dining room table and set up a single black candle in the centre, Claire wrung her hands nervously, trying to get Michael's attention. When she did, she mouthed, *What do we do?*

He shrugged. Nothing, she guessed. Well, nobody but Eve believed in it, anyway. She supposed it couldn't really hurt.

'OK,' Eve said, and sat Miranda down in a chair at the end. 'Shane, Michael, Claire – sit down.'

'This is bullshit,' Shane said.

'Just – please. Just do it, OK?' Eve looked stressed. Scared. Whatever she and Miranda had been doing upstairs with those tarot cards had really made her nervous. 'Just do it for me.'

Michael slid into the chair at the other end, as far from Miranda as he could get. Claire sat next to him, and Shane grabbed a seat on the other side, leaving Eve and Claire the closest to Miranda, who was shaking like she was about to have a fit.

'Hold hands,' Eve said, and grabbed Miranda's left, then Shane's right. She glared at Claire until Claire followed suit, taking Miranda's other hand and Michael's. That left Shane and Michael, who looked at each other and shrugged.

'Whatever,' Michael said, and took Shane's hand.

'Oh, God, guys, homophobic much? This isn't about you being manly men, it's about—'

'He's dead! I see him!'

Claire flinched as Miranda practically screamed it out. All around the table, they froze. Even Shane. And then fought the insane urge to giggle – well, Claire did, and she could see Shane's shoulders shaking. Eve bit her lip, but there were tears in her eyes.

'Somebody died in this house! I see him. I see his body lying on the floor…' Miranda moaned, and thrashed around in her chair, twisting and turning. 'It's not over. It's never over. This house – this house won't let it be over.'

Claire, unable to stop herself, looked at Michael, who was staring at Miranda with cold, slitted eyes. His hand was gripping Claire's tightly. When she started to say something, he squeezed it even more. Right. Shutting up, she was.

Miranda wasn't. 'There's a ghost in this house! An unquiet spirit!'

'Unquiet spirit?' Shane said under his breath. 'Is that politically correct for *pissed off*? You know, like *Undead American* or something?'

Miranda opened her eyes and frowned at him. 'Somebody already died,' she proclaimed. 'Right here. Right in this room. His spirit haunts this place, and it's strong.'

They all just looked at one another. Michael and Claire avoided more eye contact, but Claire felt her breath get short and her heart race faster. She was talking about Michael! She *knew*! How was that even possible?

'Is it dangerous?' Eve asked breathlessly. Claire nearly choked.

'I – I can't tell. It's murky.'

Shane said, 'Right. Dead man walking, can't tell if he's dangerous because, wow, murky. Anything else?' And again, Claire had to choke back a hysterical giggle.

There was a bitter, unpleasant twist to Miranda's face now. 'Fire,' she said. 'I see fire. I see someone screaming in the fire.'

Shane yanked his hands away from Eve and Michael, slammed his chair back, and said, 'OK, that's it. I'm outta here. Feel free to get your psychic jollies somewhere else.'

'No, wait!' Eve said, and grabbed for him. 'Shane, wait, she saw it in the cards, too—'

He pulled free. 'She sees whatever you want! And she gets off on the attention, in case you didn't notice! *And* she's a fang banger!'

'Shane, please! At least listen!'

'I've heard enough. Let me know when you want to move on to table rapping or Ouija boards – those are a lot more fun. We could get some ten-year-olds to show us the ropes.'

'Shane, wait! Where are you going?'

'Bed,' he said, and went up the stairs. 'Night.'

Claire was still holding Michael's hand, and Miranda's. She let go of both, pushed her chair back, and went up after him. She heard his door slam before she made it to the top, and raced down the hall to bang her fist on the wood. There was no answer, no sound of movement inside.

Then she noticed that the picture on the wall hallway was crooked, and moved it to stare at the button underneath. Would he?

Of course he would.

She hesitated for a second, then pressed it. The panel across the hallway clicked open, letting out a breath of cold air, and she quickly slipped inside, latched it back, and went up the stairs.

Shane was lying on the couch, feet on the curved polished-wood armrest, one arm flung over his eyes.

'Go away,' he said. Claire eased herself down on the

couch next to him, because his voice didn't sound, well, right. It was quiet and a little bit choked. His hand was shaking. 'I mean it, Claire, go.'

'The first time you met me, I was crying,' she said. 'You don't have to be ashamed.'

'I'm not crying,' he said, and moved his arm. He wasn't. His eyes were hot and dry and furious. 'I can't stand that she pretends to *know.* She was Lyssa's friend. If she knew, if she really knew, she should have tried harder.'

Claire bit her lip. 'Do you mean she—?' She couldn't even say it. *Do you mean she tried to tell you?* And he couldn't admit it if she had. If he admitted that much... maybe his sister didn't have to be dead.

No, Claire couldn't say that. And he couldn't hear it.

Instead, she just reached out and took his hand. He looked down at their clasped fingers, sighed, and closed his eyes. 'I'm drunk and I'm pissed off,' he said. 'Not the best company right now. Man, your parents would kill us all if they knew about any of this.'

She didn't say anything, because that was absolutely true. And something she didn't want to think about. She just wanted to sit here, in this silent room where time had frozen still, and be with him.

'Claire?' His voice was quieter. A little smeared with sleep. 'Don't do that again.'

'Do what?'

'Go out like you did tonight. Not at night.'

'I won't if you won't.'

He smiled, but didn't open his eyes. 'No dates? What is this, the Big Brother house? Anyway, I didn't come back to Morganville to hide.'

She was instantly curious. 'Why *did* you come back?'

'Michael. I told you. He called, I came. It's what he'd do for me.' Shane's smile faded. He was probably remembering Michael not answering the phone, not coming to the hospital. Not having his back.

'It's more than that,' she said. 'Or else you'd have just taken off by now.'

'Maybe,' Shane sighed. 'Leave it, Claire. You don't have to dig into every secret around here, OK? It's not safe.'

She thought about Michael. About the way he'd looked at Miranda across the séance table. 'No,' she agreed. 'It's not.'

They talked for hours, about pretty much nothing – certainly not about vampires, or sisters dying in fires, or Miranda's visions, obviously. Shane delved into what Claire had always thought were the Boy Classics: debates about whether Superman could take Batman ('Classic Batman or Badass Batman?'), movies they liked, movies they hated. Claire tried him on books. He was light on the classics, but who wasn't? (She wasn't, but she was a freak of nature.) He liked scary stories. They had that in common, too.

Time just didn't seem to pass at all in that little room. The talk seemed to keep going, spinning out of them on its own, gradually getting slower as the minutes and hours slipped away. She got cold and sleepy, and dragged an afghan off the arm of a nearby chair, spread it around her shoulders, and promptly dropped off to sleep sitting on the floor with her back against the settee, where Shane was lying.

She woke up with a start when the settee creaked, and she realised that Shane was getting up. He blinked, yawned, rubbed at his hair (which did very funny things when he did) and checked his watch.

'Oh, God, it's early,' he groaned. 'Hell. Well, at least I can grab the bathroom first.'

Claire jumped to her feet. 'What time is it?'

'Nine,' he said, and yawned again. She reached over him, pushed the hidden button, dashed past him to the door, barely remembering to shed the afghan on the way. 'Hey! Dibs on the bathroom! I mean it!'

She wasn't worried about the bathroom so much as being caught. After all, she'd spent the entire night with a boy. A boy who'd been *drinking.* Most of that was against the house rules, she figured, and Michael would have freaked out if he'd known. Maybe...maybe Michael was too distracted from what Miranda had been spilling to worry about it, though, because she had to admit, Miranda had known exactly what she was talking about.

Just not by name, really.

Well, Michael was back to incorporeal in the light of day, so at least she didn't have to worry about running into him...but she did need to decide what to do about school. This was already the worst academic week of her life, and she had the feeling it wasn't going to get any better unless she acted quickly. Shane had made a deal with the devil; it only made sense to take advantage of it, until she could find a way to cancel it. Monica and her girls wouldn't be after her – not in a lethal way. So there was no reason not to get her butt in the library.

She grabbed her clothes and jumped in the bathroom just as Shane, still yawning, stumbled out of the hidden room.

'But I called dibs!' he said, and knocked on the door. 'Dibs! Damn girls don't understand the rules...'

'Sorry, but I need to get ready!' She cranked up the shower and skinned out of her old clothes in record time. The jeans *really* needed washing, and she was down to her last clean pair of underwear, too.

Claire was in and out of the shower fast, trusting that the waterproof bandage they'd put on her back would hold (it did). In under five minutes she was fluffing her wet hair and sliding past Shane in a breathless rush to grab her backpack and stuff it with books.

'Where the hell are you going?' he asked from the doorway. He didn't sound sleepy now. She zipped the bag shut, hefted it on the shoulder that wasn't aching and complaining, and turned towards him without answering. He was leaning on the doorframe, arms folded, head cocked. 'Oh, you've *got* to be kidding. What've you got, some kind of death wish? You really *want* to get knocked down another flight of stairs or something?'

'You made the deal. They won't come after me.'

'Don't be dense. Leave that to the experts. You really think they don't have ways around it?'

She walked up to him, staring up into his face. He looked enormously tall. And he was big, and in her way.

And she didn't care.

'You made a deal,' she said, 'and I'm going to the library. Please get out of the way.'

'Please? Damn, girl, you need to learn how to get mad or—'

She shoved him. It was dumb, and he had the muscle to stay right where he was, but surprise was on her side, and she got him to stumble a couple of steps back. She was already out the door and heading out, shoes in hand. She wasn't about to stop and give him another chance to keep her nice and safe.

'Hey!' He caught up, grabbed her arm, and spun her around. 'I thought you said you wouldn't—'

'At night,' she said, and turned to go down the stairs. He let go...and she slipped. For a scary second she was off-balance, teetering on the edge of the stairs, and then Shane's warm hands closed around her shoulders and pulled her back to balance.

He held her there for a few seconds. She didn't turn around, because if she did, and he was right there, well, she didn't know...

She didn't know what would happen.

'See you,' she gulped, and went down the stairs as fast as she dared, on shaking legs.

The heat of the morning was like a toaster oven, only without any yummy food smells; there were a couple of people out on the street. One lady was pushing a baby stroller, and for a second, while Claire was sitting down to put on her battered running shoes, she considered that with a kind of wonder. Having babies in a town like this. What were people thinking? But she guessed they did it anywhere, no matter how horrible it was. And there was a bracelet around the woman's slender wrist.

The baby was safe, at least until it turned eighteen.

Claire glanced down at her own bare wrist, shivered, and put it out of her mind as she set off for campus.

Now that she was looking, just about every person she passed had something around his or her wrist – bracelets for the women, watchbands for the men. She couldn't tell what the symbols were. She needed to find some kind of alphabet; maybe somebody had done research and put it somewhere safe...somewhere the vampires wouldn't look.

She'd always felt safest at the library, anyway. She went straight there, watching over her shoulder for Monica, Gina, Jennifer, or anybody who looked remotely interested in her. Nobody did.

TPU's library was huge. And dusty. Even the librarians at the front looked like they might have picked up a cobweb or two since her last visit. More proof – if she'd needed it – that TPU was first, and only, a party school.

She checked the map for the shelves, and saw that the Dewey decimal system reigned in Morganville – which was weird, because she'd thought all the universities were on the Library of Congress system. She traced through the listings, looking for references, and found them in the basement.

Great.

As she started to walk away, though, she cocked her head and looked at the list again. There was something strange about it. She couldn't quite put her finger on it...

There wasn't a fourth floor. Not on the list, anyway, and Mr Dewey's system jumped straight from the third floor to the fifth. Maybe it was offices, she thought. Or storage. Or shipping. Or...coffins.

It was definitely weird, though.

She started to take the stairs down to the basement, then stopped and tilted her head back. The stairs were old-school, with massive wooden railings, turning in precise L-shaped angles all the way up.

What the hell, she thought. It was only a couple of flights of stairs. She could always pretend she'd got lost.

She couldn't hear anything or anybody once she'd left the first floor. It was silent as – she hated to think it – the grave. She tried to go quietly on the stairs, and quit gripping the banister when she realised that she was leaving sweaty, betraying handprints behind. She passed the second-floor wooden door, and then the third. Nobody visible through the clear glass window.

The fourth floor didn't even *have* a door. Claire stopped, puzzled, and touched the wall. Nope, no door, no secrets she could see. Just a blank wall. Was it possible there was no fourth floor?

She went up to the fifth floor, made her way through the silent, dusty stacks to the other set of stairs, and went down. On this side, there was a door, but it was locked, and there weren't any windows.

Definitely not offices, she guessed.

But coffins weren't out of the question. Dammit, she resented being scared in a library! Books weren't supposed to be scary. They were supposed to...help.

If she were some kick-ass superhero chick, she'd probably be able to pick the lock with a fingernail clipping or something. Unfortunately, she wasn't a superhero, and she bit her fingernails.

No, she wasn't a superhero, but she was something else. She was...resourceful.

Standing there, staring at the lock, she began to smile.

'Applied science,' she said, and ran down the stairs to the first floor.

She had a stop to make in chem lab.

Her TA was in his office. 'Well,' he said, 'if you really want to shatter a lock, you need something good, like liquid helium. But liquid helium isn't all that portable.'

'What about Freon?' Claire asked.

'No, you can't get your hands on the stuff without a licence. What you can buy is a different formulation, doesn't get as cold but it's more environmentally friendly. But it probably wouldn't do the job.'

'Liquid nitrogen?'

'Same problem as helium. Too bulky.'

Claire sighed. 'Too bad. It was a cool idea.'

The TA smiled. 'Yes, it was. You know, I have a portable liquid-nitrogen tank I keep for school demonstrations, but they're hard to get. Pretty expensive. Not the kind of thing you'd find lying around. Sorry.' He wandered off, intent on some postgrad experiment of his own, and he promptly forgot all about her. She bit her lip, stared at his back for a while, and then slowly...very slowly, moved back to the door that led to the supply room. It was unlocked so that the TA could easily move in and out if he needed to. Red and yellow signs on it warned that she was going to get cancer, suffocate, or die other horrible deaths if she opened the door...but she did it anyway.

It squeaked. The TA had to have heard it, and she froze like a mouse in front of an oncoming bird. Guilty.

He didn't turn around. In fact, he deliberately kept his back to her.

She let out a shaky breath, eased into the room, and looked around. The place was neatly kept, all its chemicals labelled and stored with the safety information for each hanging below it. He stored in alphabetical order. She found the LIQUID NITROGEN sign and saw a bulky, very obvious tank...and a small one next to it, like a giant thermos, with a shoulder strap.

She grabbed it, then read the sign. USE PROTECTIVE GLOVES, the sign said. The gloves were right there, too. She shoved a pair in her backpack, slung the canister over her shoulder, and got the hell out of there.

The librarians didn't even give her a second look. She waved and smiled and went into the stacks, all the way to the back stairs.

The door was just as she'd left it. She fumbled on the gloves, opened the top of the canister, and found that there was a kind of steel pipette that fit into a nozzle. She made sure it was in place, then opened the valve, held her breath, and began pouring supercooled liquid into the lock. She wasn't sure how much to use – too much was better than not enough, she guessed – and kept pouring until the outside of the lock was completely frosted. Then she cranked the valve shut, and – reminding herself to keep the gloves *on* – yanked on the doorknob.

Crack! It sounded like a gunshot. She jumped, looked around, and realised the knob had moved in her hand.

She'd opened the door.

Nothing to do now but go inside...but somehow, that didn't seem like such a great idea, now that she was actually able to do it.

Because...coffins. Or worse.

Claire sucked in a steadying breath, opened the door, and carefully looked around the edge.

It looked like a storeroom. Files. Stacks of cartons and wooden crates. No one in sight. *Great*, she thought.

Maybe I did just break into the file room. That would be disappointing. Still, she stuffed the gloves in her backpack, just in case.

The cartons looked new, but the contents – when she unwrapped the string tying one closed – appeared old. Crumbling books, badly preserved. Ancient letters and papers in languages she couldn't read, some of which looked like ancestors of English. She tried the next box. More of the same. The room was vast, and it was full of this kind of stuff.

The book, she thought. *They're looking for the book. Every old book they find comes here and gets examined.* Now that she looked, she saw that the crates had small red X marks on them – meaning they'd been gone through? Initials, too. Somebody was being held accountable.

Which meant...somebody was working here.

She had just enough time to form the thought when two people walked out of the maze of boxes ahead of her. They weren't hurrying, and they weren't alarmed. *Vampires.* She didn't know how she knew – they weren't exactly dressed for the part – but the way they moved, loose and sure, screamed *predator* to her fragile-prey brain.

'Well,' said the short blond girl, 'we don't get many visitors here.' Except for the pallor of her face and the glitter in her eyes, she looked like a hundred other girls out on the Quad. She was wearing pink. It seemed wrong for a vampire to be wearing pink.

'Did you take a wrong turn, honey?' The man was taller, darker, and he looked really odd…really dead. It was because of his skin tone, she realised. He was black. Being a vampire bleached him, not to white, but to the colour of ashes. He had on a TPU purple T-shirt, grey sweatpants, and running shoes. If he'd been human, she'd have thought he was old – old enough to be a professor, at least.

They split up, coming at her from two different sides.

'Whose little one are you?' purred the pink girl, and before Claire could engage her brain to run, the girl had taken her left hand, examining her bare wrist. Then examining her right one. 'Oh, my, you really *are* lost, sweetie. John, what should we do?'

'Well,' John said, and put a friendly hand on Claire's shoulder. It felt colder than the liquid-nitrogen bottle hanging across her back. 'We could sit down and have a nice cup of coffee. Tell you all about what we do in here. That's what you want to know, right? Children like you are just so darn curious.' He was steering her forward, and Claire knew – just knew – that any attempt to pull free would result in pain. Probably broken bones.

Pink Girl still had hold of her other wrist, too. Her cool fingers were pressed against Claire's pulse point.

I need to get out of this. Fast.

'I know what you do here,' she said. 'You're looking for the book. But I thought vampires couldn't read it.'

John stopped and looked at his companion, who raised pale eyebrows back at him. 'Angela?' he asked.

'We can't,' she said. 'We're just here as...observers. And you seem very knowledgeable, for a free-range child. Under eighteen, aren't you? Shouldn't you be under someone's Protection? Your family's?'

She seemed honestly concerned. That was weird. 'I'm a student,' Claire said. 'Advanced placement.'

'Ah,' Angela said, and looked kind of regretful. 'Well, then, I guess you're on your own. Too bad, really.'

'Because you're going to kill me?' Claire heard herself say it in a kind of dreamlike state, and remembered what Eve had told her. *Don't look in their eyes.* Too late. Angela's were a soft turquoise, very pretty. Claire felt a deliciously warm edge-of-sleep sensation wash over her.

'Probably,' Angela admitted. 'But first you should have some tea.'

'Coffee,' John said. 'I still like the caffeine.'

'It spoils the taste!'

'Gives it that zip.' John smacked his lips.

'Why don't you let me look through boxes?' Claire asked, desperately bringing herself back from the edge of whatever that was. The vampires were leading her through a maze of boxes and crates, all marked with red Xs and initials. 'You've got to let humans do it, right? If you can't read the book?'

'What makes you think *you* could read it, little one?' Angela asked. She had a buttery sort of accent, not quite California, not quite Midwest, not quite anything. Old. It sounded old. 'Are you a scholar of languages, as well?'

'N-no, but I know what the symbol is that you're looking for. I can recognise it.'

Angela reached down and drew her fingernails lightly over the skin of Claire's inner arm, looking thoughtful.

'No, I don't have the tattoo. But I've seen it.' She was absolutely shaking all over, terrified in a distant sort of way, but her brain was racing, looking for escape. 'I can recognise it. You can't, can you? You can't even draw it.'

Angela's fingernails dug in just a bit, in warning. 'Don't be smart, little girl. We're not the kind of people you should mock.'

'I'm not mocking. You can't see it. That's why you haven't found it. It's not just that you can't *read* it – right?'

Angela and John exchanged looks again, silent and meaningful. Claire swallowed hard, tried to think of anything that might be a good argument for keeping her unbitten (*Maybe if I don't drink any tea or coffee?*) and spared a thought for just how pissed off Shane was going to be if she went and got herself killed. On campus. In the middle of the day.

The vampires turned a corner of boxes, and there, in an open space, was a door that didn't lead out onto any stairwell she'd seen, an elevator with a DOWN button, a battered school-issue desk and chair, and...

'Professor Wilson?' she blurted. He looked up, blinking behind his glasses. He was her Classics of English Literature professor (Tuesdays and Thursdays at two) and although he was boring, he seemed to know his stuff. He was a faded-looking man, all greys – thin grey hair, faded grey eyes – with a tendency to dress in colours that bleached him out even more. Today it was a white shirt and grey jacket.

'Ah. You're—' he snapped his fingers two or three times – 'in my Intro to Shakespeare—'

'Classics of English Lit.'

'Right, exactly. They change the title occasionally, just to fool the students into taking it again. Neuberg, isn't it?' Fright in his eyes. 'You weren't assigned here to help me, were you?'

'I—' Light dawned. Maybe letting mistaken impressions lie was a good idea right now. 'Yes. I was. By...Miss Samson.' Miss Samson was the dragon lady of the English department; everyone knew that. Nobody questioned her. As excuses went, this one was thinner than paper, but it was all she had. 'I was looking for you.'

'And the door was open?' John asked, looking down at her. She kept her eyes firmly fixed on Professor Wilson, who wasn't likely to hypnotise her into not lying.

'Yes,' she said firmly. 'It was open.' The only good thing about the canister on her back was that at least it *looked* like something a college student might carry around, with soup or coffee or something in it. And it didn't exactly look like something to break locks. By now, the liquid nitrogen in the lock would have sublimated into the air, and all evidence was gone.

She hoped.

'Well then,' Wilson said, and frowned at her, 'better sit down and get to work, Neuberg. We have a lot to do. You know what you're looking for?'

'Yes, sir.' John let go of her shoulder. After a reluctant second, Angela released her, too, and Claire went to the desk, dragged up a wooden chair, and carefully placed her backpack and canister on the floor.

'Coffee?' John asked hopefully.

'No, thank you,' she said politely, and pulled the first stacked volume towards her.

It was interesting work, which was weird, and the vampires became less and less frightening the more she was in their company. Angela was a fidgeter, always tapping her foot or restlessly braiding her hair or straightening stacks of books. The vampires seemed assigned only as observers; as Professor Wilson and Claire finished each mountain of books, they took them away, boxed them, and brought new volumes to check.

'Where do these come from?' Claire wondered out loud, and sneezed as she opened the cover of something called *Land Register of Atascosa County*, which was filled with antique, neat handwriting. Names, dates, measurements. Nothing like what they were looking for.

'Everywhere,' Professor Wilson said, and closed the book he'd flipped through. 'Secondhand stores. Antique shops. Book dealers. They have a network around the world, and everything comes here for inspection. If it isn't what they're looking for, it goes out again. They even make a profit on it, I'm told.' He cleared his throat and held up the book he'd been looking at. 'John? This one is a first-edition Lewis Carroll. I believe you should put it aside.'

John obligingly took it and set it in a pile that Claire thought was probably 'rare and valuable'.

'How long have you been doing this, Professor?' she asked. He looked tired.

'Seven years,' he said. 'Four hours a day. Someone will come in to relieve us soon.'

Us, meaning that she'd get to walk out. Well, that was nice. She'd been hoping that she might at least slip a note out with the professor, something along the lines of IF YOU FIND MY BODY, I WAS KILLED BY MISS PINK IN THE LIBRARY, but that sounded too much like something out of that board game her parents liked so much.

'No talking in class,' John said, and laughed. When he did, his fangs came down. His were longer than Brandon's, and looked scarier, somehow. Claire gulped and focused on the book in front of her. The cover said *Native Grains of the New World*. A whole book about grain. Wow. She wondered how Professor Wilson had stayed sane all these years. *Corn is a member of the grass family and is native to the American continents...* She flipped pages. More about corn. She didn't know you could write so much about one plant.

Beside her, Professor Wilson swore softly under his breath, and she looked up, startled. His face had gone pale, except for two red spots high in his cheeks. He quickly faked a smile and held up a finger striped with red. 'Paper cut,' he said. His voice sounded high and tight, and Claire followed his stare to see Angela and John moving closer, watching the professor's finger with eerie concentration. 'It's nothing. Nothing at all.' He groped in his pocket, came out with a handkerchief, and wrapped it around his bloodied finger. In trying to attend to that, he knocked the book he'd been reviewing to the floor. Claire automatically bent to pick it up, but Wilson's foot hooked around it and scooted it out of her reach. He bent over and in the darkness under the desk...switched books.

Claire watched, open-mouthed. What the hell was he doing? Before she could do anything stupid that might give him away, there was a ding from the elevator across the room, then the rumble of opening doors.

'Ah,' Wilson said with evident relief. 'Time to go, then.' He reached down, picked up the hidden book, and slipped it into his leather satchel with such skill Claire wasn't absolutely sure she'd seen it. 'Come along, Neuberg.'

'Not her,' John said, smiling cheerfully. 'She gets to stay after class.'

'But—' Claire bit her lip and made desperate eye contact with the professor, who frowned and shifted his weight from one foot to the other. 'Sir, can't I go with you? Please?'

'Yes, of course,' he said. 'Come along, I said. Mr Hargrove, if you don't like it, please take it up with management. I have a class.'

He might have pulled it off, too, if Angela hadn't been

so sharp-eyed, or suspicious; she stopped him half-way to the elevator, opened up his portfolio, and took out the book he'd stashed away. She leafed through it silently, then handed it to John, who did the same.

Both of them looked at the professor with calm, cool, oddly pleased eyes.

'Well,' Angela said, 'I don't know, but I think this may be a violation of the rules, Professor. Taking books from the library without checking them out first. Shame, shame.'

She deliberately opened the first page and read, 'It was the best of times, it was the worst of times...' and then flipped carefully through, stopping at random spots, to read lines of text. It all sounded right to Claire. She flinched when Angela pushed the book at her. 'Read,' the vampire said.

'Um...where?'

'Anywhere.'

Claire recited a few lines in a faltering voice from page 229.

'*A Tale of Two Cities*,' John said. 'Let me guess, Professor...a first edition?'

'Mint condition,' Angela said, and plucked it out of Claire's trembling hands. 'I think the professor has a nice retirement plan, composed of screwing us out of our rightful profits.'

'Huh,' John said. 'He didn't look quite so dumb as that. Got all those degrees and stuff.'

'That's just paper smarts. You never can tell about

what's really in their heads until you open them up.' The two of them were talking like he wasn't even there.

Professor Wilson's pale skin had a sweaty gleam on it now. 'A moment of weakness,' he said. 'I really do apologise. It won't ever happen again, I swear that to you.'

'Apology accepted,' Angela said, and lunged forward, planted her hand on his chest, and knocked him flat to the floor. 'And by the way, I believe you.'

She grabbed his wrist, raised it to her mouth, and paused to strip off his gold wristwatch band and toss it on the floor. As it rolled, Claire's stricken eyes caught sight of the symbol on the watch face. A triangle. Delta?

Her shock broke at the sound of the professor's scream. Grown men shouldn't scream like that. It just wasn't right. Fright made her angry, and she dropped her book bag, took the canister off her shoulder, and yanked off the top.

Then she threw liquid nitrogen all over Angela's back. When John turned on her, snarling, she splashed what was left at his face, aiming for his eyes. Wilson rolled to his feet as Angela collapsed, shrieking and thrashing; John reached out for him, but she'd managed to hurt him, too – he missed. Wilson grabbed his satchel and she got her book bag; they ran for the elevator. A very surprised professor – someone she didn't recognise – was standing there, open-mouthed; Wilson yelled at him to stand aside, leapt into the cage, and pressed the DOWN button so frantically Claire was afraid it would snap or stick or something.

The doors rolled shut, and the elevator began to fall. Claire tried to get her breathing under control, but it was no good; she was about to hyperventilate. Still, she was doing better than the professor. He looked awful; his face was as grey as his hair, and he was breathing in shallow, hard gasps.

'Oh dear,' he said weakly. 'That wasn't good.' And then he slowly collapsed down the wall of the elevator until he was in a sitting position, legs splayed loosely.

'Professor?' Claire lunged forward and hovered over him.

'Heart,' he panted, and then made a choking sound. She loosened his tie. That didn't seem to help. 'Listen. My house. Bookshelf. Black cover. Go.'

'Professor, relax, it's OK—'

'No. Can't let them have it. Bookshelf. Black—'

His eyes got very wide, and his back arched, and she heard him make an awful noise, and then...

Then he just *died*. Nothing dramatic about it, no big speeches, no music swelling to tell her how to feel about it. He was just...gone, and even though she pressed her shaking fingers to his neck, she knew she wouldn't feel anything, because there was something different about him. He was like a rubber doll, not a person.

The elevator doors opened. Claire gasped, grabbed her books and the empty silver canister, and sprinted down the blank cinder-block hallway to the end, where a fire door opened into bright afternoon sunlight.

She stood there for a few long seconds, just shaking and

gasping and crying, and then tried to think where to go. Angela and John thought her name was Neuberg, which was good – she supposed not so good for Neuberg, if one existed – but they'd find out who she was eventually. She needed to be home before that happened.

Bookshelf. Black cover.

Professor Wilson had been in that room for seven years, sorting through books. Probably slipping out those he thought might be worth something on the black market.

What if...?

No. It couldn't be.

Except...what if it was? What if a year ago, or five years ago, Professor Wilson had *found* that book the vampires were so intent on having, and decided to hang on to it for a rainy day? After all, she'd been basically planning to do the same thing, only for her it was already stormy weather.

She needed his address.

It wasn't far to the Communication Arts Building, and she ran as much of the way as she could before the pain in her still-bruised ankle and still-raw back made her slow down. Two flights of steps brought her to the offices, and she passed up Professor Wilson's closed and locked office to stop next to the cluttered desk out in the open between the corridors. The nameplate read VIVIAN SAMSON, but everyone just called her Dragon Lady, and the woman sitting behind it had earned the name. She was old, fat, and legendarily bad-tempered. There was no smoking in all university buildings, but the Dragon Lady had an overflowing ashtray on the corner of her desk and a glowing cigarette hanging out of the corner of her red-painted lips. Beehive hair, straight out of old movies. She had a computer, but it wasn't turned on, and as far as Claire could tell from the two-inch-long bright red nails, the Dragon Lady didn't type, either.

She ignored Claire and kept on reading the magazine open in front of her.

'Um – excuse me?' Claire asked. She felt sticky with sweat from the run in the heat, and still kind of sick from what had happened at the library. The Dragon Lady turned a page in her magazine. 'I just need—'

'I'm on break.' The red-clawed hand took the cigarette out of the red-painted mouth for a trip to the ashtray to shed some excess. 'Not even supposed to be here today. Damn grad students. Come back in half an hour.'

'But—'

'No buts. I'm on break. Shoo.'

'But Professor Wilson sent me to get something from his house, but he didn't give me the address. *Please*—'

She slapped the magazine closed. 'Oh, for God's sake. I'm going to wring his neck when he gets back here. Here.' She grabbed a card from the holder on her desk and pitched it at Claire, glaring. 'If you're some nutcase, it's not my problem. You tell His Highness that if he wants to roll around with undergrads, he can damn well remember to tell them his own damn address from now on. Got it?'

'Got it,' Claire said in a very small voice. *Roll around with...* She wasn't going to think about that. Not at all. 'Thank you.'

The Dragon Lady puffed a cloud of smoke out of both nostrils and raised eyebrows plucked into more of a suggestion than an actual form. 'You're a polite one. Go on, get out of here before I remember I'm supposed to be off today.'

Claire escaped, clutching the card in her sweaty fingers.

Chapter Thirteen

'You know,' Shane said twenty minutes later, 'I'd feel a whole lot better about the two of us if you didn't think I was the go-to guy for breaking and entering.'

They were standing on the professor's back porch, and Claire was peering through a murky window into an equally murky living room. She felt a flash of guilt about the breaking-and-entering part – but she had called him – just before her heart did a funny little painful flip and she heard him say again in her head *the two of us*.

She didn't dare look at him. Surely he didn't mean that, exactly. That meant, you know, friendship or something. He treated her like a kid. Like his sister. He didn't – he couldn't—

But what if he could?

And she couldn't believe she was thinking this now, on the doorstep of a dead man. The memory of Professor Wilson's limp, rubbery body steadied her, and she was able to finally stand back from the window and meet Shane's eyes without fluttering like some scared sparrow. 'Well, I couldn't ask Eve,' she said reasonably. 'She's at work.'

'Makes sense. Hey, look, what's that?' Shane pointed. She whirled to stare. There was a sound of tinkling glass behind her, and when she turned back he was opening the back door. 'There. Now you can say you didn't know I was going to do it. Crime free.'

Well, not exactly. She was still carrying the metal cylinder over her shoulder. She wondered if the vampires had recovered yet, and if anybody had thought to question the TA at the chem lab. She hoped not. He was nice, and in his own way he was brave, but she had no illusions that he wouldn't sell her out in a hot second. There weren't a whole lot of heroes left in Morganville.

One of the last of them turned in the doorway and said, 'In or out, kid, daylight's burning.'

She followed Shane over the threshold into Professor Wilson's house.

It was kind of weird, really – she could see that he'd been here hours ago, living his life, and now the house seemed like it was waiting for him. Maybe not so much weird as sad. They came in through the kitchen, and there was a cereal bowl, a glass, and a coffee cup in the dish strainer. The professor had eaten breakfast, at least. When she touched the towel underneath the strainer, it was still damp.

'Hey,' Shane said. 'So what are we looking for in here?'

'Bookshelves,' she said.

'Yo. Found 'em.' He sounded odd. She followed him into the next room – the living room – and felt her stomach sink a little. Why hadn't she thought about this? He was a *professor.* Of course he'd have a jazillion books...and there were, floor to ceiling, all the way around the room. Crammed in together. Stacked on the floor in places. Stacked on tables. She'd thought the Glass House was a reader's paradise, but this...

'We have two hours,' Shane said. 'Then we're gone. I don't want to risk you out on the street after dark.'

She nodded numbly and went to the first set of shelves. 'He said it had a black cover. Maybe that will help.'

But it didn't. She began pulling out all the black-bound books and piling them on the table; Shane did the same. By the time they'd met in the middle of the shelves, an hour had passed, and the pile was huge.

'What the hell are we looking for?' he asked, staring at it. She didn't suppose *I don't know* would be an answer that would get any respect.

'You know the tattoo on Eve's arm?'

Shane acted like she'd stuck him in the butt with a fork. 'We're looking for *the* book? *Here?*'

'I—' She gave up. 'I don't know. Maybe. It's worth a try.'

He just shook his head, his expression something

between *You're crazy* and *You're amazing.* But not in a good way. She pulled up a chair and began leafing through the books, one after another. Nothing…nothing… nothing…

'Claire.' Shane sounded odd. He handed her a black leather-bound book. 'Take a look.'

It was too new. They were looking for an old book, right? This was…this was a Holy Bible. With a cross on the front.

'Look *inside*,' he said. She opened it. The first few gold-leafed pages were standard, the same familiar words she'd grown up with, and still believed. Eve had said they had a few churches in Morganville, right? Maybe they had services. She'd have to check.

Midway through Exodus, the pages went hollow, and there was a tiny little volume hidden inside the Bible. Old. Very old. The cover was water-stained dirty leather, and scratched into it was a symbol.

The symbol.

Claire pulled it out of the Bible and opened it.

'Well?' Shane demanded after a few seconds. 'What about it?'

'It's—' She swallowed hard. 'It's in Latin.'

'So? What does it say?'

'I don't *read* Latin!'

'You're kidding. I thought all geniuses read Latin. Isn't that the international language for smart people?'

She picked up a book without looking and threw it at him. He ducked. It flopped to the floor. Claire flipped pages in the small volume. It was handwritten in faded, coppery ink, the kind of beautiful perfect writing from hundreds of years ago.

She was actually holding it in her hands.

And here she'd been intending to just fake it.

'We'd better get going,' Shane said. 'Seriously. I don't want to be here when the cops come calling.'

'You think they will?'

'Well, if dear old Prof Wilson keeled over after stealing the vampires blind, yeah, I think they'll send a couple of cops over to inventory the goodies. So we'd better move it.'

She stuffed the journal back into the Bible and started to put it into her backpack, then paused in outright despair. Too much stuff. 'We need another bag,' she said. 'Something small.'

Shane came up with a plastic grocery sack from the kitchen, stuck the Bible inside, and hustled her out. She looked back at Professor Wilson's lonely living room one last time. A clock ticked on the mantel, and everything waited for a life that would never start up again.

She was right. It *was* sad.

'Run first,' Shane said. 'Mourn later.'

It was the perfect motto for Morganville.

They made it back home with half an hour or so to spare, but as they turned the corner on Lot Street, where the Gothic bulk of the Glass House pretty much dwarfed all of the other, newer houses around it, Claire's eyes went immediately to the blue SUV sitting at the kerb. It looked familiar…

'Oh my God,' she said, and stopped dead in her tracks.

'OK, stopping? Not a great idea. Come on, Claire, let's—'

'That's my parents' car!' she said. 'My parents are here! Oh my *God*!' She practically squealed that last part, and would have turned around and run away, but Shane grabbed her by the neck of her shirt and hauled her around.

'Better get it over with,' he said. 'If they tracked you this far, they're not going to drive off without saying hello.'

'Oh, *man*! Let go!' He did. She twitched her shirt down over her shoulders and glared at him, and he did an extravagant bow.

'You first,' he said. 'I'm watching your back.'

She was, at least temporarily, more worried about her front.

When she cracked open the door to the house, she could hear Eve's anxious voice. 'I'm sure she'll be here any time – she's, you know, at class, and—'

'Young lady, my daughter is *not* in class. I've *been* to her classes. She hasn't been to class the entire afternoon. Now, are you going to tell me where she is, or do I have to call the police?'

Dad sounded *pissed*. Claire swallowed hard, resisted the urge to back up and close the door and run away

– mainly because Shane was right behind her, and he was finding this way too funny to let her escape – and walked down the hall towards the voices. Just Eve and Dad, so far. Where was—

'Claire!' She'd know that shriek of relief anywhere. Before she could say *Hi, Mom*, she was buried in a hug and a wave of L'Oreal perfume. The perfume stayed longer than the hug, which morphed into Claire's being held at arm's length and shaken like a rag doll. 'Claire, *what have you been doing? What are you doing here?*'

'Mom—'

'We were so worried about you after that terrible accident, but Les couldn't get off work until today—'

'It wasn't that big a deal, Mom—'

'And we just had to come up and see you, but your room is *empty* in the dorm. You weren't in classes – Claire, what's happened to you? I can't believe you'd do something like this!'

'Like what?' she asked, sighing. 'Mom, would you quit shaking me? I'm getting dizzy.'

Mom let go and folded her arms. She wasn't very tall – just a couple of inches over Claire's height, even in mid-heeled shoes – and Dad, who was glowering at Shane in the background, was as tall and twice as broad. 'Is it him?' Dad asked. 'Did he get you into trouble?'

'Not me,' Shane said. 'I've just got that kind of face.'

'Shut *up*!' Claire hissed. She could hear that he thought all this was funny. She didn't. 'Shane's just a friend, Dad. Like Eve.'

'Eve?' Her parents looked at each other blankly. 'You mean—' As one, they cast horrified glances at Eve, who was standing with her hands folded, trying to look as demure as it was possible to look while wearing an outfit that looked like something a Goth ballerina might wear – all black netting in the skirt and red satin up top. She smiled sweetly, but it was kind of spoilt by the red lipstick (had she borrowed Miranda's?) and skull earrings.

Mom said faintly, 'Claire, you used to have such *nice* friends. What happened to Elizabeth?'

'She went to Texas A & M, Mom.'

'That's no reason not to still be friends.'

Mom logic. Claire decided that Shane had been right – there was no getting out of this one. She might as well jump into the pool; the sharks were circling no matter what she did. 'Mom, Eve and Shane are two of my roommates. Here. In this house.'

Silence. Mom and Dad looked frozen. 'Les?' Mom asked. 'Did she say she was *living here*?'

'Young lady, you are *not* living here,' Dad said. 'You live in the dorm.'

'I'm not. I'm living here, and that's my decision.'

'That's *illegal*! The rules said that you have to live *on campus*, Claire. You can't just—'

Outside the windows, night was slipping up on them, stealthy and quick as an assassin. 'I can,' Claire said. 'I did. I'm not going back there.'

'Well, I'm not paying good money just to have you

squat in some old wreck with a bunch of—' Dad was at a loss for words to describe how little he thought of Eve and Shane. '*Friends*! And are they even in school?'

'I'm currently between majors,' Shane offered.

'Shut *up*!' Claire was nearly in tears now.

'All right, that's it. Get your things, Claire. You're coming with us.'

All the amusement faded out of Shane's face. 'No, she isn't,' he said. 'Not at night. Sorry.'

Dad got red-faced and even more furious, and levelled a finger at her. 'Is this why you're here? Older boys? Living under the same roof?'

'Oh, Claire,' Mom sighed. 'You're too young for this. You—'

'Shane,' Shane supplied.

'Shane, I'm sure you're a perfectly nice boy,' – she didn't sound especially convinced – 'but you have to understand that Claire is a very special girl, and she's very young.'

'She's a kid!' Dad interrupted. 'She's sixteen! And if you took advantage of her—'

'Dad!' Claire thought her face might be just as red as his, for very different reasons. 'Enough already! Shane's my *friend*! Stop embarrassing me!'

'Embarrassing *you*? Claire, how do you think we feel?' Dad roared.

In the silence, Claire heard Michael say mildly, from the stairs, 'I think maybe we'd all better sit down.'

* * *

They didn't all sit down. Shane and Eve escaped to the kitchen, where Claire heard a clattering of pots and furious whispering; she was sitting uncomfortably on the couch between her parental bookends, looking mournfully at Michael, who was sitting in the armchair. He looked calm and collected, but then, he would. Mom, Dad, this is Michael, he's a dead guy... Yeah, that would really help.

'My name is Michael Glass,' he said, and extended his hand to Claire's dad like an equal. Dad, surprised, took it and shook. 'You've already met our other two roommates, Eve Rosser and Shane Collins. Sir, I know you're concerned about Claire. You should be. She's on her own for the first time, and she's younger than most kids coming to college. I don't blame you for being worried.'

Dad, defused, settled for looking stubborn. 'And who the heck are you, Michael Glass?'

'I own this house,' he said. 'I rent a room to your daughter.'

'How old are you?'

'A little over eighteen. So are Shane and Eve. We've known each other a long time, and to be honest, we didn't really want to let another person into the house, but...' Michael shrugged. 'We had an empty bedroom, and splitting costs four ways is better. I thought a long time about letting Claire stay here. We had house meetings about it.'

Claire blinked at him. He had? They did?

'My daughter's a minor,' Dad said. 'I'm not happy about this. Not at all.'

'Sir, I understand. I wasn't too happy about it, either. Even having her here is a risk for us, you understand.' Michael didn't have to go into it, Claire saw; her dad totally got it. 'But she needed us, and we couldn't turn her away.'

'You mean you couldn't turn her money away,' Dad said, frowning. For answer, Michael got up, went to a wooden box sitting on the shelf, and took out an envelope. He handed it to Dad.

'That's what she paid me,' he said. 'The whole amount. I kept it in case she wanted to leave. This wasn't about money, Mr Danvers. It was about Claire's safety.'

Michael glanced across at her, and she bit her lip. She'd been hoping to avoid this – desperately hoping – but she couldn't see any way out now. She nodded slightly and slumped back on the couch cushions, trying to make herself small. Smaller.

'Claire's dorm was girls-only,' Claire's mom put in. She reached over to stroke Claire's hair absently, the way she did when Claire was little. Claire endured it. Actually, she secretly liked it, a little, and had to fight not to relax against Mom's side and let herself be hugged. Protected. 'She was safe, wasn't she? That Monica girl said—'

'You talked to Monica?' Claire said sharply, and looked wide-eyed at her mother. Mom frowned a little, dark eyes concerned.

'Yes, of course I did. I was trying to find out where

you'd gone, and Monica was very helpful.'

'I'll bet,' Claire muttered. The idea of Monica standing there smiling at her mom – looking innocent and nice, probably – was sickening.

'She said you were staying here,' Mom finished, still frowning. 'Claire, honey, why would you leave the dorm? I know you're not a silly girl. You wouldn't do it if you didn't have a reason.'

Michael said, 'She did. She was being hazed.'

'Hazed?' Mom repeated the word like she had no idea what it meant.

'From what Claire told me, it started small – all the freshmen girls get it from the older ones. Nasty stuff, but not dangerous. But she got on the wrong side of the wrong girl, and she was getting hurt.'

'Hurt?' That was Dad, who now had something to hold on to.

'When she came here, she had bruises like a road map,' Michael said. 'To be honest, I wanted to call the cops. She wouldn't let me. But I couldn't let her go back there. She wasn't just getting knocked around... I think her life was in danger.'

Mom's hand had frozen in Claire's hair, and she let out a little moan.

'It's not that bad,' Claire offered. 'I mean, look, nothing broken or anything. I had a sore ankle for a while, and a black eye, but—'

'A black eye?'

'It's gone. See?' She batted her eyelashes. Mom's gaze

searched her face with agonising care. 'Honest, it's over. Done. Everything's fine now.'

'No,' Michael said. 'It's not. But Claire's handling it, and we're watching out for her. Shane especially. He – he had a little sister, and he's taken an interest in making sure Claire stays safe. But more than that, I think Claire's taking care of herself. And that's what she has to learn, don't you agree?' Michael leant forward, hands loosely clasped, elbows on his knees. In the glow of the lamps, his hair was rich gold, his eyes angel blue. If anybody *ever* looked trustworthy, it was Michael Glass.

Of course, he was dead and all, which Claire had to bite her tongue not to blurt out in sheer altered-state panic.

Mom and Dad were thinking. She knew she had to say something...something important. Something that would make them not drag her home by the ear. 'I can't leave,' she said. It came from her heart, and she meant every word. Her voice stayed absolutely steady, too – for once. 'Mom, Dad, I know that you're afraid for me, and I – I love you. But I need to stay here. Michael isn't telling you this, but they put themselves on the line for me, and I owe it to them to stay until it's settled and I'm sure they won't get in trouble for me. It's what I have to do, you understand? And I can do it. I *have* to.'

'Claire,' Mom said in a small, choked voice. 'You're *sixteen*! You're a *child*!'

'I'm not,' she said simply. 'I'm sixteen and a half, and I'm not giving up. I never have. You know that.'

They did. Claire had fought all her life against the odds, and both her parents knew it. They knew how stubborn she was. More, they knew how important it was to her.

'I don't like this,' her dad said, but he sounded unhappy now, not angry. 'I don't like you living with older boys. Off campus. And I want these people who hurt you stopped.'

'Then *I* have to stop them,' Claire said. 'It's my problem. And there are other girls in that dorm getting hurt, too, so it isn't just about me. I need to do it for them, too.'

Michael raised his eyebrows slightly, but didn't answer. Mom wiped at her eyes with a handkerchief. Eve appeared in the doorway wearing a huge apron with a red-lips emblem that read KISS THE COOK, peered uncertainly at them, and gave Claire's parents a nervous smile.

'Dinner's ready!' she said.

'Oh, we couldn't,' Mom said.

'The heck we can't,' Dad said. 'I'm starved. Is that chilli?

Dinner was uncomfortable. Dad made noncommittal grunts about the quality of the chilli. Shane looked like he was barely holding on to his laughter most of the time. Eve was so nervous that Claire thought she would jitter right out of the chair, and Michael... Michael was the calm one. The adult. Claire had never felt more like the kid at the big table in her life.

'So, Michael,' Claire's mother said, nibbling at a spoonful of chilli, 'what is it you do?'

Haunts the house where he died, Claire thought, and bit her lip. She took a fast sip of her cola.

'I'm a musician,' he said.

'Oh really?' She brightened up. 'What do you play? I love classical music!'

Now even *Michael* looked uncomfortable. Shane coughed into his napkin and drained Coke in huge gulps to drown out his hiccupping laughter.

'Piano and guitar,' he said. 'But mostly guitar. Acoustic and electric.'

'Humph,' Claire's dad said. 'Any good?'

Shane's shoulders were shaking.

'I don't know,' Michael said. 'I work hard at it.'

'He's *very* good!' Eve jumped in, eyes bright and flashing. 'Honestly, Michael, you should quit being so humble. You're really great. It's just a matter of time before you really do something big, and you know it!'

Michael looked...blank. Expressionless. That didn't quite hide the pain, Claire thought. 'Someday,' he said, and shrugged. 'Hey, Shane, thanks for dinner. Good stuff.'

'Yeah,' Eve said. 'Not bad.'

'Spicy,' Dad said, as if that was a flaw. Claire knew for a fact he ordinarily added Tabasco to half of what he ate. 'Mind if I get a refill?'

Eve jumped up like a jack-in-the-box. 'I'll get it!' But Dad was at the end of the table, closest to the kitchen, and he was already on his feet and heading that direction.

Michael and Shane exchanged looks. Claire frowned, trying to figure out what they were looking so alarmed about.

They sat in silence as the refrigerator opened, bottles rattled, and then it closed. Dad came back, one cold-frosted Coke in his hand.

In his other hand he held a beer. He sat it in the centre of the table and glared at Michael.

'You want to explain why there's beer in a refrigerator with a sixteen-year-old in the house?' he asked.

'Not to mention that none of you is old enough to be drinking it!'

Well, that was that. Some days, Claire thought, you just couldn't win.

She had two days, and only because Dad agreed to allow her to go to the admissions office and file transfer paperwork. Michael tried his best, but even angelic good looks and complete sincerity weren't good enough this time. Shane had stopped finding it amusing at some point, and started yelling. Eve had gone to her room.

Claire had cried. A lot. Furiously.

She was so angry, in fact, that she barely cared that Mom and Dad were going to be driving out of Morganville in the dark, unprotected and unwarned. Michael took care of that, though, with a story about carjackers stealing SUVs in the area. That was the best anyone could do, and more than Claire wanted, anyway.

Dad had looked at her like she was a *disappointment*.

She'd never, ever been a disappointment before, and it totally pissed her off, because she didn't deserve it, not one bit.

Michael and Shane stood in the doorway, watching her parents hurry to their SUV in the dark. Shane, she saw, had a big hand-carved cross, and he was ready to charge to the rescue, even though he was mad as hell. He didn't need to, though. Mom and Dad got in their truck and drove away, into the hushed Morganville night, and Michael closed and locked the door and turned to look at Claire.

'Sorry,' he said. 'That could have been better.'

'You think?' she shot back. Her eyes were swollen and hot, and she felt like she might vibrate apart; she was so mad. 'I'm not leaving! No way!'

'Claire.' Michael reached out and put his hands on her shoulders. 'Until you're eighteen, you really don't have the right to say that, OK? I know, you're almost seventeen, you're smarter than ninety per cent of the people in the world—'

'One hundred per cent smarter than anybody else in this house,' Shane said.

'—but that doesn't matter. It will, but it doesn't right now. You need to do what they say. If you decide to fight them, it's going to get ugly, and Claire, we can't afford it. *I* can't afford it. You understand?' He searched her eyes, and she had to nod. 'Sorry. Believe me, it isn't the way I wanted it to happen, but at least you'll be out of Morganville. You'll be safe.'

He hugged her. She felt her breath leave for a second, and then he was gone, walking away.

She looked at Shane.

'Well, I'm not hugging you,' he said. He was standing close to her, so close she had to crane her neck way up to meet his eyes. And for a long few seconds, they didn't say anything; he just...watched her. In the living room, she heard Eve talking to Michael, but here in the hallway it was very quiet. She could hear the fast pounding of her heart, and wondered if he could hear it, too.

'Claire—' he finally said.

'I know,' she said. 'I'm sixteen. Heard it already.'

He put his arms around her. Not the way Michael had, exactly – she didn't know why it was different, but it was. This wasn't a hug; it was – it felt – *close.*

He wasn't holding himself back, that was it. And she relaxed against him with a breathless sigh, cheek against his chest, almost purring with relief. He rested his chin on the top of her head. She felt so *small* next to him, but that was all right. It didn't make her feel weak.

'I'm going to miss you,' he whispered, and she leant back to look up at him again.

'Really?'

'Yeah.' She thought – really thought – that he was going to kiss her, but just then, she heard Eve call, 'Shane!' and he flinched and pulled back, and the old

Shane, the cocky Shane, was back. 'You made things exciting around here.'

He loped off down the hall, and she felt a pure burst of fury.

Boys. Why were they always such dumbasses?

The night did its usual tricks – creepy creaking sounds upstairs, wind hissing at the windows, branches tapping. Claire couldn't sleep. She couldn't get used to the idea that this room, this lovely room, was hers for only two more nights, and then she'd be carted off, humiliated and defeated, back home. No way would her parents let her go anywhere now. She'd have to wait out the next year and a half, which meant that her admission paperwork would have to be re-done, and she'd have to start all over...

At least it didn't matter now if she blew off classes, she thought, and punched her pillow into a more comfortable shape. Several times.

If she'd been asleep – even a *little* asleep – she'd have missed the knock on the door, as light as it was, but she was wired and full of restless energy, and she slipped out of bed and went to unlock it and swing it open.

It was Shane. He stood there, clearly wanting to come in, not daring to come in, as uncertain as she'd ever seen him. He was wearing a loose T-shirt and sweatpants, feet bare, and she felt a white-hot wave of – *something* – sweep over her. This had to be what he slept in. Or... maybe less than that.

OK, she *really* needed to stop thinking about that.

She became aware, a hot second later, that she was standing there in a thin oversized T-shirt – one of Michael's old ones – with bare legs from mid-thigh down. Half-naked wouldn't be overstating it.

'Hi,' she said.

'Hi,' Shane said. 'Did I wake you up?'

'No. I couldn't sleep.' She was acutely aware of the bed behind her, covers all twisted. 'Um, do you want to, um…come in?'

'Better not,' he said softly. 'Claire, I—' He shook his head, brown hair swinging loose around his face. 'I shouldn't even be here.'

But he wasn't leaving, either.

'Well,' she said, 'I'm sitting down. If you want to stand there, fine.'

She went to the bed and sat, careful how she did it. Legs together, prim and proper. Her toes barely brushed the carpet. She felt alive and tingling all over.

She looked down at her hands, at the ragged fingernails, and picked at them nervously.

Shane took two steps into the room. 'For the next two days, I don't want you leaving the house,' he said. Which was *not* what she was expecting him to say. Not at all. 'Your dad already thinks we're getting you drunk and staging orgies in the hallway. Last thing I want is to send you home with fang marks in your neck. Or in a coffin.' His voice dropped lower. 'I couldn't stand that. I really couldn't. You know that, right?'

She didn't look up. He came a step closer, and his

bare feet and sweatpants came into her vision. 'Claire. You've got to promise me.'

'I can't,' she said. 'I'm not some little kid. And I'm not your sister.'

He laughed, low in his throat. 'Oh, yeah. That, I know. But I don't want to see you get hurt again.'

His hand cupped her chin in warmth, and tilted her face up.

The whole world hushed, one perfect second of stillness. Claire didn't even think her heart beat.

His lips were warm and soft and sweet, and the sensation just blinded her, made her feel awkward and scared. *I've never...nobody ever...I'm not doing it right...* She hated herself, hated that she didn't know how to kiss him back, knew he was measuring her against all those other girls, those better girls he'd kissed.

It stopped. Her heart was beating so fast it felt like a bird fluttering in her chest. She was flushed and hot and *warm*, so warm...

Shane pressed his forehead to hers and sighed. His breath warmed her face, and this time she kissed him, letting her instincts guide her, letting him pull her to her feet. Their hands were clasped, fingers laced, and parts of her – parts she'd only ever warmed up alone – were going full blast.

This time, when they came up for air, he pulled completely back. His face was flushed; his eyes were bright. Claire's lips felt swollen, warm, utterly deliciously damp. *Oh*, she thought. *I guess I should have done the tongue thing.* Putting theory into practice was hard when her brain kept wanting to short out entirely.

'OK,' Shane said. 'That – that shouldn't have happened.'

'Probably not,' she admitted. 'But I'm leaving in two days. It'd be stupid if I never even kissed you.'

She wasn't absolutely sure who kissed whom this time. Maybe it was gravity tilting, stars exploding. It felt like it. His hands were free this time, and they cupped her face, stroked her hair, her neck, down to her shoulders...

She gasped into his open mouth, and he moaned. *Moaned.* She had no idea a sensation could go through her like that, travelling through her skin and nerves like lightning.

His hands stopped right there, at her waist.

When their tongues touched, gentle and tentative and wet, it made her knees weak. Made her whole spine rattle like dry bones. Shane put his right arm around her waist, holding her close, and cupped the back of her head with his left.

OK, this was *kissing.* Serious kissing. Not just a kiss before moving out, not a goodbye, this was *Hello, sexy*, and wow, she'd never even *suspected* that it could feel this way.

When he let go, she fell back to sit on the bed, utterly weak, and she thought that if he followed her, she'd fall back and...

Shane took two giant-sized steps backward, then turned and walked out into the hall. Facing away from her. In a kind of dreamlike trance she watched the strong, broad muscles of his back moving under his shirt as he took deep breaths.

'OK,' he said finally, and turned around. But staying well out in the hall. 'OK, that really shouldn't have happened. And we're not going to talk about that, right? Ever?'

'Right,' she said. She felt like there was light dripping from her fingertips. Spilling out of her toes. She felt full of light, in fact, warm buttery sunlight. 'Never happened.'

He opened his mouth, then closed it, and closed his eyes. 'Claire—'

'I know.'

'Lock the door,' he said.

She got up and swung it mostly closed. One last look at him through the gap, and then she clicked it shut and flipped the dead bolt.

She heard a thump against it. Shane was slumped on the other side; she just knew it.

'I am *so* dead,' he muttered.

She went back to bed and lay there, full of light, until morning.

CHAPTER FOURTEEN

No sign of Shane on Monday morning, but she got up way early – just after Michael would have evaporated into mist, in fact. She showered and grabbed a Pop-Tart from the cabinet for breakfast, washed the dishes that had been dumped in the sink from last night's disaster of Parental Dinner – hadn't that been Michael's job? – and emptied out her backpack to stuff in the metal canister (to return to the chem lab, which made it borrowing, not stealing) and the Bible with its concealed secret.

And then she thought, *It won't do any good if they just steal it from me*, and took it out again and put it on the shelves, wedged in between an old volume 10 of the *World Encyclopaedia* and some novel she'd never heard of. Then she stepped out, locked the door, and began walking towards the school.

The chem lab was busy when she arrived between

classes, and she had no trouble slipping into the supply room to put the canister back in place, after carefully wiping her fingerprints from everything she could think of. That moral duty done, she hustled to the admissions office to put in her paperwork to withdraw from school. Nobody seemed surprised. She supposed that there were a lot of withdrawals. Or disappearances.

It was noon when she walked down to Common Grounds. Eve was just arriving, yawning and bleary-eyed; she looked surprised to see Claire as she handed over the cup of tea. 'I thought you weren't supposed to leave the house,' she said. 'Michael and Shane said—'

'I need to talk to Oliver,' Claire said.

'He's in the back.' Eve pointed. 'In the office. Claire? Is there anything wrong?'

'No,' she said. 'I think something's about to be right for a change.'

The door marked OFFICE was closed. She knocked, heard Oliver's warm voice telling her to enter, and came in. He was sitting behind a small desk in a very small room, windowless, with a computer running in front of him. He smiled at her and stood up to shake her hand. 'Claire,' he said. 'Good to see you're safe. I heard there had been some...unpleasantness.'

Oliver was wearing a tie-dyed Grateful Dead T-shirt and blue jeans with faded patches on the knees – not so much style as wear, she figured. He looked tired and concerned, and she thought suddenly that there was something about him a lot like Michael. Except that he was here in the daytime, of course, and at night, so he couldn't be a ghost. Could he?

'Brandon is very unhappy,' he said. 'I'm afraid that there's going to be retaliation. Brandon likes striking from an angle, not straight on, so you'd better watch out for your friends, as well. That would include Eve, of course. I've asked her to be extra careful.'

She nodded, heart in her throat. 'Um...what if I have something to trade?'

Oliver sat down and leant back in his chair. 'Trade for what? And to whom?'

'I – something important. I don't want to be more specific than that.'

'I'm afraid you're going to have to be, if you want me to act as any kind of go-between for you. I can't trade if I don't know what I'm offering.'

She realised she was still holding her teacup, and put it down on the corner of the desk. 'Um...I'd rather do it myself. But I don't know who to go to. Whoever can order Brandon around, I guess. Or even higher than that.'

'There is a social order to the vampire community,' Oliver agreed. 'Brandon's hardly at the top. There are two factions, you know. Brandon is part of one – the darker side, I suppose you could say. It depends on your viewpoint. Certainly, from a human standpoint, neither faction is exactly lily-white.' He shrugged. 'I can help you, if you'll let me. Believe me, you don't want to try to contact these people on your own. And I'm not sure they'd even allow you to do so.'

She bit her lip, thinking about what Michael had said about the deals in Morganville. She wasn't good at it; she knew that. And she didn't know the rules.

Oliver did, or he'd have been dead a long time ago. Besides, he was Eve's boss, and *she* liked him. Plus, he'd been able to keep Brandon from biting her at least twice. That had to count for something.

'OK,' she said. 'I have the book.'

Oliver's grey eyebrows came down into a straight line. 'The book?'

'You know. The *book*.'

'Claire,' he said slowly, 'I hope you understand what you're saying. Because you can't be wrong about this, and you absolutely can't lie. Bluffing will get you, and all your friends, killed. No mercy. Others have tried, passing off fakes or pretending to have it, then running. They all died. *All of them.* Do you understand?'

She swallowed again, convulsively. Her mouth felt very dry. She tried to remember how it had felt last night, being warm and full of light, but the day was cold and hard and scary. And Shane wasn't here. 'Yes,' she whispered. 'I understand. But I have it, and I don't think it's a fake. And I'm willing to trade for it.'

Oliver didn't blink. She tried to look away, but there was something about him, something hard and demanding, and she felt a real surge of fear. 'All right,' he said. 'But you can't do this by yourself. You're too young, and you're too fragile. I'll undertake this for you, but I'll need proof.'

'What kind of proof?'

'I need to see the book. Take photographs of at least the cover and one inside page, to prove that it's legitimate.'

'I thought vampires couldn't read it.'

'They can't, at least according to legend. It's the symbol. Like the Protection symbols, it has properties that humans can't really understand. In this case, it confuses the senses of vampires. Only humans can read the words inside – but a photograph removes the confusion, and vampires will be able to see the symbol for what it is. Wonderful thing, technology.' He glanced at the clock. 'I have a meeting this afternoon that I can't postpone. I'll come to your house this evening, if that's all right. I'd like a chance to speak with Shane and Eve, as well. And your other friend, the one I've never seen come in – Michael, correct? Michael Glass?'

She found herself nodding, a little alarmed and not even sure why she should be. It was OK, wasn't it? Oliver was one of the good guys.

And she had no idea whom else she could turn to, not in Morganville. Brandon? Right. There was a good option.

'Tonight,' she echoed. 'OK.'

She stood up and walked out, feeling strangely cold. Eve looked up at her, frowned, and tried to come after her, but there were people crowding at the coffee bar, and Claire hurried to the door and escaped before Eve could corner her. She didn't want to talk about it. She was sickly certain she'd just made a terrible mistake, but she didn't know what, or why, or how. She was so caught up in it, lost in her own head and lulled by the hot safety of the sun, not to mention people on the streets, that she forgot not all the dangers came at night in Morganville. The first warning she had, in fact, was the low rumble of an engine, and then she was being knocked off-balance and stumbling against the sun-heated finish of a van door, which slid aside.

She was being pushed from one side, pulled from the other, and before she could do more than yelp, she was in the van, bodies were piling on top of her, and the van door slammed shut on the sun. She slid on the carpeted floor as the van accelerated off, and heard whoops and laughter.

Girls' laughter.

Somebody was kneeling on her chest, making it hard to breathe; she tried to twist and throw her off, but it didn't work. When she blinked away stars she saw that the person on top of her was Gina, looking freshly made-up and fashion perfect, except for the sick gleam in her eyes. Monica was kneeling next to her, smiling a tight, cruel little smile. Jennifer was driving. There were a couple of other girls in the van, too, ones she remembered from the basement confrontation at the dorm. Apparently, Monica was still recruiting, and these two had made the cut to Advanced Psycho School.

'Get off me!' Claire yelled, and tried to bat at Gina;

Monica grabbed her hands and yanked them over her head, painfully hard. 'Bitch, get *off*!'

Monica punched her in the stomach, driving out what little air she had, and Claire whooped for breath. Gina's weight made it incredibly hard to breathe. Could you kill somebody like this? Smother a person like this? Maybe if the victim was small…like her…

The van was still going, taking her farther and farther away from safety.

'You,' Monica said, leaning over her, 'really pissed me off, fish. I don't forget things like that. Neither does my boyfriend.'

'Brandon?' Claire wheezed. 'Jeez, at least get one with a pulse!'

For that, she got punched again, and this time it hurt bad enough she started to cry, furious and helpless. Gina put a hand around her neck and began to squeeze. Not enough to kill her, just enough to hurt and make it even harder to gasp for precious little air.

They could keep this up for hours if they wanted. But Claire thought they probably had a lot more in store.

Sure enough, Monica reached in her pocket and brought out a lighter, one of those butane ones with a long, bright flame. She brought it close to Claire's face. 'We're going to have a barbecue,' she said. 'Roast freak. If you live, you're going to be hideous. But you shouldn't worry about that, because you probably won't live, anyway.'

Claire screamed with whatever she had, which wasn't much; it startled Monica, and it positively scared

Jennifer, who was driving; she twisted to look back, turning the wheel while she did.

Mistake.

The van careened to the right, and smashed into something solid. Claire flew through the air, with Gina riding her like a magic carpet, crashed into the padded back of the seats, and Monica and Gina rolled in confusion as the van skidded to a stop.

Claire shook off her panic and lunged for the van door. She bailed out. The van had ploughed into the rear of another car, parked along the side, and car alarms were going off. She felt dizzy and almost fell, then heard Monica yelling furiously behind her. That pulled her together, fast. She began running.

This part of downtown was mostly deserted – shops closed, only a few pedestrians on the street.

None of them would look at her at all.

'Help!' she yelled, and waved her arms. 'Help me! Please—'

They all just kept walking, as if she were invisible. She sobbed for a second in horror, and then pelted around the corner and skidded to a stop.

A *church*! She hadn't seen a single one the entire time she'd been in Morganville, and there one was. It wasn't a big one – a modest white building, with a small-sized steeple. No cross on it, but it was unmistakably a church.

She darted across the street, up the steps, and hit the doors at a run.

And bounced off.

They were locked.

'No!' she yelled, and rattled the doors. 'No, come on, please!'

The sign on the door said that the church was open from sundown to midnight. What the hell...?

She didn't dare think too much. She jumped off the steps and ran around the side, then the back. Next to the dumpster there was a back door with a glass window in it. It was locked, too. She searched around and found a broken piece of wood, and swung it like a baseball bat.

Crash!

She scraped her arm reaching through the broken window for the lock, but she made it, and slammed the door behind her. She locked it, frantically looked around, and found a piece of black poster board to prop against the blank space where the window had been. Hopefully, it would pass a quick glance.

She backed away, sweating, aching now from the crash and the run, and turned to go into the chapel. It was unmistakably a chapel, with abstract stained-glass windows and long rows of gleaming wood pews, but there was no cross, no crucifix, no symbol of any kind. The ultimate Unitarian church, she guessed.

At least it was empty.

Claire sank down on a pew midway back through the sanctuary and then stretched full length on the red velvet padding. Her heart was beating fast, so fast, and she was still so very scared.

Nobody knew where she was. And if she tried to leave, Monica might...

They were going to burn me alive.

She shivered and wiped tears from her cheeks and tried to think, think of *something* she could do to get out of this. Maybe there was a phone. She could call Eve or Shane? Both of them, she decided. Eve for the car, Shane for the bodyguard duty. Poor Shane. He was right – she really ought to stop calling him every time she needed brute strength. Didn't seem fair, somehow.

Claire froze, unable to breathe, as she heard a soft noise in the chapel. Like fabric moving. A bare whisper, maybe just a curtain moving in the air-conditioning breeze, right? Or...

'Hello,' said the very pale woman leaning over the pew and looking down on her. 'You would be Claire, I believe.'

Once the paralysing terror receded just a little, Claire finally placed her. She knew she'd seen her; it had been just a split-second glance, but this was the woman – the vampire – who'd been brought to Common Grounds in a limousine after closing time.

What was she doing in a *church*?

Claire slowly sat up, unable to take her eyes off of the woman, who was smiling slightly. Light filtered in softly from the stained-glass windows and gave her a golden glow.

'I followed you,' the woman said. 'Although in truth, I

do like this church quite a bit. Very peaceful, don't you think? A sacred place. And one that grants those within it a certain...immunity from danger.'

Claire licked her lips and tasted salt from sweat and tears. 'You mean you won't kill me here.'

The smile stayed intact. If anything, it widened a little. 'I mean exactly that, my dear. The same goes for my guards, of course. I assure you, they're present. I am never left alone. It is part of the curse of the position I hold.' She smiled and tilted her head an elegant fraction. Everything about her was elegant, from the shining golden crown of her hair to the clothes she was wearing. Claire wasn't much for noticing fashion, unless it was worn by girls kicking the crap out of her, but this outfit looked like something out of old formal photographs from her mother's time. Or grandmother's.

'My name is Amelie,' the woman continued. 'You are, in a sense, already acquainted with me, although you might not be aware of it. Please, child, don't look so frightened. I absolutely assure you that no harm will come to you with me. I always give very clear warning before I do anything violent.'

Claire had no idea how to look any less frightened, but she clasped her hands in her lap to stop them from shaking. Amelie sighed.

'You are very new to our town,' she said, 'but I have rarely seen anyone disturb quite so many hornets in such a short time. First Monica, then Brandon, and then I hear you turn to my dear Oliver for advice...and now I see you running for your life through my streets... Well, I find you interesting. I find myself wondering about you, Claire. About who you are. *Why* you are.'

'I'm – nobody,' Claire said. 'And I'm leaving town. My parents are taking me out of school.' It suddenly seemed like a really good idea. Not so much running away as retreating.

'Are they? Well, we'll see.' Amelie made a shrug seem like a foreign gesture. 'Do you know who I am?'

'Somebody important.'

'Yes. Someone very important.' Amelie's eyes were steady in the dim light, of no real colour – grey, maybe? Or blue? It wasn't colour that made them powerful. 'I am the oldest vampire in the world, my dear. In a certain sense, I am the only vampire who matters.' She said it without any particular sense of pride. 'Although others may have differing opinions, of course. But they would be sadly, and fatally, wrong.'

'I – I don't understand.'

'No, I do not expect you to.' Amelie leant forward and put lean, elegant, white hands on the wooden pew in front of her, then rested her pointed chin on top of them. 'Somehow you have become mixed up in our search for the book. I believe you know the one I mean.'

'I – uh – yes.' No way was she going to confess what she had sitting at home. She'd made that mistake once already. 'I mean, I know about all the—'

'Vampires,' Amelie supplied helpfully. 'It is not a secret, my dear.'

'Vampires looking for it.'

'And you just happened to stumble into the operation at the library, in which we were combing through volumes to find it?'

Claire blinked. 'Does it belong to you?'

'In a way. Let's say that it belongs to me as much as it belongs to anyone alive today. If I am, strictly speaking, living. The old word was *undead*, you know, but aren't all living things undead? I dislike imprecision. I think we may have that in common, young lady.' Amelie tilted her head a little to the side. Claire was reminded, with a chill, of a nature film. A praying mantis studying its food-to-be. '*Vampire* is such an old word. I believe I shall commission the university to find another term, a more – what is the new saying? – *user-friendly* term for what we are.'

'I – what do you want?' Claire blurted. And then, ridiculously, '...sorry.' Because she knew it sounded rude, and however scary this vampire, or whatever, might be, she hadn't been *rude*.

'That's quite all right. You're under a great deal of stress. I shall forgive your breach of manners. What I want is just the truth, child. I want to know what you have found out about the book.'

'I – um, nothing.'

There was a long silence. In it, Claire heard distant noises – somebody tugging on the front door of the church.

'That's unfortunate,' Amelie said quietly. 'I had hoped

I would be able to help you. It appears that I cannot.'

'Um – that's it? That's all?'

'Yes, I'm afraid it is.' Amelie sat back again, hands folded in her lap. 'You may go the way you came. I wish you luck, my dear. You are going to need it. Unfortunately, mortal life is very fragile, and very short. Yours could be shorter than usual.'

'But—'

'I can't help you if you have nothing to offer me. There are rules to life in Morganville. I can't simply adopt strays because they seem winsome. Farewell, little Claire. Godspeed.'

Claire had no idea what *winsome* meant, but she got the message. Whatever door had been opened – whether it led to good things or bad – had slammed shut on her now. She stood up, wondering what to say, and decided that saying nothing might be the very best thing...

...and she heard the back door crash open.

'Oh, crap,' she whispered. Amelie looked at her in reproach. 'Sorry.'

'We are in a house of worship,' she said severely. 'Really, did no one teach your generation any sort of manners?'

Claire ducked behind a pew. She heard fast footsteps, and then Monica's voice. 'Ma'am! I'm sorry, I didn't know you were—'

'But I am,' Amelie said coolly. 'Morrell, aren't you? I can never keep any of you straight.'

'Monica.'

'How charming.' Amelie's voice changed from cool to ice-cold. 'I'll have to ask you to leave, Miss Morrell. You do not belong here. My seal is on this place. You know the rules.'

'I'm sorry, ma'am. I didn't think—'

'Often the case, I suspect. Go.'

'But – there's this girl – did she—?'

Amelie's voice turned to a hiss like sleet on a frozen window. *'Are you questioning me?'*

'No! No, so sorry, ma'am, it won't happen again, I'm sorry…' Monica's voice was fading. She was backing away, down the hall. Claire stayed where she was, trembling.

She almost screamed when Amelie's pale form rose up over the edge of the pew again and gazed down at her. She hadn't heard her move. Not at all.

'I suggest you go straight home, little Claire,' Amelie said. 'I would take you there, but that would imply more than I think I can afford just now. Run, run home. Hurry, now. And – if you have lied to me about the book, remember that many people might want such a valuable thing, and for many reasons. Be sure of why they want it before you give it over.'

Claire slowly took her hands away from her head and slid onto the seat of the pew, facing the vampire. She was still scared, but Amelie didn't seem…well…evil exactly. Just cold. Ice-cold.

And old.

'What is it?' Claire asked. 'The book?'

Amelie's smile was as faded as old silk. 'Life,' she

said. 'And death. I can tell you no more. It wouldn't be prudent.' The smile vanished, leaving behind only the chill. 'I believe you really should go now.'

Claire bolted up and hurried away, checking over her shoulder every other step. She saw other vampires coming out – she hadn't spotted them, not one of them. One of them was John, from the library. He grinned at her, not in a friendly way. One of his eyes was milky white.

She ran.

Wherever Monica and her friends had gone, it wasn't the way Claire ran – and run she did, the whole way to Lot Street. Her lungs were burning by the time she turned the corner, and she was nearly in tears with gratitude at the sight of the big old house.

And Shane, sitting on the front steps.

He stood up, not saying a word, and she threw herself at him; he caught her and held her close for a few seconds, then pushed her back for a survey of damage.

'I know,' she said. 'You told me not to go. I'm sorry.'

He nodded, looking grim. 'Inside.'

Once she was in, with the door safely locked, she babbled out the whole story. Monica, the van, the lighter, the church, the vampire. He didn't ask any questions. In fact, he didn't even blink. She ran out of words, and he just looked at her, expressionless.

'You,' he finally said, 'had better like the inside of your room, because I'm locking you in there, and I'm not letting you out until your parents come to load you in the car.'

'Shane—'

'I mean it. No more bullshit, Claire. You're staying alive no matter what I have to do.' He sounded flatly furious. 'Now. You need to tell me about Michael.'

'What?'

'I mean it, Claire. Tell me, right now. Because I can't find him anywhere, and you know what? I can never find him during the day – damn! Did you feel that?' She did. A cold spot, sweeping across her skin. Michael, trying to tell her something. Probably *Hell no, don't tell him*. 'We can't get through this if we're not straight with each other.' Shane's Adam's apple bobbed as he swallowed. 'Is he – you know – one of them? 'Cause I need to know that.'

'No,' she said. 'No, he's not.'

Shane closed his eyes and slumped against the wall, hands to both sides of his head. 'God, thank you. I was going nuts. I thought – I mean, it's one thing to be a night person, but Michael – I was – I thought—'

'Wait,' Claire said, and took a deep breath. Cold settled over her again – Michael, trying to stop her. She ignored it. 'Quit it, Michael. He needs to know.'

Shane took his hands away from his head and looked around, then frowned at her. 'Michael's not here. I checked. I searched the damn place from top to bottom.'

'Yes, he is. Cold spot.' She held out her hand and waved it through the refrigerated air. 'I figure he's standing...right here.' She looked at her watch. 'He'll be back in about two hours, when the sun goes down. You can see him then.'

'What in the *hell* are you talking about?'

'Michael. He's a ghost.'

'Oh, come on! Bullshit! The dude sits here and eats dinner with us!'

She shrugged, threw up her hands, and walked away. 'You wanted to know. Fine. Now you know. And by the way? I'm fine.'

'What do you mean, he's a ghost?' Shane caught up with her, came around her, and blocked her path. 'Oh, come on. Ghost? He's as real as I am!'

'Sometimes,' she agreed. 'Ask him. Better yet, watch him at dawn. And then tell me what he is, because ghost is about all I know to call him. The thing is, he can't leave the house, Shane. He can't help us. He's stuck here, and during the day, he can't even talk to us. He just – drifts.' She batted away the cold air again. 'Stop it, Michael. I know you're pissed. But he needs to know.'

'Claire!' Shane grabbed her and shook her out of sheer frustration. 'You're talking to thin air!'

'Whatever. Let go, I've got things to do.'

'What things?'

'Packing!' She pulled free and went upstairs, two steps at a time. Shane always slammed his door when he was mad; she tried it out. It helped.

The cold spot followed her. 'Dammit, Michael, get out of my room, you pervert!' Could you even be a pervert if you were dead? She supposed you could, if you had a working body half the time. 'I swear, I'm going to start taking my clothes off!'

The cold spot stayed resolutely put until she got the hem of her T-shirt all the way up to her bra line, and then faded away. 'Chicken,' she said, and paced the room, back and forth. Worried and more than a little scared.

Shane pounded on the door, but she stretched out on her bed, put a pillow over her face, and pretended not to hear him.

Dusk came, pulling a blue gauze over the sky; she watched the sun sink halfway down the horizon, then unlocked her door and stormed out. Shane was just coming out of Michael's bedroom. Still looking for someone he wasn't going to find. Not the way he thought, anyway.

'Michael!' Claire yelled from her end, and felt the cold settle around her like an icy blanket. Shane spun around, and she felt the mist gather, thick and heavy, and then she actually saw it, a faint grey shape in the air...

Eve's door flew open. 'What in the *hell* is going on around here?' she yelled. 'Could you guys keep it down to aircraft-carrier noise?'

...And then Michael just...appeared. Midway between all three of them, forming right out of a thick grey heavy mist, taking on colour and weight.

Eve screamed.

Michael collapsed to his hands and knees, retching.

He fell on his side, then rolled over to stare up at the ceiling. 'Shit!' he gasped, and just stayed there, fighting for breath. His eyes looked wet and terrified, and Claire realised that it was like this for him every day. Every night. Frightening beyond anything she could even imagine.

Claire looked down the hall at Shane. He was frozen in place, mouth open, looking like a cartoon of himself. Eve, too, from her angle.

Claire walked over, held out a hand to Michael, and said, 'Well, I guess that settles things.'

He gave her a filthy, wordless look, and took her hand to pull himself up. He staggered and leant against the wall for support, shaking his head when she tried to help. 'In a minute,' he said. 'Takes a lot out of you.'

Eve said, in a high, squeaky, airless voice, 'The ghost! You're the ghost Miranda was talking about! Oh my God, Michael, you're the *ghost*! You *bastard*!'

He nodded, still concentrating on breathing.

Eve got control of her voice and squealed, 'That is without a doubt *the coolest damn thing I have ever seen in my entire life*!'

Shane looked...pale. Pale and shaken and – how predictable was this? – pissed. Michael met his eyes, and the two of them looked at each other for a long, silent second before Shane said, 'This is why you asked me to come back.'

'I—' Michael coughed. When he sagged this time, Eve threw his arm around her shoulders. He looked surprised, then pleased. 'Not just because—'

'I get it,' Shane said. 'I get it, man. I do. What the hell happened while I was gone?'

Michael just shook his head. 'Later.'

No, it wasn't that Shane was pissed after all, Claire realised. He turned away and pounded down the stairs before she could say anything, but she'd seen his eyes.

She knew.

He lost Alyssa. Now he thinks he's lost Michael, too. She didn't know how that felt, not really; she could imagine, but she was – she knew it – sheltered. She'd never really lost anybody, not even a grandparent. Grief was something in TV shows, in movies, in books.

She had no idea what to say to him. She'd thought that he'd just take it in stride, the way Shane seemed to take things, but...

'Claire,' Michael said. 'Don't let him leave.'

She nodded and left Eve supporting Michael in the hallway, the two of them looking surprisingly comfortable with the whole living-dead-not-dead thing. She supposed that if a ghost had to have a girlfriend, well, Eve was just about the best choice there was.

Shane was standing downstairs, just...standing. Not paying much attention to her or anything else. She reached out, ready to tap him on the shoulder, let him know she was here even if she was no help at all, but just then, there was a knock on the front door.

'I swear to God, if that's Miranda—' he grated. His fists were clenched at his sides.

'No, I think it's for me,' Claire said, and darted around him to run down the hallway. She checked the peephole first, and sure enough, there was Oliver, standing on the doorstep and looking uncomfortable. She supposed he had good reason... Jeez, hanging around *anywhere* after dark in Morganville had to be like hanging an EAT ME sign on your back.

She unlocked the door and swung it open.

'I don't have a lot of time,' he said. 'Where are they? Shane and Eve?'

'Inside,' she said, and pulled it open wider, the universal signal for *Come in*. He didn't. He held up a hand instead, waved it in the air in front of him with a puzzled frown. 'Oliver?'

'I'm afraid you'll have to ask me in,' he said. 'It seems this house has some very detailed Protections in place. I can't come in unless you ask.'

'Oh. Sorry about that.' She was about to ask him inside when it occurred to her that maybe it wasn't the best idea, just asking people in without okaying it with the rest of the Glass House first. Especially since she was living here only another day. 'Um, can you wait just a second?'

'No, Claire, I really can't,' Oliver said impatiently. He was still wearing the hippie gear from Common Grounds, but somehow he looked...different. Odd. 'Please invite me in. I don't have time to wait.'

'But I—'

'Claire, *I can't help you if you won't trust me*! Now

quickly, before it's too late, let me in!'

'But I—' She pulled in a deep breath. 'All right. I invite you—'

'No!' It was a roar from behind her, absolutely terrifying, and she threw herself to one side and covered her mouth with both hands to hold in her scream. It wasn't Shane bearing down on her; it was Michael. Shane was behind him, and Eve. 'Claire, get back!'

Michael looked like an avenging angel, and nobody argued with angels. Claire scurried backward, still holding her hands over her mouth, as Michael strode past her, right up to the doorway. The edge of his territory.

Oliver looked disappointed but, she saw, not particularly surprised. 'Ah, Michael. Good to see you again. I see you're surviving nicely.'

Michael didn't say anything, but from Claire's vantage point to the side, she saw the look he was giving Oliver, and it frightened her. She hadn't thought Michael could get that angry.

'What do you want here?' he asked tightly. Oliver sighed.

'I know you won't believe me,' he said, 'but in truth, I had the best interests of your young friend at heart.'

Michael laughed bitterly. 'Yeah. I'll bet.'

'Also your friend Shane—' Oliver's eyes darted past Michael to lock on Shane, then Eve. 'And of course my dear sweet Eve. Such a fine employee.'

Michael turned slowly to look at Eve, whose eyes were wide with what Claire hoped was horror. Or at least confusion. 'You know each other?' Eve blurted. 'But – Michael, you said you didn't know Oliver, and—'

'I didn't,' Michael said, and turned back, 'until he killed me. We were never formally introduced.'

'Yes,' Oliver said, and shrugged. 'Sorry about that. Nothing personal about it; it was an experiment of sorts that didn't quite work out. But I'm pleased to see you survived, even if not quite in the form that I'd hoped.'

Michael made a sound Claire hoped never to hear again from any person, living or dead. It was Eve's turn to clap her hands over her mouth, then quickly take them away to yell, 'Oh my *God*! Oliver!'

'We can discuss my moral shortcomings later,' he said. 'For now, you need to let me inside this house, and as quickly as possible.'

'You have got to be kidding,' Michael said. 'I think one of us dead in here is good enough. I'm not letting you in to kill the rest.'

Oliver studied him silently for a long moment. 'I'd hoped to bc able to avoid this,' he finally said. 'Your little Claire is quite the prodigy, you know. She says she's found the book. I think she has quite a promising future in Morganville...provided she survives the night.'

Michael looked like he wanted to vomit. His eyes darted to Claire, then away. 'Doesn't matter. Go away. Nobody's asking you in.'

'No?' Oliver smiled widely, and his fangs came down with lazy slowness. That was absolutely the scariest thing Claire had ever seen, that and the sincerity in his eyes. 'I think someone will. Sooner or later.'

'I'd say over my dead body, but I think you already made that point,' Michael snapped. 'Thanks for the visit. Now fuck off, man.'

He started to close the door. Oliver held up a hand – not like he was trying to stop him physically, just a warning – and his fangs folded up to leave his face kind and trustworthy again. Like...the face of a really cool teacher, the kind who made school worth living through. That, Claire thought, was a bigger betrayal than anything else.

'Wait. Do they understand why they're here, Michael? Why you risked exposing your secrets to them?' Michael didn't stop. The door was swinging closed on Oliver. 'Shane, listen to me! *Michael needed someone living to activate the house Protection!* You think he cares about you, he doesn't! You're just arms and legs for him! Beating hearts! He's no different from me!'

'Except for the not-bloodsucking part, you freak!' Shane yelled, and then the door slammed shut on Oliver's face. Michael threw the bolt with shaking fingers. 'Christ, man. Why didn't you tell us?'

'I – about what?' Michael asked, not turning to face him. He looked pale, Claire saw. Scared.

'*Any damn thing!* How did this happen, Michael? How did you get to be—?' Shane made a gesture that was vague enough to mean anything. 'Was he trying to, you know, vamp you out?'

'I think so. It didn't work. This is as far as I got.'

Michael swallowed hard and turned to face him. 'He's right about the Protections. The house won't enforce any Protection unless there's someone living in it. I don't exactly count. I'm – part of it now. I did need you.'

'Whatever, man. I don't care about that. I care that you went and got yourself drained by some damn leech while my back was turned—'

'He can't be a vampire,' Eve said suddenly. 'He can't. He's my *boss*! And...and he works days! How is that even possible?'

'Ask him,' Michael said. 'Next time you go to work.'

'Oh, right, as if I didn't just quit that job!' Eve moved up beside Michael and put her arms around him. He hugged her back, like it was the most natural thing in the world. Like they'd been doing that all along which, Claire admitted, maybe they had and she just hadn't known. Michael stroked Eve's hair. 'God, I am *so* sorry!'

'Not your fault,' he said. 'Not anybody's fault except his.'

'How'd you—?'

'I played a set at Common Grounds. I didn't know he owned the place. I was dealing with a guy named Chad—'

'Oh. Right. Chad died,' Eve said.

'Wonder how *that* happened?' Shane put in acidly.

'This guy – Oliver, but I never knew his name – said he was a musician and he was looking for a room to rent. I thought it was a good idea. He came over to see the house.' Michael closed his eyes tight, like he couldn't bear to see the pictures in his head again. Not that it would help, Claire knew. 'As soon as I asked him in. I felt it. But it was too late, and – he had friends.'

Shane cursed, one harsh word that boomed off the wood floor like a gunshot, and leant back against the wall, head down. Slumped. 'I should have been here,' he said.

'Then we'd both be dead.'

'And you still will be,' said Oliver's voice through the door. 'Eve, my dear. Listen to me. Listen to my voice. Let me in.'

'Leave her alone!' Michael roared, and turned to face the door.

Claire saw something happen in Eve's face – the will go out of it, the light go out of her eyes. *Oh no*, she thought, frozen, and tried to open her mouth to warn Michael.

Before she could do it, Eve said, 'Yes, Oliver. Come inside.'

And the lock snapped on the door with a crisp, bright ringing sound, and the door drifted open on the night, and Oliver stepped over the threshold.

Chapter Fifteen

Claire didn't even see Michael move; he was that quick. Until that moment she'd thought he was just a normal guy, really… OK, one who disappeared into mist during the day. But nobody moved that fast. Nobody human.

And *nobody* was that strong, either. Michael grabbed Oliver by the shoulders, lifted him into the air, and launched him headfirst down the hall to crash into the far wall. Claire dived out of the way. So did Shane, and Eve, although Eve was diving *towards* Oliver, not away. Shane got hold of her ankle and dragged her backward, kicking and screaming.

Michael went after Oliver. As the vampire was rolling to his feet, Michael smashed into him. Oliver was strong, and fast, but in this house Michael was unstoppable, and he was really, really angry.

'You fool!' Oliver screamed at him. 'Do you understand what I said? *Claire has the book!*'

'I don't care!'

'You have to care! If you don't give it over, they'll rip all of you apart to get it! I'm trying to save you!'

Michael slammed his fist into his face two or three times, quicker than Claire could blink. Oliver went down again, scrabbling at the floor, then rolled over and stared furiously through tangled greying hair up at them. Vampires bled, after all, but it didn't quite look right – not red enough, and too thick. It trickled from the corners of Oliver's mouth as he snarled, fangs down, and tried to drag Michael close enough to bite. Michael hit him so hard that one of the fangs broke off and skittered away across the floor like an ivory dagger. Oliver shouted in surprise and pain and rolled, trying to protect himself.

'Eve!' Michael yelled, and dragged him by one foot down the hallway towards the door. 'Revoke the invitation! Do it!' Oliver was fighting him wildly now, ripping long raw scratches in the wooden floor with his fingernails, snarling and twisting to get free. '*Eve!*'

Shane lunged for Eve, pulled her to her feet, and shook her hard. That didn't work. She just stared right past him, her face still and dead.

Claire moved him out of the way and slapped Eve hard.

Eve yelped, clapped a hand to her wounded cheek, and blinked. 'Hey! What the hell...?' And then she looked past Claire to the furious battle going on in the hallway, lips parted in amazement.

'Eve!' Michael yelled again. 'The invitation! You have to withdraw it *now*!'

'But I didn't—' Eve didn't waste time arguing. 'Hey! Oliver! Get the hell out of our house!'

Oliver went still. Completely still, like a dead man. Michael picked him up by an arm and a leg, and threw him out into the dark. Claire heard the vampire hit the pavement outside and curse as he rolled back to his feet and came back at the door.

He bounced off a solid cushion of air in the doorway.

'You're not welcome,' Michael grated. He had a cut on his face, bleeding a thick thread down the side of his neck, and he was breathing hard. 'And by the way? Eve quits.'

He slammed the door in Oliver's snarling face, and collapsed against it, shaking. He didn't look all-powerful anymore. He looked terrified. 'Michael?' Eve asked, breathless. 'You OK?'

'Peachy,' he said, and got it together. 'Eve, stay away from the door. He got to you once; maybe he can do it again. Claire! You, too. Stay away from the door.' He grabbed her by the arm and pulled her down the hall – which was a mess, wow, the floor all ripped up, the walls scraped and scratched – and shoved her down to a sitting position on the couch. 'Claire.'

'Um…yes?' Things were moving too fast. She didn't know what he was waiting to hear.

'The book?'

'Oh. Yeah. Well – see, there was this floor in the

library where they were going through books, and Professor Wilson was stealing things, and—'

He held up a hand to stop her. 'Do you have the book?'

'Yes.'

'Please tell me you didn't bring it here.'

She blinked. 'Well – yes.'

Michael fell into the armchair, leant forward, and buried his face in his hands. 'Sweet baby Jesus, do you not pay any *attention* to what goes on in this town? You really have the book?'

'I...guess so.' She got up and started to retrieve it, but he raised his head and grabbed her wrist as she moved by him.

'No,' he said. 'Leave it, wherever it is. The less we know, the better. We need to figure out what we're going to do, because Oliver wasn't kidding around. He wouldn't have come here if he hadn't intended to kill us all for that book. As it was, he took a big chance. He knows how powerful the Protection is on this house.'

'That how come you could beat him?' Shane asked. 'Because you know, I'm your best friend, but you're just not that badass, man.'

'Thanks, asshole. Yeah. I'm part of the house, and that means I can use what the house has. It's strong. Really strong.'

'Good to know. So what's the plan?'

Michael took in a deep breath, then let it out. 'Wait

for daylight,' he said. 'Eve. You ever see Oliver outside in the sun?'

'Um...' She thought hard. 'No. Mostly he stays in his office, or in the bar area, away from the windows. But I didn't think vampires could be awake during the day!'

Claire thought about the church Monica had chased her into, and the elegant, ancient woman sitting in the pews. 'I think they can,' she said. 'If they're old. He must be really old.'

'I don't care how old he is – he's not tanning,' Shane said. 'We wait for dawn, and then we get Claire and the book out of here.'

'She can't go home. They'll go there first,' Eve said. Claire went cold.

'But – my parents! What about my parents?'

Nobody answered her for a second or two, and then Shane came and sat down next to her. 'You think they'll listen? If we tell them the truth?'

'What, about Morganville? About vampires?' She laughed, and it sounded hysterical. 'Are you kidding? They'd never believe it!'

'Besides,' Eve said, and sat down on her other side to take her hand, 'even if you convinced them, they'd forget all about it once they were out of town. It's hard to be paranoid when you don't remember they're out to get you.'

'Ouch,' Shane agreed. 'OK, then. Running's out – for one thing, we can't throw Claire's parents to the vampire wolves...right?'

Michael and Eve nodded.

'And besides, same problem for Claire. Even if we got her out of town, she'd forget why she was running. They'd catch her.'

More nods.

'So what do we do?'

'Trade the book,' Claire said. They all looked at her. 'What? I was going to, anyway. In exchange for some things.'

'Like what?' Michael asked, amazed.

'Like – Brandon not holding Shane to his deal. And Monica and her freaks backing off of me. And... Protection for all the dorms on campus, so that the students are safe.' She blushed, because they were all staring at her like they'd never seen her before. 'That's how Oliver knew I had the book. I messed up. I was trying to make a deal, but I thought he was just, you know, a good guy who could help. I didn't know he was one of the vampires.'

'Oh, he's not one of them,' Michael said. 'He *is* them.'

Shane frowned. 'How do you know that, man?'

'Because in a way I'm one of them,' Michael replied. 'And something in me wants to do what he says.'

'But – not a big part, right?' Eve ventured.

'No. But he's definitely in charge.'

Shane got up and walked to the windows, twitched back the curtain, and looked out. 'No kidding,' he said.

'What've you got?'

'Vamp city, man. Check it out.'

Michael joined him at the window, then Eve. When Claire squeezed in, she gasped, because there were *dozens* of people in view, all standing or sitting facing the house. Unnaturally still. Eve dashed to another set of windows. 'Same here!' she called. 'Hang on!'

'Shane,' Michael said, and jerked his head after her. Shane loped off in pursuit. 'Well, so much for sneaking out. I think we're here for the night, at least. Most of them have to go underground during the day. Those that don't won't be able to stay out in direct sunlight – I hope – so maybe we'll have more options then.'

'Michael—' Claire felt like crying. 'I didn't know. I thought I was doing something good. I really did.'

He put his arm around her. 'I know. It's not your fault. It might have been a dumb idea, but at least it was a sweet one.' He kissed her cheek. 'Better get some rest. And if you hear voices, try not to listen. They're going to be testing us.'

She nodded. 'What are we going to do?'

'I don't know,' he said quietly. 'But we'll think of something.'

Claire curled up on the corner of the couch, piled under an afghan; Eve took the other end. Nobody felt much like going upstairs to bed. Shane paced a lot, talking in low whispers with Michael, who hadn't once got out his guitar. The two of them looked wired. Ready for anything.

Claire didn't mean to fall asleep – she thought she

was too scared – but she did, eventually, as night spun on towards morning. Voices whispered to her – Michael's, she thought, and then Shane's. *Get up*, the voices said. *Get up and open the door. Open the window. Let us in. We can help you if you'll just let us in.*

She whimpered in her sleep, sweaty and sick, and felt Shane's hand on her forehead. 'Claire.' She opened her eyes and saw him sitting there next to her. He looked tired. 'You're having a nightmare:'

'Don't I wish,' she muttered, tried to swallow, and discovered she was burning-up thirsty. She felt feverish and weak, too. Well, *this* was a perfect time to be catching the flu...

'Michael!' Oliver's voice came faint through the front door. 'Something you should see, my boy! Look out your windows!'

'Trap,' Shane said instantly, and reached out to grab Michael's arm as he walked by. 'Don't, man.'

'What's he going to do? Make faces at me?'

'If you start doing what he wants, it's hard to stop. Just don't.'

Michael considered that for a few seconds, then pulled away and went on to the windows.

Where he stared out, frowning. There were red and blue flashing lights shining on the glass and reflecting on his skin.

'What is it?' Claire asked, and got up.

'Hey! Seriously, guys. Quit playing their game—'

'Cops,' Michael said. He sounded blank and shocked.

'They've got the whole street blocked off. They're moving people out.'

'What people? The vampires?' Eve wanted to know. She piled on at the window, too.

'Sheesh,' Shane said grumpily. 'Fine. Don't listen to me. If a vampire tells you to jump off a cliff...'

'They're evacuating the neighbourhood,' Michael said. 'Getting rid of witnesses.'

'Oh, shit,' Shane said, and jumped up and craned to look over Claire's shoulder. 'So just how screwed are we?'

'Well, the cops aren't vampires. And the Protections won't keep them out.'

As Claire watched, the six police cars, all with their lights running in blood-red and vein blue flashes, were joined by two long, skeletal fire trucks. One at each end of the block.

Michael said nothing, but his eyes narrowed.

'Oh, *shit*!' Shane whispered. 'They wouldn't.'

'Yeah,' Michael said. 'I think they would. If this book is that important, I think they'd do just about anything to get it.'

Oliver's face suddenly popped up in front of the window. They all screamed – even Michael – and jumped back. Shane tried to push Claire behind him. She smacked at him until he left her alone.

She wanted to hear what Oliver had to say.

'It's nearly five o'clock,' Oliver said, his voice muffled by the window glass. 'We're running out of time, Michael.

Either invite me in and give me the book, or I'm afraid this is going to get unpleasant.'

'Wait!' Claire balled her hands into fists. 'I want to trade for it!'

His eyes weighed her, and dismissed her. 'I'm very sorry, my dear, but that opportunity has come and gone. We're in much rougher waters now. Either hand over the book, or we'll come in and get it. I promise you, this is the best deal you're likely to get this side of hell.'

Michael yanked down the shade. 'Shane. You, Eve, and Claire get into the pantry room. Move it.'

'No way!' Eve declared. 'I'm not leaving you!'

He took her hand and locked eyes with her, in a way that made Claire's knees go weak even at several feet away. 'They can't hurt me, except by hurting the house itself. They can't kill me, except by destroying the house. Understand? You guys are the vulnerable ones. And I want you safe.'

He kissed her hand, darted a self-conscious look at Claire and Shane, and then kissed her lips, too.

'Huh,' Shane said. 'Thought so.' He took Claire's hand. 'Michael's right. Better get you girls someplace safe.'

'You, too, Shane,' said Michael.

'No way!'

'Not the time to be proving anything, dude. Just take care of them. I can take care of myself.'

Maybe, Claire thought. And maybe he just wanted them out of the way in case he couldn't.

Either way, she didn't have a chance to protest. Shane

steered her and Eve into the kitchen, loaded them down with water and pre-packaged food like Pop-Tarts and energy bars, and helped them stack things in the dark, gloomy hiding place where Claire had spent her first morning in the Glass House.

She didn't know if Shane really might have followed Michael's orders – it was possible, she guessed – but just as they were pushing the last of the supplies into the narrow little doorway, there was a loud crashing of glass from the living room.

'What the hell?' Shane blurted, and ducked out to see what was going on. Claire went after him, and when she looked back, Eve was following, too.

But they didn't get very far, because the kitchen window smashed into splinters, and Claire and Eve stopped and turned to look.

Oliver was standing just outside the window. They heard more glass breaking, all over the house.

'Girls,' he said. 'I'm sorry to do this. Truly I am. But you're not giving me much choice. Last chance. Invite me in, and this can end peacefully.'

'Bite me!' Eve taunted. 'Oh, wait...you can't, can you? Not from way out there!'

His eyes flared, and his fangs snapped down. *Threat display.* That was what it was called when a rattlesnake shook its tail, or a cobra spread its hood. He was giving them a clear sign that he didn't find them very funny.

'The book,' he said. 'Or your lives. That's the only deal

you're going to get, Claire. I suggest you make the right choice quickly.'

'It's OK,' Eve said. 'They can't come inside.' Oliver nodded, his faded, curling hair blowing in the hot night wind. 'That's true,' he said. 'But then, I'm hardly all alone.'

And he stepped aside as a policeman, in uniform, broke out the remaining glass with a nightstick and hopped up on the windowsill to climb through.

Eve and Claire screamed and ran.

The living room was a mess of broken furniture, scattered papers, struggling bodies – Shane punched out some guy in a black jacket, who flew back out of the window and into the arms of some waiting, snarling vampires. Michael was fighting a couple more, whom he just bodily picked up and threw out. As Eve and Claire skidded into the room and broke right and left, the cop in pursuit ran headlong into Michael and got tossed out, as well.

'They're coming in!' Eve screamed, and slammed the kitchen door and jammed a chair under the handle. Michael grabbed the nearest bookcase – not the one with the Bible on it, Claire saw – and pulled it over to block the window, then leant the sofa against it.

'Upstairs!' he yelled. 'Move it!'

Shane grabbed Claire by the hand and pounded up the steps, half dragging her; she missed a step and stumbled, and pulled him off-balance just at the right moment, because the bat that was swung at his head missed and thumped into the wall with a crack of wood. Another person hiding at the top of the stairs, this one female and tall. Shane grabbed the bat away from her and menaced her with it, driving her back down the hallway. Claire recognised her – one of the dorm girls, Lillian.

'Don't!' Lillian yelled, and put up her arms when Shane pulled back the bat.

'Hell,' Shane spit in disgust. 'I can't hit a girl. Here, Claire. *You* hit her.' He tossed her the bat. Claire grabbed it and came to a clumsy batting stance, wishing she'd paid more attention in phys ed. Lillian screamed again and ran into the open doorway of Eve's room. Eve, coming up the stairs, screamed, too, for different reasons.

'Hey! That's *my* room, bitch!' And she flew in to grab Lillian by the hair, swing her around, and throw her out into the hall, then shoved her towards the stairs. 'Michael! This one needs to go out!'

She shoved her again. Lillian tottered down the steps, and shrieked once more before leaving the building at speed, propelled by Michael-power.

'Check the rooms,' Shane panted. 'If one got in, there are probably more. Don't take chances. Yell for help.'

Claire nodded and hurried to her room. It looked quiet, thank God – the windows were unbroken, and there was no sign of anybody hiding in the closets or under the bed. Same for the bathroom, although she had a bad shower-curtain moment. She heard crashing from down the hall. Shane had found somebody. She ran out into the hall and started to come to his defence, then hesitated when she saw that Eve's door was now open a crack.

She'd left it closed.

She opened it slowly, as silently as she could, and peeked around the edge...

...and saw Eve up against the wall, and Miranda holding a knife at Eve's throat. She recognised the bruises and bite marks on her neck first, then the faded blue eyes as the girl's head turned towards her.

'Don't,' Miranda said. 'I have to do this. Charles says I need to. To make the visions stop. I want it to *stop*, Claire. You understand, right?'

'Let her go, Miranda, OK? Please?' Claire swallowed hard and stepped into the room. She could hear fighting from down the hall. Shane and Michael were busy. 'You don't want to hurt Eve. She's your friend!'

'It's too much,' Miranda said. 'So many people dying, and I can't do anything. Charles said he'd make it go away. All I have to do is—'

'What? Kill Eve? Really, don't – you don't want to – to do anything—' Panicked, she looked to Eve for help. One thing was for sure: the pallor in Eve's face wasn't make-up.

'Yeah,' Eve said faintly. 'I'm your friend, Mir. You know that.'

Miranda shook her head so hard her dark hair

flew. The knife trembled against Eve's throat, and she squeezed her eyes shut, whispering something that sounded like, '*Charles*,' and when she opened her eyes again she looked different. Not scared. Focused.

She's going to do something. I need to— Claire didn't have time to figure it out; she just moved, because Eve was moving, her arm flashing up and smacking Miranda's elbow. In the second that the knife was away from Eve's throat, Claire grabbed a thick handful of Miranda's hair and yanked, hard, dragging her backward. Miranda shrieked and slashed wildly at them. Eve's upraised arm got a bloody cut, and Claire moved backward, gasping, holding on to Miranda's hair and trying to stay out of cutting range.

Miranda swept the knife around and cut off the clump of hair a couple of inches away from Claire's knuckles. *Oh no...*

Miranda lunged at her, knife held out, and Claire ran into the black bedside table, toppled over onto the black satin comforter, and saw the knife coming for her.

'Hey!' Eve screamed, and spun Miranda around and slapped her, hard, across the face. Twice. When Miranda tried to stab her, Eve smacked the girl's hand into the wall and twisted her wrist until Miranda's fist opened and the knife dropped to the wood floor.

Miranda started crying. It was a hopeless, helpless sound, and if Claire hadn't been angry-scared, she might have actually felt sorry for her. 'No, no, I don't want to see it anymore, I don't want to – he said he'd make it stop—'

Eve grabbed her by the arm, opened up the closet door, and stuffed Miranda inside, then jammed a wooden chair under the door handle to hold it shut. She looked furious and really, really hurt. Her arm was bleeding all over the place – not spurting, but flowing pretty freely. Claire grabbed up a black towel lying on the bureau and pressed the makeshift bandage to the wound; Eve blinked, like she'd forgotten all about it, and held it in place.

'Maybe she was just under his spell. Like you were, when you—' OK, maybe it hadn't been smart to bring that up, Claire thought.

'That's why I slapped her,' Eve said. 'But I don't think that's it. Miranda's always been crazy. I just thought – well, I thought she wasn't *that* crazy.'

Eve looked better. More colour in her face, anyway... and then Claire thought, no, she looked *too* good.

Claire's eyes turned to the broken window. Outside, there was a slight edge of sunlight climbing above the horizon, and the sky had turned a deep blue-grey.

'Michael!' she blurted. 'Oh my God!'

She left Eve and ran into the hall. Shane was just coming out of his room, shaking out his right hand. His knuckles were bloody. 'Where's Michael?' she yelled.

'Downstairs,' he said. 'What the hell is that?'

Claire realised with a shock that somehow she was

still holding the handful of Miranda's severed hair. She made a face and let go, then fluttered her hand to shake off the clingy strands. 'You don't *even* want to know. Oh, Miranda's locked in Eve's closet, by the way.'

'Well, that's a bonus. Sorry, but I really don't like that kid.'

'She's not growing on me, either,' Claire admitted. 'Come on, we need to get to Michael.'

'Trust me, he's doing OK without us.'

'No, he's not,' she said grimly. 'The sun's coming up.'

He didn't get it for a second, and then he *did*, and oh, boy. He was gone before she could yell at him to wait for her.

She reached the bottom of the staircase a few seconds behind, and saw him race across to where Michael was grabbing another – presumably, human – intruder on his way in through the broken-down front door.

'I don't need you!' he yelled at them both, and tossed the guy halfway to Kansas. 'Get upstairs! Shane, show her where!'

Shane ignored him, plunged past him and into the hallway. Guarding the front door. Michael started to follow him, and stepped into the growing light from the back window.

He spun to look at it, then wordlessly at Claire. She saw the outright fear in his eyes. 'No,' he said. 'Not now!'

She couldn't say or do anything to help, and she knew it. 'How long...?'

The terrible look on his face pretty much answered the question, but he said it anyway. 'Five minutes. Maybe less. *Dammit!*'

As if the vampires knew, there was a rattle at the window behind the bookcase blocking it. It heaved uneasily, then started to topple forward. Michael got in between it and the floor, caught it, and flung it back upright, then braced it again with the sofa.

'Back up!' Michael ordered her, and she retreated to the stairs. She could hear Shane fighting in the hall again. 'Claire, you and Eve need to find a way to block everything. Seal it up. Don't let Shane—'

She wasn't sure what he was going to say, but just then he gasped and doubled over, and she knew that it was lost. He looked pale. Paler.

Mist.

Gone, along with a fading ghost of a scream.

Eve skidded to a stop beside her, eyes wide. 'He's gone,' she whispered, as if she really couldn't believe it. 'He left us.'

'He couldn't help it.' Claire took her hand. 'Come on, Eve, let's get the bookcase down the hall. We need to wedge it in the doorway.'

Eve nodded numbly. It was like all the fight had gone out of her, and Claire understood why... What hope was there now? Michael had been handling things, but without him...?

'Help me,' she said to Eve, and she meant it in every way she could.

Eve gave her a tiny little smile and squeezed her fingers. 'You know I will.'

Between the three of them, they managed to block the front door pretty thoroughly, wedging the bookcase in place and bracing it with two more at an angle. Sweaty, panting, scared, they looked at each other.

It got quiet. Weirdly quiet.

'Well?' Eve looked around the corner. 'I don't see anything...'

'Can we get to the pantry?' Claire asked. 'I mean, I don't hear anybody...'

'Too risky,' Shane said. He grabbed the phone from a pile of debris and started dialling on the fly, then dropped it. 'They cut the line.'

Eve pulled her cell phone out of a holster on her belt. Shane grabbed for it, checked the signal, and held up his hand for a high five. He was already dialling when they smacked it. 'Come on,' he muttered, pacing, listening. 'Pick up, pick up, pick up...'

He stopped in mid-step. 'Dad? Oh, damn, it's the machine – Dad, listen, if you get this, it's Shane, I'm at Michael Glass's house in Morganville, and I need shock and awe, man – come running. You know why.'

He flipped the phone shut and threw it to Eve. 'Upstairs, both of you. Get in the secret room. Michael? Are you with us?'

Claire shivered in a sudden cold draft. 'He's here.'

'Watch out for them,' Shane said. 'I – I kind of have a plan.' He said it as if he was half surprised.

'Girls. Upstairs. Now.'

'But—'

'Go!' He'd learnt how to yell orders from Michael, and it seemed to work, because Claire was moving for the stairs without any conscious decision to do it. The cold chill stayed around her, and she saw Eve shivering, too.

The upstairs was quiet, as well, except for the distant knocking sound of Miranda hammering on her door. 'I don't like this,' Claire said. 'Oliver knows Michael can't do anything after dawn, right?'

'I don't know,' Eve said, and chewed at her bottom lip. Most of her make-up had sweated off or been wiped away; even her lips were normal lip colour now, for nearly the first time Claire could remember. 'You're right. It's weird. Why would they just give up now?'

'They haven't,' said a voice that Claire's tingling spine recognised before her brain. Michael's bedroom door opened, and standing there, smiling, was Monica Morrell. Gina and Jennifer were behind her.

They were all holding knives, and that was a hell of a lot scarier than Miranda, no matter how crazy she might be.

Eve got in between Claire and Monica and began backing her away, down the hallway. 'Get in your room,' Eve said. 'Lock the door.'

'Won't do you any good,' Monica said, leaning around Eve. 'Ask me why. Go on, ask me.'

She didn't have to. She heard the door open behind her, and whipped around to see a man in a police uniform stepping out into the hallway with his gun drawn.

'Meet my brother, Richard,' she giggled. 'Isn't he cute?' He might have been, but Claire couldn't look anywhere but at the gun, which was big and shiny and black. She'd never had a gun pointed at her before, and it scared her in ways that even knives didn't.

'Shut up, Monica,' he said, and nodded towards the far end of the hall. 'Ladies. Downstairs, please. We don't have to make this bloody.' He sounded harassed more than anything else, like mass home invasion was just something standing between him and morning coffee.

Claire backed up, touched Eve, and whispered, 'What do we do?' She was asking Michael, too, for all the good it would do.

'I guess we go downstairs,' Eve said. She sounded defeated.

The chill swept across them stronger than ever.

'Um, I think that's a no?' Warm air flooded in. 'That's a yes?' More warm air. 'You're kidding me, Michael. *Stay here?*' Fine, if you were already a ghost, but how the hell were the two of them supposed to fight off three girls with knives and a cop with a gun?

Eve fainted. She did it convincingly, too, so well that Claire wasn't totally for sure that she wasn't really out. Monica, Gina, and Jennifer looked down at her, frowning, and Claire bent over her, fanning at her face. 'She got cut,' she said. 'She's lost a lot of blood.' She hoped that was an exaggeration, but she wasn't too sure, because the black towel had fallen away from Eve's arm and it looked soaked.

'Leave her,' said Monica's brother. 'We only need you, anyway.'

'But – she's bleeding! She needs—'

'Move.' He shoved her, and she nearly ran into the knife Gina was holding out. 'Monica, for God's sake, back the hell off, will you? I think I can handle some little girl!'

Monica frowned at him. 'Oliver said we could have her when it's over.'

'Yeah, when it's over. Which isn't now, so *back the hell off!*'

She shot him the finger, then stepped back to let Claire move past her. Claire did it as slowly as she could, manufacturing a crying jag and some shaking that, once started, felt too real to stop.

'See?' Monica said over her shoulder to Jennifer. 'Told you she was a punk.'

Claire doubled over, moaning, and very deliberately puked all over Monica's shoes. That was all it took. Monica screamed in horror and slapped her, Gina grabbed her, Jennifer stepped away, and Richard, confused by all the sudden girl fighting, took a couple of steps back so he wouldn't put a bullet in the wrong one.

'Hey!' Shane's voice, loud and angry. He was on the stairs, looking through the railing at them. 'Enough already. I'll give you the damn book. Just leave them alone.'

'Not fair,' Monica muttered, glaring at him. He glared right back, looking like he'd take back that hitting-a-girl rule, just once. Gladly. 'Richard, shoot him.'

'No,' Richard said wearily. 'I'm a *cop*. I only shoot who I'm told to shoot, and you aren't the chief.'

'Well, I will be. One day.'

'Then I'll shoot him when you are,' he said. 'Shane, right? Get up here.'

'Let them walk out of here first.'

'Not going to happen, so just get your ass up here before I decide I don't need either one of them.' Richard cocked the gun for emphasis. Shane slowly came up to the top of the steps and stopped. 'Where is it?'

'The book? It's safe. And it's someplace you'll never get it if you piss me off, Dick.'

Richard fired the gun. Everybody – even Monica – screamed, and Claire looked down at herself in shock.

He'd missed. There was a smoking round hole in Michael's door.

Oh. He hadn't missed.

'Kid,' Richard said wearily, 'I am *not* in the mood. I haven't slept in thirty-six hours, my sister's crazy—'

'Hey!' Monica protested.

'—and you're not *my* high school crush—'

'He is *not* my high school crush, Richard!'

'The point is, I couldn't give a crap about you, your friends, or your problems, because for me this isn't personal. Monica will kill you because she's nuts. I'll kill you because you make me kill you. Are we straight?'

'Well,' Shane said, 'that's kind of a personal question.'

Richard aimed directly at Claire. It wasn't much of a change, but she definitely felt it, like being in the centre of the spotlight instead of just on the edges, and she heard Shane say, 'Dude, I'm kidding, all right? Kidding!'

She didn't dare blink, or move her eyes away from the gun. If she could just keep staring at it, somehow, that would keep him from shooting her. She knew that didn't make sense, but...

In her side vision she saw Shane reach behind his back and pull out a book. Black leather cover. *Oh no. He's really going to...he can't. Not after all this.* Although she didn't have any answers for how he was supposed to avoid it, either.

Shane held up his left hand, showing it empty, and held out the black Bible with his right.

'That's it?' Richard asked.

'Swear to God.'

'Monica. Take it.'

She did, scowling at Shane. 'You are *not* my high school crush, idiot.'

'Great. I can die happy, then.'

'I'm shooting the next person who talks who isn't my sister,' Richard said. 'Monica?'

She opened the Bible. 'There's a hole in it. And another

book.' She stopped, staring at the inside. 'Oh my God. It really is. I thought for sure she was bull-shitting us.'

'She knows better. Let me see.'

Monica tilted the open Bible towards him, and Claire's last faint hope went away, because yes, that was the cover, with its scratchy home-engraved symbol.

Shane had done it. He'd given it up.

Somehow she'd expected better.

'So. We're square, right?' Shane asked tensely. 'No shooting or anything.'

Richard reached out, took the Bible from Monica, and flipped it close to tuck it under one arm. 'No shooting,' he agreed. 'I meant what I said. I'll only kill you if you make me. So thanks, I really didn't need the paperwork.'

He walked past Shane to the stairs, and started down.

'Hey, wait!' Shane said. 'Want to take your psycho sister with you?'

Richard stopped and sighed. 'Right. Monica? Let's go.'

'I don't want to,' she said. 'Oliver told me I could have them.'

'Oliver's not here, and I am, and I'm telling you that we have to go. Right now.' When she didn't move, he looked back. 'Now. Move, unless you want to fry.'

She blew Claire and Shane a mocking kiss. 'Yeah. Enjoy the barbecue!'

She followed her brother down. Gina went after, and that just left Jennifer standing there, looking oddly helpless even with a knife in her hands.

She bent over and put it on the floor, held up her hands, and said, 'Monica set a fire. You should get out while you can, and run like hell. It probably won't help, but – I'm sorry.'

And then she was gone. Shane stared after them for a frozen second, then moved over to kneel next to Eve. 'Hey. You OK?'

'Taking a nap,' Eve said. 'I thought maybe if I stayed down, you'd have it easier.' She sounded shaky, though. 'Help me up.'

Shane and Claire each took a hand and pulled her up; she swayed woozily. 'Did I get that right? You actually handed it over?'

'You know what? I did. And it kept you guys alive, so there you go. Hate me.' He was going to say something else, but then stopped and frowned and nodded down the hallway.

There was a thin thread of smoke curling out from underneath the door of Claire's bedroom.

'Oh my God!' she gasped, and ran for it; the knob was hot. She instantly let go and backed away. 'We have to get out of here!'

'Like they're going to let us go?' Shane asked. 'And no way am I letting this house burn. What about Michael? He can't leave!'

She hadn't even thought of that, and it hit her hard. Michael was trapped. Would he die if the house burnt? *Could* he? 'Fire trucks!' she yelled. 'There are fire trucks outside—'

'Yeah, to keep everything *else* from going up,' Eve said. 'Trust me. This is their easy answer. The Glass House goes up in flames, along with all their problem kids. Nobody's going to help us!'

'Then we have to do it,' Shane said. 'Yo, Michael! You there?'

'Here's there,' Eve said. 'I'm cold.'

'Anything you can do?'

Eve looked puzzled. 'Yes? No? Oh. Maybe. He says maybe.'

'Maybe's not good enough.' Shane opened the door to Eve's room and grabbed the black comforter off the bed. 'Blankets, towels, whatever, get it in the bathroom and soak it down. Oh, and let Miranda out, will you? We can hate her later.'

Claire kicked the chair out of the way from under the doorknob. The closet door flew open, and Miranda spilt out, coughing. She took one look at them and ran for the stairs.

'My clothes!' Eve yelped, and grabbed a double armful of hangers, then ran to Michael's room to dump them in a pile.

'Yeah, way to stay focused, Eve!' Shane yelled. He had the tap going in the bath, and seconds later he was back, dragging the soaking wet bundle. 'Stay back.'

He kicked open the door, and behind it Claire saw fire licking from the curtains up towards the ceiling. Her bed was on fire, too. It looked like that was where Monica had started it, since it was mostly in flames.

'Be careful!' she yelled, and hesitated to watch as Shane yanked the curtains down, threw the wet comforter over the bed, and began stomping down flames.

'Don't just stand there!' he said. 'Blankets! Towels! Water! *Move!*'

She dashed off.

CHAPTER SIXTEEN

The whole house smelt like smoke and burnt mattress, but on the whole, it could have been a lot worse. Claire's room was a mess, and her bed and curtains were a dead loss. Scorches on the floor and smoke damage on the ceiling.

Still.

Shane dumped more water on the mattress, which was already a sodden mess, and collapsed against the wall next to Claire and Eve.

'They've got to be wondering why we're not all screaming and burning by now,' Eve said. 'I mean, logically.'

'Go look.'

'You go look. I've had a tough night.'

Claire sighed, got up, and went to the unbroken window at the far end of the room. She couldn't see anything. No vampires, obviously, since the sun was blazing in the sky by now, but no human flunkies, either. 'Maybe they're all out front,' she said.

In the silence, she distinctly heard…the doorbell. 'You're kidding me,' Shane said. 'Hey, did you order pizza? Good thinking. I'm starved.'

'I think you have brain damage,' Eve shot back.

'Yeah, because I'm starved.'

There was a crash from downstairs, and Shane stopped smiling. His eyes went dark and focused. 'I guess this is it,' he said. 'Sorry. Last stand at the Alamo.'

Eve hugged him and didn't say a word. Claire walked over and hugged each of them in turn, Shane last so she could spend more time doing it. There really wasn't enough time, though, because she heard footsteps coming up the stairs, and she felt a strong chill sweep over her. Michael was with them. Maybe that was his version of a hug.

'Stay strong,' she heard Eve whisper in her ear. She nodded and took Eve's hand. Shane stepped out in front, which was – she knew by now – just what Shane did. He picked up the baseball bat he'd retrieved from down the hall and got ready.

'There's no need for that,' said a light, cool voice from the hallway. 'You must be Shane. Hello. My name is Amelie.'

Claire gasped and peeked around his broad back. It was the blond vampire from the church, looking perfectly cool and at ease as she stood there, hands folded.

'You can put that away,' Amelie said. 'You won't need it, I assure you.'

She turned and left the doorway. The three of them looked at one another.

Is she gone? Eve mouthed. Shane edged up to the doorway and looked out, then shook his head. *What's she doing?*

That was obvious one second later, as there was a faint click and the panelling on the other side popped free.

Amelie opened the hidden door and went up the steps.

'I think you have some questions,' she called down. 'I have some, as well, as it happens, and it would be prudent if we indulged each other. If not, then of course you are free to go but I must warn you that Oliver is not happy. And when Oliver is unhappy, he tends to be rather childish about lashing out. You are not, as they say, out of the woods quite yet, *mes petits*.'

'Vote,' Shane said. 'I'm for leaving.'

'Stay,' Eve said. 'Running won't do us any good, and you know it. We need to at least hear what she has to say.'

They both looked at Claire. 'I get a vote?' she asked, surprised.

'Why wouldn't you? You pay rent.'

'Oh.' She didn't even have to think about it. 'She saved my life today. I don't think she's – well, maybe she's bad, but she's not, you know, *bad*. I say we listen.'

Shane shrugged. 'Whatever. You go first.'

* * *

Amelie had settled herself on the antique Victorian settee. There were two other vampires in the room, standing very quietly in the corner, both wearing dark suits. Claire swallowed hard and fought an urge to back up and change her vote. Amelie smiled at her, lips closed, and gestured elegantly at the chair next to the sofa. 'Claire. Ah, and Eve, how lovely.'

'You know me?' Eve asked, surprised. She took a look around at the other two vampires.

'Of course. I always pay attention to the dispossessed. And your parents are particular favourites of mine.'

'Yeah, great. So who the hell are you?' Shane asked, blunt as ever. Amelie regarded him for an instant in surprise.

'Amelie,' she said, as if that explained everything. 'I thought you knew whose symbol you wore from birth, my dear.'

Shane looked pissed off. Of course. 'I don't wear any symbols.'

'That's true. You don't now.' She shrugged. 'But everyone in this town did once, including those from whom you sprang. One way or another, you are owned, body and soul.'

Shane, for once, didn't try a comeback. He just stared at her with dark, angry eyes. She didn't seem bothered.

'You have a question,' Amelie stated. Shane blinked.

'Yeah. How did you get in here? Oliver couldn't.'

'An excellent question, well phrased. And were I any other vampire, I would not be able to do so. However, this house is *my* house, first and foremost. I built it, as I built several such in Morganville. I live in each of them in turn, and while I am in residence the Protections will defend me from any enemy, either human or vampire. While I am absent, they will exclude vampires, if the residents are human, and of course humans if the residents are vampires. Unless the proper permissions are given.' She inclined her head. 'Does that answer your question?'

'Maybe.' Shane chewed on it a little, then said, 'Why didn't it protect Michael?'

'He gave Oliver permission to enter, and, in doing so, forfeited the house's Protection. However, the house did what it could to preserve him.' Amelie spread her hands. 'Perhaps it helped that Oliver was, in fact, not trying to destroy him but to change him.'

'Into a vampire,' Eve said.

'Yes.'

'Yes! I always wanted to ask why that doesn't work. I mean, the vampires keep on biting, but...?'

Amelie said nothing. She seemed to be thinking, or remembering; either way, it was a long and uncomfortable silence before she said, 'Have you children any concept of geometric progression?'

Claire raised her hand.

'And how many vampires would it take to turn the entire world into vampires, if it was so simple as that?' Amelie smiled as Claire opened her mouth. 'My dear, I do not expect you to answer, though if you would like to work out the math of it and tell me someday, I should be most interested to see it. The truth is that we came very near to it, in my younger years, when humans were much fewer. And it was agreed – as it has lately been agreed among you humans – that perhaps conservation of game is a wise idea. So we – removed the knowledge of how to create more vampires, simply by refusing to teach it. Over time, the knowledge was lost except to the Elders, and now it is lost altogether, except in two places.'

'Here?' Claire asked.

'Here,' Amelie said, and touched her temple. 'And there.'

She pointed at Shane.

'What?' Claire and Eve both blurted, and Claire thought, *Oh my God I kissed him and he was a vampire*, but Shane was looking odd, too. Not lost, exactly.

Guilty.

'Yeah,' he said, and put his hand in the pocket of his blue jeans. He pulled out a small book. The cover – Claire could read it from where she sat – read *Shakespeare Sonnets*. 'It was all I could think of.'

He tipped it sideways, and the pages slid out, away from the cover. Sliced neatly at both edges of the binding.

'Very clever,' Amelie said. 'You gave them the cover, filled with words they did not want, and kept for yourself what was important. But what if I told you that it was the cover they were after, and not the contents?'

He looked shaken. 'I had to play the odds.'

'Wise gamesmanship,' she said. 'In fact, I told you that Oliver is unhappy, and so he is, because he has allowed *that*' – she nodded towards the pages – 'to slip through his fingers. And so I find that I come to you for a favour.'

His eyes lit up, and he said, 'A favour? Like a deal?'

'Yes, Shane. I shall make a deal for what you hold in your hand, and I promise you that it is the only deal that matters, as I am the only vampire that matters. I will take the book, and destroy the last written record of how vampires may be created, which will ensure my continued survival against my enemies, who will not dare to move against me for fear of losing what only I know.' She sat back against the puffed cushions, studying him very calmly. 'And for this, you and all in this house will receive my Protection for as long as you should choose to have it. This will cancel any other, lesser contracts you might have made, such as the agreement you made with Oliver, through Brandon.'

'Oliver – is Brandon's boss?' Claire asked.

'Boss?' Amelie considered that, and nodded. 'Yes. Exactly. While I do not command Oliver, neither can he command me. Until he discovers the secrets I hold, he cannot unseat me in Morganville, and he cannot create his own followers to overwhelm mine. We are...evenly matched.'

Shane looked down at the book in his hand. 'And this would have changed that.'

'Yes,' she said softly. 'That book would have destroyed

us all in the end. Vampires as well as humans. I owe you a debt for this, and I will pay it as well as circumstances will allow.'

Shane thought about it for an agonising second, then looked at Eve. She nodded. Claire nodded when he checked for her approval, and then he held the book up. 'Michael?' he asked. 'Yes or no?' After another long second, he sighed. 'Guess that's a yes. Well, anything that pisses off Oliver is a good deed, so...' He held it out to Amelie.

She made no move to take it. 'Understand,' she said, and her eyes were bitter cold, 'that once this is done, it is done. Your Glass House will remain, but you are bound together. None may leave Morganville, after. I cannot risk your knowledge escaping my control.'

'Yeah, well, if we go now, we're toast anyway, right?' Shane kept holding it out. 'Take it. Oliver was right about one thing: it's nothing to us but death.'

'*Au contraire*,' she said, and her pale white fingers took it from his. 'It is, in fact, your salvation.'

She stood, looked around the room, and sighed a little. 'I have missed this place,' she said. 'And I believe it has also missed me. Someday I will come back.' She pressed the hidden catch on the arm of the settee, and without another word to them turned to leave.

'Hey, what about the cops?' Shane asked. 'Not to mention all those people who tried to kill us today?'

'They answer to Oliver. I will make it known that you are not to be troubled. However, you must not further disturb the peace. If you do, and it is your fault, I will be forced to reconsider my decision. And that would be... unfortunate.' She gave him a full smile. With fangs. '*Au revoir*, children. Do take care of the house more carefully in the future.'

Her two vamp guards went with her. Smoke and silence. There was no sound on the stairs after. Claire swallowed. 'Um...what did we just do?' she asked.

'Pretty much all we could,' Shane said. 'I'm checking the street.'

They ended up going down together, in a group – Shane with the bat, Eve with the knife Jennifer had abandoned, and Claire armed with a broken chair leg sharp on one end.

The house was deserted. The front door was standing open, and out on the street, cop cars were pulling away from the kerb around the big black Cadillac. A limousine was leaving, too. Its tinted windows cast back blinding reflections of the sun.

It was all over in seconds. No cars, no vampires, nobody hanging around. No Monica. No Richard. No Oliver.

'Crap,' Shane said. He was standing on the porch, looking at what was hanging next to the doorbell. It was a black lacquered plaque with a symbol on it. The same symbol that had been on the book cover he'd sent to Oliver. 'Does that mean she wrote the damn book, too?'

'I'll bet she did, for back-up,' Eve said. 'You know, the symbol's also on the well in the centre of town. It's the Founder symbol.'

'She's the Founder,' Shane said.

'Well, somebody had to be.'

'Yeah, but I figured it was a *dead* somebody.'

'Funny,' Claire said, 'but I think it *is* a dead somebody.'

Which made Shane laugh, and Eve snort, and Shane slung his arm over her shoulders. 'You still quitting school?' he asked.

'Not if I can't leave town.' Claire smacked herself in the head. 'Oh my *God*! I can't leave town! I can't *ever leave town?* What about school? Caltech? *My parents?*'

Shane kissed her on the forehead. 'Tomorrow's problems,' he said. 'I'm going with let's just be glad there's a tomorrow, at this point.'

Eve closed the front door. It swung open again in the breeze. 'I think we're going to need a new door.'

'I think we're going to need Home Depot.'

'Do they sell stakes at Home Depot here?' Claire asked. Shane and Eve looked blank. 'Dumb question. Never mind.'

Chapter Seventeen

Clean-up took pretty much all day, what with the broken furniture, the shattered windows, the front and back doors, and hauling Claire's damaged mattress out to the kerb. They were just sitting down to dinner when the sun went behind the horizon, and Claire heard the sound of a body hitting the floor, followed by dry retching.

'Michael's home,' Eve said, as if he'd just come back from school. 'You guys dig in.'

It took a while before she came back with Michael. Holding hands. Shane got up, smiling, and held up his hand. Michael high-fived it.

'Not bad, brother,' Michael said. 'The girls gave you enough time for the switch.'

'Even though they didn't know. Yeah. Worked out,' Shane said, pleased. 'See? My plans don't all suck. Just most of them.'

'So long as we keep on being able to tell the

difference.' Michael pulled up a chair. 'What's for – oh, you're kidding me. Chilli?'

'Nobody wanted to go to the store.'

'Yeah, I guess.' Michael closed his eyes. 'I'm saying a prayer. Maybe you ought to, too. It's going to take us a miracle to get through this.'

Whether he was serious or not, Claire sent the prayer up towards heaven, and she thought the others did, too. So it seemed kind of miraculous when the doorbell rang.

'At least they're getting more polite when they try to kill us,' Shane said. Michael got up and went to the door. After a second's hesitation, they all got up and followed.

Michael swung the new door open. Outside, in the glow of the porch light, stood a middle-aged man with a scraggy beard and a huge scar down one side of his face, dressed in black motorcycle leather. Behind him were two more guys, not quite as old and a whole lot bigger and meaner-looking.

Bikers. Claire nearly choked on her bite of chilli.

The man nodded.

'Son,' he said, looking past Michael right at Shane. 'Got your message. Cavalry's here.' He walked right in, past the threshold, and ignored Michael like he wasn't even there. 'About time you got your ass in gear. Been waiting for you to call for six damn months. What kept you? Took you this long to find the head bloodsucker?'

They followed him into the living room. Michael

turned to look at Shane, who was turning red. Not meeting anybody's eyes, really. 'Things have changed, Dad,' he mumbled.

'Nothing's changed,' Shane's dad said, and turned to face them, hands on hips. 'We came to kick us some ass and kill us some vampires, just like we planned all along. Time to get some payback for Alyssa and your mother. Nothing's going to change that.'

'Dad, things are *different* now, we can't—'

Shane's father grabbed him by the hair, quick as a snake. There were tattoos on his hand, ugly dark blue smudges, and he forced Shane's head back. 'Can't? *Can't?* We're going to burn this town down, boy, just like we agreed. And you're not changing your mind.'

'Hey!' Michael said sharply, and reached out for Shane's dad. When he touched him, something happened, something like an electric shock that flared blue white in the room and raised the hair on Claire's arms. Michael flew back and hit the wall, too stunned to do anything.

'No!' Shane yelled, and tried to pull free. He couldn't. 'Dad, no!'

Shane's dad nodded to one of his biker buddies. 'Yep. He's one of them,' he said. 'Take care of it.'

The biker guy nodded back, pulled a knife from his belt, and advanced on Michael.

'*No!*' Shane screamed it this time. Claire took a hesitant step forward, and stopped when Michael's wide blue eyes locked on hers. Eve was screaming, and so was Shane.

Miranda saw this, she thought. Michael was even standing on the rug Miranda had pointed to when she'd said, *And he died…right…there*. It hadn't been his first death.

It was his second.

'Guys, stay out of it!' Michael said sharply when Eve tried to lunge towards him and get between him and the biker. He was still backing away, and this time, he looked afraid. He hadn't been afraid of the vampires and all their minions, but this time…

The biker moved faster than anybody Claire had ever seen, except vampires; she didn't even see what happened, just heard the heavy thud as Michael hit the floor. The biker went down with him, holding him flat with one huge hand while the other one raised the knife.

'No, Dad, God, I'll do whatever you want!'

'Shut up,' Shane's dad said, and threw Shane towards the sofa. He sprawled there, and Claire ran over to him and put her arms around him. 'You bet you will. You three are going to tell me which vamps to strike first. Because it's us against them now, and don't you forget it.'

'Three?' Eve said faintly. Her huge eyes were locked on Michael, and the biker, and the knife.

'Three,' said Shane's dad, and nodded to the biker.

They all screamed as the knife came down.

Acknowledgements

Every teacher and student at Socorro High School in El Paso, Texas, and every student and professor at Texas Tech University.

None of you are in this book, but heck, if you can't acknowledge your alma maters...!

You gave me the tools and the passion.
Thank you.

The Dead Girls' Dance

For Ter, who helped lay
the cornerstone of Morganville.

For Katy, who helped me through
the plot jitters!

CHAPTER ONE

It didn't happen, Claire told herself. *It's a bad dream, just another bad dream. You'll wake up and it'll be gone like fog...*

She had her eyes squeezed tight shut. Her mouth felt dry, shrivelled-up, and she was pressed against Shane's hot, solid side, curled up on the couch in the Glass House.

Terrified.

It's just a bad dream.

But when she opened her eyes, her friend Michael was still dead on the floor in front of her.

'Shut those girls up, Shane, or I will,' Shane's father snapped. He was pacing the wooden floor, back and forth, hands clasped behind him. He wasn't looking at Michael's body, shrouded under a thick, dusty velvet curtain, but it was *all* Claire could see, now that she'd opened her eyes again. It was as big as the world, and it wasn't a dream, and it wasn't going away. Shane's dad was here, and he was terrifying, and Michael—

Michael was dead. Only Michael had already been dead, hadn't he? Ghostly. Dead during the day...alive at night...

Claire realised she was crying only when Shane's dad turned on her, staring with red-rimmed eyes. She hadn't felt that scared when she'd stared into vampire eyes... well, maybe once or twice, because Morganville was a scary place, generally, and the vampires were pretty terrifying.

Shane's father – Mr Collins – was a tall, long-legged man, and his hair was wild and curly and going grey. Long enough to reach the collar of his leather jacket. He had dark eyes. Crazy eyes. A scruffy beard. And a huge scar running across his face, puckered and liver coloured.

Yeah, definitely scary. Not a vampire, just a man, and that made him scary in whole different ways.

She sniffled and wiped her eyes and quit crying. Something in her said, *Cry later; survive now.* She figured that voice had spoken inside of Shane, too, because Shane wasn't looking at the velvet-covered sprawl of his best friend's body. He was watching his father. His eyes were red, too, but there were no tears.

Now Shane was scaring her, too.

'Eve,' Shane said softly, and then, louder, 'Eve! Put a sock in it!'

Their fourth roommate, Eve, was collapsed in an

awkward heap against the far wall by the bookcases, as far from Michael's body as she could get. Knees up, head down, she was crying hard and hopelessly. She looked up when Shane yelled her name, and her face was streaked with black from running mascara, half her Goth white make-up gone. She had on her death's-head Mary Jane shoes, Claire noticed. She didn't know why that seemed important.

Eve looked completely lost, and Claire slipped off the couch and went to sit beside her. They put their arms around each other. Eve smelt of tears and sweat and some kind of sweet vanilla perfume, and she couldn't seem to stop shaking. Shock. That was what they always said on TV, anyway. Her skin felt cold.

'Shhhh,' Claire whispered to her. 'Michael's OK. It's all going to be OK.' She didn't know why she said that – it was a lie; it had to be a lie; they'd all seen… what happened…but something told her it was the right thing to say. And sure enough, Eve's sobbing slowed, then stopped, and she covered her face with shaking hands.

Shane hadn't said anything else. He was still watching his dad, with the kind of intense stare most guys reserved for people they'd like to pound into hamburger. If his dad noticed, he clearly didn't care. He continued to pace, up and down. The guys he'd brought with him – walking slabs of muscle in black motorcycle leather, shaved heads and tattoos and everything – were standing in the corners, arms folded. The one who'd killed Michael looked bored as he flipped the knife in his fingers.

'Get up,' Shane's dad said. He'd stopped pacing, and was standing right in front of his son. 'Don't you dare give me any crap, Shane. I told you to stand up!'

'You didn't have to do that,' Shane said, and slowly stood, feet slightly apart. Ready to take (or give) a punch, Claire thought. 'Michael wasn't any threat to you.'

'He's one of them. Undead.'

'I said he wasn't a threat!'

'And *I* say that you just don't want to admit your friend's turned freak of nature on you.' Shane's dad reached out and awkwardly punched Shane on the shoulder. It was supposed to be a gesture of affection, Claire supposed. Shane just rode with the blow. 'Anyway, done is done. You know why we're here. Or do you need a reminder?'

When Shane didn't answer, his father reached into his leather jacket and took out a handful of photographs. He threw them at Shane. They bounced off of Shane's chest, and he reflexively tried to catch them, but some drifted free and fell to the wood floor. Some slid over towards Claire and Eve.

'Oh God,' Eve whispered.

They were pictures of Shane's family, Claire guessed – Shane as a cute little boy, arm around an even tinier little girl with a cloud of curly black hair. A pretty woman standing behind them, and a man she could barely recognise as Shane's dad. No scar, back then. Hair cut short. He looked...normal. Smiling and happy.

There were other pictures, too. Eve was staring at one of them, and Claire couldn't make any sense of it. Something black and twisted and—

Shane bent over and snatched it up, fumbling it back into the pile.

His house burnt. He got out. His sister wasn't so lucky.

Oh *God*, that twisted thing was Alyssa. That was Shane's sister. Claire's eyes filled up with tears, and she covered her mouth with both hands to hold in a scream, not because what was in the picture was gross – it was – but Shane's *own father* had made him look at it.

That was cruel. Really cruel. And she knew it wasn't the first time.

'Your mother and sister are both dead because of this place, because of the *vampires*. You didn't forget that, did you, Shane?'

'I didn't forget!' Shane shouted. He kept trying to make the pictures fit into a neat stack, but he didn't look at them at all. 'I dream about them every night, Dad. Every night!'

'Good. It was you got this started. You'd better remember that, too. Can't back out now.'

'I'm not backing out!'

'Then what's all this crap, *Things have changed, Dad*?' Shane's dad mimicked him, and Claire wanted to punch him, never mind that he was about four times her size and probably a whole lot meaner. 'You hook up with your old friends and next thing I know, you lose your nerve. That thing was Michael, right? The Glass kid?'

'Yes.' Shane's throat worked hard, and Claire saw tears glitter in his eyes. 'Yeah, it was Michael.'

'And these two?'

'Nobody.'

'That one looks like another vamp.' Shane's father fixed his red-rimmed glare on Eve, and took a step towards where Claire and Eve were huddled on the floor.

'You leave her alone!' Shane dropped the pictures into a pile on the couch and jumped into his father's path, fists clenched. His dad's eyebrows raised, and he gave Shane a scar-twisted grin. 'She's not a damn vampire. That's Eve Rosser, Dad. Remember Eve?'

'Huh,' his father said, and stared at Eve for a few seconds before shrugging. 'Turned into a wannabe, then, just about as bad in my book. What about the kid?'

He was talking about Claire.

'I'm not a kid, Mr Collins,' Claire said, and clambered to her feet. She felt awkward, all strings and wires, nothing working right. Her heart was hammering so hard, it hurt to breathe. 'I live here. My name is Claire Danvers. I'm a student at the university.'

'Are you.' He didn't make it a question. 'You look a little young.'

'Advanced placement, sir. I'm sixteen.'

'Sweet sixteen.' Mr Collins smiled again, or tried to – the scar pulled the right side of his mouth down. 'Never been kissed, I'll bet.'

She felt her face go red. Couldn't stop it, or keep herself from looking at Shane. Shane's jaw was set tight, muscles fluttering. He wasn't looking at anything in particular.

'Oho! So it's like that. Well, you watch yourself around the jailbait, my boy.' Still, Shane's dad looked weirdly pleased. 'My name's Frank Collins. Guess you figured out that I'm this one's father, eh? Used to live in Morganville. I've been gone a few years now.'

'Since the fire,' Claire said, and swallowed hard. 'Since Alyssa died. And...Shane's mom?' Because Shane had never said a word about her.

'Molly died later,' Mr Collins said. 'After we left. Murdered by the vamps.'

Eve spoke for the first time – a soft, tentative voice. 'How did you remember? About Morganville, after you left town? I thought nobody did, once they left.'

'Molly remembered,' Mr Collins replied. 'Little bit at a time. She couldn't forget Lyssa, and that opened the door, inch by inch, until it was all there. So we knew what we had to do. We had to bring it down. Bring it all down. Right, boy?'

Shane nodded. It didn't look like agreement so much as a wish not to get smacked for disagreeing.

'So we spent time preparing, and then I sent Shane here back to Morganville to map the town for us, identify targets, do all the stuff we wouldn't have time to do once we rolled in. Couldn't wait any longer once he yelled for help, though. Came running.'

Shane looked sick. He wouldn't look at Eve, or Claire, or Michael's body. Or his father. He just – stared. There were tear tracks on his cheeks, but Claire couldn't remember seeing him cry, really.

'What are you going to do?' Claire asked faintly.

'First thing, I guess we bury that,' Mr Collins said, and nodded towards Michael's shrouded body. 'Shane, best you stay out of the way—'

'No! No, don't you touch him! I want to do it!'

Mr Collins gave him a long frowning look. 'You know what we're going to have to do' – he glanced at Eve and Claire – 'to make sure he doesn't come back.'

'That's folklore, Dad. You don't have to—'

'That's the way we're going to do things. The right way. I don't want your friend coming back at me next time the sun goes down.'

'What is he talking about?' Claire whispered to Eve. Sometime in the last few minutes, Eve had got up to stand next to her, and their hands were clasped. Claire's fingers felt cold, but Eve's were like ice.

'He's going to put a stake in his heart,' Eve said numbly. 'Right? And garlic in his mouth? And—'

'You don't need all the details,' Mr Collins interrupted. 'Let's get this done, then. And once we're finished, Shane's going to draw us a map of where to find the high-rolling vampires of Morganville.'

'Don't you know?' Claire asked. 'You lived here.'

'Doesn't work like that, little girl. Vamps don't trust us. They move around, they have all kinds of Protection to keep themselves safe from retribution. But my boy's found a way. Right, Shane?'

'Right,' Shane said. His voice sounded absolutely flat. 'Let's get this done.'

'But...Shane, you can't—'

'Eve, *shut up.* Don't you get it? There's nothing we can do for Michael now. And if he's dead, it won't matter what we do to him. Right?'

'You *can't*!' Eve yelled it. *'He isn't dead!'*

'Well,' Mr Collins said, 'I guess that'll be his problem when we plant a stake in him and chop off his head.'

Eve screamed into her clenched fists, and collapsed to her knees. Claire tried to hold her up, but she was more solid than she looked. Shane instantly whirled and crouched next to her, hovering protectively and glaring at his father and the two motorcycle dudes standing guard over Michael's body.

'You're a bastard,' he said flatly. 'I told you, Michael was no threat to you before, and he's no threat now. You killed him already. Let it go.'

For answer, Shane's father nodded to his two friends – accomplices? – who then reached down, seized hold of Michael's body, and dragged him out and around the corner to the kitchen door. Shane bolted back to his feet.

His father stepped into his path and backhanded him across the face, hard enough to stagger him. Shane put up his palms – defence, not offence. Claire's heart sank.

'Don't,' Shane panted. 'Don't, Dad. Please don't.'

His father lowered the fist he'd raised for a second

blow, looked down at his son, and turned away. Shane stood there, shaking, eyes cast down, until his father's footsteps moved away, towards the kitchen.

Then Shane spun around, lunged forward, and grabbed Claire and Eve by the arms. 'Come on!' he hissed, and towed them both stumbling towards the stairs. 'Move!'

'But—,' Claire protested. She looked over her shoulder. Shane's father had gone to look out the window, presumably at whatever they were doing in the backyard (oh God) to Michael's body. 'Shane—'

'Upstairs,' he said. He didn't leave them much choice; Shane was a big guy, and this time he was using his muscle. By the time Claire got herself together, they were upstairs, in the hallway, and Shane was shoving open the door to Eve's room. 'Inside, girls. Lock the door. I mean it. Don't open it for anybody but me.'

'But…Shane!'

He turned to Claire, took hold of both of her shoulders in those big hands, and leant forward to plant a warm kiss on her forehead. 'You don't know these guys,' he said. 'You're not safe. Just…stay in there until I get back.'

Eve, looking dazed, murmured, 'You have to stop them. You can't let them hurt Michael!'

Shane locked eyes with Claire, and she saw the grim sadness. 'Yeah,' he said. 'Well, that's pretty much done. Just – I have to look out for you now. It's what Michael wants.'

Before Claire could summon up anything else in

protest, he pushed her back over the threshold and slammed the door. He banged on it once with his fist. 'Lock it!'

She reached up and flipped the dead bolt, then turned the old-fashioned key, as well. She stayed where she was, because she could feel, somehow, that Shane hadn't moved away.

'Shane?' Claire pressed herself against the door, listening. She thought she could hear his uneven breathing. 'Shane, don't let him hurt you again. *Don't.*'

She heard a breathless sound that was more like a sob than a laugh. 'Yeah,' Shane agreed faintly. 'Right.'

And then she heard his footsteps moving away, down the hall to the stairs.

Eve was sitting on her bed, staring into space. The room smelt like a fireplace, thanks to the fire that had raged next door, in Claire's room, but there was only some smoke damage, nothing really serious. And besides, with all the black Goth stuff everywhere, you couldn't even really tell.

Claire sat down on the bed beside Eve. 'Are you OK?'

'No,' Eve said. 'I want to go look out the window. But I shouldn't, right? I shouldn't see what they're doing.'

'No,' Claire agreed, and swallowed hard. 'Probably not a good idea.' She rubbed Eve's back gently and thought about what to do...and that wasn't much. It wasn't like allies were exactly falling off the trees around here... Besides Shane, they had nobody else. Their second-best choice was a vampire.

How scary was *that*?

Still, she *could* call Amelie. But that was a little like arming a nuclear weapon to take care of an ant problem. Amelie was so badass, the other badass vampires backed down without a fight. She'd said, *I will make it known that you are not to be troubled. However, you must not further disturb the peace. If you do, and it is your fault, I will be forced to reconsider my decision. And that would be…*

'Unfortunate,' Claire finished aloud, in a whisper. Yeah. Pretty unfortunate. And there was no way that this didn't constitute disturbing the peace – or wouldn't, as soon as Shane's dad got rolling. He'd come to kill vampires, and he wasn't going to be stopped by any little considerations like, oh, his son's life and safety.

No, not a good idea to call Amelie.

Who else? Oliver? Oliver wasn't exactly at the top of Claire's Best Friends Forever list, although in the beginning she'd thought he was pretty cool, for an old guy. But he'd been playing her, and he was the second-most badass vamp in town. Who'd use them, and this situation, against Amelie if he could.

So no. Not Oliver, either. The police were bought and paid for by the vampires. Her teachers at school… no. None of them had impressed her as being willing to stand up to pressure.

Mom and Dad? She shuddered to think what would happen if she put in a frantic yell to them… For one thing, they'd already had their memories altered by

Morganville's strange psychic field, or so she assumed, since they'd forgotten all about ordering her home for living off campus. With boys. Mom and Dad weren't exactly the kind of backup she needed, not up against Shane's dad and his bikers.

Her cousin Rex...now, there was an idea. No, Rex had been sent to jail three months ago. She remembered Mom saying so.

Face facts, Danvers. There's nobody. Nobody coming riding to the rescue.

It was her, Eve, and Shane against the world.

So the odds were about three billion to one.

CHAPTER TWO

It was a long, long day. Claire eventually stretched out on one side of the bed, Eve on the other, each wrapped in her own separate cocoon of misery and heartache.

They didn't talk much. There didn't seem to be a lot to talk about.

It was almost dark when the doorknob rattled, sending Claire into a heart-pounding terror seizure; she advanced slowly, and whispered, 'Who is it?'

'Shane.'

She unlocked fast and opened up. Shane came in, head down, carrying a tray on which sat two bowls of chilli – which made sense, because it was nearly the only thing Shane knew how to fix. He set it down on the edge of the bed, next to Eve, who was sitting like an unstuffed rag doll, limp with grief and dejection.

'Eat something,' he said. Eve shook her head. Shane picked up a bowl and shoved it in her direction; she took it just to avoid wearing it, and glared at him.

Claire saw her expression change into something else. Blank at first, then horrified.

'It's nothing,' Shane said as Claire came around to see. It wasn't nothing. It was bruises, dark ones, spilling over his cheek and jaw. Shane avoided looking at her. 'My fault.'

'Jesus,' Eve whispered. 'Your dad—'

'My fault,' Shane snapped back, got up, and headed for the door. 'Look, you don't understand. He's right, OK? I was wrong.'

'No, I don't understand,' Claire said, and grabbed his arm. He pulled free without any effort at all and kept walking. 'Shane!'

He paused in the doorway and looked back at her. He looked bruised, beaten, and sullen, but it was the desperation in his eyes that scared her. Shane was always strong, wasn't he? He had to be. She needed him to be.

'Dad's right,' he said. 'This town is sick, it's poisoned, and it's poisoning us, too. We can't let it beat us. We have to take them out.'

'The vampires? Shane, that's stupid! You can't! You know what'll happen!' Eve said. She put the bowl of chilli back on the tray and got off the bed, looking tear-streaked and forlorn but more like herself. 'Your dad's crazy. I'm sorry, but he is. And you can't let him drag you down with him. He's going to get you killed, and Claire and me, too. He already—' She caught her breath and gulped. 'He already got Michael. We can't let him do this. Who knows how many people are going to get hurt?'

'Like Lyssa got hurt?' Shane asked. 'Like my mom? *They killed my mom, Eve!* They were willing to burn us up in this house yesterday, don't forget, and that included Michael.'

'But—'

'This town is bad,' Shane said, and looked at Claire, almost pleading. 'You understand, right? You understand that there's a whole world out there, a whole world that isn't like this?'

'Yes,' she said faintly. 'I understand that. But—'

'We're doing this. And then we're getting out of this place.'

'With your father?' Eve managed to put a whole dictionary of contempt into that. 'I don't think so. I look good in black, but not so great in black and blue.'

Shane flinched. 'I didn't say... Look, just the three of us. We get out of town while my dad and the others—'

'We run?' Eve shook her head. 'Brilliant. And when the vamps have a big party and roast your dad and his buddies, what then? Because they're definitely going to come looking for us. Nobody escapes who had any part in killing a vampire, you know that. Unless you really believe that your dad and his idiot muscle are going to be able to take down hundreds of vamps, all their human allies, the cops, and, for all I know, the U.S. Marines.'

'Eat your damn chilli,' Shane said.

'Not without something to drink. I know your chilli.'

'Fine! I'll get you Cokes!' He slammed the door behind him. 'Lock it!'

Claire did. This time, Shane didn't linger in the hall; she heard the hard thump of his boots as he went downstairs.

'Did you have to do that?' she asked Eve. She leant against the door and folded her arms.

'Do what, exactly?'

'He's confused. He lost Michael, his dad's got him—'

'Say it, Claire: his dad's got him brainwashed. Worse. I think his dad's beaten the fight out of him. He's certainly beaten the brains out of him.' Eve wiped at her face impatiently; there were more tears streaming down her cheeks, but it was more like water escaping under pressure than real sobs. 'His dad wasn't always like this. He used to be...well, not nice, because he was kind of a drunk, but better. Way better than this. After Lyssa he just went...crazy. I didn't know about Shane's mom. I thought she just, you know...killed herself. Shane never really said.'

Claire hadn't heard any footsteps on the stairs, but she heard and felt a soft knock through the door, and then a rattle of the doorknob. She unlocked and swung it open, holding out her hands for the Cokes she expected Shane to thrust at her...

...and there was a grinning, smelly mountain of a man in the doorway. The one who'd stabbed Michael.

Claire let go of the door and stumbled back, thinking

only an instant later, *Stupid, that was stupid – you should have slammed it*...but it was too late; he was already inside, closing the door behind him.

And locking it.

She looked in terror at Eve. Eve lunged forward, grabbed Claire, and hustled her around to the far side of the bed...and stepped in front of her. Claire looked frantically around for a weapon. Anything. She picked up a heavy-looking skull, but it was plastic, light and utterly useless.

Eve yanked a field hockey stick from under her bed.

'Let's do this nice,' the man said. 'That little stick isn't going to do you any good, and it's only going to piss me off.' His lips widened in a grin, revealing big, square, yellow teeth. 'Or get me all excited.'

Claire felt sick and faint. This wasn't like Shane coming into her room the other night, not at all. This was the flip side of men, and although she'd heard about it – you couldn't grow up without that – she'd never really *seen* it. Some jerks, sure, but there was something horrible about this guy. Something that looked at her and Eve like pieces of meat he was about to devour.

'You're not touching us,' Eve said, and raised her voice. 'Shane! Shane, get your ass up here *now*!'

There was a touch of panic in her voice, although she was putting on a good front. Her hands were shaking where they gripped the hockey stick.

The man glided around the end of the bed, prowling like a cat. Six feet tall, at least, and as broad as two of Eve, maybe bigger. His bare arms were ripped with muscle. His blue eyes looked shallow and hungry.

Claire heard the thump of footsteps outside, and then a *bang* as Shane fetched up against the locked door. He rattled the knob and pounded hard. 'Eve! Eve, open up!'

'She's busy!' the biker yelled, and laughed. 'Oh yeah, gonna be *real* busy.'

'No!' Shane screamed it, and the door shook with the strength of the blows he put into it. 'Stay away from them!'

Eve backed Claire up, all the way to the window. She took a swipe at the biker, who just stepped back out of range, still laughing.

'Get your dad!' she yelled at Shane. 'Make him do something!'

'I'm not leaving you!'

'Do it, Shane, *now*!'

Footsteps pounded down the hall. Claire swallowed, feeling suddenly even more alone and vulnerable. 'Do you think his dad will come?' she whispered. Eve didn't answer.

'Swear to God, you come near us and—'

'Like this?' The biker sidestepped a slash from the hockey stick, grabbed it on the way, and yanked it out of Eve's hands. He tossed it over his shoulder to land on the floor with a clatter. 'This near enough? Whatcha gonna do, doll girl? Cry all over me?'

Claire hid her eyes as the biker reached out for Eve with one tattooed hand.

'No,' Eve said breathlessly. 'I'm going to let my boyfriend beat the crap out of you.'

There was a dull *thunk* of wood meeting flesh, and a howl. Then another, harder *thunk*, and a crash as a body hit the floor.

The biker was down. Claire stared at him in disbelief, then looked past him, to the figure standing there with the field hockey stick in both hands.

Michael Glass. Back from the dead, again, a gorgeous blond avenging angel, breathing hard. Flushed with anger, blue eyes flashing. He glanced at the two girls, making sure they were OK, and then put the blade of the hockey stick on the biker's throat. The biker's eyes fluttered and tried to open, but didn't make it. He relaxed into unconsciousness.

Eve flew towards Michael, leapt over the biker's body, and fastened herself around Michael like she was trying to be sure he was all there. He must have been; he winced from the force of the impact, then kissed her on the top of her head without looking away from the man lying limp at their feet.

'Eve,' he said, and then glanced at her and gentled his tone. 'Eve, honey, go open the door.'

She nodded, stepped away, and followed instructions. Michael handed her the hockey stick, grabbed the biker by the shoulders, and towed him quickly out into the hallway. He closed the door again, locked it, and said, 'Right, here's the story. Eve, you knocked him out with the hockey stick and—'

He didn't finish, because Eve grabbed him and pushed him back against the door, wrapping herself around him like a Goth-girl coat. She was crying again, but silently; Claire could see her shoulders shaking. Michael sighed, put his arms around her, and bent his blond head to rest against her dark one.

'It's OK,' he murmured. 'You're OK, Eve. We're all OK.'

'You were *dead*!' she wailed, muffled by the fact that her face was still pressed against his chest. 'Damn you, Michael, you were *dead*, I saw them kill you, and...they—'

'Yeah, it wasn't too pleasant.' Something passed fast and hot across Michael's eyes, the reflection of a horror that Claire thought he didn't want to remember or share. 'But I'm not a vampire, and they can't kill me like a vampire. Not while the house owns my soul. They can do pretty much anything to my body, but it just...gets fixed.'

The prospects of that made Claire sick, like standing on the edge of a huge and unexpected drop. She stared at Michael, wide-eyed, and saw he understood the same things she did: that if Shane's father and his merry band of thugs found out, they might decide to test that out. Just for fun.

'That's why I'm not here,' Michael said. 'You can't tell them. Or Shane.'

'Not tell Shane?' Eve pulled back. 'Why not?'

'I've been watching,' he said. 'Listening. I can do that when I'm, you know—'

'A ghost?' Claire supplied.

'Exactly. I saw—' Michael didn't go on, but Claire thought she knew what he'd been about to say.

'You saw Shane's dad hit him,' she said. 'Right?'

'I don't want to make him keep secrets from his dad. Not now.'

Footsteps pounding up the stairs, then slowing when they hit the hallway. Michael touched his finger to his lips and eased out from Eve's frantic grip. He pressed his lips silently to hers.

'Hide!' Claire whispered. He nodded and opened the closet, rolled his eyes at the mess inside, and forced his way in. Burying himself in piles of clothes, Claire hoped.

Miranda had been trapped in that closet after trying to knife Eve, before the house had caught fire; she'd really done a job of messing things up. Eve was going to be furious.

Both girls jumped at a hard blow on the door. Eve hastily unlocked the door and stepped back as it flew open, and Shane charged through.

'How—?' He was breathing hard, and he had a crowbar in his hand. He'd have broken through the locks, Claire realised, if he'd had to. She came towards him slowly, trying to figure out what he was feeling, and he dropped the crowbar and wrapped his arms around her, lifting her up off the ground. His face was buried in the crook of her neck, and the warm, fast pump of his breath on her skin made her shiver in raw delight.

'Oh Christ, Claire. I'm sorry. I'm so sorry.'

'Not your fault,' Eve said. She held out the field hockey stick. 'Look! I hit him. Um, twice.'

'Good.' Shane kissed Claire's cheek and let her slide back down to the floor, but he kept hold of her arms. His eyes, bright under the bruises and swelling, surveyed her carefully. 'He didn't hurt you? Either of you?'

'I hit him!' Eve repeated brightly, and brandished the stick again for emphasis. 'So, no, he didn't hurt us. We hurt him. You know, all alone. Without any help. Um, so...where's your dad? He charges to the rescue pretty slow.'

Shane closed the door and locked it again as the biker in the hall groaned and rolled over on his side. He didn't answer, which was answer enough. Shane's dad needed his bikers more than he needed Eve or Claire. They were expendable. Worse, they'd probably just become rewards.

'We can't stay here,' Eve said. 'It isn't safe. You know that.'

Shane nodded, but he looked bleak. 'I can't come with you.'

'Yes, you can! Shane—'

'He's my dad, Eve. He's all I've got.'

Eve snorted. 'Yeah, well, what you've got I'd give back.'

'Sure, you just walked away from your folks—'

'Hey!'

'Didn't even care what happened to them—'

'*They* didn't care what happened to *me*!' Eve almost

shouted it. Suddenly, the hockey stick in her hands wasn't so much for display. 'Leave my family out of this, Shane – you don't have a clue. Not a *clue*.'

'I've met your brother,' Shane shot back.

They both went quiet. Dangerously quiet. Claire cleared her throat. 'Brother?'

'Leave it alone, Claire,' Eve said. She sounded dead calm, not at all like herself. 'You *really* don't want to get into it.'

'Bones in every family closet in Morganville,' Shane said. 'Yours rattle pretty loud, Eve. So don't judge me.'

'Here's a thought: why don't you *get the hell out of my room, you asshole!*'

Shane picked up his crowbar, opened the door, and stepped outside. He reached down and hauled the biker to his feet, and shoved him towards the stairs. The biker went, still groaning and weaving.

Claire peeked through the gap in the door until she was sure they were gone, then nodded to Eve, who dumped the hockey stick and opened the closet door. 'Oh, crap,' she sighed. 'I hope nothing's torn in there. It is *not* easy to get clothes in this town. Michael?'

Claire looked over her shoulder. A pile of black and red netting stirred, and Michael's blond head appeared. He sat up, brushing off Goth, and silently held up a pair of black lace panties. Thong.

'Hey!' Eve yelped, and grabbed them from his fingers. 'Personal! And...laundry!'

Michael just smiled. For a guy who'd been stabbed,

hacked up, and buried less than twenty-four hours ago, he looked remarkably composed. 'I'm not even going to ask what you wore them with,' he said. 'It's more fun to imagine.'

Eve snorted and gave him a hand up. 'Shane's taken our new boyfriend downstairs. What now? We can't exactly shimmy down a drainpipe.'

'Not in fishnets, you can't,' he agreed, straight-faced. 'Get changed. The less attention you attract from these guys, the better.'

Eve grabbed a pair of blue jeans from the floor of the closet, and a baby-doll T that must have been a gift; it was aqua blue, with a sparkle rainbow over the chest. Very *not* Eve. She glared at Michael and tapped her foot.

'What?' he asked.

'Gentlemen turn around. Or so I've heard.'

He faced the corner. Eve stripped off her spiderweb-lace shirt and the red top beneath, and stepped out of the red and black tartan skirt. The fishnets were garters – *totally* sexy. 'Not a word,' she warned Claire, and rolled them down. She didn't take her eyes off of Michael. There was red burning hot in her cheeks.

Dressing took thirty seconds, and then Eve grabbed up the scattered clothes, the garter belt, and the fishnets, and stuffed them into the closet before saying, 'OK, you can turn around.'

Michael did, leaning against the wall with his arms folded. He was smiling slightly, eyes half-closed.

'What?' Eve demanded. She was still blushing. 'Don't I look stupid enough now?'

'You look great,' he said, and crossed to kiss her lightly on the lips. 'Go wash your face.'

Eve went to the bathroom and shut the door. Claire said, 'You've got some kind of a plan, right? Because we don't. Well, Shane thinks we should let his dad do whatever, and run, but Eve doesn't think it's a good idea—'

'It's suicide,' Michael said flatly. 'Shane's dad is an idiot, and he's going to get Shane killed. You, too.'

'But you've got a plan.'

'Yeah,' Michael said. 'I have a plan.'

When Eve came back from the bathroom, Michael put his finger to his lips again, unlocked the door, and walked them across the hall. He reached behind the picture frame and pushed the hidden button, and the panelling creaked open to reveal one of the secret rooms of the Glass House. Amelie's room, Claire remembered. The one the vampire liked the best, probably because there were no windows and the only exit was from a concealed button. How weird was it to be living in a house built – and, really, owned – by a vampire?

'Inside,' Michael whispered. 'Eve. Cell phone?'

She patted her pockets, held up a finger, and dashed back to her room. She came back holding it up. Michael hustled them up the narrow staircase, and the door hissed shut behind them. No knob on this side, either.

Upstairs, the room was just as Claire had last seen it

– elegant Victorian splendour, a little dusty. This room, like all of the house, seemed to have a sense of something present in it, something just out of sight. *Ghosts*, she thought. But Michael seemed to be the only ghost, and he was as normal as could be.

Then again, the house was alive, kind of, and it was keeping Michael alive, too. So maybe not so normal.

'Phone,' Michael said, and held out his hand as he sat down on the couch. Eve handed it over, frowning.

'Just who are you planning to call?' she asked. 'Ghostbusters? It's not like we have a lot of options...'

Michael grinned at her and pressed three keys, then activated the call. The response was nearly immediate. 'Hello, 911? This is Michael Glass, 716 Lot Street. I have intruders in my house. No, I don't know who they are, but there are at least three of them.'

Eve's mouth flopped open in surprise, and Claire blinked, too. Calling the police seemed so...*normal*. And so wrong.

'You might want to tell the officers that this house and its occupants are under the Founder's Protection,' he said. 'They can verify that, I guess.'

He smiled and hung up a moment later, handed the phone back, and looked *very* smug.

'And Shane?' Claire asked. 'What about Shane?'

Michael's self-assurance faded. 'He's making his own choices,' he said. 'He'd want me to look out for the two of you first. And the only way I can do that is to get these guys out of my house. I can't protect you twenty-four/seven – in the daytime, you're vulnerable. And I'm not going to float around and watch while you get—' He didn't finish, but Claire – and Eve – knew where that was going. They both nodded. 'Once they're out of the house, I can keep them from coming back, unless Shane lets them in. Or one of you, though I can't see that happening.'

More headshakes, this time more violent. Michael kissed Eve's forehead with obvious affection, and ruffled Claire's hair. 'Then this is the best way,' he said. 'It'll shake them up, anyway.'

'I'm sorry,' Eve said in a small voice. 'I didn't think. I'm so used to thinking of the cops as enemies, and besides, they were just trying to kill us. Right?'

'Things change. We have to adapt.'

Michael was pretty much the king of that, Claire thought. He'd gone from a serious musician with his whole focus on making a name for himself, to a part-time ghost trapped in a house, to a part-time ghost trapped in a house forced to take in roommates to make the bills. And now he was trying to save their lives, and he still couldn't escape himself.

Michael was just so...responsible. Claire couldn't even imagine how someone got that way. Maturity, she guessed, but that was a lot like a road through fog to her. She had no idea how she was supposed to get there. Then again, she supposed nobody really did know, and you just stumbled through it.

They waited.

After about five minutes there was a wail of sirens in the distance – very faint, because the room was well soundproofed. That meant the sirens were close. Maybe even by the house already. Claire rose and pressed the button concealed in the lion's-head arm of the couch, and the sirens immediately increased in volume as the secret door opened. She hurried down the steps and peered out. No one in the hallway, but from downstairs she heard angry shouting, and then the sound of a door banging open. Motorcycle engines roaring, tyres squealing.

'They're going,' she yelled up, and pelted out into the hallway, down the stairs, breathless to find Shane.

Shane was up against the wall, and his father was holding him by the throat. Outside, police sirens suddenly cut off.

'Traitor,' Shane's dad said. He had a knife in his hand. 'You're a traitor. You're *dead* to me.'

Claire skidded to a stop, found her voice, and said, 'Sir, you'd better get out of here unless you want to end up talking to the vampires.'

Shane's father turned his face towards her, and his expression was twisted with fury. 'You little *bitch,*' he said. 'Turning my son against me.'

'No—' Shane grabbed at his father's hand, trying to pry it free. 'Don't—'

Claire backed up. For a second, neither Shane nor his dad moved, and then Shane's father let him go, and raced for the kitchen door. Shane dropped to his knees, choking, and Claire went to him...

…just as the front door banged open, splintering around the lock, and the police charged in.

'Oh man,' Shane whispered, 'that *sucks*. We just fixed that door.'

Claire clung to him, terrified, as the police swarmed through the house.

Chapter Three

Shane wasn't talking to the cops. Not about his dad, and not about anything. He just sat like a lump, eyes down, and refused to answer any questions from the human patrol officers; Claire didn't know *what* to say – or, more importantly, what not to – and stammered out a lot of 'I don't know' and 'I was in my room' sort of answers. Eve – more self-possessed than Claire had ever seen her – stepped in to say that she'd heard the intruders downstairs breaking things, and she'd pulled Claire into her room and locked the door for protection. It sounded good. Claire supported it with a lot of nodding.

'Is that so?' A new voice, from behind the cops, and they parted ranks to admit two strangers. Detectives, it looked like, in sport jackets and slacks. One was a woman, frost pale, with eyes like mirrors. The other one was a tall man with grey close-cropped hair.

They were wearing gold badges on their belts. So. Detectives.

Vampire detectives.

Eve had gone very still, hands folded in her lap. She looked carefully friendly. 'Yes, ma'am,' she said. 'That's what happened.'

'And you have no idea who these mysterious intruders might have been,' said the male vamp. He looked – scary. Cold and hard and scary. 'Never saw them before.'

'We didn't see them at all, sir.'

'Because you were...locked in your room.' He smiled, and flashed fang. Clear warning. 'I can smell fear. You give it off like the stench of your sweat. Delicious.'

Claire fought back an urge to whimper. The human cops had backed up a step; one or two looked uncomfortable, but they weren't about to interfere with whatever was about to happen. Which was nothing, right? There were rules and stuff. And they were the victims!

Then again, she didn't suppose the vamps cared all that much for victims.

'Leave them alone,' Shane said.

'It speaks!' the woman said, and laughed. She sank down into a crouch, elegant and perfectly balanced, and tried to peer into Shane's face. 'A knight-errant, defending the helpless. Charming.' She had an old-world accent, sort of like blurred German. 'Do you not trust us, little knight? Are we not your friends?'

'That depends,' Shane said, and looked right at her.

'You take your orders from Oliver, or the Founder? Because if you touch us – any of us – you have to take it up with her. You know who I mean.'

She lost her amused expression.

Her partner made a noise, halfway between a bark of laughter and a growl. 'Careful, Gretchen, he snaps. Just like a half-grown puppy. Boy, you don't know what you're saying. The Founder's mark is on the house, yes, but I see no bands on your wrists. Don't be stupid and make bold claims you can't back up.'

'Bite me, Dracula,' Shane snapped.

Gretchen laughed. 'A wolf pup,' she said. 'Oh, I like him, Hans. May I have him, since he's a stray?'

One of the uniformed cops cleared his throat. 'Ma'am? Sorry, but I can't allow that. You want to file the paperwork, I'll see what I can do, but—'

Gretchen made a frustrated noise and came back to her feet. 'Paperwork. Fah. In the old days we would have run him down like a deer for insolence.'

'In the old days, Gretchen, we were starving,' Hans said. 'Remember? The winters in Bavaria? Let him howl.' He shrugged and gave Eve and Claire a smile that looked a little less terrifying than before. 'Sorry. Gretchen gets carried away. Now, you're sure none of you knew these intruders? Morganville's not that big a town. We're all pretty close-knit, especially the human community.'

'Strangers,' Eve said. 'I think they might have been strangers. Maybe just...passing through.'

'Passing through,' Hans repeated. 'We don't get a lot

of casual visitors. Even biker gangs.' He studied them each in turn, and while his eyes were on her Claire felt as if she were being x-rayed. Surely he couldn't really see her thoughts, right? Hans finished with his gaze on Shane, fixed and dark. 'Your name.'

'Shane,' he said. 'Shane Collins.'

'You left Morganville with your family a few years ago, yes? What brought you back?'

'My friend Michael needed a roommate.' Shane's eyes flickered, and Claire realised that he'd just made a mistake. A big one.

'Michael Glass. Ah, yes, the mysterious Michael. Never around when anyone comes calling during the day, but always present at night. Tell me, is Michael a vampire?'

'Wouldn't you know?' Shane shot back. 'Last I heard, nobody had made a new vampire in fifty years or more.'

'True.' Hans nodded. 'Yet it's curious, isn't it? That your friend seems so hard to keep around?'

They knew. They knew *something*, anyway; Claire supposed Oliver would have no reason to keep secrets, especially Michael's secrets. He'd probably blabbed it to all of his minions that Michael was a ghost, caught between worlds – not quite vampire, not quite human, not quite anything.

'It's night,' Gretchen pointed out. 'So where is he? Your friend?'

Shane swallowed, and it was hard to miss the wave of misery that went through him. 'He's around.'

'Around where, exactly?'

Claire exchanged a look of dread with Eve. Shane still thought Michael was dead, buried in the backyard... and Michael had been pretty firm on the idea that Shane shouldn't know...

'I don't know,' Shane said. The tips of his ears were turning red.

Hans the Detective smiled slowly. 'You don't know much, son. And yet you look like you're not completely stupid, so how exactly does that work? Did you hide in the room with the girls?' He leant on the last word, and his vampire partner laughed.

Shane got up. There was something insane in his eyes, and Claire felt her heart stop beating because this was bad, very bad, and Shane was going to do something horribly unwise, and there was no way they could stop him...

'You're looking for me?'

They all turned.

Michael was standing at the top of the stairs. He was pulling on a plain black T-shirt with blue jeans, and he looked like he'd just rolled out of bed. His feet, Claire saw, were bare as usual.

Shane sat down. Fast and hard. Michael took his time coming down the stairs, making sure they were all focused on him instead of Shane, to give Shane time to get through what he was feeling – which was, Claire thought, a lot to pack into less than thirty seconds. Relief, of course, which brought a sheen of tears to his eyes. And then, predictably, he got pissed, because, well, he was a guy, he was Shane, and that was how he handled being scared.

So, really, by the time Michael padded down the last step to the wooden floor and crossed over to the couch through the circle of police, things were pretty much just as they'd been, except that Shane wasn't about to push the button on his nuclear temper.

'Hey,' Michael said to him. Shane moved over on the couch to make room. Guy room, which left plenty of empty space. 'What's up?'

Shane looked at him like he might be crazy, not just nearly dead part-time. 'Cops, man.'

'Yeah, man, I can see that. How come?'

'You're telling me you actually slept through all that? Dude, you need to see a doctor or something. Maybe you have a disease.'

'Hey, I need the sleep. Lisa, you know.' Michael grinned. They were good at this, Claire realised – good at playing normal, even if there wasn't a normal thing in the world about their situation. 'So what happened?'

'You weren't aware of intruders in your home?' asked Gretchen, who'd been watching the exchange – and the correspondingly shrinking chance of bloodshed – with disappointment. 'The others described it as quite loud.'

'He can sleep through World War Three,' Shane said. 'I told you, it's some kind of sickness or something.'

'I thought you said you didn't know where he was,' Hans said. 'Wasn't he in his room?'

Shane shrugged. 'I'm not his keeper.'

'Ah,' Gretchen said, and smiled. 'That is where you are wrong, little knight. You are all your brothers' keepers here in Morganville, and you can all suffer for their crimes. Which you should know and remember.'

Hans looked bored now. 'Sergeant,' he said, and the most senior uniformed cop stepped out of the ranks. 'I leave this in your hands. If you find anything out of the ordinary, let us know.'

Just like that, the vamps were gone. They moved fast, and silently; they didn't seem to want to blend in much, Claire thought, and tried not to tremble. She sank down on the couch beside Shane, nearly crawling into his lap. Eve crowded in between the two boys.

'Right.' The sergeant didn't look happy with having the whole thing dumped in his lap again, but he also looked resigned. Couldn't be the easiest thing, Claire thought, having vamps for bosses. They didn't seem to have a long attention span. 'Glass, right? Occupation?'

'Musician, sir,' Michael said.

'Play around town, do you?'

'I'm rehearsing for some upcoming gigs.'

The cop nodded and flipped pages in a black leather book. He ran a thick finger down a list, frowned, and said, 'You're behind on your donations, Glass. About a month.'

Michael threw a lightning-fast glance at Shane. 'Sorry, sir. I'll get out there tomorrow.'

'Better, or you know what happens.' The cop ran

down the roster. 'You. Collins. You still unemployed?' He gave him a stare. A long one. Shane shrugged, looking – Claire thought – as dumb as possible. 'Try harder.'

'Common Grounds,' Eve volunteered before he could start in on her. 'Eve Rosser, sir, thank you.' She was vibrating all over – she was so nervous – which was funny; when she'd been on her own, she'd been cool and calm. She had hold of both Michael's and Shane's hands. 'Although, um, I'm thinking of making a change.'

The cop seemed bored now. 'Yeah, OK. You, the kid. Name?'

'Claire,' she said faintly. 'Um...Danvers. I'm a student.'

He looked at her again, and kept looking. 'Shouldn't you be in the dorm?'

'I have permission to live off campus.' She didn't say from whom, because it was primarily herself.

He watched her for another few seconds, then shrugged. 'You live off campus, you follow the town rules. Your friends here'll tell you what they are. Watch on campus about how much you pass along – we got enough problems without panicking students. And we're real good at finding blabbermouths.'

She nodded.

That wasn't the end of it, but it was the end of her discussions with them; the police poked around a little, took some pictures, and left the house a few minutes later without another word to any of them.

For a good ten seconds after the police closed the

front door – or closed it as much as was possible with a busted lock – there was silence, and then Shane turned to Michael and said, 'You fucking bastard.' Claire swallowed hard at the tight fury in his voice.

'You want to take this outside?' Michael asked. *He* sounded neutral, almost calm. His eyes were anything but.

'What, you can leave the house now?'

'No, I meant another room, Shane.'

'Hey,' Eve said, 'don't—'

'Shut up, Eve!' Shane snapped.

Michael came off the couch like somebody had pushed him; he reached down, grabbed Shane by the T-shirt, and yanked him upright. 'Don't,' he said, and gave him one hard shake. 'Your father's an asshole. It's not a disease. You don't have to catch it.'

Shane grabbed him in a hug. Michael rocked back a little from the impact, but he closed his eyes and hung on for a moment, then slapped Shane's back. And of *course* Shane slapped his back, too, and they stepped way apart. Manly. Claire rolled her eyes.

'I thought you were dead,' Shane said. His eyes looked suspiciously bright and wet. 'I saw you die, man.'

'I die all the time. It doesn't really take.' Michael gave him a half smile that looked more grim than amused. 'I figured it was better to let your dad think he'd taken me out. Maybe he wouldn't be so hard on the rest of you.' His gaze swept over the bruises on Shane's face. 'Brilliant plan. I'm sorry, man. Once I was dead, I couldn't do much until night came around again.'

He said it so matter-of-factly that Claire felt a shiver. 'Do you remember…you know, what they did to you?'

Michael glanced at her. 'Yeah,' he said. 'I remember.'

'Oh hell.' Shane collapsed back on the sofa and put his head in his hands. 'God, man, I'm sorry. I'm so sorry.'

'Not your fault.'

'I called him.'

'You called him because it looked like we were all pulling an Alamo. You didn't know—'

'I know my dad,' Shane said grimly. 'Michael, I want you to know, I wasn't… I didn't come here to do his dirty work. Not…not after the first week or so.'

Michael didn't answer him. Maybe there was no answer to that, Claire thought. She scooted closer to Shane and stroked his ragged, shoulder-length fine hair. 'Hey,' she said. 'It's OK. We're all OK.'

'No, we're not.' Shane's voice was muffled by his hands. 'We're totally screwed. Right, Mike?'

'Pretty much,' Michael sighed. 'Yeah.'

'The cops will find them,' Eve said in an undertone to Claire as both girls stood in the kitchen making pasta. Pasta, apparently, was a new thing that Eve wanted to try. She frowned down at the package of spaghetti, then at the not-yet-bubbling pot of water. 'Shane's dad and his merry band of assholes, I mean.'

'Yeah,' Claire agreed, not because she thought they would, but because, well, it seemed like the thing to say. 'Want me to warm up the sauce?'

'Do we do that? I mean, it's in a jar, right? Can't you just dump it over the pasta?'

'Well, you *can*, but it tastes better if you warm it up.'

'Oh.' Eve sighed. 'This is complicated. No wonder I never cook.'

'You make breakfast!'

'I make two things: bacon and eggs. And sometimes sandwiches. I hate cooking. Cooking reminds me of my mother.' Eve took another pot from the rack and banged it down onto the massive stove. 'Here.'

Claire struggled with the top on the spaghetti sauce jar, and finally got it to release with a *pop*. 'You think they're going to stay mad at each other?' she asked.

'Michael and Shane?'

'Mmm-hmmm.' The sauce plopped into the pot, chunky and wet and vaguely nauseating. Claire considered the second jar, decided that if two of the four of them were boys, more was better. She got it opened and in the pot, as well, then turned on the burner and set it to simmer.

'Who knows?' Eve shrugged. 'Boys are idiots. You'd think Shane could just say, "Oh man, I'm glad you're alive," but no. It's either guilt or amateur night at the Drama Queen Theatre.' She blew out a frustrated breath. '*Boys*. I'd turn gay if they weren't so sexy.'

Claire tried not to laugh, but she couldn't help it, and after a second Eve smiled and chuckled, too. The water started boiling. In went the pasta.

'Um...Eve...can I ask...?'

'About what?' Eve was still frowning at the pasta like she suspected it was going to do something clever, like try to escape from the pot.

'You and Michael.'

'Oh.' A surge of pink to Eve's cheeks. Between that and the fact that she was wearing colours outside of the Goth red and black rainbow, she looked young and very cute. 'Well. I don't know if it's...God, he's just so—'

'Hot?' Claire asked.

'Hot,' Eve admitted. 'Nuclear hot. Surface of the sun hot. And—'

She stopped, the flush in her cheeks getting darker. Claire picked up a wooden spoon and poked the pasta, which was beginning to loosen up. 'And?'

'And I was planning on putting the moves on him before all this happened. That's why I had on the garters and stuff. Planning ahead.'

'Oh, wow.'

'Yeah, embarrassing. Did he peek?'

'When you were changing?' Claire asked. 'I don't think so. But I think he wanted to.'

'That's OK, then.' Eve blinked down at the pasta, which had formed a thick white foam on top. 'Is it supposed to be doing that?'

Claire hadn't ever seen it happen at her parents' house. But then again, they hadn't made spaghetti much.

'I don't know.'

'Oh crap!' The white foam kept growing, like in one of those cheesy science fiction movies. The foam that ate the Glass House...it mushroomed up over the top of the pot and down over the sides, and both girls yelped as it hit the burners and began to sizzle and pop. Claire grabbed the pot and moved it. Eve turned down the burner. 'Right, pasta makes foam, good to know. Too hot. Way too hot.'

'Who? Michael?' Claire asked, and they dissolved in giggles.

Which only got worse when Michael walked in, went to the refrigerator, and retrieved the last two beers from his birthday pack. 'Ladies,' he said. 'Did I miss something?'

'Pasta boiled over,' Claire gulped, trying not to giggle even harder. Michael looked at them for a second, curious, and then shrugged and left again. 'Do you think he's telling Shane right now that we're insane?'

'Probably.' Eve managed to control herself, and put the pasta back on the burner. 'Is this shock? Are we in shock right now?'

'I don't know,' Claire said. 'Let's see, we've been barricaded in the house, attacked, nearly burnt to death. Michael was murdered right in front of us, then came back, and we got interrogated by the big, scary vampire cops? Yeah, maybe shock.'

Eve choked on another snort/giggle. 'Maybe that's why I decided to cook.'

They watched the pasta bubble in silence. The whole room was starting to smell warm with spices and tomato sauce, a comforting and homey sort of smell. Claire stirred the spaghetti sauce, which was looking delicious now that it was simmering.

The kitchen door banged open again. Shane, this time, a beer in one hand. 'What's burning?'

'Your brain. So, did you two girls kiss and make up?' Eve asked, stirring the pasta.

He glowered at her, then turned to Claire. 'What the hell is she making?'

'Spaghetti.' And technically, it was Claire mostly, but she decided not to mention it. 'Um, about your dad – do you think they're going to catch him?'

'No.' Shane hip-bumped Eve out of the way at the stove and did some spaghetti maintenance. 'Morganville's got a lot of hiding places. That's mostly for the vamps' benefit, but it'll work for him, too. He'll go to ground. I've been sending him maps. He'll know where to go.'

'Maybe he'll just leave?' Eve sounded hopeful. Shane dragged a piece of spaghetti out of the tangle in the pot and pressed it against the metal with the spoon. It sliced cleanly.

'No,' Shane said again. 'He definitely won't leave. He's got no place else to go. He always said that if he crossed the border into Morganville again, he was here until it was done.'

'You mean until *he's* done.' Eve crossed her arms, not as if she was angry, more like she was cold. 'Shane, if he goes after even one vampire, we are dead. You know that, right?'

He picked up the beer bottle and drank, avoiding an answer. He flipped off the burner under the spaghetti, took the pot to the sink, and drained it with the edge of a lid. Like a real chef or something.

Which, Claire had to admit, was pretty much totally hot, the way he moved so confidently. She liked to cook, but he had *authority.* In fact, she was paying a lot more attention to what Shane did today – the way he moved, the way his clothes fit – or didn't, in his case, because Shane was wearing his jeans loose and just baggy enough to give her fantasies about them sliding down. Which made her blush.

She concentrated on getting down the bowls from the cupboard. Mismatched bowls, two out of four of them chipped. She put them out on the counter as Shane returned with the spaghetti and began portioning it out. Eve grabbed the sauce and followed him down the line, ladling.

It looked pretty tasty, actually. Claire picked up two bowls and carried them into the living room, where Michael was tuning his guitar as if nothing had happened, as if he hadn't been stabbed through the heart and dragged outside and – oh my God, she didn't want to finish that thought at all.

She handed him the bowl. He set the guitar carefully back in its case – somehow, with all the mayhem that had gone on in the past two days, it had escaped damage – and dug in as Eve and Shane trailed in with their own dinner. Eve had two chilled bottles of water under one arm. She tossed one to Claire as she sat down cross-legged on the floor, next to Michael's knee.

Shane settled on the couch, and Claire joined him. For a few minutes nobody said anything. Claire hadn't realised that she was hungry, not really, but the second the sauce hit her tongue and exploded into flavours, she was *starving*. She couldn't gobble it fast enough.

'Hell's put in a skating rink,' Shane said. 'This is actually edible, Eve.'

Again, Claire had the impulse to claim credit...and managed not to, mostly because that would have required her to stop shovelling pasta into her mouth.

'Claire,' Eve said. 'She's the cook, not me. I just, you know, supervised.' Which gave Claire a pleasant little spurt of gratitude and surprise.

'See? I knew that.'

Eve flipped him off and noisily sucked some spaghetti into her mouth.

Claire got to the bottom of the bowl first – even before Michael or Shane – and sat back with a sigh of utter contentment. *Nap*, she thought. *I could take a nap.*

'Guys,' Michael said. 'We're still in trouble. You know that, right?'

'Yeah,' Eve said. 'But now we have *catered* trouble.'

He ignored her, except for a brief little quirk of a smile, and focused on Shane. 'You need to tell me everything,' Michael said. 'No bullshit, man. Every last thing, from the time you left Morganville.'

Shane seemed to lose his appetite.

Which, for Shane, was not a good sign *at all.*

* * *

The vampires had offered them money. Cash compensation. It was Morganville's version of Allstate, only it wasn't insurance – it was blood money for a dead child.

And the Collins family – Dad, Mom, and Shane – had packed up whatever had survived the fire that had taken Alyssa, and left town in the middle of the night. Running. That probably would have been that, Shane explained; people did leave town from time to time, and it was rarely any trouble. Michael's own parents had taken off. But... something went wrong with Molly Collins.

'At first, she'd just space,' Shane said. He'd drained his beer, and now he was just rolling the bottle between his palms. 'Stare at things, like she was trying to remember something. Dad didn't notice. He was drinking a lot. We ended up in Odessa, and Dad got a job at the recycling plant. He wasn't home much.'

'That must have been an improvement,' Eve muttered.

'Hey, let me get through it, OK?'

'Sorry.'

Shane took another deep breath. 'Mom...she kept talking about Alyssa. You have to understand, we didn't... I couldn't remember anything, except that she'd died. It was all just sort of a blur, but not the kind of blur you worry about, if you know what I mean...?'

Claire was fairly certain nobody did, but she remembered her conversation with her own parents. They'd forgotten things, and somehow, they hadn't really cared. So maybe she did understand.

'I started working, too. Mom...she just stayed in the motel. Wouldn't do anything except eat, sleep, sometimes take a bath if we yelled at her long enough. I figured, you know, depression...but it was more than that. One day, out of nowhere, she grabs me by the arm and she says, "Shane, do you remember your sister?" So I go, "Yeah, Mom, of course I do." And she says the weirdest thing. She says, "Do you remember the vampires?" I didn't remember, but it felt...like something in me was trying to. I got a bad headache, and I felt sick. And Mom...she just kept on talking, about how there was something wrong with us, something going wrong in our heads. About the vampires. About Lyssa dying in the fire.'

He fell silent, still rolling the beer bottle like some kind of magic talisman. Nobody moved.

'And I remembered.'

Shane's whisper sounded raw, somehow, vulnerable and exposed. Michael wasn't looking at him. He was looking down, at his own beer bottle, and the label he was peeling off in strips.

'It was like some wall coming down, and then it all just flooded in. I mean, it's bad enough to live through it and sort of cope with it, but when it comes back like that...' Shane visibly shuddered. 'It was like I'd just watched Lyss die all over again.'

'Oh,' Eve said faintly. 'Oh God.'

'Mom—' He shook his head. 'I couldn't handle it. I left her. I had to get away, I couldn't just... I had to *go*. You know? So I left. I ran.' A hollow rattle of a laugh.

'Saved my life.'

'Shane—' Michael cleared his throat. 'I was wrong. You don't have to—'

'Shut up, man. Just shut up.' Shane tipped the bottle to his lips for the last few drops, then swallowed hard. Claire didn't know what was coming, but she could see from the look on Michael's face that he did, and it twisted her stomach into a knot. 'So anyway, I came back a few hours later and she was in the tub, just floating there, and the water was red...razor blades on the floor—'

'Oh, honey.' Eve got up and stood there, hovering next to him, reaching out to touch him and then pulling back in jerky motions without making contact, like he had some force field of grief shielding him. 'It wasn't your fault. You said she was depressed.'

'Don't you get it?' He glared up at her, then at Michael. 'She didn't do it. She wouldn't. It was *them*. You know how they work: they close in; they kill; they cover it up. They must have got there right after I left. I don't know—'

'Shane.'

'—I don't know how they got her in the tub. There weren't any bruises, but the cuts were—'

'*Shane!* Christ, man!' Michael looked outright horrified this time, and Shane stopped. The two of them looked at each other for a long, wordless moment, and then Michael – visibly tense – eased back into his chair. 'Shit. I don't even know what to say.'

Shane shook his head and looked away. 'Nothing to say.

It is what it is. I couldn't… Shit. Let me just finish, OK?'

As if they could stop him. Claire felt cold. She could feel Shane's body shaking next to her, and if *she* felt cold, how must he be feeling? Frozen. Numb. She reached out to touch him and, like Eve, just…stopped. There was something about Shane right now that didn't want to be touched.

'Anyway, my dad came home, eventually. Cops said it was a suicide, but after they were gone I told him. He didn't exactly want to hear it. Things got…ugly.' Claire couldn't imagine how ugly that had been, for Shane to actually admit it. 'But I made him remember.'

Eve sat on the floor, hugging her knees close to her chest. She looked at him with anime-wide eyes. 'And?'

'He got drunk. A lot.' Bitterness ran black through Shane's voice, and all of a sudden the beer bottle in his hand seemed to get a whole lot of significance for him, beyond just something to occupy his nervous hands. He set it down on the floor and wiped his palms on his blue jeans. 'He started hooking up with these bikers and stuff. I…wasn't in a real good place; I don't remember some of that. Couple of weeks later we got a visit from these guys in suits. Not vamps, lawyers. They gave us money, lots of it. Insurance. Except we both knew who it was from, and the point was, they were trying to figure out what we knew and remembered. I was too drugged out to know what was going on, and Dad was drunk, so I guess that saved our lives. They decided we were no threat.' He wiped his forehead with the heel of his hand and laughed – a bitter, broken sound like glass in a blender.

Shane on drugs. Claire saw that Michael had caught it, too. She wondered if he was going to say something, but maybe it wasn't the best time to say, *Hey, man, you using now?* Or something like that.

He didn't need to ask, as it turned out. Shane answered anyway. 'But I kicked it, and Dad sobered up, and we planned this out. Thing is, even though we remembered a lot of stuff, the personal stuff, we couldn't remember things about how to find vamps, or the layout of the town, or even who we were looking for. So that was my job. Come back, scout it out, find out where the vamps hide during the day. Report back. It wasn't supposed to take this long, and I wasn't supposed to... get tangled up.'

'With us,' Eve supplied softly. 'Right? He didn't want you to have any friends.'

'Friends get you killed in Morganville.'

'No.' Eve put a pale hand on his knee. 'Shane, honey, in Morganville, friends are the only things that keep you alive.'

Chapter Four

Claire couldn't believe how much had poured out of Shane – all that grief and horror and bitterness and anger. He'd always seemed sort of, well, *normal*, and it was a shock to see all the emotional bloodshed…and a shock to hear him talk so much, about things so personal. Shane wasn't a talker.

She collected the dishes and did them alone, comforted by hot water and the fizz of soap on her hands; she cleaned up pots and pans and splashes of red sauce, and thought about Shane finding his mom dead in a bloody bathtub. *I wasn't in a real good place*, Shane had said. The master of understatement. Claire wasn't so sure that she'd ever have been able to smile again, laugh again, function again, if that had happened to her, especially after losing a sister and winning the Drunk-Asshole Lottery with Dad. How did he do it? How did he keep it together, and stay so…brave?

She wanted to cry for him, but she was almost sure that he'd have been embarrassed, so she kept the misery inside, and scrubbed dishes clean. *He doesn't deserve this. Why don't they all just leave him alone? Why does he have to be the one everybody beats on?*

Maybe just because he'd shown he could take it, and make himself stronger for it.

The kitchen door swung open, and she jumped, expected Shane, but it was Michael. He walked over to the sink, ran some cold water in his hands, and splashed it over his face and the back of his neck.

'Bad night,' Claire said.

'Tell me about it.' He cut a sideways look towards her.

'Do you think he's right? About them, you know, killing his mother?'

'I think Shane's carrying around a load of guilt the size of Trump Tower. And I think it helps him to be angry.' Michael shrugged. 'I don't know. It's possible. But I don't think we can know one way or the other.'

That felt...sick, somehow. No wonder Shane was so reluctant to talk about it. She tried to imagine living with that kind of uncertainty, those memories, and failed.

She was glad she did.

'So,' Michael said. 'I've got about three hours until morning. We need to make some plans about what we're going to do, and what we're *not* going to do.'

Claire nodded and set a plate aside to dry.

'First thing is, none of you leave the house,' Michael said. 'Got it? No school, no work. You stay indoors. I can't protect you if you go outside.'

'We can't just hide!'

'We can for a while, and we will. Look, Shane's dad can't run around out there forever. It's a temporary problem. Someone's going to find him.' The unspoken subject of what would happen to Shane's dad after he was caught was a whole other issue. 'As long as we don't do anything directly that ties us to whatever his dad does, we're OK. Amelie's word is good for that.'

'You're putting a lot of trust in—'

'A vampire, yeah, I know.' Michael shrugged and leant a hip against the counter, looking down on her. 'What choices do we have?'

'Not too many, I guess.' Claire studied him more closely. He looked tired. 'Michael? Are you OK?'

Now he looked surprised. 'Sure. Shane's the one who's got issues. Not me.'

No, Michael was all good. Killed, dismembered, buried, reborn…yeah, just another day in the life. Claire sighed. 'Guys,' she said mournfully. 'Michael, I'll stay home today, but I really do have to go to school, you know. Really.' Because her missing school was like a caffeine addict going without a daily jolt.

'Your education or your life, Claire. I'd rather you be alive and a little bit dumber.'

She met his eyes squarely. 'Well, I wouldn't. I'll stay home today. I don't promise about tomorrow.'

He smiled, leant forward, and put a warm sloppy kiss on her forehead. 'That's my girl,' he said, and left. She sighed again, this time happily, and found herself grinning. Michael might be Eve's new main crush, but he was still available as an oh-my-God-how-cute-is-*he* thrill.

Claire finished the dishes and went back to the living room. The TV was on, tuned to some forensics show, and Shane was slumped on the couch staring at it. No sign of Eve or Michael. Claire hesitated, thinking longingly about bed and forgetting about all this for a while, but Shane just looked so...alone.

She went and settled in next to him. She didn't say anything, and neither did he, and after a while his arm went around her and that was all right.

She fell asleep there, braced against his warm body.

It was nice.

Claire supposed that she should have known Shane might have nightmares – bad ones – but she'd never really thought about it. When Shane jerked and rolled off the couch, she thumped flat onto the cushions. The TV was still on – a flickering confusion of colour – and Claire flailed and scrambled for some grasp of what was going on through the fog of interrupted sleep.

'Shane?'

He was on his side on the floor, shuddering, curled up into a ball. Claire slid down next to him and put her hands on his broad back. Under the thin T-shirt his skin was clammy, and his muscles were as tense as steel cable. He was making these *sounds*, agonising gasps that weren't quite sobs but weren't quite not, either.

She didn't know what to do. She'd felt helpless a lot in the past few hours, but this was worse, somehow, because Michael and Eve were nowhere to be seen, and she wasn't sure if Shane would have wanted them to see him like this. Or if he wanted *her* to see him like this. Shane was all about the pride.

'I'm OK,' he gasped out. 'I'm OK. I'm OK.' He didn't sound OK. He sounded scared, and he sounded like a little boy.

He managed to sit up. Claire wrapped her arms around him, hugging him tight, and after a few seconds of resistance she felt him sag against her, and hug her back. His hand stroked her hair as if she might break. 'Shhh,' she whispered to him, the way her mother had whispered it to her when things got bad. 'You're here. You're safe. You're OK.' Because wherever he'd been in his dreams, he hadn't been any of those three things.

If she expected him to talk about it, she was disappointed. He pulled back, avoided looking at her, and said, 'You should go to bed.'

'Yeah,' she agreed. 'You first.'

'Can't sleep.' Didn't want to, more likely; his eyes were red and blurred with exhaustion. 'I just need some coffee or something.'

'Coke?'

'Whatever.'

She fetched it for him, and Shane downed it like a frat boy at a mixer, belched, and shrugged an apology. 'Where's Michael?' She spread her hands. 'Eve?' She did another silent pantomime of ignorance. 'Well, at least somebody's getting a good night's sleep. They together?'

Claire blinked. 'I...don't know.' She hadn't thought about it, actually. She hadn't seen them go, didn't know if they'd gone to separate rooms or if Eve had finally worked up the courage to proposition Michael. 'Cause he'd never make the first move. That just wasn't Michael, somehow.

'Christ, I hope so,' Shane said. 'They deserve a little fun, even in hell.' He was kidding, but not. He *did* see Morganville as hell. Claire had to admit, he had a point.

It was hell, and they were the lost souls, and it was coming on towards morning and she'd been scared for what felt like a very, very long time...

He was watching her closely, in a way that made her feel warmth all over her skin, like a light sunburn.

'How about us?' she heard herself ask. 'Don't we deserve a little fun?'

I did not just say that.

Only she had.

He smiled. She wondered if the shadows were ever going to leave his eyes again. 'I could do something fun.'

'Ummm...' She licked her lips. 'Define fun.'

'Quit doing that, jailbait. It's distracting.'

The whole idea that somebody would even *think* of her as jailbait was tremendously exciting. Especially Shane.

She tried to hide that, and act like she wasn't quaking on the inside like a Jell-O fruit salad. 'So now you want me to stay up? I thought you said I should go to bed.'

'You should.' He didn't put any particular emphasis on it. ''Cause if you stay down here, there's going to be fun. I'm just saying.'

'Video game fun?'

His eyes widened. 'You want to play video games?'

'Do you?'

'You are the weirdest girl.'

'Please. You live with *Eve*.' She was *not* doing this right. How did girls seduce boys? What did they say? Because she was pretty sure that talking about video games and bringing up roommates wasn't in the have-fun game plan. She was hyperaware of her body, too. How was she supposed to move? She felt awkward, all angles, and she wanted to be one of those graceful girls, all delicacy and elegance. Like in the movies.

Eve would know. She'd had those garter hose on, and those thong panties, and Claire didn't even own those things, or have any idea how to get them. And Eve had worn them for Michael, or maybe just as a secret little excitement for herself around Michael. Yeah, Eve would know what to say.

Say something sexy, she commanded herself, and in a blind panic, she opened her mouth and blurted, 'Do you think they're doing it?' She was so appalled that she clapped both hands over her mouth. She'd never in her life wanted to take back words so much, and so fast...and for a second, Shane just looked at her, like he couldn't figure out what she was talking about.

And then he laughed. 'Man, I hope. Those two could use a good…uh—' He blinked and she saw her age flash in front of his eyes. 'Hell. Never mind.'

Words weren't working for her. She leant forward and kissed him. It felt weird, and awkward, and he didn't immediately respond – maybe he was too surprised. Maybe she was doing it wrong, or she'd been wrong to make the move on him…

His lips parted under hers, damp and soft and warm, and she forgot all of that. Her entire life focused in on the sensations, the gentle pressure that grew more intense the longer the kiss went on.

Chaste kisses, then dirtier ones, and man, those tasted good. They tasted better the wider her mouth opened, and especially after his tongue touched hers.

She could have done a whole semester of kissing with Shane. Intense personal study. With lab classes.

Time really wasn't happening for her, but eventually Claire realised that there was a soft glow coming from the windows, and she was numb and sore from sitting on the floor. She winced as a muscle in her back protested, and Shane reached out, pulled her up, and settled himself on the couch.

He stretched out, and extended a hand to her. She stared, tingling and confused. 'There's no room.'

'Plenty of room,' he said.

She felt breathless and kind of wild, stretching out

on the tiny area of sofa cushion available next to him, and then smothered a yelp as Shane picked her up and draped her over his chest and, *oh my God*, over all the rest of him, too.

'Better?' he asked, and raised his eyebrows. It was a real question, and he was looking for a real answer. Claire felt a blush building a fire in her cheeks, but she didn't look away from his gaze.

'Perfect,' she said.

It felt like being naked, except for all the clothes. The kisses this time were wet and urgent and deep, and the feeling of Shane's muscles tensing and relaxing under her was incredibly exciting. *This should be illegal*, she thought. Well, it was kind of illegal. Or would be, if any clothes came off.

Shane might not have been Michael, with all the responsibility, but he definitely wasn't that impulsive. At least, not with her. His hands roamed, but never to places where she wanted them to – badly – and some of the places they roamed made her wonder why she'd never wanted someone to touch her there before. Like the small of her back, where the skin dipped into a shallow valley. Or the back of her neck. Or the inside of her arms. Or...

As he was bringing his hands up her sides, his fingers just *barely* brushed the outer curve of her breasts, and she gasped into his mouth.

Shane immediately sat her upright, and moved to the other end of the couch. His face was flushed; his eyes were bright and no longer looked even a little bit tired. 'No,' he said, and held out his hand like a traffic cop when she tried to scoot closer. 'Red flag. If you make that sound again, we are in trouble. Or I am, anyway.'

'But—' Claire felt that blush creeping in again, and had no idea what it was going to be like to put this into words. 'What about you? You know—' She made a vague gesture that could have been anything. Or nothing. Or anything.

'Don't worry about me. I needed this.' He was still breathing deeply, but he did look better. Steadier. More like...Shane, instead of that lost and hurt little boy terrified of his nightmares. 'So? Did we have fun?'

'Fun,' she agreed faintly. So much fun she felt like a fizzed-up soda, ready to burst. 'Um, I need to—'

'Yeah, me, too.' But Shane made no move to go. Claire swallowed hard and took the course of the better part of valour, up the stairs to her room. She shut the door and locked it, threw herself on her brand-new mattress – she hadn't even put sheets on it yet, and they were a little light on blankets after using most of them to fight the fire – and bounced. The room smelt like a wet smoky dog, but she didn't care.

Not at all.

Fun.

Oh yes.

Around noon, Claire heard the doorbell, and ran downstairs. Shane was lying on the couch, sound asleep. Still no sign of Eve, and she didn't expect to have any

Michael sightings, given the daylight hours. She raced down the hall to the door, which was braced with a wooden chair as a temporary lock, and hesitated.

'Michael? You there?' A chilly breeze swept across her, ruffling her hair. Wow. He was strong today. 'Can I open the door? One for yes, two for no.'

Apparently, yes. She pulled the chair away and peered outside. There were two men standing on the porch, both tall; one was lean and hard-looking, with black hair; the other one was a little pale (but not vamp pale) and heavyset, and where he wasn't balding, his very short hair looked brown.

They both displayed badges. Police.

'You're Claire, right?' the lean one said, and extended his hand. 'Joe Hess. This is my partner, Travis Lowe. How you doing?'

'Um...' She fumbled for the handshake. 'Fine, I guess.' Lowe also shook her hand. 'Is something... I mean, did you find—?' Because she both hoped that Shane's dad was in a holding cell, and was afraid of what that would mean for Shane. She rocked nervously back and forth on her heels, her eyes darting from one of them to the other.

Joe Hess smiled. Unlike most smiles she'd seen since coming to Morganville, this one seemed...uncomplicated. Clean, sort of. Not happy, because that would have been weird, but comforting. 'It's OK,' he said. 'No, we haven't found them, but you've got nothing to be afraid of. May we come inside?'

She heard shuffling footsteps behind her. Shane had woken up, and was standing in the hallway, barefoot and rumpled, with a fierce bed-head that got worse as he yawned and ran fingers through his hair, standing part of it on end.

How sick was it that she found that sexy?

Claire collected herself and pointed at the cops on the doorstep. Shane's eyes focused fast.

'Officers,' he said, and came towards the door. 'Anything you need?'

'I was just asking if we can come in and talk,' Detective Hess said. He'd stopped smiling, but he still looked kind. 'Informally.'

A chill moved softly over Claire's skin. A single wave of chill. *Yes.* Michael was OK with it.

'Sure,' Claire said, and stepped back to swing the door wider. The cops stepped over the threshold, Hess first, then Lowe, and Shane shot Claire a look she couldn't quite figure out and led the men back to the living room.

Lowe studied the place more than the two of them; he seemed to really appreciate it. 'Nice,' he murmured, which was the first thing he'd said. 'Great use of wood in here. Real organic.'

She couldn't really say *thank you*, because, hey, she didn't build it. She didn't even own it. But on Michael's behalf she said, 'We think so, too, sir.' Claire settled nervously back on the sofa, perched on the edge. Shane remained standing, and Hess and Lowe moved around, not exactly searching, but cataloguing everything. Hess stayed focused on the two of them, and after a moment, he bent his knees and sat down in the chair that Michael had occupied last night. Déja vu, Claire thought. Hess seemed to shiver a little, and he looked up, maybe trying to locate the source of the draft that had just brushed past him.

Michael liked that chair.

'You had some trouble here last night,' Hess said. 'I know you had a talk with our colleagues Gretchen and Hans. I read the report this morning.'

No harm in admitting to that. Both Shane and Claire nodded.

'A little scary, huh?'

Claire nodded. Shane didn't. He gave the detective a narrow little smile. 'I'm a Morganville lifer. Define scary,' he said. 'Anyway, if you're playing good cop, bad cop—'

'I'm not,' Hess said. 'Trust me, you'd know if I was, because I'd be the bad cop.' And there was something in his eyes that – oddly – made Claire believe it. 'Look, I won't lie to you. Gretchen and Hans, they've got their own agendas. But so do we. We want to make sure you're protected, understand me? That's our job. We serve and protect, and Travis and I believe in that.'

Lowe paused in his slow amble to nod.

'We're neutral. There's a few of us in town who did enough good for each side to earn a little freedom, as long as we're careful.'

'What Joe means,' Detective Lowe said, 'is that they

ignore us as long as we keep it on our side of the tracks. Humans are the slave race here; forget about skin colour. So we have to take care of our own when we can.'

'And when we *can't*,' Hess said, as smoothly as if they'd rehearsed all this, 'things get ugly. It ain't like the two of us are free agents. We're Switzerland. If you cross the line, you're on your own.'

Shane frowned at him. 'What can you do for us, if you're Switzerland?'

'I can make sure that Gretchen and Hans don't make any follow-up visits,' Hess said. 'I can keep most of the cops away from you, maybe not all. I can put out the word widely that you're not just under a Founder's seal; Travis and I are keeping an eye on you. That'll keep anybody else from trying to win friends by smacking you around.'

'Anybody human, he means,' Lowe amended. 'The vamps, they'll scare the shit out of you if they can, but they won't hurt you. Not unless you screw up and that Founder's seal goes away. Got me?'

Which had already happened, really. The screwing-up part. Well, technically, she supposed Shane's dad hadn't broken any laws – yet – because Michael hadn't really died.

Except that he had.

God, Morganville made her head hurt.

A door slammed upstairs, and Eve came clattering down the stairs, fully dressed in Goth finery: a purple sheer shirt over a black corset thingy, a skirt that looked like it had got caught in a shredder, hose with skulls woven in, and her black Mary Janes. Very fierce. Her make-up was back in full force, ice white face, black-rimmed eyes, lips like three-day-old bruises.

'Officer Joe!' Eve practically flew across the room to hug him. Shane and Claire exchanged a look. Yeah, this wasn't something they were going to see every day. 'Joe Joe Joe! I've been wondering where you were!'

'Hi, Skippy. You remember Travis, right?'

'Big T!' Another hug. This, Claire thought, had tipped over the edge into the surreal, even for Morganville. 'I'm so glad to see you guys!'

'Ditto, kid,' Lowe said. He was smiling, and it transformed his face into something that was almost angelic. 'You've still got the numbers, right?'

Eve slapped her hand on the mobile phone strapped to her belt in a coffin-shaped holder. 'Oh yeah. Speed dial. But there hasn't been...um—'

Claire had the sudden weird feeling that Eve had something she couldn't talk about in front of them. The cops seemed to think so, too, because their eyes met briefly, and then Hess said, 'You want an update? How about showing us to your coffee pot?'

'Sure!' Eve said brightly, and led them off into the kitchen.

'Well,' Shane said as the door shut behind them, 'that's bizarre.'

'Did I miss a chapter?' Claire asked. 'And are there Cliff's Notes?'

'No idea.'

The sound of conversation drifted in from the kitchen, music without words. Claire fidgeted, then got up and tiptoed over.

'Hey!' Shane protested, but he followed.

Hess was talking about somebody named Jason. Shane reacted, putting his hand on Claire's shoulder and lifting his finger to his lips.

What? she mouthed silently.

I want to hear.

Detective Lowe was talking. '—you probably would want to know that he's getting out today. Now, before you say anything, he's been warned. He's not about to go near you or your parents. He'll be monitored.'

'Monitored.' Eve sounded shaken. 'But…I thought he was going to be in jail for a long time! What about that girl…?'

'She withdrew the complaint,' Hess said. 'We couldn't keep him locked up forever, honey. I'm sorry.'

'But he's *guilty*!'

'I know. But now it's your word against his, and you know how that gets decided. You're not sworn to anybody, Eve. He is.'

Eve cursed. It sounded like she was trying not to cry. 'Does he know where I am?'

'He'll find out,' Hess said. 'But like I said, he's being monitored, and we'll keep an eye on all of you kids here. You leave Jason alone, he'll leave you alone. OK?'

If Eve agreed, she did it silently. Claire nearly tipped

backward as Shane tugged on her shoulder; then she caught her balance and followed him back to the couch.

'Who's Jason?' She couldn't even wait until they were seated to ask.

'Crap,' he sighed. 'Jason's her brother. Last I heard, he was in jail for stabbing somebody. He's kind of a psycho, and Eve turned him in. No wonder she's freaked.'

'Her older brother?' Because Claire was picturing some Gothed-out muscular football type about ten feet tall, with a steroid habit.

'Younger,' Shane said. 'Seventeen, I guess. Skinny, creepy kid. I never liked him.'

'Do you think—?'

'What?'

'Do you think he'll come *here*? Try to hurt Eve?'

Shane shrugged. 'If he does, he'll be regretting it all the way to the hospital.' He said it in a matter-of-fact kind of way that made Claire feel strangely warm. She fought to catch her breath. If Shane noticed, he didn't show it. 'As long as we stay here, we're safe.' He looked up at the blank ceiling. 'Right, Michael?'

A chill drifted over Claire's skin. 'Right,' she said, on Michael's behalf.

But she wondered.

CHAPTER FIVE

The cops left, Shane played some video games, and Claire studied. It was a normal kind of day, all things considered. Shane had the TV on, looking for any news that might show a clue as to what his dad was up to, but Morganville's local station (it had only one) seemed bland, vanilla, and content-free even on the newscast.

The night came; Michael drifted back into human form; they had dinner.

Normal life, such as it passed for in a place like Morganville. In the Glass House.

It was only at midnight, when Claire was drifting off to sleep to the distant, sweet sound of Michael's guitar, that she started wondering about what she was going to do in the morning. She couldn't just *hide*, no matter what Michael thought. She had a life – sort of – and she'd already missed enough classes this semester. It was go or withdraw, and withdrawing would make things worse.

She'd never get her academic life together and go on to the Ivy League schools she was dreaming about.

She fell asleep thinking of vampires, fangs, pretty girls with mean smiles and cigarette lighters. Of fires and screaming. Of Shane's mom floating in the bathtub.

Of Shane, huddled in a corner, crying.

Not a great night. She woke up at first light, wondering if Michael was already gone again, and yawned and struggled her way out of bed and to the bathroom. Nobody else was up, of course. The shower felt good, and by the time she'd dried her hair and pulled on a plain white shirt and blue jeans and sneakers, and loaded up her backpack with the daily essentials, she felt ready to face the outside world.

Shane was asleep on the couch downstairs. She tiptoed past him, but a squeaky floorboard made it a useless exercise; he came bolt upright and stared at her with wild, uncomprehending eyes for a few seconds before he blinked and sighed. 'Claire.' He swung his legs off, sat up, and rested his head on the palms of his hands. 'Ow. Man, remind me that two hours of sleep doesn't really cut it.'

'I think you just reminded yourself. What were you doing up?'

'Talking,' he said. 'Michael needed to talk.'

Oh. Guy stuff. Stuff Michael hadn't wanted to share with the girls. OK, fine, not her business. Claire hitched up her backpack and edged towards the hallway.

'Where are you going?' Shane asked without lifting his head.

'You know where I'm going.'

'Oh no, you're not!'

'Shane, I'm *going*. Sorry, but you don't get to tell me what to do.' Technically, she supposed he could; he was older, and in Michael's absence he was sort of the owner and operator of the house. But…no. Not even then. Once she started letting that happen – or happen again – she'd lose whatever independence she'd earned. 'I have to go to class. Look, I'll be fine. Amelie's Protection's still good, and the campus is neutral ground, you know that. Unless I screw up, I'll be OK.'

'It's not neutral ground for Monica,' he said, and looked up. 'She tried to kill you, Claire.'

True. Claire gulped down a hard little bubble of fear. 'I can handle Monica.' She didn't think she could, but at least she could avoid her. Running was always an option.

Shane stared at her with bloodshot, tired eyes for a few long seconds, then shook his head and flopped back against the couch cushions, arms spread wide. 'Whatever,' he said. 'Call if you get into trouble.'

Something in his tone made Claire want to shed the backpack and crawl up on the couch next to him, cuddling close, but she straightened her spine and said, 'I will,' and marched to the door.

Two hard, fast chills swept over her. Michael, telling her a firm *no*.

'Bite me,' she said, shot the brand-new locks that Shane had installed, and exited into the warm Texas morning sun.

* * *

English class was boring, and she'd already read through everything in the curriculum, so Claire spent her time writing out her thoughts in the back of her journal. A lot of them centred on Shane, and Shane's lips, and Shane's hands. And curses, on the fact that she wasn't eighteen yet, and that it was a stupid rule anyway.

She was still thinking about the injustice of all that after class, when she ran into trouble.

Literally.

Claire turned the corner, head down, and collided with a tall, firm body that instantly grabbed her by the shoulders and shoved her, *hard*, backward. Claire nearly lost her balance, but skidded to a shaky and upright halt, bracing herself against the wall. 'Hey!' she yelled, more in shock than anger, and then her brain caught up with her eyes and she thought, *Oh, crap.*

It was Monica.

Monica Morrell looked polished and perfect, from her shining straight hair to her flawless make-up to the cute, trendy sheer top over baby doll T she was wearing. No backpack for Monica. She had a designer bag, and she looked Claire up and down, glossed lips twisting in disdain. Of course, she wasn't alone. Monica never went anywhere without an entourage, and today it was her usual wing girls, Jennifer and Gina, as well as a hovering flock of hard-bodied boys, most of them athletes of some kind or other.

Everybody was taller than Claire.

'Watch it, freak!' Monica said, and glared at her. And

then started to smile. It didn't lessen the menace in her pretty eyes. 'Oh, it's you. You ought to watch where you're going.' She half turned to her little gaggle of followers. 'Poor Claire. She's got a syndrome or something. Falls down stairs, hits her head, nearly burns down her house...' She focused back on Claire as Jennifer and Gina giggled. 'Isn't that right? Didn't your house burn?'

'Little bit,' Claire said. She was shaking, deep down, but she knew that if she backed down, she risked a lot worse. 'But I heard it's not the first time that's happened when you stop by for a visit.'

Monica's clique made a low *ooooooooooh* sound, a no-she-didn't murmur evenly split between appreciation and anticipation. Monica's eyes turned cold. – Er.

'Don't even go there, freak. Not my fault you live with a bunch of losers and jerks. Probably that Goth whore lighting candles all over the place. She's a walking fire hazard, not to mention a fashion disaster.'

Claire bit the inside of her lip and swallowed her reply, which would have had to do with who the real whore was in the conversation. She just raised her own eyebrows – well aware they weren't plucked, or perfect, or anything – and smiled like she knew something Monica didn't.

'She's not the only one. Isn't that top from Wal-Mart? The Trailer Park collection?' She turned around to go as Monica's friends *oooooh*ed again, this time with an edge of laughter.

Monica grabbed her by the backpack, yanking her off-balance. 'Tell Shane I said hi,' she said, her breath hot against Claire's ear. 'Tell him I don't care who's put out the truce flag... I'm going to get him, and you, and he's going to be sorry he *ever* screwed with me.'

Claire pulled herself free from Monica's highly polished manicured grip and said, 'He wouldn't screw you if you were the last girl on earth and it was survival of the species.'

She thought that Monica was going to scratch her eyes out with those perfectly manicured talons, and backed off fast. Monica, strangely, let her go. She was even smiling, a little, but it was a weird kind of smile, and it made Claire's stomach lurch when she looked back.

'Bye now,' Monica said. 'Freak.'

Chem class was already under way when Claire breathlessly slid into an empty seat and unpacked her notebook and text. She kept an eye out for Monica, Gina, Jennifer, or any random chemicals being flung her way – it had happened before – but she didn't run into Monica there, or on her way to her next class, or the next. By mid-afternoon she was aching from the tension, but her heart rate was pretty normal, and she'd got back into the groove of listening for comprehension. Not that she wasn't way ahead in the classes – she had a habit of reading the whole book at the beginning of the semester – but it was always nice when professors dropped some titbit that wasn't in the book or the published notes. Even the classes she didn't much like seemed relatively interesting. History had a quiz, which she finished in five minutes and handed in, then escaped with a silent thumbs-up from the professor.

It was late afternoon when she exited into the quadrangle outside of the science building; the crowds of students had thinned, since a lot of people tried to finish classes early and get on with the all-important party schedule. Texas Prairie University wasn't exactly Harvard on the Plains; most of the students were here to plough through two years of required courses, then transfer out to a legitimate university. So it was 'Party till you puke,' mostly.

It was funny as she looked around now, knowing what she knew about Morganville. She'd never realised what an insulated little world college was; she'd be willing to bet that ninety per cent of the kids attending had no idea what the real score was in town, or ever would. TPU was like a wildlife park, and the students were the wildlife.

And sometimes, the herd got culled.

Claire shivered, looked around for any signs of lurking Monicas, and took off for home. It wasn't a long walk, but it took her over the nicely tended (though sun-seared) grounds and out into Morganville proper's 'business district' – which really wasn't. It was a side-show for the students, all coffee shops (she wondered what poor fool Oliver had got to fill Eve's empty barista apron) and bookstores and trendy clothing emporiums. Buildings sported school colours – green and white – and usually had STUDENT DISCOUNT signs fading in the windows.

There was a weedy-looking guy in black standing at

the corner, watching her with burning dark eyes. He looked familiar, but she couldn't think why...somebody from class, maybe? Scary, anyway. She wondered why he was staring at *her*. There were other girls on the street. Prettier ones.

Claire walked faster. When she looked back, he wasn't there anymore. Was that better, or way creepier?

Walking even faster seemed like a great idea suddenly.

As Claire passed Common Grounds, the coffee shop, she glanced inside and saw someone she thought she recognised...but what the hell would Shane's dad be doing *here*? In the middle of the day? He didn't exactly blend in with the college crowd, and every cop in town was shaking the trees for him, right?

But there he was. Granted, she'd got only a quick look, but how many Frank Collins look-alikes could there be in Morganville?

I should get the hell out of here, she thought, but then she wondered. If she could find out what he was doing, maybe that would help Michael and Shane with planning what to do next. Besides, it was the middle of the day, broad daylight, and it wasn't like Mr Collins didn't know where to find her if he wanted – he knew where she lived, after all.

So Claire opened the door and slipped inside, hiding behind a couple of big jocks with bulky laptop-laden backpacks who were having some earnest conversation about whether baseball stats were legitimate during the steroid years, or had to be thrown out. Yes, that *was* Shane's dad, and he was sitting in the corner of the coffee bar, sipping from a cup. Plain as day.

What the *hell*...?

She caught her breath as Oliver slipped into the seat opposite him. Oliver was a lanky guy, tall and a bit stooped, with long curling hair that was sprinkled and shot through with grey. Not very threatening, Oliver, until you saw the fangs and the real personality lurking underneath what he put on for the public. Oliver was terrifying, and she had no desire *at all* to get into any position where she'd have to deal with him again.

Claire turned to go, and ran into a broad chest clad in a soft grey T-shirt. She looked up, and saw a guy she didn't recognise – a little older than Shane, maybe, but not much. He had soft, short red hair, and he was fair-skinned and freckled. Big blue eyes, the kind of blue that made her think of clear skies or deep oceans. He was just...pretty. And kind of peaceful.

Big and solid, and wearing – of all things, in this Texas late-summer heat wave – an old, worn brown leather jacket. No backpack, but he looked like a student.

He smiled down at her. She expected him to step out of the way, but he didn't; instead, he reached down, took her hand, and said, 'Hello, Claire. I'm Sam. Let's talk.'

His fingers felt cool, like clay. And he was, under the freckles, a little *too* pale. And there was something fey and sad in his eyes, too.

Oh, crap. Vampire.

Claire tried to pull free. He held on effortlessly. He could break bones if he wanted to – she sensed it – but he used just enough strength to keep her from getting loose. 'Don't,' Sam said. 'I need to talk to you. Please, I promise not to hurt you. Let's sit down, OK?'

'But—' Claire looked around, alarmed. The two jocks were moving away, heading for the bar to get drinks. The place was busy, and there were students everywhere – chatting, laughing, playing games, tapping away on laptops, talking on cell phones. And, of course, nobody was paying attention to her. She could make a scene and probably get away, but that would draw the attention of Oliver, not to mention Shane's dad, and she didn't want that. Low-pro was the order of the day.

Claire swallowed and let the vampire pull her to a secluded table near the window. He sat far from the hard white line of sunshine that had crept in across the wooden floor. The canopy outside screened most of it, but there was a tiny little area of risk left, she supposed.

Sam kept hold of her hand. She sat down, tried to make her voice strong and steady, and said, 'Would you mind letting go now? Since I'm sitting?'

'What? Oh. Sure.' He released her, and gave her a smile that even her biased, suspicious (verging on paranoid) mind interpreted as...sweet. 'Sorry. You're just so warm. It feels good.'

He sounded wistful. She couldn't afford to feel sorry for him, no way in hell. *Couldn't.* 'How do you know my name?' she asked.

His blue eyes narrowed when he smiled. 'You're kidding. Everybody knows your name. You, Shane, Eve, Michael. The Founder put out a Directive. First time in, oh, I guess about thirty years, maybe forty. Pretty dramatic stuff. We're all on our best behaviour around you, don't worry.' His gaze flicked around, touched on Oliver, and came back to her. 'Well, except for people who don't really have a best behaviour.'

'People,' Claire said, and crossed her arms. She hoped it made her look tough and strong, but she really did it because she was feeling cold. 'You're not *people*'

Sam looked a bit hurt. 'Harsh, Claire. Of course we're people. We're just...different.'

'No, you *kill people.* You're...parasites!' And she had no idea why she was getting into a debate about it with a total stranger. A vampire, at that. At least he hadn't done that thing to her like Brandon had done, that mesmerising thing. Oh, and she wasn't supposed to be looking him in the eye. Crap. She'd forgotten. Sam seemed kind of, well, normal. And he did have lovely eyes.

Sam was thinking over what she'd said, as if it was a serious argument. 'Food chain,' he offered.

'What?'

'Well, humans are parasites and mass murderers, from the point of view of vegetables.'

That…almost made some kind of weird sense. Almost. ‘I'm not a carrot. What do you want from me? Besides the obvious, I mean.’ She mimed fangs in the neck.

He looked a little ashamed. ‘I need to ask you a favour. Can you give something to Eve for me?’

She couldn't imagine anything Eve would want less than a gift from a vampire. ‘No,’ she said. ‘Is that it? Can I go?’

‘Wait! It's nothing bad, I swear. It's just that I always thought she was a lot of fun. I'm going to miss her coming in here. She always brightened up the place.’ He reached in his pocket and took out a small black box, which he handed over. Claire frowned and fidgeted with it for a second, then snapped the cover open. Not that it was any of her business, but…

It was a necklace. A pretty one, silver, with a shiny coffin-shaped locket. Claire raised her eyes to Sam's, reminded herself *again* not to do that, and focused somewhere in the middle of his chest. (He had a nice chest. Kind of built, actually.) ‘What's in it?’

‘Open it,’ he said, and shrugged. ‘I'm not trying to hide anything. I told you, it's nothing dangerous.’

She snapped the lid of the coffin open. Inside, there was a tiny silver statue of a girl with her arms crossed over her chest. Creepy, but kind of cool, too. Claire had to admit, Eve would probably be delighted.

‘Look, I'm not stalking her,’ Sam said. ‘We're just… friends. She's not the biggest fan of the not quite breathing, thanks to that asshole Brandon – I get that.

I'm not trying to be her boyfriend. I just thought she might like it.'

Sam was *not* fitting into Claire's recently built pigeon-holes, so new they still smelt of mental sawdust. VAMPIRES – BAD, one said. The one next to it said VAMPIRES – DOWNRIGHT EVIL. Those were pretty much the only two vampire slots available.

She didn't know where to put him. Sam just looked like a guy with sad eyes and a sweet smile, who could use some sun. A normal guy, one she'd probably get her heart rate up over talking to in class.

But that was probably how he got his victims, she reminded herself. She snapped the cover shut on the locket, closed the case, and slid it back across the table to him. 'Sorry,' she said. 'I'm not taking anything. If you want her to have it, give it to her yourself. Not that I think she'll ever come in here again.'

Sam looked taken aback, but he took the case and put it in the pocket of his leather jacket. 'OK,' he said. 'Thanks for listening. Can I ask you something else? Not a favour, just information.'

She wasn't sure, but she nodded.

'It's about Amelie.' Sam had lowered his voice, and his eyes were suddenly fierce and intense. Not so normal-guy. This was what he'd really wanted, not just the gift to Eve. This was *personal*. 'You talked to her, I heard. How is she? How did she seem?'

'Why?'

He didn't break the stare. 'She doesn't talk to me

anymore. None of them do. I don't care about the others, but…I worry about her.'

Claire couldn't believe what she was hearing. A vampire wanted her to talk about his vampire queen? Weirdy McWeird. 'Um…she seems…fine… She doesn't talk to you anymore? Why not?'

'I don't know,' he said, and sat back. 'She hasn't spoken to me for fifty years, give or take a few months. And no matter how many times I ask, I can't see her. They won't accept messages.' Something dark and wounded flickered in those innocent-looking eyes. 'She made me, and she abandoned me. Nobody's seen her in public in a long time. Now suddenly she's talking to you. Why?'

Fifty years. She was talking to an at-least-seventy-year-old man, with skin finer than hers. With a gorgeous, unlined face, and eyes that had seen…well…more than she ever would, most likely. *Fifty years?* 'How old are you?' she blurted, because it was seriously freaking her out.

'Seventy-two. I'm the youngest,' he said.

'In town?'

'In the world.' He fiddled with the sugar container on the table. 'Vampires are dying out, you know. That's why we're here, in Morganville. We were being slaughtered out there, in the world. But even here, Amelie's only made two new vampires in the last hundred and fifty years.' He looked up slowly and met her eyes, and this time, she felt an echo of that thing

Brandon did, that compulsion that held her in place. 'I know how it looks to you, because I've been there. I was born in Morganville; I grew up Protected. I know it sucks to be you around here. You're slaves. Just because you don't wear chains and get branded doesn't make you any less slaves.'

She flashed on an image of Shane's mother, dead in the bathtub. 'And if we run, you kill us,' she whispered. She would have expected him to flinch, or have some kind of reaction to that, but Sam's expression didn't change at all.

'Sometimes,' he said. 'But Claire, it isn't like we want to. We're trying to survive, that's all. You understand?'

Claire could almost see him standing there, looking down at Shane's mom as she bled to death. He'd have that same gentle, sad look in his eyes. Molly Collins would have been just a pet he had to put down, that was all, and it wouldn't matter to him enough to make him lose a night's sleep. If vampires slept. Which she was starting to doubt.

She stood up so fast, her chair hit the wall with a clatter. Sam leant back, surprised, as she grabbed up her backpack. 'Oh, I understand,' Claire said through gritted teeth. 'I can't trust *any* of you. You want to know how Amelie is? Go ask. There's probably a good reason why she won't talk to you!'

'Claire!'

She stiff-armed open the door and escaped into the day. She looked back to see Sam standing there at the edge of the strip of sunlight inside Common Grounds, staring after her with an expression on his face like he'd lost his best – his only – friend.

Dammit, she was *not* any vampire's friend. She couldn't be. And she wasn't going to be, ever.

Chapter Six

Claire decided on the way home that maybe it wouldn't be a good idea to blurt all of it out to Shane – not about Monica, or his dad, or the vampire Sam. Instead, she made dinner (tacos) and waited for Michael to rejoin the world. Which he did, as soon as the sun was safely under the horizon, and looked just as normal and angelic as ever.

She somehow got the message across to him that she needed to talk in private, which resulted in Michael drying dishes in the kitchen while she washed up. How that happened, she wasn't sure – it wasn't her turn – but the warm water and smooth suds were kind of soothing.

'Did you tell Shane about Monica?' Michael asked when she was done relating the day's events. He didn't seem bothered, but then, it took a lot to faze Michael. He might have been wiping the plates a little too thoroughly, though.

'No,' she said. 'He gets a little, you know, about her.'

'Yeah, he does. OK, you need to be careful, you know that, right? I'd ask Shane to go with you to class, but—'

'But that's probably what she wants,' Claire finished, and handed him another plate. 'To get us both together so she can use us against each other. Right?'

Michael nodded, eyebrows going up. 'All she has to do is grab you and she's got him. So be careful. I'm...not much use, outside of here. Or any use, actually.'

She felt bad for the flash of anger in his eyes – it wasn't directed at her but at himself. He hated this. Hated being trapped here while his friends needed him.

'I'll be fine,' she said. 'I got a new cell phone. Mom and Dad sent it.'

'Good. You've got us all on speed dial?'

'One, two, and three. And 911 on four.'

'Sweet.' Michael hip-bumped her. 'How are classes?'

'OK.' She couldn't work up any enthusiasm for them right at the moment. 'We're not talking about Shane's dad?'

'Nothing to talk about,' he said. 'You stay out of Common Grounds, and stay away from Oliver. If Shane's dad was in there, he was probably just taking a look around. Oliver might have sent him on his way. He does a good regular-guy act.' Michael ought to know, Claire reflected. Oliver had done a good enough regular-guy act to charm his way into the house, where he'd killed Michael, trying to make him a vampire. The house had saved Michael – partly. A kind of supernatural apology for having failed to protect him in the first place. The house did things like that. It was creepy, and occasionally flat-out scary, but it was at least mostly loyal to whoever was in residence.

Oliver, though...Oliver was loyal to Oliver. And that was about it.

'So we do nothing?' Claire asked.

'We do the best nothing you've ever seen.' Michael put the last plate away and tossed the towel over his shoulder like a bartender going on break. 'Meaning, *you* do nothing, Claire. That's an order.' She gave him a cockeyed mock salute. 'Yes, sir, sorry, sir.'

He sighed. 'I liked you better when you were this timid little kid. What happened?'

'I started living with you guys.'

'Oh, right.'

He fluffed her hair, smiled, and ambled off towards the living room. 'It's game night,' he said. 'I made Shane swear, no video games tonight. I think he's blowing the dust off of Monopoly. I wouldn't let him have Risk. He gets crazy with Risk.'

Didn't they all?

'So, I got a new job,' Eve said brightly as they sat on the floor around the Monopoly board. Shane was kicking ass, but Michael had the railroads; Eve and Claire were just mostly watching their money stacks dwindle. *No wonder people like this game*, Claire thought. *It's just like life.*

'You got a job already?' Shane asked as Michael rattled the dice in his hand and then tossed them out on the faded, warped board. 'Jeez, Eve, throw the brakes on full employment. You're making me look bad.'

'Shane Collins, permanent slacker. If you'd book more than one interview a month, and actually, you know, *show up* to them, you might get a job, too.'

'Oh, so now you're a career counsellor?'

'Bite me. You're not even going to ask me where?'

'Sure,' Michael said as he moved his cannon across four squares. 'Where?...Oh, crap.'

'That'll be five hundred, my man. And extra for clean towels in the hotel.' Shane held out his palm.

'I got hired at the university,' Eve said, watching Michael count out cash and hand it over to Shane. 'In the student union coffee shop. I even got a raise.'

'Congratulations!' Claire said. 'And you're not working for an evil vampire. Bonus.'

'Boss-wise, a definite step up. I mean, he's a slack-jawed loser with bad breath and a drinking problem, but that pretty much describes most of the male population of Morganville...'

'Hey!' both Shane and Michael chorused, and Eve gave them both a brilliant grin.

'Excluding the hotties in the room, of course. And cheer up, guys, it includes most of the *female* population, too. Anyway. Better hours – I'm working days, so not a lot of vamp worries – and bigger pay-cheques. Plus, I get to check out campus life. I hear they party hard.'

'From the other side of the counter, all you're going to see is people dissing you and complaining about their drinks,' Shane said without looking up. 'You watch yourself, Eve. Some of those assholes on campus think that if you're wearing a name badge, you're their own personal toy.'

'Yeah, I know. I heard about Karla.'

'Karla?' Claire asked.

'She works at the university,' Eve said. 'Karla Gast. We went to school with her.' Michael and Shane both looked up and nodded. 'She was kind of a party girl in high school, you know? Real pretty, too. She went to work on campus – I don't know what she was doing – but anyway, she's missing.'

'It was in the paper,' Michael said. 'Abducted last night walking to her car.'

Claire frowned. 'Why would it be in the paper? I mean, they don't usually put stuff like that in the papers, right?' Because in Morganville, murder was sort of legitimate, wasn't it?

'They do if it wasn't vampires,' Eve said, and nibbled on a carrot stick as she rolled the dice. 'Oooooh, pay me my two hundred, Mr Banker. If she'd been dragged off by vamps, even rogue vamps, it would have just been swept under the carpet like usual. Pay-offs to the family, end of the story. But this is different.'

'Is that, you know, unusual? Crime? Crime that isn't vampire related, I mean?'

'Kinda.' Eve shrugged. 'But people tend to get nasty

around Morganville. Nasty, or drunk, or timid. One of those.'

'Which are you?' Shane asked. Eve bared her teeth at him and growled. 'Ouch. Right. Gotcha.'

'So... Eve, I heard your brother's out of jail,' Michael said. Claire was rolling dice for her move, and by the time the plastic hit the board it sounded as loud as plates shattered on a tile floor. Nobody was making a sound. Nobody was *breathing*, so far as she could tell. From the expression on his face, Michael was clearly rethinking having brought up the subject, and Eve looked...hard and fierce and (deep down) scared.

Shane was just watching, no expression at all.

Awkward.

'Um...' Claire cautiously slid her Scottie dog the six squares that she'd rolled. 'You haven't said much about your brother.' She was curious what Eve would say. Because clearly Eve was *not* happy Michael had brought it up.

'I don't talk about him,' Eve said flatly. 'Not anymore. His name is Jason, and he's a dick, and let's drop the subject, OK?'

'OK.' Claire cleared her throat. 'Shane?'

'What?' He looked down at the board where she was pointing. 'Oh. Right. Three hundred.'

She mutely handed over her last bills as Shane took the dice in hand.

'Eve, you know what he went to jail for. You don't think—,' Michael began, very slowly.

'Shut up, Michael,' Eve said tensely. 'Just shut up, OK? Is it possible he did it? Sure. I wouldn't put it past him, but he just got out yesterday morning. That's pretty fast work, even for Jason.' But she looked shaken, under the fierce expression, and even paler than normal. 'You know what? I have to get up early.

'Night.'

'Eve—'

She jumped up and headed for the stairs. Michael followed, two steps behind as she climbed towards her room, black tattered-silk skirt fluttering. Claire watched them go, eyebrows raised, and Shane continued to shake the dice.

'Guess the game's over,' he said, and rolled anyway. 'Heh. Boardwalk. I think that completes Shane's real estate empire, thank you for playing, goodnight.'

'What was Michael talking about?' Claire asked. 'Does he think Eve's brother might have taken that girl?'

'No, he thinks Eve's brother might have *killed* that girl,' Shane said. 'And the cops probably think so, too. If he did, they'll get him, and this time, he won't be getting out of jail. In fact, he probably won't even make it to jail. One of Karla's brothers is a cop.'

'Oh,' Claire said in a small voice. She could hear the murmur of conversation upstairs. 'Well...I guess I should get to bed, too. I have early classes tomorrow.'

Shane met her eyes. 'Might want to give them some privacy for a while.'

Oh. Right. She jiggled her foot under the table and

started gathering up the cash and cards from the table. Her hands brushed Shane's, and he let go of the cards and took hold.

And then, somehow, she was in his lap, and he was kissing her. Hadn't meant to do that, but…well. She couldn't exactly be sorry about it, because he tasted amazing, and his lips were so soft and his hands were so strong…

He leant back, eyes half-shut, and he was smiling. Shane didn't smile all that much, and it always left her breathless and tingling. There was a secrecy about it, like he only ever smiled with her, and it just felt… perfect. 'Claire, you're being careful, right?' He smoothed hair back from her face. 'Seriously. You'd tell me if you got into trouble.'

'No trouble,' she lied, thinking about Monica's not-so-veiled threats, and that glimpse of Shane's dad seated across from Oliver in the coffee shop. 'No trouble at all.'

'Good.' He kissed her again, then moved down her jawline to her neck, and, wow, neck nibbles that took her breath away again. She closed her eyes and buried her fingers in his warm hair, trying to tell him through every touch how much she liked this, liked *him*, loved…

Her eyes came open, fast.

She did *not* just think that.

Shane's warm hands moved up her sides, thumbs grazing the sides of her breasts again, and he traced his fingers across the thin skin of her collarbone...down to where the neck of her T-shirt stopped him. Teasing. Pulling it down an inch, then two.

And then, maddeningly, he let go and leant back, lips damp. He licked them, watching her, and gave her that slow, crazy sexy smile again.

'Go to bed,' he said. 'Before I decide to come with.'

She wasn't sure she could stand up, but somehow, she got her legs to steady under her, and made it up the stairs. Michael was in Eve's room, the door was open, and they were sitting together on her bed. Michael was so bright, with his golden hair and china-blue eyes, and he didn't match the room all draped in dramatic black and red. He looked like an angel who'd taken a massive wrong turn.

He was holding Eve in his arms and rocking her, very gently, back and forth. As Claire looked in, he met her eyes and mouthed, *Close the door.*

She did, and went to her own bed.

Sadly, alone.

It occurred to Claire that she'd be smart to know what Jason Rosser looked like, in order to avoid him, but she had the strong feeling that it wouldn't be a very good idea to ask Eve for a peek at the family album. Eve was pretty touchy just now about anything to do with her brother...which, if Shane's pessimistic assessment was right, probably wasn't the wrong attitude.

So Claire went researching. Not the university

library, which – while not too bad – didn't really have a lot of info about Morganville itself. She'd checked. There was some history, all carefully blanded down, and some newspaper archives.

But there was a Morganville Historical Society. She found the address in the phone book, studied the map, and calculated the time it would take to walk the distance. If she hustled, she could get there, find what she needed, and still make it to her noon class.

Claire showered, dressed in blue jeans and a black knit top with a screen-printed flower on it – one of her thrift-shop buys – and grabbed her backpack on the way to the door. She set herself a blistering pace once she hit the sidewalks, heading away from the university and into the unexplored guts of Morganville. She had the map with her, which was handy, because as soon as she was out of sight of the Glass House, things became confusing. For having been master planned, Morganville was not exactly logical in the way its streets ran. There were cul-de-sacs, dead ends, lots of unlit deserted areas.

But then again, maybe that *was* logical, from a vampire's planning perspective. Even in the hot beat of the sunlight, Claire shuddered at that idea, and moved faster past a street that ended in a deserted field littered with piled-up lumber and assorted junk. It even smelt like decay, the ugly smell of dead things left to rot in the heat. Having too much imagination was sometimes a handicap. *At least I'm not walking it at night...*

No power on earth was going to make her do that.

The residential areas of Morganville were old, mostly run-down, parched and beaten by summer. It was bound to get cooler soon, but for now, Indian summer was broiling the Texas landscape. Cicadas sang in dull dental-drill whines in the grass and trees, and there was a smell of dust and hot metal in the wind. Of all the places to find vampires, this was pretty much the last she would have expected. Just not...Goth enough. Too run-down. Too... American.

The next street was her turn, according to the map. She made it, stopped in the shade of a live oak tree, and took a couple of drinks from her water bottle as she considered how much longer a walk it would be. Not long, she thought. Which was good, because she was *not* going to miss another class. Ever.

The street dead-ended. Claire came to a stop, frowning, and checked; nope, according to the map, it went all the way through. Claire sighed in frustration and started to turn back to retrace her path, then hesitated when she saw a narrow passage between two fences. It looked like it went through to the next street.

Lose ten minutes or take a chance. She'd always been the lose-ten-minutes kind of girl, the prudent one, but maybe living in the Glass House had corrupted her. Besides, it was hot as hell out here.

She headed for the gap between the fences.

'I wouldn't do that, child,' said a voice. It was coming from the deep shadow of a porch, on a house to her right. It looked better cared for than most houses in

Morganville – freshly painted in a light sea-blue, some brick trim, a neatly kept yard. Claire squinted and shaded her eyes, and finally saw a tiny bird-like old lady seated on a porch swing. She was as brown as a twig, with drifting pale hair like dandelion fuzz, and since she was dressed in a soft green sundress that hung on her like a bag, she looked like nothing so much as a wood spirit, something out of the old, old storybooks.

The voice, though, was pure warm Southern honey.

Claire backed up hastily from the entrance to the passageway. 'I'm sorry, ma'am. I don't mean to trespass.'

The tiny little thing cackled. 'Oh, no, child, you're not trespassin'. You're bein' a fool. You ever heard of ant lions? Or trap-door spiders? Well, you walk down that path, you won't be comin' out the other side. Not this world.'

Claire felt a pure cold bolt of panic, followed by a triumphant crow from the prudent side of her brain: *I knew that!* 'But…it's daytime!'

'So it is,' the old woman said, and rocked gently back and forth on her swing. 'So it is. Day don't always protect round Morganville. You should know that, too. Now, go back the way you came like a good child, and don't come here again.'

'Yes, ma'am,' Claire said, and started to back away.

'Granma, what are you— Oh, hello!' The screen door to the house opened, and a younger version of the Stick Lady stepped out – young enough to be a granddaughter.

She was tall and pretty, and her skin was more cocoa than wood brown. She wore her hair in braids, lots of them, and she smiled at Claire as she came to lay a hand on the old lady's shoulder. 'My granma likes to sit out here and talk to people. I'm sorry if she bothered you.'

'No, not at all,' Claire said, and nervously fiddled with one of the loose adjustment straps of her backpack. 'She, um, warned me about the alley.'

The woman's eyes moved rapidly, from Claire to the old lady and back again. 'Did she?' she said. She didn't sound warm anymore. 'Granma, you know better than that. You need to quit scaring people with your stories.'

'Don't be a damn fool, Lisa. They ain't just stories, and you know it.'

'Granma, there hasn't been any…trouble around here for twenty years!'

'Doesn't mean it wouldn't happen,' Granma said stubbornly, and pointed a stick-thin shaking finger at Claire. 'You don't go down that alley, now. I meant what I said.'

'Yes, ma'am,' she said faintly, and nodded to both women. 'Um, thanks.'

Claire turned to go, and as she did, she noticed something mounted on the wall next to the old woman's porch swing. A plaque, with a symbol.

The same symbol as was on the Glass House. The Founder's symbol.

And now that she was looking at the house, really

looking, it had some of the same lines to it, and it was about the same age.

Claire turned back, smiled apologetically, and said, 'I'm sorry, but could I use your restroom? I've been chugging water out here—'

She thought for a second that Lisa was going to say no, but then the younger woman frowned and said, 'I suppose,' and came down the steps to open the white picket gate for Claire to enter. 'Go on inside. It's the second door off the hall.'

'Offer the child some lemonade, Lisa.'

'She's not staying, Granma!'

'How you know if you don't ask?'

Claire let them argue it out, and stepped inside. She didn't feel anything – no tingle of a force field or anything – but then, she didn't going in and out of the Glass House, either.

Still, she recognised it immediately...There was something about this house. It had the same quality of stillness, of *weight*, that she always felt at home. Not the same at all inside from a decorating point of view – Granma and Lisa seemed to like furniture, lots of it, all in fussy floral patterns and chintz, with rugs everywhere and a smothering amount of curtains and lace. Claire walked slowly down the hardwood hallway, trailing her fingers lightly over the panelling. The wood felt warm, but all wood did, right?

'Freaky,' she muttered, and opened the bathroom door.

It wasn't a bathroom.

It was a study, a large one, and it couldn't have been more different from the overblown frilly living room… severe polished wood floors, a massive dark desk, a few glowering portraits on the walls. Dark red velvet curtains blocking out the sun. The walls were lined with books, old books mostly, and in the cabinet there was something that looked like a wine rack, only it held…scrolls?

Amelie was seated at the desk, signing sheets of paper with a gold pen. One of her assistants, also a vampire, was standing attentively next to her, taking each sheet out of the way as she wrote her name.

Neither of them looked up at Claire.

'Close the door,' Amelie said in a gentle voice accented with an almost-French sort of pronunciation. 'I dislike the draft.'

Claire thought about running, but she wasn't stupid enough to believe she could run far enough, or fast enough, and even though the idea of shrieking and slamming the door from the *other* side was pretty tempting, she swallowed her fear and stepped all the way in before she shut it with a quiet *click*.

'Is this your house?' Claire asked. It was the only thing she could think of to ask, frankly; every other question had been shaken right out of her head because *this couldn't be happening.*

Amelie glanced up, and her eyes were just as cool and intimidating as Claire remembered. It felt a little like being frostbitten. 'My house?' she echoed. 'Yes, of course.

They are all my house. Oh, I see what you ask. You ask if the particular house you entered is my home. No, little Claire, it is not where I hide myself from my enemies, although it would certainly be a useful choice. Very...' Amelie smiled slowly. 'Unexpected.'

'Then...how...?'

'You'll find that when I need you, Claire, you will be called.' Amelie signed the last paper, then handed it to her assistant – a tall, dark young man in a black suit and tie – and he bowed slightly and left the room through another door. Amelie sat back in her massive carved chair, looking more like a queen than ever, including the golden coronet of hair on top of her head. Her long fingers tapped lightly on the lion-head arms of the chair. 'You are not in the house where you were, my dear. Do you understand that?'

'Teleportation,' Claire said. 'But that's not possible.'

'Yet you are here.'

'That's *science fiction*!'

Amelie waved her graceful hand. 'I fail to understand your conventions of literature these days. One impossible thing such as vampires, this is acceptable, but two impossible things becomes science fiction? Ah well, no matter. I cannot explain the workings of it; that is a subject for philosophers and artisans, and I am neither. Not for many years.' Her frost-coloured eyes warmed just a fraction. 'Put down your pack. I've seen tinkers carrying lighter loads.'

What's a tinker? Claire wondered. She started to

ask, but didn't want to sound stupid. 'Thank you,' she said, and carefully lowered her backpack to the wooden floor, then slid into one of the two chairs facing the desk. 'Ma'am.'

'So polite,' Amelie said. 'And in a time when manners are forgotten…you do understand what manners are, don't you, Claire? Behaviours that allow humans to live closely together without killing each other. Most of the time.'

'Yes, ma'am.'

Silence. Somewhere behind Claire, a big clock ticked away minutes; she felt a drop of sweat glide down her neck and splash into the fabric of her black knit shirt.

Amelie was staring at her without blinking or moving, and that was weird. *Wrong.* People just didn't *do* that.

But then, Amelie wasn't people. In fact, of all the vampires, in many ways she was the most not-people.

'Sam asked about you,' Claire blurted, just because it popped into her head and she wanted Amelie to stop staring at her. It worked. Amelie blinked, shifted her weight, and leant forward to rest her pointed chin on her folded hands, elbows still braced on the arms of the chair.

'Sam,' she said slowly, and her gaze wandered up and to her right, fixed on nothing. Trying to remember, Claire thought; she'd noticed how people – even vampires, apparently – did that with their eyes when remembering things. 'Ah yes. Samuel.' Her gaze snapped back to Claire with unnerving speed. 'And how did you come to chat with dear young Samuel?'

'Claire shrugged. 'He wanted to talk to me.'

'About?'

'He asked about you. I…think he's lonely.'

Amelie smiled. She wasn't trying to impress Claire with her vampiness – no need for that! – so her teeth looked white and even, perfectly normal. 'Of course he's lonely,' she said. 'Samuel is the youngest. No one older trusts him; no one younger exists. He has no ties to the vampire community, save me, and no ties left to the human world. He is more alone than anyone you will ever meet, Claire.'

'You say that like you…want him that way. Alone, I mean.'

'I do,' Amelie said calmly. 'My reasons are my own. However, it is an interesting experiment, to see how someone so alone will react. Samuel has been intriguing; most vampires would have simply turned brutal and uncaring, but he continues to seek comfort. Friendship. He is unusual, I think.'

'You're *experimenting* on him!' Claire said.

Amelie's platinum eyebrows slowly rose to form perfect arches over her cold, amused eyes. 'Clever of you to think such a thing, but attend: a rat who knows it is running a maze is no longer a useful subject. So you will keep your counsel, and you will keep your distance from dear sweet Samuel. Now. Why did you come to me today?'

'Why did I…?' Claire cleared her throat. 'I think

maybe there's been a mistake. I was, you know, looking for a bathroom.'

Amelie stared at her for a frozen second, and then she threw back her head and laughed. It was a full, living sound, warm and full of unexpected joy, and when it passed, Claire could see the traces of it still on her face and in her eyes. Making her look almost...human. 'A bathroom,' she repeated, and shook her head. 'Child, I have been told many things, but that may yet prove the most amusing. If you wish a bathroom, please, go through that door. You will find all that you require.' Her smile faded. 'But I think you came to ask me something more.'

'I didn't come here at all! I was going to the Morganville Historical Society—'

'I *am* the Morganville Historical Society,' Amelie said. 'What do you wish to know?'

Claire liked books. Books didn't talk back. They didn't sit there in their fancy throne chairs and look all queeny and imposing and *terrifying*, and they didn't have fangs and bodyguards. Books were *fine*. 'Um...I just wanted to look something up...?'

Amelie was already losing patience. 'Just tell me, girl. Quickly. I am not without duties.'

Claire cleared her throat nervously, coughed, and said, 'I wanted to find out about Eve's brother, Jason. Jason Rosser.'

'Done,' Amelie said, and although she didn't seem to do anything, not even lift a finger, the side door opened and her cute but deathly pale assistant leant in. 'The Rosser family file,' she told him. He nodded and was gone. 'You would have wasted your time,' Amelie said to Claire. 'There are no personnel files of any kind in the Historical Society building. It is purely for show, and the information there is inaccurate, at best. If you want to know the true history of things, little one, come to someone who has lived it.'

'But that's just perspective,' Claire said. 'Not fact.'

'All fact is perspective. Ah, thank you, Henry.' Amelie accepted a folder from her assistant, who silently left again. She flipped it open, studied what was inside, and then handed it over to Claire. 'An unexceptional family. Curious that it produced young Eve and her brother.'

It was their whole lives reduced to dry entries in long-hand on paper. Dates of births, details of school records…there were handwritten reports from the vampire Brandon, who gave them Protection. Even those were dry.

And then not so dry, because between the ages of sixteen and eighteen, Eve changed. Big-time. The school photograph at fifteen was of a pretty, fragile-looking girl dressed in conservative clothes – something even Claire would have worn.

Eve's photograph at sixteen was Goth City. She'd dyed her dark hair a flat glossy black, whited her face, raccooned her eyes, and generally adopted a 'tude. By seventeen she'd started getting piercings – one showed in the tongue she stuck out at the camera.

By eighteen, she looked pensive and defiant, and then the photographs stopped, except for some that looked like surveillance photos of Eve in Common Grounds, pulling espresso shots and chatting with customers.

Eve with Oliver.

You're supposed to be looking up Jason, Claire reminded herself, and flipped the page.

Jason was just the same, only younger; about the time that Eve had turned Goth, so had Jason, although on him it looked less like a fashion choice and more like a serious turn to the dark side. Eve always had a light of humour and mischief in her eyes; Jason had no light in his eyes at all. He looked skinny, strong, and dangerous.

And Claire realised with an icy start that she'd seen him before… He'd been on the street, staring at her just before she'd gone into Common Grounds and talked to Sam.

Jason Rosser knew who she was.

'Jason likes knives, as I recall,' Amelie said. 'He sometimes fancies himself a vampire. I should be quite careful of him, were I you. He is not likely to be as… polite as my own people.'

Claire shivered and flipped pages, speed-reading through Jason's not-very-impressive academic life, and then the police reports.

Eve had been the witness who'd turned him in. She'd seen him abduct this girl and drive away with her – a girl who was later found wandering the streets bleeding from a stab wound. The girl refused to testify, but Eve had gone on record. And Jason had gone away.

The file showed he'd been released from prison the day before yesterday at nine in the morning. Plenty of time for him to have grabbed Karla Gast on campus and...

Out with the bad thoughts, Claire. In with the good.

She flipped pages and looked at Eve's mother and dad. They looked...normal. Kind of grim, maybe, but with a son like Jason, that probably wasn't too strange.

Still, they didn't look like the kind of parents who'd just toss their daughter out on her ear and never write or call or visit.

Claire closed the file and slid it back across the desk to Amelie, who put it in a wooden out-box at the corner of her desk. 'Did you find what you wished to know?' Amelie asked.

'I don't know.'

'What a wise thing to say,' Amelie said, and nodded once, like a queen to a subject. 'You may go now. Use the door that brought you.'

'Um...thanks. Bye.' Which sounded like a dumbass thing to say to someone a billion years old, who controlled the town and everything in it, but Amelie seemed to accept it fine. Claire grabbed her backpack and hurried through the polished wood door...

...into a bathroom. With lots of floral wallpaper and really yak-worthy frilly doll-skirt toilet paper covers.

Reality whiplash.

Claire dropped her backpack and yanked open the door again.

It was the hallway. She looked right, then left. The room even smelt different – talcum powder and old-lady perfume. No trace of Amelie, her silent servants, or the room where they'd been.

'Science fiction,' Claire said, deeply unhappy, and – feeling strangely guilty – flushed the toilet before trudging back the way she'd come. The house was warm, but the heat outside was like a slap from a microwaved towel.

Oh, she was *so* going to figure that trick out. She couldn't stand the idea of it being, well, *magic*. Sure, vampires she could accept...grudgingly...and the whole mind-control thing. But not instantaneous transportation. Nope.

Lisa was sitting next to Granma on the porch swing now, sipping lemonade. There was an extra one gathering beads of sweat on the small table next to her, and she nodded Claire to it without speaking.

'Thanks,' Claire said, and took a deep, thirsty gulp. It was good – maybe too sweet, but refreshing. She drained it fast and held on to the cool glass, wondering if it was bad manners to crunch the ice cubes. 'How long have you lived here?'

'Granma's been in this house all her life,' Lisa said, and gently rubbed her grandmother's back. 'Right, Granma?'

'Born here,' the old woman said proudly. 'Gonna die here, too, when I'm good and ready.'

'That's the spirit.' Lisa poured Claire another glass of lemonade from a half-empty pitcher. 'I find anything missing in Granma's house, college girl, and you can't hide from me in Morganville. You feel me?'

'Lisa!' Granma scolded. 'I'm so sorry, honey. My granddaughter never learnt proper manners.' She smacked Lisa on the hand and gave her the parental glare. 'This nice girl here, she never would steal from an old lady. Now, would you, honey?'

'No, ma'am,' Claire said, and drank half of the second serving of lemonade. It tasted as tart and sweet and wonderful as the first. 'I was just wondering, about the symbol next to your door...'

Lisa and Granma both looked at her sharply. Neither one of them replied. They were both wearing bracelets, she noticed, plain silver with the Founder's symbol on a metal plaque, like those MedicAlert bracelets. Finally, Lisa said, softly, 'You need to leave now.'

'But—'

'Go!' Lisa yelled it, grabbed the glass out of Claire's hand, and thumped it down on the table. 'Don't you make me throw you down the stairs in front of my granma!'

'Hush, Lisa,' Granma said, and leant forward with a creaking sound, from either the wooden porch swing or her old bones. 'Girl's got no better sense than God gave a sheep, but that's all right. It's the Founder's symbol, child, and this is the Founder's house, and we're the Founder's people. Just like you.'

Lisa looked at her, open-mouthed. 'What?' she finally said when she got control of her voice.

'Can't you see it?' Granma waved her hand in front

of Claire. 'She shines, baby. *They* see it, I guarantee you they do. They won't touch her, mark or no mark. Worth their lives if they do.'

'But—' Lisa looked as frustrated and helpless as Claire felt. 'Granma, you're seeing things again.'

'I do *not* see things, missy, and you better remember just who in this family stayed alive when everybody else fell.' Granma's faded eyes fixed on Claire, who shivered despite the oppressive, still heat. 'Don't know why she marked you, child, but she did. Now you just got to live with it. Go on, now. Go home. You got what you came for.'

'She did?' Lisa scowled fiercely. 'Swear to God, if you lifted anything from our house—'

'Hush. She didn't steal. But she got what she needed, didn't you, girl?'

Claire nodded and nervously ran a hand through her hair. She was sweating buckets; her hair felt sticky and wet. Home suddenly sounded like a real good idea.

'Thank you, ma'am,' she said, and extended her hand. Granma looked at it for a few seconds, then took it in a bird-like grip and shook. 'Can I come back and see you sometime?'

'Long as you bring me some chocolate,' Granma said, and smiled. 'I'm partial to chocolate.'

'Granma, you're diabetic.'

'I'm old, girl. Gonna die of something. Might as well be chocolate.'

They were still arguing as Claire retreated down the steps, through the neatly kept front garden, and out through the gate in the white picket fence. She looked at that alley, the one she'd almost taken, and this time she felt a shiver of warning. *Trap-door spiders.* No, she no longer had any desire to take shortcuts. And she'd learnt about as much as she could stomach about Jason Rosser. At least she knew now who to watch out for, if he started following her around again.

Claire hitched her backpack to a more comfortable position, and began walking.

Chapter Seven

There was no sign of Shane's dad or the bikers. In fact, it was very quiet in Morganville, despite Claire's fears. Travis Lowe and Joe Hess dropped by early the next morning to deliver the no-news-is-good-news party line to Eve and the house in general; they were polite and kind, and generally seemed like OK guys for cops, but they made Claire feel scared and paranoid. She supposed all cops were like that, when they were on Official Business. It didn't seem to bother Eve at all; she was up, bleary-eyed and yawning, fresh out of the shower and still wrapped in a Hello Kitty bathrobe, free of the Goth mask. Shane was, predictably, asleep, and who knew where Michael was? Watching, Claire thought. Always watching. She supposed that should have been creepy, except that in Michael's case, it was just...comforting.

'Hey, guys,' Eve said after wandering down the stairs

into the living room. She plopped on the couch, bounced, and yawned again. 'Coffee. Need coffee.'

'I made some,' Claire said, and went into the kitchen to get it. Travis Lowe followed her silently and carried the cups back out. He and his partner drank it black; Claire could barely stand it even with more milk and sugar than actual coffee. Eve was cream only, no sugar, and she sucked it down like Gatorade after a hard work-out, then collapsed against the couch cushions and sighed happily.

'Morning, Officers,' she said, and closed her eyes. 'It's too early for this.'

'Heard you got a job on campus,' Hess said. 'Congratulations, Eve.'

'Yea, me.' She made a lazy woo-hoo gesture. 'You come all this way to say that?'

'Not a long way in Morganville.' Hess shrugged. 'But no. Like I told Claire, there's no sign of your intruders. So I think you're in the clear on that. Hope that makes your day better.'

Eve shot Claire a fast, tentative look. 'Sure,' she said. 'Um…about…the other thing…?'

'You want to talk in private?' Claire asked, and stood up with her coffee cup in hand. ''Cause I can go on to school—'

'Sit,' Hess said. 'You're not going anywhere yet. And you're not going anywhere by yourself.'

'I'm…what?'

'We're giving you girls a ride to school,' Lowe said,

and sipped his coffee. 'And a ride home when you're done. Consider us your Thin Blue Line Taxi Service.'

'No!' Claire blurted, appalled. 'I mean, you can't...you shouldn't...why?'

'Eve knows why,' Hess said. 'Don't you, Eve?'

Eve put her coffee cup on the side table and crossed her arms against her chest. She looked very young in pink and white, and very scared. 'Jason.'

'Yeah, Jason.' Hess cleared his throat, glanced at Claire, and continued. 'We found Karla Gast late last night. Well, actually, some of our more night-inclined colleagues found her. Dumped in a vacant lot about six blocks from here behind some piled-up lumber.'

In a flash, Claire remembered walking past the empty lot on her way to her unintended visit with Amelie. She'd even *smelt decay.* She put her coffee cup down and put both hands over her mouth, fighting an impulse to gag.

'You think—' Eve looked tense and pale. She licked her lips, swallowed, and continued. 'You think Jason was involved.'

'Yeah,' Hess said softly. 'We think. No proof, though. No witnesses, no forensic evidence, but she was definitely not killed by a vampire. Look, Jason's been spotted in the area, so I don't want you out there by yourself for now, OK? Either one of you.'

'He's my *brother*!' Eve sounded angry now, voice shaking. 'How could he do this? What kind of...of—'

'It's not your fault,' Lowe said. 'You tried to get him help. He just got sicker.'

'It *is* my fault!' she shouted. 'I'm the one who turned him in! I'm the one who didn't stop Brandon from—'

'From what?' Lowe asked, very quietly.

Eve didn't answer. She looked down at her black-painted fingernails, and picked at them restlessly.

'From moving on to an easier target,' she said. 'Once I made sure he couldn't get to me.'

'Christ,' Lowe muttered in weary disgust. 'Someday, that goddamn vamp's going to get his—'

'Trav,' Hess said. 'It ain't laundry day. Let's not air it in public.'

'Yeah, I know, but *Jesus Christ*, Joe, it ain't like this is the first time...'

It took Claire a few seconds to work out what they were all talking about, but then she remembered Eve's poetry that she'd looked through on the computer...all romantic *Aren't vampires great?* stuff until she was about fifteen, and then...no more romance. *Brandon. Brandon tried to mess with her when she was fifteen.*

And Jason was her younger brother.

'What did he do to him?' Claire asked in a very small voice. 'Brandon, I mean. Did he...bite him?'

Eve didn't look up, but her cheeks went pink to match her robe. 'Sometimes,' she said. 'And sometimes it was worse than that. We're just toys to him, you know. Dolls. We're not *real*. People aren't real at all.'

'I'm afraid the same goes for Jason now,' Hess said. 'Can't really blame the kid. He didn't have much of a chance. But I repeat, Eve, you can't blame yourself, either. You saved yourself, and that's important.'

'Yeah, I saved myself by screwing over my brother. What a hero.'

'You be careful with all that guilt,' Lowe said. 'It'll pound you down. Your parents were the ones who should have stepped in, and you know it. Anybody willing to let their kids become toys, just to get ahead...'

Claire reached out and took hold of Eve's hand. Eve, surprised, looked up – she wasn't crying, which was kind of surprising because Eve cried a *lot*. Her eyes were dry, clear, and hard. Angry.

'Why do you think I left?' she asked. 'As soon as I could. Between my parents and what Brandon made out of Jason...'

Claire couldn't think of anything to say. She just sat there, holding Eve's hand. She'd never been through any of that... She'd grown up warm and safe in a house where her parents loved her. In a town where there were no such things as vampires, where child abuse and molestation were something that happened on the evening news, and if anybody had brothers who killed people, it happened in big cities, to people she didn't know.

All this was just...too much to take in. And much too painful.

'It's going to be OK,' she finally said. Eve smiled at her sadly, but her eyes were still fierce.

'No,' she said. 'Don't think so, Claire. But thanks.'

She took a deep breath, let go of Claire's hand, and

turned back to the two cops. 'Right. You guys hang out here while I get dressed.'

'Oh, sure,' Hess said, and raised an eyebrow. It made his face look crooked, but maybe that was just the way his nose was; Claire wasn't sure. 'Not like we're protecting or serving or anything.'

'You're not even on duty,' Eve said.

'Busted,' Lowe said, smiling. 'We're on our own for this. Hurry up, kid – I'd like to get to sleep sometime today before I have to fight for truth and justice again.'

Eve padded up the stairs, one hand on the railing, and Claire let out a slow, careful breath. Eve was kind of like an unexploded bomb right now. Claire ached to make it all better, but there was no way she could do that…and no way that Eve would even let her try, she thought.

She wished Shane would wake up. She needed…well, *something*. A hug, maybe. Or one of those deliciously warm kisses. Or just to look at him, all rumpled and grumpy with his hair sticking up at odd angles, sheet creases on his face, his bare feet looking so cute and soft…

She had never thought of a guy's *feet* as sexy before. Not even movie-star feet. But Shane…there was no part of him that wasn't sizzle hot.

'More coffee?' Hess asked, and waggled his empty mug. Claire sighed and took his and Lowe's into the kitchen for refills.

She had just set the two ceramic cups down on the

counter, and was reaching for the coffee pot, when a big, thick, sweaty hand closed over her mouth, and irresistibly strong arms yanked her backward. She tried to scream, and kicked, but whoever had her, really had her. She squirmed, but it didn't do any good.

'Quiet,' a rough male voice whispered in her ear. 'Shut up, or this gets ugly.'

It was already ugly, at least from Claire's terrified side of things. She went still, and the man holding her lowered her down enough to let her sneakered toes touch the floor. Didn't let her go, though.

She'd already figured out who it was – the speaker, not the one holding her – before Shane's dad stepped out into her view and leant forward, scary-close. 'Where's my son?' he asked. His breath was nasty, and stank of booze. Breakfast of Collins champions. 'Just nod. Is he in the house?' She nodded slowly. The hand muffling her mouth let her do it. 'Upstairs?' She nodded again. 'Those cops in the living room?' She nodded vigorously, and tried to think what she could do to get Detective Hess's attention. Screaming wasn't doing any good; the kitchen door was pretty solid, and it was useless to try to get sound past a hand that was about two inches thick. If they'd grabbed her when she was holding the mugs, at least she could have dropped them...

'My kid likes you,' Shane's dad said. 'That's all that keeps you alive right now, you get me? So don't push your luck. I could always change my mind, and you could get buried out back with your little friend Michael. Now, my buddy here is going to let go of your mouth, and you'd better not scream, because if you do, we're just going to have to do some killing, starting with you and ending with the cops. And that vampire-wannabe girlfriend of yours. You get me? My son is all that matters to me.'

Claire swallowed hard and nodded again. The hand pulled slowly away from her mouth.

She didn't scream. She pressed her lips together to hold in the urge.

'Good girl,' Shane's dad said. 'Now tell me what the cops are doing here. They looking for us?'

She shook her head. 'They think you're gone,' she said. 'They're here to take me and Eve to school.'

'School.' He poured contempt into the word. 'That's not a school. It's a holding pen for cattle.'

She licked her lips and tasted the sweat of the guy who was holding her. Disgusting. 'You need to go. Right now.'

'Or?'

'You can't do what you're here to do if everybody's still looking for you,' she said. She was making it up, but suddenly it made sense to her. 'If you have to kill me, and everybody here, they turn the town upside down until they find you. And they'll put Shane in jail, or worse. If you let me go and take Shane, I'll just tell them everything anyway, and they turn the town upside down—'

'Are you trying to scare me, little girl?'

'No,' Claire whispered. She could barely get the word

out. 'I'm trying to tell you what will happen. They've kind of given up looking for you, but if you kill me, you lose. And if you let me go, I'm going to tell them everything.'

'Then why shouldn't I kill you?'

'Because I'll keep my mouth shut if you promise to leave Shane alone.'

He glared at her, but she could see he was thinking about it.

'Boss,' said the man holding her. He had a deep voice, rough like his throat was lined with gravel. 'Bitch got no reason to keep her word.'

'What makes you think I like the vamps any more than you do?' she shot back. 'Did Shane tell you about Brandon? I saw you in Common Grounds. Were you looking for him? Because if you weren't, you should be. He's a dick.'

Frank Collins's eyes drifted half-shut, and she was reminded sickly of Shane, somehow. 'You telling me which vamps to kill now?'

'No.' She swallowed again, acutely aware that at any second the kitchen door could swing open, and someone could come stumbling in, and everything could go to hell on the express train. 'Just a suggestion. Because as far as I can tell, he's just about the worst one. But you're going to do what you want, I know that. I just want me and my friends out of it.'

Shane's dad smiled at her. *Smiled.* And it seemed, for the first time, like a mostly genuine expression, not just a freaky twist of his lips. 'You're tougher than you look, kid. That's good. You're going to need to be, you stick around here.' He looked past her, at the biker (or so she thought – she could feel leather squeaking behind her when she struggled). 'Let her down, man. She's OK.'

The biker released her. She jerked forward, spun, and set her back to the refrigerator. She scrambled for a knife in the drawer next to her, found a wicked-looking cleaver, and held it out in front of her. 'You need to go,' she said. 'Right now. And don't come back here, or I swear, I'll tell them everything.'

He wasn't smiling anymore. Well, not as much. The biker behind him, though, was grinning.

'Girl, you don't know my son at all, do you?' he asked. 'I don't have to come back here. He's going to come to me. Eventually.'

He made a *Let's go* gesture to his six-foot bodyguard, and together they went back out the side door of the kitchen. Claire ran to pull it shut and lock it, both locks plus the newly installed sliding bolts.

Which made her wonder why it hadn't been locked before...oh. Of course. The cops had come in through the kitchen.

She took some deep breaths, rinsed the taste of that sweaty hand off her lips, and picked up the coffee cups.

Her hands were shaking so badly, there was no way she could carry anything liquid. She put them back down and went back to the door to call through, 'Making some fresh!'

She poured out the rest of the pot, loaded it again, and, by the time the machine finished, had mostly got herself under control.

Mostly.

Claire had a break between classes – it couldn't really be called a lunch break, because it fell at ten a.m. and she walked over to the University Centre for coffee. The UC was large and kind of seedy; the carpet was ancient, and the furniture had seen the eighties, at least, and maybe the seventies. It was one large, open atrium filled with couches, chairs, and even – tucked in one corner – a grand piano. Student-activity banners, most badly painted, draped overhead and fluttered in the weak air-conditioning.

Most of the couch groupings were already claimed by students talking or separately studying. Claire had her eye on an open study table near the corner, but she'd have to hurry; there were plenty of people looking for places to settle.

She hurried to the coffee bar at the back of the atrium, and smiled and waved as she spotted Eve behind the espresso machine. Eve waved back, pulled two shots at the same time, and dumped them into steamed milk. The line was about five deep, and Claire had plenty of time to think about what Shane's dad had said. And what he hadn't.

What was he doing there today? Really? Maybe he'd come to fetch Shane, but she wasn't sure. Shane's dad seemed to have a plan, but she had no idea what it was.

Maybe Shane would know, but she didn't want to ask.

Michael. She'd tell Michael everything, as soon as he appeared.

'Large mocha,' Claire said, and dug out the required three-fifty from her jeans pocket. It was a huge expense for her, but she figured it was only right to celebrate

Eve's first day on the job. The cashier – a bored-looking guy who was probably wishing he were anywhere else – took her cash and waved her on to the line for drinks.

She was standing there, thumbing through her English-lit book, when she heard muffled laughter, and then a wet dull thud as a drink tipped over on the counter. She looked up to see a ring of guys standing around a spilt drink, which was dripping off both sides of the counter.

'Hey, zombie chick,' one of them said to Eve, who was standing next to the counter, still pulling shots and very obviously ignoring them. 'Wanna clean that up?'

A muscle fluttered in Eve's jaw, but she silently got a handful of paper towels and began to mop up the mess. Once the counter was clean, she raised the hinged section of the bar and cleaned the floor on both sides.

The boys continued to snigger. 'You missed a spot,' said the one who'd spilt the drink. 'Over there.'

Eve had to bend over to get to the spot where he was pointing. He quickly stepped up behind her and began banging his crotch against her butt. 'Oh, baby!' he said, and they all laughed. *Laughed.* 'You're so fucking hot for a dead girl.'

Eve calmly straightened up, turned around, and stared at him. Not a word. One thing Claire could say for Goth make-up, at least it covered up blushes... She was blushing, furiously, on Eve's behalf. And shaking.

'Excuse me,' Eve finally said, and moved him aside with one hand flat against his chest. She got behind the bar again and slammed down the hatch, took the two espresso shots and dumped them into a fresh cup, stirred, put a lid on it, and put it on the bar. 'Here. On the house.'

The creep reached out, grabbed the cup, and *squeezed.* The top popped off. Coffee went everywhere, splattering Eve, the counter, the floor, the guy holding it. His buddies burst into open laughter when he said, 'Oops. Guess I don't know my own strength.'

Eve looked at the guy at the register, but he just shrugged. She took a deep breath, smiled – not, Claire saw, her normal smile *at all* – and said, 'You ought to see a doctor about that, Bullwinkle. Plus the crotch rash. *Next!* I have a mocha for Claire!' Eve thumped down another cup and vigorously scrubbed the counter.

Claire hurried up. 'Oh my God!' she whispered. 'What do you want me to do? Get somebody?'

'Who?' Eve rolled her eyes. 'It's my first day – it's a little early to run tattling like a girlie girl. Leave it alone, Claire. Just take your coffee and go on. I'll be fine.

I've got a PhD in taking shit from jocks.'

'But Shane? Should I call Shane?'

'Only if you want to be cleaning up blood instead of coffee—'

'Hey, bitch, where's *my* drink?' the guy asked loudly from behind Claire. She felt him crowding up against her a second before he body-slammed her hard against the bar. 'Oops, sorry, little girl, didn't see you there.' He didn't move back. 'Since when do we have kindergarten classes, anyway?'

Her mocha had – of course – tumbled out of her hand and was rolling across the counter, bleeding coffee. Eve caught it and set it back upright. 'Hey!' Claire squirmed to get free; he just kept her pinned.

'Hey! Asshole!' Eve echoed, louder, and pointed a finger over Claire's head, glaring. 'Back off, man, or I call the campus cops.'

'Yeah, they'll really come running.' Still, he backed up enough to let Claire twist away from him, clutching her mocha. He wasn't even looking at her. He was a big guy – Shane-big – with black gelled hair in the latest cool style and fierce blue eyes. A nice face, good lips, high cheekbones. Altogether too pretty for his own good, Claire thought. 'Get me my damn coffee. Some of us have class around here.'

Claire grabbed paper towels and began mopping up the spill on the customer side of the counter, so Eve didn't have to come around. Eve gave her a grateful look and began to pull shots. She assembled the drink in record time, slapped the top on it, and handed it to her tormentor.

Who grinned at her, tasted it, and put it back on the counter. 'Sucks,' he said. 'Keep it.'

He high-fived with his friends, and they all walked away.

'What a *jerk*!' Claire said, and Eve just raised her eyebrows, took the latte, and poured it out down the sink.

'No, he was right, it *did* suck,' she said. 'But then, he paid three bucks for it, so I win. How's the mocha?'

Claire swallowed a mouthful and gave her a thumbs-up. 'I'm sorry. I wish there was something—'

'Gotta fight our own battles, Claire Bear. Go on. I'm sure you've got some kind of studying to do.'

Claire backed away as Eve began to pull another set of drinks; the line continued to queue up in front of the register.

The guy picking up his latte next – a tall, kind of awkward-looking boy with a round face and big brown eyes – made a point of thanking Eve, who dimpled at him and winked. He looked *much* nicer than the hard-bodied jerks who'd just left, although Claire noticed that he was wearing a fraternity shirt.

'Epsilon Epsilon Kappa?' she read out loud. 'EEK?'

He gave her an apologetic smile. 'Yeah, well, it's kind of a joke. Because of the town. You know, creepy.' He blinked and focused on her, and smiled wider. 'I'm Ian, by the way. Ian Jameson. From, ah, Reno.'

'You're a long way from home, Ian Jameson,' Claire

said, and stuck out her hand. He shook it. 'Claire Danvers. From Longview.'

'I'd say you were a short way from home, but everything's far from this place,' he said. 'So, you're a freshman?'

'Yes.' She felt the dreaded blush creeping up again. 'Early admission.'

'Yeah? How early?'

She tried to shrug it off. 'Couple of semesters. No biggie.'

'What's your major?' Ian took the top off his coffee and blew on it to cool it down, then took a sip. 'Thanks again, by the way, this is really good.'

'No problem,' Eve said. She sounded much more cheerful now, and gave the sorority girls their skinny-half-caff-no-sugar lattes with a sunny, slightly manic grin.

Nobody had actually bothered to ask Claire what her major was before. Of course, it was customary for a freshman to change three or four times before settling on something, but Claire had always been pretty definite. 'Physics.'

'Really?' Ian blinked. 'Wow. That's pretty intense. You must be good at maths.'

She shrugged. 'I guess.' Modesty in action; she'd never failed to land an A, ever.

'Gonna transfer out of here, I suppose. I mean, a degree in physics from Nowhere U isn't going to do you all that much good, right?'

'I'm hoping for MIT,' Claire said. 'What about you?'

Ian shook his head. 'CE. Civil engineering. Yeah, I've got to take physics, but no way would I volunteer to take *more*. And I've got one more semester. Then I transfer out to UT Austin.'

A lot of students transferred out to the University of Texas; it was a major school for just about everything. Claire nodded. She'd considered it herself, but...MIT? Caltech? If she had a chance, she'd take it.

'So...what's EEK? A professional fraternity?' Because there were some on campus; you paid your dues and went to some meetings and put it on your résumé later.

'It's a bunch of guys who like to party, really.' Ian looked embarrassed. 'I'm in it because I've got a couple of friends...anyway, they do throw this really cool party every year – it's a big bash. It's called the Dead Girls' Dance. All zombie-freaky scary-movie stuff.' He glanced over at Eve, who was steaming milk. 'Your friend there would fit right in as is. Most people wear costumes, though.'

Was he asking her out? No, he couldn't be. For one thing, she'd just met him. For another...well, *nobody* ever asked her out. It just didn't happen.

'It sounds neat,' Claire said, and thought, *I just used the word* neat *in a conversation with a cute boy, and I should walk away now and shoot myself.*

'It's at the EEK frat house tomorrow night. Listen, if you give me your number, I can text you the details...'

'Um...sure.' Nobody had *ever* asked before. She

stumbled over the digits; he keyed it into his cell phone and smiled at her. A nice smile. A really nice smile, actually. 'Um, I don't know if I can come, though.'

'Well, if you can, you'd save my life. We geeks have to stick together while everybody else goes nuts, right? See you there tomorrow night at eight?'

'Right,' she echoed. 'Um...sure. I'll be there. Thanks. Um, Ian, right?'

'Ian.'

'Claire,' she said, and pointed at herself. 'Oh. Did I already say that?'

He laughed and walked away, sipping his latte.

It was only when he did that she realised she'd just agreed to go out on a date. An actual *date*. With a boy who *was not Shane*. How had that happened? She'd meant only to be nice, because he seemed like an OK guy, and then he'd been all charming, especially by comparison with the other guys...

She had a date.

With a boy who was not Shane.

Not good.

'Hey,' Eve said, and motioned her closer. 'So, what was that? Is he giving you a hard time or what?'

'Ummm...' Claire's mind went blank. 'No. He just... Never mind.'

Eve's eyes turned from concerned to shrewd. 'He hitting on you?'

Claire settled for a shrug. She had no idea how to tell, actually. 'I think he was just being nice.'

'Guys aren't nice,' Eve said. 'What did you tell him you'd do?'

OK, that was scary, how quickly she'd nailed it. Claire shifted her weight uncomfortably, and fiddled with her heavy backpack. 'Maybe I said I might go to this party. But it totally wasn't a date.'

'Oh, totally not,' Eve agreed. And rolled her eyes. 'Next up! Vanilla latte!...which totally describes you, by the way.'

'I'll, um, be over there,' Claire said. 'Studying.'

Eve might have wanted to stop her, but the drinks kept coming, and Claire was able to fade away and go in search of her study table. Which, miraculously, was still unoccupied. She thunked down her backpack on the battered wood and sat, sipping her mocha. The UC seemed safer than most places in Morganville... Any place packed with people reading couldn't be that bad.

Almost like a real university.

Claire was reading ahead in her history text when a shadow fell over the page. She looked up and saw a girl she slightly knew from her old dorm, Howard Hall – a freshman, like herself. Lisa? Lesley? Something like that.

'Hey,' the girl said. Claire nodded towards the empty chair opposite her, but Lisa/Lesley didn't sit. 'That Goth at the coffee bar, the one who used to work at Common Grounds – is she your friend?'

Word got around fast. Claire nodded again.

'Might want to keep her from getting herself killed,

then,' Lisa/Lesley said. ''Cause she's just pulled the pin from the Monica grenade over at the counter.'

Claire winced and closed her book. She checked her watch; well, it was probably close to time to leave for class anyway. It was bad, and shallow, but she wished that Lisa/Lesley had decided *not* to do her good deed of the day. It would have been nice to leave without another crisis.

Claire repacked her book bag and walked back towards the coffee bar. *I'm just going to tell her goodbye*, she thought. *No agenda here at all. Totally staying out of it.*

Monica, Gina, and Jennifer were leaning on the bar, blocking coffee pickup. The counter was all that separated them from Eve, who was steadily ignoring them.

'Hey, Walking Dead, I'm talking to you,' Monica was saying. 'Is it true your brother tried to kill you?'

'Yeah, was that before or after he tried to do you?' Hand gestures and everything. Wow, that was low even for Jennifer.

'Tried?' Gina snickered. 'That's not what *I* heard. I heard they were getting it on all through high school. No wonder they both turned out to be freaks.'

Eve's face was a still white mask, but her eyes…she looked crazy. In control, but just barely. Her hands were steady as she pulled espresso shots and mixed drinks; she thumped the finished products down on the counter, three across, and said, 'If you don't go away, I'm going to call my manager.'

'Ooooh,' Monica said. 'Your *manager*. Wow, I'm terrified. You think some barely-over-minimum-wage brain donor stupid enough to work *here* is going to scare me? Do you?' She leant to the side, trying to catch Eve's eyes. 'I'm talking to you, freak face.'

Gina noticed Claire standing a few feet away, and drew Monica's attention with a hand on her shoulder. 'Two freaks for one,' she said. 'They must be having some kind of special.'

'Claire.' Monica's smile widened. 'Sure, why not? You angry I'm ragging on your little lesbo girlfriend?'

'Make up your mind,' Claire said. Her voice sounded low and kind of cool, actually. Maybe it was easier doing this here in public, where she felt more comfortable. Or maybe she was actually getting used to facing down Monica. 'Are we gay, or did she sleep with her brother? 'Cause you know, kind of not making much sense.'

Monica actually *blinked.* Logic wasn't her strong suit, anyway. Claire could almost see the *Don't confuse me with facts* flicker across her brain. 'You laughing at me?'

'Yeah,' Claire said. 'A little.'

Monica smiled. A big, genuine smile. 'How about that?' she said. 'Claire's grown a pair. I guess having a badass Protector hanging over your shoulder must be a real comfort.' She threw a glance at Eve. 'But it won't last. My family means something around here. You freaks are just temporary. And...sad.'

She flipped her hair back over her shoulders, picked

up her latte, and walked away. Guys' heads turned as she passed, with Gina and Jennifer in a flying-V formation behind her.

'Huh,' Eve said as she wiped down the machines with maybe a little bit more force than was necessary. 'She doesn't usually back down that easily.'

'Maybe she's got class.'

Eve snorted. 'Trust me,' she said. 'That girl's got no class at all.'

'How weird is it that we have our own personal cop limo service?' Eve asked. She and Claire were standing on the sidewalk in front of the UC, and the campus looked mostly deserted – it was seven o'clock, and the sky had darkened to a deep twilight. There were even a few premature stars out already. The sun had just gone down, and there was still a fiery orange and yellow glow on the western horizon. 'I mean, it's not like I don't have a car. I can drive.'

'I don't think they'll keep it up,' Claire offered. 'I mean, it's just a special thing. Until they catch…whoever killed that girl.'

Eve sighed and didn't answer. A blue car turned and cruised around the circular drive, pulling to a halt in front of them. Joe Hess was driving, and Travis Lowe got out and opened the back door with a dumb-looking overdone bow. It was kind of cute, actually. Claire climbed in and slid over, and Eve got in next to her.

'Hello, girls,' Hess said, and turned to look back at

them. He had dark circles under his eyes, and he seemed like he hadn't slept at all. 'Thanks for the coffee.'

Claire and Eve looked at each other. 'Sorry,' Eve said. 'I always smell like coffee; it's the perfume of the barista. I didn't actually bring any for you. But if you want, I'll go back and—'

'No way,' Lowe said as he got into the shotgun seat. 'Dark already. Let's get you gals home. Joe and me, we'll grab some later.'

'Thank you,' Claire said. 'For the ride.'

Neither of the cops answered. Detective Hess drove the other half of the circle, turned out onto the campus main drag, and within two blocks was off campus and into the dark Morganville night. Most shops were tightly closed already. As they passed Common Grounds, Claire and Eve both looked. It was full, of course, an oasis of light in the dark, empty street. No sign of Oliver. No sign of Shane's dad, either, which made Claire's conscience twinge hard. *I need to tell Shane. Soon.* She didn't see how blabbing it to Eve would help, except to make Eve even more worried. And from the pensive way Eve was staring out into the dark, there was enough of that going on already.

They were only one block from the house when a sleek black car – with tail fins, like a shark – pulled in front of them and, with shocking speed, turned sideways. Hess jammed on the brakes, and the sound of screeching tyres was like a banshee's wail. He didn't hit the other car...

quite. Claire thumped back against the vinyl upholstery, panting from shock, and exchanged a wide-eyed look with Eve.

In the front seat, Hess and Lowe were doing the same things. Only with a full helping of grim, and a side of tense.

'What's happening?' Eve asked, and leant forward. 'Detectives?'

'You stay here,' Hess said, and popped his door.

'Trav. Stay with them.'

'Joe—'

'I'll be fine.' He got out, slammed the door, and walked towards the other car. A dark-tinted window rolled down, and in the glare of the headlights, Claire saw a dead-pale face she recognised.

'Hans,' she whispered. The vampire detective. She looked at Detective Lowe, and saw something strange; he had his gun out, held in his lap. And a cross in his left hand. 'Right? It's Hans.'

'You girls stay put,' Lowe said. His eyes didn't move from the scene playing out in front of him. 'Just a routine check.'

Claire didn't know much about police procedure, but she was pretty sure it wasn't routine for one cop to block another one off in the road, right? Not even here. And it wasn't routine procedure for a detective to have his gun out, either.

Whatever conversation Hess was having, it wasn't making him happy. It was also short. He shook his head a couple of times and then finally nodded.

As he walked back to the car, Claire had a real bad feeling. His expression was too serious and too angry for it to be good news. *Shane. Oh God, maybe it's about Shane – something's happened to Shane...*

Hess opened the back door – Claire's side – and leant in. 'Girls,' he said. 'You're going to have to come with me.'

'The hell!' Lowe barked. 'I thought we were taking them home.'

'Change of plans,' Hess said. He was trying not to look angry, or worried, but Claire could still see it in his eyes. 'You're wanted downtown, girls. I'll come with you. Trav, I need you to take the car in.'

The two men exchanged a long look, and then Lowe let out a slow breath. 'Right,' he said. 'Sure. You look after them.'

'You know I will.'

Claire got out of the car, feeling more exposed and vulnerable even than usual. Hess was right there, big and comforting, but still...she saw Hans's eyes on her, and it made her feel cold.

His partner, Gretchen, got out of the passenger side and came around to open the back door. 'In,' she snapped. Claire swallowed hard and moved forward, but Eve got there first, sliding inside and all the way across.

Hess followed Claire. When Gretchen slammed the door, the three of them barely fit in the back seat.

'You all keep your mouths shut until you're asked to speak,' Hans said, and put the car in gear as Gretchen got back in. He turned the big car with a squeal of warm rubber and accelerated fast down the street.

They passed 716 Lot Street. All the lights were on, and the door was open, and someone was standing in the doorway, watching them roar by. It was too quick to tell whether it was Shane or Michael, but Claire hoped it was Shane.

She hoped that if something happened, she at least had got to see him before the end.

'I thought we were going to the police station,' Eve whispered as the car took some turns and wound through the confusing maze of streets.

'We're not?' Claire whispered back.

'Passed it back there. I guess we're going somewhere else.' Eve sounded flat-out scared, and when Claire reached over, she found Eve's hand was cold and shaking. They held on to each other as the car made more turns, and then slowed for some kind of barricade. 'Oh *God*. We're going to the square.'

'The square?'

'Founder's Square. It's, like, vamptown this time of night.' Eve swallowed and gripped Claire's hand more tightly. 'I'm trying to think of any way this could be a good thing.'

'Hush,' Detective Hess said quietly. 'You're OK. Trust me.'

Claire did. She just didn't trust the two vampire

detectives sitting in the front seat, who were obviously more in charge.

The barricade lifted. Hans drove them through, brought the big car to a stop in an unlit parking lot, and turned to look at them. Claire first, then Eve. Hess, last of all.

Gretchen turned, too. She was smiling.

'Something we want you to see,' Hans said. Gretchen exited the car and opened the back door on Eve's side. 'Out.'

They clambered out into the cooling night air. The moon was up, casting a sickly yellow glow that didn't illuminate much. The dark seemed very deep, even though there was still some indigo lining the horizon. Not even really full night yet...

A cold, strong hand closed over Claire's upper arm. She squeaked breathlessly, and heard Eve making a sound of surprise, too. Gretchen had somehow got between them, holding them both by the arms.

Hans threw a look at Detective Hess. 'Stay with the car,' he said.

'I'm coming with the girls.'

'You're taking orders like a good little neutral,' Hans said. 'Unless you want to lose that status for both you and your partner. This isn't some minor incident. This has the attention of the Elders. If the girls don't cause trouble, they'll come back unharmed, but *you stay here*.'

Gretchen said, 'No, Hans. Let him come. It'll be good for him to attend.'

Hans frowned at her, then shrugged. 'Fine. But get in the way, Hess, and you're meat.'

Gretchen hustled the girls forward.

'What's going on?' Eve asked. Neither of the vampires answered. Claire turned her head and saw that Hess was behind them, but somehow, that didn't give her all that much comfort. Gretchen frog-marched them around the corner of a blank-faced brick building, and into...

A park.

Claire blinked, surprised, because this was actually very...nice. Green grass, big shady trees rustling in the darkness. There were lights, too, strung through the tree branches and shining on flowers and bushes and walking paths.

The area that bordered the park was more alive than anything she'd seen yet in Morganville. Where the stores bordering the campus were run-down and dingy, the ones facing the square were shining, polished, beautifully maintained. Beautiful in an old-world kind of way, all stone and marble and pillars. There were gargoyles, too, built onto the roofs as drain spouts.

It looked like pictures Claire had seen of old European towns, only...nicer.

Every business facing the square was open. Two outdoor restaurants were serving, and the smell of roasting meats and fresh bread made Claire's mouth water. All she'd really had for the day was coffee, and that was long gone.

And then she remembered what Eve had said. If downtown at night was vamptown, why the restaurants?

She knew when they passed close to one of them. There were groups dining, mixed vampire and human; the vampires had plates of food and were eating just as enthusiastically as the humans. 'You eat!' Claire blurted, astonished. Gretchen glanced at her with those cold, alien eyes.

'Of course,' she said. 'It provides us no nutrition, but the taste is still attractive. Why? You'll find that poisons will do you no good, if you're searching for a way to kill us.'

Claire hadn't even thought that far, actually. She was just...weirdly intrigued.

The stores they passed were incredible. Jewellers, with displays of gems and gold. Book dealers carrying ancient volumes as well as new best sellers. Clothing stores, lots of them, with tasteful and expensive styles. It was like a rich neighbourhood from a major city, like Dallas or Houston or Austin, had been transplanted directly in.

Weird.

And all the shoppers were vampires. In fact, there were lots of them around, more than Claire had ever imagined lived in Morganville; the more she saw, the more scared she felt. They were staring at her and Eve like the girls were cows on the way to the slaughterhouse, and she felt horribly alone. *I want to go home. I swear, if you let me get out of this, I'll move back with Mom and Dad. I'll never leave again...*

Gretchen steered them towards a black marble building with gold lettering at the top. ELDERS' COUNCIL, it said.

'It's OK,' Hess said quietly from behind them. 'You'll be OK, girls. Just cooperate. If they ask questions, tell the truth.'

Claire barely felt her feet on the polished black marble steps. It was a little like moving in a dream, helpless and numb, but Gretchen's grip on her arm was all too real. And painful. Ouch. Bruises later.

Hans opened the big polished door, and they went inside.

Of all the things Claire expected to see, she somehow hadn't expected a television set, but there one was, tuned to a twenty-four-hour news channel showing flickering pictures of a war – bombs exploding, soldiers shooting. And standing in front of it, arms folded, was Oliver. He wasn't wearing his hippie-dippie Coffee Shop Guy clothes; he was wearing a suit, black, tailored, and sharp as a knife. His greying hair had been pulled back into a ponytail, and he was wearing a tie. No, not a tie, exactly. Kind of like a scarf, with a diamond pin through it to hold it in place. Maybe it had been fashionable when Oliver was younger.

'Some things never change,' he said, staring at the television. 'People continue to kill over the stupidest possible excuses. And they call *us* monsters.'

On the last word, his gaze snapped to Claire, and she shivered. Oliver had nice eyes, but somehow, they scared her even more than Gretchen's ice-cold ones. Maybe it was because she still wanted to like him, no matter what he'd done. *He killed Michael!* she reminded herself. Well, he'd mostly killed him, anyway.

'Hello,' Oliver said to her, and nodded. He moved his stare to Eve. 'Eve. We've missed you at the shop.'

'B—' Eve swallowed what she'd been about to say, which Claire was ninety-nine per cent sure was *Bite me*. 'Thanks.' Which for Eve was amazingly cautious. If anybody had been shocked and angry about Oliver turning out vampire, it had been Eve.

Oliver nodded and walked across the large, empty room – empty except for the silently playing television and thick plush maroon carpet – and opened a set of double doors. He wasn't the doorman; he walked on through and into the next room. Gretchen pushed Claire and Eve forward. The carpet was squishy soft under Claire's feet, and she caught the scent of fading flowers. Roses. Lots of roses.

It hit her full force when they entered the next room, which was a big circular place with burgundy velvet curtains all around, with pillars in between. A low-key chandelier cast a medium-bright glow. Same carpet, but this room had furniture – chairs laid out in neat rows, in three sections with aisles between.

It took Claire a second to realise that she was walking into a *funeral parlour*. When she did, she stopped, and stumbled as Gretchen continued to drag her relentlessly onward, past the rows of empty folding chairs, all the way to the front, where Oliver was standing near another velvet curtain.

'Sir,' Joe Hess said, coming out from behind Claire and Eve. 'I'm Detective Hess.'

Oliver nodded. 'I know you.'

'Shouldn't there be others present here for this?' The tension in Hess's voice, and his body, warned Claire that Oliver's interrogating them on his own was a very bad thing.

'There are others present, Detective Hess,' said a light, cool voice from the far corner of the room, which Claire could have *sworn* was empty one second before.

She gasped and looked, and there was Amelie, standing there as if she'd been carved in stone before the building came up around her. And her bodyguards – or servants – were standing in a group near her. She'd brought four of them. Claire wondered if that was a signal of how much trouble she and Eve were in.

'There is a third coming,' Amelie said, and settled herself in a chair as if it were a golden throne. She was wearing black, like Oliver, but her attire was a long elegant suede skirt suit, with a severe white shirt under the tailored jacket. She crossed her legs, which were pale and perfect, and folded her hands in her lap.

Oliver wasn't looking happy. 'Who are we waiting for?' he asked.

'You know the laws, Oliver, even if you choose to find ways to cheat them,' Amelie said. 'We are waiting for Mr Morrell.'

They didn't have to wait long; in a matter of less than a minute, Claire heard voices coming from the anteroom outside, and a jingle of keys. She'd never seen the man who walked in, flanked by two uniformed cops, but she knew one of the cops: Richard Morrell, Monica's brother. So the portly, balding man with the smug expression was probably her dad.

The mayor of Morganville.

He was dressed in a suit, too – blue, pin-striped, with wide lapels. Kind of pimpish, really, and the pants were a little too long. He had too many rings on his fingers, all in gold, and he was smiling.

'Oliver,' he said cheerfully. The smile vanished fast when he spotted Amelie sitting so quietly off to the side, with her entourage. His face composed itself into something a whole lot more...respectful. 'Founder.'

'Mayor.' She nodded to him. 'Good. We can begin.'

Gretchen let go of Claire's arm. She winced at the returning flow of blood to her tingling hand, and rubbed at the place where Gretchen had been gripping her. Yeah, that was going to be a bruise. Definitely. She risked a look at Eve, who was doing the same thing. Eve looked dead scared.

Oliver reached over and pulled a hidden cord, and the burgundy velvet curtain behind him opened.

There was a body lying on the marble slab, surrounded by rich red roses, bunches of them in floor vases. The corpse looked blue-white, rubbery, and utterly, horribly *dead*. Claire felt a cloud creep over her, heard a buzzing in her ears, and nearly collapsed, but somehow she managed not to faint.

'Oh my God,' Eve whispered, and brought both hands to her mouth.

'It's Brandon,' Claire said, and looked at Oliver. 'It's Brandon, right?' Because that cold, white face didn't look human anymore, and she couldn't match it up to the living person – vampire – she'd feared. The one who'd threatened her, chased her home, nearly killed her and Eve...

Oliver nodded. He pulled back the velvet covering Brandon from the neck down, revealing black open wounds. Some of them still smoked. Claire caught the smell of cooking meat, and this time, her knees buckled. Detective Hess caught her arm and steadied her.

'He was tortured,' Oliver said. He sounded neutral – disinterested, even. 'It took a long time. Someone very much enjoyed this. Almost as if there was a...personal agenda at work.'

Mayor Morrell motioned his son forward. Richard wasn't nearly the psycho his sister was. In fact, Claire kind of liked him, as much as she could like anybody from his family who worked for vampires. He seemed almost fair.

Richard examined the wounds in Brandon's body. He actually *touched* them, which made Claire throw up in her head, if not actually through her mouth. 'Looks like some kind of weapon straight to the heart. Probably a stake,' Richard said, and looked up at his father. 'Whoever did this was serious. This wasn't just random; this was done slowly. I don't know what they wanted out of him, but whatever it was, they probably got it. I can see shadows of wounds that closed over before he died. That's hours, at least.'

Silence. Deep, dark silence. Richard straightened up and glanced at Claire and Eve. If he recognised them, he gave no sign. 'These two girls have something to do with it?'

'Perhaps,' Oliver said. Claire didn't see him move, but all of a sudden he was right in front of her, looking down. 'Perhaps they know something. You didn't like Brandon very much, did you, Claire?'

'I—' She didn't know what to say. *Don't lie*, Hess had said. Did the vamps have some kind of lie detector power? Maybe even mind-reading? 'No, I didn't like him. But I wouldn't want to see this happen to anybody.' *Not even you.* She said that to herself, though.

He had such kind eyes. That was the horrible thing about him, this warm feeling that she could trust him, *should* trust him, that somehow she was letting him down by not—

'Don't,' Eve said sharply, and pinched her arm. Claire yelped and looked at her. 'Don't look him in the eye.'

'Eve,' Oliver sighed. 'I'm very disappointed in you. Don't you understand that it's my responsibility, as Brandon's Patron, to get to the bottom of this? To find the ones responsible? You're not the innocent Claire may be; you know the penalties for killing one of us. And you know the lengths to which we'll go to find out the truth. If I can get it from her without pain, don't you want me to do that?'

Eve didn't answer. She kept her eyes focused somewhere around the middle of his chest. 'I think you'll do whatever you want,' she said grimly. 'Just like vamps always do. You didn't ask me, but I'm glad Brandon's dead. And I'm glad he suffered, too. However much it was, it wasn't enough.'

That was when Nice Oliver vanished. Just…gone. Claire saw a flicker of movement, nothing more, and then he had hold of Eve's black-dyed hair and he was yanking her head back at a painful angle.

And there was nothing human in his eyes. Unless pure, flaming rage was human.

'Oh,' he breathed into Eve's ear. 'Thank you for saying that. Now I don't have to be so careful anymore.'

Detective Hess stepped forward, fists clenched; Richard Morrell got in his way. 'Easy, Joe,' he said. 'It's under control.'

Didn't look that way to Claire. She was breathing too fast, feeling faint again, and she could see Eve's knees buckling. The menace in the room – the body on the table – it was all just…terrifying.

Shane's dad did that. Claire felt sick and even more terrified once she had the thought, because now somehow she had to keep it to herself.

And she knew they were going to ask.

Oliver sniffed at Eve's exposed neck. 'You've been working at a coffee shop,' he said. 'On campus, I suppose. Funny. I wasn't asked for any references.'

'Let go,' Eve said faintly.

'Oh, I can't do that. It makes it harder to hurt you.' Oliver smiled, then opened his mouth, and his fangs – snake fangs, deadly sharp – snapped down into place. They weren't like teeth, really; they were more like polished bone, and they looked *strong*.

He licked Eve's neck, right over the pulse.

'Oh God,' she whispered. 'Please don't do that. Please don't let him do that.'

'Ask the girl a question, Oliver. We don't have time for your hobbies.' Mayor Morrell said it in a bored tone, like all of this was keeping him from something more important. He inspected his manicure and buffed his fingernails against his suit jacket. 'Let's move this train down the track.'

Amelie wasn't saying or doing *anything*.

'I'm Protected,' Eve said. 'You can't hurt me.' She didn't sound very confident, though, and Claire looked at Amelie, sitting in the front row of chairs, studying the scene closely, as if it was all some show put on for her benefit. Her expression was polite, but cool.

Please help, Claire thought. Amelie's pale gold eyebrow raised just slightly. *Can you hear me?*

If she could, Amelie gave no other sign. She simply sat, calm as Buddha.

'Let's just say that Amelie and I have an understanding in matters such as this,' Oliver said. 'And Eve, love, that understanding is that I can use any methods to pursue humans who break the peace. Regardless of Protection. Regardless of *who* that Protection is from. Now, I think we should have a little talk about your home invaders.'

'Our...what?' Eve was struggling not to meet his eyes, but he was so close, it was almost impossible to avoid him. 'I don't know who they were.'

'You don't. You've very sure about that,' he said. His voice had dropped to a low, lethal whisper, and Claire tried to think of something to say, something to do, that would help Eve. Because clearly, Eve wasn't going to help herself, and she couldn't just stand by and see her...hurt. She *couldn't*.

'I know,' she said, and she felt everyone shift their collective attention onto her. Scary. Claire cleared her throat. 'They were bikers.'

'Bikers.' Oliver let go of Eve's hair and turned towards Claire. 'I see. You're attempting to distract me with the obvious, and, Claire, that is not a good idea. Not a good idea at all. We know all that, you see. We know when they came to town. We even know who called them.'

Claire felt all the blood drain from her head. Her stomach flipped over, and kept flipping, and Oliver walked away from Eve and yanked another cord.

Another curtain slid aside, next to Brandon's body.

Two men, on their knees, bound and gagged and held in place by really scary-looking vampires. One of the prisoners was a biker.

Shane was the other.

Claire screamed.

CHAPTER EIGHT

In the end, they sat her down in a chair and had Gretchen hold her down with those strong, iron-hard hands pressing on her shoulders. Claire continued to struggle, but fear and shock were winning out over anger. And Shane wasn't moving. He was watching her, but he couldn't say anything around the gag, and if Shane wasn't struggling, maybe there wasn't anything to be gained from it.

Eve spun around and slapped Oliver. An open-hand, hard smack that echoed like a gunshot off of all the marble in the room. There was a collective intake of breath. 'You son of a bitch!' she spit. 'Let Shane go! He has nothing to do with this!'

'Really.' A flat word, not even really a question. Unlike a human's, Oliver's face didn't show any sign of a handprint from the slap, and it had definitely been hard enough. He barely looked as if he'd felt it at all.

'Sit down, Eve, while I tell you the facts of your rather pathetic life.'

She didn't. Oliver put his hand flat on her chest, right at the notch of her collarbone, and shoved. Eve sprawled in a chair, glaring at him.

'Detective Hess,' Oliver said. 'I suggest you explain to my dear ex-employee exactly what she risks the next time she touches me in anger. Or, come to think of it, touches me at all.'

Hess was already moving, sitting in the chair beside Eve and leaning towards her. He whispered to her, urgent words that Claire couldn't catch. Eve shook her head violently. A trickle of sweat ran from her messy hair down the side of her face, making a flesh-coloured track through the white make-up.

'Now,' Oliver continued once Hess stopped, and Eve was sitting still. 'We're not technological idiots, Eve. And we do own the telephone providers in this area, particularly the cell phone providers. Shane placed a call from your home to a number that, much to our surprise, we found to be assigned to a device we located on his friend Mr Wallace.' Oliver pointed to the biker. 'GPS is a marvellous invention, by the way. We're quite grateful for all the hard work humanity has put into keeping track of itself. It makes finding people so much easier than it used to be in the old days.'

'Shane didn't do anything,' Claire said. 'Please. You have to let him go.'

'Shane was found at the crime scene,' Oliver said.

'With Brandon's body. And I hardly think we can say he wasn't involved, if he was friendly enough with Mr Wallace to be exchanging telephone calls.'

'No, he didn't—!'

Oliver slapped her. She never saw it coming, just felt the impact and saw red for a second. Her whole body shook with the force of how much she wanted to hit him back, and she felt the stinging imprint of his hand on her cheek like a brand.

'You see, Eve?' Oliver asked. 'An eye for an eye. Of course, my interpretation is a bit free of the Scriptures.'

Shane was screaming around his gag, and now he was fighting, but the vampires were holding him down on his knees without breaking a sweat. Eve's eyes were huge and dark, and Hess was holding her down in the chair as she struggled to come after Oliver.

Don't, Claire thought wildly. Because her friends had just told Oliver exactly what he wanted to know: that hurting her would get something out of them.

'Oliver,' Amelie said. Her voice was soft and very gentle. 'Is there a question you are posing to the children? Or are you merely indulging yourself? You say you already know the boy called this man. What more information do you need?'

'I want to know where his father has gone,' Oliver said. 'One of them knows.'

'The girls?' Amelie shook her head. 'It seems unlikely that someone like Mr Collins would trust in either of them.'

'The boy knows, then.'

'Possibly.' She tapped her lips with one pale finger. 'Yet somehow, I doubt he will tell you. And there is no need for any cruelty to discover the truth, I believe.'

'Meaning?' Oliver turned fully towards her, crossing his arms.

'Meaning that he will come to us, Oliver, as you very well know. In order to save the boy from the consequences of his actions.'

'So you withdraw your Protection from the boy?'

Amelie looked at the body lying on the slab. After a moment of silence, she rose gracefully and walked to what was left of Brandon, trailed ghost-white fingers over his distorted face, and said, 'He was born before King John, did you know that? Born a prince. All those years, ending. I grieve for the loss of all that he saw that we will never know. All the memories that can never enrich us.'

'Amelie.' Oliver sounded impatient. 'We can't allow his killers to run free. You know that.'

'He was yours, Oliver. You might spare a moment for his loss before you run baying after blood.'

Amelie's back was to him, so she couldn't have seen it, but Claire did: there was hate in Oliver's eyes, hate twisting his face. He got it under control before Amelie turned towards him.

'Brandon had his flaws,' Oliver said. 'Of all of us, he was the one who enjoyed the hunt the most. I don't think he ever came to terms with the rules of Morganville. But it's those rules we have to observe now. By sentencing these criminals.'

Sentencing? What about a trial? Claire started to ask, but a cold hand clapped over her mouth from behind, and she looked up to see Gretchen bending over her, fangs out, holding a hushing finger to her own mouth. Eve was likewise gagged by Hans. Next to them, Detective Hess folded his arms and looked deeply troubled, but he didn't speak.

Amelie looked at Oliver, then past him, at Shane.

'I warned you,' she said quietly. 'My Protection can only extend to you so far. You betrayed my trust, Shane. For the sake of kindness, I will not break faith with your friends; they remain under my Protection.' She shifted her pale gaze to Oliver, and gave him a slow, regal incline of her head. 'He is yours. I withdraw Protection.'

Claire screamed out a protest, but it was lost against the gag of Gretchen's hand. Amelie bent over and placed a kiss on Brandon's waxy forehead.

'Goodbye, child,' she said. 'Flawed as you were, you were still one of the eternal. We won't forget.'

Claire heard someone yell outside the room, and Amelie whipped around so quickly that she was a blur, then *moved*...and something hit the marble pillar next to where she'd been and exploded with a sharp popping sound.

A bottle. Claire smelt gas, and then heard a thick, whooshing sound.

And then the curtains exploded into flame.

Amelie snarled, bone-white and utterly not *people*, all of a sudden, and then she was dragged out of the way and down, with a moving bunker of bodyguards crowding around her. Gunfire exploded in the room, and somebody – Detective Hess? – shoved Claire forward to the carpet and covered her, too. Eve was down, too, curled into a protective ball, her black-fingernailed hands covering her head.

And then, there was fighting – grunts and smacks and wood being thrown against walls and smashed during struggles. Claire couldn't get any sense of what was going on, except that it was brutal and it was over fast, and when the choking fog of smoke began to clear, Hess finally backed off and let her sit up.

There were two men dead in the entrance of the room. Big guys, in leather. There was one still moving.

Amelie pushed aside her bodyguards and stalked past Claire as if she didn't exist. She glided down the aisle and to the one biker still feebly trying to crawl away. He was trailing a dark streak on the maroon carpet. Claire got slowly to her feet, grateful for Detective Hess's arm around her, and exchanged a look of sheer horror with Eve, on his other side.

Amelie never got to the biker. Oliver was there ahead of her, dragging the wounded man up and, before Claire could blink, snapping his neck with a dry sound.

The body dropped to the carpet with a limp thump.

Claire turned and hid her face against Hess's jacket, trying to control a surge of nausea.

When she looked back, Amelie was staring at Oliver. He was staring right back. 'No point in taking chances,' he said, and gave her a slow, full smile. 'He might have killed you, Amelie.'

'Yes,' she said softly. 'And that wouldn't have been in anyone's best interests, would it, Oliver? How fortunate I am that you were here to...save me.'

She didn't move or gesture, but her bodyguards swarmed and surrounded her, and the whole mass of them moved out, walking around (or over) the dead men.

Oliver watched her go, then turned back to sweep a glare around the entire room, stopping on Shane.

'Your father thinks he can act without consequences, I see,' he said. 'How sad for you. Put these two where they belong. In cages.'

The biker and Shane were pulled to their knees and dragged off, behind the curtains. Claire lunged forward, but Gretchen grabbed her and put her hand over Claire's mouth. Claire winced as her arm was twisted up behind her back, and she realised she was crying, unable to breathe for the pressure of the hand on her mouth and the stuffiness building up in her nose.

Eve wasn't crying. Eve was staring at Oliver, and even when Detective Hess let go of her, she didn't move.

'What are you going to do to them?' she asked. She sounded unnaturally calm.

'You know the laws,' Oliver said. 'Don't you, Eve?'

'You can't. Shane had nothing to do with this.'

Oliver shook his head. 'I won't debate my judgement with you. Mayor? You'll sign the papers? If you're done cowering, that is.'

The mayor had been down in a defensive crouch behind an urn; he got up now, looking flushed and angry. 'Of course I'll sign,' he said. 'The nerve of these bastards! Striking *here?* Threatening—'

'Yes, very traumatic,' Oliver said. 'The papers.'

'I brought a notary. It'll be all nice and legal.'

Gretchen let go of Claire, sensing her will to fight was trickling away. 'Legal?' Claire gasped. 'But...there hasn't even been a *trial*! What about a jury?'

'He had a jury,' Detective Hess told her. His tone was gentle, but what he was saying was harsh. 'A jury of the victim's peers. That's the way the law works here. Same for humans. If a vampire ever got brought up on murder charges, it would be humans deciding whether he lived or died.'

'Except no vampire has ever been brought up on charges,' Eve said. She looked nearly cold and pale enough to be a vampire herself. 'Or ever will. Don't kid yourself, Joe. It's only the humans who get the sharp end of justice around here.' She looked at the dead guys lying on the carpet at the entrance to the room. 'Scared the shit out of you, though, didn't they?'

'Don't flatter them. They had no hope of succeeding,'

Oliver said. He looked at Hans. 'I have no further use for these two.'

'Wait! I want to talk to Shane!' Claire yelled. Gretchen propelled her towards the exit with a shove. It was move, or fall over the dead, bloody bodies.

Claire moved. Behind her, she heard Eve doing the same.

She blinked away tears, wiped angrily at her face and nose, and tried to think what to do next. *Shane's dad*, she thought. *Shane's dad will save him*. Although, of course, the dead guys she was stepping over indicated that rescue had already been attempted, and that hadn't gone so well. Besides, Shane's dad wasn't here. He hadn't stuck around when Shane got caught. Maybe he didn't care. Maybe nobody cared but her.

'Easy,' Detective Hess said, and stepped in beside her to take her by the elbow. He managed to make it feel like escorting, instead of arresting. 'There's still time. The law says that the convicts have to be displayed on the square for two nights so that everyone can see them. They'll be in cages, so they'll be safe enough. It's not the Ritz, but it keeps Brandon's friends from ripping them apart without due process.'

'How—' Claire's throat closed up on her. She cleared it and tried again. 'How are they going to—?'

Hess patted her hand. He looked tired and worried and grim. 'You won't be here when it happens,' he said. 'So don't think about it. If you want to talk to him, you can. They're putting them in cages now, at the centre of the park.'

'Oliver said take them back,' Gretchen said from behind them. Hess shrugged.

'Well, he didn't say when, did he?'

The Founder's Park was a large circle, with walkways like spokes in a wheel, all leading to the centre.

And at the centre were two cages. Cells just big enough for a man to stand up, not wide enough to stretch out. Shane would have to sleep sitting up, if he slept, or curled in a foetal position.

He was sitting, knees up, head resting on his arms, when Eve and Claire arrived. The biker was yelling and rattling his bars. Not Shane. He was...quiet.

'Shane!' Claire almost flew across the open space, grabbed the cold iron bars in both hands, and pressed her face between them. 'Shane!'

He looked up. His eyes were red, but he wasn't crying. At least, not now. He managed to move around in the small, cramped cage until he was sitting closer to her, and reached through the bars to lay his hand against her cheek, stroking it with his thumb. It was the cheek that Oliver had slapped, she realised. She wondered if it was still red.

'I'm sorry,' Shane said. 'My dad... I had to go. I couldn't let him do this. I had to try to stop it, Claire, I had to—'

She was crying again, silently. With his thumb, he

wiped away the tear that fell. She could feel his hand shaking. 'You didn't do anything, did you? To Brandon?'

'I didn't like the son of a bitch, but I didn't hurt him, and I didn't kill him. That was already done when I got there.' Shane laughed, but it sounded forced. 'Just my luck, huh? Charging off to be the hero, I get to be the villain instead.'

'Your dad—'

He nodded. 'Dad'll get us out. Don't worry, Claire. It'll be OK.'

But the way he said it, she knew he didn't believe it, either. She bit her lip to hold back a fresh wave of sobbing, and turned her head to kiss his palm.

'Hey,' he said softly. He moved closer to the bars, pressing his face between them. 'I always said you were jailbait, but this is ridiculous.'

She tried to laugh. She really did.

His smile looked broken. 'I'm going to consider this protective custody. At least this way, I can't do anything that'd get me in real trouble, right?'

She leant forward to kiss him. His lips felt just the same, soft and warm and damp, and she didn't want to move away. Not ever.

He sat back first, leaving her stranded there tingling and once again on the verge of tears. *Dammit!* Shane could *not* be blamed for this. It wasn't *fair*!

'I'll talk to Michael,' she said.

'Yeah.' Shane nodded. 'Tell him...well, hell. Tell him I'm sorry, OK? And he can have the PlayStation.'

'Stop it! Stop it... You're not going to die, Shane!'

He looked at her, and she saw the bright spark of fear in his eyes. 'Yeah,' he said softly. 'Right.'

Claire clenched her fists until they ached, and looked at Eve, who'd been standing quietly in the background. As Eve came towards the cage, Claire turned away and went to Detective Hess. 'How?' she asked again. 'How are they going to kill him?'

He looked deeply uncomfortable, but he looked down and said, 'Fire. It's always fire.'

That nearly made her cry again. Nearly. Shane already knew, she thought, and so did Eve. They'd known all along. 'You have to help him,' she said. 'You have to! He didn't do *anything*!'

'I can't,' he said. 'I'm sorry.'

'But—'

'Claire.' He put both hands on her shoulders and pulled her into a hug. She realised she was trembling, and then the tears came, a huge flood of them, and she held to the lapels on his coat and cried like her heart was breaking. Hess stroked her hair. 'You bring me proof that he had nothing to do with Brandon's death, and I swear to you, I'll do everything I can. But until then, my hands are tied.'

The idea of Shane burning in that cage was the most horrible thing she had ever imagined. *Get hold of yourself*, she thought furiously. *You're all he has!* So she pulled in deep, shaking breaths and stepped back from Hess's embrace, scrubbing the tears from her face with the sleeve of her T-shirt. Hess offered her a tissue. She took it and blew her nose, feeling stupid, and felt Eve's hand on her shoulder before she even knew Eve was there behind her.

'Let's go,' Eve said. 'We've got things to do.'

It had been Michael in the doorway when they'd driven by on their way to Founder's Square, and it was Michael in the doorway when the car pulled to a halt at 716 Lot Street. Gretchen opened the back door to allow Eve and Claire to scramble out. Claire looked back; Hess was still in the back seat, watching them go. He wasn't making a move to get out with them. 'Detective?' she asked. Eve was already halfway up the walk, moving fast. Claire knew that the first rule of Morganville was 'Never hang around out in the dark,' but she did it anyway.

'I'm going back to the station,' he said. 'Hans and Gretchen will drop me off. It's OK.'

She didn't like the idea of leaving anybody alone with Hans and Gretchen, but he was the adult, and he had to know what he was doing, right? She nodded, backed up, and then turned and ran the rest of the way up the steps and into the house.

Michael had pulled Eve inside, but not far in; she nearly ran into the two of them when she charged over the threshold. She slammed the door and locked it – Shane or Michael had replaced the locks again, and added more – and spun around to see that Michael had Eve in a bear hug, pressing her against him so tight that she nearly disappeared. He looked at Claire in total misery over Eve's shoulder. 'What the hell is going on? Where's Shane?'

Oh God, he didn't know. Why didn't he know? 'What happened?' she blurted. 'Why did you let him leave?'

'Shane? I didn't *let him* do anything. Any more than I let you go running off unprotected in the middle of the day. His dad called. He just...left. It was still daylight. There wasn't anything I could do.' Michael pushed Eve back a little and looked at her. 'What happened?'

'Brandon's dead,' Eve said. She didn't try to soften it, and her voice was as hard as an iron bar. 'They've got Shane in a cage on Founder's Square for his murder.'

Michael sagged back against the wall as if she'd punched him in the stomach. 'Oh,' he whispered. 'Oh my God.'

'They're going to kill him,' Claire said. 'They're going to burn him alive.'

Michael closed his eyes. 'I know. I remember.' Oh, *crap*, he'd seen it done before. So had Eve. She remembered them saying so before, though they'd spared her the details. Michael just breathed for a few seconds, and then said, 'We have to get him out.'

'Yeah,' Eve agreed. 'I know. But by *we*, you mean me and Claire, right? Because you're of no damn use at all.'

She might as well have punched him *again*, Claire thought; Michael's mouth dropped open, and she saw the agony in his eyes. Eve must not have seen it. She turned and clomped away, brisk and efficient.

'Claire!' she called back. 'Come on! Move it!'

Claire looked miserably at Michael. 'I'm sorry,' she said. 'She didn't mean that.'

'No, she did,' he said faintly. 'And she's right. I'm no use to you. Or to Shane. What good am I? I might as well be dead.'

He turned and slammed his hand into the wall, hard enough to break bones. Claire yelped, scrambled backward, and ran after Eve. When Michael went all avenging-angel, well, it was definitely scary. And he didn't look like he wanted witnesses to whatever was happening inside.

Eve was already going up the stairs. 'Wait!' Claire said. 'Michael...shouldn't we—?'

'Forget about Michael. Are you in or out?'

In. She guessed. Claire cast another look back at the hallway, where the sound of flesh hitting wood continued, and winced. Michael couldn't hurt himself, not permanently, but it sounded painful.

Probably not as painful as what he was feeling.

When Claire reached the doorway, Eve was yanking open drawers, pulling out frilly stuff, and throwing it aside. Black lace. Netting. Fishnet hose. 'Ah!' she said, and brought out a big, black box. It must have been heavy. It made a hollow *thunk* as she slammed it down on top of the dresser, rattling her collection of Evil Bobbleheads, which all started nodding uneasily. 'Come here.'

Claire went, worried; this was a brand-new Eve, one she wasn't sure she liked. She liked the vulnerable Eve, the one who cried at the drop of a hat. This one was harsh and hard and liked to order people around.

'Hold out your hand,' Eve said. Claire did, tentatively. Eve slapped something round and wooden into it.

Pointed on one end.

A home-made stake.

'Vampire killer's best friend,' Eve said. 'I made a bunch when Brandon was bothering me. I let him know, the next time he came sniffing around me he was going to get a woody. A *real* one.'

'Aren't these...illegal?'

'They'll get you thrown *under* the jail. Or killed and dumped in some empty lot somewhere. So don't get caught holding.'

She pulled out more stakes, and set them on the top of the dresser. Then some crude home-made crosses, extra large. She passed one to Claire, who gripped it in numbed fingers. 'But...Eve, what are we *doing*?'

'Saving Shane. What, you don't want to?'

'Of course I do! But—'

'Look.' Eve pulled out some more stuff and dumped it on the pile of stakes – lighter fluid, a Zippo lighter. 'The time for playing nice is over. If we want to get Shane out of there, vampires have to die. That means we start a war nobody wants, but tough. I'm not watching Shane burn. I won't do that. *They* want this. Oliver wants it. Fine, he can have it. He can choke on it.'

'Eve!' Claire dropped the cross and stake, grabbed her shoulders, and shook her. 'You *can't*! You know it's suicide – you've told me that before! You can't just...kill vampires! You'll end up in a cage right next to—'

Oh, God. She hadn't seen it before, but now she knew what was different about Eve. What was missing in her eyes.

'You want to die,' Claire said slowly. 'Don't you?'

'I'm not afraid of it,' Eve said. 'No big deal, right? Tra-la, off to paradise just like my parents always told me, pearly gates and all that. Besides, nobody's going to help us, Claire. We have to stick together. We have to help ourselves.'

'What if I find some evidence?' Claire asked. 'Detective Hess said—'

'Detective Hess stood there and did *nothing*. That's what they're all going to do. *Nothing*. Just like Michael.'

'God, Eve, stop it! That's not fair. Michael can't leave the house! You know that!'

'Yeah. Not much help, is it?' Eve began stuffing her arsenal of vampire-killing equipment into a black gym bag. 'It's time for a little payback around here. There are other people who're tired of sucking up to the vamps. Maybe I can find them if you're going to punk out on me. I need people I can rely on.'

'Eve!'

'With me or out of the way.'

Claire retreated to the doorway, and bumped into a warm body. She yelped and lunged forward, turning to face...

Michael.

His face was like a chalky mask, and his eyes were big and wounded and angry. He took Claire's hand and pulled her through the doorway, out into the hall.

Then he took hold of the doorknob, and looked at Eve. 'You're not going anywhere,' he said. 'Not while I can stop you.'

He slammed the door and locked it with an old-fashioned key. Seconds later, Eve hit the other side with a bang and began rattling the knob. 'Hey!' she screamed. 'Open it! Right now!'

'No,' Michael said. 'I'm sorry, Eve. I love you. I'm not letting you do this.'

She screamed and battered harder. 'You *love me*? You *asshole*! *Let me go!*'

'Can you really keep her in there?' Claire asked anxiously.

'I can for tonight,' Michael said, his eyes fixed on the door as it vibrated under the force of her kicks and blows. 'The windows won't open, or the doors. She's stuck. But when the sun comes up...' He turned to look at Claire. 'You said if you could find evidence, Detective Hess would step in for Shane?'

'That's what he said.'

'It's not enough. We need Amelie on his side. And Oliver.'

'Oliver's the one who put him in the cage! And Amelie – she walked away. I don't think we can get anything from her, Michael.'

'Try,' he said. 'Go. You have to.'

Claire blinked. 'You mean...go out there? At night?'

Michael looked exhausted suddenly. And very young. 'I can't do it. I can't trust Eve enough to let her out of her room, much less go out and talk to some of the most powerful vampires in town. Call Detective Hess, or Lowe. Don't go alone...but Claire, I need you to do this. I need you to make it right. I can't—'

It was written all over his face, the things he couldn't do. The limits he'd crashed into with so much force it had left him broken and bleeding in the wreckage.

'I know,' Claire said. 'I'll try.'

It was dark, it was Morganville, and she was sixteen years old. Not the best idea ever, going out of the house again, but Claire put on her darkest pair of jeans, a black shirt, and a big, gaudy cross that Eve had given her. She felt queasy at the idea of stakes. Doubly queasy at the idea of actually stabbing somebody with one.

I still have Protection, Amelie said so.

She hoped that would actually mean something.

Claire called Detective Hess's number from the card Eve had left pinned to the board in the kitchen. He answered on the second ring, sounded tired and depressed.

'I need a ride,' Claire said. 'If you're willing. I need to talk to Amelie.'

'Even I don't know how to get to Amelie,' Hess said. 'Best-kept secret in Morganville. I'm sorry, kid, but—'

'I know how to get to her,' she said. 'I just don't want to walk. Given...the time.'

There was a second of silence, and then the sound of a pen scratching against paper. 'You shouldn't be out at all,' Hess said. 'Besides, I don't think you're going to get anywhere. You need to find somebody who can back up Shane's story. That means one of his dad's biker buddies. There may be one or two running around loose, but I don't think talking sweet to them's going to get you much.'

'What about his dad?'

'Trust me, you're not going to find Frank Collins. Not before the powers that be do, anyway. Every vampire in town is out tonight, combing the streets, looking for him. They'll find him eventually. Not a lot of places he can hide when it's an all-out effort.'

'But...if they catch him, that's kind of a good thing. He could tell them Shane didn't do it!'

'He could,' Hess agreed. 'But he's just crazy enough to think burning in a cage alongside his kid is going out in a blaze of glory. Some kind of victory. He might say Shane was part of it just to punish him. We can't know.'

She couldn't deny that. Claire swallowed hard. 'So... are you going to give me a ride or not?'

'You're determined to go out,' Hess said. 'In the dark.'

'Yes. And I'll walk if I have to. I just hope I don't – have to.'

His sigh rattled the phone speaker. 'All right. Ten minutes. Stay inside until I honk the horn.'

Claire hung up the phone and turned, and nearly bumped into Michael. She yelped, and he reached out and steadied her. He kept hold of her arms even after she didn't need the steadying support anymore. He felt warm and real, and she thought – not for the first time – how weird it was that he could seem so *alive* when he really wasn't. Not exactly. Not all the time.

He looked like he had something he wanted to say, but he didn't know how to say it. And finally, he looked away. 'Hess is coming?'

'Yeah. Ten minutes, he said.'

Michael nodded. 'You're going to see Amelie?'

'Maybe. I've got exactly one shot. If that doesn't work, then…' She spread her hands. 'Then I guess I talk to Oliver instead.'

'If…you do see Amelie, tell her I need to talk to her,' he said. 'Will you do that for me?'

Claire blinked. 'Sure. But…why?'

'Something she said to me before. Look, obviously I can't go to her. She has to come here.' Michael shrugged and gave her a tiny curve of a smile. 'Not important why.'

That raised a little red flag in the back of her mind. 'Michael, you're not going to do anything, well, crazy, right?'

'Says the sixteen-year-old about to walk out the door in the dark to go see a vampire? No, Claire. I'm not going to do anything crazy.' Michael's eyes glittered suddenly with some fierce emotion. It looked like rage, or pain, or some toxic mix of both. 'I hate this. I hate letting you go. I hate Shane for getting himself caught. I hate *this*—'

What Michael was really saying, Claire understood, was *I hate me*. She totally got that. She hated herself on a regular basis.

'Don't punch anything, OK?' Because he had that look again. 'Take care of Eve. Don't let her go crazy, OK? Promise? If you love her, you need to take care of her. She needs you now.'

Some of the fierceness faded out of his eyes, and the way he looked at her made her go all soft and warm inside. 'I promise,' he said, and rubbed his hands gently up and down her arms, then let go. 'You tell Hess that if anything happens to you – anything – I'm killing him hard.'

She smiled faintly. 'Ooooh, tough guy.'

'Sometimes. Look, I didn't ask before – is Shane OK?'

'OK? You mean, did they hurt him?' She shook her head. 'No, he looked pretty much in one piece. But he's in a cage, Michael. And they're going to kill him. So no, he's not *OK*.'

The look in his eyes turned a little wild. 'That's the only reason I'm letting you go. If I had any choice—'

'You do,' she said. 'We can all sit here and let him die. Or you can let Eve go on her wild-ass rescue mission and get herself killed. Or you can let sweet, calm, reasonable Claire go do some talking.'

He shook his head. His long, elegant hands, which

looked so at home wrapped around a guitar, closed into fists. 'Guess that means there's no choice.'

'Not really,' Claire agreed. 'I was kind of lying about that choice thing.'

Detective Hess was surprised when she gave him the address. 'That's old-lady Day's house,' he said. 'She lives there with her daughter. What do you want with them? Far as I know, they're not involved in any of this.'

'It's where I need to go,' Claire said stubbornly. She had no idea where Amelie's house was, but she knew of one door into it. She'd been thinking about ways to explain how you could open a bathroom door and be in a house that might be halfway across town, but all she could think of was folded space, and even the most wild-haired physicists said that was nearly impossible.

But she liked folded space better as an explanation than crazy booga-booga vampire magic.

'You going prepared for trouble?' he asked. When she didn't answer, he reached into the glove compartment of the car and pulled out a small jewellery-type box.

'Here. I always carry spares.'

She opened it and found a delicate silver cross on a long chain. She silently put it around her neck and dropped it down the neck of her shirt. She already had a backup, one of Eve's handmade wooden ones, but this one felt...real, somehow. 'I'll give it back to you,' she said.

'No need. Like I said, I've got more.'

'I don't take jewellery from older men.'

Hess laughed. 'You know, I thought you were a mousy little thing when I first saw you, Claire, but you're not, are you? Not underneath.'

'Oh, I am mousy,' she said. 'All this scares the hell out of me. But I don't know what else to do, sir, except try. Even a mouse bites.'

Hess nodded, the laughter fading out of his face. 'Then I'll try to give you the chance to show some teeth.'

He drove the half mile or so, navigating dark streets with ease. She saw glimpses of people moving in the dark, pale and quick. The vampires were out in force, he'd said, and he was right. She caught a burning reflection of eyes as the car turned a corner. Vampire eyes reflected light like a cat's. Disturbing.

Hess pulled to a halt in front of the old Victorian-style house. 'You want me to come up with you?' he asked.

'You'd just scare them,' Claire said. 'They know me. Besides, I'm not exactly threatening.'

'Not until they get to know you,' Hess said. 'Stay out of the alley.'

She paused, her hand on the door. 'Why?'

'Vampire lives at the end of it. Crazy old bastard. He doesn't come out of there, and neither does anybody who wanders in. So just stay out.'

She nodded and ducked out into the dark. Outside, the Morganville shadows had a character all their own. A neighbourhood that had been a little shabby in the daytime was transformed into a freak-show park at night, gilded by cold silver moonlight. The shadows looked like holes in the world; they were so black. Claire looked at the house, and felt its *presence*. It was like the Glass House, all right. It had some kind of living soul, only where the Glass House seemed mildly interested in the creatures scuttling around inside of it, this place... she wasn't sure it even liked what was going on.

She shuddered, opened the picket gate, and hurried up to knock on the door. She kept knocking, frantic, until a voice shouted through the wood, 'Who the hell's that?'

'Claire! Claire Danvers, I was here, you remember? You gave me some lemonade?' No answer. 'Please, ma'am, please let me in. I need to use your bathroom!'

'You *what*? Girl, you better step off my granma's porch!'

'Please!' Claire knew she sounded desperate, but then...she was desperate. Not to mention just one step shy of crazy. '*Please, ma'am, don't leave me out here in the dark!*'

That was only a little bit of acting, frankly, because the dark kept getting heavier and closer around her, and she couldn't stop thinking about the alley, the crazy vampire hiding at the end like some giant tarantula waiting to jump—

She nearly screamed as the door was suddenly opened, and a hand closed around her arm.

'Oh, for God's sake, get in!' snapped Lisa. She looked irritated, tired, and rumpled; Claire had clearly rattled her right out of bed. She was wearing pink satin pyjamas and fluffy bunny slippers, which didn't make her look any less pissed off. She yanked, Claire stumbled forward across the threshold, and Lisa slammed and multiply locked the door behind her.

Then she turned, crossed her arms, and frowned at Claire. It was a formidable frown, but the pink pj's and bunny slippers undermined it.

'What the *hell* are you doing here? Do you know what time it is?' Lisa demanded. Claire took a deep breath, opened her mouth...and didn't have to say anything.

Because Granma was standing in the hallway entrance, and with her was Amelie.

The contrast couldn't have been more striking. Amelie looked every inch the glorious, perfect ice queen, from her carefully braided and coiled hair to her unlined face to the sleek white dress she wore – she'd changed from the black suit she'd worn to the Elders' Council building. She looked like one of those Greek statues made out of marble. Next to her, Granma seemed ancient, exhausted, and breakable.

'The visitor is here for me,' Amelie said calmly. 'I've been expecting her. I do thank you, Katherine, for your kindness.'

Who's Katherine? Claire looked around, and realised after a few seconds that it had to be Granma. Funny, she couldn't imagine Granma ever having had a first name, or being young; Lisa looked kind of thrown by it, too.

'And I appreciate your vigilance, Lisa, but your caution is unnecessary,' Amelie continued. 'Please return to your—' For a second, Amelie hesitated, and Claire couldn't imagine why until she saw that the vampire's gaze was fixed on the sight of Lisa's bunny shoes. It was only a second, a little crack in the marble, but Amelie's eyes widened just a bit, and her mouth curved. *She has a sense of humour.* That, more than anything else, made Claire feel lost. How could vampires have a sense of humour? How exactly was that fair?

Amelie recovered her poise. 'You may return to your sleep,' she said, and bowed her head gracefully to Lisa and her granma. 'Claire. If you would attend me.'

She didn't wait to see if Claire would, or explain what 'attend me' meant; she just turned and glided down the hallway. Claire exchanged a look with Lisa – this time, Lisa looked worried, not angry – and hurried after Amelie's retreating figure.

Amelie opened the bathroom door and stepped through into the same study Claire had visited before, only now it was night, and a fire was roaring in the enormous hearth to warm the chilly room. The walls were thick stone, and looked very old. The tapestries looked old, too – faded, tattered, but still keeping a sense of magnificence, somehow. The place looked way spookier by firelight. If there were electric lights, they weren't on. Not even the books crowding the shelves made the place warm.

Amelie crossed to a chair near the hearth and gracefully motioned Claire to one across from her. 'You may sit,' she said. 'But be warned, Claire, what I expect you want from me is not in my power to grant.'

Claire settled carefully, not daring to relax. 'You know why I'm here.'

'I'd be a fool if I thought it was any reason other than young Shane,' Amelie said, and smiled very sadly. 'I can recognise loyalty when I see it. It shines strongly from you both, which is one reason I have trusted you so much on insignificant acquaintance.' She lost her smile, and her pale eyes turned to frost again. 'And that is why I cannot forgive what Shane has done. He broke faith with me, Claire, and that is intolerable. Morganville is founded on trust. Without it, we have nothing but despair and death.'

'But *he didn't do anything*!' Claire knew she sounded like a whiny little girl, but she didn't know what else to do. It was that or cry, and she didn't want to cry. She had the feeling she'd be doing plenty of that, no matter what. 'He didn't kill Brandon. He tried to save him. You can't punish him for being in the wrong place!'

'We have no one's word of that save Shane's. And make no mistake, child, I know why Shane returned to Morganville in the first place. It is regrettable that his sister was so brutally and unnecessarily killed; we tried to make amends with his family, as is custom. We even allowed them to leave Morganville, which you understand is *not* common, in hopes that Shane and his parents might heal their grief in less...difficult surroundings. But it was not possible. And his mother broke through the block surrounding her memories.'

Claire shifted uncomfortably in her chair. It was too

big, and too high up; her toes barely touched the ground. She gripped the arms firmly, tried to remind herself that she was strong and courageous, that she *had* to be, for Shane. 'Did you kill her? Shane's mother?' she asked, as bluntly as she could. It still sounded timid, but at least she'd got the question out.

For a second she thought Amelie wasn't going to answer her, but then the vampire looked away, towards the fire. Her eyes looked orange in its glow, with dots of reflective yellow in the centre. She shrugged, a gesture so small, Claire barely even saw it. 'I have not lifted a hand against a human in hundreds of years, little Claire. But that is not what you ask, is it? Am I responsible for his mother's death? In a larger sense, I am responsible for anything that is done in Morganville, or even beyond its borders if it relates to vampires. But I think you ask if I gave an explicit order.'

Claire nodded. Her neck felt stiff, and her hands would have been shaking if they hadn't been grabbing the arms of the chair so hard her knuckles cracked.

'Yes,' Amelie said, and turned her head back to meet Claire's eyes. She looked cool, merciless, and absolutely without conscience. 'Of course I did. Shane's mother was one of the rare cases who, by focusing on a single event in their past, are able to overcome the psychic block that is placed on them when they depart this place. She remembered her daughter's death, and from that, she remembered other things. Dangerous things. As soon as we became aware this was happening, it was brought to my attention, and I gave the order to kill her. It was to be done quickly and without pain, and it was a mercy, Claire. Shane's mother had been in so much pain for so long, do you understand? She was damaged, and some damages cannot be healed.'

'Nothing heals if you're dead,' Claire whispered. She remembered Shane on the couch, blurting out all the horror of his life, and she wanted to throw up on Amelie's perfect lap. 'You can't do things like that. You aren't God!'

'For the safety of all who live here? Yes, Claire, I can. I must. I am sorry my decisions do not meet with your approval, but nevertheless, they are mine, and the consequences are also mine. Shane is a consequence. My agents warned me at the time that they believed the boy might have been tainted by his mother, that his block was slipping, but I chose not to expand the tragedy by killing a boy who might not have been a threat.' Amelie shrugged again. 'Not all of my decisions are cruel, you see. But the ones which are not are usually wrong. Had I killed Shane then, and his father, as well, we would not now be facing this...bloody and painful farce.'

'Because he'd be *dead*!' Claire felt tears sting hard in her eyes and at the back of her throat. 'Please. Please don't let this happen. You can find out the truth, can't you? You have powers. You can tell that Shane didn't kill Brandon...'

Amelie said nothing. She turned back towards the fire.

Claire watched her miserably for a few seconds, and felt tears break free to run down her cheeks. They felt ice-cold in the overly warm room. 'You can tell,' she repeated. 'Why won't you even *try*? Is it just because you're angry at him?'

'Don't be infantile,' Amelie said distantly. 'I do nothing out of anger. I am too old to fall into the trap of emotion. What I do, I do for expedience, and for the sake of the future.'

'Shane *is* the future! He's *my* future! And he's innocent!'

'I know all that,' Amelie said. 'And it does not matter.'

Claire stopped, stunned. Her mouth was open, and she tasted woodsmoke on her tongue until she closed it and swallowed. 'What?'

'I know Shane is innocent of the crime of which he is accused,' Amelie said. 'And yes, I could countermand Oliver. But I will not.'

'*Why?*' It burst out of Claire like a scream, but it was really just a whimper, all the fight kicked out of it.

'I have no reason to explain myself. Suffice to say that I have chosen to place Shane in that cage for a purpose. He may live, or he may die. That is no longer in my hands, and you may save both your breath and your hopes; I shall not stand up dramatically at the last moment as they light the pyres, and save your lover. Should it come to that, Claire, you must be prepared for the harsh reality that the world is not a fair or just place, and all your wishing cannot make it so.' Amelie sighed, very lightly. 'A lesson I learnt long, long ago, when the oceans were young, and sand was still rock. I am old, child. Older than you can possibly understand. Old enough that I play with lives like counters in a game. I wish this was not so, but damn me if I can change what I am. What the world is.'

Claire said nothing. There didn't seem to be anything left to say, so she just cried, silently and hopelessly, until Amelie pulled a white silken handkerchief from her sleeve and gracefully held it out to her. Claire dabbed at her face with it, honked her nose, and hesitated with the silken square clutched in her hand. She'd grown up with disposable tissues; she'd never actually held a handkerchief before. Not one like this, all beautiful embroidery and monogramming. You didn't throw these away, right?

Amelie's lips curved into that distant smile. 'Wash it and return it to me someday,' she said. 'But go now. I grow tired, and you will not change my mind. Go.'

Claire slid off the chair and stood up, turned, and gasped. There were two of Amelie's bodyguards standing *right there*, and she hadn't even known they were behind her the whole time. If she'd tried anything...

'Go to sleep, Claire,' Amelie said. 'Let things be. We shall see how the cards fall in our game.'

'It's not a game: It's Shane's life,' Claire shot back. 'And I'm not sleeping.'

Amelie shrugged and folded her hands neatly in her

lap. 'Then go about your quest,' she said. 'But do not come back to me, little Claire. I will not be so well-disposed to you again.'

Claire didn't look back, but she knew the bodyguards followed her all the way to the door.

'Was there not something else you wanted to tell me?' Amelie asked, just before she went out. Claire glanced back; the vampire was still staring into the fire. 'Did you not have another request?'

'I don't know what you're talking about.'

Amelie sighed. 'Someone asked you for a favour.'

Michael. Claire swallowed hard. 'Michael wants to talk to you.'

Amelie nodded. Her expression didn't change.

'What do I tell him?' Claire asked.

'That is entirely your affair. Tell him the truth – that you did not care enough to deliver his message.' Amelie waved a hand without even looking towards her. 'Go.'

Lisa was sitting in the living room, frowning, arms folded, when Claire came back down the hall. She still looked fierce, never mind the bunny slippers, as she stood up to open the locks on the front door. *Warrior princess on vacation*, Claire thought. She guessed you grew up tough in Morganville, especially if you lived in a house Amelie could visit any time she felt like it.

'Bad news,' Lisa said. 'Right?'

Did it show that much? 'Right,' Claire said, and wiped at her eyes again with the handkerchief. She shoved it in her pocket and sniffled miserably. 'But I'm not giving up.'

'Good,' Lisa said. 'Now, when I open this door, you're gonna want to hurry. Go straight to the car out there. Don't look left or right.'

'Why? Is there something...?'

'Morganville rules, Claire. Learn them, live them, survive them. Now *go*!' Lisa yanked open the door, put a hand flat on Claire's back, and propelled her out onto the porch. A second later, Lisa slammed the door, and Claire heard the rattle of the locks being turned. She got her balance, jumped down the steps, and hustled down the dark path and through the picket gate, and yanked open the passenger door of the car. She scrambled in and hit the lock, and then relaxed.

'I'm OK,' she said, and turned to Detective Hess.

He wasn't there.

The driver's seat was empty. The keys were still in the ignition, the engine was idling, and the radio was playing softly. But the car was completely empty, except for her.

'Oh God,' Claire whispered. 'Oh God, oh God, oh God.' Because she *could* drive the car, but that would mean stranding Detective Hess, if he'd gone off doing police things. Stranding him without his partner to help him. She'd seen enough cop shows to know that wasn't a good idea. Maybe he'd just gone off to talk to somebody and was coming right back...or maybe he'd been snatched out of the car by some hungry vamp. But didn't Hess have some kind of special Protection?

She had no idea what to do.

While she was thinking about it, she heard voices. Not loud, but a steady stream of conversation. It sounded like Detective Hess, and he wasn't far away. Claire cautiously rolled down the window and listened hard; she couldn't make out any words, but there were definitely voices.

Claire unlocked her door and eased it open, straining to catch the words, but they were just sound, no meaning. She hesitated, then slipped out of the car, eased the door shut, and hurried towards the sound of the voices. Yes, that was Detective Hess; she recognised his voice. No question about it.

She didn't even realise where she was going – she was so intent on listening – until she realised how *dark* it was, and the words weren't getting any clearer, and she wasn't at all sure now that *was* Detective Hess's voice after all.

And she was halfway down an alley with tall, rough board fence on both sides, trapping her.

She'd gone into the alley. Why the hell had she done that? Hess had warned her. Granma had warned her. And she hadn't listened!

Claire tried to turn around, she really tried, but then the whispers came again, and yes, for sure that was Detective Hess, there was no safety back there in the car, the car was a trap waiting to spring, and if she could just get to the end of the alley she'd be safe,

Detective Hess would keep her safe, and she'd be—

'Claire.'

It was a cold, clear voice, falling on her like ice down her back, and it shocked her right out of the trance she'd fallen into. Claire looked up. On the second story of Granma's house, bordering the alley, a slender white figure stood in the window, staring down.

Amelie.

'Go back,' she said, and then the window was empty, curtains blowing in the wind.

Claire gasped, turned, and ran as fast as she could out of the alley. She could feel it at her back, pulling at her – *it*, whatever *it* was, it wasn't a vampire as she understood vamps in Morganville; it was something else, something worse. *Trap-door spider*, that was how Granma and Lisa had described it. Panic whited out its song in her head, and she made it – somehow – to the end of the alley and burst out into the street.

Detective Hess was standing at the car, looking straight at the alleyway. Gun drawn and held at his side. He visibly relaxed at the sight of her, came around, and hustled her to the passenger side of the car. 'That was dumb,' he said. 'And you're lucky.'

'I thought I heard you,' she said faintly. Hess raised his eyebrows.

'Like I said. Dumb.' He shut the door on her, came around, and put the car in gear.

'Where'd you go?'

He didn't answer. Claire looked back. There was

something in the shadows in the alley, but she couldn't tell what it was.

Just that its eyes reflected the light.

It was coming up on deep night, when most sensible people were fast asleep in their beds with their doors bolted and windows securely locked, and Claire was knocking on the door of Common Grounds. It had a CLOSED sign in the window, but the lights were on in the back.

'You're sure you want to do this,' Hess said.

'You sound just like my subconscious,' Claire said, and kept knocking. The blinds twitched and tented; locks rattled.

Oliver opened the door of the coffee shop, and the smell of espresso and cocoa and steamed milk washed over her. It was warm, welcoming, and so very wrong, considering what she knew about him.

He looked very humanly harassed at her arrival. 'It's late,' he said. 'What is it?'

'I need to talk to you about—'

'No,' he said very simply, and looked at Hess over her head. 'Detective Hess, you need to take this child home. She's lucky to still be alive today. If she wants to continue that winning streak, then she ought to be a little more cautious than to run around Morganville in the dead of night, knocking on my door.'

'Five minutes,' Claire promised. 'Then I'll go. Please. I never did anything to hurt you, did I?'

He stared at her for a few cool seconds, and then stepped back and held the door open. 'You, too, Detective. I hate to leave anyone with a pulse outside of shelter this evening.'

I'll bet, she thought. Oliver's peace-and-love hippie act no longer worked on her. Amelie had a kind of noble dignity that let her get away with pretending concern; Oliver was different. He was trying to be like Amelie, but not quite making it.

And I'll bet that pisses him off, too.

Hess urged her across the threshold and followed her in. Oliver locked up, walked to the coffee bar, and, without being asked, began to put together three drinks – cocoa for Claire, strong black coffee for Detective Hess, and a pale tea for himself. His hands were steady and sure, the activity so normal that it lulled Claire into relaxing just a little as she sat down at a table. She ached all over with exhaustion and the tension she'd run through her body at Amelie's.

'Miles to go before you sleep,' Oliver said, as he stirred the cocoa. 'Here. Steamed milk and spiced cocoa. Hot peppers. It does have an amazing effect.'

He brought it to the table and handed it off to her, put Hess's coffee down, and retrieved his own brewing teacup before sitting. All very normal-life casual.

'You're here about the boy, I would suppose,' Oliver said. He dunked his tea bag and watched the results critically. 'I really must get a new supplier. This tea is pathetic. America just doesn't understand tea at all.'

'He's not *the boy*. His name is Shane,' Claire said. 'And he's not guilty. Even Amelie knows that.'

'Does she?' Oliver raised his gaze to fix it on hers. 'How interesting, because I, in fact, don't. Brandon was hideously and cruelly tortured, then murdered. He might have had his flaws—'

'What, like molesting children?'

'—but he was born into a different time, and some of his habits were difficult to change. He had his bright side, Claire, as do we all. And now that's gone, along with any harm he might have done.' Oliver wouldn't let her look away. 'Hundreds of years of memory and experience, poured out like water. Wasted. Do you think it's so simple to forget such a thing for me? For any of us? When we look at Brandon's body, we see ourselves at the mercy of humans. At *your* mercy, Claire.' He glanced at Detective Hess. 'Or yours, Joe. And you must admit, that's a terrifying prospect.'

'So you'll just kill anyone who frightens you. Who *could* hurt you.'

'Well...yes.' Oliver took the tea bag out of his cup and set it aside on the saucer, then sipped. 'A habit we learnt from you, really. Humans are all too ready to slaughter the innocent with the guilty, and if you were older, Claire, you would know this. Joe, I'm sure, is not so naive.'

Hess smiled thinly and sipped coffee. 'Don't talk to me. I'm just the driver.'

'Ah,' Oliver said. 'How generous of you.' They

exchanged some kind of a look that Claire didn't know how to interpret. Was that anger? Amusement? A willingness to get up and beat the crap out of each other at a moment's notice? She couldn't even figure out what Shane and Michael were thinking, and she knew them. 'Is she then aware of the price of your services?'

'He's trying to get you rattled, Claire. There's no price.'

'How interesting. And what a departure.' Oliver dismissed Hess and got back to Claire, who hastily took a sip of her cocoa. *Ohhhhhh*...it just kind of exploded in her mouth, rich cocoa, warm milk, and a spicy edge that she didn't expect. Wow. She blinked and took another sip, carefully. 'I see you like the cocoa.'

'Um...yeah. Yes, sir.' Because somehow, when Oliver was being civilised, she felt compelled to still call him *sir*. Mom and Dad had a lot to answer for, she decided. She couldn't even be rude to evil vampires who'd caged her boyfriend and were preparing to roast him alive. 'What about Shane?'

Oliver leant back, and his eyelids drifted down to half-mast. 'We've covered this subject, Claire. Quite thoroughly. I believe you might even have the bruises to remind you of my opinion.'

'He didn't do it.'

'Let us deal in facts. *Fact*, the boy came back to Morganville with the clear intention of disrupting the peace, at the very least, and more likely killing vampires, which is an automatic death sentence. *Fact*, he concealed himself from us, along with his intentions. *Fact*, he communicated with his father and his father's friends both before they came to Morganville and after. *Fact*, he was at the scene of the crime. *Fact*, he has offered little in his own defence. Need I go on?'

'But—'

'Claire.' Oliver sounded sad and wounded. He leant forward, braced his elbows on the table, and placed his chin on top of his folded hands. 'You're young. I understand that you have feelings for him, but don't be a fool. He'll drag you down with him. If you force me to it, I'm sure I could uncover evidence that you knew about the presence of Shane's father in Morganville, and you had knowledge of their agenda. And that, my dear girl, would mean the end of your precious Protection, and put you in a cage alongside your boyfriend. Is that what you want?'

Hess put a warning hand on her arm. 'Enough, Oliver.'

'Not nearly enough. If you came to bargain, I think you have nothing to offer me that I can't get elsewhere,' Oliver said. 'So please take yourselves—'

'I'll sign whatever you want,' Claire blurted. 'You know, swear myself to you. Instead of Amelie. If you want. Just let Shane go.'

She hadn't been planning to do it, but when he'd mentioned *bargain* it had just taken on a life of its own inside her, and leapt right out of her mouth. Hess groaned and ran a hand over his hair, then covered his mouth, evidently to keep himself from telling her what an idiot she was.

Oliver continued to gaze at her with those steady, kind eyes.

'I see,' he said. 'It would be love, then. For love of this boy, you would tie yourself to me for the rest of your life. Give me the right to use you as I see fit. Do you have any idea what you're offering? Because I would not offer you the conditional contracts that most in Morganville sign, Claire. No, for you, there would be the old ways. The hard ways. I would own you, body and soul. I would tell you when to marry and whom to marry, and own your children and all their issue. I was born in a time when this was custom, you see, and I am not in a charitable mood just now. Is this what you want?'

'Don't,' Hess said sharply. He gripped Claire's forearm and pulled her up to her feet. 'We're going, Oliver. Right now.'

'She has the right to make her own choices, Detective.'

'She's a *child*! Oliver, she's sixteen years old!'

'She was old enough to conspire against me,' he said. 'Old enough to find the book that I spent half a hundred years pursuing. Old enough to cut off my one and only chance to save my people from Amelie's intolerable iron grip. *Do you think I care about her age?*' Oliver's friendly courtesy was all gone, and what was left was like a man-sized snake, with a cruel light flickering behind his eyes, and fangs flicking down in warning. Claire let Hess pull her out from behind the table, towards the door. He'd drawn his gun.

'I may not let you leave,' Oliver said. 'You realise that?'

Hess spun and raised the gun, pointed it straight at Oliver's chest. 'Silver bullets washed in holy water, with a cross cast right in.' He clicked back the hammer. 'You want to test the line, Oliver? Because it's right here. You're standing on it. I'll take a lot of shit from you, but not this. Not that kind of contract, and not with a kid.'

Oliver hadn't even bothered to stand up.

'I take it you don't want your coffee poured to go? A pity. Do watch your back, Detective. You and I will have a talk, one of these days. And Claire…come back anytime. If the hours run thin, and you want to make that deal, I will listen.'

'Don't even think about it,' Hess said. 'Claire, open the door.' He held his gun trained on the vampire, unblinking, while Claire unlocked the three dead bolts and swung it open. 'Get in the car. Move.' He backed out behind her as she ran to the car and dived inside. Hess banged the door to Common Grounds closed, hard enough to crack glass, and slid over the hood of the car in a move she'd only ever seen in action movies, and was in the car and starting it before she could take a breath.

They raced off into the night. Claire checked the back seat, suddenly terrified she'd turn around to see Oliver grinning at her, but it was empty.

Hess was sweating. He wiped at the drops with the back of his hand. 'You don't fool around when you get yourself in trouble, I'll give you that,' he said. 'I've lived here all my life, and I've never seen anybody get that out of Oliver. Ever.'

'Um...thanks?'

'It wasn't a compliment. Listen, under no circumstances do you *ever* go back to Common Grounds, get me? Avoid Oliver at all costs. And no matter what happens, don't make that deal. Shane wouldn't want it, and you'd live to regret it. You'd live a long time, and you'd hate every horrible second of it.' Hess shook his head and took a deep breath. 'Right. That's the end of the line for you tonight. You're going home, I'm seeing you safe inside, and I'm going home to hide in a closet until this blows over. I suggest you do the same.'

'But Shane—'

'Shane's dead,' Hess said, so quietly and matter-of-factly that she thought he meant it, that somehow someone had slipped in and killed him and *she hadn't even known*...but then he went on. 'You can't save him. Nobody can save him now. Just let go and watch yourself, Claire. That's all you can do. You've pissed off both Amelie and Oliver in one night. Enough already. A little common sense would be welcome from you right about now.'

She sat in dull, grim silence the rest of the way home.

* * *

Hess was as good as his word. He walked her from the car up the steps, watched her open the front door, and nodded wearily as she stepped inside. 'Lock it,' he said. 'And for God's sake, go get some rest.'

Michael was right there, warm and comforting, when she closed the door. He was holding his guitar by the neck, so he'd clearly been playing; his eyes were red-rimmed, his face tense. 'Well?' he asked.

'Hello, Claire, how are you?' Claire asked the air. 'No death threats, right? Thanks for going out in the dark to bargain with two of the scariest people on earth.'

He at least had the good manners to look embarrassed about it. 'Sorry. You OK?'

'Duh. No fang marks, anyway.' She shuddered. 'I do *not* like those people.'

'Vampires?'

'Vampires.'

'Technically, not people, but then, neither am I, now that I think about it. So never mind.' Michael put an arm around her and steered her towards the living room, where he sat her down, put a blanket around her shoulders. 'I'm guessing it didn't go well.'

'It didn't go at all,' she said. She'd been depressed on the ride home, but having to actually report on her failure was a whole new level of suck. 'They're not letting him go.'

Michael didn't say anything, but the light died in his eyes. He went down on one knee next to her and fussed with the blanket, tucking it tighter around her. 'Claire. *Are* you OK? You're shaking.'

'They're cold, you know,' she said. 'They make me cold, too.'

He nodded slowly. 'You did what you could. Rest.'

'What about Eve? Is she still here?'

He glanced up at the ceiling, as if he could see through it. Maybe he could. Claire really didn't know what Michael could and couldn't do; after all, he'd been dead a couple of times already. Wouldn't do to underestimate somebody like that. 'She's asleep,' he said. 'I...talked to her. She understands. She won't do anything stupid.' He didn't look at Claire when he said that, and she wondered what kind of talking that might have been.

Her mother had always said, when in doubt, ask. 'Was it the kind of talk where you gave her something to live for? Like maybe, um, you?'

'Did I... What the hell are you talking about?'

'I just thought maybe you and her—'

'Claire, *Jesus*!' Michael said. She'd actually made him flinch. Wow. That was new. 'You think banging me is going to make her forget about charging out to commit cold-blooded vampire slaying? I don't know what kind of standards you have on sex, but those are pretty high. Besides, whatever's between me and Eve...well, it's between me and Eve.' *Until she tells me about it later*, Claire thought. 'Anyway, that's not what I meant. I... persuaded her. That's all.'

Persuaded. Right. The mood Eve had been in when Claire left? Not too likely…

And then Claire remembered the voices whispering to her in the alley, and her blind, stupid assumption of safety leading her into danger. Could Michael do that?

Would he?

'You didn't—' She touched her temple with one finger.

'What?'

'Screw with her head? Like *they* can?'

He didn't answer. He fussed with the blanket around her shoulders some more, fetched her a pillow, and said, 'Lie down. Rest. It's only a couple of hours until dawn, and I'm going to need you.'

'Oh, God, Michael, you didn't. You *didn't*! She'll never forgive you!'

'As long as she lives to hate me later,' he said. 'Rest. I mean it.'

She didn't intend to sleep; her brain was whirling like a tyre rim scraping pavement, shooting off sparks in every direction. Lots of energy being expended, but she wasn't going anywhere fast. *Have to think of something. Have to…*

Michael started playing, something soft that sounded melancholy, all in minor keys, and she felt herself begin to drift…

…and then, without any sense of going, she was gone.

* * *

The blanket around her smelt like Shane.

Claire burrowed deeper into its warmth, murmuring something that might have been his name as she woke; she felt good, relaxed, safe in his embrace. The way she'd been the other night when they'd spent it here on the couch, kissing...

All that faded fast when the events of the past day flooded back, stripping away the comfort and leaving her cold and scared. Claire sat up, clutching the blanket, and looked around. Michael's guitar was back in its case, and the sun was over the horizon. So, he was gone again, and she and Eve...she and Eve were on their own.

'Right,' she whispered. 'Time to get to work.' She still needed to find some kind of viable strategy to break Shane out of that cage on Founder's Square. Which meant research...maybe Detective Hess could tell her something about how many guards there were, and where. Clearly, there was some kind of security process for keeping out the human losers like her, but any security could be broken, right? At least, that's what she'd always heard. Maybe Eve knew something that could help.

If Eve wasn't back on suicide watch this morning, anyway. Claire thought wistfully about a hot shower, decided maybe it could wait, and wandered into the kitchen to put on coffee. Eve wasn't going to be happy, but she'd be even less happy without caffeine. Claire waited while the pot filled, then carried a black mug full of the stuff upstairs. The key to Eve's door was hanging on a hook, with a note taped to it. Michael's handwriting.

It read, *Don't let her leave the house.* By implication, of course, it meant Claire was supposed to stay here, too.

As if she could even think about doing that, with Shane's last hours running out. And who knew what was happening to him out there? She thought about the cold fury in Oliver, the indifference in Amelie, her stomach twisting. She grabbed the key, turned it in the lock, and opened Eve's bedroom door.

Eve was sitting, fully dressed and made-up in zombified glory, on the edge of her bed. She'd put her hair into two pigtails, one on each side, and she'd done her make-up with great care. She looked like a scary porcelain doll.

An *angry* scary porcelain doll. The kind that they made horror movies about, with stabby knives.

'Coffee?' Claire asked weakly. Eve looked at her for a second, took the coffee, got up, and walked out of the bedroom towards the stairs. 'Oh boy.'

By the time Claire made it downstairs, Eve was standing in the middle of the living room, looking up at nothing. She'd put the coffee down, and her hands were on her hips. Claire paused, one hand still clutching the banister, and watched Eve turn a slow circle as if she was looking for something.

'I know you're there, you coward,' she said. 'Now hear this, crazy supernatural boy. *If you ever fuck with me again, I swear, I will walk out this door and never come back*. You get me? One for yes, two for no.'

He must have said yes, because some of the stiffness

went out of Eve's shoulders. She was still mad, though. 'I don't know what's lower, you playing vamp tricks on me, or locking me in my room, but either way, you are so busted, man. Being dead can't save you. When you get back tonight, I am completely kicking your ass.'

'He was sorry,' Claire said. She sat down on the first step as Eve turned a glare of righteous anger in her direction. 'He knew you were going to be mad, but he couldn't... He cares about you, Eve. He couldn't just let you go out and get yourself killed.'

'Last time I checked, I was over eighteen and nobody's *property*!' Eve yelled, and stomped her foot. 'I don't care if you're sorry, Michael... You're going to have to work really hard to make this up to me! Really hard!'

Claire saw the breeze ruffle Eve's hair. Eve closed her eyes for a second, swaying, mouth open in a round, red O.

'OK,' she said weakly. 'That was different.'

'What?' Claire asked, and jumped to her feet.

'Nothing. Um, nothing at all. Right.' Eve cleared her throat. 'What happened last night? Did you get them to let Shane go?'

Claire's throat just locked up on her in misery. She shook her head and looked down. 'But it's no use going out there with stakes and crosses,' she said. 'They'd be ready. We need another plan.'

'What about Joe? Detective Hess?'

Claire shook her head again. 'He can't.'

'Then let's go talk to some people who can,' Eve said

reasonably. She picked up her coffee and drained it in long, chugging gulps, set the mug aside, and nodded. 'Ready.'

'Who are we going to see?'

'It may shock you, but living in Morganville my entire pathetic life isn't a complete waste. I know people, OK? And some of them actually have backbones.'

Claire blinked. 'Um...OK. Two minutes.'

She dashed upstairs for the fastest shower and change of clothes in her life.

Chapter Nine

It stood to reason that Eve would know places to go that Claire didn't, but for some reason it surprised Claire where those places were. A Laundromat, for instance. And a photo-processing place. In each case, Eve made her wait in the car while she talked to somebody – a human somebody, Claire was almost sure. But nothing came out of it, either time.

Eve got back in her big, dusty Cadillac looking grim and already wilting in the morning's heat. 'Father Jonathan's on a trip,' she said. 'I was hoping we could get him to talk to the mayor. They go back.'

'Father Jonathan? There's a priest in town?'

Eve nodded. 'The vampires don't care about whether or not he celebrates Mass, as long as he doesn't display any crosses. Communion's kind of interesting; the vamps keep the wafers and wine under guard. Oh, and forget about the holy water. If they ever caught him making the sign of the cross over anything liquid, they'd make sure his next congregation has an address behind the pearly gates.'

Claire blinked, trying to get her head around it. 'But...he's on a trip? Out of town? What?'

'Gone to the Vatican. Special dispensation.'

'The *Vatican* knows about Morganville?'

'No, idiot. When he leaves town, he's like anybody else: no memory of the vamps. So I don't think we can count on the Vatican Strike Team storming in to save Shane, if that's what you were thinking.'

It wasn't, but it was kind of comforting to imagine paramilitary priests in bullet-proof armour, with crosses on the vests. 'So what now, then? If you can't get to Father Jonathan?'

Eve started the car. They were parked in the tiny photo-store parking lot, next to a big industrial-sized Dumpster. They were the only car in the parking lot, although a white van was just turning into the lot and squealing to a stop, in the space next to them. It was still pretty early – before nine a.m. – and what passed for traffic in Morganville was slowly filtering around the streets. The photo-processing place claimed to be open twenty-four hours; now, that was a job Claire figured she didn't want. Did vampires take pictures? What kind? Maybe the trick was not to look at what came spitting out of the machine, just shuffle the prints into an envelope and hand them over...but then, that was probably the trick outside of Morganville, too.

She checked the clock again. 'Eve! What about your job?'

'I can get another one.'

'But—'

'Claire, it wasn't that good of a job. Look at what I had to put up with. Jocks. Jerks. Monica.'

Eve started to back out of the parking lot, then slammed on the brakes when another car pulled in behind her, blocking her in. 'Dammit,' she breathed, and fumbled for her cell phone. She pitched it to Claire. 'Call the cops.'

'Why?' Claire twisted to look out the back, but she couldn't see who was driving the other car.

She was looking in the wrong place. The threat wasn't the car behind them; it was the white van next to the passenger side of the Cadillac, and as she started punching 911, a sliding panel came open, and someone reached out and pulled on the handle of Claire's door.

It was locked. She wasn't a total idiot. But two seconds later, it didn't matter, because a crowbar hit the window behind her, smashing it into a million little sparkly pieces, and Claire reflexively jerked forward, hands over her head. She fumbled the phone into the floorboards, and tried frantically to find it. Eve was cursing breathlessly.

'Get us out of here!' Claire yelled.

'I can't! We're blocked in!'

Claire grabbed the phone triumphantly, finished pushing buttons for 911, and pressed SEND just as a hand reached in from the back seat and slammed her face-first into the dash.

After that, things got a little distant and fluffy around the edges. She remembered being taken out of the car. Remembered Eve yelling and fighting, then going quiet.

Remembered being bundled into the van and the door sliding shut.

And as her head began to clear up again, except for a monster-sized headache centred right over her eyes, she remembered the van, too. She'd seen it before. She'd *been* in it before.

And just like before, Jennifer was driving, and Monica and Gina were in the back. Gina was holding her down. The girls looked flushed. Crazy. Not good.

'Eve,' Claire whispered.

Monica leant closer. 'Who, the freak? Not here.'

'What did you do to her?'

'Just a little cut, nothing too serious,' Monica said. 'You ought to be worried about yourself, Claire. My daddy wanted to get a message to you.'

'Your...what?'

'Daddy. What, you don't have one of those? Or do you just not know which John was the sperm donor?' Monica sneered. She was wearing a tight pair of blue jeans and an orange top, and she looked as glossy as a magazine page. 'Oh, don't bother, mouse. Just stay down... You won't get hurt.'

Gina pinched Claire, hard. Claire yelled, and Monica grinned in response. 'Well,' she amended, 'maybe hurt a *little*. But a tough chick like you can take it, right, genius?'

Gina pinched Claire again, and Claire gritted her teeth and managed to keep it to just a whimper this time. Easier, since she was already prepared for the pain. Gina looked disappointed. Maybe she should scream her lungs out no matter what, save herself the trouble of Gina having to work harder for it...

'You were following us,' Claire said. She felt nauseated, probably from smacking her head into the dashboard, and she was deeply worried about Eve. *A little cut.* Monica wasn't the type to do anything halfway.

'See? I told you she was a genius, didn't I?' Monica sat down in one of the padded leather seats that lined the van, and crossed her legs. She had on cute platform shoes that matched her orange tank top, and she inspected her nails – also done in orange – for signs of chipping. 'You know what, genius? You're right. I was following you. See, I wanted to bring you in quietly, but no, you and Zombie Girlfriend had to make it all difficult. Why aren't you in class, anyway? Isn't that, like, against your religion or something, cutting class?'

Claire struggled to sit up. Gina glanced at Monica, who nodded; Claire edged away from Gina and put her back up against the sliding door of the van. She rubbed her stinging arm where Gina had given her pinches. 'Shane,' she said. 'That's what your dad wants to see me about, isn't it?'

Monica shrugged. 'I guess. Look, I don't like Shane; that's no secret. But I never intended for his sister to get killed in that fire. It was a stupid school thing, OK? No big deal.'

'No big deal?' Of everything Monica had ever said to her – and there'd been some jaw-droppers – that was maybe the worst. '*No big deal?* A kid died, and you destroyed their whole family! Don't you get it? Shane's mom—'

'Not my fault!' Monica was suddenly flushed. Not used to being blamed, Claire guessed; maybe nobody ever had blamed her except Shane. 'Even if she remembered, if she'd kept her mouth shut, she'd have been fine! And Alyssa was an accident!'

'Yeah,' Claire said. 'I'm sure that makes it all better.' She felt gritty and tired, never mind the sleep she'd had, or the shower. The floor of the van was filthy. 'What the hell does your father want with me, anyway?'

Monica stared at her in silence for a few seconds, then said, 'He doesn't think Shane killed Brandon.'

'You're kidding.'

'No. He thinks it was Shane's dad.' Monica's perfectly lipsticked mouth curved into a slow smile. 'He'd like for you to tell Shane's dad that and see what happens. 'Cause if he was any kind of a father, he wouldn't stand by and let his baby boy take the heat for him. Literally.'

'So he wants me to tell Shane's dad the mayor is willing to make a deal?'

'Shane's life for his father's,' Monica said. 'No real dad

could resist something like that. Shane's not important, but Dad wants this over. Now.'

Claire had a very bad feeling squirming in the pit of her stomach, like she'd swallowed earthworms. 'I don't believe it. They'd never let Shane go!' Not if Oliver had any say in it, anyway.

Monica shrugged. 'I'm just delivering a message. You can tell Frank whatever you damn well want, but if you're smart, you'll tell him something to get him out in the open. Get me? Amelie's Protection only goes so far. You can still be hurt. In fact, Gina would probably enjoy that a lot, even if she gets a slap on the wrist for punishment.'

'And think about your friend, back there all by herself,' Gina said. She was smiling, a wet, crazy sort of smile. 'All kinds of things can happen to girls out on their own in this town. All kinds of *bad* things.'

'Yeah, well, Eve should know,' Monica said. 'Look who her brother is.'

Claire's head knocked back against metal as the van bumped over what felt like railroad tracks, setting off a nuclear vibration in her head with the already-fierce headache in the front. 'So,' Monica said. 'You know what you have to do, right? Go to Shane's dad. Convince him to trade himself for Shane. Or...you may find out just how unfriendly Morganville can really be.'

Claire didn't say anything. The things she wanted to say would, she figured, get her killed; whether or not

Monica and Gina would be punished for it later wasn't much of a comfort.

She finally gave them one sharp, unwilling nod.

'Home, James!' Monica called up to Jennifer, who gave the OK sign and turned a corner. Claire tried to peer out, but she didn't recognise the street. Somewhere close to campus, though. She saw the bell tower next to the UC rising up on the right-hand side.

She grabbed for a handhold as Jennifer slammed on the brakes. Monica wasn't so lucky; she spilt out of her seat and onto the floor, screaming and cursing. 'Dammit! What the hell was that, Jen, Driving for Dummies?'

Jen didn't say anything. Her hands slowly came up in a position of surrender.

The door behind Claire slid open, and a big hand grabbed her by the back of the neck and hauled her backward into the hot sunlight. *Not a vampire*, she thought, but that wasn't much of a comfort, because a burly, muscular arm stretched out past her, and it was holding a sawn-off shotgun. She recognised the blue flame tattoos licking down his arm and onto the back of his hand.

One of the bikers.

She looked around and saw three more, all armed, pointing weapons at the van – and then, she saw Shane's father walking up, as easy as if the whole town and every vampire in it hadn't been hunting him through the night. He even looked rested.

'Monica Morrell,' he said. 'Come on down! See what you've won.'

Monica froze where she was, holding on to one of the hanging leather straps. She looked at the guns, at Gina, who was kneeling with her hands in the air, and then helplessly at Claire.

She was afraid. Monica – crazy, weird, pretty Monica – was actually scared. 'My father—'

'Let's talk about him later,' Frank said. 'You get your sweet ass down here, Monica. Don't make me come and get you.'

She retreated farther into the van. Shane's dad grinned and motioned two of his bikers inside. One grabbed Gina by the hair and dragged her out to sprawl in the street.

The other one grabbed Monica, struggling and spitting, and handcuffed her to the leather strap in the back. She stopped fighting, amazed. 'But—'

'I knew you were going to do the opposite of what I told you,' Frank said. 'Easiest way to keep you in the van was to tell you to get out.' He opened the driver's-side door and stuck a gun in Jennifer's face. 'You, I don't need. Out.'

She slid down, fast, and kept her hands high as Frank pushed her towards the bikers. She sat down next to Gina on the kerb and put her arms around her. Funny, Claire had never thought of those two as being friends in their own right, just as hangers-on for Monica. But now they seemed...real. And really scared.

'You.' Shane's dad turned to look directly at Claire. 'In the back.'

'But—'

One of the bikers put his gun close to her head. She swallowed and scrambled into the van, claiming the leather seat that Monica had so recently tumbled out of. Shane's father got in after her, then a sweaty load of bikers. One of them got in the driver's seat, and the van lurched into gear.

It hadn't taken but a minute, Claire figured. In Morganville, at this hour, nobody probably even noticed. The streets looked deserted.

She looked at Monica, who stared back, and for the first time, she thought she really understood what Monica was feeling, because she felt it, too.

This was a very bad thing.

The van lurched through a long series of turns, and Claire tried to think of an easy way to get to her cell phone, which was in the pocket of her jeans. She'd dropped Eve's back at the car, when Monica had slammed her face-first into the dashboard... She managed to get her fingers hooked in her pocket, casual-like, and touched the metal case. *All I have to do is dial 911*, she thought. Eve had probably already reported the abduction, if Eve was OK enough to talk. They could trace cell phones, right? GPS tracking or something?

As if he'd read her mind, Shane's dad came to her, stood her up, and patted her down. He did it fast, not lingering like some dirty old man, and found the phone in her pocket. He took it. Monica was yelling again, and trying to kick; one of the bikers was doing the same thing as Frank, although Claire thought it was more feeling up than patting down. Still, he found her cell, too – a Treo – and slid open the van door to pitch them out into the street. 'Kill 'em!' he yelled to the driver, who pulled the van into a U-turn and went back the other way. Claire didn't hear the crunch, but she figured the phones were nothing but electronic bits.

The turning and lurching continued. Claire just hung on, head down, thinking hard. She couldn't get word out, but Eve would have. Detective Hess, Detective Lowe? Maybe they'd come running.

Maybe Amelie would send her own people to enforce her Protection. That would be pretty fabulous right about now.

'Hey,' Monica said to Shane's dad. 'Stupid move, asshole. My dad's going to have every cop in Morganville on you in seconds. You're never going to get away, and once they have you, they'll throw you in a hole so deep, even the sewer will seem like heaven. *Don't touch me, you pig!*' Monica writhed to get away from the stroking hands of the biker next to her, who just smiled and showed gold-capped teeth.

'Don't touch her,' Shane's dad said. 'We're not animals.' Claire wondered where all this sudden White Knight syndrome came from, because he'd been willing to let his boys do whatever to her and Eve back at the Glass House. 'Take her bracelet.'

'What? No. *No*! It doesn't come off, you know that!'

The biker reached down and took a small pair of bolt cutters from a pouch on his belt. Claire gasped in horror as the biker grabbed Monica's arm. *Oh God*, she thought, *he's going to cut off her hand...*

But he just sliced through the metal bracelet, instead, yanked it off her wrist, and tossed it to Shane's father. Monica glared at him, trembling, and slapped him. Hard.

He drew back a hand to slap her back. 'Leave it,' Shane's father said. He was staring at the bracelet. The outside was the symbol, of course; Claire couldn't read it, but she figured it was Brandon's symbol, and now that Brandon was dead, she wondered who picked up his Protection duties. Maybe Oliver...

On the inside was inscribed Monica's full name: MONICA ELLEN MORRELL. Shane's dad grunted in satisfaction.

'You want a finger, too?' the biker asked, snipping the shears. 'No trouble.'

'I think this makes the point for us,' Shane's dad said. 'Get us underground, Kenny. Move.'

The guy driving – Kenny, at least now Claire knew one of their names – nodded. He was a tall man, kind of thin, with long black hair and a blue bandanna. His leather vest had a naked girl on a Harley on the back, and it matched the tattoos down the arm that Claire could see. Kenny expertly navigated the confusing streets and turns of Morganville, moving fast but not dangerously fast, and then all of a sudden...darkness.

Kenny flicked on the lights. They were in a storm drain, a huge concrete tunnel big enough to fit the van – though barely – and it was heading down at a steep angle into the dark. Claire fought to get her breath. She didn't really like closed-in places, or the dark... She remembered how freaked-out she'd been sealed in the hidden pantry room at the Glass House, not so many days ago. No, she didn't like this. She didn't like it at all.

'Where are you taking us?' she asked. She meant it to sound tough, but instead it sounded like what she was: a scared sixteen-year-old, trying to be brave. Great.

Frank Collins, hanging on to one of the leather straps, looked at her with something strange in his eyes – almost, she thought, respect. 'Not taking *you* anywhere,' he said. 'You get to deliver the message.' And he pitched her Monica's severed bracelet. 'Tell the mayor that if I don't hear that my son's been set free before tomorrow at dawn, pretty little miss here gets to find out what fire is really like. We've got us a nice blowtorch.'

She didn't like Monica. In fact, she kind of hated her, and she thought Morganville would be a much better place if Monica just...disappeared.

But nobody deserved what he was talking about.

'You can't do that,' she said. 'You can't.' But she knew,

looking around at the grinning, sweaty crew he'd brought with him, that he could do that, and a lot worse. Shane was right. His dad was seriously sick.

'Kenny up there's going to pull up to a ladder soon,' Frank continued. 'And I'm going to want you to get out of the van, Claire. Go up the ladder and push open the grate. You'll be right in front of the Morganville City Hall. You walk up to the first cop you see and you tell him you need to see the mayor about Frank Collins. And you tell him that Frank Collins has his daughter, and she's going to pay for the life she already took, not to mention the one they're about to. Got it?'

Claire nodded stiffly. Monica's bracelet felt cold and heavy in her fingers.

'One more thing,' Frank said. 'I'm going to need you to tell them just how serious I am. And you'd better be persuasive, because if I don't hear something from the mayor before dawn, we'll be using those bolt cutters to send him some more reminders. And she's fresh out of bracelets.'

The van lurched to a stop, and Frank threw open the sliding door. 'Out,' he said. 'Better make it good, Claire. You want to save my son, don't you?'

He didn't say anything about saving Monica, she noticed. Nothing at all.

Monica looked at her, no longer sleek and magazine glossy. She seemed small and vulnerable, alone in the van with all those men. Claire hesitated, then got up from her seat and grabbed a leather strap to steady herself. Her knees felt like water. 'This is crazy,' she said. 'Hang in there. I'll get help.'

Tears glittered in Monica's eyes. 'Thanks,' she said softly. 'Tell my dad—' She didn't finish, and she sucked in a deep breath. The tears cleared away, and she gave Claire a half-crazy smile. 'Tell my dad that if anything happens to me, he can hold you personally responsible.'

The door slammed shut between them, and the van sped off into the dark. Claire was glad she had her hand on the ladder, because the lights went away fast, and she was left in a dark so close and hot and filthy that she wanted to curl up into a ball.

Instead, she climbed, feeling for the slimy rungs in the dark and waiting for something – something with teeth – to lunge onto her back at any second. Vampires lived down here, they had to. Or at least, they used these tunnels as highways; she'd always wondered how they got around during the day. These weren't sewer tunnels, just storm drains built extra large. And since Morganville wasn't exactly built on a floodplain, chances were, the water had never been more than ankle-high in these things since they'd been constructed.

Claire climbed, and when she squinted just right, she saw flickers of what looked like daylight. There was a grate overhead, covered with some kind of protective material to keep the sun from filtering down into the tunnel. She braced herself on the rungs, hooked her left arm through one of the iron bars, and heaved with her right to push the grate up.

Hot Texas sun washed over her in a warm, sticky flood, and Claire gasped and raised her face to it in gratitude. After taking a few fast breaths, she pushed herself up another rung and thumped the grate back on its hinges to climb out.

Just as Shane's dad had said, she was standing in front of the Morganville City Hall – which was, unfortunately, *not* on Founder's Square. It was a big Gothic castle of a building, all red sandstone in rough-cut blocks, and people were coming and going on their way to or from work, or filing paperwork – just carrying out their daily lives, whatever that meant in Morganville.

She rolled out onto the grass and flopped there, breathing hard. A couple of faces appeared overhead, blocking out the sun. One of them was wearing a policeman's uniform cap.

'Hello,' Claire said, and shaded her eyes. 'I need to talk to the mayor. Tell him I have information about his daughter, and Frank Collins.'

The mayor had changed out of the suit he'd worn to put Shane in a cage the night before; he was wearing a green golf shirt with black slacks and loafers. Very preppy. He was in the hallway, talking into his cell phone, looking tense and angry. Claire was escorted past him, into his office, and deposited in a big red leather chair by two members of Morganville's finest; she didn't recognise either of them. When she asked after Detectives Hess and Lowe, she got nothing.

Nobody even admitted to knowing their names.

Claire was feeling more than a little light-headed. She had no idea how long it had been since she'd eaten, but the world was starting to take on a surreal melty edge that really wasn't a very good sign. Between the stress, the poor sleep, and the lack of food, she was going to be loopy soon.

Keep it together, Claire. Pretend you're cramming for a test. She'd gone without sleep for three days once, prepping for her SAT, and she hadn't eaten much beyond Jolt cola and Cheetos. She could do this.

'Here,' said a voice from beside her, and a red can of Coca-Cola appeared, held in a big male hand. 'You look like you could use something to drink.'

Claire looked up. It was Richard, Monica's cop brother. The cute one. He looked tired and worried. He pulled up another chair close to hers and leant forward, elbows on his knees. Claire busied herself with the Coke, popping the top and taking a fast chug of the icy sweet contents.

'My sister got carjacked,' he said. 'You know that, right?'

Claire nodded and swallowed. 'I was there. I was in the van.'

'That's exactly why I wanted to talk to you before I let you see my dad,' Richard said. 'You were in the van with Jennifer and Gina and Monica.'

Claire nodded again.

'Let me ask you this, then. How did you signal them?'

She blinked. 'How did I what?'

'How did you plan the set-up? What was your system? Did you text message them? You know, we can pull those records, Claire. Or was it some kind of trap you led my sister into?'

'I don't know what you're—'

Richard looked up at her, and she fell silent, because he didn't look so friendly this time. Not friendly at all. 'My sister's a crazy psycho – I know that. But she's still *my sister*. And nobody lays their hands on a Morrell in this town, or somebody – maybe a whole bunch of somebodies – pays for it. Get the point? So whatever you know, whatever your relationship is with these invaders, you'd better come to it quick, or we're going to start digging. And Claire, that's going to be a fast, bloody kind of process.'

She wrapped both hands around the Coke can and raised it to her mouth for another trembling gulp, then said, 'I didn't lead them to your sister. Your sister abducted *me*. Right out of the Photo Finish parking lot. Ask Eve. Oh God...Eve...Gina cut her. Is she OK?'

Richard frowned at her. 'Eve's all right.'

That eased a terrible knot in her stomach. 'What about Gina and Jennifer?'

'Also fine. They called in the carjacking. Gina said—' He turned something over in his mind, and then said, more slowly, 'Gina said a lot of things. But I should have remembered who I was talking to. If there's anybody in Morganville crazier than my sister, it's Gina.'

She couldn't disagree with that. 'The guys who took over the van—'

'Shane's father,' Richard interrupted. 'We already know all that. Where is he now?'

'I don't know,' she said. 'I swear! He let me out in the storm drain and told me to climb the ladder and talk to your father. That's why I'm here.'

'Leave the kid alone, Richard.' Mayor Morrell stalked in, slamming the office door behind him, and paused to glare at the two extra police officers standing guard. 'You. Out. If my son can't handle some sixteen-year-old stick of a girl, he deserves what he gets.'

They left, fast. Claire put the Coke can aside on a table as the mayor sank into his big, plush leather chair. He no longer looked quite as smug as he had back at Founder's Square, and he definitely looked angry.

'You,' he snapped. 'Talk. Now.'

She did, spilling it out in a tumbling stream of words. Shane's father hijacking the van and pitching Gina and Jennifer out. Destroying the cell phones. Threatening Monica and sending Claire as his messenger of doom. 'He's serious,' she finished. 'I mean, I've seen him do things. He's seriously not afraid to hurt people, and he definitely doesn't like Monica.'

'Oh, and suddenly you're her bestest little friend? Please. You hate her guts, and you've probably got reason,' Richard said. He got up to pace the room. 'Dad, look, let me do this. I can find these guys. If we put every available man and vampire on the streets—'

'We did that last night, son. Wherever these guys go, they're going someplace we can't follow.' The mayor's red-rimmed eyes fastened back on hers. He cracked his knuckles. He had big hands, like his son. Hard hands. 'Oliver wants this over. He wants to move up the timetable, burn the kid tonight and get them out in the open. It's not a bad plan. Call their bluff.'

'You think Frank Collins is bluffing?' Richard asked.

'No,' the mayor said. 'I think he'll do exactly what he said he'd do, only a whole lot worse than we can imagine. But what Oliver wants...'

'You're just going to let him do it? What about Monica?'

'Oliver doesn't know they've got her. Once I tell him—'

'Dad,' Richard said. 'It's *Oliver*. He's not going to give a crap and you know it. Acceptable losses. But it's not acceptable to me, and it shouldn't be to you, either.'

Father and son exchanged looks, and Richard shook his head and continued to pace. 'We need to find a way to get her back. Somehow.'

'You.' The mayor pointed a thick finger at Claire. 'Tell me the whole thing again. Everything. Every detail, I don't care how minor. Start from the first time you saw these men.'

Claire opened her mouth to answer, and caught herself just in time. *No, you idiot! You can't tell them the truth! The truth gets Shane fried for sure...* She wasn't a good liar, she knew that, and there was too much time slipping by while she was scrambling around in her head, trying to pick up the threads of where to start the story...

'I guess... I saw some of them when they broke into the house,' she said tentatively. 'You know, when we called the cops about the home invasion? And then I saw...'

She froze and closed her eyes. She'd seen something important. *Very* important. What was it? Something to do with Shane's dad...

'Start with the van,' Richard said, and short-circuited her attempt at catching the memory. She dutifully recounted it all again, and then again, answering specific questions as fast as she could. Her head ached, and despite the cold Coke, her throat did, too. She needed sleep, and she wanted to roll up in blankets and cry herself into a coma. *Oliver wants to move up the timetable, burn the kid tonight.* No. No, they couldn't let it happen, they couldn't...

But they could. Without question.

'Let's start over,' Richard said. 'From the beginning.'

She burst into despairing tears.

It took hours before they were done with her. Nobody offered to drive her home.

Claire walked, feeling like she was drifting half out of her body, and made it all the way home without a single incident. It was still daylight, which helped, but the streets seemed unnaturally quiet and deserted. Word was out, she guessed. Humans were keeping their heads down, hoping the storm would pass.

As Claire slammed the door, Eve came bolting down the stairs, raced to her, and wrapped her in a breathless full-body hug. 'Bitch!' she said. 'I can't believe you scared the crap out of me like that. Oh my *God*, Claire. Can you believe those jerks at the police station wouldn't even take my statement? I even had a wound! A real wound with blood and everything! How'd you get away? Did Monica hurt you?'

Eve didn't know. Nobody, had told her at the police station.

'Shane's dad stopped the van,' Claire said. 'He took Monica as a hostage.'

For a second, neither one of them moved, and then Eve whooped and held up her hand for a high five. Claire just stared at her, and Eve compensated by clapping both hands over her head. 'Yesssss!' she said, and did a totally geeky victory dance. 'Couldn't happen to a nicer psycho!'

'Hey!' Claire yelled, and Eve froze in mid-celebration. It was stupid, but Claire was angry; she knew Eve was right, knew she had no reason at all to think Monica was ever going to be anything but a gigantic pain in the ass, but… 'Shane's dad's going to burn her if they go through with the execution. He has a *blowtorch*.'

The glee dropped out of Eve's expression. 'Oh,' she said. 'Well…still. Not like she didn't ask for it. Karma's a bitch, and so am I.'

'Oliver's trying to get them to kill Shane *tonight*. We're

out of time, Eve. I don't know what to do anymore.'

That knocked the last of Eve's smugness right out from under her. She didn't seem to know, either. She licked her lips and said, 'There's still time. Let me make some phone calls. And you need to get some food. And some sleep.'

'I can't sleep.'

'Well, you can eat, right?'

She could, as it turned out – and she needed to. The world had taken on a grey colour, and her head was aching. A hot dog – plain except for mustard – chips, and a bottle of water solved some of that, though not the ache in her heart, or the sick feeling that had nothing to do with hunger.

What are we going to do?

Eve was on the phone, calling people. Claire slumped on the couch, tipped over, and curled up under the blanket. It still smelt like Shane's cologne.

She must have slept for a while, and when she woke it was almost as though someone had flipped a switch or whispered in her ear, *Wake up!* Because she was upright in seconds, heart racing, and her brain was running to catch up. The house was quiet, except for the usual ticks and pops and moans that old houses got. A breeze rattled dry leaves outside.

And it took Claire a second to realise that she couldn't see the tree that shaded the window because *it was dark.*

'No!' She catapulted off the couch and raced to find

a clock. It was exactly what she'd feared. No eclipses or sudden unexplained collapses of the normal day-night continuum; no, it was just dark because it was night.

She'd slept for hours. *Hours.* And Eve hadn't woken her up. In fact, she wasn't even sure Eve was still in the house.

'Michael!' Claire went from room to room, but he was nowhere to be seen. 'Michael! Eve! Where are you?'

They were in Michael's room. He opened the door, and he was half-dressed – shirt open, jeans hanging low-slung around his hips, revealing a chest and abs that even now Claire *had* to notice – and Eve was curled up in the bed, under the covers.

Michael quickly stepped out, buttoning his shirt. 'You're awake.'

'Yeah.' Claire suppressed a burst of pure fury. 'If you're done screwing around, maybe we can talk about Shane *dying tonight*.'

Michael dipped his chin a little, staring her straight in the eyes. 'You do *not* want to go there, Claire,' he said flatly. 'You really don't. You think I don't know? I don't care? *Fuck.* What do you think Eve's been doing all day while you—'

'Slept? Yeah, I fell asleep! You could have woken me up!'

He came forward a step. She backed up a step, then another, because his eyes...not Michael's usual expression. Not at all.

'So you could sit and rip your guts out, too?' he asked

softly. 'Enough of that going around, Claire. You needed to sleep. I let you sleep. Get over it.'

'So what's the brilliant plan you guys came up with while I was napping, then? What is it, Michael? What the hell do we do now?'

'I don't know,' he said, and whatever tight control he'd been hanging on to ripped loose at the roots. 'I don't know!' It was a yell, and it came right out of his guts. Claire backed up another step, feeling an icy flush race over her skin. 'What the hell do you want me to do, Claire? What?'

Her eyes filled up with tears. 'Anything,' she whispered. 'God, please. Anything.'

He grabbed her and hugged her. She sagged against him, trembling, not quite crying but...not quite not, either. It was a hopeless sort of feeling, as if they were loose and drifting and there was no land in sight.

Like they were lost. All lost.

Claire sniffled and stepped back, and when she did, she saw Eve standing in the doorway, watching them. Whatever Eve was thinking, it wasn't good, and it wasn't anything that Claire ever wanted to see again.

'Eve—'

'Whatever,' Eve said flatly. 'There's still one vampire who might help us. If we can find him and get him to agree. He could get into Founder's Square without any problem. He might even be willing to open up Shane's cage if we create some kind of diversion.'

Michael turned towards her. 'Eve.' He didn't sound

guilty, at least. He sounded worried, though. 'No. We talked about this.'

'Michael, it's the last thing we can do. I know that. But we need to go for it now, if we're going to do it at all.'

'What vampire?' Claire asked.

'His name is Sam,' Michael said, 'and this is going to sound weird, but he's my grandfather.'

'*Sam?* He's your...your—'

'Grandfather. Yeah. I know. Freaks me the hell out, too. It has all my life.'

Claire had to sit down. Fast.

When she recovered her breath, she told Eve and Michael about running into Sam at Common Grounds. About the present Sam had tried to give her for Eve.

'I didn't take it,' she said. 'I didn't know...well, it just didn't seem...right.'

'Damn straight,' Michael said.

Eve wasn't looking at him. 'Sam's OK,' she said.

'I thought you hated vampires.'

'I do! But... I guess if there's a most-hated-vampire list, he's at the bottom. He always seems so lonely,' Eve said. 'He came into Common Grounds pretty much every night and just talked for hours. Just talked. Oliver always watched him like a hawk, but he never did anything, never threatened anybody. Not like Brandon. In fact, I sometimes wondered—'

'Wondered what?'

'If Sam was there keeping an eye on Brandon. Maybe on Oliver, although I didn't know that at the time. Looking out for...'

'For the rest of us?' Michael nodded slowly. 'I don't know how true it is, because I always avoided him, but family talk always said Sam was a good guy, before he was changed. And he is the youngest of all of them. The most like...well, like us.'

Eve had gone over to the dark window, and was looking out, hands behind her back. 'You know anything else about him? Family secrets, I mean?'

'Just that supposedly he took on the vampires and won.'

'Won? He's one of them! How exactly is that winning?'

Michael shook his head, moved up behind her, and put his hands on her shoulders. He kissed the nape of her neck gently. 'I don't know, Eve. I'm just telling you what I heard. He got some kind of agreement out of the vampires. And it was because Amelie loved him.'

'Yeah, loved him enough to kill him and turn him into a bloodsucking fiend,' Eve said grimly. 'How sweet. Romance isn't dead. Oh, wait. It is.'

She pulled free of Michael and walked into the kitchen. Michael looked at Claire mutely. She shrugged.

When they got downstairs, they found that Eve was making bologna and cheese sandwiches. Claire wolfed down one in about six bites, then took a second sandwich.

The other two looked at her. 'What?' she asked. 'I'm starved. Honest.'

'Be my guest,' Michael said. 'I hate bologna. Besides, not like I can starve.'

Eve snorted. 'I made you roast beef, genius.' She handed him one. 'So go on. This is the first I've heard from you about the History of Sam. What made him so special to be the last vampire ever?'

'I don't really know,' Michael said. 'The only thing Mom ever told me was what I just told you. The point is, Sam's never really fit in with the vampires. Amelie doesn't like to be reminded of weakness, and he was a constant neon sign. She really cared about him. So she cut him off... Last I heard, she wouldn't see him or talk to him. He hangs around humans a lot more than other vampires.'

'And that's why I said he could help us,' Eve said. 'Or at least, he'd be willing to listen. Bonus if he's family.'

'So where do we find him?' Claire looked from Michael to Eve, then back again. 'At Common Grounds?'

'Off-limits to you,' Eve said. 'Hess told me what happened with you and Oliver.'

'Something happened?' Michael mumbled around his roast beef. 'Why don't I know this? God, I needed this. Tastes great.'

Eve rolled her eyes. 'Yeah, sandwiches take great skill. I'm thinking of teaching a class. Meanwhile, back on the subject, Claire is not going anywhere near Common Grounds. I said so. If anybody's going, it's me.'

'No,' Michael said. Eve glared at him.

'We had this talk,' she said. 'You may be dead sexy, and I mean, like, really dead and really sexy, but you don't get to tell me what to do. Right? And no head-shrinker stuff, either, or I swear to God, I'll pack my shit and move!'

Claire scraped her chair back, walked over to the cordless phone lying on the counter, and dialled from the business card still stuck to the refrigerator with a magnet. Four rings, and a cheerful voice answered on the other end and announced she'd reached Common Grounds. 'Hi,' Claire said. 'Can I talk to Sam, please?'

'Sam? Hold on.' The phone clattered, and Claire could hear the buzz of activity in the background – milk being steamed, people chatting, the usual excitement of a busy coffee shop. She waited, jittering one leg impatiently, until the voice came back on the line. 'Sorry,' it said. 'He's not here tonight. I think he went to the party.'

'The party?'

'You know, the zombie frat party? Epsilon Epsilon Kappa? The Dead Girls' Dance?'

'Thanks,' Claire said. She hung up and turned to face Michael and Eve, who were staring at her in outright surprise. She held up the phone. 'The power of technology. Embrace it.'

'You found him.'

'Without going into Common Grounds,' Claire pointed out. 'He's at a party on campus. The big frat thing. The one—' She paused, felt a chill, then a rush of heat.

'The one I was invited to. It was kind of a date. I was supposed to meet this boy there. Ian Jameson.'

'Guess what?' Eve said. 'We're both going. Time to put on the dead look, Claire.'

'The...what?'

Eve was looking at her critically while she munched her sandwich. 'Size one, maybe two, right? I've got some things that would fit you.'

'I'm not getting dressed up!'

'I don't make the rules, but everybody knows you don't get into the Dead Girls' Dance without making an effort. Besides, you'll look way cute as a teeny little Goth girl.'

Michael was frowning at them both now. 'No,' he said. 'It's too dangerous for you to be out at night without an escort.'

'Well, we're fresh out of escorts. I think Claire broke Detective Hess last night. And I'm *not* going to just sit and wait, Michael. You know that.' Eve locked eyes with him, and softened as he reached across the table and took her hand. 'No head stuff. You promised.'

'I promised,' he agreed. 'Never happen again.'

'Cute as you are when you worry, it's a party – there are hundreds of people there. It's safe enough.' Eve held his gaze steadily. 'Safer than Shane is, in that cage, waiting to die. Unless you're giving up on him.'

Michael let go of her hand and walked away. He stiff-armed his way out of the kitchen door.

'Guess not,' Eve said softly. 'Good. Claire. We need to find out what the timeline is. Whether they've moved it.'

'I'll do it,' Claire said, and punched in the number from another card. It was Detective Hess's private number, the one pencilled in on the back, and it rang four times before he picked up. He sounded bleary and exhausted. 'Sir? It's Claire. Claire Danvers. I'm sorry to wake you—'

'Not asleep,' he said, and yawned. 'Claire, whatever you're thinking, don't. Stay home, lock the doors, and keep your head down. I mean it.'

'Yes, sir,' she lied. 'I just want to know – there was talk about moving up the...the execution?'

'The mayor said no,' Hess said. 'Said he wanted due process, and called for Shane's dad to give himself up. Looks like a Mexican stand-off to me: he's got Shane;

Shane's dad has Monica. Nobody wants to blink.'

'How long...?'

'Before sunrise. Five in the morning,' Hess said. 'It'll all be over before dawn. For Monica, too, if Shane's dad isn't just bluffing.'

'He's not bluffing,' Claire said numbly. 'Oh God. That's not much time.'

'Better than what Oliver wanted. He wanted to do it at sunset tonight. The mayor backed him off, but only to the legal deadline. There won't be any last-minute stays of execution.' Hess shifted; his chair creaked. 'Claire, you need to prepare yourself. There's no miracle coming; nobody's going to have a change of heart. He's going to die. I'm sorry, but that's the way it is.'

She didn't have the heart to argue with him, because

she knew, deep down, that he was right. 'Thank you,' she whispered. 'I have to go now.'

'Claire. Don't try. They'll kill you.'

'Goodbye, Detective.'

She hung up, put the phone down on the counter, and braced herself with stiffened arms. When she looked up, Eve was watching her with bright, strange eyes.

'All right,' Claire said. 'If I have to be a zombie, I'll be a zombie.'

Eve smiled. 'Cutest zombie ever.'

Claire had never worn this much make-up in her life, not even at Halloween. 'You wear this every day?' she asked as Eve stepped back to look at her critically, make-up sponge still in hand. 'It feels weird.'

'You get used to it. Close your eyes. Powder time.' Claire obeyed, and felt the feathery touch of the powder brush as it glided over her face. She fought back an urge to sneeze.

'OK. Now, eyes,' Eve said. 'Hold still.'

It went on like that for a while, with Claire passively sitting and Eve working whatever dark magic she was working. Claire didn't know. There was no mirror, and she was weirdly reluctant to see what was happening to her, anyway. It felt a little like she was losing herself, although that was stupid, right? How you looked wasn't *you*. She'd always believed that, anyway.

Eve finally stepped back, studied her, and nodded. 'Clothes,' she said. Eve herself had put on a black corset thing, a tattered black skirt, and a necklace of skulls with matching earrings. Black lipstick. 'Here you go.'

Claire took off her blue jeans and T-shirt with great reluctance, then sat down to put on the black hose. They had white death's-head symbols in a line, and she couldn't figure out if they were supposed to go front or back. 'Where do you find this stuff?' she asked.

'Internet. Skulls go in the back.'

After the adventure of the hose, the black leather skirt – knee-length, jingling with zippers and chains – seemed almost easy. Claire's legs felt cold and exposed. She hadn't been in a skirt in…when? Not since she was twelve, probably. She'd never liked them.

The top was a black net thing, stretchy and tight, see-through with a black skull and crossbones printed on it. 'No way,' she said. 'It's transparent!'

'You wear it over a camisole, genius,' Eve said, and tossed a black silky thing to her. Claire slipped it over her head, then fought her way into the clingy embrace of the skull shirt. 'Watch the make-up!' Eve warned. 'OK, you're good. Excellent. Ready to take a look?'

She wasn't, but Eve didn't seem to notice. She steered her into the bathroom, turned on the light, and put her arm around Claire. 'Ta da!' Eve said.

Oh my God, Claire thought. *I can't believe I'm doing this.*

She looked like Eve's skinny little sister. A dead-on junior freak in training.

Well, at least she'd blend in, and if anybody was

looking for her, they'd never, ever recognise her. She wouldn't recognise herself. And somehow she just *knew* there'd be pictures on the Internet later.

Claire sighed. 'Let's go.'

Eve drove the black Cadillac onto campus and parked in the faculty lot – a blatant violation, but then, Eve didn't give a crap about campus tickets, either. It was the closest parking to the frat house. So close, in fact, that Claire could see the lights blazing from every window, and hear the low thudding thump of the bass rattling through the car.

'Wow,' Eve said. 'They've gone all out this year. Good old EEK.'

There was a graveyard around the house – tilting tombstones, big creepy-looking mausoleums, some decaying statues. There were also zombies – or, Claire guessed, party guests – lurching around and doing their best *Night of the Living Dead* parody for their friends' cameras.

The dull roar of the party was audible even through the car's closed windows.

'Stay close,' Eve said. 'Let's find Sam, yeah? In and out.'

'In and out.' Claire nodded.

They got out and ran the short distance to the graveyard.

At close range, the tombstones were either foam rubber or Styrofoam, and the mausoleum was a dressed-up storage building, but it looked great. Zombie hands were reaching up out of the dirt. Nice touch, Claire thought. She came close to one, and it turned and groped her ankle. Claire screamed and jumped back into Eve, who caught her. 'Jesus, guys, grow up,' Eve said, and crouched down to look at the ground. 'Where are you?'

'Right here!' A trapdoor covered with sod lifted up, and a geeky-looking frat boy wearing a pledge board stuck his head out. 'Uh, sorry. Just kidding. I have to—'

'Grope girls and look up their skirts. Yeah. Tough work, pledge.' Eve stood up and brushed dirt from her knees. 'Carry on.'

He grinned at her and thumped the trapdoor back down. His hand came up again through a hole in the ground.

'Wow,' Claire said. 'How many of them are there? In the ground?'

'Just the pledges,' Eve said. 'Come on. If Sam's here, he'll be talking to people. He loves to talk.'

If Sam could talk, and anyone could hear him, it was more than Claire could imagine. The music was pounding so loud that she felt it like physical waves through her body, and she had to fight back an urge to cover her ears. Eve had put Claire's hair up in little pigtails, and she missed having it over her ears to block out the roar. 'I need earplugs!' she yelled in Eve's ear. Eve mimed a *What did you say?* 'Never mind!'

The Epsilon Epsilon Kappa fraternity house was trashed. Claire suspected it was usually trashed, but this was extra special – plastic cups everywhere, drinks soaking into carpet, a chair broken in the corner, and drunks sleeping on the sofa. And this was just the foyer. Two guys stepped into their path and held out their hands in the universal gesture for *Don't even think about it*; they were big, muscular guys dressed in white face paint with black T-shirts that said UNDEAD SECURITY on them. 'Invitations?' one of them yelled. Claire exchanged a look with Eve.

'Ian Jameson invited me!' she screamed back. 'Ian Jameson!'

The security guys had a list. They checked it, and nodded. 'Upstairs!' one yelled. 'Last door on the left!'

She didn't intend to find Ian, but she nodded anyway. She and Eve pressed between the two security guys – who were maybe a *little* too close and stepped over the threshold into the wildest party Claire had ever seen in her entire life.

Not that her experience was wide, but still...she was pretty sure Paris Hilton would have classified this as wild. Despite the fact that alcohol was banned on campus, she was also pretty sure the punch that was being ladled out of gigantic coolers was alcoholic (it also had severed hands, eyeballs, and assorted plastic gross-outs floating in it, and was blood red). A lot of the people at the party already showed the telltale signs of being wasted – stumbling, laughing too loud, making wild gestures. Spilling drinks all over themselves and others, which really didn't seem to bother people because, hey, zombies! Not neat freaks. Everybody wore white make-up, or had some kind of rubbery disgusting mask (though that was mostly the guys).

The main room was kind of a dance floor, people pressed up against each other and swaying. Claire stood in the doorway, frozen with sudden dread. It looked like a room full of dead people. Worse – dead, drunk, *horny* people.

'Come on,' Eve yelled impatiently, and grabbed her by the hand. She plunged into the crowd without hesitation, craning her head to look around. 'At least he's a redhead!' Because most of those at the party were wearing black wigs, or had dyed their hair like Eve's. Claire's had suffered a temporary blacking from some kind of spray-on stuff Eve had assured her would wash right out. Claire tried to shield herself from unnecessary body-to-body contact, but it was pretty much useless; she was closer to a whole bunch of guys than she'd ever been in her life.

A hand tried to go up her skirt as she pressed through the crowd. She yelped and jumped, moving faster. Somebody else swatted her on the ass.

'Faster!' she yelled at Eve, who had slowed down to get her bearings. 'God, I can't breathe in here!'

'This way!'

Claire felt filthy – not just from getting groped, which continued to happen, but because she was sopping with other people's sweat by the time Eve squirmed them through to a small clear space on the other side of the room, next to the stairs. It must have been the Wallflower Corner; there were some shy-looking girls, all dressed in mock-Goth finery, grouped together for comfort and (Claire suspected) protection. She felt an instant sympathy for them. 'Great party!' Eve screamed over the pounding beat of the music. 'Wish I could enjoy it!'

'Any sign of Sam?'

'No! Not in here! Let's try the other rooms!'

After the chaos of the main dance room, the kitchen felt like a study hall, even though it was still filled with people talking too loud and gesturing too much. More punch-filled coolers in here, which was driving Claire crazy; she was thirsty, but no way was she adding being drunk to her problems just now. Too much was at stake.

Her ears were still ringing. At least, in here, there was room to breathe. Claire reflexively searched for her cell phone, remembered it getting crunched under the wheels of the white van, and cursed under her breath. 'What time is it?' she asked Eve, who consulted her own black Razr (decorated, of course, with skulls).

'Ten,' she said. 'I know. We have to hurry.'

Somebody grabbed Claire by the arm, and she recoiled in fright, but then she recognised him under the make-up – Ian, the guy who'd told her about the party. The one whose name they'd used to get inside. 'Claire?' he asked. 'Wow. You look great!'

He looked less geeky now, more edgy, with spiked black hair and vampire-style make-up. Claire wondered uneasily how many actual vampires were infiltrating this party tonight. Not a pleasant thought. 'Oh...hi, Ian!' Eve was scanning the room, and as Claire glanced at her, Eve shook her head and mimed going to the next room. Claire begged her not to go, at least with her eyes, but the thick make-up probably disguised her desperation.

'I'm so glad you came!' Ian said. He hardly had to raise his voice at all to be heard over the roar; he just had that kind of voice, and plus, it was a blessedly dull roar in here. 'Can I get you some punch?'

'Um...do you have anything that's not, you know...?'

'Right, yeah. How about some water?'

'Water would be wonderful.' Where the hell was Eve? She'd ducked behind two tall guys and now Claire couldn't see her, and she felt alone and very vulnerable just standing here in her fake Goth get-up, and God, this make-up itched; how did Eve stand it? Claire wanted a shower, wanted to scrub her face clean, and wanted to put on plain jeans and a plain T-shirt and never be adventurous again.

Shane. Think about Shane. She felt an uncomfortable twist of guilt that she'd ever let him slip out of her thoughts, even for a minute.

Ian came back with a bottle of water, the top already off. 'Here you go,' he said, and handed it over. He was drinking water, too, not the punch stuff. 'Crazy, huh?'

'Crazy,' she agreed. In a town full of vampires, this was just about the craziest idea she could imagine, putting a bunch of drunk, horny college kids in a place where vampires could blend right in. 'Did you see where my friend went?'

'Girls,' Ian sighed. 'Always travel in packs. Yeah, she went into the library. Come on.'

Claire gulped water as she followed him, stepping carefully over the legs of several people who'd decided the kitchen floor looked like a good place to sit down for a chat. And oh God, what was that couple in the corner doing? She blushed under the make-up and looked quickly away, focusing on the back of Ian's neck. He'd missed a spot on the make-up. It looked pink.

The next room had people, too, but not quite as many as the kitchen and it was practically deserted compared to the dance room. *Library* was a generous word. It had books, but not as many as Claire would have thought, and most of them were old textbooks. Some were being defaced by people wielding black markers and pens, giggling with one another over the results.

No sign of Eve.

'Huh,' Ian said. 'Hang on.' He went to ask a question of another guy, taller, dressed in a silky-looking black shirt open halfway down to reveal a strong, muscular chest. It took a while. Claire swigged more water, grateful for the moisture because even the library was steaming hot, and almost wiped at her face before she remembered the careful make-up job.

There was no sign of Sam in this room, either. While Ian was talking, Claire went over to one of the girls defacing books. She looked vaguely familiar – maybe somebody from chemistry? Anna something?

'Hi...Anna?' It must have been right; the girl looked up. 'Have you seen Sam? Red hair...maybe wearing a brown leather jacket...?' Although he had to have taken it off, in this heat. 'Blue eyes?'

'Oh, sure. Sam. He's upstairs somewhere.' Anna went back to her book sabotage, which seemed to involve drawing devils and pitchforks. *Upstairs*. Claire needed to get upstairs, but most importantly, she needed to find Eve. Fast.

Ian came back. 'She went upstairs,' he said. 'She's looking for a guy named Sam, right?'

'Yeah,' Claire said. 'Would you mind if—?'

'No, sure, I'll go with you.' He looked at the drained bottle in Claire's hand. 'Want some more?'

She nodded. He grabbed a bottle from an ice-filled cooler and handed it over. She cracked the seal and took another life-giving mouthful as Ian led the way to the stairs.

The heat was making her feel slow and disconnected. She wanted to pour the cold water over her face, but realised just in time – again – about the make-up. Stupid make-up.

The stairs seemed to go on forever, and it was like dancing around land mines; people were sitting on just about every step, some talking, some mumbling to themselves, some passing joints back and forth. *Oh man*. She really needed to get out of here, fast.

The upstairs landing seemed like a paradise of open space, and Claire clung to the handrail and breathed for a few seconds. Ian came back to get her. 'You OK?' he asked. She nodded. 'I don't know which room he's in. We'll just have to look.'

She followed him. He swung open the first door on the hall, and behind him she saw about ten people talking very intensely. They all looked at Ian with a definite *Get out* vibe, and as he shut the door, Claire realised that all ten of them were vampires.

Not Sam, though, but given what Sam had told her, and what she'd heard from Michael and Eve, that made sense. He'd be hanging around the humans, right? The vampires didn't want any part of him.

'Wrong room,' Ian said unnecessarily, and moved to the next one. She couldn't see over his shoulder, but he closed it in a hurry. '*Really* wrong room. Sorry.'

There were about ten doors on the hallway, but they didn't get that far. Claire was feeling kind of light-headed – in fact, she was dizzy. Maybe it was the heat. She took another gulp from the bottle, but that just seemed to make her feel nauseous. As Ian opened the fourth door, she said, 'I don't feel so good.'

Ian smiled and said, 'Well, that was fast,' and shoved her into the room. 'I thought I was going to have to work a little harder, but you're pretty easy.'

There were three other guys in the room. She didn't know any of them... No, wait, one looked familiar.

The jerk from the UC coffee bar, the one who'd been

so mean to Eve. He was one of them. She turned towards Ian, confused, but he was locking the door.

Her knees felt wobbly, and so did her head. Something was wrong. Something was very, very wrong…but she hadn't had anything to drink. She'd been careful…

Not careful enough. The first water bottle he'd brought her, he'd opened it first.

Stupid, Claire. Stupid, stupid, stupid. But he'd seemed so…nice.

'You don't want to do this,' she said, and backed up as one of the guys reached for her. There wasn't a lot of space. It was somebody's bedroom, most of it taken up by a bed, a dresser with the drawers hanging half-open. Dirty laundry piled in a corner. *Oh God.* It hit her hard that Eve had no idea where she was, she had no cell phone, and even if she screamed, no one would hear her over the music. Or care.

She remembered what Eve had done that terrible evening after the biker shoved his way in. *You need a weapon.* Yeah, but Eve was older and bigger, and wasn't drugged at the time…

She nearly tripped over a baseball bat sticking out from under the bed. She grabbed it and took up a bleary, weaving batting stance. 'Don't touch me!' she said, and screamed at the top of her lungs. 'Eve! *Eve!* I need help!'

She took a wild swing at Ian, who was strolling forward, and he ducked it easily. She reversed and slammed the butt end of the bat towards him, and that one, he didn't duck. It hit him squarely in the mouth, and he staggered back, bleeding.

'You *bitch*!' he said, and spit blood. 'Oh, you are gonna pay for that.'

'Hold up,' said the coffee bar jerk, who was leaning against the door with his arms folded. 'You put the full dose in her bottle, right? And she drank it?'

Ian nodded. He fished around in the laundry pile and found a sock to press against his mouth and nose. Good. She hoped it was filthy. And had athlete's foot on it.

'Then all we have to do is wait a couple of minutes,' the jerk said. 'She's not going anywhere except to la-la land.' He high-fived his buddies. Ian continued to glare at her. They were all between her and the door. There was a window, but it was the second floor and she wasn't even steady enough to stand, much less free-climb. Claire gripped the bat in sweaty, numbed hands, and saw sparkles at the edges of her vision. Everything looked bleary. She felt waves of heat sweep over her, and then an icy chill. Michael? Was Michael here? No, Michael couldn't leave the house...

Somehow, she was sliding down to a sitting position on the floor. The bat was still clutched in her hands, but she was tired, very tired, and she felt so sick and hot...

Somebody rattled the doorknob. Claire summoned up whatever was left of her strength and screamed, 'Help! Get help! Eve!'

Ian said, and grinned at Claire with bloody teeth, 'Just somebody looking for a place to screw. Don't worry, baby. We won't hurt you. Not that you'll remember, anyway.'

She pretended to be worse off than she really was (although truthfully, she was pretty bad) and, mumbling, let her eyes drift half-closed.

'That's it,' the coffee bar jerk said. 'She's out. Get her on the bed.'

She'd never really done this before, but she was imagining hard how Eve would have handled it. She let the bat kind of wobble and fall to rest in her lap, aligned with her leg, as if it had got too heavy to hold up. (Not quite. Just nearly.)

And when Ian walked up to grab her, she brought the bat straight up with as much force as she could manage. It smacked him right where it would hurt the most, and Ian crumpled with a high-pitched, breathless scream, huddled in on himself.

Claire forced her legs to hold her, and slid back up to a standing position. She was leaning for support, and lucky to be in a corner, where the two angled walls let her look like she wasn't about to topple over. Her arms were shaking, and the guys would have seen that if she'd tried to raise the bat, so she tapped it casually against her leg. 'Who wants some?' she asked. 'I won't hurt you. Much.'

It was all show, and they only had to wait. Coffee Bar Jerk knew that, all too well, and she could feel the drug

– what the hell was it? – stealing away her concentration, her strength, making her slow and stupid and all-too-easy prey.

Shane, she thought, and forced herself to stand upright just a little longer. *Shane needs me. I'm not letting this happen.*

'You're bluffing,' Coffee Bar Jerk said, and came around the bed. Claire took a swing at him, missed, and smacked the bat into the wood so hard it rattled her teeth.

He grabbed the bat on the backswing and easily twisted it out of her grip. He tossed it to one of the other two guys, who caught it one-handed. 'That,' he said, 'was really stupid. This could have been real nice and easy, you know that, right?'

'I have Amelie's Protection,' Claire said.

He grabbed her by the throat of her sheer black skull-printed shirt, and dragged her forward. Her legs folded when she tried to pull away.

'I don't care,' he said. 'I'm not from this stupid town. None of us are. Monica said that was the way to go, to get around the dumbass rules, whatever they are. Whoever Amelie is, she can kiss my ass. After you're done doing it.'

The door to the hall gave a dry, metallic pop, and swung slowly open. Claire blinked and tried to focus her eyes, because there was someone standing there. No, two someones. One had red hair. Wasn't there something about red hair...? Oh yeah. Sam had red hair. Sam the vampire. Sam I Am. Michael's grandpa, wasn't that just too weird?

The door no longer had a knob on the outside. The one on the inside fell out with a dull thud to the carpet and rolled under the bed.

'Claire!' Oh, that was *Eve*. 'Oh my God...'

'Excuse me,' Sam said, 'but what did you say about Amelie?'

Coffee Bar Jerk let go of Claire's top, and she slid back down the wall. She fumbled around for something to use for a weapon, but all she came up with was another set of filthy socks that had missed the laundry. For some reason, that seemed funny. She giggled and rested her head against the wall to let her neck relax. Her neck was working too hard.

'I said that Amelie can kiss my ass, Red. And what are you going to do about it? Stare me to death?'

Sam just stood there. Claire couldn't see anything about him change, but it was like the room just went... cold. 'You really don't want to do this,' Sam said. 'Eve, go get your friend.'

'Yeah, Eve, come on in, we've got a nice big bed!' Ian giggled. 'I hear you know how to have a real good time.' He tossed the bloody sock he'd been pressing to his nose down on the floor and got ready to grab Eve if she came inside. Sam looked at the discarded sock for a second, then picked it up and squeezed it, drizzling blood into the palm of his hand.

And then he licked it up. Slowly. Meeting the eyes of every guy facing him.

'I said,' he whispered, 'you really don't want to do this.'

Claire heard a great big buzzing in her head, like a hive full of bees. *Oh, I'm going to pass out, because that was gross.*

'Shit,' Ian whispered, and backed up. Fast. 'You're sick, man!'

'Sometimes,' Sam agreed. 'Eve, go get her. Nobody's going to touch you.'

Eve cautiously edged past him, hurried to Claire, and gave her a fast embrace before she hauled her upright again. 'Can you walk?'

'Not very well,' Claire said, and gulped down nausea. The world kept coming in hot and cold flashes, and she felt like she was going to throw up, but somehow it was all smeared and funny, even the terror in Eve's eyes.

Not so funny when Coffee Bar Jerk decided to grab Eve, though.

He lunged over the bed, reaching for Eve's wrist – Claire was too fuzzy to know why he was doing it. Maybe he was hoping to use her as some kind of shield against Sam. But whatever he meant, it was a bad decision.

Sam moved in a flicker, and when Claire blinked, Coffee Bar Jerk was up against the wall, eyes wide, staring at Sam's face from a distance of about three inches.

'I said,' Sam whispered, 'nobody was going to touch her. Are you *deaf*?'

Claire didn't see it, but she imagined he probably flashed some fang right about then, because Coffee

Bar Jerk whimpered like a sick dog.

The other boys moved out of Eve's way without even trying to stop her.

'Monica,' Claire said. 'I think it was Monica. She got Ian to ask me.'

'What?'

'Monica got him to ask me. Told them to do this.'

'*Bitch!* OK, I take it all back. She needs a good blowtorching.'

'No,' Claire said faintly. 'Nobody deserves that. Nobody.'

'Great. Saint Claire, the patron saint of the kick-me sign. Look, keep it together, OK? We need to get out of here. Sam! Come on! Leave them!'

Sam didn't seem inclined to listen. 'Manners, boys,' he said. 'Looks to me like nobody ever taught you any. It's time you had a lesson before somebody else gets hurt.'

'Hey, man—' Ian was holding out his hands in surrender. 'Seriously. Just having fun. We weren't going to hurt her. No need to go all Charles Bronson. We didn't even really touch her. Look. Clothes still on.'

'Don't even try.' Sam continued to stare at Coffee Bar Jerk, who was looking less like a predator, and more and more like a scared kid faced with the big, bad wolf. 'I like these girls. I don't like you. Do the maths. Consider yourself subtracted.'

'Sam!' Eve's voice was loud and flat. 'Enough with the

macho hero stuff. We came to find you. Let's get out of here and talk.'

'I'm not leaving,' Sam said, his eyes fixed on the boy he was holding. 'Not until Disney Princess here apologises, or his head comes off, one of the two.'

'Sam! What we need to talk about is *important*, and Disney Princess is *not*!'

For a second Claire thought nothing Eve could say would get through, but then she saw Sam smile – it wasn't a nice smile – and he let Coffee Bar Jerk slide back to the floor. 'Fine,' he said. 'Consider yourself horribly tortured. Make sure you think about all the ways I could have hurt you, because if I hear about anything like this happening again, I want you to know what's coming.'

Coffee Bar Jerk nodded shakily, and kept his back to the wall as he slid over to join his posse.

Sam turned towards the girls, and came forward to touch Claire lightly on the shoulder. 'Are you all right?'

Claire nodded, a loose flop of her head. That was a mistake; she nearly pitched over, and it took all of Eve's strength to keep her on her feet.

When she was able to open her eyes and focus again, Sam had moved away, to the door.

'What?' Eve asked. 'And by the way, you're blocking the escape hatch.'

'Hush,' Sam said softly, barely loud enough to be heard over the pounding, relentless beat of the music.

And then Claire heard the screaming.

In a blink, Sam was gone from the doorway. Eve moved out into the hallway, craning her head to look over the rail, and Claire looked, too.

It was chaos down there, and not the happy chaos of a dance. Knots of screaming, pushing people, desperately jamming up the exits from the big open room, all in black clothes, white faces, some splashes of red here and there...

Blood. There was *blood.*

Sam grabbed both her and Eve by the shoulders, swung them around, and pushed them back inside the room. He looked at Ian, who was still cowering against the wall. 'You. O Positive. How many exits?'

'What?... Oh *shit*, did you just call me by my blood type?'

'*How many exits?*"

'The stairs! You have to take the stairs!'

Sam cursed under his breath, went to the closet, and yanked it open. It was a walk-in, pretty large, filled with junk. He shoved Claire and Eve inside and held the door open. 'You,' he said to the four boys. 'If you want to live, get in. Touch these girls and I'll kill you myself. You know I'm serious, yeah?'

'Yeah,' Ian said faintly. 'Not a finger on 'em. What's happening? Is it, like, one of those shooting things?'

'Yes,' Sam said. 'It's like that. Get in.'

The boys piled into the closet. Eve dragged Claire to the farthest corner, shoving piles of rank-smelling athletic shoes out of the way, and sat her down. Eve crouched next to her, ready for action, and glared at the guys. They kept their distance.

Sam slammed the door.

Darkness.

'What the hell is going on?' Coffee Bar Jerk demanded. His voice was shaking.

'People are getting hurt,' Eve said tightly. 'Could be you if you don't shut up.'

'But—'

'Just *shut the hell up*!'

Silence. The music was still pounding downstairs, but over it Claire could hear the screaming. She started to go into that funny grey place, but jerked herself back with an effort and squeezed Eve's tense hand. 'It's OK,' Eve whispered to her. 'You're OK. I'm so sorry.'

'I was doing OK,' Claire said. Surprised, actually, that it was true. 'Thanks for saving me.'

'I didn't do anything but find Sam. He found you.' Eve stopped. 'All right, who's touching me?'

A high-pitched male voice out of the darkness. 'Oh shit! Sorry!'

'Better be.'

There was a tense silence in the dark.

And then Claire heard heavy footsteps coming down the hallway.

'Quiet,' Eve whispered. She didn't need to say it. Claire felt it, and she knew everybody else did, too. There was something bad out there, something worse than four horny, stupid, cruel boys.

She felt something brush against her. A hand. One of the boys, she didn't know which one – was it Ian who'd slumped against the wall nearest to her?

She took it and squeezed. He squeezed back, silently.

And Claire waited to see if they were going to die.

CHAPTER TEN

The screaming stopped, and the music cut off in mid-rave. That was worse, somehow. The silence felt…cold. Claire held on grimly to consciousness. The effects seemed to be coming and going. Maybe she was going to be OK.

A floorboard creaked *right outside the closet door.*

Claire felt a tremor go through the boy whose hand she held, and she pressed herself harder against the wall and stared at the closet door. It was a big black rectangle outlined in warm yellow.

There was a flicker of shadow, and a snarl, and a man's full-throated yell, and the sound of a body hitting the floor.

Then the boom of a gun going off. Claire jumped, and felt Eve and the boy jump, too. 'Oh God,' he whispered. He was shaking all over. Claire supposed that was one thing that being roofied was good for – it kept your heart rate down in an emergency. She felt pretty calm, all things considered. Or maybe she was just getting used to being scared out of her mind.

Running footsteps. The banister in the hall creaked. More shouts from downstairs, feet pounding on the stairs, heading down…

And then the distant, shrill sound of sirens.

'Cops,' somebody whispered, maybe Coffee Bar Jerk. He sounded a whole lot less arrogant. 'We'll be OK. We're going to be OK.'

'Yeah, until these two turn us in,' muttered another boy. 'For, you know. The thing.'

'You mean for *attempted rape*?' Eve whispered fiercely. 'Jesus, listen to you. *The thing*. Call it what it is, you asshole.'

'Look, it was just… I'm sorry, OK? We didn't want to hurt her. We just—'

'She's *sixteen*, man.'

'What?'

'Sixteen. So you can thank me now for saving you serious jail time, because attempted rape is a hell of a lot better than *actual* rape. The statutory kind. Did Monica put you up to it?'

'I…uh…yeah. She said…she said Claire was good to go, that she just needed it rough. She wanted to be sure we got her here.'

'Shhhhhh,' Claire whispered frantically. She heard another floorboard creak. Everybody fell silent.

The door swung open, blinding them with a wash of

light, and Claire squinted at the man standing there.

Red hair.

'Out,' Sam said. 'Move.'

The boys got up and filed out, looking a whole lot less arrogant than before and clustered together in the corner. It had been Ian whose hand she'd held, after all,

Claire saw. He was looking at her in a weird, new way, as if he actually saw her for the first time.

'I'm sorry about your nose,' she said. He blinked.

'It's not so bad,' he offered. 'Look, Claire—'

'Don't.'

'You still going to tell the cops?' That was Coffee Bar Jerk.

'No,' Claire said.

'Bullshit! Yes,' Eve said. 'A world of yes. So you'd better not try this again. Ever. And besides, if you do, the last thing you have to worry about is the cops. Right, Sam?'

Sam nodded without speaking.

'Let's get out of here. Claire? Can you walk?'

'I can try.'

But the world just slipped out from under her when she got up, and she fell into Eve's arms. Eve juggled her awkwardly, trying to find the right way to hold her up, and suddenly Claire was floating about four feet off the ground.

Oh. Sam had her, and he was holding her as if she were as heavy as a bag of feathers.

'Hey,' Coffee Bar Jerk said. Sam stopped on his way

to the door. 'Sorry, seriously. It was just…Monica said—'

'Stop, man,' Ian said. 'Monica just gave us the idea. We were the ones who did it. No excuses.'

'Yeah,' Coffee Bar Jerk said. 'Whatever, man. Won't happen again.'

'If it does,' Sam said, 'never mind the police. I'll find you.'

Things were melting into one another. Claire felt sick and disoriented, and only having her arms around Sam's cool, strong neck kept her from floating away on a tide of chemicals. When she opened her eyes she caught flashes… The EEK frat house was trashed. Furniture broken, walls bashed, people lying on the floor…

And some of them were bloody.

Eve stopped and pressed her fingers to the throat of a boy wearing full vamp gear, including the teeth; his blue eyes were open, staring at the ceiling. He didn't move.

'He's dead,' she whispered.

There was a wooden stake in his chest.

'But…he wasn't a vampire,' Claire said. 'Right?'

'They didn't care. He looked like one, and he must have got in the way,' Sam said. 'There are two vampires dead in the other room. This one was a mistake.'

'In the other room?' Claire asked. 'How do you know?'

'I know.' Sam stepped over the body and moved around a busted-up couch. Glass crunched under his feet. The sirens were getting closer now, late to the party as usual.

'Was it Frank's guys?' Eve asked. 'The bikers?'

Sam didn't answer, but he didn't really have to. How many rampaging anti-vamp gangs could there be in Morganville?

Claire closed her eyes and let her head drop against Sam's chest, meaning just to rest for a second.

And...she just left the world for a while.

Claire woke up to the sound of voices and a headache the size of Cleveland inside of her skull; her mouth was dry as a bone, and her tongue a thick roll of felt covered in sandpaper. Also, hello, nausea.

She was lying in her own bed, at home.

Claire rolled out, ran to the bathroom, and took care of the sickness first, then looked in the mirror. It was horrible. Her face was smeared with make-up, her black eyeliner smudged every which way, her black-sprayed hair sticking up in thick clumps.

Claire started the shower, stripped off the Goth disguise, and sat in the tub with the water pounding down. There wasn't enough soap in the world, really, but she tried, scrubbing hard. Scrubbing until her skin was stinging.

She froze at the sound of a knock on the bathroom door. 'Claire? It's Eve. You OK?'

'Yeah,' she said. 'I'm OK.' Her voice sounded thick and weak.

Eve must have taken her at her word, because she went away. Claire wished she hadn't, somehow; she needed somebody to ask; she needed somebody to be there for her. *I was almost...*

The worst part of it was that they weren't monsters, those guys. In fact, they were probably OK most of the time. How was that even possible? How could people be good and bad at the same time? Good was good; bad was bad – you had to draw a line, right? *Like with the vampires?* some part of her mind whispered. *Where's Amelie, then? Where's Sam? Sam saved your life. Which side of the line do you put him on?*

She didn't know. And she didn't want to think about it anymore. Claire sat under the pounding hard rain of the hot water and let it all go for a while, until the water started to run cool and she remembered that Eve probably wanted to shower, too. *Crap*. She jumped up, turned off the taps, and dried off, realised she hadn't brought more clothes in with her, and wrapped in the towel for the fast trip to her room.

When she opened the bathroom door, Michael was standing right outside. He looked up, saw she wasn't dressed, and looked briefly conflicted.

He solved it by turning his back. 'Go get some clothes on,' he said. 'Then I need to talk to you.'

'What time is it?' she asked. He didn't answer, and she felt something sick take hold in her stomach. 'Michael? *What time is it?*'

'Just get dressed,' he said. 'And come downstairs.'

She raced to her room, dropped the towel, and grabbed her little travel clock.

It was *four a.m.* Dawn was just a couple of hours away. 'No,' she whispered. 'No...' She'd been asleep for *hours.*

No time to waste, then. Claire put on underwear, jeans, and a T-shirt, grabbed her shoes and socks, and hurried to the stairs.

She stopped on the first step down when she heard Amelie's voice. *Amelie? In the house? Why?* Sam, she kind of expected – not that Michael liked any vampires, but hey, he was family, right? And besides, Sam seemed OK. And sure enough, she caught sight of Sam's copper-coloured hair when she eased down another step; he was standing in the far corner, near the kitchen, with his arms folded.

Amelie and Michael were in the centre of the room.

'Hey!' Eve's voice, coming from behind her, made her jump. Claire turned and saw Eve standing there in a thick black bathrobe, clothes in her arms. 'I'm taking my shower. Tell them I'll be there soon, OK?'

Eve looked tired, her make-up sweated or smeared away. Claire felt guilty about using all the hot water. 'OK,' she said, and edged another step down towards the living room. Eve's footsteps creaked behind her, and the bathroom door closed. The water went on.

Claire heard Amelie say, '...can't take it back. Do you understand? Once you make this choice, it is done. There can be no returning.'

That didn't sound good. No, that didn't sound good at all. Claire still felt shaky and sick, as if she'd drunk half a gallon of that red punch at the party, and she didn't feel in any shape to face Amelie again. Only so much scary she could deal with in one day. Maybe she'd just wait for Eve...

'I understand,' Michael said. 'But there isn't a lot of choice anymore. I can't live like this, trapped in this house. I need to *leave*. I can't help Shane if I'm stuck here.'

'You may not be able to help Shane at all,' Amelie said coolly. 'I would not base such a choice on the love of one friend. It may turn out badly for you both.'

'Life is risk, right? So I have to risk it.'

She shook her head. 'Samuel, please speak to him. Explain.'

Sam stirred from where he stood in the corner, but he didn't come closer. 'She's right, kid. You don't know what you're getting into. You think you do, but...you don't. You've got a good thing here: you're alive; you're safe; you have friends who care about you. Family. Stay where you are.'

Michael let out a hollow laugh that sounded a little crazy. '*Stay where I am?* Jesus Christ, what choice do I have? This house is twenty-five hundred square feet of tomb. I'm not alive. I'm *buried* alive.'

Sam shook his head and bent his head, avoiding Michael's stare.

Amelie stepped closer to him. 'Michael. Please think what you are asking. It is not only difficult for you; it is difficult for *me*. If I give you your freedom from this house, it comes at a terrible price. There will be great pain, and the loss of things that neither you nor I can fully name. What you are will change, and change forever. You would live and die at my command, do you understand? And you would never be even the half human you are now, never again.' She shook her head slowly. 'I believe you will regret this, and regret is like cancer to us. It rots our will to live.'

'Yeah? What do you think it's like, being trapped here when people need me?' Michael asked. His fists were clenched, his face tense and flushed. 'I've watched my girlfriend nearly get killed five feet away from me, and I couldn't do anything because she was outside the house. Now it's Shane, and he's all alone out there. It couldn't be worse than this, Amelie. Trust me. If you're not going to save Shane, then you have to do this for me. Please.'

He was asking Amelie for…what? Something she could do that would set him free? Claire eased down another step, and saw Sam's eyes shift and lock on her. She expected him to say something, but he just gave her a very small shake of his head. Warning her.

She retreated back to the top of the stairs, hesitating. Maybe she should get Eve… No, the shower was still running. She should wait. Michael wouldn't do anything stupid…would he?

While she was hesitating, she heard Amelie say something that she couldn't quite understand, except for one word.

'Vampire.'

And she heard Michael say, 'Yes.'

'No!' Claire jumped up and pelted down the steps, fast as she could, but before she could get to the bottom Sam was standing there, looking up at her. Blocking her path. She looked over the railing at Michael and Amelie, and saw Michael watching her.

He looked scared, but he gave her a smile – broken, like the one Shane had put on for her in the cage. Trying to show it didn't matter.

'It's OK, Claire,' he said. 'I know what I'm doing. This is the way it has to be.'

'No, it doesn't!' She edged down another step, clinging to the rail with both hands. She felt hot and disoriented again, but she figured if she was going to fall, at least Sam was there to cushion her. 'Michael, *please*. Don't do this!'

'Oliver tried to make me a vampire. He made me into—' Michael made a disgusted gesture at himself. 'I'm half-alive, Claire, and there's no going back. I can only go forward.'

She couldn't say anything to that, because he was right. Right at every point. He couldn't go back to being just a regular guy; he couldn't live with being stuck here, helpless. Maybe he could have, if Shane hadn't been taken, but now...

'Michael, please.' Her eyes were filling up with tears. 'I don't want you to change.'

'Everybody changes.'

'Not as you will,' Amelie said. She was standing there

like the Snow Queen, all perfect and white and smooth, nothing really human about her at all. 'You will not be the man she knows, Michael. Or the one Eve loves. Will you risk that, too?'

Michael took in a deep breath and turned back towards her. 'Yes,' he said. 'I will.'

Amelie stood in silence for a moment, then nodded. 'Sam,' she said. 'Take the child away. This wants no witnesses.'

'I'm not leaving!' Claire said.

Yeah, good plan. Sam walked up three steps, scooped her into his arms, and carried her upstairs. Claire tried to grab for the railing, but her fingers slipped away. 'Michael! Michael, *no*! Don't do this!'

Sam carried her to her room and dumped her on the bed, and before she could struggle up to a sitting position he was already outside, closing the door.

Later, thinking back on it, Claire couldn't say if she heard the scream or felt it; either way, it seemed to vibrate through the bones and boards of the Glass House, through her head, and she moaned and clapped her hands over her ears. That didn't stop it. The scream just went on and on, shrill and painful as a steam whistle, and Claire felt something...pull at her, like she was made of cloth, and a gigantic, malicious kid was yanking at her loose threads.

And then it just...stopped.

She slid off the bed, ran to the door, and opened it. Sam was nowhere to be seen. Eve was rushing out of the bathroom, clutching her bathrobe around her dripping body, her black hair plastered wet against her face. 'What's happening?' she yelled. 'Michael? Where's Michael?'

The two girls exchanged a desperate look, and then ran for the stairs.

Amelie was sitting in an armchair, the one Michael usually used; she looked drawn and tired, and her head was bent. Sam was crouched next to her, holding her hand, and he rose to his feet when Eve and Claire arrived breathlessly at the bottom of the stairs.

'She's resting,' he said. 'It takes a lot to do what she did. A lot of strength, and a lot of will. Leave her alone. Let her recover.'

'Where's Michael?' Eve demanded. Her voice was shaking. 'What did you do to Michael, you bastard?'

'Easy, child. Sam had nothing to do with it. I set him free,' Amelie said. She raised her head and let it rest against the back of the chair, eyes closed. 'So much pain in him. I thought he could be happy here, but I see I was wrong. One such as Michael can never stay caged for long.'

'What do you mean, you set him free?' Eve was stammering now, her face ashen without any Goth cosmetics to help. '*You killed him?*'

'Yes,' Amelie said. 'I killed him. *Sam!*'

Claire couldn't see why she snapped the other vampire's name until Sam turned in a blur, and met another blur coming at them from across the room. That turned into a struggle, two bodies moving too fast for Claire's eyes to follow until it ended and one was flat on his back on the floor.

That was Michael on his back...but not the Michael she knew. Not the one she'd seen five minutes before, talking to Amelie, making this choice. This Michael was *terrifying*. Sam was having trouble holding him; Michael was struggling, trying to throw him off, and he was *snarling*, oh God, and his skin – his skin was the pale colour of marble and ashes...

'Help me up,' Amelie said quietly. Claire looked at her, stunned. Amelie was holding out a queenly hand, clearly expecting to be obeyed. Claire gave her help up to her feet, just because she'd always been taught to be polite, and braced the vampire, as she seemed about to lose her balance. Amelie found her balance and gave her a weary, thin smile. She let go of Claire's arm, and walked slowly – painfully – to where Sam was fighting to keep Michael down.

Claire looked at Eve. Eve was backed into the corner, her hands in fists covering her mouth. Her eyes were huge.

Claire put her arm around her.

Amelie put one white hand on Michael's forehead, and he instantly stopped struggling. Stopped moving at all, staring straight up at the ceiling with fierce, strange eyes. 'Peace,' Amelie whispered. 'Peace, my poor child. The pain will pass; the hunger will pass. This will help.' She reached into a pocket of her dress and took out a very small, very thin silver knife – no bigger than a fingernail – and sliced a gash across her palm. She didn't bleed like a normal person; the blood seeped out, thicker than normal, and darker. Amelie put it to Michael's lips, pressed it, and closed her eyes.

Eve screamed beneath the cover of her hands, then turned blindly and hid her face against Claire. Claire wrapped her in a tight, shaking hug.

When Amelie withdrew her hand, the gash was closed, and there was no blood on Michael's lips. He closed his eyes, swallowing, gasping. After a few long seconds, Amelie nodded to Sam, who let go and stepped back, and Michael slowly rolled over on his side and met Claire's horrified stare.

His *eyes*. They were the same colour, and...not the same at all. Michael licked his pale lips, and she saw the bright white flicker of snake fangs in his mouth.

She shuddered.

'Behold,' Amelie said softly, 'the youngest of our kind. From this day on, Michael Glass, you are one of the eternal of the Great City, and all will be yours. Rise. Take your place among your people.'

'Yeah,' Sam said. 'Welcome to hell.'

Michael got to his feet. Neither of them helped him up.

'That's it?' Michael asked. His voice sounded strange – deep in his throat, deeper than Claire remembered. It gave her a little shiver at the base of her spine. 'It's done?'

'Yes,' Amelie said. 'It's done.'

Michael walked towards the door. He had to stop and brace himself against the wall on the way, but he looked stronger every second. Stronger than Claire felt comfortable with, in fact.

'Michael,' Amelie said. 'Vampires can be killed, and many know the ways. If you grow careless, you will die, no matter how many laws Morganville holds to protect us from our enemies.' Amelie glanced at the two girls, standing together in the corner. 'Vampires cannot live among humans. It is too difficult, too tempting. You understand? They must leave your house. You must have time to learn what you are.'

Michael looked at Eve and Claire – more at Claire than Eve, as if he couldn't stand to really face her yet. He looked more like himself now, more in control. Except for the pale skin, he might nearly have been normal.

'No,' he said. 'This is their home, and it's my home, and it's Shane's home. We're a family. I'm not giving that up.'

'Do you know why I stopped you?' Amelie said. 'Why I ordered Sam to stop you? Because your instincts cannot be trusted, Michael, not at this point. You cannot care, because your feelings for them will hurt them. Do you understand? Were you not moving towards these two girls with the intention of feeding on them?'

His eyes went wide and, suddenly, very dark. 'No.'

'Think.'

'*No.*'

'You were,' Sam said quietly, from behind him. 'I know, Michael. I was there once. And there was no one to stop me.'

Michael didn't try to deny it again; he looked at Eve, right at her, with such terrible dawning pain that it hurt to see it.

'It won't happen again.' Eve hadn't said a word since all this had started, so it was a little shocking to hear her say that, so calmly. So...*normally*. 'I know Michael. He wouldn't have done this if he was going to hurt any of us. He'd die first.'

'He did die,' Amelie said. 'The human part of him is gone. What is left is mine.' She said it with a little regret, which didn't surprise Claire much; she'd seen it in Amelie's infinitely weary eyes as she'd helped her up. 'Come, Michael. You need food. I will show you where to go.'

'Wait a minute,' he said. 'Please.' And he stepped away from her, and held out his hand to Eve.

Amelie drew breath to tell him something – probably *no* – but she didn't speak. Sam didn't, either, but he turned and walked away, aimlessly circling the room. Claire reluctantly let go of Eve, and Eve walked directly to Michael, no hesitation at all.

He took both of her hands in his.

'I'm sorry. There wasn't any other way.' Michael swallowed, his eyes fixed on Eve's. 'I've been feeling it, more and more. Like this...pressure inside. It's not just that I needed to do this to help Shane. I just...needed it to stay sane. And I'm sorry. You're going to hate me.'

'Why?' Eve asked. It was half bravado, it had to be, but she sounded certain. 'Because you're vamped? Please. I loved you when you were only halfway here at all. As long as you're with me, I can deal, Michael. For you, I can deal.'

He kissed her, and Claire blinked and looked away. There was a lot of hunger in that kiss, and desperation, and it was way too personal.

Eve wasn't the first one to pull away, either.

When he stepped back from her, he was the old Michael after all, never mind the paler skin and the odd shine to his eyes. That smile...he was *Michael*, and everything was going to be OK.

He wiped away Eve's silent tears with his thumbs, kissed her again, very lightly, and said, 'I'll be back. Amelie's right, I need to—' He hesitated, glanced at Amelie, and then back down at Eve. 'I need to feed. I guess I need to get used to saying that.' His smile looked a little dimmer this time. 'I'm going to miss dinners.'

'You won't,' Sam said. 'You can still eat solid foods if you want. I do.'

For some reason, that seemed really important. It was something they could hold on to.

'I'll make dinner tonight,' Claire said. 'To celebrate getting Shane home.'

'It's a deal.' Michael let go of Eve and stepped back. 'I'm ready.'

'Then come outside,' Amelie said. 'Come back to the world.'

Michael might have become a vampire, but watching him stand outside in the night air, breathing in his freedom… Claire thought that was as human as it could get.

CHAPTER ELEVEN

Eve changed into what Claire thought of as 'Goth camo'...black pants, a black silk shirt with red skulls embroidered at the collar, and a black vest with loads of pockets that could hold things. Things like stakes and crosses, as it turned out. 'Just in case,' Eve said, catching Claire's look. 'What?'

'Nothing,' she sighed. 'Just don't use them on Michael.'

Eve stopped for a second, stricken, and then nodded. She was still getting her head around it, Claire knew. Well, Claire was doing the same thing. She kept expecting to hear Michael's guitar downstairs; she kept wondering about what time it was. Not dawn yet – she checked the Internet and found out that they still had time, but if Michael didn't come back soon...

The front door opened and closed. Eve snatched a stake from her pocket, wide-eyed, and Claire motioned to her to stay where she was, then sneaked carefully to the corner.

She nearly ran into Michael, who was moving way more quietly than she was used to. He looked nearly as surprised as she did. Behind him was Sam, but there was no sign of Amelie.

'You OK?' she asked. Michael nodded. He looked... better, in some strange sort of way. At peace. 'Not going to...?' She mimed fangs in her neck. He smiled.

'No way, kid.' He ruffled her hair lightly. 'There's a deal on the table for Shane.'

'A deal?' Eve sounded tense as she came around into view, and Claire didn't blame her. Deals hadn't gone especially well for them so far.

'If we get Monica back safely, Shane goes free. The Morrells still have influence in this town, even with the vamps.' Of which Michael was one now, but he didn't seem to be lumping himself in quite yet. 'Oliver was willing to trade. Or maybe not willing – convinced.'

'Shane for Monica? Sweet!' Eve realised she was holding a stake in her hand, blushed, and put it away. Neither Sam nor Michael seemed all that bothered. 'Ah, sorry. Nothing personal...so it's you two and us against the world, or what?'

'No,' Sam said, and looked at Michael. 'It's the three of you. I can't go with you.'

'What? But...you—'

'I'm sorry.' Sam honestly sounded like he meant it. 'Amelie's orders. Vampires stay neutral – Michael's the only exception because of his agreement with Amelie. I can't help you.'

'But—'

'I can't,' he repeated, with emphasis, and sighed. 'You'll get some help from the human community – that's all I can tell you. Good luck.' He started to walk away, towards the door, then turned back. 'Thank you, Claire. Eve.'

'What for?'

Sam's smile was suddenly luminous, and it looked just like Michael's. 'You brought me to Amelie. And she talked to me. That counts.'

There was a story behind that, Claire was sure, full of heartbreak and longing; she could see it, for a second, written all over his face. Amelie? He loved *Amelie*? That was kind of like loving the *Mona Lisa* – the painting, not the person. Presuming Amelie even had enough emotion in her to feel something for Sam these days.

Maybe once she had. Wow.

Sam nodded to Michael, equal to equal, and he left, closing the door behind him.

'Hey,' Eve said. 'Did he have an invitation? To get into the house?'

'He didn't need one,' Michael said. 'The house adjusted itself once I…changed. Now humans need an invitation. Except for you, since you live here.'

'OK, that's stupid.'

'It's Protection,' Michael said. 'You know how it works.'

Claire didn't, but she was fascinated. Not the time, though. 'Um, he said the town was sending help...?'

'Richard Morrell,' Michael said. 'Monica's cop brother. And he's bringing Hess and Lowe with him.'

'That's it?' Claire squeaked. Because there were a lot of bikers. Like, a *lot*. Not to mention Shane's dad, who frankly scared her worse than most of the vampires just because he didn't seem to have any rules.

Funny, the vampires seemed to be all about rules. Who knew?

'I'm going to want you both to stay here,' Michael said.

'No,' Eve said flatly. Claire echoed it.

'Seriously, you need to stay. This is going to get dangerous.'

'Dangerous? Dude, they *killed kids*. On campus!' Eve shot back. 'We were *there*! Don't you get it? We're not safe here, and maybe we can help you. At the very least, we can grab Monica and hustle her skanky ass back to her dad while all you brave, strong menfolk hold off the bad guys. Right?'

'Not Claire, then.'

'Claire,' Claire said, 'decides for herself. In case you forgot.'

'Claire *doesn't* decide when it's something like this, because Claire is sixteen and Michael doesn't want to be explaining her tragic accidental death to her parents. So, no.'

'What're you going to do?' Eve asked, and cocked her head to one side. 'Lock her in her room?'

He looked from one of them to the other, his frown deepening. 'Oh, crap. What is this, Girl Solidarity?'

'Bet your ass,' Eve said. 'Somebody's got to keep you in line.' Her smile faded, because that was true now, not just a funny idea. Michael cleared his throat.

'Did you hear that?'

'What?'

'A car. Brakes. Outside.'

'Great,' Eve said. 'Vampire hearing, too. I'm never going to be able to keep a secret around here. Bad enough when you were a ghost...' She was doing a good job of looking like she wasn't freaked-out, but Claire thought she was. So did Michael, apparently, because he reached out and touched her cheek – just one small gesture, but it said a lot.

'Stay here,' he said.

He should have known they wouldn't – not completely, anyway. Claire and Eve followed him partway down the hall, enough to watch him unlock the front door and swing it open.

Richard Morrell stood on the doorstep in his police uniform. Next to him were Detectives Hess and Lowe, both looking even more exhausted than normal.

'Michael,' Richard said, and nodded to him.

He tried to move across the threshold, and was stopped cold. Hess and Lowe exchanged a curious look and tried to come across, as well. Nothing.

'Come in,' Michael said, and stepped back. This time, all three men could enter.

Richard was looking at Michael closely. 'You're kidding,' he said. 'You've got to be kidding. All this time, and she picks *you*?'

Hess and Lowe exchanged looks, a second behind the curve, and both appeared startled.

'Yeah,' Michael said. 'What about it?'

Richard smiled, all teeth. 'Nothing, man. Congratulations, and all that. You're going to be the talk of the town. Get used to it.'

Michael shut the door behind them. 'Whatever. How much time do we have to get to Shane?'

'Not much,' Hess said. 'And the thing is, we don't have anyplace to start. No leads.'

'Well, we've got one. We know the van went through the Underground,' Richard said. 'We've got an eyewitness. Right?' He looked straight at Claire, who nodded. 'We pulled all the surveillance tapes, and we tracked the van in and out of the Underground half a dozen times, but it finally disappeared. Problem is, one white van looks a lot like other white vans, especially on NightSight surveillance cameras.'

'We know that Shane's dad had maps of Morganville. Shane provided them. You're sure he didn't say *anything* about where his father might be making his base of operations?' Hess asked. 'Any of you?'

'He never said anything,' Claire said. 'Not to me. Michael?' Michael shook his head. 'God, I can't believe *nobody* knows where these guys are! They have to be somewhere!'

'Actually, two people probably know exactly where they are,' Richard said. 'Shane, and the biker, Des. One of them, maybe both, has to know the places Frank was using.'

'And nobody's asked them?' Eve questioned, and then her expression turned blank with horror. 'Oh *God*. Somebody *has*.'

'It's not so bad as that,' Lowe offered. 'I was there observing. They're all right.'

'That doesn't mean they'll stay that way,' Michael said. 'Especially now. Or was that the plan, Richard? Get the two neutral cops here with you so your guys could beat the information out of Shane?'

Richard smiled slowly. 'You know, that's not a bad idea, but no. I honestly thought you guys would have a place for us to start looking. We can go with that plan B if you come up empty, though. I never liked that kid anyway.'

Michael's eyes were narrowing, and Claire felt the whole barely reasonable alliance starting to come apart.

'Wait!' she said. 'Um, I think I have something. Maybe.'

'Maybe?' Richard turned to her. 'Better be good. It's your boyfriend on the line, and if anything happens to my sister, I swear I'll torch him myself.'

Claire looked at Michael, then Eve. 'I saw him,' she said. 'Shane's dad. He was in Common Grounds.'

'He was *what*?'

'In Common Grounds. It was the same day I met Sam

for the first time. I wondered what he was doing there, but—'

Richard interrupted her, grabbing the neck of her T-shirt and hauling her forward. 'Who was he talking to? Who?' He shook her.

'Hey!' She smacked at his hand, and to her surprise, he let go. 'He was talking to Oliver.'

Silence. They all stared at her, and then Hess put a hand to his forehead. Lowe said, 'Whoa, whoa, whoa, hang on a second. Why would the Fearless Vampire Killer be talking to Oliver? He knows, right? Who Oliver is? What Oliver is?'

Claire nodded. 'Shane must have told him. He knows.'

'And Oliver knows who Frank Collins is,' Hess said. 'He'd know him on sight. So we've got two mortal enemies sitting down together, and we don't know why. When was it, Claire?'

'Right before Brandon was killed.'

Another silence, and this one was deep. Lowe and Hess were staring at each other. Richard was frowning. After a long moment, Lowe said slowly, 'Anybody want to take a bet?'

'Spit it out, Detective,' Richard said. 'If you know something, say so.'

'I'm not saying I know. I'm saying I've got a hundred dollars that says Oliver knew all about Frank Collins rolling back into town, and he used Frank to get rid of a troublemaking child-molesting bastard who'd outlived his usefulness.'

Claire asked, 'Why didn't he just kill him, if he wanted him dead?'

'Vampires do not kill each other. They just don't. So this way, he and Frank both get what they want. Oliver gets Morganville in chaos, Amelie losing control and I heard about the attack on her downtown. Maybe Oliver was hoping they'd take her out, leave him in charge. Brandon was probably a small price to pay.' He paused for thought. 'I'm guessing here, but I'll bet Oliver made Frank a whole lot of promises he never intended to keep. Brandon was a sign of good faith, to get Frank to commit. And holding on to Shane was insurance. No way would Oliver have let Frank keep on killing, though. Chaos is one thing. A bloodbath is another.'

'How does this help?' Michael asked. 'We still don't know where they are.'

Hess reached in his pocket and pulled out a folding pocket map – a Morganville map. It was marked in grids, colour-coded: yellow for the university, pale red for the human enclaves, blue for the vampires. The centre of town, Founder's Square, was black. 'Here,' he said, and walked to the dining room table. Michael moved his guitar case out of the way, and Hess spread the map out. 'Travis, you know who owns what near the square, right?'

'Yeah.' Lowe leant forward, fished some reading glasses out of his coat pocket, and looked closer. 'OK, these are warehouses here. Vallery Kosomov owns some of them. Most of these belong to Josefina Lowell.'

'Anything owned by Oliver down there?'

'Why down there?' Lowe asked.

'You want to answer that one, Officer Morrell?' Hess asked. Richard edged in to consider the map, and marked out something with his finger.

'Underground runs right through here,' he said. 'This is the only area of the Underground where we *didn't* see the van come and go.'

'Which tells you what?' Hess asked.

'*Crap.* They were faking the video. Showing us where they weren't, sending us all over town. And hiding where they were.' Richard looked up at Hess, then Lowe. 'Oliver's warehouses are off of Bond Street. It's mostly storage.'

'Gentlemen, we have exactly' – Hess consulted his watch – 'fifty-two minutes. Let's get moving.'

They all moved to the door, and it was going fine until Richard Morrell glanced at Claire and Eve, put his arm up like a barricade, and said, 'Oh, I don't think so, kids.'

'We've got a right to—'

'Yeah, I'm getting all choked up about your rights, Eve. You stay here.'

'Michael's going!' Claire said, and winced, because she sounded like a disappointed little kid instead of the responsible, trustworthy adult she'd intended.

Richard rolled his eyes nearly as well as Eve. 'You sound like my sister,' he said. 'That's really not attractive. And it's not going to work. Michael can take care of himself on a whole bunch of levels you can't, kid, so you. Stay. Here.'

And Hess and Lowe backed him up.

Michael just looked vaguely sorry to be in the middle of it, but relieved all the same that they weren't going. It was Michael who took Eve's car keys from the tray on the hall table, where she always left them. 'Just in case,' he said, and dropped them, in his pocket. 'Not that I don't trust you or anything, just that I know you never listen to me.'

He slammed the door on Eve's frustrated cry.

And that, Claire thought, was that.

'I can't believe they left us,' Claire said numbly, staring at the door. Eve kicked it hard enough to leave a black mark on the wood and stalked away, into the living room. She stood at the window until the police cruiser pulled away from the kerb and glided off into the night. Then she turned and looked at Claire.

She was smiling.

'What?' Claire asked, confused, as Eve grinned wider. 'Are we happy about getting left behind?'

'Yes, we're happy. Because now I know where they're going,' Eve said, and reached in her pocket. She pulled out a second key ring and shook it with a merry, metallic jingle. 'And I've got a spare set of keys. Let's go save their asses.'

It was a good thing the Morganville police force was otherwise occupied, because Claire thought that Eve probably broke every traffic law that was on the books.

Twice. She couldn't bring herself to open her eyes very often – just peeks every other block or so – but it seemed like they were going very, very fast, and taking corners at speeds that would have given a driver's-ed instructor a heart attack. Not much traffic, at least, in this predawn darkness. That was something, Claire supposed. She clung to the stiff aftermarket shoulder belt as Eve screeched the big black Cadillac through a hairpin right-hand turn, then another, and into one of the storm-drain tunnels.

'Oh God,' Claire whispered. If she'd been in danger of motion sickness before, it was ten times worse in the tunnel. She squeezed her eyes tight shut and tried to breathe. Between the dark, the panic, and the closed-in spaces, it wasn't exactly her best rescue attempt ever.

'Almost there,' Eve said, but Claire thought she said it to herself. Eve wasn't calm, either. That was...not comforting. 'Left turn up ahead...'

'That's not a turn!' Claire yelped, and braced herself against the dashboard as Eve slammed on the brakes and the big car shimmied and sprayed shallow water as it skidded. 'That's a dead end!'

'Nope, that's a turn,' Eve panted, fought the wheel, and somehow – Claire had no idea how – got the car to make the impossible corner with only a little bang and scrape up against the concrete wall. 'Ouch. That's gonna leave a mark.' And she laughed, high and wild, and hit the gas again. 'Hold on, Claire Bear! Next stop, Crazytown!'

Claire thought they were already there, actually.

She lost track of the nauseatingly twisty course they were following. In fact, she started to think that Eve didn't know where she was going at all, and was just making random turns hoping to find an exit, when suddenly the tunnel ended, and the car hit an upslope, and they rocketed out into the open darkness again.

'Bond Street,' Eve said. 'Home of upscale vampire shopping, fine restaurants, and…oh shit.'

She hit the brakes and brought them to a fast, complete stop that tossed Claire painfully against the restraints. Not that Claire noticed all that much, because like Eve, she was pretty much horror-struck by what she was seeing ahead.

'Tell me that's not the place,' she said.

Because if it was, the place was on fire.

Richard Morrell's police cruiser was parked at the wrought-iron gates, its doors hanging open. The guys had bailed out fast. Eve moved the Caddy closer, then shut off the engine, and the two girls looked in dawning horror at the flames shooting out from the windows and roof of the big stone building.

'Where's the fire department?' Claire asked. 'Where are the cops?'

'I don't know, but we can't count on help. Not tonight.' Eve opened the door on her side and stepped out. 'Do you see them? Anywhere?'

'No!' Claire flinched as glass exploded from one of the upper windows. 'Do you?'

'We have to go in!'

'*Go in?*' Claire was about to point out how crazy that was, but then she saw someone inside the gates, lying very still. 'Eve!' She ran to the gate and rattled it, but it was locked tight.

'Up!' Eve yelled, and scrambled up on the wrought iron. Claire followed. It was slippery and sharp, and cut her hands, but somehow she made it to the top, then dangled from the crossbar and let herself fall on the other side. She hit hard, and rolled clumsily back to her feet. Eve, who'd come down a lot more gracefully, was already moving towards the guy lying on the ground…

…who was one of Frank's guys. Dead. Eve looked up at Claire wordlessly and showed her the blood on her hand, shaking her head. 'He was shot,' she said. 'Oh, God. They're inside, Claire. *Michael's inside!*'

Only he wasn't, because between one blink and the next, as Eve tried to rush into the open smoke-filled door, Michael plunged out of it, and he grabbed her and hauled her back. 'No!' he yelled. 'What the hell are you doing here?'

'Michael!' Eve turned and threw herself into his arms. 'Where's Monica?'

'In there.' Michael looked terrible – smoke-stained and red-eyed, with little burnt patches in his shirt. 'The others went in to get her. I…I had to come out.'

Vampires could be killed by fire. Claire remembered that from the list she'd made shortly after moving to Morganville. She couldn't believe he'd risked his just barely begun life to get as far as he'd gone.

'Damn right you can't!' Eve yelled. 'If you go and get yourself killed for *Monica Morrell*, I'll never forgive you!'

'It wouldn't be for Monica,' he said. 'You know that.'

They stared at the flames, waiting. Seconds ticked by, and there was no sign of anyone: no Monica, and no cops, either. The horizon was getting lighter in the east, Claire realised, going from dark blue to twilight.

Dawn was coming, and they were almost out of time to get Monica to Founder's Square, if they could get her at all.

If she was still alive.

'Sun's coming!' Michael shouted over the roar of the fire.

Claire didn't ask how he knew. He'd known when he was a ghost; she figured it was probably the same time sense as a vampire's. Made sense. It would be a survival trait, to know when to get under cover. 'You need to get out of here!' she yelled back. A thick, black billow of smoke belched out of the doorway and made her double over, coughing. They all retreated. 'Michael, you have to go! Now!'

'No!'

'At least get in the police car!' Eve pointed to it, on the other side of the fence. 'Tinted windows! We'll wait here, I swear!'

'I'm not leaving you!'

The sun crested the far horizon in a tiny sliver of gold, and where it touched him, Michael's pale skin started to sizzle and smoke. He hissed in pain and slapped at it. A pale, licking flame took hold on his hand.

Claire and Eve screamed, and Eve tackled him into the shadows. That helped, but not much; he was still burning, just more slowly. Michael groaned and looked like he was trying not to scream.

'Claire!' Eve tossed her the car keys. 'Ram the gate! Get it open! Do it!'

'But…your car!'

'It's just a freakin' *car*! Come on, move it! We'll never get him over the fence!'

Claire scrambled back over the slick, warm iron of the fence, slicing her hands in two or three more places, and barely felt the impact when she fell this time. She was up and running for the Caddy –

– and then she changed course, threw herself into the driver's seat of the police car, and started it with the keys hanging from the ignition.

This had to be some kind of crime, right? But in an emergency…

She backed it up almost to the end of the block, put the car in drive, and pressed the gas pedal to the floor.

She screamed and managed to hang on to the wheel somehow as the gate rushed up at her; there was a bone-jarring *crunch*, and she slammed on the brakes. The gates flew open, bent and mangled, and the police car gave a roar and died, sputtering. Claire got out and opened the back door as Eve rushed Michael towards her; Michael dived in, and Claire slammed the door behind him. Eve was right – the windows were heavily tinted, probably to protect vampire cops from the sun. He'd be OK in there.

Claire hoped.

'What about the others?' she yelled at Eve, who shook her head. They both turned to look at the warehouse, which was fully on fire now, shooting flames twenty or thirty feet into the morning sky. 'Oh God. Oh *God*! We have to do something!'

Just then, two figures staggered out of the side door, bathed in black smoke, and collapsed to the pavement. Eve and Claire dashed to them. For a second, Claire didn't even know who they were, so blackened were they by smoke, and then she recognised Joe Hess under the grime.

The other one was Travis Lowe. They were both coughing and retching up black stuff.

'Get up!' Eve ordered, and grabbed Hess's arm to drag him away from the building. 'Come on, get up!'

He did, weaving badly, and Claire managed to get Lowe to do the same. They made it about halfway to the police car, and then Lowe sat down in the open parking lot, coughing his lungs out, gasping. Claire crouched down next to him, wishing she could do something, wishing the damn fire department would come, wishing…

'We're too late,' Eve said. She was watching the sun climb over the horizon. 'It's dawn. We're too late.'

Hess gasped, 'No. Not yet. Richard…had Monica—'

'What? Where?' Claire spun to look at him. Hess was

nearly as badly off as his partner, but he was able to form words, at least. 'They're still alive?'

'Should have been right behind us,' Lowe wheezed.

Claire didn't think about it. If she'd given herself time, she would have talked herself out of it, but her brain was on hold and all that was left was instinct. It wasn't just that there was still hope to save Shane; it was that she couldn't leave anybody to die like that.

She just couldn't.

She heard Eve yelling her name, but she didn't stop, couldn't stop; she kept running until she was in the smoke, and then she dropped to her knees and crawled into the hot, suffocating darkness. She flailed with her hands, trying to find something, anything, and kept her eyes tight shut. She could barely breathe, even close to the ground, and every breath she did manage to take was tainted and toxic, more harm than good.

OK, this was a really bad idea.

She didn't dare crawl too far; in the chaos and darkness, she'd never find her way out again. Something fell near her with a huge crash, and fire roared overhead. Claire went flat on the floor and curled into a ball, then – when she wasn't roasted or crushed – forced herself to keep moving. *One minute. One minute and then straight back out.*

She wasn't sure she could survive a minute in here.

Her searching fingers brushed cloth. Claire opened her eyes and was instantly sorry, because the smoke burnt and stung, and she couldn't see a thing anyway.

But she had her hand on cloth, and yes, that was a leg, a pant leg...

And that was a hand that turned and gripped hers. An unrecognizable voice rasped, 'Get Monica out!'

A new burst of fire lit up the darkness, and she saw Richard Morrell lying there, curled around his sister. Protecting her. Monica looked up, and there was sheer terror in her face. She reached out blindly. Claire took her hands and pulled her back the way she'd come in, straight back. She felt the draft of air coming in the door, and that helped guide her. 'Grab your brother!' she yelled. Monica took Richard's hand, and Claire hauled with all her strength, dragging them both.

She didn't make it.

She wasn't sure how it happened exactly... One minute she was pulling; the next she was down, and she couldn't breathe, couldn't stop coughing. *Oh no. No no no.* But she couldn't get up, couldn't force her body to move.

Shane...

Somebody grabbed her by the ankles and yanked, hard. Claire had just enough presence of mind left to hold on to Monica's wrist.

'Shit!' Eve was groaning, coughing, and all of a sudden Claire was outside lying in the sun, watching black smoke billow into the air. 'Claire! Breathe, dammit!'

It wasn't so much breathing as hacking up a lung, but at least air was moving in and out. She heard someone else coughing next to her, and raised her head to see Monica on her hands and knees, spitting out black phlegm.

And now Eve was dragging Richard Morrell out by his feet.

Eve collapsed next to them, coughing, too, and somewhere on the distant edges of the fire's roar, as if somebody had flipped a switch, Claire heard sirens. Oh, *now* they were coming. Perfect. Someone's tax dollars at work, even if it wasn't hers...

Claire rolled painfully to her feet. There were burnt patches in her clothes, and she smelt burnt hair, too. She was going to hurt later, but for now, she was just glad to be alive.

'Get Monica,' she wheezed at Eve, and grabbed one of Monica's arms. Eve grabbed the other, and they half dragged her across the parking lot to the shattered gate. Hess and Lowe were leaning up against the police car. Lowe, incredibly, was smoking a cigarette, but he dropped it and managed to get to his feet to stumble over to where Richard was lying, and help him up.

'Michael!' Eve rapped on the window of the police car. Claire blinked her watering eyes; she could just barely see his shadow through the tinted glass. 'Move over!' Eve opened the back door carefully, making sure he was out of the direct sun, and loaded Monica into the back seat, then got in with them. Monica made a groan of protest. 'Oh, shut up already and be grateful.'

Claire went around to the front seat, got in, and asked blankly, 'Who's driving?'

Richard Morrell slid in behind the wheel. 'Joe and Travis will stay here,' he said. 'I'll bring you back for your car. Everybody, hold on.'

As Richard backed the car out and then accelerated towards Founder's Square, lights and sirens going, Monica managed to get her first coherent words out between coughs.

'Claire…bitch!' Her voice sounded raw and hoarse. 'You…think this…makes us…friends?'

'God, no,' Claire said. 'But I think you kinda owe me.'

Monica just glared.

'I'll call it even if Shane walks away.'

Monica coughed again. 'You wish.'

Chapter Twelve

Founder's Square was insane. Richard had to stop the car almost a block away, just outside of a cordon of police cars with flashing lights. Claire got out and had another coughing fit, bad enough that Eve patted her nervously on the back and did the talking for her to the grim-faced uniformed policewoman standing guard at the barricade. 'We need to see Mayor Morrell,' she said.

'Mayor's busy,' the policewoman said. 'You'll have to wait.'

'But—'

Monica got out of the back seat, and the cop's eyes widened. 'Miss Morrell?' Well, Claire admitted, the smoke-stained scarecrow with frizzed hair didn't look much like the usual Monica. She secretly hoped somebody would take pictures. And put them on the Internet.

When Richard got out, as well, the policewoman gulped. 'Jesus. Sorry, sir. Hang on, I'll get someone here.' The policewoman got on her radio and passed on information; while they waited, she passed out bottled water from her squad car. Claire took two bottles and ducked back into the patrol car's back seat, where Michael was sitting, eyes shut tight. He stirred and looked at her when she called his name. He didn't look good – paper pale, burnt in places, and apparently sick, too. She handed him the water. 'I don't know if it'll help, but...?'

Michael nodded and gulped some down. Claire cracked her own bottle and swallowed, nearly moaning in ecstasy. Nothing had ever tasted so good in Claire's entire life as that lukewarm, flat water washing away the smoke from her throat.

'I thought—' Michael licked his lips and let his head flop back against the seat. 'I thought I'd be stronger. I've seen other vampires in the daytime.'

'Older ones,' Claire said. 'I think it must take time. Amelie can even walk around in the daylight, but she's really old. You just have to be patient, Michael.'

'Patient?' He closed his eyes. 'Claire. Today's the first day I've been outside of my house for nearly a year, my best friend's still under a death sentence, and you're telling me to be *patient*?'

It did sound stupid, when he put it that way. She drank her water silently, wiping sweat from her forehead and then grimacing at the sooty mess.

It's going to be all right, she told herself. *We'll get Shane. We'll all go home. It'll be fine.*

Which even now she knew wasn't very likely, but she had to have something to hold on to.

It was only about a five-minute wait, and the mayor came himself, trailed by an anxious entourage and two uniformed paramedics, who swooped in on Monica and Richard, ignoring Claire and Eve. 'Hey, we're fine, thanks,' Eve said sarcastically. 'Flesh wounds. Look, we kept our part of the bargain. We want Shane. Right now.'

The mayor, hugging his soot-stained daughter, barely even glanced their way. 'You're too late,' he said.

Claire's knees went out from under her. It came to her in a blinding rush – the fire, the smoke, the terror. *Shane.* Oh no, no, it couldn't be...

The mayor must have realised what she was thinking, and what Eve was thinking, too, from the expressions on their faces, because he looked momentarily annoyed.

'No, not that,' he said. 'Richard said you were en route. I said I'd wait. I don't break my word.'

'Much,' Eve muttered, and covered it with a fake cough. 'OK, then why are we too late?'

'He's already gone,' the mayor said. 'His father staged an attack just before dawn, when our attention was on the warehouse fire. Broke Shane and the other one out of the cages, killed five of my men. They were heading out of town, but we've got them cornered this time. It'll all be over soon.'

'But...Shane!' Claire looked at him pleadingly. 'We kept our part of the bargain – please, can't you just let him go?'

Mayor Morrell frowned at her. 'Our agreement was that I'd let him go if you brought my daughter back. Well, he's free. If he gets himself killed trying to save his no-good father, that's no business of mine,' the mayor said. He put his arm around Monica and Richard. 'Come on, kids. You can tell me what happened.'

'*I'll* tell you what happened,' Eve said angrily. 'We saved both of their lives. You can thank us for that anytime, by the way.'

From the glare he threw Eve, the mayor really didn't find that funny. 'If you hadn't put them in danger in the first place, none of this would have happened,' he said. 'Consider yourselves lucky that I don't toss you in jail for aiding and abetting a vampire hunter. Now, if you want my advice, go home.' He kissed his daughter's filthy hair. 'Come on, princess.'

'Dad,' Richard said. 'She's right. They did save our lives.'

The mayor looked more than just annoyed now, at this minor rebellion in the family ranks. 'Son, I know that you may feel some gratitude towards these girls, but—'

'Just tell us where Shane is,' Claire said. 'Please. That's all we want.'

The two Morrell men exchanged long looks, and then Richard said, 'You know the old hospital? The one on Grand Street?'

Eve nodded. 'Our Lady? I thought they tore that thing down.'

'Scheduled for demolition at the end of the week,' Richard said. 'I'll take you there.'

Claire almost cried; she was so relieved. Not that the problem was solved – it wasn't – but at least they had another step to take.

'Richard,' the mayor said. 'You don't owe them anything.'

'I do, though.' Richard looked from Eve, to Claire. 'And I won't forget it.'

Eve grinned. 'Awww. Don't worry, Officer. We won't let you.'

There were vampires out in the daytime. Claire figured that was unusual, but she realised just how unusual when Richard Morrell, slowing the police car to a crawl, whistled. 'Oliver's called out the troops,' he said. 'Not good for your friend. Or his father.'

The streets around the massive bulk of the old hospital were lined with cars...big cars, dark-tinted windows. Lots of police cars, too, but it was those other autos that looked...menacing.

As did the people standing in shadows, surrounding the building. Some wore heavy coats and hats, even in the oppressive heat. There had to be at least a hundred gathered, and a lot of them were vampires.

And right in the centre, standing right at the edge of the border of sunlight and shadow, stood Oliver. He was wearing a long black leather coat, and a leather broad-brimmed hat, and his hands were cased in gloves.

'Oh, man. I don't think you guys are going to do any good here,' Richard said. Oliver's head turned towards them, and he stepped out into the sunlight. The vampire approached, moving at a slow, leisurely pace. 'Maybe I ought to take you on home.'

In less time than it took to tell Richard no, Oliver had crossed the open space and jerked open the back door of the police cruiser. 'Maybe you should join us instead,' Oliver said, and bared his teeth in a smile. 'Ah, Michael. Out of the house at last, I see. Felicitations on your birthday. I would suggest, for your own safety, that you stay strictly in the shadows this morning. Not that you'll have the strength to do anything else.'

And he grabbed Claire, who was sitting nearest the door, by the throat.

Claire heard Michael and Eve yelling, and felt Eve trying to hold on to her, but there was no way Eve could match Oliver's strength. He simply pulled Claire out of the car like a rag doll, his fingers wrapped cruelly tight around her throat, and dragged her out into the street.

'Shane! Shane Collins!' he shouted. 'I have something for you! I want you to watch this very carefully!'

Claire grabbed at his hand with both of her own, trying to pry his grip free, but it was no good. He knew just how tightly to hold on without *quite* crushing her throat or cutting off her breathing. She fought back another panicked bout of coughing, and tried to think of something, anything, to do.

'I'm going to kill this girl,' Oliver continued, 'unless

she swears herself to me and my service, in front of all of these witnesses. Shane, you can save her by making the same deal. You have two minutes to consider your decision.'

'Why?' Claire whispered. It came out as a mouse squeak, barely audible. Oliver, who was staring at the decaying facade of the old hospital, with its weather-stained weeping angels and moulding baroque stonework, turned his attention briefly to her. The morning was warm and cloudless, the sun a hot brass penny in a bright blue sky. It seemed wrong for a vampire to be out here.

He wasn't even sweating.

'Why what, Claire? It's an imprecise question. You have a better mind than that.'

She fought for breath, helplessly clawing at his fingers. 'Why...kill Brandon?'

He lost his smile, and his eyes turned wary. 'Clever,' he said. 'Cleverness may not be good for you after all. The question you should be asking is, why do I want your service?'

'All right,' she wheezed. 'Why?'

'Because Amelie has some use for you,' he said. 'And I am not accustomed to giving Amelie what she wants. It has nothing to do with you, and everything to do with history. But, sadly, I'm making it your problem. Cheer up; if your boyfriend swears on your behalf, I'll keep him alive. Let you see him from time to time. Star-crossed lovers are so entertaining.'

Amelie didn't seem to have much of a use for her, Claire reflected, but she didn't argue about it. Couldn't, in fact. Couldn't do much of anything but stand on tiptoe, gag for each breath, and hope that somehow, she'd figure a way out of this stupid situation that she'd got herself into. Again.

'One minute!' Oliver called. There was movement inside of the building, flickers at the windows. 'Well. It appears we have a domestic disturbance.'

What he meant was, Shane's dad was kicking the crap out of him. Claire struggled to see what was going on, but Oliver's grip was too tight. She could see only from the corner of her eye, and what she could see wasn't good. Shane was in the doorway of the hospital, trying to get free, but someone dragged him back.

'Thirty seconds!' Oliver announced. 'Well, this is coming down to the wire. I'm a bit surprised, Claire. The boy really is fighting for the chance to save you. You should be very impressed.'

'You should take your hands off of her, Oliver,' said a voice from behind them, accompanied by the unmistakable sound of a shotgun being pumped. 'Seriously. I'm not in a good mood, I'm tired, and I just want to go home.'

'Richard,' Oliver said, and turned to regard him. 'You look like hell, my friend. Don't you think you should go be with your family, instead of worrying about these... outcasts?'

Richard stepped forward and put the shotgun under Oliver's chin. 'Yeah, I should. But I owe them. I said—'

Oliver backhanded him. Richard went flying and rolled to a limp stop on the pavement, the shotgun clattering to the ground.

'I heard you the first time,' Oliver said mildly. 'My, you do make friends in strange places, Claire. I suppose you'll have to tell me all about that later.' He raised his voice. 'Time's up! Claire Danvers, do you swear your life, your blood, and your service to me, now and for your lifetime, that I may command you in all things? Do say yes, my dear, because if you don't, I'll simply close my hand. It's a very messy way to go. Takes minutes for you to choke to death, and Shane gets to watch the whole thing.'

Claire couldn't believe she'd ever thought Oliver was kind, or reasonable, or *human*. She stared at his cold, cold eyes, and saw a thin, blood-coloured trickle of sweat run down his face under the hat.

She was no longer standing on tiptoe, she realised. Her feet were flat on the ground.

He's getting weaker!

Not that it would do her any good.

'Wait.' Shane's voice. Claire breathed in a shallow gasp and saw him limping across the open ground from the hospital building towards her. His face was bloody, and there was something wrong with his ankle, but he wasn't stopping. 'You want a servant? How about me?'

'Ah. The hero appears.' Oliver turned towards him, and as he did, Claire got a better look at Shane. She saw the fear in his eyes, and her heart just broke for him.

He'd been through so much; he didn't deserve this, too. Not this. 'I thought you might say that. What if I take you both, then? I'm a generous, fair boss. Ask Eve.'

'Don't believe anything he says. He's working with your dad,' Claire wheezed. 'He's been working with him the whole time. He arranged for Brandon to be killed. Shane—'

'I know all that,' Shane said. 'Politics, right, Oliver? Mind games, you and Amelie. We're just pawns to you. *Well, she's not a pawn.* Let her go.'

'All right, my young knight,' Oliver said, and smiled. 'If you insist.'

He was going to kill her, he really was...

Shane had something in his hand, and he threw it right in Oliver's eyes.

It looked like water, but it must have burnt like acid. Oliver let go of Claire and screamed, stumbling backward, tearing the hat from his head and bending over, clawing at his face...

Shane grabbed Claire's hand, and pulled her with him in a limping run.

Straight into the old hospital building.

With a roar, the cops, the vampires, and their servants came rushing across the open sunlit parking lot. Some of the vampires went down, hammered by the hot sun, but not all of them. Not nearly all of them.

Shane pushed Claire through the doorway and yelled, 'Now!'

A huge, heavy wooden desk dropped down on its side,

blocking the doorway with a crash, and then another one dropped on top of it from the balcony above.

Shane, breathing hard, grabbed Claire and pulled her into a hug. 'You OK?' he asked. 'No fang marks or anything?'

'I'm fine,' she gasped. 'Oh, *God*, Shane!'

'So this charcoal look, that's just fashion. You're OK.'

She clung to him tightly. 'There was a fire.'

'No kidding. Dad makes one hell of a diversion.' Shane swallowed and pushed her back. 'Did you get Monica out of there? Dad told me – well, he meant to leave her in there.' She nodded. Shane's eyes glittered with relief. 'I tried to stop this, Claire. He won't listen to me.'

'He never did. Didn't you know that?'

He shrugged, and looked around. 'Funny, I keep thinking he will. Where's Eve? In the police car?'

With Michael, she almost said, and realised it probably wasn't the best moment to announce that Shane's best friend was now a full-fledged vampire. Shane was just barely warming up to the whole ghost issue. 'Yeah. In the police car.' She took a corner of his shirt and lifted it to wipe at the blood on his face.

'Ouch.'

'Where's your dad?'

'They've been moving out,' he said. 'He tried to get me to go. I said I'd damn well go when I had you back. So… I guess now would be a good time.'

There was a clatter of metal off to the side, and Claire's world gradually expanded past the miracle of seeing Shane again to take in the room where she stood. It was a big lobby, floored in scarred, ugly green plastic tile. What little furniture remained in the room was mostly bolted down, like the reception desk; the walls were black and furry with thick streaks of mould, and lights hung at odd angles overhead, clearly ready to fall at the slightest jolt. There was a creaky-looking second floor overlooking the lobby, and around it dented filing cabinets blocked the windows.

It smelt like dead things – worse, it *felt* that way, like terrible things had been done here over the years. Claire was reminded of the Glass House, and the energy stored inside of it...What kind of energy was stored here? And what had it come from? She shuddered even thinking about it.

'They're coming!' someone called from up above, and Shane raised a hand in acknowledgment. 'Time to get the hell out, man!'

'Coming.' He grabbed Claire's hand. 'Come on. We have a way out.'

'We do?'

'Morgue tunnels.'

'What?'

'Trust me.'

'I do, but...*morgue tunnels*?'

'Yeah,' Shane said. 'They were sealed off in the mid-fifties, but we opened up one end. It's not on the maps. Nobody's watching it.'

'Then who's in here with you?'

'Couple of Dad's guys,' Shane said.

'That's it?' She was horrified. 'You know there are about a hundred angry people outside, right? And they have guns?'

Behind them, the battering at the doors strengthened. The desks blocking access grated across the floor, one torturous inch at a time. She could see daylight spilling inside.

'We'd better move,' Shane said. 'Come on.'

Claire let him tow her along, and looked back over her shoulder to see the desks shuddering under the impact of bodies. They slid across the tile with another groan, and one of them cracked in half, drawers spilling out in a noisy clatter.

Shane waved to a big guy in black leather as they passed, and the three of them ran down the second-floor hallway. It was dark, filthy, and scary, but not as scary as the sounds coming from the lobby behind them. Shane had a flashlight, and he switched it on to pick out obstacles in the way – fallen IV stands, an abandoned, dust-covered wheelchair, a gurney tipped over on its side. 'Faster,' she gasped, because she heard a final crash from the lobby.

They were inside.

Claire didn't think more than half the vampires had made it successfully across the sun-drenched parking lot, but those who'd been strong enough were inside now, and it was nice and dark for them. No contest.

Shane knew where he was going. He turned right at a

corner, then left, yanked up a fire exit door, and pushed Claire inside. 'Up!' he said. 'Two flights, then go left!'

There were things on the stairs; Claire couldn't see them very well, even in the glow of Shane's flashlight, but they smelt dead, sickly rotten. She tried not to breathe, avoided the sticky puddles of dried – whatever that was, she couldn't think of it as blood – and kept running up the steps. First landing, then another set of stairs, these clear except for some broken bottles she vaulted over.

She yanked the fire door two flights up, and nearly dislocated her shoulder.

It was blocked.

'Shane!'

He pushed her out of the way, grabbed the handle, and pulled. 'Shit!' He kicked it furiously, looked blank for a second, then turned to the next flight of stairs. 'One more! Go!'

The fifth-floor door was open, and Claire darted through it into the dark.

Her foot caught on something, and she toppled foward, hit the floor, and rolled. Shane's flashlight bounced a ball of light towards her, lighting up scarred linoleum tile, stacks of leaning boxes...

...and a skeleton. Claire yelped and scrambled back from it, then realised that it was one of those medical teaching skeletons, scattered out on the floor from where she'd tripped over it.

Shane grabbed her by the arm, hauled her up, and pulled her along. Claire looked over her shoulder. She couldn't see the biker guy, the one who'd been following them. Where had he—

She heard a scream.

Oh.

Shane hurried her down the long hall, then turned left and pulled Claire after him. There was another set of fire stairs. He opened the door, and they raced down one flight.

This exit was open. Shane pulled her out into another long, dark hallway and moved fast, counting doorways under his breath.

He stopped in front of number thirteen.

'Inside,' he said, and kicked it open. Metal gave with a shriek, and the door flew back to slam against tile. Something broke with a clatter like dropped plates.

Claire felt a chill take hold, because she had walked into what looked like a morgue. Stainless steel trays, stainless steel lockers on the wall, some gaping open to reveal sliding trays.

Yes, she was pretty sure it was the morgue. And pretty sure it was going to feature prominently in her nightmares from now on, provided she ever got to sleep again.

'This way,' Shane said, and pulled open what looked like a laundry chute. 'Claire.'

'Oh, hell, *no*!' Because if she hated tight spaces, there couldn't be anything much worse than this. She had no idea how long it was, but it was small, it was dark, and had he said something about *morgue tunnels*? Was this a body chute? Maybe there was a corpse still stuck in it! Oh God...

There were noises coming from outside the mob, coming fast.

'Sorry, no time,' Shane said, and picked her up and dumped her into the chute feet-first.

She tried not to scream. She thought she might have actually succeeded as she slid helplessly through the dark down a cold, metal tunnel meant only for the dead.

Chapter Thirteen

She landed hard, on stone, in the dark, and suppressed a burning need to whimper. A hand closed on her arm and helped her up. She heard a thumping clatter behind her, and got out of the way just in time as Shane – she thought it was Shane, anyway – tumbled out of the chute after her.

And the lights came on.

Well, not *lights* exactly...one light, and it was a flashlight.

And Shane's dad was holding it.

He took one fast, cold look at his son, then one at Claire, and said, 'Where's Des?'

Shane looked shocked. 'Dad – you were supposed to go! That was the whole point!'

'Where the hell is Des?'

'He's gone!' Shane shouted. 'Dammit, Dad—'

Frank Collins looked blackly furious, face twisting,

and he swung the flashlight away from them. Claire blinked spots away, and saw that he was aiming it at two of his guys standing in the dark. 'Right,' he said. 'Let's do this.'

'Do what?' Shane demanded, getting to his feet. He winced as he put his weight on his wounded ankle. 'Dad, what the hell is going on? You said you were leaving!'

'Didn't kill enough vampires to leave,' Frank Collins said. 'But I'm about to even the score.'

The two guys he had trained his light on were crouched next to a makeshift circuit board built out of what looked like old computer parts. It was hooked up to a car battery. One of the two guys held two wires by the insulated parts, but the tips were bare copper, freshly stripped.

Things fell together.

Shane's dad had used him, again. Used him as bait, letting him think he was being the hero, distracting the vampires to give his dad time to escape.

Used him to get a large number of vampires in one place. But they weren't just vampires; there were people there, too. Cops, and wannabe vampires. And people who were just there because they owed Oliver.

It was cold-blooded murder.

Richard had said it. *Demolition this week.* The explosives were already in place.

'They're going to blow the building!' Claire screamed, and lunged. She couldn't fight the bikers, but she didn't need to.

All she had to do was yank at the wires under the circuit board.

They gave with a blue white *pop*, and she was lucky not to be fried. One of the bikers reached her then, grabbed her, and threw her back, looking at the mess and shaking his head. 'Got a problem!' he yelled. 'She trashed the board! Gonna take time to rewire!'

Frank's face went scarlet with fury, and he ran towards her, fist in the air. 'You stupid little—'

Shane caught his fist in an open palm and held it there. 'Don't,' he said. 'Enough, Dad. No more.'

Frank tried to hit him. Shane ducked. He caught the second blow in an open palm again.

The third one, he blocked, and punched back. Just once.

Frank went down, flat on his ass, something like fear in his face.

'Enough,' Shane said. Claire had never seen him look taller, or more frightening. 'You've still got time to run, Dad. You'd better do it while you can. They'll figure out where we are soon, and you know what? I'm not dying for you. Not anymore.'

Frank's mouth opened, then closed. He wiped blood from his mouth, staring at Shane, as he got to his feet.

'I thought you understood,' he said. 'I thought you *wanted*—'

'You know what I want, Dad?' Shane asked. 'I want my life back. I want my girlfriend. And I want you to leave and never come back.'

Frank's eyes went flat, like a shark's. 'Your mother's turning over in her grave, watching you betray your own kind. Your own *father*. Siding with the parasites that infest this sick town.'

Shane didn't answer him. The two of them stared at each other in tense, angry silence for a few seconds, and then Claire heard metal clattering from up above. She tugged on Shane's arm urgently. 'I think they found the chute,' she said. 'Shane—'

Shane's dad said, 'I should have left you in the damn cage to fry, you ungrateful little bastard. You're no son of mine.'

'Hallelujah,' Shane said softly. 'Free at last.'

His dad turned off the flashlight, and Claire heard running footsteps in the dark.

Shane grabbed Claire's sweating hand, and they ran the opposite direction, with Shane breathlessly counting steps, until there was a golden glow of light at the end of the tunnel.

Shane wanted to run, but escape was impossible. Unless they made it out of Morganville, and even then, Claire understood – finally – that the vampires wouldn't let them leave. Not with what they'd done, or nearly done.

She needed to make it right.

Claire worked it out in her head before she said anything to him; Shane was talking in a breathless monologue, spinning a plan to steal a car, head out of town, maybe out of state.

Claire kept quiet until she saw the cherry red and blue flashers of a Morganville police cruiser coming down the darkened street, and then she let go of Shane's hand and said, 'Trust me.'

'What?'

'Just trust me.'

She stepped out in front of the police car, which came to a fast, controlled stop. A floodlight blinded her, and she stood still for it. She sensed Shane retreating, and said, sharply, 'Shane, no! Stay where you are!'

'What the hell are you doing?'

'Surrendering,' she said, and put her hands in the air. 'Come on. You, too.'

She didn't think he would, for a long terrifying second, and then he stepped out into the street with her, put his hands up, and laced his fingers behind his head. The police cruiser's doors popped open, and Shane dropped to his knees. Claire blinked at him, then followed suit.

She was on the ground in seconds, pinned by someone's hot, hard hand, and she heard a male voice say, 'Heller here. We've got Danvers and the Collins kid. They're alive.'

She didn't hear the reply, but she was too busy wondering if she'd made an awful mistake as cold steel handcuffs clicked shut around her wrists. The policeman hauled her upright by her elbow, and she winced at the pull on her sore muscles. Next to her, Shane was getting the same treatment. He wasn't resisting. He looked... tense.

'It's OK,' she told him. 'Trust me.'

His eyes were wild, but he nodded.

Better be right, she thought, and swallowed hard as they were shoved inside the back of the police car.

The police didn't talk to her or Shane at all. The ride was short, and silent, and when the cruiser pulled into the parking garage at City Hall, there was a welcoming committee standing there waiting. Claire almost cried at the sight of Michael and Eve – smoke-stained but standing side by side, holding hands. They looked worried. Next to them was Richard Morrell, with a bandage on his head.

And Mayor Morrell. She couldn't read his expression at all – annoyed, but she thought that was usual for him. Claire caught a glimpse of red hair, and saw Sam leaning against a pillar up on the dock. Apart from Michael, he was the only vampire present. At least, the only one she could see.

The cruiser's doors were opened, and Claire slid out. The mayor looked her over, then Shane. His eyes narrowed.

'My sources say somebody set up a spark board down under the hospital,' he said. 'Connected up the wires and got ready to blow the building. Looks like somebody trashed it before anything happened.'

Shane said, 'Claire pulled the wires. My dad was going to blow it and kill everybody inside.'

The Morrells, father and son, exchanged a look. Even Sam raised his head, though he stayed where he was, arms folded, looking relaxed and neutral. 'And where's your dad?' Richard asked. 'Shane, you don't owe him. You know that.'

'Yeah,' Shane said. 'I know. He's gone. I wish I could tell you he wouldn't be back, but—' He shrugged. 'Let Claire go, man. She saved people. She didn't hurt anybody.'

Mayor Morrell nodded at the cop standing behind Claire. She felt her handcuffs jiggle, then loosen, and gratefully folded her arms across her chest.

'What about Shane?' she asked.

'The vampires caught two of Frank's men. They admitted that Frank murdered Brandon. Shane's in the clear,' Richard said.

Shane blinked at him. 'What?'

'Go home,' Richard said, and the cop unlocked Shane's handcuffs, as well. 'Sam's taken care of getting word out to the vampires. They don't like you much, so watch your step, but you're not guilty of any crimes. Not major ones.'

'Great!' Eve said, and grabbed Claire's hand, then Shane's. 'We're outta here.'

Eve's Cadillac was parked a few spaces away. The back and side windows had been blacked out, Claire realised, and there was a fresh smell of paint in the air, and two cans of spray enamel lying on the ground. She got in the front seat, and Michael slid into the back seat. Shane hesitated, looking in at him, then climbed in and slammed the door.

Eve started the car. 'Shane?'

'Yeah?'

'I'm freaking *killing* you when we get home.'

'Good,' Shane said. 'Because right now, death seems like a better idea than talking about any of this.'

The town was strangely quiet – fires out, mobs dispersed, nothing to see here, move along. But Claire didn't really think it was over. Not at all. She leant against the window on the ride home, exhausted and unhappy. There was an ominous silence coming from the back seat, a feeling like thunderclouds rolling in and ready to break. Eve rambled on nervously about Shane's dad, and where he might have gone; nobody responded. *I hope he leaves*, Claire thought. *I hope he gets away.* Not because he shouldn't pay – he should – but because if he did, all it meant for Shane was more grief. Losing the last member of his already destroyed family. Better if his dad just… disappeared.

'Have you told Shane?' Eve asked. Claire sat up, blinking and yawning, as Eve pulled the Caddy to a halt in front of their house.

'About what?'

Eve pointed at Michael. 'You know.'

Claire turned to look at him. Shane was staring straight ahead, his face like stone. 'Let me guess,' he said. 'You came up with some magical fairy who granted you your freedom, and now you can come and go whenever you want,' he said. 'Tell me that's it, Michael. Because I've been thinking about why you're sitting in this car the whole way, and I can't really come up with any other answer that won't make me vomit.'

'Shane—' Michael said, and then shook his head. 'Yeah. My fairy godmother came and granted me a wish. Let's just get past this.'

'Get past it?' Shane said. 'How exactly do I do that? Fuck off.'

He got out of the car and stalked up the walkway. Eve grabbed a huge black umbrella and hurried around to Michael's side of the car; she opened it like a valet, and he stepped out, grabbed the umbrella, and ran after Shane. Even with the thin shade, his skin began to smoke lightly as it cooked.

Michael made it to the shade of the porch, he dropped the umbrella, and Shane turned and punched him.

Hard.

Michael rode the punch, caught the second one in his open palm, stepped in, and hugged him.

'Get off me!' Shane yelled, and shoved him back. '*Damn!* Get off!'

'I wasn't going to bite you, idiot,' Michael said wearily. 'Jesus. I'm just glad you're alive.'

'Wish I could say the same, but since you're *not*—' Shane slammed open the door and vanished inside, leaving Michael leaning against the wall.

Claire and Eve came slowly up the walk.

'I'll—' Claire swallowed hard. 'I'll talk to him. I'm sorry. He's just a little... It's been a long day, you know? He'll be OK.'

Michael nodded. Eve put an arm around him and helped him into the house.

Shane was nowhere to be seen when Claire entered the living room, but she heard his door slam upstairs. Damn, he was fast when he wanted to be. And bitter.

Who said *girls* were moody? She eyed the couch – it was the first comfortable spot to lie down – with weary longing. Maybe she should just let Shane get through it alone. Not like he wasn't used to dealing with trauma.

Then again...just because he could do it alone didn't mean he ought to have to.

There was something odd about the room, and for a long second, Claire couldn't put her finger on it. Then it dawned on her.

The room smelt like flowers. Roses, to be exact.

Claire frowned, turned, and saw a huge bunch of red roses lying on the side table. There was an envelope next to it with her name on it in old-fashioned copper-plate handwriting.

She tore it open and unfolded the papers inside.

Dear Claire,

My informal Protection is no longer sufficient for you and your friends, and I think you know that now. More drastic steps must be taken, and soon, or your friends will pay the price. Oliver will not allow today's events to go unanswered. You have been brave, but extremely foolish in your enemies.

Consider my proposal carefully.

I shall not offer it again.

There wasn't a signature, but Claire didn't have any doubt who had written it. Amelie. The letter was watermarked with her seal.

The other papers in the stack looked legal. She read them, frowning, trying to understand what they meant, and some of the language leapt out at her.

I, Claire Elizabeth Danvers, swear my life, my blood, and my service to the Founder, now and for my lifetime, that the Founder may command me in all things.

It was the same thing Oliver had said, back at the hospital, when he'd been trying to make her…

…make her his slave.

Claire dropped the paper like it had caught on fire. No, she couldn't do that. She couldn't.

Or your friends will pay the price.

Claire swallowed, stuffed the contract back into the envelope, and shoved it in her pocket just as Eve came around the corner and said, 'Roses! Jeez, who died?'

'Nobody,' Claire said hoarsely. 'They're for you. From Michael.'

Michael looked surprised, but his back was to Eve, and if he had any sense at all, he'd play along.

Claire went upstairs to take a shower.

* * *

Being clean made it better. Not a whole lot better, but some. She sat for a while, staring at the white envelope with her name on it, wishing she could talk to Shane about it, or Eve, or Michael, but not daring to do any of that because this was *her choice*. Not theirs. And she knew what they'd say, anyway.

Not enough no in the world, that's what they'd say.

It was after dark when Shane finally knocked on her door. She opened it and stood there looking at him. Just looking, because somehow she didn't think she'd ever see enough of him. He looked tired, and rumpled, and sleep creased.

And he was so beautiful she felt her heart break into a million little sharp-edged pieces.

He shifted uncertainly. 'Can I come in? Or do you just want me to—?' He pointed back down the hall. She stepped back and let him inside, then shut the door behind him. 'I freaked about Michael.'

'Yeah, you think?'

'Why didn't you tell me?'

'Well, it didn't exactly seem like the right time,' she said tiredly, and sat down on the bed, back to the headboard. 'Come on, Shane. We were running for our lives.'

He granted that argument with a shrug. 'How did this happen?'

'You mean, who? Amelie. She was here, and Michael asked.' Claire looked at him for a long second before she added the coup de grace. 'He asked because he wanted to be able to leave the house.'

Shane looked stricken. He lowered himself down on the corner of the bed, staring at her with those wounded, vulnerable eyes. The ones that made her heart break all over again. 'No,' he said. 'Not because of me. Tell me it wasn't—'

'He said it wasn't. Not, you know, completely, anyway. He had to do this, Shane. He couldn't live like this, not for ever.'

Shane looked away. 'Christ. I mean, he knows how I feel about vampires. Now I'm living with one. Now I'm *best friends* with one. That's not good.'

'Doesn't have to be bad, either,' she said. 'Shane, don't be angry, OK? He did what he thought he had to do.'

'Don't we all?' He flopped back on the bed, hands under his head. Staring up at the ceiling. 'Long day.'

'Yeah.'

'So,' he said. 'You got plans for tonight? Because suddenly I'm free.'

He made her laugh, even though she thought she didn't have any of that left. Shane rolled up on one elbow, and the gentleness in the way he smiled at her made her breath catch in her throat.

He reached out and tugged at her hair, smiling. 'You're all wild today,' he said. 'Hero.'

'Me? No way.'

'Yeah, you. You saved lives, Claire. Granted, some people I'd just as soon see gone, but...still. I think you even saved my dad. If he'd blown up that building, killed all those people...he couldn't have walked away from it.

I couldn't have let him.' They just looked at each other, and Claire felt tension coiling up between them, pulling them closer. She saw him leaning towards her, drawn by the same thing. He reached out and traced one hand slowly along her bare foot. 'So. What's the plan, hero? Want to watch a movie?'

She felt odd. Crazy and strange and full of uncertainty. 'No.'

'Kill some video zombies?'

'No.'

'If we get down to canasta, I'm jumping... off...the... what are you doing?'

She stretched out across the bed on her side, facing him. 'Nothing. What do you want to do?'

'Oh, let's not go there.'

'Why not?'

'Don't you have school tomorrow?'

She kissed him. It wasn't an innocent kiss – anything but. She felt like those roses downstairs, dark and red and full of passion, and it was new to her, so new, but she couldn't stop the feeling that she had to do this, *now*, because she'd almost lost him, and—

Shane leant his forehead against hers and broke the kiss with a gasp, like a drowning man. 'Hang on,' he said. 'Slow down. I'm not going anywhere. You know that, right? You don't have to put out to keep me here. Well, as long as you eventually—'

'Shut up.'

He did, mainly by pressing his lips back to hers. A

slower kiss this time, warm and then hot. She thought she'd never get enough of the *taste* of him; it just jolted through her like raw current and lit her up inside. Lit her up in ways she knew weren't good, or at least weren't completely legal.

'Want to play baseball?' she asked. Shane's eyes opened, and he stopped stroking her hair.

'What?'

'First base,' she said. 'You're already there.'

'I'm not running the bases.'

'Well, you could at least steal second.'

'Jeez, Claire. I used to distract myself with sports stats at times like these, but now you've gone and ruined it.' Another damp, hot kiss, and his hands trailed down her neck, feather-light. Over her shoulders, brushing skin her thin jersey nightshirt left bare. Down...

'Dammit.' He rolled over on his back, breathing hard, staring at the ceiling again.

'What?' she asked. 'Shane?'

'You could have died,' he said. 'You're sixteen, Claire.'

'Nearly seventeen.' She moved up against his side, cuddling close.

'Yeah, that makes it all better. Look—'

'You want to wait?'

'Yeah,' he said. 'Well, obviously, not my first choice, but I'm all about second thoughts right now. But the thing is...I don't want to leave you.' His arm was around her, and there was nothing in the world to her but the warmth of his body against her, and his whisper, and the utterly vulnerable need in his eyes. 'But it's not going to be easy for me to say no. So help me out here.'

Her heart was pounding. 'You want to stay?'

'Yes. I—' He opened his mouth, then closed it, then tried again. 'I need to stay. I need you.'

She kissed him, very gently. 'Then stay.'

'OK, but so far as baseball goes, second base is as far as I go.'

'You're sure about that?'

'I swear.'

And somehow, he kept his word, no matter how hard she tried to convince him.

Shane was still asleep, curled in a heap among the pillows, snoring lightly. She'd got his shirt off at some point, and Claire lay in the soft glow of the rising sun, watching the light gleaming on the strong muscles of his back. She wanted to touch him...but she didn't want him to wake up. He needed to sleep, and she had something she had to do.

Something he wasn't going to like.

Claire eased out of bed, moving very carefully, and found her blue jeans crumpled on the floor. The envelope was still in the back pocket. She opened it and slipped out the stiff, formal paper, unfolded it, and read the note again.

She put the contract on the desk, looked at Shane, and thought about the risk of losing him. Of Eve and Michael, too.

I, Claire Elizabeth Danvers, swear my life, my blood, and my service...

Shane had said she was a hero, but she didn't feel like one. She felt like a scared teenager with a whole lot to lose. *I can't watch him get hurt,* she thought. *Not if there's anything I can do to stop it. Michael – Eve – I can't take the risk.*

How bad could it be?

Claire opened the drawer and found a pen.

Acknowledgments

Musical inspiration from Joe Bonamassa,
a genius at his art.

Editorial excellence from Liz Scheier,
truly a master.

And a special shout-out to my friends at
Mysterious Galaxy bookstore in San Diego!

Midnight Alley

For the people who got me through
my own personal Morganville years:
Elizabeth Sandlin, Andy Sealy, Mona Fluitt,
Bruce Tinsley, Luis Hernandez, Gary Wiley,
Scott Chase, Marsha McNeill, Rachel Scarbrough,
and many more who made the days bright.
Also to the memory of sitting next to
Stevie Ray Vaughn, hearing him make magic
when few people were even listening.

For the people who are getting me
through these Morganville years: Cat Conrad,
Kelley Walters, Maria Stair, Katy Hendricks,
Claire Wilkins and Baby Griff, Becky Rocha,
Laurie Andrews and her lovely girls, PN Elrod,
Jackie Leaf, Bill Leaf, Joanne Madge, Irene Ferris,
Ter Matthies, the Alphas, ORAC, Douglas Joseph,
Sharon Sams and her son Boardman,
Ann Jackson and her son Trey, and literally
too many LiveJournal and MySpace friends
to even attempt to list. Every one of
them a special, undeserved gift.
And to Charles Armitage and Kevin Cleary,
for making Morganville an even
more exciting place.

CHAPTER ONE

The instant the phone rang at the Glass House, Claire knew with a psychic flash that it had to be her mother.

Well, it wasn't so much a psychic flash as simple logic. She'd told Mom that she would call days ago, which she hadn't, and now, of course, it could only be her mother calling at the most inopportune moment.

Hence: had to be a call from Mom.

'Don't,' her boyfriend – she couldn't believe she could actually call him that, *boyfriend*, not a boy friend – Shane murmured without taking his mouth off of hers. 'Michael will get it.' And he was giving her a very good argument in favour of ignoring the phone, too. But somewhere in the back of her mind that little voice just wouldn't shut up.

She slid off of his lap with a regretful sigh, licked her damp, tingling lips, and dashed off in the direction of the kitchen door.

Michael was just rising from the kitchen table to head for the phone. She beat him to it, mouthing a silent apology, and said, 'Hello?'

'Claire! Oh my goodness, I've been worried sick, honey. We've been trying to call you on your cell for days, and—'

Crap. Claire rubbed her forehead in frustration. 'Mom, I sent you guys an email, remember? My cell got lost; I'm still working on getting another one.' Best not to mention how it had got lost. Best not to mention anything about how dangerous her life had become since she'd moved to Morganville, Texas.

'Oh,' Mom said, and then, more slowly, 'Oh. Well, your father forgot to tell me about that. You know, he's the one who checks the email. I don't like computers.'

'Yes, Mom, I know.' Mom really wasn't *that* bad, but she was notoriously nervous with computers, and for good reason; they had a tendency to short out around her.

Mom was still talking. 'Is everything going all right? How are classes? Interesting?'

Claire opened the refrigerator door and retrieved a can of Coke, which she popped open and chugged to give herself time to think what, if anything, to tell her parents. *Mom, there was a little trouble. See, my boyfriend's dad came to town with some bikers and killed people, and nearly killed us, too. Oh, and the vampires are angry about it. So to save my friends, I had to sign a contract, so now I'm basically the slave of the most badass vampire in town.*

Yeah, that wouldn't go over well.

Besides, even if she said it, Mom wouldn't understand it. Mom had been to Morganville, but she hadn't really seen. People usually didn't. And if they did, they either never left town or had their memories wiped on the way out.

And if by some chance they started to remember, bad things could happen to them. Terminally bad things.

So instead, Claire said, 'Classes are great, Mom. I aced all my exams last week.'

'Of course you did. Don't you always?'

Yeah, but last week I had to take my exams while worrying that somebody was going to stick a knife in my back. It could have had an effect on my GPA. Stupid to be proud of that...'Everything's fine here. I'll let you know when I get the new cell phone, OK?' Claire hesitated, then asked, 'How are you? How's Dad?'

'Oh, we're fine, honey. We miss you is all. But your father's still not happy about your living in that place, off campus, with those older kids...'

Of all the things for Mom to remember, she had to remember *that*. And of course Claire couldn't tell her *why* she was living off campus with eighteen-year-olds, especially when two of them were boys. Mom hadn't got around to mentioning the boys yet, but it was just a matter of time.

'Mom, I told you how mean the girls were to me in the dorm. It's better here. They're my friends. And really, they're great.'

Mom didn't sound too convinced. 'You're being careful, though. About those boys.'

Well, that hadn't taken long. 'Yes, I'm being careful about the boys.' She was even being careful about Shane, though that was mostly because Shane never forgot that Claire was not quite seventeen, and he was not quite nineteen. Not a huge age difference, but legally? Huger than huge, if her parents got upset about it. Which they definitely would. 'Everybody here says hello, by the way. Ah, Michael's waving.'

Michael Glass, the second boy in the house, had settled down at the kitchen table and was reading a newspaper. He looked up and gave her a wide-eyed, *no-you-don't* shake of his head. He'd had a bad enough time of it with her parents the last time, and now...well, things were even worse, if that was possible. At least when he'd met them, Michael had been half-normal: fully human by night, an incorporeal ghost by day, and trapped in the house twenty-four/seven.

For Morganville, that *was* half-normal.

In order to help get Shane out of trouble, Michael had made a terrible choice – he'd gained his freedom from the house and obtained physical form at the time, but now he was a vampire. Claire couldn't tell if it bothered him. It had to, right? But he seemed so...normal.

Maybe a little too normal.

Claire listened to her mother's voice, and then held out the phone to Michael. 'She wants to talk to you,' she said.

'No! I'm not here!' he stage-whispered, and made waving-off motions. Claire wiggled the phone insistently.

'You're the responsible one,' she reminded him. 'Just try not to talk about the—' She mimed fangs in the neck.

Michael shot her a dirty look, took the phone, and turned on the charm. He had a lot of it, Claire knew; it wasn't just parents who liked him, it was...well, everybody. Michael was smart, cute, hot, talented, respectful...nothing not to love, except the whole undead aspect. He assured her mother that everything was fine, that Claire was behaving herself – his eye roll made Claire snort cola up her nose – and that he was watching out for Mrs Danvers's little girl. That last part was true, at least. Michael was taking his self-appointed older-brother duties way too seriously. He hardly let Claire out of his sight, except when privacy was required or Claire slipped off to class without an escort – which was as often as possible.

'Yes ma'am,' Michael said. He was starting to look a little strained. 'No ma'am. I won't let her do that. Yes. Yes.'

Claire had pity on him, and reclaimed the phone. 'Mom, we've got to go. I love you both.'

Mom still sounded anxious. 'Claire, are you sure you don't want to come home? Maybe I was wrong about letting you go to MIT early. You could take the year off, study, and we'd love to have you back home again...'

Weird. Usually she calmed right down, especially

when Michael talked to her. Claire had a bad flash of Shane telling her about his own mother, how her memories of Morganville had started to surface. How the vampires had come after her to kill her because the conditioning didn't stick.

Her parents were in the same boat now. They'd been to town, but she still wasn't sure just how much they really knew or understood about that visit – it could be enough to put them in mortal danger. She had to do everything she could to keep them safe. That meant not following her dreams to MIT, because if she left Morganville – assuming she could even get out of town – the vampires would follow her, and they'd either bring her back or kill her. And the rest of her family, too.

Besides, Claire *had* to stay now, because she'd signed a contract pledging herself directly to Amelie, the town's Founder. The biggest, scariest vampire of them all, even if she rarely showed that side. At the time, she'd been Claire's only real hope to keep herself and her friends alive.

So far signing the contract hadn't meant a whole lot – no announcements in the local paper, and Amelie hadn't shown up to collect on her soul or anything. So maybe it would just pass by...quietly.

Mom was still talking about MIT, and Claire didn't want to think about it. She'd dreamt of going to a school like MIT or CalTech her whole life, and she'd been smart enough to do it. She'd even got early acceptance. It was drastically unfair that she was stuck in Morganville now, like a fly in a spider's web, and for a few seconds she let herself feel bitter and angry about that.

Nice, the brutally honest part of her mocked. *You'd sacrifice Shane's life for what you want, because you know that's what would happen. Eventually, the vampires would find an excuse to kill him. You're not any better than the vampires if you don't do everything you can to prevent that.*

The bitterness left, but regret wasn't following bitterness any time soon. She hoped Shane never knew how she felt about it, deep down.

'Mom, sorry, I've got to go; I have class. I love you… Tell Dad I love him, too, will you?'

Claire hung up on her mother's protests, heaved a sigh, and glanced at Michael, who was looking a little sympathetic.

'That's not easy, talking to the folks,' he offered. 'Sorry.'

'Don't you ever talk to your parents?' Claire asked, and slid into the chair at the small breakfast table across from him. Michael had a cup of something; she was afraid it was blood for a second, but then she smelt coffee. Hazelnut. Vampires could, and did, enjoy food; it just didn't sustain them.

Michael looked suspiciously good this morning – a little colour in his face, an energy to his movements that hadn't been there last night.

He'd had more than coffee this morning. How did that

happen, exactly? Did he sneak off to the blood bank? Was there some kind of home delivery service?

Claire made a mental note to check into it. Quietly.

'Yeah, I call my folks sometimes,' Michael said. He folded the newspaper – the local rag, run by vampires – and picked up a smaller, rolled bundle of letter-sized pages secured by a rubber band. 'They're Morganville exiles, so they have a lot to forget. It's better if I don't keep in contact too much; it could make trouble. I mostly write. The mail and email get read before they're sent; you know that, right? And most of the phone calls get monitored, especially long-distance.'

He stripped off the rubber band and unfolded the cheap pages of the second newspaper. Claire read the masthead upside down: *The Fang Report*. The logo was two stakes at right angles making up a cross. Wild.

'What's that?'

'This?' Michael rattled the paper and shrugged. 'Captain Obvious.'

'What?'

'Captain Obvious. That's his handle. He's been doing these papers every week for about two years now. It's an underground thing.'

Underground in Morganville had a lot of meanings. Claire raised her eyebrows. 'So...Captain Obvious is a vampire?'

'Not unless he's got a serious self-image problem,' Michael said. 'Captain Obvious hates vampires. If somebody steps out of line, he documents it—' Michael froze, reading the headline, and his mouth opened, then closed. His face set like stone, and his blue eyes looked stricken.

Claire reached over and took the newspaper from his hands, turned it, and read.

New Bloodsucker in Town

Michael Glass, once a rising musical star with too much talent for this twisted town, has fallen to the Dark Side. Details are sketchy, but Glass, who's been keeping to himself for the past year, has definitely joined the Fang Gang.

Nobody knows how or where it happened, and I doubt Glass will be talking, but we should all be worried. Does this mean more vamps, fewer humans? After all, he is the first newly risen undead in generations.

Beware, boys and girls: Glass may look like an angel, but he's got a demon inside now. Memorise the face, kibbles. He's the newest addition to the Better-Off-Dead club!

'The *Better-Off-Dead* club?' Claire repeated aloud, horrified. 'He's kidding, right?' There was Michael's picture, probably directly out of the Morganville High yearbook, inset as a graphic into a tombstone.

With crudely drawn-in fangs.

'Captain Obvious never comes out and tells anyone

to kill,' Michael said. 'He's pretty careful about how he phrases things.' Her friend was angry, Claire saw.

And scared. 'He's got our address listed. And all your names, too, though at least he points out none of you are vampires. Still. That's not good.' Michael was getting past the shock of seeing himself outed in the paper, and was getting worried. Claire was already there.

'Well...why don't the vampires do something about him? Stop him?'

'They've tried. They've arrested three people in the last two years who said they were Captain Obvious. Turned out they didn't know anything. The captain could teach the CIA a thing or two about running a secret operation.'

'So he's not that obvious,' Claire said.

'I think he means it in the ironic sense.' Michael swallowed a quick gulp of coffee. 'Claire, I don't like this. Not like we didn't have enough trouble without this kind of—'

Eve slammed in through the kitchen door, which hit the wall with a thunderous boom, startling both of them. She clomped across the kitchen floor and leant on the breakfast table. She wasn't very Goth today; her hair was still matte-black, but it was worn back in a simple ponytail, and the plain knit shirt and black pants didn't have a skull anywhere in view. No make-up, either. She almost looked...normal. Which was so *wrong*.

'All right,' she said, and slapped down a second copy of *The Fang Report* in front of Michael. 'Please tell me you have a snappy comeback for this.'

'I'll make sure the three of you are safe.'

'Oh, *so* not what I was looking for! Look, I'm not worried about us! We're not the ones Photoshopped into tombstones!' Eve looked at the picture again. 'Although yes, better dead than that hairdo...God, was that your prom photo?'

Michael grabbed the paper back and put it face-down on the table. 'Eve, nothing is going to happen. Captain Obvious just loves to talk. Nobody's going to come after me.'

'Right,' a new voice said. It was Shane. He'd come in behind Eve, clearly wanting to watch the fireworks, and now he leant against the wall next to the stove and crossed his arms. 'By all means, let's keep on shovelling the bull,' he said. 'It's trouble, and you know it.' Claire waited for him to come over to the table and join the three of them, the way things used to be.

He didn't. Shane hadn't willingly stayed long in the same room with Michael since...the change. And he wouldn't look at him, except in angles and side glances. He'd also taken to wearing one of Eve's silver crosses, although just now it was hidden beneath the neck of the grey T-shirt he was wearing. Claire found her eyes fixing on its just-visible outline.

Eve ignored Shane; her big, dark eyes were fixed on

Michael. 'You know they'll all be gunning for you now, right? All the would-be Buffys?' Claire had seen *Buffy the Vampire Slayer*, but she had no idea how Eve had managed; it was contraband in Morganville, along with every other movie or book featuring vampires. Or vampire killing, more to the point. Internet downloads were strictly controlled, too, though no doubt there was a hot black market in those kinds of things that Eve had tapped into.

'Like you?' Michael said. He still hadn't forgot the arsenal of stakes and crosses that Eve kept hidden in her room. In the old days, that had seemed like good sense, living in Morganville. Now, it seemed like a recipe for domestic violence.

Eve looked stricken. 'I'd never—'

'I know.' He took her hand gently in his. 'I know.'

She softened, but then she shook it off and went back to frowning at him. 'Look, this is *dangerous*. They know you're an easier target than those other guys, and they're going to hate you even more, because you're one of us. *Our* age.'

'Maybe,' Michael said. 'Eve, come on, sit. Sit down.'

She did, but it was more like a collapse, and she didn't stop jittering her heel up and down in agitation, or drumming her black-painted fingernails on the table. 'This is bad,' she said. 'You know that, right? Nine point five on the ten point scale of make-me-yak.'

'Compared to what?' Shane asked. 'We're already

living with the enemy. What does that score? Not to mention you probably get extra points for banging him—'

Michael stood up so fast his chair tipped and hit the floor with a clatter. Shane straightened, ready for trouble, fists clenched.

'Shut up, Shane,' Michael said, deathly quiet. 'I mean it.'

Shane stared past him at Eve. 'He's going to bite you. He can't help it, and once he starts, he won't stop; he'll *kill* you. But you know that, right? What is that, some freak-ass Goth idea of romantic suicide? You turning into a fang-banger?'

'Butt out, Shane. What you know about Goth culture you got from old episodes of *The Munsters* and your Aryan Brotherhood dad.' Great, now Eve was angry, too. That left Claire the only sane one in the room.

Michael made an effort to dial it back. 'Come on, Shane. Leave her alone. *You're* the one hurting her, not me.'

Shane's gaze snapped to Michael and focused. Hard. 'I don't hurt girls. You say I do, and you'd better back it up, asshole.'

Shane pushed away from the wall, because Michael was taking steps in his direction. Claire watched, wide-eyed and frozen.

Eve got between them, hands outstretched to hold both of them back. 'Come on, guys, you don't want to do this.'

'Kinda do,' Shane said coolly.

'Fine. Either hit each other or get a room,' she snapped,

and stepped out of the middle. 'Just don't pretend it's all about protecting the itty-widdle girl, because it isn't. It's about the two of you. So get it together, or leave; I don't care which.'

Shane stared at her for a second, eyes gone wide and oddly hurt, then looked at Claire. She didn't move.

'I'm out,' he said. He turned and walked through the kitchen door. It swung shut behind him.

Eve let out a little gasp. 'I didn't think he'd go,' she said, so unsteadily that for a second Claire thought she was going to cry. 'What a freaking *idiot*.'

Claire reached over and took her hand. Eve squeezed, hard, and then leant back into Michael's embrace. Vampire or not, the two of them seemed happy, and anyway, this was *Michael*. She just couldn't understand Shane's anger. It seemed to bubble up when she least expected it, for no reason at all.

'I'd better…' she ventured. Michael nodded.

Claire slipped out of her chair and went to find Shane. Not like it was difficult; he was slumped on the couch, staring at the PlayStation screen and working the controls on yet another zombie-killing adventure.

'You taking his side?' Shane asked, and splattered the head of an attacking undead monster.

'No,' Claire said and settled in carefully next to him, with enough open space between so he didn't feel pressured. 'Why are there sides, anyway?'

'What?'

'Michael's your friend; he's our housemate. Why do there have to be sides?'

He snapped his fingers. 'Um, wait, I've got this one... because he's a bloodsucking, night-crawling leech who *used* to be my friend?'

'Shane—'

'You think you know, but you don't. He's going to change. They all change. Maybe it'll take time, I don't know. Right now, he thinks he's just human plus, but that's not what it is. He's human *minus*. And you'd better not forget it.'

She stared at him, a little bit stunned and a whole lot saddened. 'Eve's right. That sounds like your father talking.'

Shane flinched, paused the game, and threw the controller down. 'Low, Claire.' He wasn't exactly his dad's biggest fan at the best of times – he couldn't be, with the number of cruel things his dad had done to him.

'No, it's just true. Look, it's *Michael*. Can't you give him the benefit of the doubt? He hasn't hurt anybody, has he? And you have to admit, having a vampire on our side, *really* on our side, couldn't hurt. Not in Morganville.'

He just glared at the screen, jaw set. Claire was trying to think of another way to get through to him, but she was derailed by the ringing of the doorbell. Shane didn't move. 'I'll get it,' she sighed, and went down the hall to open the front door. It was safe enough – midmorning, sunny, and relatively mild. Summer was finally starting a slide towards fall, now that it had burnt all the green out of the Texas landscape.

Claire squinted against the brilliance. For a second she thought that there was something deeply wrong with her eyes.

Because her arch-enemy, Queen Bitch Monica Morrell, flanked by her ever-present harpies Gina and Jennifer, was standing on the doorstep. It was like seeing Barbie and her friends, blown up life-sized and dressed like Old Navy mannequins. Tanned, toned, and perfect, from lip gloss to toenail polish. Monica had on a forced, pleasant expression. Gina and Jennifer were trying, but they looked like they were smelling something rotten.

'Hi!' Monica said brightly. 'Got plans today, Claire? I was thinking we could hang.'

That's it, Claire thought. *I'm dreaming. Only this is a nightmare, right? Monica pretending to be my friend? Definitely a nightmare.*

'I...what do you want?' Claire asked, because her relationship with Monica, Gina, and Jennifer had started with being pushed down the stairs at the dorm, and hadn't improved since. She was a crawling bug to the Cool Girls. At best. Or...a tool. *Was this about Michael?* Because his status had changed from 'hermit musician' to 'hottie vampire' in one night, and Monica was definitely a fang-banger, right? 'You want to talk to Michael?'

Monica gave her an odd look. 'Why would I want to

do that? Can he go shopping in broad daylight?'

'Oh.' She had no idea what else to say to that.

'I thought a little retail therapy, and then we all go study,' Monica said. 'We're going to check out that new place, not Common Grounds. Common Grounds is so last century. Like I *want* to be under Oliver's thumb all the time. Now that he's taken over as Protector for our family, he's been all hands-on, wanting to see my grades. Sucks, right?'

'I—'

'C'mon, save my life. I really need help with economics, and these two are boneheads.' Monica dismissed her two closest friends with an offhand wave. 'Seriously. Come with. Please? I could really use your brainpower. And I think we should get to know each other a little better, don't you? Seeing as how things have changed?'

Claire opened her mouth, then closed it without saying anything. The last two times she'd gone anywhere with Monica, she'd been flat on her back on the floor of a van, getting beaten and terrorised.

She managed to stammer, 'I know this is going to sound rude, but...what the hell are you doing?'

Monica sighed and looked – how weird was this? – contrite. 'I know what you're thinking. Yes, I was a bitch to you, and I hurt you. And I'm sorry.' Gina and Jennifer, her constant Greek chorus, nodded and repeated *sorry* in whispers. 'Water under the bridge, all right? All is forgiven?'

Claire was, if anything, even more mystified. 'Why are you doing this?'

Monica pursed her glossy lips, leant forward, and dropped her voice to a low, confidential tone. 'Well...all right, yeah, it's not like I had a head injury or something and woke up thinking you were cool. But you're different now. I can help. I can introduce you around to all the people you really need to know.'

'You're kidding. I'm different *how*?'

Monica leant even closer. 'You signed.'

So...this wasn't about Michael. Claire had just become...popular. Because she'd become Amelie's property.

And that was terrifying.

'Oh,' she managed, and then, more slowly, 'Oh.'

'Trust me,' Monica said. 'You need somebody in the know. Somebody to show you the ropes.'

If the only other person left on the planet was Jack the Ripper, Claire would have trusted him first. 'Sorry,' she said. 'I have plans. But...thank you. Maybe some other time.'

She shut the door on Monica's surprised face, then locked it. She jumped when she turned to find Shane standing right behind her, staring at her as though he'd never seen her before.

'*Thank you?*' he mimicked. 'You're thanking that bitch? For what, Claire? For beating you? For trying to kill you? For killing my sister? Christ. First Michael, then you. I don't know any of you anymore.'

In true Shane fashion, he just took off. She listened to the heavy tread of his footsteps cross the living room and then go up the stairs. Heard the familiar slam of his door.

'Hey!' she shouted after him. 'I was just being polite!'

CHAPTER TWO

'So,' Eve said as she drove Claire to school, 'what was up with the Monica thing? I mean, maybe you ought to watch your back with her. Even more than you already do.'

'She sounded like she really kind of meant it. It took a lot for her to come eat crow like that.'

Eve shot her a look. One of *those* looks, doubly effective coming from a girl wearing rice-powder make-up and flawless eyeliner and black-cherry lips. 'In Monica's world, being friends means doing whatever Monica wants, when Monica wants to do it. Somehow, I can't see you as one of her brain-dead back-up singers.'

'No! That's not...I didn't say I was *going* to be her friend, just...you asked.' Claire crossed her arms and settled back in the bucket seat of Eve's ancient black Caddy, shooting for a stubborn look. 'She's not my friend, OK? You're my friend.'

'So when Monica starts bringing the in-crowd to hang at your study table, you'll get up and leave? No way. You're too nice. Before you know it, you're tagging along with them, and then you start to actually feel sorry for them. You'll tell me how Monica's not bad, she's just misunderstood, and before you know it you're braiding each other's hair and giggling over boy bands.'

Claire made a retching sound. 'I wouldn't do that.'

'Please. You like everybody. You even like me. You like *Shane*, and let's face it, Shane's kind of an idiot, at least right now.' Eve's eyes narrowed as she thought about that. 'And about Shane, I swear, if he doesn't snap out of it, I'm going to punch him in the face. Well, punch him in the face and then run like hell.'

Claire played that out in her head and nearly laughed. Eve's best possible punch wouldn't do more than surprise Shane, she figured, but she could just picture the wounded look of confusion on his face. *What the hell did I do?*

'I'm not popular,' she declared. 'Monica's not my friend, and I'm not hanging with her, ever, end of story.'

'Swear?'

Claire held up her hand. 'Swear.'

'Huh.' Eve didn't sound convinced. 'Whatev.'

'Look, if we're friends, how about buying me a mocha?'

'Mooch.'

'You're the one with the job.'

* * *

Mid-afternoon, and it was raining, which was kind of a rarity – a cold, early-fall rain that came down in glittering sheets. Claire, like about ninety per cent of the other students, hadn't thought to bring an umbrella, so she sloshed along miserably along the Quadrangle, past the empty benches and rain-soaked message boards, towards her chem lab. She loved Chem Lab. She hated rain. She hated being soaked to the skin and frankly, living in this part of Texas made it usually not that much of a risk. There was no room in her backpack for anything frivolous, like a raincoat. She worried her books were getting soggy, but the backpack was supposed to be waterproof...

'You look cold,' said a voice from behind her, and then the rain cut off, and she heard the hollow thump of raindrops hitting the thin skin of an umbrella.

Claire looked up, blinked water out of her eyes, and saw she was walking under a golf umbrella big enough for four or five of her...or one of her, plus the guy holding the umbrella. Because he was *huge*. Also cute, in that big-boned football player kind of way. He would have made Shane look small. Well proportioned, though, so the height (had to be at least six feet five, Claire thought) and weight just seemed right on him. He had chocolate brown skin and gorgeous brown eyes, and he seemed... kind of nice.

'I'm Jerome,' he said. 'Hey.'

'Hey,' she said back, still amazed that *somebody* who was clearly somebody would stop to hang an umbrella over her head. 'Thanks. Um, I'm Claire. Hi.'

She juggled her dripping backpack to her other hand and offered him her right. He took it and shook. His was about three times as large, big enough (she bet) to cup most of an entire football.

He was wearing a TPU athletic department T-shirt. No mystery about his major.

'Where're you heading, Claire?'

'Chem Lab,' she said, and pointed at the building, which was about a football field-length away, on the other side of the Quad. He nodded and steered that direction. 'Look, it's nice of you, but you don't have to—'

'It's no problem.' He smiled at her. He had dimples. 'I hear the Science Building is nice this time of year. And anything for a friend.'

'But I'm not—'

Jerome nodded to a group of girls standing huddled together under the awning of the Language Arts Building. Pretty girls. In the centre of them was Monica Morrell, and she blew Jerome a flirty sort of kiss.

'Oh,' Claire said. '*That* friend.' Her estimate of Jerome fell by several dozen notches, hit bottom, and started digging for China. 'Look, I appreciate it, but I'm not sugar. I won't melt.'

She veered away and walked fast. Jerome took about two long strides and put the umbrella over her again without comment. She glared at him.

He lifted an eyebrow. 'I can play this game all day.'

'Fine,' she said. 'But I don't need favours from Monica.'

'Girl, it's an umbrella, not a Lamborghini,' he pointed out. Way too reasonably. 'I'm not even lending it to you. It's not really that much of a favour.'

She kept her mouth shut, head down, and walked fast. Jerome stopped at the foot of the Science Building's stairs, and she bounded up and darted under the concrete porch, which was already choked with other students hiding from the rain. She looked back down. Jerome smiled and waved, and a bronze or copper bracelet caught her eye.

He was Protected. Probably a native of Morganville.

'I'm not her friend. That was not my fault,' she complained, defending herself to an Eve who wasn't even there.

And then she sneezed, sniffled, and dragged her soggy butt to class.

The rain kept up all day and all night, but the next day dawned bright and shiny, with a pale silver sun not quite as fierce as Claire expected. Kind of nice, actually. She'd already showered by the time Eve stumbled into the bathroom, looking more like the walking dead than most vampires. Eve mumbled something and ignored Claire as she started up the shower again. Claire finished at the sink and hurried downstairs. She found Michael at the coffee-pot, emptying the filter of cold grounds. Deeply weird that he was *more* of a morning person as a vampire. Maybe he was just enjoying having a morning again, instead of becoming a floaty ghost at dawn.

'Eve's up. You'd better make it so dark the spoon melts.'

Michael shot her a half smile, still almost lethal enough to stop a girl's heart. Luckily he knew just how much current to use on his charm. 'That bad, huh?'

She thought about it for a second as she took down a bowl and the box of Rice Krispies, and found the milk behind the bottles of beer – contraband, from Shane – in the fridge. 'You've seen that movie where the zombies eat people's brains?'

'*Night of the Living Dead*?'

'The zombies would run if they got a look at her.'

Michael spooned extra coffee into the fresh filter. He looked good, she thought. Strong, tall, confident. He had on a nice blue shirt and some not-so-ratty blue jeans, and he was wearing shoes. Running shoes, sure, but shoes. Claire stared at his feet. 'You're going out,' she said.

'Got a job,' Michael said. 'Working at JT's Music over on Third Street, ten to close. Mostly I'll be demoing guitars and selling them, but JT said he'd let me do some private lessons if I wanted.'

That was so...normal. *Really* normal. And he sounded happy, too. Claire bit her lip and tried to organise the explosion of questions in her brain.

'Ah...what about the sun?' she asked. Because that seemed to be the first hurdle.

'They issued me a car,' Michael said. 'It's in the

garage. Fully sunproofed. And there's underground parking at JT's. There is most places.'

'Issued...who issued you a car?' He shot her a *you're not stupid* look. 'The town? Amelie?'

He didn't answer directly as he slid the filter compartment shut and turned on the *brew* switch. The machine began wheezing and trickling into the pot. 'They tell me it's standard procedure,' he said. 'For new vampires.'

'Not that there have been any for fifty years, right?'

He shrugged. It was obvious that she was making him uncomfortable with the questions, but Claire couldn't help herself. 'Did you ever find out why...why there haven't been any in so long?'

'I don't think it's a great idea to be too curious right now.'

She understood that – and understood he meant it for her as well – but she couldn't stop asking questions, somehow. 'Michael...did they get you the job, too?'

'No. I know JT. I got the job all by myself. They offered—' He stopped, clearly thinking he'd already said too much.

Claire finished it out, guessing. 'They offered you some kind of job in the vampire community. Right? Or—' Oh God. 'Or they offered to make you a Protector?'

'Not right off the bat,' he said, still staring at the coffee-maker. 'You have to work up to that. So they say.'

Michael. Owning people. Skimming off their wages like some Mafia don. She tried not to let him see how sick that idea made her feel, that he'd ever really consider doing it.

His eyes suddenly cut towards her, as if he'd read her mind. 'I didn't do it. I found the job at JT's, Claire,' Michael said, and suddenly moved towards her. She flinched, and he took a deep breath and held out his hand in clear apology. 'Sorry. I forget sometimes...it's hard, OK, learning how to move around people when I can go so much faster. But I wouldn't hurt you, Claire. No way.'

'Shane thinks—'

Light caught and flared in Michael's eyes, eerie and frightening, and then he blinked and it was gone. He obviously made a real effort to keep his voice quiet.

'Shane's wrong,' he said. 'I'm not changing, Claire. I'm still your friend. I'll look after you. All of you. Even Shane.'

She didn't answer him. Truthfully, as much as she liked him – and it verged on love – she felt something different about him today. Something complicated and agitated and strange.

Was he...hungry? He was staring at her. No, he was staring at the thin skin of her neck, wasn't he? Claire put her hand to it, involuntary but irresistible, and Michael got a very slight pink flush in his pale cheeks and looked away.

'I wouldn't,' he said, in a far different tone than before. It almost sounded scared to her. 'I wouldn't, Claire. You have to believe me. But...this is hard. It's so hard.'

She did believe him, mostly because she could hear all the heartbreak and sorrow in his voice. She took a breath, stepped forward, and hugged him. He was tall; the top of her head only brushed his chin. His arms felt strong and comforting, and she told herself that he wasn't warm because it was chilly in the kitchen. It wasn't really true, but that helped.

'I wouldn't hurt you,' he murmured. 'But I've got to admit, I want to. I spent all my life hating vampires, and now...now look at me.'

'You had to,' Claire said. 'You didn't have a choice.'

She felt his sigh go through both of them. 'Not true,' he said. 'Shane's right... I did have a choice. But this is the choice I made, and now I have to live with it.'

He let go when she stepped back. Neither of them knew what to say, so Claire busied herself by opening kitchen cabinets to get down the four mismatched cups they used in the morning. Michael's was plain chunky stoneware, oversized, like a diner cup on steroids. Eve's was a petite black thing with a yawning cartoon vampire on it. Shane's had a happy face with a bloody bullet hole in the centre of its forehead. Claire had taken one with Goofy and Mickey on it.

'How's school?' Michael asked. Neutral subjects. He didn't want to talk it out; he wanted to keep it inside. She wasn't too surprised. Michael had always been too self-contained for his own good, as far as she could tell.

'Too easy,' she sighed, and poured coffee.

They were sitting down and sipping from their mugs

when the kitchen door opened, and Shane – wearing pyjama bottoms and a ratty old faded T-shirt came into the kitchen. He avoided Michael, picked up his cup off the counter, and filled it to the brim. He left without a word.

Michael watched him go, face set and hard.

Claire felt the need to apologise. 'He's just—'

'I know,' Michael said. 'Believe me. I know exactly how Shane is. Doesn't mean I have to like it right now.'

I really need to stop being the Glass Goodwill Ambassador, Claire thought, but she knew she'd keep on doing it. Somebody had to, after all. So after she'd finished her coffee, she went to talk to Shane.

Shane's door was unlocked and slightly open. Claire pushed it and stepped inside, then stopped short. All her carefully prepared speeches flew right out of her head, because Shane was getting dressed.

The sight of him short-circuited her thought processes and completely grounded her better judgement. He'd already hauled on his blue jeans, and his back was to her. No shirt yet. She was spellbound by the ripples of muscles on his back, the gorgeous smoothness of his skin, the way his shaggy hair brushed the tops of his shoulders and begged to be smoothed back...

The sound of his zipper being pulled up snapped her back to sanity. She stepped hastily back, out into the hall, and pulled the door almost shut, then knocked.

'What?' It wasn't a friendly response.

'It's me,' she said. 'Can I come in?'

She heard something halfway between a grunt and a sigh, and opened the door to find him dragging a dark grey, form-fitting shirt over his head. It looked very good on him. Not as good as the no-shirt thing, but she was trying hard not to think about that. It had made her warm and fluttery inside.

'Is that a new shirt?' she asked, desperate to get her mind off the vivid mental pictures that kept bubbling up. That got another indefinite grunt. 'It looks nice.'

Shane gave her an ironic look. 'We're talking clothes now? Wait, let me get my *Fashion for Dummies* book.'

'I...never mind. About Michael—'

'Stop.' Shane stepped forward and kissed her on the forehead. 'I know, you don't want me ripping him, but I can't help it. Give me some time, OK? I need to figure some things out.'

Claire tipped her head back, and this time he found her lips. It was, she thought, supposed to be a fast and sweet little kiss, but somehow it slowed down, got warmer and deeper. His lips were damp and soft as silk, and that was such a contrast to the hard lines of his body pressed against her, the strength of his hands sliding around her waist and pulling her even closer. She heard him growl low in his throat, a wild and hungry sound that made her go weak and faint.

He broke the kiss and leant against her, breathing hard. 'Good morning to you, too. Man, I just can't stay mad when you do that.'

'Do what?' she asked innocently. She didn't feel innocent. She also didn't feel sixteen-nearly-seventeen, not at all. Shane always made her feel older. Much older. Ready for anything. It was a good thing Shane wasn't as dumb as her hormones seemed to be.

'Unless you want to stay home and cut class, we don't really have time to talk about it,' he said, and waggled his eyebrows. 'So. Wanna cut class and make out?'

She socked him on the arm. 'No.'

'You are such a strange girl. Ow,' he said, in the way that meant he hadn't felt it at all. 'You riding with Eve?'

'When she passes the snarling cannibal phase, yeah. Another two cups of coffee, probably.'

'You sure you don't want a bodyguard?' He meant it. Shane didn't have a job – she wasn't really sure he could get one, after what his dad had been up to in Morganville recently. Probably better he kept it low profile for a while. The fewer vampires – and vampire loyalists – he came in contact with right now, the better. He was still thought of as an unindicted co-conspirator to his dad's revenge rampage, and even though the mayor had officially signed his pardon, nobody had much liked it.

Accidents happened.

'I don't need a bodyguard,' Claire said. 'Nobody's out to get me. Even Monica's got all friends-making with me.'

That earned her a too-sharp look, which didn't go well with his reddened, kissable lips. 'Yeah. Why is that?'

She shrugged and avoided his eyes. 'I don't know.'

He tipped her chin up with one finger. 'So, are we at the lying part of the relationship already? Usually that comes after the exciting, hot and sexy honeymoon period.'

She stuck out her tongue at him, and he leant forward and – to her horror – licked it. 'Ewwww!'

'Then don't stick it out.' Shane smiled. 'If you're going to hang out in my room and tempt me, there's a penalty. One item of clothing per minute comes off.'

'Perv.'

He pointed to himself. 'Male and eighteen. What's your point?'

'You are *so*—'

'Say, you got any pleated miniskirts and knee socks? I really get off on—'

She squealed and dodged his grabby hands, then checked her watch. 'Oh, crap – I really do have to go. I'm sorry. Look, you'll be...you're OK, right?'

The smile disappeared, leaving only a trace in his dark, secretive eyes. 'Yeah,' Shane said. 'I'll be OK. Watch your back, Claire.'

'You too.' Claire started for the door, but she heard his footsteps behind her and turned; he moved her back to the wall, tipped up her chin, and kissed her so thoroughly that she felt her head fill with light and her knees turn to rubber.

When she could breathe again, and he pulled back to give her just an inch or so of space between their lips, she gasped, 'Was that a goodbye?'

'That was a come-home-soon,' he said, and pushed off from the wall. 'Seriously, Claire. Watch yourself. I worry.'

'I know,' she said, and smiled. Her knees were still weak, and the chorusing light in her head just didn't seem to be fading. 'Best kiss so far, by the way.'

His eyebrows rose. 'You're keeping score?'

'Hey, you raised the bar. I don't grade on a curve.'

She left him, reluctantly, to grab her backpack and see if Eve was in the mood to eat brains, or to give her a ride to school.

Chapter Three

Morning classes went pretty well, and Claire spent her breaks hanging at the coffee bar at the University Centre, where Eve barista'd her way through the day. Eve was good at it – calm, efficient, seemingly impervious to the pissy demands and bitchiness of a lot of the students. Claire had figured out that the rude ones were mostly Protected, so it was a class thing; Eve had elected not to sign up with a vampire for protection, and those who had looked down on her.

Or else they were just bitchy. Which was equally possible. People didn't have to have a vampire connection to be arrogant jerks.

Eve was working today with another girl, somebody Claire didn't know; she had long, straight brown hair that shimmered like a curtain when she moved. She wore it loose around her shoulders, which Claire guessed was OK because she wasn't working directly with the drinks or anything, just taking orders and cash. Her name tag said AMY, and she looked cheerful and sweet. She and Eve were talking like friends, which was good; Eve needed that. Claire killed time between classes by skimming through her English Lit – boring – and reading a book she'd checked out from the library on advanced string theory – not boring. She liked the whole idea of vibrating strings being the basis of everything, that there were all kinds of surfaces that vibrated. It made the world more...exciting. Always in motion.

Her watch beeped to let her know she was going to be late for class if she didn't hurry, so she packed it up, waved to Amy and Eve, and jogged out of the UC and into the warm afternoon sunshine.

As she was blinking in the glare, she ran into Monica. Literally, as Monica was coming up the steps while she was going down. Claire automatically reached out to steady the other girl when she wavered, and then thought, *What am I doing?* Because Monica had once laughed as Claire tumbled down the stairs and cracked her head halfway open.

'Hey, *watch it*, bitch!' Monica snapped, and then did a double take. 'Claire? Oh, hi. Cute shirt!'

Claire looked down at herself, mystified. It wasn't. She didn't really own any clothes she'd classify as cute, and even the best of them would never match Monica's standards, which were much higher.

'You on your way to class?' Monica continued brightly. 'Too bad, I'd buy you a mocha or something.'

'I...uh...yeah, I've got class.' Claire edged around and tried to descend the steps, but Monica got in her way. Monica's smile was friendly, but it didn't really warm up her big, pretty eyes. 'I'll be late.'

'One thing,' Monica said, and lowered her voice. It occurred to Claire that it was almost the first time she'd seen Monica alone, not flanked by Gina and Jennifer, not trailing an entourage of the Popular. 'I'm having a party on Friday night. Can you come? It's at my parents' house. Here's the address.' Before Claire could react, Monica pressed a slip of paper into her hand. 'Keep it quiet, all right? I'm asking only the best people. Oh, and wear something nice; it's formal.'

And then Monica was gone, breezing by her up the steps, where she fell in with a group of girls and went into the UC's glass atrium, chatting and laughing.

The best people? Claire eyed the slip of paper, thought about throwing it away, and then shoved it in her pocket.

Maybe this was a golden opportunity to convince Monica that she wasn't ever going to be anything like a friend.

She headed out for class, moving quickly, but keeping her eyes peeled. When she spotted the guys she was looking for, she veered off the sidewalk and onto the grass.

Gamers. Nerds. They sat around outside most of the afternoon moving counters around on complicated-looking boards and rolling dice. She'd seen them every day for weeks, and in all that time she'd never seen any kind of girl with them, or even approach them. In fact, when she cleared her throat they stared at her as though she were an alien from one of the planets on their game board.

'Hi,' she said, and thrust out the slip of paper. 'My name's Monica. I'm having a party on Friday night. If you guys want to come. Tell your friends.'

One of them reached out and gingerly took the slip of paper. Another snatched it away from him, read it, and said, 'Wow. Really?'

'Really.'

'Mind if we invite some other people?'

'Knock yourself out.'

Claire headed off to class.

'Claire Danvers?'

Last class of the day, and Claire, startled, looked up from writing the date in her notebook. The professor didn't usually take roll. In fact, he seemed pretty much indifferent to who showed up, which was sometimes next to nobody. Like today – she was one of about twelve people. Showing up was really kind of useless in this particular course, since Professor What's-His-Name lectured from PowerPoint slides, bullet by bullet, and then made them available on his website right after the lecture. No wonder most people skipped.

She raised her hand, wondering what was going on. She had a guilty flash of handing over the party invitation to the Nerd Squad, but no, how could they find out so soon? And besides, who'd care, besides Monica?

The professor – grey, wrinkled, tired, and unenthusiastic – stared at her for a second without recognition, then said, 'You're wanted in Administration, room three-seventeen. Go now.'

'But—' Claire started to ask what was going on, but he'd already dismissed her and turned back to his PowerPoint, droning on in a monotone. She stuffed books into her bag, wondered again what was going on, and left without much regret.

She'd been in the Administration Building exactly three times – once to register, once to file the official paperwork to move off campus, once to do add/drop. It looked just like any administration building at any school – grubby and utilitarian, with tired, crabby employees and desks piled high with file folders. She avoided the first-floor Registrar's Office and went up the steps. The second floor was quieter, but still full of people talking, keys clicking on computers, printers running.

The third floor was whisper-quiet. Claire started down the hallway, and the silence sank deeper. She couldn't even hear sounds from outside the windows, although she could clearly see people out there walking and talking, and cars tooling around the street below. Room 317 was at the end of the hall. All of the glossy wooden doors were firmly closed.

She knocked on 317, and thought she heard someone say 'Come in,' so she turned the knob and stepped inside...into darkness. Complete, velvety darkness that disoriented her immediately. The knob slipped out of her hand and the door clicked shut, and she couldn't find it again. Her hand moved over what felt like a featureless, smooth wall.

A light bloomed behind her and she turned to see the flare of a match, and a candle wick catching fire. In the glow, Amelie's face shone like perfect ivory.

The elder vampire looked exactly the same as before: cool, queenly, pale, with her white-blonde hair twisted back in an elegant updo that must have required servants to achieve. She was wearing a white silk suit, and her skin was flawless. If she wore make-up, Claire couldn't tell. Her eyes were eerie in the near-dark...luminous and not quite human, and very beautiful.

'My apologies for the dramatics,' Amelie said, and smiled at her. It was a very nice smile, cool and polite. Claire's mother had always loved the Hitchcock movie *Rear Window*, and Claire was struck by the thought that if Grace Kelly had ended up a vampire, this was how she'd have looked. Icy and perfect. 'Don't bother looking for the door. It's gone until I wish it to be there again.'

Claire's heartbeat sped up, and she knew Amelie could tell, though the vampire didn't comment on it; she just shook out the match and dropped it in a silver dish on the table next to the candle. Claire's eyes adjusted gradually to the dimness. She was standing in a fairly small room, some kind of library crammed with books. *Crammed* was an understatement – the books were double-stacked on the shelves, leaning in towers on the top of the bookcases, filling the corners in untidy ziggurats. So many books that the whole room smelt like ancient paper. There wasn't any wall space, except where Claire had come in, that wasn't blocked up by packed, groaning shelves.

'Hi,' Claire said awkwardly. She hadn't seen Amelie since signing the Protection papers and putting them, as instructed, in the mailbox outside. She'd expected some kind of visit, but...nothing. 'Um...what should I call you?'

Amelie's delicate brows rose, pale on pale. 'I know that the concept of manners has declined, but I should think you would know at least some polite form of address that would be appropriate.'

'Ma'am,' Claire stammered. Amelie nodded.

'That will do.' She lit another candle. The light strengthened, flickering but casting a warm and welcome glow. Claire spotted another door in the shadows, small and fitted with an antique-style doorknob. There was a big skeleton key in the massive lock.

Nobody else in the room, just she and Amelie.

'I have called you to discuss your studies,' Amelie said, and sat down in a chair on the other side of the table. There wasn't any seat on Claire's side, so she stood there, awkwardly. She put her backpack down and folded her hands.

'Yes ma'am,' she said. 'Aren't my grades OK?' Because usually a 4.0 GPA was OK by most standards.

Amelie dismissed it with a wave. 'I did not say classes; I said studies. No doubt you are finding the local college beneath your abilities. You are said to be quite exceptional.'

Claire didn't know what to say to that, so she didn't say anything. She wished she had a chair. She wished she could say something nice and get back to class and never, ever see Amelie again, because as superficially polite and kind as the old vampire was, there was something ice-cold about her. Something unsettlingly *not human.*

'I would like you to study privately with a friend of mine,' Amelie said. 'For credit, of course.' She looked around, smiling very slightly. 'This is his library. Mine is far more orderly.'

Claire's throat felt tight and uncomfortable. 'A...uh... vampire friend?'

'Is that an issue?' Amelie folded her white hands together on the table. The candlelight flickered in her eyes.

'N-no ma'am.' *Yes.* God, she couldn't imagine what Shane was going to say.

'I believe you will find him most interesting, Claire. He is indeed one of the most brilliant minds I have ever encountered in my long life, and he has learnt so much through his lifetime that he could never teach it all. Still, he has much to pass along. I have been seeking the right pupil, one who can quickly grasp the discoveries he has made, and assist him in his research.'

'Oh,' Claire whispered faintly. *So*...an old vampire. Her experience wasn't so good with the older ones. Like Amelie, they were cold and strange, and most of them were cruel, too. Like Oliver. Oh God, she wasn't talking about Oliver, was she? 'Who—?'

Amelie looked down. Just for an instant, and then she met Claire's eyes and smiled. 'You have not met,' she said. 'Not formally, at any rate. His name is Myrnin. He is one of my oldest friends and allies. Understand, Claire, that your actions since you came to Morganville, including your agreement with me, have won my trust. I would not grant this honour to any but those I found worthy.'

Flattery. Claire recognised it, and knew the slight warmth in Amelie's voice was probably calculated, but it still worked. It made her feel less scared. 'Myrnin,' she repeated.

'It is an old name,' Amelie agreed, in response to the question in Claire's tone. 'Old and forgot, now. But once he was a great scholar, known and revered. His works should not be forgot as well.'

There was something strange in that, but Claire was too nervous to figure out what Amelie could be trying to say. Or not say. She was working hard to swallow a lump in her throat, but it was about the size of a poisoned apple and seemed to be growing larger. She could only nod.

Amelie smiled. It looked kind of artificial, like an expression she'd practised in a mirror rather than learnt as a child. Smiling was something her face just didn't naturally do, Claire decided. And sure enough, the smile was gone in seconds, without a trace.

'If you're ready...?'

'Now?' Claire cast an involuntary, helpless look at the blank wall behind her. There wasn't a door, and that meant there was no way to retreat. So she didn't really have a choice.

Amelie wasn't waiting for her answer, anyway. The ice queen stood up and walked – oh so very undead Grace Kelly – to another small, low doorway with the key in the lock. She turned the key, withdrew it, and looked down at it for a moment before holding it out to Claire. 'Keep it,' she said. 'Leave your book bag here, please. I shouldn't want you to forget it. You will leave through the same door that brought you.'

Claire's fingers closed around the key, registering rough, cold, heavy metal. She shoved it in the pocket of her blue jeans as Amelie swung open the door, and leant her backpack against a convenient bookcase.

'Myrnin?' Amelie's voice was low and gentle. 'Myrnin, I've brought the girl I told you about. Her name is Claire.'

Claire knew that tone of voice. You used it with old, sick people, people who didn't really understand what was happening anymore. People you didn't think were really going to be around for long. Coming from Amelie, it was really odd, because she could also hear the love in that low voice. Could vampires love? Well, sure, she guessed; Michael could, right? So why not Amelie, too?

Claire stepped out from behind Amelie at the vampire's imperative gesture, and anxiously scanned the room. It was big, full of the weirdest mixture of equipment and junk she'd ever seen. A brand-new widescreen laptop computer with a shimmying belly dancer as a screen saver. An abacus. A chemistry set that looked straight out of some old Sherlock Holmes movie. More books, carelessly piled around as trip hazards, leaning in columns on every table. Lamps – some electric, some oil. Candles. Bottles and jars and shadows and angles and...

And a man.

Claire blinked, because she was expecting an old, sick person; expecting it so much she looked around again, trying to find him. But the only man in the room sat in a chair, peacefully reading a book. He marked the spot with a finger, closed it, and looked up at Amelie.

He was young, or at least he looked it. Shoulder-length curly brown hair, big, dark puppy-dog eyes, flawless, faintly golden skin. Frozen at the age of maybe twenty-five, just enough for creases to be forming at the corners of his eyes. Also, he was really, really...*pretty*.

And he didn't look sick. Not at all.

'Ah, good, I've been waiting for you,' he said. He spoke English, but with some kind of accent, nothing that Claire could identify. It sounded a little bit like Irish, a little bit like Scottish, but more...liquid, somehow. Welsh? 'Claire, is it? Well, come forward, girl, I won't bite.' He smiled, and unlike Amelie's cool attempt, it was a warm, genuine expression, full of merriment. Claire took a couple of steps towards him. She sensed Amelie tensing behind her, and wondered why. Myrnin seemed OK. Seemed more OK than any vampire she'd seen so far, except maybe Sam, Michael's grandfather – and Michael, the youngest vampire in Morganville.

'Hello,' she said, and got an even wider smile.

'She speaks! Excellent. I have no use for someone without a backbone. Tell me, young Claire, do you like the sciences?'

That was an antique way of saying it...*the sciences*. People usually said *science* or mentioned a specific thing, like biology or nuclear studies or chemistry. Still, she knew the right answer. 'Yes, sir. I love the sciences.'

His dark eyes glittered, full of slightly wicked humour. 'So very polite, you are. And philosophy?'

'I...I don't know. We didn't study it in high school. I just got to college.'

'Science without philosophy is nonsense,' he said, very seriously. 'And alchemy? Do you know anything of it?'

She just shook her head to that one. She knew what it meant, but wasn't it all about turning lead into gold or something like that? Sort of con-man science?

Myrnin looked tragically disappointed. She almost wanted to lie to him and tell him that she'd got an A in Alchemy 101.

'Don't be difficult, Myrnin,' Amelie said. 'I told you, this age doesn't regard the subject with much respect.

You won't find anyone with a working knowledge of the Hermetic arts, so you'll have to use what's available. From all accounts, this girl is quite gifted. She should be able to understand what you have to teach, if you are patient.'

Myrnin nodded soberly and put the book aside. He stood up – and up – and up. He was tall, gawky, with long legs and arms – like a human stick bug. He was wearing a weird mixture of clothes, too – not homeless-guy weird, but definitely funky. A vertically striped knit shirt under what looked like some kind of frock coat, and blue jeans, old ones, with holes in the knees. And flip-flops. Claire stared at his exposed toes. Somehow, with that outfit, flip-flops looked almost indecent.

But he had pretty feet.

He extended his hand to Claire, bending over to do it. She carefully took it and shook. Myrnin looked surprised, then delighted. He pumped the handshake enthusiastically enough to make her shoulder ache.

'A handshake, is that the correct way to greet these days?' he asked. 'Even for such a lovely young woman? I know it's common among men, but among women it seems quite a violent gesture—'

'Yes,' Claire said quickly. 'It's fine. Everybody does it.' God, he wasn't going to try to kiss her hand or anything, was he? No, he was letting go and crossing his arms. Studying her.

'Quickly,' he said. 'What's the elemental designation for rubidium?'

'Um...Rb.'

'Atomic number?'

Claire frantically called to mind the periodic table. She'd played with it the same way other kids played with puzzles, back when she was young; she'd known every detail. 'Thirty-seven.'

'Group number?'

She could see the square on the table now, as real as if it were a card in her hand. 'Group one,' she said confidently. 'Alkali metal. The period number is five.'

'And what are the dangers of working with rubidium, young Claire?'

'It spontaneously burns when exposed to air. It also reacts violently to water.'

'Solid, liquid, gas, plasma?'

'Solid to forty degrees centigrade. That's the melting point.' She waited for the next question, but Myrnin only cocked his head and watched her. 'How did I do?'

'Adequately,' he said. 'You've memorised well. But memorisation is not science, and science is not knowledge.' Myrnin stalked over to a leaning stack of books, tossed some carelessly to the floor, and found a threadbare volume that he flipped open without much regard for the fragile pages. 'Ah! Here. What is this, then?'

He held the book out to her. Claire squinted at the dim illustration. It looked a little like a small square sail, full of wind. She frowned and shook her head. Myrnin snapped the book closed with a sharp clap, making her jump.

'Too much to teach her,' he said to Amelie. He began to pace, then got distracted and fiddled with a glass retort full of some noxious green liquid. 'I don't have time to coddle infants, Amelie. Bring me someone who at least understands the basics of what I am trying to—'

'I've told you before, there is no one available who would recognise that symbol, and in any case, the field has never attracted the most trustworthy of characters.

'Give Claire a chance. She's a quick study.' Her voice cooled to a measured, icy tone. 'Do not force me to make it an order, Myrnin.'

He stopped moving, but he didn't raise his head. 'I don't want another student.' He sounded resentful.

'Nevertheless, you must have one.'

'Have you explained the risks?'

'I leave that to you. She is yours, Myrnin. But make no mistake, I will hold you responsible for her performance, and for her safety.'

Claire heard the click of metal, and when she looked behind her, Amelie was…gone.

She'd left her alone. With *him*.

When Claire turned back to him, Myrnin had raised his head and was staring straight at her. Warm, brown eyes no longer amused. Very serious.

'It seems neither of us has much choice,' he said. 'We'll just have to make the best of it, then.' He fumbled through the stacks of books and came up with one that looked just as threadbare and fragile as the first one he'd mishandled, but this one was much thinner. He thrust it towards her, and Claire took it. The inscription on the cover was in English. *Metals in Egyptian Inscriptions.*

'The symbol I showed you is for copper,' Myrnin said. 'Know the rest when you come back tomorrow. I will also expect you to read Basil Valentine's *Last Will and Testament*. I have a copy here...' He shoved books around, almost frantic, and located something with a cry of satisfaction. He held that out to her as well. 'Pay special attention to the alchemical symbols. You'll be expected to copy them out until you know them by heart.'

'But—'

'Take them! Take them and get out! Out! I'm busy!'

Myrnin rushed past her, bowling over stacks of books in his haste, to fling open the door through which Amelie had disappeared. He was at least a foot taller than the door itself, like a human in a hobbit house. He stood there, jittering his foot in impatience, the flip-flop making plastic slaps between flesh and floor.

'Did you hear me?' he snapped. 'Go. No time now. Get out. Come tomorrow.'

'But...I don't know how to get home. Or back here.'

He stared for a second, and then he laughed. 'Someone will have to bring you. I can't configure the system just for you!'

Configure the system? Claire stopped, staring back. 'What system? These...doorways?' The implications were dizzying. If Myrnin understood the doorways, controlled the doorways, the ones that appeared and disappeared out of nowhere in Morganville...*I need to know. I need to know how that works.*

'Yes, I am responsible for that, among many other things, though it's hardly the most important thing right now,' he said. 'Later, Claire. Go now. Talk tomorrow.'

He took hold of her, bodily shoved her through the doorway, and slammed it behind her. She heard his hand hit the wood with stunning force.

'Lock it!' he shouted. Claire dug the key out of her pocket. She could barely get it in the lock; the light was bad here, and her hands were shaking. But she managed, and heard the solid click as the tumblers fell. 'Take the key!' Myrnin yelled.

'But—'

'You're responsible for me now, Claire. You must keep me safe.' Myrnin's voice had fallen lower now, as if he'd got tired. 'Keep me safe from everyone.'

And then he started...crying.

'Myrnin?' Claire said, bending closer to the door. 'Are you OK? Should I come in and—'

The whole door vibrated with the force of his blow. Claire scrambled backward, shocked.

And the crying continued. Lost, little-boy crying.

Claire hesitated for a few seconds, then turned to see that Amelie hadn't left after all. She was standing quietly by the desk, in the glow of the single candle, and her expression was composed, but sad.

'Myrnin's mind is not what it once was. He has periods of lucidity, however. And at all costs, you must take full advantage of these to learn what he has to teach. It can't be lost, Claire. It *must not* be lost. There are things he does that—' Amelie shook her head. 'There are projects in motion that must continue.'

Claire's heart was racing, her whole body shaking. 'He's crazy, he's a vampire, and you want me to be his student.'

'No,' Amelie said. 'I *require* you to be his student. You will comply, Claire, by the rules of the contract you signed of your own free will. This is valuable work. I would not risk you unnecessarily.'

Have you explained to her the risks? Myrnin had asked that. 'What are the risks?' Claire demanded.

Amelie merely pointed to the bookcase, where her backpack still leant. Claire grabbed it and hauled it to her shoulder – and paused, because a doorway had formed in the blank area of the wall. A solid wooden door, with a plain knob. Identical to those at the university. 'Open it,' Amelie said.

'But—'

'Open the door, Claire.'

Claire did, and the glare of fluorescent lights and the dead, air-conditioned smell of the Administration Building swept over her in a rush.

Amelie blew out the light. In the darkness, Claire couldn't see her anymore.

'Be ready at four o'clock tomorrow in the University Centre,' Amelie said. 'Sam will fetch you. I suggest you do the reading Myrnin requires of you. And Claire...tell no one what you're doing here. Absolutely no one.'

It wasn't until Claire was in the hall, with the door shut, that she realised Amelie hadn't answered her question. She opened the door again, but – there was just a room piled with discarded, broken furniture. Something moved furtively in the corner. There was a window with crooked blinds, but no Amelie. No cave of books. No Myrnin.

'He's sick,' Claire said aloud, to whatever was rustling in the corner behind a three-legged desk. 'That's why she talked to him like that. He's old, and he's sick. Maybe even dying.' Vampires could get sick. Vampires could *die*? Somehow she'd never even considered that.

She shut the door gently, adjusted the weight of her backpack, and looked down at the two ancient books in her hand.

Last Will and Testament.

She hoped that wasn't a sign of her future.

Eve chattered on about her day on the drive back, talking about some boy who had totally tried to ask her out, and Amy's boyfriend, Chad, who'd come by to help clean up and was a total sweetheart, and how her boss was a toe-rag, but at least he'd given her a twenty-cent-an-hour raise. 'I think that's just for not quitting in the first couple of weeks,' Eve said, but she sounded pretty jacked about it, and Claire was pleased for her. 'Yeah, it's only a couple more dollars a week, but—'

'But it's something.' Claire nodded. 'Congratulations,

Eve. You deserve it. You're really good at this. I'll bet you could run the whole thing if you wanted.'

'Me? Manager?' Eve laughed so hard she snorted. 'Yeah, like I want to become Tinpot Dictator of the coffee bar. Get serious.'

'No, I mean it. You're nice, people like you; you know what you're doing. You could. You'd be good at it.'

Eve shot her a sideways look that was almost a frown. 'You're serious.'

'Yep.'

'I don't know if I'm ready for management. Don't you have to wear a tie for that?'

'You've got one,' Claire said solemnly.

'Only one with the Grim Reaper on it. Hey, wait. That could be my management style! Screw up and I'll kill you, maggot.' Eve grinned. 'They ought to teach that in business school.'

'They probably do here,' Claire sighed.

'What's up with you, CB?' CB stood for Claire Bear, which was Eve's funny nickname for her. Claire didn't think she much resembled a bear, not even the stuffed Gund variety. 'You seem really, I don't know, thoughtful.'

'Yeah, well—' She couldn't talk to Eve about Myrnin. 'Homework and stuff.' Yeah, it was just that she'd never had quite *this* kind of pass/fail pressure before. She'd flipped through the book on Egyptian inscriptions. That was pretty straightforward, though she wasn't sure how actually Egyptian it all was. Interesting, though. The other one, *Last Will and*

Testament, was lots tougher. Tons of symbols in some weird notation she didn't understand. She'd be up all night trying to make sure she remembered even the basics. 'Eve...has anybody ever broken their contract in Morganville? I mean, and lived?'

'Contract?' Eve shot her yet another look, this one definitely coming with a side order of frowning. 'You're talking about a vamp contract? Sure. People have tried everything, at one time or another. But not very successfully.'

'What happened?'

'Back in the old days, they got hanged. These days, I think they just throw 'em in jail until they rot, if the vampires don't eat 'em. But hey, not like you and me have to worry about it, right? Live free or die!' Eve held up her hand. 'High five!'

Claire slapped it, without much enthusiasm. She was thinking about the way the pen had felt in her hand, moving across that stiff paper. Signing her life away. And she felt ashamed.

'Why?' Eve asked.

'Huh?'

'Why are you asking?' Eve made the turn onto Lot Street, and the glow of the windows of the Glass House – home – spilt out into the street. 'C'mon, Claire. Someone you know thinking about it?'

'Um...there's this guy at school. I just heard him say... I wondered, that's all.'

'Well, quit wondering. His problem, not yours. Ready

for the fire drill? Quick like a bunny. Go!' Eve braked the black Caddy hard, Claire threw open her passenger-side door and jogged around the back of the car, banged open the white picket gate, and raced up the walk to the steps with her house keys in her hand. She heard the engine die, and the noisy clatter of Eve's shoes behind her.

Eve's steps stopped. Stopped dead. Claire whirled, scared and expecting to see a vampire on the prowl, but Eve was just checking the mailbox, grabbing a small handful of stuff, and then hurrying up the steps as she sorted through it. Claire stepped over the threshold, and Eve followed, hip-bumping the door shut behind them and shooting the bolt with her elbow, a feat Claire would never have tried – or been able to accomplish with half that grace.

'Electric bill, water bill...Internet bill. Oh, and something for you.' Eve pulled out a small bubble-padded mailer from the pile and handed it over. 'No return address.'

Who'd send her anything? Well, Mom and Dad, sure, and the occasional card from another relative. Her former BFF Elizabeth had sent a postcard from Texas A&M, but only the one. Claire didn't recognise the neat handwriting on the outside of the envelope. Eve left her to it and walked down the hallway, yelling to let Shane and Michael know they were back, to which Michael yelled back, 'Get in here and make me some dinner... now, woman.'

'News flash, Michael, you're supposed to have turned evil, not redneck!'

Claire ripped open the package and upended it, and a small jewellery box slid into her hand. A nice one – red velvet, with some kind of gold crest embossed into it. She felt the skin tighten up on the back of her neck. *Oh no.*

Her suspicions were confirmed as she flipped up the lid and saw the gold bracelet nestled on blood-red velvet. It was pretty, and it wasn't too big; delicate enough to circle one of her small wrists.

The Founder's Symbol was embossed discreetly in a small gold cartouche.

Oh no.

Claire bit her lip and stared at the bracelet for a long time, then snapped the lid shut, put it back in the envelope, and went to join Eve and Michael in the kitchen.

'So?' Eve was getting down pots, and Michael was rummaging in the refrigerator. 'Spaghetti OK with you?'

'Fine,' Claire said. She wondered if she looked spooked. She hoped not, but even if she did, Eve was looking at Michael, and he was looking back, and she was safe from any kind of major inspection while they were making eyes at each other.

Until she turned, and ran into Shane, who'd come in the kitchen door behind her. The package felt hot and heavy in her right hand, and she took an involuntary step back.

Which hurt him. She saw the flash of it in his eyes. 'Hey,' he said. 'You all right?'

She nodded, unable to speak, because if she said anything, it would have to be a lie. Shane stepped closer and put a warm hand on her face; it felt good, so very good that she leant into it, then further, into his arms. He made her feel small and loved, and for just a second, what was in the package in her hand didn't matter.

'You're working too hard,' he said. 'You look pale. School OK?'

'School's fine,' she said. That wasn't a lie, school was definitely not what scared her anymore. 'I guess I need more sleep.'

'Just a few more days until the weekend.' He kissed the top of her head, bent closer, and whispered, 'My room. I need to talk to you.'

She blinked, but he was already stepping back and heading out the door. She looked over her shoulder at Eve and Michael, but they were happily talking as Eve adjusted the flame under the pots, and they hadn't noticed anything.

Claire shoved the package into her backpack, zipped it up, and followed Shane upstairs.

Shane's room was very utilitarian – his bed was never made, though he made an attempt as she came in to straighten out the sheets and toss the blanket over it. A couple of posters on the wall, nothing special. No photos, no mementos. He didn't spend a lot of time here, except to sleep. Most of his stuff was crammed into the closet.

Claire leant her backpack against the wall and sat down next to him on the bed. 'What?' she asked. If she'd expected a wild pre-dinner make-out session, she was disappointed. He didn't even put his arm around her.

'I'm thinking of leaving,' he said.

'Leaving? But Eve's making dinner—'

He turned and made eye contact. 'Leaving Morganville.'

She felt a surge of utter panic. 'No. You can't!'

'Done it before. Look, this place, it's...I didn't come back here because I missed it. I came back because my dad sent me, and now that he's been and gone and I'm not doing his dirty work anymore...' Shane's eyes were begging her to understand. 'I want a life, Claire. And you don't belong here. You can't stay. They'll kill you. No, worse. They'll make you into one of them, one of the walking dead. I'm not talking about the vampires, either. Nobody who lives here has a pulse, not really.'

'Shane—'

He kissed her, and his lips were warm and damp and soft and urgent. 'Please,' he whispered. 'We need to leave this town. It's going to get bad. I can feel it.'

God, *why* was he doing this? Why now? 'I can't,' she said. 'I...school, and...I just can't, Shane. I can't leave.' Her signature on a piece of paper. Her soul on a platter. It had been the price to keep them safe, but she'd have to keep on paying, right? As apprentice to Myrnin. And she guessed that wouldn't be a long-distance study course.

'Please.' It was barely a whisper from him, his lips brushing hers, and honestly, she would have done almost anything for him when he used that tone, but this time...

'What happened?' she asked.

'What?'

'Was it something with Michael? Did he...did you...?' She didn't even know what she was asking, but something had deeply disturbed Shane, and she had no idea what it was.

He looked at her for a long few seconds, then pulled away, stood up, and walked to his window to look down on the backyard they never really used. 'My dad called,' he said. 'He told me that he was coming back, and he wanted me to be prepared to take out some vampires. If I stay, I'm going to have to kill Michael. I don't want to be here, Claire. I can't.'

He didn't want to make the choice, not again. Claire bit her lip, hard; she could hear the pain in his voice, although he wasn't going to let her see it in his expression. 'You really think your dad will come back?'

'Yeah. Eventually. Maybe not this month, maybe not this year, but...someday. And next time, he'll have what he needs to start a real war around here.' Shane shivered; she saw the muscles in his back tense up under the tight grey shirt he was wearing. 'I need to get you out of here before you get hurt.'

Claire got up, walked to him, and put her arms

around him from behind. She leant against him, her head on his back, and sighed. 'I'm more worried about you,' she said. 'You and trouble…'

'Yeah.' She heard the smile in his voice. 'We're like that.'

CHAPTER FOUR

The spaghetti was good, and a little pleading got Shane to sit down and eat. He sat across from Michael, but they didn't talk, and they didn't make eye contact. All in all, pretty polite. Claire was just starting to relax when Shane asked, blandly, 'You put extra garlic in this, Eve? You know how I like the garlic.'

She shot him a dirty look. 'Oh, the *neighbourhood* knows.' And then an apologetic one towards Michael. 'It's OK, right? Not too much?' Because garlic wasn't something vampires were especially fond of. That was why Shane tended to use it as garnish on everything he ate.

'It's fine,' Michael said, but he was picking at his food, and he looked a little pale. 'Monica stopped by today. Looking for you, Claire.'

Both Shane and Eve groaned. For once, all three of her housemates were entirely in agreement. And they were all looking at her.

'What?' she asked. 'I swear, it's not…I'm not sucking up to her or anything! She's just…crazy, OK? I'm not her friend. I don't know why she's coming around.'

'She's probably going to set you up again,' Eve said, and scooped more spaghetti into her bowl. 'Like she did at the frat dance. Hey, she's throwing a party this Friday, did you hear? Super-exclusive, flying in out of towners and everything. I guess it's her birthday, or Daddy-gave-me-money day, or whatever. We should crash.'

'I like the sound of that,' Shane said. 'Crashing Monica's party.' He glanced at Michael, then quickly away. 'What about you? That break some kind of vampire rules of conduct or something?'

'Blow me, Shane.'

'Boys,' Eve said primly. 'Language. Minor at the table.'

'Well,' Shane said, 'I wasn't actually planning to do it.'

Claire rolled her eyes. 'Not like it's the first time I've heard it. Or said it.'

'You shouldn't say it,' Michael said, all seriousness. 'No, I mean it. Girls should say "eat me," not "blow me." Wouldn't recommend "bite me," though. Not around here.'

Eve choked on her spaghetti. Shane pounded her on the back, but he was laughing, too, and so was Michael, and Claire glared at them for a little bit before giving in and admitting it was funny, after all.

Everything was all right.

'So. Friday night?' Eve asked, wiping her eyes and gasping through her giggles. 'Par-tay? Because I could so use a good blowout.'

'I'm in,' Michael said, and took a manful bite of spaghetti. Claire wondered if it burnt him. 'I think if I'm with you, there's no way she can keep us out. Vampire VIP status. Might as well be good for something.'

Shane looked at him, and for a second there was that warmth that Claire missed so much, but then it was gone again, and the wall was back firmly in place between the two of them.

'Must be nice,' he said. 'We should all go, if it's going to ruin Monica's night.'

They finished the rest of the meal in uncomfortable silence. Claire realised that she kept thinking about that red velvet box sitting upstairs in her room, and struggled not to look guilty. Probably didn't succeed. She caught Michael watching her with a strange intensity; whether he was picking up on her discomfort or still wondering about why she didn't jump at the chance to go to Monica's party.

She ate too fast, cleaned her dishes, and dashed upstairs with a mumbled excuse about homework. Well, it wasn't as though they weren't used to her studying. It was Shane's turn for dishes, so that would keep him busy for a while...

The box was right where she'd left it, sitting on the dresser. She grabbed it, put her back against the wall, and slid down to a cross-legged sitting position as she weighed the box in her hand.

'You're wondering whether or not to wear it,' Amelie said, and Claire yelped in surprise. The elegant older vampire, completely at her ease, was seated in the antique old velvet chair in the corner, her hands folded primly in her lap. She looked like a painting, not a person; there was something about her – now more than ever – that seemed antique and cold as marble.

Claire scrambled to her feet, feeling stupid about it, but you just didn't sit like that in Amelie's presence. Amelie acknowledged the courtesy with a graceful nod, but didn't otherwise move.

'I apologise for surprising you, Claire, but I needed to speak with you alone,' she said.

'How can you get in here? I mean, this is our house; aren't vampires...?'

'Prevented from entry? Not into another vampire's home, and even were you all human, this house ultimately belongs to me. I built it, as I built all of the Founder Houses. The house knows me, and so I need no permissions to enter.' Amelie's eyes glinted in the dark. 'Does that disturb you?'

Claire swallowed and didn't answer. 'What did you want?'

Amelie raised one long, slender finger and pointed at the velvet box in Claire's hand. 'I want you to put that on.'

'But—'

'I am not asking. I am instructing.'

Claire shivered, because although Amelie's voice stayed level, it sounded...hard. She opened the box and shook the bracelet out. It felt heavy and warm in her hand, and she peered at it carefully.

There wasn't a catch, but it was clearly too small to fit over her hand. 'I don't know how—'

She saw a flash in her peripheral vision, and by the time she looked up, Amelie was taking the bracelet out of her palm, and cold strong fingers were holding her arm.

'It's made for you,' Amelie said. '*Hold still.* Unlike the bracelets most of the other children wear, yours cannot be removed. The contract you signed gives me this right, do you understand?'

'But...no, I don't want—'

Too late. Amelie moved, and the bracelet seemed to pass *through* Claire's skin and bone, and settle heavily around her wrist. Claire tried to yank free, but there was no way, not as strong as Amelie was. Amelie smiled and held her still for another second, just to make the point, before she let go. Claire turned the bracelet frantically, pressing, looking for the trick.

It looked seamless, and it wasn't coming off.

'It must be done this way, the old way,' Amelie said. 'This bracelet will save your life, Claire. Mark me. It is a favour I have given rarely in my life. You should be grateful.'

Grateful? Claire felt like a dog on a leash, and she hated it. She glared at Amelie, and the vampire's smile intensified. She couldn't really say it brightened – there was something in it that undermined the whole concept of comfort.

'Perhaps you'll be grateful at a later date,' Amelie said, and raised her eyebrows. 'Very well. I'll leave you now. No doubt you have studies.'

'How am I supposed to hide this from my friends?' Claire blurted, as the vampire walked towards the door.

'You aren't,' Amelie said, and opened the door without unlocking it. 'Don't forget. You should be well prepared for Myrnin tomorrow.' She stepped out into the hall and closed it behind her. Claire lunged forward and turned the knob, but it refused to open. By the time she twisted the thumb lock and swung it back, Amelie was gone. The hall was empty. Claire stood there, listening to the clatter of dishes from downstairs, the distant laughter, and wanted to cry.

She scrubbed at her eyes, took a deep breath, and went to her desk to try to study.

The next day was a busy whirl of classes, quizzes, and discussion groups, and Claire was grateful for the afternoon break when it finally arrived. She felt stupid, dressed in her long-sleeved T, but it was the only thing she had that could hide the bracelet, and she desperately wanted to hide it. So far, so good. Eve hadn't noticed, Shane hadn't been awake when they'd left for school. No sign of Michael, either. She'd got desperate last night and tried a couple of ways to break the gold band – scissors, then a pair of rusty old bolt-cutters from the basement – but she broke the blade on the scissors, and the bolt-cutters were clumsy and slid right off the metal. She couldn't do it alone, and she couldn't ask for help.

Can't hide it for ever.

Well, she could try.

Claire headed for the UC and the coffee bar, and she found Eve harassed, pink-cheeked under the rice-powder make-up, all alone behind the counter. 'Where's Amy?' Claire asked, and handed over three dollars for a mocha. 'I thought she was working all week?'

'Yeah, no kidding, me too. I called my boss, but he's sick and so's Kim, so it's just me today. Not enough coffee in the world to make this easy.' Eve blew hair from her sweaty forehead and zipped over to the espresso machine, where she pulled shots. 'Ever have one of those dreams where you're running and everybody else is standing still, but you can't catch up?'

'No,' Claire said. 'Usually mine are about being naked in class.'

Eve grinned. 'For that, you get a free caramel shot. Go sit down. I don't need you hovering like the rest of these vultures.'

Claire claimed a study desk and spread out her books, got her mocha when Eve called her name, and yawned as she cracked open *Last Will and Testament* again. She'd spent most of the night memorising the symbols, but they were tricky. She'd got all of the Egyptian ones down, but these were a whole lot less straightforward, and she had the sense that Myrnin wouldn't be too forgiving of mistakes.

A shadow fell over her book. She looked up and saw Detective Travis Lowe, and his partner, Joe Hess, standing close behind him. She knew both of them pretty well; they'd helped her during that crazy time when Shane's dad had been skulking around Morganville, trying to kill vampires (and succeeding). They didn't wear bracelets, and they weren't Protected; as she understood it, they'd earned some kind of special status. She wasn't sure how they'd managed that, but it had to be something really brave.

'Morning, Claire,' Hess said, and pulled up a chair. Lowe did the same. They weren't all that similar in body types – Hess was tall and kind of wiry, with a long face; Lowe was chubby and balding. But the expressions in their eyes were identical – careful, hidden, wary. 'How have you been?'

'Fine,' she said, and resisted the nearly overwhelming urge to touch her bracelet, fiddle with it. She looked from one to the other, feeling less secure all the time. 'What's going on? Is something wrong?'

'Yeah,' Lowe said. 'You could say that. Look, Claire, there's… I'm sorry to tell you this, but there was a dead girl out back of your house. She was found this morning by the trash collectors.'

A dead girl? Claire swallowed hard. 'Who is she?'

'Amy Callum,' Hess said. 'She's a local girl. Family lives just a few blocks from you. Her people are pretty broken up about it.' He shifted his gaze towards the coffee bar. 'She worked here.'

Amy? Coffee Bar Amy? Oh no...'I knew her,' Claire said faintly. 'She worked with Eve. She was supposed to be here today. Eve was saying—' Eve. Claire looked over and saw that Eve was still chattering away brightly, filling orders, taking cash. They hadn't told her yet. 'You're sure it was our house?'

'Claire...' The two detectives exchanged a look, not a good one. 'Her body was stuffed inside your trash can. We're sure.'

Claire felt faint. That close...she'd put out trash just two days ago, right? Dumped garbage bags into the can. Amy had been alive then. And now...

'Did you see anything last night?' Hess continued.

'No, I was...it was dark when I got home. And then I studied all night.'

'Hear anything, maybe some racket out by the garbage cans?'

'No, sir. I had headphones on. I'm sorry.'

Shane had been looking out the window, she remembered. Maybe he'd seen someone. But he'd have said, right? He wouldn't hide something like that.

An awful thought struck her, and she looked up into Joe Hess's calm, impartial eyes. 'Was it—' Too many people around. She mimed fangs in the neck. He shook his head.

'It's the same as the last one we found,' Lowe said. 'Can't rule out our toothy friends, but it doesn't fit their style. You know whose style it fits, though?'

'Jason's,' Claire said numbly. 'Eve's brother. He's still out?'

'Haven't caught him doing anything illegal yet. But we will. He's too crazy to live sane.' Lowe studied her. 'Haven't seen him, have you?'

'No.'

'Good.' Like there'd been some signal between them, Hess and Lowe got up from their chairs. 'We'd better go tell Eve. Look, you think of anything, you call, all right? And don't go out alone. Protection doesn't cover this.' Lowe cast a significant look at her wrist, and she felt herself blush, as though he'd guessed what colour panties she had on. 'You need to go out, you go with one of your friends, all right? Same goes for Eve. We'll try to keep an eye on you, but caution is your best defence.'

Claire watched as the cops walked away. They exchanged nods with a tallish young man who was coming in her direction. For a second she thought it was Michael – he had the same walk, the same basic shape – but then his hair caught the light. Red hair, not blond like Michael's.

Sam. Sam Glass, Michael's grandfather. Amelie had told her that Sam would escort her to see Myrnin; she'd just forgot about it. Well, that was OK. Claire liked Sam. He was quiet and kind and didn't seem much like a vampire at all, except for the pale skin and the slight weird shine to his eyes. Exactly like

Michael, now that she thought of it. But then, they were the two youngest, and – weirdly – related. Maybe the older the vampires got, the farther they moved from normal.

'Hey, Claire,' Sam said, as if they'd just talked five minutes before, although she hadn't seen him for nearly a week, at least. She supposed that time was different for vampires. 'What'd they want?' He was wearing a TPU T-shirt and jeans, and it made him look kind of hot. Hot for a redheaded vampire, anyway. And he had a nice, if absent, smile. She wasn't his type. As far as Claire knew, Sam was still totally in love with Amelie, a concept she found harder to wrap her brain around than curved-surface string theory.

He was still waiting for an answer. She scrambled to put one together. 'There's a dead girl. She was found in our garbage cans. Amy. Amy Callum?'

Sam's mobile, earnest face took on a grim look. 'Dammit. I know the family, they're good folks. I'll stop by and see them.' He sat down and leant closer, dropping his volume. 'She wasn't a vampire kill, I know that much. I'd have heard by now if someone had stepped out of line.'

'No,' Claire agreed. 'It sounded as though she was killed by one of us.' She realised, with a rush of horror, that he wasn't *us*, exactly, and blushed. 'I mean one of the...humans.'

Sam smiled at her, but his eyes were a little sad. 'That's all right, Claire; I'm used to it by now. It's an us-and-them town.' He looked down at his hands, loose and relaxed on the tabletop. 'I'm supposed to take you to your appointment.'

'Yeah.' She hastily closed up her books and began loading her backpack. 'Sorry, I didn't realise what time it was.'

'No rush,' he said. Still not looking at her. Very softly, he continued, 'Claire. Are you sure you know what you're doing?'

'What?'

His hand flashed out and grabbed her wrist – the one with the bracelet hidden under the long sleeve. It dug painfully into her skin. 'You know what.'

'Ow,' she whispered, and he let go. 'I had to. I didn't have a choice. I had to sign if I wanted to keep my friends safe.'

Sam didn't say anything to that; he was looking at her now, but she didn't dare meet his eyes. She didn't like him knowing about her agreement with Amelie.

What if he told Michael? What if Michael told Shane? *He's going to find out, sooner or later.* Well, she'd much rather it be later.

Sam said, 'I know that. I wish you wouldn't do this other thing. With Myrnin. It's...not safe.'

'I know. He's sick or something. But he won't hurt me. Amelie—'

'*Amelie* isn't in the business of worrying about individuals.' That, for Sam, was surprisingly bitter, especially when it came to Amelie. 'She's using you the way she uses all humans. It's not personal, but it's not in your best interest, either.'

'Why? What is it you're not telling me?'

Sam looked at her for a long time, clearly trying to decide, and finally said, 'Myrnin's had five apprentices in the past few years. Two of them were vampires.'

Claire blinked, surprised, as Sam got to his feet. 'Five? What happened to them?'

'You're asking the right questions. Now ask the right people.'

He walked away. Claire gasped, grabbed her bag, and followed.

Over at the coffee bar, the two detectives were breaking the news to Eve. As Claire looked back, she saw the precise second that Eve realised her friend was dead. Even from across the room, it hurt to see the pain in her face, quickly masked and locked away. In Morganville, losing someone was something you got used to, Claire supposed.

God, this town *sucked* sometimes.

Sam had a car, a sleek, dark red sedan with dark-tinted windows. It was parked in the underground garage beneath the UC, in a reserved spot marked SPONSORS ONLY, with a graphic of a sticker that had to appear in the corner of the windshield for the parking to be legal.

A sticker that Sam, of course, had. 'So that means what, you donate money or something?'

Sam opened the passenger door for her, a bit of

chivalry she wasn't really used to, and Claire climbed inside. 'Not exactly,' he said. 'Amelie gives them to vampires who have campus business.'

Once he was in the car, turning the key, Claire said, 'You have campus business?'

'I teach night classes,' Sam said, and grinned. He looked about twelve, when he did that. She had the feeling it wasn't something vampires were into, looking that endearingly goofy. Maybe if they were, they'd be more popular with the local breathing population. 'Sort of an outreach programme.'

'Cool.' The tinting was so dark it was like midnight outside. 'You can see through this?'

'Like daylight,' Sam said, and she gave up, buckled her seat belt, and let him drive. It wasn't a long trip – nothing in Morganville was – but she had time to notice some things about Sam's car. It was clean. *Really* clean. No trash at all. (Well, he wouldn't be chowing down on burgers in the car, now, would he? Wait. He could...) It also didn't smell like most cars. It smelt new and kind of sterile. 'How are classes going?'

Oh, Sam was going to do the interested-adult thing now. 'Fine,' Claire said. Nobody ever wanted to really hear the truth, to a question like that, but fine wasn't a lie, either. 'They're not very hard.' Also not a lie.

Sam shot her a glance, or so she thought, in the dim lights from the dashboard. 'Maybe you're not getting all you can out of them,' he said. 'Ever thought of that?'

She shrugged. 'I've always been ahead. It's better than

high school, but I was hoping for something harder.'

'Like working for Myrnin?' Sam's voice had gone dry. 'That's a challenge, all right. Claire—'

'Amelie didn't exactly give me a choice.'

'But you still want to do it, don't you?'

She did. She had to admit that. Myrnin had been scary, but there had been something so bright in him, too. She knew that spark. She felt it herself, and she was always looking for someone, something to feed it. 'Maybe he just needs someone to talk to,' she said.

Sam made a noncommittal noise that somehow sounded amused, too, and pulled the car to a stop. 'I have to move fast,' he said. 'It's the door at the end of the alley; I'll meet you there in the shade.'

He opened his door and just...vanished. The door slammed shut, but it did it on its own. Claire gaped, unbuckled her seat belt, and got out, but there was no sign of Sam at all on the street, in the brilliant sunlight. The car was parked at the kerb of a cul-de-sac, and it took her a second, but then she recognised the house in front of her. A big Gothic ramble of a house, nearly a mirror image of the Glass House where she lived, but this one belonged to a lady named Katherine Day and her granddaughter.

Granma Day was on her porch, rocking peacefully and stirring the warm air with a paper fan. Claire raised her hand and waved, and Granma waved back. 'You come to see me, girl?' Granma called. 'Come on up; I'll get some lemonade!'

'Maybe later!' Claire called back. 'I have to go—'

She realised, with a jolt of horror, where Sam had told her to go.

Into the alley. The alley where everybody, Granma Day included, had told her *not* to go. The alley with the trap-door spider vampire who'd tried before to lure her inside.

Granma pulled herself to her feet. She was a tiny, wrinkled woman who looked as dry and tough as old leather. Had to be tough, to be old in Morganville, Claire thought. 'You all right, girl?' she asked.

'Yeah,' Claire said. 'Thanks. I'll…I'll be back.'

She headed off down the alley. Behind her, Granma Day called out, 'Girl, what you playin' at? Ain't you got good sense?'

Probably not.

The alley was narrow, with fences on both sides, and it seemed to get even more narrow the farther she went, like a funnel. She didn't feel any strange attraction, though, or hear voices.

She also didn't see Sam.

'Here,' a voice said, as she turned a slight corner. And there he was, leaning back in a patch of black shade next to an overhanging doorway, which was attached to what looked like a shack. Not a really well-made shack, either. Claire wondered if it was supposed to lean like that.

'It's Myrnin,' she said. 'He's the trap-door spider.'

Sam looked thoughtful at that, and then nodded. 'Most people know not to come down this way,' he said.

'He only takes Unprotecteds. He can tell the difference, so he wouldn't try it with you. Not now.'

Cheery. Sam opened the door, which didn't look sturdy enough to keep out a cool breeze, and stepped inside. A smell washed out into the still air, something old and bitter. Chemicals. Ancient paper. Unwashed clothes.

Well?

Claire sucked in a breath that tasted of all those things, and stepped into Myrnin's lair.

CHAPTER FIVE

Myrnin was in a mood. A *good* mood.

'Claire!' As she came down the steps – the only thing in the shack itself were the steps leading down – into his main chamber, he flashed across the room in a blur and stopped just an inch away from her, close enough that she flinched back into Sam's broad chest and he steadied her. Myrnin's eyes were wide, blazing with enthusiasm. 'I've been waiting! Late, late, late, you're very late, you know. Come on, come on, we haven't got time for nonsense. Did you bring the books? Good. What about *Last Will and Testament?* Are you familiar with the symbols? Here, take this.'

Chalk, pressed into her hand. Myrnin moved again, fast as a grasshopper, and rolled an ancient stained chalkboard closer. He had to shove over some stacks of books to do it, which he did with cheerful disregard for how much of a mess he was making.

Sam, almost inaudibly, whispered, 'Be careful. He's dangerous when he's like this.'

Yeah, no kidding. Claire nodded, swallowed, and smiled as Myrnin turned towards her with those crazy, delighted eyes. She wanted to ask what came after the manic phase, but she didn't dare.

'I'll be in the other room,' Sam said. Myrnin waved him off impatiently, barely sparing him a glance.

'Yes, yes, fine, go. Here. First let's start with the Egyptian inscription for *asem. Asem.* You know what element that represents?'

'Electrum,' Claire said, and carefully chalked the symbol. Sort of a bowl, with a big staff through the middle. 'How's that?'

'Excellent! Yes, that's it. Now, something difficult. *Chesbet.*'

Sapphire. That was a hard one. Claire bit her lip for a second, getting the order in her mind, and then drew it out. Circle above a double-slashed line, next to a leg, next to a thing that looked kind of like a car with no wheels over two separated circles.

'No, no, no,' Myrnin said, grabbed an eraser, and rubbed out the car. 'Too modern. Look.'

He drew it again, this time more roughly, and it still looked like a car to her. She copied it, twice, until he was satisfied.

There were a lot of symbols, and he quizzed her on just about all of them, growing more and more excited. Her arm ached from holding up the chalk to the board, especially when, after she screwed up the symbol for lead, he made her repeat it a hundred times.

'We should do this on computer,' she said, chalking it carefully for the eighty-ninth time. 'With a drawing pad.'

'Nonsense. You're lucky I don't make you inscribe it with a stylus on a wax tablet, like the old days,' Myrnin snorted. 'Children. Spoilt children, always playing with the shiniest toy.'

'Computers are more efficient!'

'I can perform calculations on that abacus faster than you can solve them on your computer,' Myrnin sneered.

OK, now he was pissing her off. 'Prove it!'

'What?'

'Prove it.' She backed off on her tone, but Myrnin wasn't looking angry; he was looking strangely interested. He stared at her for a second in silence, and then he broke into the biggest, oddest smile she'd ever seen on the face of a vampire.

'All right,' he said. 'A contest. Computer versus abacus.'

She wasn't at all sure now that was a good idea, even if it had been *her* idea, essentially. 'Um...what do I win?' *More importantly, what do I lose?* Making bargains was a way of life in Morganville, and it was a lot like making deals with man-eating fairies. Better be careful what you ask for.

'Your freedom,' he said solemnly. His eyes were wide and guileless, his too-young face shining with honesty. 'I will tell Amelie you were not suited to the work. She'll let you go about your life, such as it is.'

Good prize. *Too* good. Claire swallowed hard. 'And if I lose?'

'Then I eat you,' Myrnin said.

With absolutely no change in expression.

'You...you can't do that.' She pulled up the sleeve on her shirt and held up her wrist so the gold bracelet caught the light.

'Don't be ridiculous,' he said. 'Of course I can do it. I can do anything I want, child. Without me, there is no future. No one, especially Amelie, begrudges me the occasional titbit. You're hardly large enough to qualify as a meal in any case, and besides, I'm making it well worth your while.'

She took a step back from him. A big one. That crazy smile... She glanced towards the door of the other room, where Sam was waiting for her. No wonder Amelie had told him to stay.

Myrnin gave a sad, theatrical sigh. 'Mortals simply aren't what they used to be,' he said. 'A thousand years ago, you would have bartered your immortal soul for a crust of stale bread. Now I can't even get you to gamble at all, even for your freedom. Really, people have become so...*boring*. So, no bet? Really?'

She shook her head. His expression fell into utter disappointment. 'All right,' he said. 'Then you will write me an essay for tomorrow on the history of alchemy. I can't expect it to be scholarly, but I do expect you to understand the basis of what it is that I am trying to teach you.'

'You're teaching me *alchemy*?'

He seemed surprised, and looked around his laboratory. 'Can you not see what I'm doing here?'

'But alchemy – it's crap. I mean, it's like magic, not science.'

'Alchemy's accomplishments are sadly forgot, and yes, magic is an excellent description for things for which you have no basis to understand. As for science...' Myrnin made a rude noise. His eyes had taken on that hectic shine again. 'Science is a method, not a religion, yet it can be just as close-minded. Open minds here, Claire. Always open minds. Question everything; accept nothing as fact until you prove it for yourself. Yes?'

She nodded hesitantly, more afraid to disagree with him than convinced. Myrnin grinned at her and slapped her back with stinging force.

'That's my girl,' he said. 'Now. What do you know of this theory of Schrödinger's? The one about the cat?'

Myrnin didn't go weird until the very end of Claire's time with him, when he was – she thought – getting tired. She had to admit, there was something fun about working in his lab; he had so much passion, so much enthusiasm for everything. Even for scaring her silly. He was like a little kid, all nervous energy and fiddling hands, quick to laugh, quick to cut her down if she made a mistake. He liked to mock, not correct. He thought if she had to figure it out for herself, she'd learn it properly.

She checked her watch and found it was almost eight o'clock – late. She was supposed to be home by now. Myrnin was ignoring her, temporarily, as she copied out tables of incomprehensible symbols from a book he said was so rare his was the only copy left. She yawned, stretched, and said, 'I need to be going.'

He had his eye fixed to what looked like a clunky, ancient microscope. 'Already?'

'It's late. I should go home.'

Myrnin straightened, stared at her, and she saw the storm forming in his expression. 'You are dictating to me now?' he snapped. 'Who is the master? Who is the student?'

'I...sorry, but I can't stay here all night!'

Myrnin walked towards her, and she couldn't even recognise him. No more manic energy, no more humour, no more sharp, brilliant anger. He looked troubled and clouded.

'Home,' he repeated. 'Home is where the heart is. Why don't you leave yours here? I'll take very good care of it.'

'M-my...heart?' She dropped the pen and backed up, putting a big lab table full of chemical equipment between them. Myrnin bared his teeth and put down his fangs. *Discovery Channel. King cobra. Oh God, can he spit venom or something?* His eyes flared bright, fuelled with something that looked to her like...fear.

'Don't run,' he said, and sounded annoyed. 'I hate it when they run. Now, tell me what you're doing here!'

he demanded. 'Why do you keep following me? *Who are you?*'

'It's Claire, Myrnin. I'm your apprentice. I'm supposed to be here, remember?'

That was the wrong thing to say, and she had no idea why. Myrnin stopped, and the light in his eyes intensified to insanity. Ugly, and very scary. When he moved, it was a smooth, sinuous glide. 'My apprentice,' he said. 'So I own you, then. I can do as I wish.'

King cobra.

'Sam!' Claire yelled, and bolted for the stairs.

She didn't get more than two steps. Myrnin came *over* the table, scattering glass instruments to shatter in glittering sprays on the floor, and she felt his cold, impossibly strong hands close on her ankles and jerk backward. She flailed for something to grab on to, but it was only a tower of books, and it collapsed as she fell.

She hit the floor hard enough to put the world on a sparkling, unsteady hold for a few seconds, and when she blinked away the stars, Myrnin had taken hold of her shoulders and was staring down at her, inches away.

'Don't,' she said. 'Myrnin, don't. I'm your friend! I won't hurt you!'

She didn't know why she said it, but it must have been the right thing to do. His eyes widened, white showing all around, and then the glitter of crazy was replaced by a flood of tears. He patted her cheek, soft and confused, and the fangs folded up in his mouth. 'Dear child,' he said. 'What are you doing here? Is Amelie making you come here? She shouldn't. You're far too young and kind. You should tell her you won't come back. I don't want to hurt you, but I will.' He tapped his forehead. '*This* is betraying me. This stupid, stupid flesh.' The tapping became violent slaps to his forehead, and tears broke free to run down his cheeks. 'I need to teach someone, but not you. Not you, Claire. Too young. Too small. You bring out the beast.'

He stood up and wandered away, *tsk*ing over the broken glass, righting the fallen books. As if she'd ceased to exist. Claire sat up and rolled to her feet, shaky and scared.

Sam was standing just a few feet away. She hadn't seen or heard him approach, and he hadn't acted to save her. His face was tense, his eyes uneasy.

'He's sick,' Claire said.

'Sick, sick, sick, yes, I am,' Myrnin said. He had his head in his hands now, as if it hurt him. 'We're all sick. All doomed.'

'What's he talking about?' Claire turned to Sam.

'Nothing.' He shook his head. 'Don't listen to him.'

Myrnin looked up and bared his teeth. His eyes were fierce, but they were sane. Mostly sane, anyway.

'They won't tell you the truth, little morsel, but I will. We're dying. Seventy years ago—'

Sam moved Claire out of his way, and for the first time since she'd met him, Sam actually looked threatening. 'Myrnin, *shut up*!'

'No,' Myrnin sighed. 'It's time for talking. I've been

shut up enough.' He looked up, and his eyes were red-rimmed and full of tears. 'Oh, little girl, do you understand? My race is dying. My race is dying and I don't know how to stop it.'

Claire's mouth opened and closed, but she couldn't find anything to say. Sam turned towards her, fury still radiating off him like heat. 'Ignore him,' he said. 'He doesn't know what he's saying. We should go, before he remembers what he was about to do. Or forgets what he shouldn't.'

Claire cast a look back over her shoulder at Myrnin, who was holding a broken glass pipe in his hands, trying to fit the two pieces back together. When it wouldn't go, he dropped it and covered his face with both hands. She could see his shoulders shaking. 'Can't…shouldn't somebody help him?'

'There's no help,' Sam said in a voice flat with anger. 'There's no cure. And you're not coming back here again if I can do anything about it.'

Chapter Six

Claire kept her silence for about half the ride home, and Sam didn't offer anything, either. The pressure of questions finally was too much for her. 'He was telling the truth, wasn't he?' she asked. 'There's some kind of disease. Amelie tried to make me think that not making more vampires was her choice, but that's not really true, is it? You *can't*. She's the only one who isn't sick.'

Sam's face went tight and still in the glow of the dashboard lights. Sitting in the car was like travelling through space; the dark-tinted windows refused even starlight, so it was just the two of them in their own pocket universe. He had the radio on, and it was playing classical music, something light and sweet.

'No use telling you to shut up, is there?'

She said regretfully, 'Probably not. And I wouldn't stop trying to find out.'

Sam shook his head. 'Do you even have a sense of self-preservation?'

'Shane asks me that all the time.'

That made Sam smile, despite his obvious unease. 'All right,' he said. 'Amelie's sick, too. It's getting harder and harder for her to create new vampires – she was barely able to bring Michael over; I was terrified it would kill her this time. The truth is, we're all sick. Myrnin's been searching for the cause – and the cure – for seventy years now, but it's too late now. He's too far gone, and the chance that anyone else could help him through it is too small. I can't let her sacrifice you like this, Claire. I told you that he's had five assistants. I don't want you to become another statistic.'

Oh God. *The vampires were all dying.* Claire felt a rush of pure adrenalin, enough to make her hands tremble with the force of it. She felt a fierce surge of something like...satisfaction. And then another one, right on top of it, of guilt. *What about Sam? What about Michael?* Yeah, and what about Oliver and all those scary vamps like him? Wouldn't it be great to see them go?

'What if he doesn't find the cure?' Claire asked. She tried not to give away any of what she was feeling, but she was sure Sam could hear her elevated heartbeat. 'How long—?'

'Claire, you need to forget you ever heard any of this. I mean it. There are a lot of secrets in Morganville, but this one could kill you. Say *nothing*, understand? Not to your friends, and not to Amelie. *Do you understand?*'

His intensity was even more terrifying than Myrnin's, because it was so controlled. She nodded.

It didn't stop the questions from swirling in her brain, or the possibilities.

Sam let her out at the kerb and watched her until she was inside the house – it was full dark, and there were plenty of hunting vampires out on a clear, cool night like this. Nobody would hurt her – probably – but Sam wasn't in the mood to take chances.

Claire shut the door and locked it, leant against the wood for a long few seconds, and tried to get her head together. She knew her friends would bombard her with questions – where had she been, was she crazy being out alone in the dark – but she couldn't answer them, not without violating some order from either Amelie or Sam.

They're dying. It seemed impossible; the vampires seemed so strong, so frightening. But she'd seen it. She'd seen the way Myrnin was decaying, and how afraid Sam was. Even Amelie, perfect icy Amelie, was doomed. Wasn't that a good thing? And if it was, why did she feel so sick when she thought about Amelie going slowly mad, like Myrnin?

Claire took a few more deep breaths, willed her mind to shut up for a while, and pushed off to walk down the hall.

She didn't get far. There was stuff piled everywhere. It took her a second, but she recognised it with a shock of horror. 'Oh no,' she whispered. 'Shane's stuff.' It was blocking the hallway. Claire shoved a path through the boxes and suitcases piled there. *Oh crap.* There was the PlayStation, unplugged and looking mournful, in a heap with its game controllers.

'Hey? Hey guys? What's going on?' Claire called, edging around the barricades. 'Anybody here?'

'Claire?' Michael's shadow appeared at the end of the hall. 'Where the *hell* have you been?'

'I...got held up late at the lab,' she said. Which wasn't a lie. 'What's happening?'

'Shane says he's moving out,' Michael said. He looked deeply angry, but it was covering up hurt, too. 'Glad you're here. I was about to come looking for you.'

Claire heard the indistinct buzz of voices upstairs. Eve's voice, high and strident. Shane's rumbling low. There was about a sixty second delay, and then Shane came down the stairs carrying a box. His face was pale but determined, and although he hesitated for a second when he saw Claire was back, he kept coming down.

'Seriously, dumbass, what the *hell* are you doing?' Eve demanded from the top of the stairs. She darted around and got into his path, forcing him to back up and try to get around her. 'Yo, village idiot! Talking to you!'

'You want to live here with him, fine,' Shane said tightly. 'I'm going. I've had enough.'

'You're moving *at night*? Do you have a head wound?'

He faked Eve to the right and moved past her to the left.

And ran into Claire, who didn't move. She didn't say

anything, and after a few seconds of silence he said, 'I'm sorry. Got to do it. I told you.'

'Is this about your dad?' she asked. 'About this prejudice you've got against Michael now?'

'Prejudice? Jesus, Claire, you act like he's still really Michael. Well, he's not. He's one of them. I'm done with this crap. If I need to I'll go break some laws and get my ass thrown in jail. Better that than living here, looking at him—' Shane stopped dead and shut his eyes for a second. 'You don't understand. You just don't understand, Claire. You didn't grow up here.'

'But I did,' Eve said, stepping up closer. 'And I don't get your paranoid bullshit, either. Michael hasn't hurt *anybody*! Especially you, you jerk. So lay off.'

'I am,' Shane said. 'I'm leaving.'

Claire didn't move out of his way. 'What about us?'

'You want to go with me?'

She slowly shook her head, and saw the pain in his face for a split second before it turned hard again.

'Then we've got nothing to talk about. And sorry to break it to you, but there's no *us*. Get it straight, Claire, it's been fun, but you're not really my type—'

Michael *moved*. He smacked the box out of Shane's hands, and it flew halfway across the room, skidded across the wood floor the rest of the way, and slammed into the baseboard, where it tipped over and spilt things all over the place.

'Don't,' he said, and grabbed Shane by the shoulders and flattened him against the nearest convenient wall.

'Don't you disrespect her. Be an asshole to me, fine. Be an asshole to Eve if you want to; she can give it right back. But don't you take it out on Claire. I've had enough of your crap, Shane.' He stopped and took a breath, but the anger wasn't burning out of him, not yet. 'You want to go, get the hell out, but you'd better take a good hard look at yourself, my man. Yeah, your sister died. Your mom died. Your dad's a violent, prejudiced asshole. Your life has *sucked*. But you don't get to be the victim anymore. We keep cutting you breaks, and you keep screwing up, and it's *enough*. I'm not letting you whine anymore about how your life sucks worse than ours.'

Shane's face went dead white, then red.

And he socked Michael in the face. It was a solid, painful punch, and Claire winced and covered her mouth in sympathy, moving back.

Michael didn't move. Didn't even react. He just stared into Shane's eyes.

'You're just like your dad,' he said. 'You want to stake me now? Cut my head off? Bury me out back? That work for you, *friend*?'

'Yes!' Shane screamed, right in his face, and there was something so frightening in his eyes that Claire couldn't move. Couldn't breathe.

Michael let him go, walked over, and picked up a couple of things from the pile that had spilt from the box Shane had been carrying out.

A pointed stake.

A wickedly sharp hunting knife.

'You came prepared,' he said, and tossed them to Shane, who caught them out of the air. 'Go for it.'

Eve screamed and threw herself in front of Michael, who gently but firmly moved her out of the way.

'Go on,' he said. 'We do this now, or we end up doing it later. You want to move out so you can kill me with a clear conscience. Why wait? Come on, man, do it. I won't fight.'

Shane turned the knife in his hand, the edge slashing the light with every agitated move. Claire felt frozen, winter-cold, unable to think of anything to say or do. What had happened? How did things get this bad? What—

Shane took a step towards Michael, a sudden long lunge, and Michael didn't move. His eyes – they weren't cold at all, and they weren't vampire-scary, either. They were human, and they were afraid.

For a long breath, nobody moved, and then Michael said, 'I know you feel like I betrayed you, but I didn't. This wasn't about you. It was for me; it was so I didn't have to be trapped here anymore. I was dying here. I was buried alive.'

Shane's face twisted, as if that hunting knife had slid into his own guts. 'Maybe you should have stayed dead.' He raised the stake in his right hand.

'Shane, *no*!' Eve was screaming, trying to get between them, but Michael was holding her off. She turned on him in a fury. 'Dammit, stop it! You don't really want to die!'

'No,' Michael said. 'I don't. He knows I don't.'

Shane paused, trembling. Claire watched his face, his eyes, but she couldn't tell what he was thinking. What he was feeling. It was just a face, and she didn't know him at all.

'You were my friend,' Shane said. He sounded lost. 'You were my best friend. How screwed up is this?'

Michael didn't say anything. He took a step forward, took the knife and stake out of Shane's hands, and pulled him into a hug.

And this time, Shane didn't resist.

'Asshole,' Michael sighed, and slapped his back.

'Yeah,' Shane muttered, stepped back, and scrubbed at his eyes with the heel of his hand. 'Whatever. You started it.' He looked around and focused on Claire. 'You. You were supposed to be home already.'

Crap. She'd hoped they'd forget all about her late arrival, in the explosion of Shane's freak-out. But of course, he'd try to find a way to shift attention away, and there she was, a sitting duck.

'Right,' Eve said. 'Guess you forgot the number to call and tell us you weren't dead in a ditch.'

'I'm fine,' Claire said.

'Amy wasn't. She was murdered and stuffed in our trash can, so excuse me if I got a little bit worried that you might be *dead*.' Eve crossed her arms, her dark stare getting even more fierce. 'I already checked out there for you, before Shane decided to pull this crap.'

Oh man. Somehow, in all of the stress of her afternoon

with Myrnin, Claire had forgot about Amy's death. Of *course* Eve was angry; not so much angry, really, as plain terrified.

Claire didn't dare meet Shane's gaze. She looked at Michael instead, helplessly. 'I'm sorry,' she said. 'I got... I was at the lab, and...I should have called, I guess.'

'And you walked home? In the dark?' Another question she had to avoid. She just shrugged. 'You know what we call pedestrians in Morganville? Mobile blood banks.' Michael sounded cold, too. Cold and angry. 'You scared the shit out of us. That's not like you, Claire. What happened?'

Shane moved to her side, and she felt a moment of relief that at least *he* wasn't angry at her. But then he yanked her shirt away from her neck on the left, then on the right, an efficient rough search that surprised her too much to fight him. He skinned up her right sleeve all the way to the elbow and turned her arm to inspect it.

As he reached for the left, she felt an electric bolt of alarm. *The bracelet. Oh God.*

She yanked free and shoved him back. 'Hey!' she said. 'I'm fine, OK? I'm fine! Fang-free!'

'Then show me,' Shane said. His eyes were steady and scared, and that broke her heart. 'C'mon, Claire. Prove it.'

'Why do I have to prove anything to you?' She knew she was wrong, and it made her stupidly angry that he cared so much. 'You don't own me, like some vampire! I just *said* I'm fine! Why can't you just trust me?'

She would have done anything to take it back, but it was too late, and it hit him like a punch in the face. *He's been hurt so much. Why did I do that? Why...*

Michael stepped in between them. He threw a glance over his shoulder at Shane. 'I'll do it.' He was blocking Eve and Shane's view. Before Claire could do anything to stop him – as if she *could* do anything – he grabbed her left hand and pulled the sleeve up to her elbow.

He stared at the gold bracelet for a paralysing second before turning her arm first one way, then the other. Then pulling her sleeve back down over the telltale jewellery evidence.

'She's fine,' he said, and met her eyes. 'She's telling the truth. I'd know if a vampire had bitten her. I'd feel it.'

Shane's mouth opened, then closed. He took another step back, stared at her for a second, then walked away. Eve called, 'Hey, how about taking some of your crap back upstairs, if you're planning on staying?'

'Later,' Shane snapped, and went upstairs without looking back.

'I'd better go talk to him,' Claire said. Michael kept hold of her arm.

'No,' he said. 'First, you'd better talk to me.'

He hustled her towards the kitchen. Behind them, Eve said, 'Just another great family dinner. Whatever! I'm taking the last hot dog!'

Even with the kitchen door shut, Michael wasn't taking any chances. He pulled Claire along with him to the pantry, opened the door, and turned on the light. 'Inside,' he ordered. She stepped in, and he shut the door after her. It was cramped with two people, and it smelt like old spices and vinegar, from where Shane had dropped the bottle a few weeks back. Michael's voice dropped to a fierce hiss. 'What the *hell* do you think you're doing?'

'What I had to,' she said. She was shaking all over, but she wouldn't let Michael intimidate her. She was tired, and besides, *everybody* seemed to be trying to intimidate her these days. She was small; she wasn't weak. 'It was the only way. Amelie—'

'You should have talked to me. Talked to *us*'

'Like *you* came clean with us, when you were a ghost? And did you have a house meeting before you decided to go all the way to vampire?' Claire shot back. 'Right. Well, you're not the only one who can make choices, Michael. This was mine; I made it; I'll live with it. And it'll keep all of you safe.'

'Who says?' Michael asked bluntly. 'Amelie? You're trusting vampires now?'

She didn't look away from his big blue eyes. 'I trust you.'

He suppressed a smile. 'Dumbass.'

'Dork.' She shoved him, just a little, and he let her do it. He even pretended to stagger, although she didn't imagine vampires got knocked off balance very often, except by other vampires. 'Michael, she didn't give me any choice. Shane's dad – even though he left, he did damage. Shane wasn't going to be trusted here, and you know what happens if—'

'If they don't trust him,' Michael said sombrely. 'Yeah. I know. Look, don't worry about Shane. I'll protect him. I told you—'

'You may not be able to. Look, no offence, but you've only been a vampire for a couple of weeks. I have library books that have been out longer. You can't promise—'

Michael reached out and put one cool finger across her lips, stilling them instantly. His blue eyes were intense, narrow, and very focused.

'Shhhh,' he whispered, and turned out the light.

Claire heard the kitchen door thump, and then the hard-heeled clonk of Eve's shoes crossing the wood floor. 'Hello? Hellllooooooo? Great. Why do all my housemates sulk like little girls or vanish when the dishes are dirty? If you can hear me, Michael Glass, I'm talking to *you*!'

Claire snorted, almost laughed. Michael's hand closed over her mouth, stifling her. He tugged on her arm, and she followed him, moving carefully so as not to knock anything off the shelf. She heard the scrape of the door opening at the rear of the pantry, the tiny little bolt-hole, and bent down to go through it. The other side was pitch-black, with not even the tiny crack of light that the pantry had enjoyed, and Claire felt a flutter of panic. Michael's hand pushed her onward, and she stepped hesitantly into the close, thick dark. Behind her, she heard him close the door with a very soft *click*, and bright electric light flooded over the floor.

'Here,' Michael said, and handed her the flashlight. 'She might come looking for us here, but not for a while.'

It was a secret hidey-hole, one that Claire had been shoved into on her very first morning in the Glass House; no exits, only the one entrance. She'd thought from the beginning it looked like someplace a vampire might stash a couple of handy coffins, but it was empty. And as far as she knew, Michael slept on a Serta.

'I meant to ask you. What is this?'

'Root cellar,' he said. 'This house was built before refrigerators, and ice deliveries were only so-so. This was where they kept most of their vegetables.'

'So...not a vampire hideout?'

Michael stretched his long legs out with a sigh and leant against the wall. God, he was pretty. No wonder Eve was willing to overlook the lack of pulse. 'Not so far as I've ever known, but the vampires in Morganville never really had to hide. Only the humans did.'

Which wasn't what they were here to talk about, she supposed. She crossed her arms and felt the bracelet bite into the skin of her wrist under the shirt. 'Whatever lecture you were going to give me, it's too late. I signed, it's done, I've got the souvenir bracelet.' Which made her suddenly, strangely want to cry. 'Michael—'

'What's she asking you to do?' Which was so right-on that she felt the pressure of tears behind her eyes and in her nose get even higher.

'Um...' She couldn't tell him; Amelie and Sam had

both made it clear. 'It's just extra schoolwork. She wants me to study some things.'

'What things?' Michael's voice got sharp and worried. 'Claire—'

'It's nothing. Science stuff. I would have probably been doing it anyway, but it's just…it's a lot more time, and I don't know how I'm going to—' *Keep it from Shane.* Because she had to, right? Bad enough he hated Michael for being a vampire, but what was he going to think about *her*, selling herself to Amelie? 'I just don't know how I'm going to do all this.'

And suddenly, she was crying. She didn't mean to, but there it was, boiling out of her. She expected Michael to do the Shane thing, come and comfort her, but he didn't. He sat right where he was and watched her. When her sobs died down, and she swiped her hands across her wet cheeks, he said, 'Finished?'

She gulped and nodded.

'You made the choice; now you want to have it both ways – the benefits, but not the consequences. You can't, Claire. It's coming home to roost, and you'd better handle it now rather than later.' Michael's tone softened, just a little. 'Look, I'm not an asshole; I know how scared you are. But you're a player in this town now. You're not the fragile little thing we took in for protection. You're trying to protect *us*. That means you may not be as well liked anymore, and you're going to have to sack up about that.'

'What?' She felt dazed. Somehow, this wasn't how

she'd expected all this to go. Especially Michael's cool, challenging look, and the lack of hugging.

'Signing the contract isn't the last choice you're going to have to make,' he said. 'It's the choices you make from now on that show whether you did the right thing or not.' He stood up, pale and strong and as gorgeous as an angel in the glow of Claire's flashlight. 'And stop lying to me. You ought to get off to a better start.'

'I...what?'

'You said what Amelie has you doing is just more studying,' he said grimly. 'And I can tell when you're lying. No, I'm not going to ask, because I can tell it scares you, but just remember, vampires know, all right?'

He swung the door open and ducked out. Claire stared after him, open-mouthed, but by the time she'd scrambled through and switched off the flashlight, Michael was already gone, out of the pantry. In fact, by the time Claire followed, Michael was already sitting on the couch, Eve curled next to him with her head on his chest. They were watching something on TV, and Eve's gaze followed Claire as she hurried past them, mumbling an apology.

She stopped on the stairs and looked back at them. Two people she cared about, wrapped in a moment of warmth and happiness.

Michael was a vampire, and that meant that Michael was *dying*. Like Myrnin. He was going to suffer and lose his mind and hurt people.

He could even hurt Eve, no matter how much he cared about her.

Tears pricked at her eyes, and she felt suddenly short of breath. When it had been just an abstract problem, just Morganville minus vampires equals safety, then that had been one thing, but it wasn't abstract. It was people she knew, liked, even loved. She wouldn't shed any tears over Oliver, but how could she not care about Michael?

Or Sam? Or even Amelie?

Claire picked up her book bag and went upstairs.

Shane's door was shut. She knocked. He didn't answer for a long moment, and then said, 'If I ignore you, will you go away?'

'No,' she said.

'Might as well come in, then.'

He was flopped on the bed, staring at the ceiling, hands under his head, and he didn't look at her as she entered and closed the door behind her.

'So is this how it's going to go?' she asked. 'I do something dumb like stay out late; you get mad and run away; I come and apologise and make everything better?'

Shane, surprised, looked at her, then said, 'Well, that kinda works for me, yeah.'

Claire thought about Michael, about the suddenly grown-up way he'd treated her. She sat down on the bed next to Shane, staring down at the floor for a few seconds to gather her courage, and then she pulled back her sleeve to expose the bracelet.

Shane didn't make a sound. He slowly sat up, staring at the shiny gold band with its Founder's Symbol.

'We need to talk,' she said. She felt sick and terrified, but she knew it was the right choice. The only other thing to do was lie, but she couldn't keep on lying. Michael was right about that.

Shane could have done anything – he could have run away, he could have thrown her out of his room.

He could even have hit her.

Instead, he took her hand in his, bent his head, and said, 'Tell me.'

Eve wasn't so understanding. 'Are you *out of your mind*?' She picked up the handiest thing to throw – it happened to be the PlayStation controller – and Shane quickly, carefully de-gamed her. Claire thought he probably wouldn't have moved that fast if Eve had grabbed, oh, say, a book.

'Let's be adults about this,' Michael said. They were downstairs again, together, although Shane and Michael were still clearly standing at opposite poles. It was getting late – eleven already – and Claire was feeling the strain of a very long, hard day. In fact, she yawned, which only made Eve shoot her a look of absolute exasperation.

'Oh, I'm sorry, are we *keeping you awake*? Michael, how the hell do we be adults about this when one of us *isn't an adult*?' Eve levelled a shaking finger at her. 'You're a *kid*, Claire. As in, you're still a wet-behind-the-ears dumbass who hasn't even been in this town a couple of months. You have no idea what you're doing!'

'Maybe I don't,' Claire agreed. Her voice was almost steady, which pleased and surprised her. She didn't like having Eve angry at her. She didn't like having *anyone* angry at her. 'The thing is, it's done. I made the choice; that discussion was over before we had it. I wanted you to know, though. I didn't want to' – her eyes met Michael's briefly – 'lie to you.'

'Why the hell not? Everybody around here lies. Michael lied about being a ghost. Shane lies about shit all the time. Why not you, too?'

Shane groaned. 'Yo, Drama Princess, want to tone it down a little? Somewhere, Sandra Bernhard wants her tantrum back.'

'Oh, like *you* don't throw a hissy every time somebody trips your angst switch!'

Claire looked helplessly at Michael, who was having a hard time not smiling. He shrugged and took a step forward. That meant, of course, that Shane backed up. 'Eve,' Michael said, ignoring Shane for the moment. 'Give the girl some credit. At least she told you, instead of letting you figure it out on your own.'

'Yeah, and she told me *last*!' Eve glared at the two boys, hands on her hips.

'Boyfriend,' Shane said, holding up his hand.

'Landlord,' Michael chimed in.

'Crap,' Eve sighed. 'Right, next time you sell your soul to the devil, *I get first contact*! Girl solidarity, right?'

'Um...OK?'

'Dumbass,' Eve sighed, defeated. 'I can't believe you did that. I worked so hard to get away from that Protection crap, and here you are, all... Protected. I just wanted you to be...safe. And I'm not sure this is.'

'Yeah,' Claire said. 'Me neither. But I swear, it was the best thing I could think of. And at least it's Amelie. She's OK, right?'

They all looked at each other. Shane said, 'But you won't tell us what she's got you doing that keeps you out late.'

'No. I...I can't do that.'

'Then she's not OK,' Shane said. 'And neither are you.'

But none of them had any good suggestions for how to fix it, and Claire fell asleep on the couch with her head in Shane's lap as he and Michael and Eve kept talking, and talking, and talking. It was three a.m. when she woke up. Shane hadn't moved, but she was covered with a blanket, and he was sound asleep, sitting straight up.

Claire yawned, groaned at sore muscles, and rolled to her feet. 'Shane. Up. You need to go to bed.'

He woke up cute, softened by sleep. 'Come with?' He was only half joking. She remembered being curled up with him in her bed the night she'd been so scared; he'd been careful then, but she wasn't sure she could count on that kind of self-restraint at three a.m., when he was half-awake.

'I can't,' she said reluctantly. 'Not that I don't want to...'

He smiled and stretched out on his side on the couch, leaving a narrow space between his warm, solid body and the cushions. 'Stay,' he said. 'I promise, no clothes will come off. Well, maybe shoes. Do shoes count as clothes?'

She kicked hers off and climbed over him to slip into that small pocket, and sighed in relief as his body pressed against hers. She didn't even need the blanket, but he put it over the two of them, anyway, and then combed her hair back from her neck and kissed her on the soft, vulnerable skin.

'You were leaving,' she whispered. He stopped moving. As far as she could tell, he stopped breathing. 'You were leaving, and you didn't even know if I was OK.'

'No. I was going to go look for you.'

'After you packed.'

'Claire, I didn't even know you hadn't come home until Eve came upstairs to yell at me. *I was going to look for you.*'

She looked back at him, over her shoulder, and saw the desperation hiding in his eyes.

'Please,' he said. 'Please believe me.'

Against her will, even against her better judgement, she did believe him. She felt safe, anchored against the troubled world by the heat of his body against hers.

His arm went around her waist, and she felt absolutely protected.

'I won't let anything happen to you,' he said. It was

a promise he probably couldn't keep, but in the night, in the dark, it meant everything to her. 'Hey.'

'What?'

'Wanna fool around?'

She did.

She must have drifted off to sleep, because she woke up with her heart pounding, and feeling like there was something really, really wrong. For a second, as she came awake, she thought she smelt smoke, and that propelled her upright in a surge of panic. The house had almost burnt once already...

No, not fire, but something was definitely wrong. There was something in the whole atmosphere of the house. The smoke had been some kind of signal, from it to her. *A get your butt out of bed* signal.

Shane was still lying next to her on the couch, but he was already awake, too, and in the next second he rolled off to his feet as if he'd also felt it.

'What's happening?' Claire felt a jolt go through her like electricity. 'Shane?'

'Something's wrong.'

They both froze as they heard the sudden loud blare of a siren. It sounded as though it was right in front of the house.

Claire heard feet on the stairs and saw Eve hurrying down in a satin nightgown and fluffy black robe. Eve's face was bare of any Goth make-up, and she looked flushed and anxious and scared.

'What is it?' Eve called. 'What's going on?'

'I don't know,' Shane said. 'Something bad. Can't you feel it?'

This was an event; they were all up and it was barely six a.m.

Eve plunged down the steps and yanked up the cord to raise the blinds on the window that faced the front yard. They all looked out. A police car was in the middle of the street, siren still wailing, and its headlights cast a hot circle of light on a maroon sedan stopped on the street, its driver's-side door open. Its lights were still on, and there was a body slumped on the road next to it.

The windows were dark-tinted.

It was a vampire's car.

Eve screamed, spun, and looked at them with wide, terrified eyes. 'Where's Michael?' she asked, and Claire stupidly looked behind her, as if she were going to find him standing there.

They all looked back at the street, the car, the body.

'It can't be,' Claire whispered. Shane was already moving for the door at a flat run, but Eve just stood there staring, frozen. Claire put her arm around her and felt her shaking.

She saw Shane blow through the gate at the fence and run towards the body; the cop who'd just emerged from the patrol car grabbed him, slung him around, and slammed him face-first onto the hood. Shane was yelling something.

'I need to go out there,' Claire said. 'Stay here.'

Eve nodded numbly. Claire hated leaving her there, but Shane was going to get himself arrested if he kept it up, and who knew what could happen to him in jail?

She was only to the porch when another police car turned the corner, lights flashing, siren adding its howl to the chaos. It braked beside the first one, and another policeman got out and moved to where Shane was being restrained.

Claire didn't recognise the cop who had Shane facedown on the hood, but she knew the new arrival. It was Richard Morrell, Monica's big brother. He wasn't a bad guy, although he was definitely from the same icky gene pool. He took over for the other cop, who backed away.

'Shane! Dammit, Shane, calm the hell down. This is a crime scene; I can't let you run out there, do you understand? Calm down!'

Richard was occupied with keeping Shane under control, so the other policeman went to crouch next to the body on tho street. *The body.* Claire took a step closer, and the policeman produced a flashlight and focused it on the face of the man lying in the street. Red hair flared in the light.

Not Michael.

Sam.

There was a stake in his chest, and he was still and white and *not moving.*

'Richard!' the cop yelled. 'It's Sam Glass! Looks dead to me!'

'Sam,' Claire whispered. 'No.'

Sam had been kind to her, and somebody had dragged him out of his car and put a stake through his chest.

'Shit!' Richard spat. 'Shane, sit your ass down. Down, right now. Don't make me handcuff you.' He yanked Shane by the collar of his T-shirt and sat him down on the kerb, glared at him for a second, then came over to look at the body. 'Holy Mother of— Grab his feet.'

'What?' The other cop – his name tag said FENTON – looked at him with a frown. 'It's a crime scene; we can't—'

'He's still alive, you idiot. Grab his damn feet, Fenton! If he burns, he's dead.'

The first rays of sun crept over the horizon and fell on Sam's still form.

And Claire saw him start to smoke.

'What are you waiting for?' Richard shouted. 'Pick him up!' The other cop, after a blank hesitation, grabbed Sam by the feet. Richard took him under the arms, and together they bodily threw him into the maroon sedan, the one with tinted windows, and slammed the door shut. Fenton started for the driver's side, but Richard got there first. 'I'll drive,' Richard said. 'The wound's still fresh. He's got a chance if I can get him to Amelie.'

Fenton backed off. Richard gunned the engine and slammed the door even as he was peeling rubber towards the end of the street.

Officer Fenton glared at Shane. 'You going to give me trouble, boy?' he demanded. Claire sure hoped not. This man was twice the size of Richard Morrell, twice as old, and he looked like a human pit bull.

Shane held up his hands. 'No trouble from me, Officer. Sir.'

'You two see what happened here?'

'No,' Claire said. 'I was asleep. We all were.'

'All in the same room?' the cop grunted, and looked her over, from her bed-head to the wrinkled clothes. 'Didn't take you for the type.'

She couldn't figure out what he meant for a few seconds, and then felt a wave of hot embarrassment sweep over her. 'No, I mean Eve was in her own room. We were asleep on the couch.'

Shane said, 'Yeah, we were all asleep. Woke up when we heard the siren.' Which wasn't quite true, was it? They'd woken up, and *then* heard the siren. But Claire wasn't sure why that would be important.

The cop tapped on a handheld device, still frowning. 'Ought to be four of you in the house. Where're the other two?'

'Eve's still inside. And Michael—' Where the hell was Michael? 'I don't know where he is.'

'I'll go see if he's in his room,' Shane volunteered, but the cop froze him in place with another thunderous scowl.

'You'll sit your ass down on that kerb and be quiet. You, what's your name?'

'Claire Danvers.'

'Claire, get in there, find out if Michael Glass is

inside. If he's not, find out if his car is missing.'

Claire stared at him, wide-eyed. 'You don't think...?'

'I don't think anything until I have facts. I need to know who's here, who isn't, and work from there.' The cop transferred his dark stare to Shane, who was starting to get up. 'I already told you, sit your ass down, Collins.'

'I didn't have anything to do with this!'

'If I had to put together a list of prime suspects out to stake some vampires, you'd be right at the top, so yeah, you do. *Sit down*.'

Shane sat, looking furious. Claire silently begged him not to do anything stupid, and hurried back into the house. Eve was upstairs dressing – black baby-doll T with a bling-enhanced cartoon Elmer Fudd on the front, and black jeans with clunky Doc Martens.

'It wasn't—'

'I know. I saw,' Eve said. Her voice sounded stuffy, as though she'd been crying, or was about to. 'It was Sam, right? Is he alive? Or...whatever?'

'I don't know. Richard said something like he could still be OK.' Claire gripped the doorknob tightly, and glanced down the hall. Michael's door was closed. It was always closed. 'Did you look—?'

'No.' Eve took a deep breath and stood up. 'I'll go with you.'

Michael's door was unlocked, and it was completely dark inside. Claire flipped on the lights. Michael's bed was empty, neatly made, and the room looked absolutely normal. Eve checked the closets, under the bed, even the master bathroom.

'No sign of him,' she said breathlessly. 'Let's check the garage.'

The garage was a shed in the back, not attached to the house; the two of them went out the back kitchen door and crossed the rutted driveway. The shed's doors were closed.

Eve opened one side, Claire the other.

Michael's car was gone.

'What about work? Could he be at work?'

'JT's doesn't open until ten,' Eve said. 'Why would he be in there at six?'

'Inventory?'

'You think they're going to call a vampire in at six a.m. to do *inventory*?' Eve slammed the shed door and kicked it for good measure. 'Where the hell is he? And why the *hell* don't I have a working cell phone? Why don't you?'

Hers had been lost, Eve's had been smashed; both of them miserably looked at each other for a few seconds, then, without a word, walked to the front yard where Shane was still sitting on the kerb. If anybody could sit rebelliously, he was doing it.

'Give me your phone,' Eve demanded and held out her hand. Shane looked at her with a frown. 'Now, dumbass. Michael's not inside, and his car's gone.'

'Michael's got a car? Since when?'

'Since the vampires issued him one. He didn't tell you?'

Shane just shook his head. A muscle jumped in his jaw. 'He doesn't tell me shit, Eve. Not since—'

'Not since you started treating him like the Evil Dead? Yeah. Imagine that.'

He silently handed over his cell phone and looked away, staring at the street where Sam's body had been tossed. Claire wondered if he was thinking about his dad's crusade, about how *the only good vampire is a dead vampire.*

Claire wondered if he really, deep down, still agreed.

Eve dialled and put the phone to her ear. For a tense few seconds nothing happened, and then Claire saw relief melt the tension out of Eve's face and body. 'Michael! Where the hell are you?' Pause. '*Where?*' Pause. 'Oh. OK. I need to tell you—' Pause. 'You know.' Pause. 'Yeah, we'll…talk later.'

Eve closed the phone and handed it back. Shane slipped it in his pocket again, eyebrows up and signalling questions.

'He's OK,' she said. Her eyes had gone dark and narrow.

'And?'

'And nothing. He's fine. End of story.'

'Bullshit,' Shane said, and tugged her down to sit next to him on the kerb. 'Spill it, Eve. Now.'

Claire sat, too, on Eve's other side. The kerb felt cold and hard, but the good thing was that the patrol car blocked Fenton's view of them. He was talking to the occupants of another car, vampire-tinted, who had pulled up behind the cruiser.

'He was downtown,' Eve said. 'At the Elders' Council.

They pulled him in there early this morning.'

'Who did?'

'The Big Three.' Oliver, Amelie and the mayor, Richard and Monica's dad. 'Amelie just got word about Sam. But Michael's not hurt or anything.' An unspoken *for now* was at the end of that. Eve was worried. She bent her head closer to Shane's, lowered her voice even further, and said, 'You didn't have anything to do with what happened to Sam, right?'

'Jesus, Eve!'

'I'm only asking because—'

'I know why you're asking,' he whispered back fiercely. 'Hell no. If I were going to go after some vampire, it wouldn't have been *Sam*. I'd be staking somebody like Oliver, make it worth my time. Speaking of Oliver, he'd be my number one suspect.'

'Vampires don't kill their own.'

'He arranged for Brandon to die,' Claire offered. 'I think Oliver's capable of anything. And he'd love to see Amelie even more isolated.' She swallowed hard. 'She told me once that Sam was safer if she didn't keep him close. I guess she was right.'

'Doesn't matter. Oliver keeps his hands clean, no matter what. Some broke-ass human is going to burn for this, and you know it,' Shane said. 'And it happened in front of our house, and nobody's forgot what happened with my dad. You don't think we're being set up?'

Crap. Shane was right. The fact that Michael was safe was good, but it was also a double-edged sword; it meant that Michael had been gone when Sam had been attacked.

And Michael was the only one of them whose word might be worth anything to the vampires.

Sure enough, Fenton came back around the cruiser and stared at the three of them for a few seconds, then said, 'You're being taken in for questioning. All three of you. Get in the back seat.'

Shane didn't move. 'I'm not going anywhere.'

The policeman sighed and leant against the quarter panel. 'Son, you've got a lot of attitude, and I respect that. But get it straight: either you get in my car, or you get in *their* car.' He pointed towards the silent dark sedan, the one with vampires inside. 'And I promise you, that won't end so well. You get me?'

Shane nodded, stood, and gave Eve a hand up.

Claire stayed seated. She pulled up the sleeve on her left arm. The bracelet glittered and glimmered in the morning light, and she held it up for Fenton's clear view.

His eyes widened. 'Is that…?'

'I want to see my Patron,' Claire said. 'Please.'

He went off to talk on his radio, then came back and jerked his head at Shane and Eve. 'In the back seat,' he said. 'You're going to the station. You, kid…' He nodded towards the other sedan. 'They'll take you to Amelie.'

Claire swallowed hard and exchanged a look with Shane, then Eve. That hadn't been her plan. She wanted them all to stay together. How could she keep them safe if they got separated?

'Don't,' Shane said. 'Come with us.'

Truthfully, that was starting to sound like a better idea. The vampires weren't going to be happy, and her shiny gold bracelet didn't exempt her from suspicion. Amelie could still order her hurt, or killed.

'OK,' Claire said. Shane looked massively relieved as he ducked his head and entered the back seat of the cruiser. Eve followed him in.

The cop slammed the door after Eve, before Claire could get in the patrol car.

'Hey!' Shane yelled, and hit the car window. He and Eve were both trying to get out, but the doors weren't opening.

Fenton grabbed her by the arm and hustled her over to the other sedan, opened the door, and put her in the back seat before she could protest. Claire heard the faint click of locks engaging, and sat very still, trying to see through the gloom.

One of the vampires flicked on the overhead light. *Oh crap.* It was two of her not-favourite people. The woman was pale as snow, with white-blonde hair and eyes of palest silver. Gretchen. Her partner, Hans, was a hard man made of angles, with greying short hair, and a stony expression.

'I wish we'd got the boy instead,' Gretchen said, clearly disappointed. Her voice was low-pitched, throaty, with a heavy foreign accent. Not quite German, but not quite anything else, either. An old accent, Claire thought. 'He was so rude to us when last we spoke. And surely his father deserves a lesson, even if the boy does not.'

'Amelie says just bring this one,' Hans said, and put the car in gear. He looked at Claire in the rear-view mirror. 'Seat belt, please.'

She had trouble wrapping her head around that – why did he care? – but she clicked the safety restraint shut and sat back. Like the ride in Sam's car the day before, she couldn't see a thing outside the windows except a faint grey dot where the sun was rising.

'Where are you taking me?' she asked. Gretchen laughed. Claire caught the flash of fangs, but Gretchen didn't really need them to be scary. Not at all.

'To the Elders' Council,' she said. 'You remember it, Claire. You had such a good time there when last we visited.'

CHAPTER SEVEN

There was Morganville – the dry, dusty, run-down town that was all most people ever saw – and then there was Founder's Square, a lush little piece of Europe where people with a pulse weren't welcome. Claire had been inside once, and it wasn't a fond memory; no matter how cute the little cafes were, or how nice the shops, she could see only the centre of the square in the park, with the cage where they'd locked up Shane.

Where they'd been meaning to burn him alive as punishment for something he hadn't even done.

For some reason, Claire had expected to be parked in the same place as last time – outside of the square, at the police checkpoint – but of course that wasn't possible, was it? A few of the older vampires might be able to stand the sun, but they wouldn't willingly stroll around in it. Morganville was built for the convenience of vampires, not humans, and when Claire's door opened, and Gretchen impatiently gestured for her to get out, they were in an underground parking garage. It was full of cars, all nice ones, with darkened windows. Like a Beverly Hills mall or something.

There were armed guards. One of them started towards them as Gretchen pulled Claire out of the car, but Hans flashed him a badge, and the other guy – vampire, presumably – backed off.

'Let's go,' Hans said. 'Your Patron is waiting.'

Gretchen chuckled. Not a happy sound. Claire stumbled over her own feet trying to keep up as the two vampires set off at a brisk walk, Gretchen's iron-hard grip on her upper arm setting in with bruising force. Claire was short of breath by the time they got to a long double flight of stairs, which the vampires took at a jog. At the top of the stairs was some kind of fire door, with a code panel. Claire didn't dare try to sneak a look at what Hans entered; knowing the vampires' paranoia, it wouldn't do her any good. The machines were probably calibrated to exclude anybody with a heartbeat.

Which made her wonder: was Myrnin behind the town's security, too? Was that something else she was supposed to learn? It could really come in handy if she could persuade him to show her...

She was obsessing on technicalities to avoid feeling the terror, but as soon as the door lock released, she had nothing else to focus on except fear, and it washed over her in a sticky, cold wave. Gretchen seemed to sense it. She looked down at Claire with those cool, mirror-grey eyes, and smiled. 'Worried, little one?' she asked sweetly. 'Worried for yourself, or for your friends?'

'Worried for Sam,' Claire said. Gretchen lost her smile, and for just an instant, she seemed honestly off balance and surprised. 'Is he alive?'

'Alive?' Gretchen's armour slid firmly back in place, and she raised a slender arched eyebrow. 'He may yet be saved, if that is what you mean. I suppose your friend Shane will have to try again.'

'Shane didn't do anything!'

This time, Gretchen's smile got positively cruel. 'Perhaps not,' she said. 'Perhaps not *yet*. But be patient. He will. It's in his nature, as much as killing is in ours.'

Claire had to save her breath, because they were walking again, big strides across thick maroon carpet. Claire's first impression of the Elders' Council building had been that it was a funeral home; it still felt like that to her, all hushed and quiet and elegant. They'd had roses in the last time, when the vampire they'd thought Shane killed had been lying in state. She didn't see any flowers this time.

Gretchen led her down a hallway and through thick double doors, into the round entry hall. There were four armed vampire guards in the room, and Gretchen and Hans had to stop and show ID, and surrender their weapons. Claire got searched – quick, competent pats from cold hands that made her shiver.

And then the doors opened, and she was pulled into a big round room with a high ceiling, chandeliers like falls of ice, and dim, expensive paintings on the walls. She hadn't imagined the smell of roses. In the centre of the room stood a massive round conference table, surrounded by chairs, and in the centre was a vase filled with red, red blooms.

Nobody was at the table. Instead, a group of at least ten was standing at the other side of the room, looking down.

Some of them turned, and Claire's gaze fixed irresistibly on Oliver. She hadn't seen him since he'd threatened her life, trying to lure Shane out of hiding, and as he stood up, now she had a flash of that again, how icy and hard his hands had been around her throat. How scared she'd been.

Oliver snarled, low in his throat but loud enough to be heard, and his eyes were like a wolf's. Not human at all.

'I see you brought us a criminal for punishment,' he said, and moved towards them.

Gretchen looked at Hans, and then shoved Claire behind her. 'Stop,' she said. Oliver did, mostly in surprise. 'The girl asked to come, to see her Patron. We have no proof she is guilty.'

'If she lives in that house, then she's guilty,' Oliver said. 'You surprise me, Gretchen. When did you begin taking the side of the breathers?'

She laughed, but it had a bright, false sound to it. She said something in a language that Claire didn't recognise; Oliver spat something back, and Hans put a big hand on Claire's shoulder.

'She's our responsibility,' he said. 'And she's Amelie's property. Nothing to do with you, Oliver. Move.'

Oliver, smiling, raised his hands and backed away. Hans moved Claire forward, past him, and she felt his stare on the back of her neck, as sharp as knives.

The circle of people parted as Hans approached. It was mostly (Claire guessed) vampires; they didn't wear tags or anything, but most of them had the same cool, pale skin, the same whip-snake quickness when they moved. In fact, the only two humans – breathers? – she saw were Mayor Morrell, looking miserably uncomfortable as he stood near the edge of the group, and his son Richard. Richard's uniform was damp in places, and it took Claire a few seconds to realise that it was wet with blood.

Sam's blood.

Sam was lying on his back on the carpet, with his head cradled in Amelie's lap. The elder vampire was kneeling, and her hands were stroking gently through Sam's bright copper hair. He looked pale and dead, and the stake was still in his chest.

Amelie's eyes were closed, but opened as Hans pushed Claire towards her. For a long second the older vampire didn't seem to recognise Claire at all, and then weariness flashed through her expression; she looked down at Sam, her fingers trailing across his cheek.

'Claire, assist me,' she said, as if they were continuing a conversation Claire hadn't even been in on. 'Give her room, please.'

Hans let go, and Claire felt a wild urge to run, run

out of this room, get Shane and just go, anywhere but here. There was something too big to understand in Amelie's eyes, something she didn't want to know. She started to take a step back, but Amelie's hand flashed out and grabbed her wrist and pulled, and Claire fell to her knees on the other side of Sam's body.

He looked dead.

Really, really dead.

'When I tell you, take hold of the wood and pull,' Amelie said, her voice low and steady. 'Not until I tell you.'

'But...I'm not very strong...' Why wasn't she asking Richard? Asking one of the vampires? Oliver, even?

'You are strong enough. When I tell you, Claire.' Amelie closed her eyes again, and Claire scrubbed her damp palms nervously over her blue jeans. The wooden stake in Sam's chest was round, polished wood, like a spike, and she couldn't tell how deep it was in his body. Was it in his heart? Wouldn't that kill him, once and for all? She remembered they'd talked about other vampires who'd been staked, and they'd died...

Amelie's expression suddenly twisted in pain, and she said, 'Now, Claire!'

Claire didn't even think. She fastened her hands around the stake and pulled, one massive yank, and for a terrifying second she thought it wouldn't work, but then she felt it sliding free, scraping against bone as it went.

Sam's whole body arched, as though he'd been

shocked with one of those heart machines, and the circle of vampires moved back. Amelie kept hold of him, her fingers white as bone where they pressed on the sides of his head. Her eyes flew open, and they were pure blazing silver.

Claire scrambled backward, clutching the stake in both hands. Someone plucked it out of her grip – Richard Morrell, looking grim and tired. He put it into a plastic bag and zipped it shut.

Evidence.

Sam went limp again. The wound in his chest was bleeding a steady, slow trickle, and Amelie took off her jacket – white silk – and folded it into a pad to press it against the flow. Nobody spoke, not even Amelie. Claire sat there feeling helpless, watching Sam. He wasn't moving, not at all.

He still looked dead.

'Samuel,' Amelie said, and her voice was low and quiet and warm. She bent closer to him. 'Samuel. Come back to me.'

His eyes opened, and they were all pupil. Scary owl eyes. Claire bit her lip and thought again about running, but Hans and Gretchen were at her back and she knew she didn't have a chance, anyway.

Sam blinked, and his pupils began to shrink slowly to a more normal size. His lips moved, but no sound came out.

'Breathe in,' Amelie said, in that same quiet, warm tone. 'I'm here, Samuel. I won't leave you.' She stroked fingers gently over his forehead, and he blinked again and slowly focused on her.

It was as though there was nobody else in all the world, just the two of them. *Amelie was wrong, Claire thought. It isn't just that Sam loves her. She loves him just as much.*

Sam looked from Amelie to the circle of people, searching it for someone. When he didn't find the right one, he looked at Amelie again. His lips formed a name. *Michael.*

'Michael is safe,' Amelie said. 'Hans. Fetch him here.'

Hans nodded and left, walking quickly. *Michael.* Claire realised with a jolt that she'd forgot he'd be here, forgot all about him in the shock of all that had happened. Sam was, at least, looking better with every passing second, but Amelie continued to press the makeshift bandage to the wound in his chest.

Sam's hand crept up, clumsy and slow, to cover hers, and for a long few seconds they looked at each other silently, and then Amelie nodded and let go.

Sam held the bandage in place and, with Amelie's help, pulled himself to a sitting position. She helped him lean against the wall.

'Can you tell us what happened?' she asked him. Sam nodded, and Claire looked up to see Richard Morrell crouching down, notebook and pen at the ready.

Sam's voice, when it finally came, was soft and thin, and it was clearly an effort for him to speak at all. 'Went to see Michael,' he said.

'But Michael was here, with us,' Amelie said. 'We summoned him during the night.'

Sam's hand – the one not occupied holding the jacket to his chest – rose and fell helplessly. 'Sensed he wasn't home, so I backed out of the drive. Someone pulled open the car door – Taser, couldn't fight back. Staked me while I was down.'

'Who?' Richard asked. Sam's eyes closed briefly, then opened.

'Didn't see. Human. Heard the heartbeat.' He swallowed. 'Thirsty.'

'You must heal first,' Amelie said. 'A few more moments. Is there anything at all you can tell us about this human who attacked you?'

Sam's eyes opened again, with an effort. 'He called me Michael.'

Michael arrived just in time to hear that last part. He looked at Claire, wide-eyed, then crouched down beside Sam. 'Who did? The one who did this?'

Sam shook his head. 'I don't know who. Male, that's all I know. He used your name. I think he thought I was you.' Sam's lips curled in the pale ghost of a smile. 'Guess he didn't see the hair before he staked me.'

The article in the newspaper. *Captain Obvious*. Somebody had decided to take out the newest vampire in town, and it was sheer luck that they'd got Sam instead. It could have been Michael lying in the street.

And from the look on Michael's face, he was thinking the exact same thing.

* * *

Amelie was agitated. It wasn't really obvious, but Claire had seen her enough to know the difference. She moved more swiftly, and there was something less calm than usual in her eyes. Claire shivered a little when Amelie summoned her into a side room. It was small and empty, probably some kind of meeting room. Amelie didn't come alone; a tall blond vampire guy followed along and stood with his back to the door, a flesh-and-blood deadbolt. No getting out quickly, or at all, really.

'What happened?' Amelie demanded.

'I don't know,' Claire said. 'I was asleep. I woke up when—' *When I heard the sirens*, she'd been about to say, but again, that wasn't really true. She'd felt something, a flash of alarm that had come out of nowhere. And Shane and Eve had felt it, too. It normally would take a nuclear explosion to blast Shane out of sleep in the predawn hours, but he'd been wide-awake. 'It was like some alarm went off in the house.'

Amelie's face went very still and smooth. 'Indeed.'

'Why? Is that important?'

'Maybe. What else?'

'Nothing...we went downstairs. The sirens were going outside, and by the time we got down there it was all over, I guess. Sam was down on the road, and the cop was already there.'

'You saw no one else?'

Claire shook her head.

'And your friends?' Amelie asked. 'Where were they?'

It wasn't a casual question. Claire felt her pulse speed

up, and tried to stay calm. If Amelie didn't believe her... 'Asleep,' she said firmly. 'Shane was with me, and I saw Eve come out of her own room. They couldn't have done it.'

Amelie shot her a look. Not one that made her feel any too secure. 'I know how much you value their lives. But understand, Claire, if you lie for them, I will not forgive it.'

'I'm not lying. They were in their rooms when I came out. The only one missing was Michael, and he was here with you.'

Amelie turned away from her and paced the length of the room in slow, graceful steps. She looked so perfect, so...*together*. Unable to help it, Claire blurted out, 'Aren't you worried about Sam?'

'I am more concerned about whoever attacked him not receiving another chance to do such harm,' Amelie said. 'Sam was old enough to survive such a thing – but only barely. If the stake had remained in his chest much longer, or the sun had burnt him, he could not have survived. Had the assassin succeeded in attacking Michael, he would have died almost instantly. It would take decades for him to build up an immunity.'

Claire's mouth opened, shut, and opened again when she found the words. 'You mean...vampires *don't* die from stakes in the heart?'

'I mean that it takes quite a lot to kill one of us,' Amelie said. 'More every year we survive. You could put a stake through *my* heart, and I would simply pull it out and be very annoyed with you for ruining my wardrobe. If I failed to remove it within a few hours, it would damage me, perhaps seriously, but it would not destroy me in the way you're thinking. We are not so fragile, little Claire.' Her teeth gleamed for a second like pearls as she smiled. 'You would do well to tell your friends. Especially Shane.'

'But...Brandon—'

Amelie's smile faded. 'He was tortured,' she said. 'Burnt with sunlight to reduce his resistance. By the time he was murdered, he had no more strength than a newborn. Shane's father understands us too well, you see.'

And now, so did Claire. Which probably wasn't good. 'The cops took Shane and Eve to the police station. I don't want anything to happen to them.'

'I'm sure you don't. As I did not want anything to happen to my dear Samuel, who would willingly die for the rights of breathers in this town.' Amelie's tone had gone cold and dark, and it gave Claire a deep-down trembling in her stomach. 'I wonder if I have been too lenient. Allowed too much freedom.'

'You don't own us,' Claire whispered, and it seemed like the bracelet around her wrist tightened all of a sudden, pinching. She grabbed at it, wincing.

'Do I not?' Amelie asked coolly. She exchanged a glance with the vampire at the door. 'Let her leave. I am done with her.'

He bowed slightly and stepped out of the way. Claire resisted the urge to lunge for the exit. Being in the same room with Amelie, never mind her guard, was scary and intense, but she needed to at least try. 'About Shane and Eve—'

'I don't interfere in human justice,' Amelie said. 'If they are innocent, then they will be released. Go now. I shall expect you to attend to Myrnin today, and I have arranged for some additional classes at university for you to attend. A list has been provided to you at your home this morning.'

Claire hesitated.

'Sam was supposed to take me to Myrnin... who's going to—'

Amelie spun on her, and there was something wild and terrible in her eyes. 'Little fool, don't bother me with trivia! Go *now*!'

Claire ran.

The house was empty when she arrived. No Shane, no Eve, and she hadn't seen Michael again at the Elders' Council building before Hans and Gretchen had bundled her off. Claire felt very alone, and she locked all the doors and made sure of all the windows.

The house felt...warm, somehow. Not in the hot-air sense, but cosy. Welcoming. Claire put her hand flat on the wall in the living room. 'Can you hear me?' she asked, and then felt stupid. It was just a house, right? Just wood and bricks and concrete and wiring and pipes. How could it hear her?

But she couldn't shake the feeling that the house had

jabbed her awake this morning, her and Shane and Eve. That it had been trying to warn them. The house had saved Michael, after all, when he'd been killed by Oliver; it had given him what life it could, as a ghost. It *wanted* to help.

'I wish you could talk,' she said. 'I wish you could tell me who tried to kill Sam.'

But it couldn't, and she was talking to a dumbass *wall.* Claire sighed, turned away, and caught a glimpse of a piece of paper stirring in a breeze.

A breeze that wasn't there.

The paper was lying on the table, on top of Michael's guitar case. Claire grabbed it and read it, barely daring to believe—

What was she thinking? That the house was going to provide her with the name of Sam's would-be Van Helsing? Of course not. It wasn't an answer to her question.

It was a class schedule printout, stamped AMENDED in big red letters. Her core classes were mostly gone; the notation next to them showed that she'd tested out.

What caught her attention, though, was what had been scheduled in their place. *Advanced Biochem. Philosophical Studies. Quantum Mechanics. Honours Myth and Legend.*

Wow. Was it wrong that she felt her heart skip a beat over that? Claire checked the times, then her watch. She barely had an hour until the first new class, but she couldn't go yet. Not until she'd heard from Shane and Eve.

Thirty minutes later she was on the phone, trying to get somebody to answer her questions at the police station, when she heard the locks rattle on the door and Eve's voice saying, ' – dumbass,' and the knot of fear in Claire's chest began to loosen. 'Yo, Claire! You here?'

'Here,' she said, and hung up to come down the hall towards them.

Eve had her arm around Shane, half supporting him. Claire blinked and focused on his face. At the swelling and bruises. 'Oh God,' she said, and hurried to his side to help Eve. 'What happened?'

'Well, Big Man here decided to get a little shirty with Officer Fenton. You ever see *Bambi Versus Godzilla*? It was like that, only with more punches,' Eve said. She sounded false and bright, like tinsel. 'I tried to take him to the hospital and get checked out, but—'

'I'm fine,' Shane gritted out. 'I've had worse.'

Probably true, but Claire still felt painfully helpless. She wanted to *do* something. Anything. She and Eve got Shane to the couch, where he collapsed against the cushions and closed his eyes. He looked pale, under the bruises. Claire stroked his matted hair anxiously, silently asking Eve what to do; Eve shrugged and mouthed, *Just let him rest.* She looked scared, though.

'Shane,' Eve said aloud. 'Seriously, I don't want to

leave you here alone. You need to go to the hospital.'

'Thanks, *Mom,*' he said. 'It's bruises. I think I'll live. Go on, get out of here.' He reached up and captured Claire's hand, and his dark eyes opened. Well, one of them. The other was swelling shut. 'What happened to you? You OK?'

'Nothing happened, I'm fine. I talked to Amelie.' Claire pulled in a deep breath. 'Sam's going to be OK, I think.'

'And Michael? Michael was all right?' Eve asked.

'Yeah, he was all right. I'm sorry I couldn't get you out any earlier. Amelie—' Probably best not to get into how not-bothered Amelie had been by the idea of Eve and Shane behind bars. 'She was busy with Sam.'

Eve shrugged and shot Shane an exasperated look. 'We probably would've been out of there in ten minutes if he'd behaved himself,' she said. 'Look, Shane, I know you're a hard-ass, but do you have to pick a fight with *every* jerk in the world? Can't you just choose half or something?'

'The scary thing? I *do* only pick fights with half of them. That's how many there are.' He groaned and adjusted himself to a more comfortable position on the couch. 'Crap. Officer Asshole can really hit.'

'Shane,' Claire said, 'really. Are you OK? I can take you to the hospital if you're not.'

'They'd just give me an ice pack and send me home, minus a hundred bucks I don't have.' He caught her hand in his. His knuckles were scraped. 'What about you? Nothing bitten or broken, right?'

'No,' she said softly. 'Nothing bitten or broken. They're angry, and they're worried, but nobody tried to hurt me.' She checked her watch, and her heart skipped and hammered faster. 'Um...I have to go. I have class. You're sure you're—'

'If you ask me if I'm OK again, I'm going to smack myself in the face just to punish you,' he said. 'Go on. Eve, make sure she doesn't go wandering off by herself, OK?'

Eve already had her keys in her hand, and she was jingling them impatiently. 'I'll do my best,' Eve said. 'Hey. This came special delivery for you.' She tossed Claire a package with her name neatly lettered on it. Same handwriting, Claire thought, as the package that had held her bracelet.

This one held a sleek new cell phone, complete with MP3 player and a tiny little flip-open keypad for texting. It was on, and it was fully charged.

The note said, simply, *For safety.* The signature, of course, was Amelie's. Eve saw it, and raised her eyebrows. Claire quickly crumpled it up.

'Do I even want to know what that is?' Shane asked.

'Probably not,' Eve said. 'Claire, little girls who take candy from strangers in Morganville get hurt. Or worse.'

'She's not a stranger,' Claire said. 'And I really need a phone.'

* * *

The classes were nothing like Claire had experienced before. It was as if she'd finally come to school.

From the first moment of the first class, the professors seemed bright, engaged; they seemed to *see* her. Even better, they *challenged* her. She fumbled her way nervously through Advanced Biochem, made notes of the books she needed, and did the same in Philosophy. There was a lot of talking in Philosophy, and she didn't understand half of it, but it sounded a lot more interesting than the droning voices of her core class instructors.

She felt exhilarated by the time her late lunch break rolled around...she felt, in fact, *alive.* She was happy as she hunted for used copies of the textbooks she needed, and even happier when she discovered that, mysteriously, she had a scholarship account set up to cover the costs. It even came with its own cash card.

She bought a new long-sleeve T-shirt, too. And some disposable razors. And some shampoo.

Scary, how good it felt having money in her pocket.

By the time three p.m. rolled around, she was starting to wonder if she was expected to head out for Myrnin's house on her own, but she decided to wait.

Nobody had told her of a change of plan, so she headed over to the UC to get in some study time while she waited. The big main study room was packed, and somebody was playing guitar in the corner of the room – quite a big crowd over there, clapping between songs. Whoever it was played well – something complicated and classical, then a pop song right after. Claire was spreading out her books on the table when she heard a song that sounded familiar, and stood up on her chair to get a better look over the heads of the people gathered in the corner.

As she'd suspected, it was Michael. He was sitting down to play, but she could see his head and shoulders. He looked up and met her eyes, nodded, then went back to focus on the music. Claire jumped down, wiped her dusty footprints off the wooden chair, and sat. Her brain was racing. *Michael* was here. Why? Was it just a coincidence? Or was it something else?

She sat down and tried to concentrate on the properties of low frequency wave modes in magnetised plasma, which was frankly pretty cool. The physics of stars. She couldn't wait for the lab demonstrations... the reading was slow going, but interesting. It linked to another thing about plasma physics that had caught her attention: confinement and transport. It might have been coincidence, but somehow she felt there was something there she ought to understand. Something that related to what Myrnin had been telling her about recomposition, which was a key element in alchemy. Was it possible there really was a link between the two?

Plasma is charged particles. It can be controlled and influenced by shaped magnetic fields. Plasma was the raw state between matter and energy...between one form and another.

Reconstitution.

It hit her, suddenly, what Myrnin had discovered. *The doorways.* They were shaped magnetic fields, holding a tiny, pliable field of plasma held in a steady state. But how did he make them into portable wormholes? Because that was what they had to be, to bend space like that... and the plasma couldn't be regular plasma, could it? Low-heat plasma? Was that even possible?

Claire was so absorbed that she didn't even hear the chair scrape back across from her, didn't know someone had sat down, until a hand grabbed the book propped in front of her and pushed it down.

'Hey, Claire,' said Jason, Eve's nutty brother. He looked weaselly and pale – not Goth-pale, sick-pale. Anaemic. There were crusty sores on his neck, and his eyes were wide and red-veined, and he looked high. Really, crazy high. He also hadn't had a bath or been near a Laundromat in a few days or weeks; he smelt filthy and rotten. Ugh. 'How you doing?'

She couldn't quite think what the right move would be. Scream? She closed the book and held on to it – it was pretty heavy, and would make a decent blunt object – and darted a look around. The UC was filled with people. Granted, Michael's playing was the centre of attention at the moment, but there were plenty of others walking around, talking, studying. From where she sat, Claire could see Eve at the coffee bar, smiling and pulling espresso shots.

It was as though Jason were invisible or something. Nobody was paying him the slightest bit of attention.

'Hi,' she said. 'What do you want?'

'World peace,' he said. 'You're pretty.'

You're really not. She didn't, and couldn't, say it. She just waited. *I'm perfectly safe here. There are a lot of people, Michael's right over there, and Eve...*

'Did you hear me?' Jason asked. 'I said, you're pretty.'

'Thank you.' Her mouth felt dry. She was scared, and she couldn't even think why, really, except what Eve had told her about Jason. He did look dangerous. Those scabs on his throat – had he been bitten? 'I have to go.'

'I'll walk you to class,' Jason said. Somehow, he made that sound filthy, like some porn movie come-on. 'I always wanted to carry some hot college girl's books.'

'No,' she said. 'I can't. I mean...I'm not going to class. But I have to go.' And why couldn't she just tell him to leave her alone? *Why?*

Jason blew her a kiss. 'Go on. But don't blame me when the next dead girl shows up in the trash because you wouldn't do me a simple favour.'

She was in the act of standing up when he said it, and she just...stopped. Stopped moving, and stared. 'What?' she asked, stupidly. Her brain, which had been moving at light speed while skipping from one physics problem to the next, felt sluggish now. 'What did you say?'

'Not that I did anything. But if I had, I'd be planning another one. Unless somebody talked to me and convinced me to stop, for instance. Or I made a deal.'

Claire felt cold. Worse, she felt *alone.* Jason wasn't doing anything – he was just sitting there, talking. But she felt violated, and horribly exposed. *Michael's right over there. You can hear him playing. He's right there. You're safe.*

'All right,' she said, and swallowed a mouthful of what felt like dust and tacks. She sank slowly back into her chair. 'I'm listening.'

Jason leant forward, rested his arms on the table, and lowered his voice. 'See, it's like this, Claire. I want my big sister to understand what she did to me when she sent me to that place. You know what a jail is like in Morganville? It's as though some third-world country threw it out for prisoner abuse. *Eve put me there.* And she didn't even try to save me.'

Claire's fingers felt numb, she was holding her book so tightly. She forced herself to relax. 'I'm sorry,' she said. 'That must have been bad.'

'Bad? Bitch, are you even *listening*?' He kept on staring at her, and, as though he were dead, he never blinked. 'I was supposed to be his, you know. Brandon's. He was going to make me a vampire someday, but now he's dead, and I'm screwed. Now I'm just waiting around for somebody to put me back in jail, and guess what, Claire? I'm not going. Not without a little fun first.'

He grabbed her wrist, and she opened her mouth to scream...

All of a sudden he had a knife, and he was pressing it to her wrist. 'Hold still,' he said. 'I'm not done talking. You move, you bleed.'

She was going to yell anyway, but when it made it to her lips it died into a weak little yelp. Jason smiled, and he tossed a filthy-looking handkerchief on top of her wrist and the knife, covering it up. ‘There,’ he said. ‘Now nobody’s going to notice, not that they’d care. Not in Morganville. But just in case there are any dumbass heroes, let’s keep this between just us.’

She was shaking now. ‘Let me go.’ Somehow, her voice stayed low and steady. ‘I won’t say anything.’

‘Oh, come *on*. You’ll run to your friends, and then you’ll run to the cops. Probably those two dicks Hess and Lowe. They’ve been out to get me since I was a kid, did you know that? Sons of bitches.’ He was sweating. A milky drop ran down the side of his pale face and splashed on his camouflage jacket. ‘I hear you’re in good with the vamps. That true?’

‘What?’ The knife pressed harder against her wrist, hot and painful, and she thought about how easy it would be for him to cut right through her veins. Her whole arm was shaking, but somehow, she managed to hold still against an overwhelming urge to try to yank her wrist away. It would only do the job for him.

‘I’m…yes. I’m Protected. You’ll get in trouble for this, Jason.’

He had a truly creepy smile, a rubbery snarl that didn’t affect his hot, strange eyes at all. ‘I was born in trouble,’ he said. ‘Bring it on. You tell whatever vamp put the mark on you that I know something. Something that could blow this town in half. And I’ll sell it for two things: rights to do whatever I want to my sister, and a ticket out of Morganville.'

Oh God oh God oh God. He wants to bargain. For Eve's life.

'I'm not making any deals,' she said, and knew it was probably a death sentence. 'I'm not going to let you hurt Eve.'

He actually blinked. It made him look almost human, for a second, and Claire remembered that he wasn't much older than she. 'How you going to stop me, cupcake? Hit me with your book bag?'

'If I have to.'

He sat back, staring at her, and then he laughed. Loudly. It was a harsh, metallic clatter of a laugh, and she thought, *Oh God, he's going to kill me*, but then he lifted up the handkerchief covering her wrist and like a magic trick, the knife was gone. There was a trickle of blood dripping from the shallow cut in her skin, and she was starting to feel the burn.

'You know what, Claire?' Jason asked. He got up, stuck his hands in his jacket pockets, and smiled at her again. 'I'm going to like you a lot. You're a scream.'

He strolled off, and Claire tried to get up and see where he was going, but she couldn't. Her knees wouldn't cooperate. He was out of sight in seconds.

Claire looked at the coffee bar. Eve was standing there, motionless, staring right at her with huge dark eyes, and even without the Goth rice powder she'd have been pale as death.

Eve mouthed, *You OK?*

Claire nodded.

She really wasn't, though, and the cut on her wrist wouldn't stop bleeding. She dug in her backpack and found an adhesive bandage – she always kept them, just in case she got blisters on her feet from all the walking. That seemed to do the trick.

She was smoothing it in place when she felt someone standing over her, and jumped, expecting the return of Jason, complete with psycho stabbing attack.

But it was Michael. He had his guitar case in his hand, and he looked – great. Relaxed, somehow, in a way that she'd never really seen him. There was even a slight flush of colour in his face, and his eyes were shining.

But that quickly faded, and he frowned. 'You're bleeding,' he said. 'What happened?'

Claire sighed and held up her wrist to show him the bandage. 'Man, you would be so embarrassed if I said it was something else.' Michael looked blank. 'I'm a girl, Michael, it could have been all natural, you know. Tampons?'

Vampire or not, he was *such* a guy, and his expression was priceless – a combination of embarrassment and nausea. 'Oh crap, I hadn't really thought that through. Sorry. Not really used to this yet. So...what happened?'

'Paper cut,' she said.

'Claire.'

She sighed. 'Don't freak, OK? It was Eve's brother, Jason. I think he just wanted to scare me.'

Michael's eyes widened, and his head turned fast, searching the coffee bar for Eve. When he saw her, the relief that spread over his face was painful and it didn't last long before it curdled into something grim. 'I can't believe he'd come here. Why can't they catch this jerk?'

'Maybe somebody doesn't want to,' she said. 'He's only killing human girls. *If* he's the one doing it.' Although he'd pretty much confessed, hadn't he? And the knife was a big clue. 'We can talk about it later. I need to get—' She remembered, just in time, that she couldn't talk to Michael about Myrnin. 'Get to class,' she said. She hadn't really thought Amelie would make her go alone, and she wasn't sure she could do it. Myrnin was fascinating, most of the time, but then when he turned… no, she couldn't go alone. What if something happened? Sam wouldn't be there to help get him off her.

Michael didn't move. 'I know where you're going,' he said. 'I'm your ride.'

She blinked. 'You're my…what?'

He lowered his voice, even though nobody was paying attention. 'I'll take you where you're supposed to go. And I'll wait for you.'

Amelie had told him, Claire found out on the way to Michael's new car. She'd needed to, apparently; she hadn't trusted any vampire but Sam with the information and access to Myrnin, but Michael had an investment in Claire's well-being, and Sam was going to be out of action for a couple of days at least. 'But he's OK?' Claire asked.

Michael opened the door to the parking garage for her, an automatic gesture that he'd probably learnt from his grandfather, once upon a time. He had some of Sam's mannerisms, and they had the same walk. 'Yeah,' Michael said. 'He nearly died, though. People – vampires – are pretty wired right now. They want the one who staked him, and they don't really care how it happens. I made Shane promise to keep his ass inside, and not to go out alone.'

'You really think he'll keep his word?'

Michael shrugged and opened the door of a standard-issue, dark vampire-tinted sedan, exactly the same as the one Sam had driven. A Ford, as it happened. Nice to know the vamps were buying American. 'I tried,' he said. 'Shane doesn't listen to much of anything I have to say. Not anymore.'

Claire got into the car and buckled in. As Michael climbed in the driver's side, she said, 'It's not your fault. He's just not dealing with it very well. I don't know what we can do about that.'

'Nothing,' Michael said, and started the car. 'We can't do anything about it at all.'

It was a short drive, of course, and as far as Claire could tell from the dimly seen streets outside, Michael took the same route Sam had to the alley, and Myrnin's cave. Michael parked the car at the kerb. When she got out, though, Claire realised something, and bent to look into the dim interior of the car, then ducked back inside.

'Crap,' she said. 'You can't come inside, can you? You can't go out in the sun!'

Michael shook his head. 'I'm supposed to wait out here for you until the sun goes down; then I'll come in. Amelie said she'd make sure you were safe until then.'

'But—' Claire bit her lip. It wasn't Michael's fault. There were about three hours of sun left, so she was just going to have to watch her own back for a while. 'OK. See you after dark.'

She closed the car door. When she straightened she saw that Granma Katherine Day was on the porch of her big Founder House, rocking and sipping what looked like iced tea. Claire waved. Granma Day nodded.

'You bein' careful?' she called.

'Yes ma'am!'

'I told the queen, I don't like her putting you down there with that thing. I told her,' Granma Day said, with a fierce stab of her finger for emphasis. 'You come on up here and have some iced tea with me, girl. That thing down there, he'll wait. He don't know where he is half the time, anyway.'

Claire smiled and shook her head. 'I can't, ma'am. I'm supposed to be there on time. Thank you, though.' She turned towards the alley, then had a thought. 'Oh…who's the queen?'

Granma made an impatient fly-waving gesture. '*Her*, of course. The White Queen. You're just like Alice, you know. Down the rabbit hole with the Mad Hatter.'

Claire didn't dare think about that too much, because the phrase *Off with her head!* loomed way too close. She gave Granma Day another polite smile and wave, hitched her backpack higher on her shoulder, and went to night school.

CHAPTER EIGHT

Amelie had made sure she was safe, all right. She'd done it by locking Myrnin up.

Claire dropped her backpack at the bottom of the stairs – where it was easy to grab in mid-run – and spotted a new addition to the lab: a cage. And Myrnin was inside it.

'Oh my God—' She took a few steps towards him, navigating around the usual haphazard stacks of books, and bit her lip. It was, as far as she could tell, the same cage that the vampires had used to lock up Shane in Founder's Square – heavy black bars, and the whole thing was on wheels. Vampire-proof, hopefully.

Whoever had locked Myrnin in had been nice enough to give him a whole pile of books, and a comfy (if threadbare) tangle of blankets and faded pillows. He was lounging in the corner on the cushions, with a pair of old-fashioned, Benjamin Franklin-style glasses perched on the end of his hooked nose. He was reading.

'You're late,' he said, as he turned a page. Claire's mouth opened and closed, but she couldn't think of a thing to say. 'Oh, don't fret about the cage. It's for your precaution, of course. Since Samuel isn't here to watch over you.' He turned another page, but his eyes weren't moving to follow text. He was pretending to read, and somehow that was worse than heartbreaking. 'Amelie's idea. I can't say that I really approve.'

She finally was able to say, 'I'm sorry.'

Myrnin shrugged and closed the book, which he dropped with a bang on the pile next to him. 'I've been in cages before this,' he said. 'And no doubt I will be let out once your appointed guardian is here to chaperone. In the meantime, let's continue with our instruction. Pull a chair close. You'll excuse me if I don't get up, but I'm a bit taller than—' He reached up and rapped the bars overhead. 'Amelie tells me you have enrolled in advanced placement classes.'

Claire gratefully took that as an opportunity not to think about how disturbingly reassuring this was, seeing him locked up like an animal in a cage, because of *her*. She read off her class schedule, and answered his questions, which were sharply worded and a strange mix of expert knowledge and complete ignorance. He understood philosophy and biochem; he didn't know anything at all about quantum mechanics, until she explained the basics, and then he nodded.

'Myth and Legend?' he echoed, baffled, when she read

off the class title. 'Why would Amelie feel it necessary… ah, no matter. I'm sure she has reason. Your essay?' He held out his hand. Claire dug the stapled computer printout from her bag and handed it over. Six pages, single spaced. The best she could do on the history of a subject she was only just now starting to understand. 'I'll read it later. And the books I gave you?'

Claire went to her backpack and pulled them out, then came back to her chair. 'I read through *Aureus* and *The Golden Chain of Homer*.'

'Did you understand them?'

'Not…really.'

'That's because alchemy is a very secretive field of study. Rather like being a Mason…are there still Masons?' When she nodded, Myrnin looked oddly relieved. 'Well, that's good. The consequences would be quite terrible, you know, if there weren't. As to alchemy, I can teach you how to translate the codes that were spoken and written, but I'm more concerned that you learn the mechanics than the philosophy. You do understand the methods outlined in the texts for constructing a calcining furnace, yes?'

'I think so. But why can't we just order what we need? Or buy it?'

Myrnin flicked the silver ring on his right hand into the bars of his cell, setting up a metallic ringing. 'None of that. Modern children are fools, slaves to the work of others, dependent for everything. Not you. You will learn how to build your tools as well as use them.'

'You want me to be an *engineer*?'

'Is it not a useful thing for one who studies physics to understand such practical applications?'

She stared at him doubtfully. 'You're not going to make me get an anvil and make my own screwdrivers or anything, are you?'

Myrnin smiled slowly. 'What a good idea! I'll consider it. Now. I have an experiment I'd like to try. Are you ready?'

Probably not. 'Yes sir.'

'Move that bookcase—' He pointed to a leaning monstrosity of shelves that looked ready to collapse. It was groaning with volumes, of course. 'Push it out of the way.'

Claire wasn't at all sure the thing would hold together to *be* pushed, but she did as he said. It was better built than it looked, and to her surprise, when she'd pushed it aside, she found a small arched doorway. It was secured with a big heart-shaped iron lock.

'Open it,' he said, and picked up the book he'd dropped upon her entrance, leafing randomly through the pages.

'Where's the key?'

'No idea.' He flipped faster, frowning at the words. 'Look around.'

Claire looked around the lab in complete frustration. 'In *here*?' Where was she supposed to start? It was all piles and stacks and half-open drawers, nothing in any order at all that she'd been able to determine so far. 'Can you give me a hint, at least?'

'If I remembered, I would.' Myrnin's voice was dry, but just a little sad, too. She shot him a glance out of the corner of her eye. He folded the book closed again and stared out of the cage – not at her, or at anything, really. There was a careful blankness to his face. 'Claire?'

'Yeah?' She pulled open the first drawer near the door. It was full of bottles of what looked like dust, none of them labelled. A spider scuttled frantically out of sight into the darker recesses, and she made a face and slammed it shut.

'Can you tell me why I'm in this cage?' He sounded odd now, strangely calm with something underneath. Claire pulled in a deep breath and kept looking in the drawers. She didn't look directly at him. 'I don't like cages. Bad things have happened to me in cages.'

'Amelie says you have to stay in there for a while,' she said. 'Remember? It's to help us.'

'I don't remember.' His voice was warm and soft and regretful. 'I'd like to get out of here. Could you open it, please?'

'No,' she said. 'I don't have the—'

Keys, except that she did. There was a ring of them sitting right there in front of her, half-hidden by a leaning tower of loose, yellowing pages. Three keys. One was a great big iron skeleton key, and she was instantly almost sure that it fit the big heart-shaped lock on the door behind the bookcase. The other one was newer, still big and clunky, and it had to be the key to Myrnin's cage.

The third was a tiny, delicate silver key, like the kind that opened diaries and suitcases.

Claire reached out for the key ring and pulled it towards her, trying to do it silently. He heard, of course. He got up from the corner of the cage and came to the front, where he held on to the bars. 'Ah, excellent,' he said. 'Claire, please open the door. I can't show you what you need to do if I'm locked in this cage.'

God, she couldn't look at him, she just couldn't. 'I'm not supposed to do that,' she said, and sorted out the big iron skeleton key. It felt cold and rough to her fingers, and old. Really old. 'You wanted me to open this door, right?'

'Claire. Look at me.' He sounded so *sad*. She heard the soft ringing chime of his ring on the bars when he gripped them again. 'Claire, *please*.'

She turned away from him and put the key into the heart-shaped lock.

'Claire, *don't open that*!'

'You told me to!'

'*Don't!*' Myrnin rattled the bars of his cage, and even though they were solid iron, she heard them rattle. 'It's *my* door! *My* escape! Come here and release me! *Now*!'

She checked her watch. Not enough time, not nearly enough; it was still at least an hour to sunset, maybe more. Michael was still stuck in the car. 'I can't,' she said. 'I'm sorry.'

The sound Myrnin made then was enough to make her glad that she was across the room. She'd never heard a lion roar, not in person, but somehow she imagined that it would sound like that, all wild animal rage. It shredded her confidence. She closed her eyes and tried not to listen, but he was talking; she couldn't understand what he was saying now, but it was a constant, vicious stream in a language she didn't know. The tone, though – you couldn't *not* get the evil undercurrents.

He'd kill her if he got hold of her now. Thank God, the cage was strong enough to...

He snarled something low and guttural, and she heard something metal snap with a high, vibrating sound.

The cage wasn't strong enough.

Myrnin was bending the bars away from the lock.

Claire spun, key still in her hand, and saw him rip at a weak point in the cage as though it were wet paper. How could he do that? How could he be that strong? Wasn't he hurting himself?

He was. She could see blood on his hands.

It came to her with a jolt that if he got out of that cage, he could do the same thing to *her*.

She needed to get out.

Claire moved around the lab table, squeezed past two towering stacks of volumes, and tripped over a broken three-legged stool. She hit the floor painfully, on top of a pile of assorted junk – pieces of old leather, some bricks, a couple of withered old plants she guessed Myrnin was saving for botanical salvage. Man, that hurt. She rolled over on her side, gasping, and climbed to her feet.

She heard a long, slow creak of metal, and stopped

for a fatal second to look over her shoulder.

The cage door was open, and Myrnin was out. He was still wearing his little Ben Franklin glasses, but what was in his eyes looked like something that had crawled straight out of hell.

'Oh crap,' she whispered, and looked desperately towards the stairs.

Too far. *Way* too far, too many obstacles between her and safety, and he could move like a snake. He'd get there first.

She was closer to the door with the lock on it than the stairs, and the key was still clutched tightly in her hand. She'd have to abandon her book bag; no way to get to it now.

She didn't have time to think about it. The cut Jason had put on her wrist was still fresh; Myrnin could still smell it, and it was ringing the dinner bell loud and clear.

She kicked stacks of books out of the way, jumped over the pile of junk, and, with the key outstretched, raced for the locked door. Her hands were shaking, and it took two tries to get the oversized key into the hole; when she started to turn it there was a terrible moment of utter panic because *it wouldn't turn…*

And then it did, a smooth metallic slide of levers and pins, and the door swung open.

On the other side was her own living room, and Shane was sitting on the couch with his back to her, playing a video game.

Claire paused, utterly off balance. That couldn't be real, could it? She couldn't be seeing him, right there, but she could hear all of the computerised grunts and punches and wet bloody sounds from whatever fight game he had on. She could *smell* the house. Chilli. He'd made chilli. He still hadn't taken some of his boxes back upstairs. They were piled in the corner.

'Shane,' she whispered, and reached out, through the doorway. She could feel something there, like a slight pressure, and the hair on her arm shivered and prickled.

Shane put the game on pause, and slowly stood up. 'Claire?' He was looking in the wrong place; he was looking up, at the staircase.

But he'd heard her. And that meant she could just step right through and she'd be safe.

She never got the chance.

Myrnin's hand landed on her shoulder, dragged her back, and as Shane started to turn towards them, Myrnin slammed the door and turned the key in the lock.

She didn't dare move. He was crazy; she could see it. There was nothing in him that recognised her at all. Amelie's warnings screamed through her head, and Sam's. She'd underestimated Myrnin, and that was what had got all the other would-be apprentices killed.

Myrnin was shaking, and his broken hands were crunched into fists. His blood was dripping on an open copy of an old chemistry textbook that lay by his feet.

'Who are you?' he whispered. The accent she'd noted the first time she'd met him was back, and strong. Really strong. 'Child, what brings you here? Do you not understand your danger? Who is your Patron? Were you sent as a gift?'

She closed her eyes for a second, then opened them and looked right into his eyes and said, 'You're Myrnin, and I'm Claire; I'm your friend. I'm your friend, OK? You should let me help you. You hurt yourself.'

She pointed to his injured fingers. Myrnin looked down, and he seemed surprised, as if he hadn't felt it at all. Which maybe he hadn't.

He took two steps backward, ran into a lab table, and knocked over a stand that held empty glass test tubes. They fell and shattered on the dirty stone floor.

Myrnin staggered, then sank down to sit against the wall, his face covered by bloody hands, and began to rock back and forth. 'It's wrong,' he moaned. 'There was something important, something I had to do. I can't remember what it was.'

Claire watched him, still scared to death, and then sank down to a crouch across from him. 'Myrnin,' she said. 'The door. The one I opened. Where does it go?'

'Door? Doorways. Moments in time, just moments, none of it stays; it flows like blood, you know, just like blood. I tried to bottle it, but it doesn't stay fresh. Time, I mean. Blood turns, and so does time. What's your name?'

'Claire, sir. My name's Claire.'

He let his head fall back against the wall, and there were bloody tears running down his cheeks. 'Don't trust me, Claire. Don't ever trust me.' He bounced the back of his head off the wall with enough force to make Claire wince.

'I... No, sir. I won't.'

'How long have I been your friend?'

'Not that long.'

'I don't have friends,' he said hollowly. 'You don't, you know, when you're as old as I am. You have competitors, and you have allies, but not friends, never. You're too young, far too young to understand that.' He closed his eyes for a moment, and when he opened them, he looked mostly sane. Mostly. 'Amelie wants you to learn from me, yes? So you are my student?'

This time, Claire just nodded. Whatever the fit was, it was leaving him, and he was empty and tired and sad again. He took off his glasses, folded them, and put them in the pocket of his coat.

'You won't be able to do it,' he said. 'You can't possibly learn quickly enough. I nearly killed you tonight, and next time I won't be able to stop. The others—' He stopped, looked briefly sick, and cleared his throat. 'I'm not... I wasn't always like this, Claire. Please understand. Unlike many of my kind, I never wanted to be a monster. I only wanted to learn, and this was a way to learn for ever.'

Claire bit her lip. 'I can understand that,' she said.

'I... Amelie wants me to help you, and learn from you. Do you think I'm smart enough?'

'Oh, you're smart enough. Could you master the skills, given enough time? Perhaps. And you'll have no choice in the matter; she'll keep you coming until you learn, or I destroy you.' Myrnin slowly lifted his head and looked at her. Rational again, and very steady. 'Did I remind you not to trust me?'

'Yes, sir.'

'It's good advice, but just this once, ignore it and allow me to help you.'

'Help...?'

Myrnin stood up, in that eerie boneless way that he seemed to have, and rummaged around through the glass jars and beakers and test tubes until he found something that looked like red salt. He shook the container – it was about the size of a spice jar – and opened it to extract one red crystal. He touched it to his tongue, shut his eyes for a second, and smiled.

'Yes,' he said. 'I thought so.' He recapped it and held it out to her. 'Take it.'

She did. It felt surprisingly heavy. 'What is it?'

'I have no idea what to call it,' he said. 'But it'll work.'

'What do I do with it?'

'Shake a small amount into your palm, like so.' He reached out for her hand. She pulled away, curling her fingers closed, and Myrnin looked briefly wounded. 'No, you're right. You do it. I apologise.' He handed her the shaker and made an encouraging gesture. She hesitantly turned the shaker upside down over her palm. A few red chunky crystals poured out. He wanted her to keep going, so she did, making quick jerks with the container until there was maybe half a teaspoon of the stuff piled up.

Myrnin took the shaker from her, set it back where he'd found it, and nodded at her. 'Go on,' he said. 'Take it.'

'Excuse me?'

He mimed popping it into his mouth.

'I...um...what is it, again?'

This time, Myrnin rolled his eyes in frustration. 'Take it, Claire! We don't have much time. My periods of lucidity are shorter now. I can't guarantee I won't slip again. Soon. This will help.'

'I don't understand. How is this stuff supposed to help?'

He didn't tell her again; he just pleaded silently with her, his whole expression open and hopeful, and she finally put her hand to her mouth and tentatively tasted one of the crystals.

It tasted like strawberry salt, with a bitter after-flavour. She felt an instant, tiny burst of ice-cold clarity, like a strobe light going off in a darkened room full of beautiful, glittering things.

'Yes,' Myrnin breathed. 'Now you see.'

This time, she licked up more of the crystals. Four or five of them. The bitterness was stronger, barely offset by the strawberries, and the reaction was even faster. It was as though she'd been asleep, and all of a sudden she was awake. Gloriously, dizzyingly awake. The world was so sharp she felt as though even the dull battered wood of the table could cut her.

Myrnin picked up a book at random and opened it. He held it up in front of her, and it was like another burst of light in the darkness, brilliant and beautiful, *oh, so pretty*, the way the words curved themselves around each other and cut into her brain. It was painful and perfect, and she read as fast as she could.

The essence of gold is the essence of Sun, and the essence of silver is the essence of Moon. You must work with each of these according to its properties, gold in the daylight, silver in the night…

It all made sense to her. Total sense. Alchemy was nothing but a poet's explanation of the way matter and energy interacted, the way different surfaces vibrated at different speeds; it was physics, nothing but physics, and she could understand how to use it now.

And then…then it was as though the bulbs all dimmed again.

'Go on, take it,' Myrnin said. 'The dose in your hand will last for an hour or so. In that time, I can teach you a great deal. Enough, perhaps, for us to understand where we should be going.'

This time, Claire didn't hesitate licking up every last bit of the red crystals.

* * *

Myrnin was right; the crystals lasted for a little more than an hour. He took some as well, one at a time, carefully measuring them out and making them last until finally even a red crystal couldn't drive the growing confusion out of his eyes. He was getting anxious by the end. Claire started closing the books and stacking them up on the table – the two of them were sitting cross-legged on the floor, practically buried in volumes. Myrnin had jumped her from one book to another, pulling out a paragraph here, a chapter there, a chart from physics, and a page from something so old he had to teach her the language before she could understand.

I learnt languages. I learnt...I learnt so much. He'd shown her a diagram, and it hadn't been just a diagram – it had been three-dimensional and as intricate as a snowflake. Morganville hadn't just happened; it had been planned. Planned around the vampires. Planned *by* the vampires, carried out by Myrnin and Amelie. The Founder Houses, they were part of it – thirteen bright, hard nodes of power in the web, holding together a complex pattern of energy. It could move people from one place to another, via the doorways, although Claire didn't yet understand how to control them. But the web could do more. It could change memories. It could even keep people away, if Amelie wanted it to do that.

Myrnin had shown her the journals, too, with all his research conducted over the last seventy years into the vampire's sickness. It was chilling, the way his notes degenerated from meticulous to scrawls at the end, and sometimes into nonsense.

Some part of her still wondered if she shouldn't just stand by and let it happen, but Myrnin...what he knew, what he'd accomplished – and she'd never learnt so much, never, not from anyone.

Maybe just a little. *Maybe I could help him just a little.*

The influence of the crystals was dimming now, and Claire felt horribly tired. There was a steady ache in her muscles, a feverish throb that told her this stuff wasn't exactly kind to the human body. She could feel every heartbeat pounding through her head, and everything looked so *dark*. So...so confusing.

She felt a breath of air stir against her cheek, and she turned towards the stairs. Michael was descending, moving faster than she'd ever seen him, and he came to a fast halt when he saw her sitting beside Myrnin.

'He's supposed to be—'

'Locked up in a cage? Yeah, I know.' Claire knew she sounded bitter. She didn't care. 'He's sick, Michael. He's not an animal. And anyway, even if you lock him up, he'll get out.'

Michael looked young to her, all of a sudden, although he was older than she was. And a vampire, on top of that. 'Claire, get up and come to me. Please.'

'Why? He's not going to hurt me.'

'He can't help what he does. Look, Sam told me how many people he's killed—'

'He's a *vamp*, Michael. Of course he's—'

'How many he's killed *in the last two years*. It's more than all the other vampires in Morganville combined. *You're not safe*. Now, get up and walk over here.'

'He's right,' Myrnin said. He was losing it, Claire could see that, but he was desperately hanging on to being the man who'd been with her for the last hour.

The gentle, funny, sweet one, ablaze with excitement and passion for showing her his world. 'It's time for you to go.' He smiled, showing teeth – not vampire teeth. It was a very human kind of expression. 'I do all right on my own, Claire, or at least there's rarely anyone for me to harm. Amelie will send someone to look after me. And I usually can't leave here, once I...forget things. It's too difficult for me to find the keys, and I can't remember how to use them once I have them. But I never forget how to kill. Your friend is right. You should go, please. Now. Continue your studies.'

It was stupid, but she hated leaving him like this, with all the light going out in his eyes and the clouds of fear and confusion rolling in.

She didn't mean to do it; it just happened.

She hugged him.

It was like hugging a tree; he was so surprised, he was as stiff as a block of wood. She wasn't actually sure how long it had been since anybody had touched him like this. For a second he resisted her, and then his arms went around her, and she felt him heave a great sigh. Still not a hug, not really, but it was as close as he was likely to get.

'Go away, little bird,' he whispered. 'Hurry.'

She backed away. His eyes were strange again, and she knew they were out of time. *Someday, he won't come back. He'll just be the beast.*

Michael was beside her. She hadn't heard him cross the room, but his hand closed around hers, and there was real compassion in his face. Not for Myrnin, though. For her.

'You heard him,' Michael said. 'Hurry.'

She bumped into the table, and the small jar of red crystals shuddered a little, nearly tipping over. She grabbed it to put it back upright, and then thought, *What if he loses this? He loses stuff all the time.*

She would only be keeping it safe, that was all. It helped him, right? So she ought to make sure he didn't knock it over or throw it away or something.

She slipped it into her pocket. She didn't think Myrnin saw, and she knew Michael didn't. Claire felt a hot burst of something – shame? Embarrassment? Excitement? *I should put it back.* But really, she'd never find it again if he moved it around. Myrnin wouldn't remember. He wouldn't even know it was gone.

She kept looking back, all the way up the stairs. By the time they were halfway out, Myrnin had already forgot them, and he was restlessly flipping through a pile of books, muttering anxiously to himself.

Gone already.

He looked up at them and snarled, and she saw the hard glint of fangs.

She hurried to the door at the top of the stairs.

Chapter Nine

Michael wasn't talking to her, and that was bad. He wasn't sullen, like Shane got from time to time; he was just thoughtful. That made the drive uneasily quiet. It was fully dark out, not that she could see through the window tinting, anyway.

The world didn't seem real to her anymore, and her head ached.

'This is the deal you made with Amelie,' Michael said. 'To work for him.'

'No. I made the deal with Amelie; *then* she told me to work for him. Or learn from him.'

'Is there a difference?'

Claire smiled. 'Yeah. I don't get paid.'

'Brilliant plan, genius. Is *anybody* paying you?'

Actually, she had no idea. The thought hadn't occurred to her, to ask Amelie for money. Was that normal, to get paid for a thing like this? She supposed it was, if she was supposed to risk her life with Myrnin on a regular basis. 'I'll ask,' she offered.

'No,' Michael said grimly. '*I'll* ask. I want to talk to Amelie about this whole thing, anyway.'

'Don't get all older-brother on me, Michael. It's not safe. You may be one of them now, but you're not—'

'One of them? Yeah, I know that. But you're way too young for this, Claire, and you don't know what you're doing. You didn't grow up in this town; you don't understand the risks.'

'What, death? I understand that one pretty well already.' She was feeling tired and achy, but also strangely annoyed with Michael's protectiveness. 'Look, I'm fine, OK? Besides, I learnt a lot today. She'll be happy, trust me.'

'Amelie's mood isn't what bothers me,' Michael said. 'It's you. You're changing, Claire.'

She looked straight at him. 'Like you haven't?'

'Cheap shot. Look, I'm sick of having to tiptoe around Shane. Don't make me do it with you, too.' Ah, now Michael was annoyed, too. Great.

'Tell you what? I'll stop nagging you about your life if you'll stay out of mine. You're not my brother, you're not my dad—'

'No,' he interrupted. 'I'm the guy who says if you get to stay in the house.'

He wouldn't. He *wouldn't*. 'Michael—'

'You made a deal with Amelie without talking to anyone, and then you covered it up. Look, the only reason you even came clean was because I saw the bracelet. If I hadn't, you'd still be lying to us. That doesn't exactly make you the ideal housemate.' Michael paused for a second. 'And then there's Shane.'

'How am I to blame for *Shane*?'

'You're not. But I can't deal with both of you, not now. So just straighten up, Claire. No more lying, and no more risk-taking, all right? I'll convince Amelie to let you out of these sessions with Myrnin. You're too young to be doing this; she ought to know that.'

No more lying. No more risk-taking. Claire shifted and felt the bottle in her pocket, and had a flash of that perfect clarity again. She wondered what Michael would have to say about her letting Myrnin give her the crystals. Probably nothing. He was talking about throwing her out of the house, right? So he probably didn't care at all.

The car slowed and turned, then bumped down a rutted drive. Home.

Claire bolted before Michael could say anything else to her.

Shane was in the kitchen, pouring himself a beer. He toasted her silently, took a sip, and nodded towards a pot on the stove. 'Chilli,' he said. 'Extra garlic.'

Michael was closing the kitchen door, and he sighed. 'When is this going to stop?'

'When you quit sucking blood?'

'Shane—'

'Don't get pissy. I made yours garlic-free.' Shane

looked at her again, and frowned a little. 'You OK?'

'Sure. Why wouldn't I be?'

'Just… I don't know. Whatever.' He slung an arm over her shoulders and kissed her on the forehead. 'Bad day, probably.'

Let's see, she'd been threatened by Eve's brother, had her wrist cut, and then played keep-away with Myrnin for hours. Did that qualify as a bad day in Morganville? Probably not. No body count.

Not yet, anyway.

Michael pushed past them and through the door into the living room. Claire pulled free of Shane's arm and went to the stove to ladle herself a bowl of chilli. It smelt hot and delicious. But mostly hot. She tasted a drop and nearly choked; was it usually this molten-lava wicked spicy? Everything felt raw to her right now. She supposed that was a side effect of the crystals.

'I thought I heard you,' Shane said. 'Weirdest thing, I heard your voice today. Right out of the air. I thought you… I kept thinking about Michael, how he used to be during the daytime…'

When he was a ghost. 'You thought I was—?'

'I thought maybe something happened,' he said. 'I called your cell number, the new one.'

She'd left it in her backpack. Claire reached down and unzipped the pocket, then checked the phone. Three calls, all from Shane. With voice mails. 'Sorry,' she said. 'I didn't hear it. Guess I need to turn the ringer up.'

He looked at her very steadily, and she felt the cold spot in her centre, the place that had chilled while she'd been with Myrnin, slowly warm. 'You worry me,' he said, and put his hand on her cheek. 'You know that, right?'

She nodded, and hugged him. Unlike Myrnin, he was warm and solid, and his body just moulded right into hers, perfect and sweet. When he kissed her she tasted beer and chilli, but only for a second. After that, it was pure Shane, and she forgot all about Myrnin, and any kind of physics except friction. Shane backed her up against the stove. She felt the low heat of the burner at her back, but she was too preoccupied to worry much about bursting into flames from outside sources. Shane just had that effect on her.

'I missed you,' he whispered, brushing her damp lips with his. 'Want to go upstairs?'

'What about my chilli?'

'Get it to go.'

There were good things about the way she felt tonight, she decided; her nerves might be raw, but that only made his touch all the sweeter. She would have felt awkward, usually, and uncertain, and scared, but it seemed like the afternoon that had started with Jason and ended with Myrnin's snarl had burnt all that out of her.

'Not hungry,' she said breathlessly. 'Come on.'

She felt as wild and free as a little kid, running up the steps with Shane in hot pursuit, and when he grabbed her around the waist, spun her around into his room, and kicked the door shut, she squealed in delight. And wiggled to fit herself against his warm, hard body as she kissed him again, breathless and flying.

He kissed as though their lives depended on it. As though it were an Olympic event and he intended to earn a medal. Somewhere in the back of her head she was chattering to herself, warning that this was going to go too far, that she was just making things worse for both of them, but she couldn't help it. Before long they were stretched out together on Shane's bed, and his big, warm hands were teasing under the hem of her shirt, stroking the fluttering skin of her stomach and stealing her breath. She lost it all when he spread his fingers out, pressing his palm flat against her, and she felt an almost irresistible impulse to feel those hands all over. Everywhere. Her heart was hammering hard enough to make her dizzy, and it was all just so...

Perfect.

She reached down and pulled up her shirt. Slowly, feeling the cool air slip over tender skin.

Up, to the bottom line of her bra. Then up.

Shane stopped.

'I want to,' she whispered against his mouth. 'Please, Shane. I want to.' She sat up and reached for the clasp on her bra, and unhooked it. 'Please.'

He pulled back from her and sat up, head down. When he looked up he licked his lips, and his eyes were wide and dark, and she could fall into them, fall for ever.

'I know,' he said. 'Me too. But I made promises, and I'm going to keep them. Especially the one to your parents, because your dad said he'd hunt me down like a dog.' Shane gave her a wild, bitter smile. 'Sucks to be me.'

'But—' She felt her bra slipping, and quickly grabbed to hold it in place. She felt ridiculous now, and wounded.

He sighed. 'Don't, Claire. It's not like I'm a saint or anything; I'm not, and trust me, for you, a saint would buy a condom and go to confession. But it's not about that. It's about keeping my word, and around here, my word is all I've got.'

She wanted him with a red fury that was all out of character for her, but somehow, the way he said it, the way he looked her straight in the eyes, she felt all that fall away and the fury turn into something pure, hot, and silver.

'Besides,' Shane said, 'I'm all out of condoms, and I hate confession.'

He put his arms around her and hooked her bra with an ease that showed he had plenty of practice.

She threw a pillow at him.

Somebody was rummaging around outside the house.

Claire woke up with a start, instantly tense, as she heard the distant rattle of metal. She rolled out of bed and peeked out of the blinds. Her bedroom window looked out on the back, a glorious corner vantage point, and she had a clear view of the fence, and the trash cans on the other side.

Somebody was definitely out there, a black shape in the moonlight. Claire could see him moving around but couldn't tell what he was doing. She reached for her cell phone and dialled 911, and told the operator she needed either Joe Hess or Travis Lowe. Detective Lowe picked up the call, sounding wide-awake even at three in the morning; Claire described what she was seeing in a whisper, as if whoever was across the yard might hear her.

'It's probably Jason,' she said. She heard the scratch of pen on paper on the other end of the phone.

'Why Jason? Can you see his face?'

'No,' she admitted, 'but Jason told me – he practically admitted it. About the dead girl. I think it's Jason, honest.'

'Did he threaten you, Claire?'

The cut on her wrist was still throbbing. 'I guess you could say so,' she said. 'I was going to tell you about it, but I…I had things to do.'

'More important than keeping us in the loop? Never mind. What happened?'

'Shouldn't I tell you when you get here?'

'Patrol car's already en route. Where did you see him today?'

'At the university,' she said, and told the story. He didn't interrupt her, just let her talk, and she could hear him continuing to take notes.

When she paused for breath, Lowe said, 'You know that was stupid, right? Look, next time you see him, you start screaming bloody murder. And put me and Hess on speed dial. Jason's nobody to play around with.'

'But…we were in public. He wouldn't have—'

'Ask Eve about why he ended up in jail in the first place, Claire. Next time, don't hesitate. This isn't about you being strong; this is about you living through the day, all right? Trust me.'

She swallowed hard. 'I do.'

'Is he still there?'

'I don't know. I can't see him. He might've gone.'

'The patrol car ought to be there in just a couple of seconds; they're doing a silent approach. You see them yet?'

'No, but my room faces the alley.' Something moved in the yard, and she felt a lurch of pure adrenalin. 'I think…I think he's in the yard now. Coming to the house. To the back.'

'Go wake up Michael and Shane. Make sure Eve's OK. Go now, Claire.'

She wasn't dressed, but she supposed it didn't really matter; the oversized T-shirt she was wearing came to her knees, anyway. She unlocked her door and swung it open, and yelled in shock.

Tried to, anyway. She couldn't quite get the sound out, because Oliver's hand clapped over her mouth, spun her around, and dragged her backward over the threshold. She screamed, but it was barely a buzz in her throat. Her bare heels scraped on the wood as she tried to get her feet under her, but he had her helpless and off balance. She dropped the phone.

She could hear Lowe's voice distantly whispering her name, but it was blotted out by Oliver's soft voice in her ear as he bent close and said, 'I only want to talk. Don't make me hurt you, girl. You know I will if you force me.'

She went still, breathing hard. Had *he* been out there in the yard? How had he got up here so fast? Didn't the protections on the house keep him out?

No. They only work against uninvited humans now, because Michael's – Michael's a vampire. Oliver had some way in and out. Easy access. *God.*

'Good girl. Stay quiet,' Oliver whispered. He looked up and down the hall, moved the painting next to the doorway, and pressed the hidden switch. The secret doorway across from Eve's room opened with a soft sigh, and he dragged her inside, then shut it. No knob on the inside. The release switch was up a flight of stairs, and he'd never let her get there if she tried to run. When he let her go, Claire stayed where she was.

He let his voice return to normal levels. Not afraid of being overheard, not here. 'I thought it was time we had a talk. You signed an agreement with Amelie. That hurts me, Claire. I thought we had a special friendship, and after all, I did offer first.' Oliver smiled at her, that cold and oddly kind smile that had suckered her in the first few times she'd met him. 'You turned me down. So why, I wonder, did you decide that Amelie would be a better choice?'

He might know about Myrnin, but not what Myrnin did. Amelie had been pretty specific: he could *never* know that.

'She smells better,' Claire said. 'And she made me cookies.' Somehow, after the day she'd had, Oliver just didn't seem all that terrifying anymore.

Until he bared his fangs, and his eyes went a strange, wide black. 'No games,' he said. 'The room's soundproofed. Amelie used to play with her victims here, you know. It's a killing jar, and you're inside. So perhaps you should be more polite, if you intend to see morning.'

Claire held up her left wrist. The golden bracelet glinted in the light. 'Bite it, Oliver. You can't touch me. You can't touch anybody in this house. I don't know how you got in, but—'

He grabbed her right wrist and ripped away the bandage covering the cut Jason had made. It broke open, and a red trickle ran from it down the interior of her arm.

Oliver licked it off.

'OK, that's just *gross*,' Claire said faintly. 'Let go. *Let go*!'

'You belong to Amelie,' he said, and let her go. 'I can taste it. Smell it on you. You're right, I can't touch you, not anymore. But the others, you're wrong about them. While they're in the house they're safe, but not out there, not in *my* town. Not for long.'

'I made a deal!'

'Did you? Did you see in writing that your friends would be protected from all attacks? Because I very much doubt that, little Claire. We've been writing agreements for thousands of years, and you're only sixteen years old. You have no idea what kind of deal you've made.' Oliver actually sounded a little sorry for her, and that *was* scary. He folded his arms and leant against the door. He was in his usual good-guy disguise tonight: a tie-dyed T-shirt, battered cargo pants, his greying, curling hair pulled back in a pony-tail. He'd probably just closed up Common Grounds, she figured. He smelt like coffee. She wondered what Oliver wore on his days off, if he wasn't trying to intimidate. Pyjamas? Fuzzy slippers? One thing she'd figured out about the vampires in Morganville, they were never exactly what they seemed to be, even the bad ones.

'Fine,' she said, and backed away from him until her heels hit the first step. She sat down. 'You tell me what I've done.'

'You've upset the balance of power in the town, and that's a terrible thing, little Claire. You see, Amelie intended to be queen of this little kingdom. She thought I was safely dead when she did so. When I came here a year ago, many people decided that they'd rather listen to me than to her. Not all, of course, and not even a majority. But she's won no real friends during her long existence, and it isn't only the humans who are trapped here, you know. It's the vampires as well.'

This was a new idea to her. 'What are you talking about?'

'We can't leave,' he said. 'Not without her permission. As I said, she fancies herself the cold White Queen, and most are content to let her. Not all. I was working to come to some...arrangements with her, to let a number of us leave Morganville and set up a community outside of her influence. Things had been static here for fifty years, you see, since she made the last vampire. Now Amelie feels the need to protect her position. She's blocked me. She won't allow me to make a move without her permission.' He lowered his chin and stared at her, and it chilled her deep inside. 'I don't like to be controlled. I tend to get... unhappy.'

'Why are you talking to me? What can I do?'

'*You*, stupid little child, are her pet. When you want something, she indulges you. I want to know why.'

Amelie hadn't exactly indulged her the last time they'd talked, although the cell phone sitting abandoned in her room might argue otherwise. 'I don't *know*!'

'She thinks you have something she needs, or she'd hardly bother. She's seen whole cities die without shedding a tear or lifting a finger. It's not altruism.'

Myrnin. It's about Myrnin. If I weren't learning from him...She couldn't say that, didn't even dare to really think it through. Oliver was unnerving, and sometimes he seemed downright psychic. 'Maybe she's lonely.'

He laughed, a harsh bark of sound with no amusement in it. 'She certainly deserves to be.' He took a step forward. 'Tell me why she needs you, Claire. Tell me what she's hiding, and I'll make a deal, a perfectly straightforward one: I'll give your friends my direct Protection. No one will hurt them.'

She didn't say anything this time; she just looked back at him. She didn't dare *not* look at him; even when she was watching him she had the eerie feeling that somehow he was creeping up behind her, ready to do something awful to her when she least expected it.

Oliver made a sound of deep frustration. 'You stupid, stupid girl.' He shoved past her, going up the stairs so lightly the wood hardly even creaked. After a second, the hidden, knobless door sighed open. Claire got up, steadied herself for a second, and then stepped out into the hallway. Nobody else had heard a thing, apparently. It was quiet as the grave.

Oliver's hands closed around her shoulders, and he moved her out of his way by simply picking her up and putting her down, as if she weighed nothing. He didn't let go once he'd done it; he stepped up behind her, bent down, and whispered, 'Not a sound, Claire. If you wake your friends and they come against me, I'll destroy you all. Understand?'

She nodded.

She felt the cold pressure of his hands go away, but not his presence, and she was surprised when she looked back and saw that he was gone.

As if he'd never been there at all.

She pressed the button behind the painting, and the

hidden door sealed itself. Then she picked up her phone from the floor of her bedroom. The call had ended; Travis Lowe was probably on his way over, burning sirens all the way.

She sat down to wait for the panic to start.

There just had to be something out there in the alley, given the response. It wasn't only a couple of cops, some yellow tape, and a write-up in Captain Obvious's underground newspaper; it looked, from Claire's window, like a full-blown *CSI*-style investigation, with people in white jumpsuits collecting evidence and everything. There was a big blocky van with heavily tinted windows that she guessed housed vampire detectives or forensics people or something, with the emblem of the Morganville police on the side, and she guessed the majority of people roaming around in Michael's backyard this morning were, in fact, the undead.

Crime-solving undead. That was new.

She wasn't sure what she was feeling anymore. Light-headed, disconnected, looped. Last night had felt like a dream, and it had passed in a blur from the time she and Shane had come upstairs until she'd heard the rattle of trash cans in the alley.

Someone was ringing the doorbell downstairs. She didn't move away from the window – couldn't seem to convince herself to move at all, in fact. It was probably the cops. Travis Lowe had, as she'd thought, already come racing to the rescue, but on finding her unfanged and still alive, he'd called in the full-on police assault.

So those were probably the detectives, Gretchen and Hans, or maybe Richard Morrell coming to take her statement.

Claire looked down at herself. *I should probably get dressed.* Her wrist was a mess, smeared with slow-leaking blood, and she pressed her T-shirt against it before she could think about what she was doing. Great, now she wasn't only undressed, she was undressed in bloody nightclothes.

It took ten minutes to shower, change, and bandage up her arm, and then she padded down the stairs in bare feet to face the music.

Her housemates were all standing in the living room, and they all looked at her with identical expressions, blank enough that she came to a stop on the steps. 'What?' Claire asked. 'What'd I do now?'

Michael stepped aside so Claire could see who was sitting cross-legged in the chair, flipping through a bubble-gum pink edition of *Teen People*.

Monica Morrell.

She was dressed in a tight-fitting pink top with diamonds that spelt out BITCH/PRINCESS, and white short-shorts that even Daisy Duke would have thrown out as too trashy. Her tan was deep and dark, and she was lazily dangling a pink flip-flop with a yellow flower on top from her perfectly manicured toes.

'Hey, Claire!' she said, and stood up. 'I thought we could grab some breakfast.'

'I...what?'

'Break...fast,' Monica said, drawing out the word. 'Most important meal of the day? Do you even *have* parents?'

Claire felt ridiculously off balance. 'I don't understand. Why are you here?'

Shane leant against the wall, glaring at Monica. He had a serious bed-head thing going on, and Claire wanted to run her hands through his thick, soft hair and return it to its usual shaggy mess. 'What a good question. The second best one being, who let her inside? And we're going to have to throw out that chair. The smell's never coming out.'

'I let her in,' Michael said quietly, and that got him a stare from Shane. 'Lay off the daggers. It was better to let her in than have her pitch a fit on the porch with all the cops around. We've already got enough trouble.'

'What's this *we*, paleface? I mean that in the vampire sense, not—'

'Shut up, man.'

Claire rubbed her forehead, feeling her headache blooming back to hot, throbbing life. She ignored Michael and Shane with an effort and focused on Monica, who had a malicious smile curving her lips. 'You're enjoying this,' Claire said. Monica shrugged.

'Of course. They're jackasses to me most of the time; it's nice to see them take it out on each other for a change. Not that I care.' Monica arched one perfectly groomed eyebrow. 'So? I know you like coffee. I've seen you drinking it.'

Eve stepped in between them, and for a second Claire thought her friend honestly looked...dangerous. 'You're not taking Claire anywhere. And you're sure not taking her anywhere near that son of a bitch,' she said.

'Which son of a bitch would that be, exactly? Because hey, she lives *here*. It's not like she's choosy about who she hangs out with.'

Eve bunched up a fist, and for a second Claire thought she was going to haul off and slug Monica right in her perfect, pouty mouth. But Eve checked herself. Barely.

'You *so* need to leave our house,' Eve said. 'Now. Before something bad happens that I won't really regret.'

Monica gave her a look. 'I'm sorry, were you talking? Because I think I dropped off. Claire? I'm not here to banter with the mentally challenged. I'm just trying to be friendly. If you don't want to go, just say so.'

Claire felt ridiculously like laughing, it was so weird. Why was this happening to her?

'What do you really want?' she asked, and Monica's lovely, crazy eyes widened. Just a little.

'I want to talk to you without the Losers Club hanging over my shoulder. I figured we could have breakfast, but if you're allergic to caffeine and pastry...'

'Anything you can say to me, you can say in front of

my friends,' Claire said. That brought *both* of Monica's eyebrows up.

'Oooookay. Your funeral,' she said, and glanced at Shane. 'So where was your boyfriend last night after midnight?'

'Who? *Shane?*' What time had she left his room, anyway? Late. But...not after midnight.

'None of your damn business where I was,' Shane said to Monica. 'Eve told you to get out. The next step is I throw your skanky ass and see if you bounce when you hit the porch. I don't care whose pet you are; you don't come here and—'

'Shane,' Monica interrupted with elaborate calm, 'shut the hell up. I saw you, idiot.'

Claire waited for Shane to give her a biting comeback, but he just sat there. Waiting. His eyes had gone very dark.

'They don't know, do they?' Monica continued, and tapped her rolled-up copy of *Teen People* against her hip. 'Wow. Shocker. Bad boy keeps secrets. That *never* happens.'

'Shut up, Monica.'

'Or you'll *what*? Kill me?' She smiled. 'There wouldn't even be DNA left when they were done with you, Shane. And the rest of you, too. *And* your families.'

'What's she talking about?' Eve asked. 'Shane?'

'Nothing.'

'*Nothing*,' Monica mocked. 'Deny everything. That's

a brilliant plan. Then again, it's what I'd expect from someone like you.'

Michael was frowning at Shane now, and Claire couldn't resist, either. Shane's dark eyes darted to each of them in turn, Claire last.

'The cops aren't going to find any bodies out there in the alley. And they're not going to find one anywhere else in your house,' Monica said, 'because Shane moved a body last night, out the back door.'

Shane *still* wasn't saying anything. Claire covered her mouth with her hand. 'No,' she said. 'You're lying.'

Monica folded her arms. 'Why exactly would I do that? Why would I admit to hanging around watching your house unless I had to? Embarrassing! Look, if I'm lying, all it takes is for him to deny it. Ask him. Go on.' She was staring right at Shane.

Shane's eyes narrowed, but he didn't say anything. For a frozen second or two, nobody moved, and then Michael said, '*Christ*, Shane, what the hell?'

'Shut up!' Shane snapped. 'I had to! I thought I heard something down in the basement last night, when I was getting some water in the kitchen. So I went to check it out. And—' He stopped, and Claire saw his Adam's apple bob as he swallowed, hard. 'She was dead down there. At the bottom of the stairs, as if somebody had just…thrown her. For a second I thought it was' – he glanced at Eve, then away – 'I thought it was you. I thought you'd tripped and fallen down the stairs or something. But when I got down there, it wasn't you.

And she was dead, not just knocked out.'

Eve sank down on the arm of the sofa, looking as stunned as Claire felt. 'Who? Who was it?'

'I didn't recognise her. Some college girl, I guess. She didn't look local and she wasn't wearing a bracelet.' Shane took in an audible deep breath. 'Look, we've been in enough trouble as it is. I had to get rid of her. So I wrapped her up in one of the blankets out of the boxes down there and carried her out. I put her in the trunk of your car—'

'You *what*?' Michael snapped.

'And I drove her to the church. I left her there, inside. I didn't want to just...dump her. I thought' – Shane shook his head – 'I thought it was the right thing to do.'

Monica sighed. She was checking out her fingernails with exaggerated boredom. 'Yeah, yeah, touching. The point is, when I saw you, you were hauling a dead chick into the trunk of *his* car. And I just can't *wait* to tell my brother. You know my brother, right? The cop?'

Unbelievable. 'What do you *want*?' Claire practically yelled it at her.

'I told you. Breakfast.' Monica gave her a sunny movie-star smile. 'Please. If you say yes, I just could forget all about what I saw. Especially since I was, you know, out after curfew, and I don't want to get asked about why. Think of it as mutually assured destruction.'

It sounded like a deal, but it wasn't, not really. Monica had all the cards, and they had none. None at all.

'There's no body in the alley,' Claire said. 'The police

aren't going to find anything. You're sure?'

'Don't think so, but wouldn't that suck for you if they did?' Monica shrugged, puckered her lips, and blew Shane a mocking kiss. 'You've got guts, Shane. No brains, but a whole lot of guts. You thought it out, right? Now that Michael's one of the chosen undead, humans can't get in this house without an invitation. So you have to either blame it on a vampire, or face up to the fact that one of you killed her. Either way, it's not going to be pretty, and somebody's going down.' She held up her hand. 'I vote for Shane. Anybody else?'

'Leave him alone!' Claire said sharply. 'You want to go out, fine. We'll go. No, don't you even start!' Eve hadn't even had a chance to do more than open her mouth, and now she shut it, fast. 'You guys work it out between the three of you. I won't be long. Believe me, I probably won't be able to keep anything down, whatever I manage to eat.'

Monica nodded, as if she'd known it would happen all along, and did a runway model's walk down the hall towards the front door. From the back, her shorts were barely legal.

And however much they hated her, Shane and Michael were watching her go.

'Guys,' Claire muttered, and grabbed her backpack.

Claire hadn't been inside Common Grounds in a while, but it hadn't changed. It was bohemian, warm, packed to the gills with college types grabbing their morning ventiwhatever, and if Claire hadn't known better – known very well – she'd never have believed that the nice, smiling hippie type behind the counter was a vampire.

Oliver locked gazes with her and nodded slightly. His face stayed pleasant. 'Nice to see you back,' he said. 'What'll it be?'

Much as she hated to admit it, he made the best drinks in town. Better than Eve, actually. 'White mocha,' she said. 'With whip.' She managed to hold back from adding anything more, because she didn't like being nice to him. God, he'd been licking blood off her wrist two hours ago! The least she could do was not say *please* and *thank you*.

'No charge,' he said, and waved away the five dollar bill she dug out of her jeans pocket. 'A welcome-back present, Claire. Ah, Monica. Your usual?'

'Half-caf no foam double pump latte, with pink sugar,' she said. 'In a real cup, not that foam stuff.'

'A simple yes would suffice,' he said. As Monica started to turn away, he reached out and grabbed her wrist. He did it in such a way that nobody but Claire would notice, but it was unmistakably threatening. 'She doesn't pay. You do, Monica. You may think of yourself as a princess, but trust me, I've met them, and you don't qualify.' He grinned just a little, but there was no humour in his eyes. 'Well, perhaps *met* isn't quite the right word.'

'Eaten?' Claire supplied acidly. His smile turned darker.

'Oh, the charm and eloquence of the younger

generation. It does warm my heart.' Oliver let go of Monica's arm and stepped away to make the drinks. Monica backed away, looking flushed. She threw a dirty look at Claire – *Yeah, like it's my fault*, Claire thought and stalked to the table in the corner. The one the deceased vampire Brandon had once staked out – pun intended – as his own. There were two young college girls sitting there, with books and papers piled up. Monica folded her arms and took up a belligerent pose.

'You're in my chair,' she said. 'Move.'

The two girls – shorter and pudgier than Monica – stared up with saucer-huge eyes. One of them stammered, 'Which one of us?'

'Both,' Monica snapped. 'I like my space. Get out.'

They gathered up papers and books and hurried away, nearly dumping coffee all over Claire in their haste to go. 'Did you have to do that?' Claire asked.

'No. It was just fun.' Monica sat, crossed her smooth tanned legs, and patted the table. 'Come on, Claire. Have a seat. We have so much to talk about.'

She didn't want to, but it was stupid to stand there, looking obvious. So she sat, dumped her backpack on the floor next to her feet, and concentrated on the scarred wood of the tabletop. She could see Monica's flip-flop living up to its name as the other girl casually jiggled her foot. Ridiculously, it reminded her of Myrnin.

'That's better.' Monica sounded way too pleased with

herself. Not cool. 'So. Tell me all about it.'

'About what?'

'Whatever Amelie's got you doing,' Monica said. 'Your super-secret stuff. I mean, she picked you for a reason, and it's not for your charm and good looks, right? Obviously. It's for your brains. You don't have any family here; you've got nothing anybody wants other than that.'

Monica was smarter than she looked. 'Amelie's not asking me to do anything,' Claire lied. 'Maybe she will later, I don't know. But she hasn't yet.' She nervously twisted the gold bracelet circling her left wrist. It was starting to remind her of those bands biologists put on endangered species.

And lab animals.

Monica's eyes were half-closed when Claire risked a glance upward. 'Huh,' she said. 'Really. Well, that's disappointing. I really thought you'd have something good I could use. Oh well. Then let's talk about making a deal.'

'A deal?' First Jason, now Monica. How had Claire stepped into the role of negotiator?

'I want to talk to Amelie about Protection. You can give me an introduction. And a recommendation.'

Claire nearly laughed. 'Ask her yourself!'

'I would, but she won't let me near her. She doesn't like me.'

'I'm shocked,' Claire muttered under her breath.

Monica gave her a long look, one strangely missing the usual hip, ironic, contemptuous features. It looked almost...earnest. 'Since Brandon died, Oliver took over his contracts. The thing is, he's not keeping most of them. He's trading them for favours with other vampires. If I don't make a better deal, there's no telling what could happen to me.' Monica pointed at Claire's bracelet. 'Might as well start at the top.'

Claire drummed her short fingernails on the table, glaring at the bar where it seemed like Oliver was taking for ever to deliver their drinks. It occurred to her to wonder if it was really safe to drink something prepared by a vampire who'd been threatening her just a couple of hours before, but honestly, if Oliver wanted to get her, it wasn't as though it would be hard for him.

And she really wanted the white mocha.

'Oliver's your Patron now?'

'For now. Until he finds something he wants more than holding on to my contract, anyway.'

'Is he behind your asking about why Amelie signed me up?'

'Do I look like I run somebody else's errands?'

Claire glanced back again at the bar. 'Maybe.'

Monica went quiet. It wasn't the comfortable kind of silence, and Claire was glad when Oliver called out their orders. She jumped up to get hers, hesitated, and then picked up Monica's as well. She managed to do it without making eye contact with Oliver. He was just a dark shape at the corner of her eye, and she turned her back on him as soon as she could.

Monica got up, and she looked honestly surprised

when Claire handed her the drink. 'What?' Claire asked. 'It's called being polite; they probably didn't teach you that at home. Doesn't mean I like you or anything.'

Monica seemed to have to think hard about what to say to that, and finally came up with a simple 'Thanks.' Which, Claire had to admit, might have been the nicest thing Monica had ever managed to say to her. Claire gave her a nod and sat down again.

Peace in our time, she thought wryly. And promptly blew it by asking again, 'Did Oliver put you up to it?'

Monica didn't even glance in his direction. 'No.' But somehow, Claire didn't believe her.

'Do you have to do everything he says?' she asked, as if Monica hadn't just lied. And Monica lifted one shoulder in a half shrug. No other answer. 'So you don't really want to talk to me, do you? You've just been told to do it.'

'Not exactly. I thought it was a good chance to get my name in front of Amelie, too.' Monica smiled slightly, and very bitterly. 'Besides, check it out: you're a star. Everybody wants to know about you, vampires and humans. They're looking into your history, your family's history. If you farted in grade school, somebody in Morganville knows it now.'

Claire almost choked on her first mouthful of white mocha. '*What?*'

'The Founder isn't what you might call accessible. And most of the vamps don't understand her any better than we do. They're always looking for clues about who she is, what she's doing here, with this town. This isn't normal, you know. The way they live here.' Monica's gaze flicked to Oliver, then away. '*He's* old enough to know more than most, but he still needs inside information. And the word is, you could be the way to get it. If I can't get Protection from Amelie, at least I can get in good with him if I have something new and valuable to tell him.'

Claire rolled her eyes. 'I'm nobody. And if she cared about me at all – which she doesn't – she'd never let anybody know it. I mean, look how she treats—'

She stopped herself cold, heart suddenly hammering fast. She'd almost said *Myrnin*, and that would have been bad. 'Sam,' she finished lamely. Which was also true, but Monica had to have noticed her stumble.

Which Monica emphasised by waiting for a full ten seconds of silence before she continued. 'Whatever. The point is, you're sort of famous, and by hanging with you, I get seen by the right people doing the right thing, and I do what Oliver wants. Which is all I care about. You're right, I don't care if we're BFFs. We're not going to trade clothes and get matching tattoos. I've got friends. I need allies.' She sipped her complicated drink, her eyes steady on Claire. 'Oliver wants what you know, yeah. And this' – she tapped her own bracelet – 'this says that I do what he says, or else.'

'Or else what?'

Monica looked down. 'You've met him. Best case,

it means he hurts me. Bad. Worst case...he trades me down.'

'That's *worse*?'

'Yeah. That means I get handed to the bottom-of-the-barrel vamps, the ones too lame to get the good earners and the pretty people. That means I'm a loser.' She looked down and fidgeted with her ceramic coffee cup, frowning at it. 'Sounds shallow, maybe, but around here, it's survival. If Oliver blackballs me, I can't get anything but the freaks and the skanks, the ones who get their fix the hard way. They'll kill me, if I'm lucky. If not, I end up some strung-out junkie fang-banger.'

She said it with such dry, matter-of-fact intensity that Claire could tell she'd spent a lot of time thinking about it. It was a long way to fall, from the darling daughter of the mayor to some addict trying to please a kinky freak for protection.

'You could be neutral,' Claire blurted. She felt oddly sympathctic, even after everything Monica had done. She *had* been born here, after all. Not like she'd ever had a real choice in what she was going to be, or do. 'Some people are, right? They're left alone?'

Monica sneered, and the second or two of humanity Claire had imagined she'd seen in that pretty face vanished. 'They're left alone until they're not. Look, officially, they're untouchable because they've done favours, big favours, and their Patrons let them out of contracts. By big favours, I mean the kind they were lucky to live through, get it? I'm not interested in that kind of hero crap.'

Claire shrugged. 'Then go without a contract.'

'Yeah, *right.* That works. I'm really looking forward to a future as second assistant fry wrangler at the Dairy Queen, and decomposing in some ditch before I'm thirty.' Monica rested her elbows on the table, coffee cup cradled in both hands. 'I thought about leaving. I actually went to Austin for a semester, you know? But...it wasn't the same.'

'Meaning you flunked out of school.'

That earned Claire a filthy look. 'Shut up, bitch. I'm here only because I need to be, and you're here only because you have to be. Let's not get too touchy-feely.'

Claire swallowed a mouthful of sweet, rich mocha. If it was poisoned, she'd die happy, at least. 'Fine by me. Look, I can't help you get to Amelie. I don't even know how to get to her myself. And even if I did, I don't think she'd take your contract.'

'Then just shut up and smile. If I don't get anything else out of this wasted morning, at least Oliver can see that I tried.'

'How long do I have to do this?'

Monica checked her watch. 'Ten minutes. Suck it up that long, and I won't call my brother about your boyfriend's little indiscretion.'

'How can I be sure?'

Monica slapped both hands to her cheeks and looked overdramatically horrified. 'Oh no! You don't trust me!

I'm crushed.' She dropped the act. 'I don't care if Shane has opened his own corpse taxi service; I care only about what I can get out of it.'

'Maybe you want revenge,' Claire said.

Monica smiled. 'If I'd wanted that, I'd have already turned him in. Besides, I hear it's best served cold.'

Claire pulled out a book. 'All right. Ten minutes. I need to study, anyway.' Monica sat back and began a running, acidly accurate monologue on the outfits of the girls standing in line for coffee, which Claire tried earnestly not to find funny. Which she was able to do, until Monica pointed out a girl wearing a truly horrible polka-dot-leggings-under-shorts ensemble. 'And somewhere in heaven, Versace sheds a single, perfect tear.'

Claire couldn't control a snort of laughter, and hated herself for it. Monica cocked an eyebrow.

'See?' she said. 'I'm so good I can even charm a hard case like you. It's a waste of my talent, but I need to keep myself sharp.' She finished her coffee and picked up her little pink purse with the *Teen People* magazine sticking out of it. 'Gotta fly, loser. Tell your boyfriend as far as I'm concerned, we're even. Well, OK, I'm a little bit more than even, and that's the way I like it. Consider this his restraining order: if I see him within fifty feet of me, I'll not only tell my brother about Shane's midnight adventure, but I'll get some football types to pay his kneecaps a visit.'

She walked out, hips swaying dangerously. People

got out of her way, and they watched her go. Fear and attraction, in just about equal measure.

Claire sighed. She supposed people always did like that sort of girl, and always would. And secretly? She envied Monica's confidence. Maybe just a little, traitorous bit.

Chapter Ten

The dead girl that Shane had taken to the church was Jeanne Jackson, a sophomore who'd gone missing from a sorority party two nights before. The papers said that she'd been raped and strangled, but nothing about suspects, and no cops showed up to interrogate Shane, much to Claire's relief. He'd done a dumbass thing, but she could understand his paranoia. In Morganville, he was one suspicion away from taking up residence in Jason's old cell, whether he'd actually done anything or not.

That was if the vampires didn't decide to hold their own brand of frontier justice.

Captain Obvious's *Fang Report* had a much more detailed article on the killings, linking the other two that Claire knew about with this one, and speculating that instead of a vampire menace, they might be dealing with a human one this time. He didn't seem as enthusiastic about forming vigilante parties for someone with a pulse, Claire noticed. Not that it mattered to the dead girls which type of monster had killed them.

She got a note from Amelie giving her time off from working with Myrnin for the rest of the week, so she devoted herself to keeping up with classes. They were tougher than she was used to, which was kind of a relief. She loved a good challenge, and the professors seemed to actually care whether or not their students had a clue. Myth and Legend wasn't what she'd expected, not at all; it wasn't Greek gods, or even Native American Trickster stories. No, it was about...vampires. Comparative vampires, actually, examining the literature and folklore from earliest recorded history to the latest vampire-as-hero in pop culture. (Which, now that Claire thought about it, kind of was the modern-day version of myth and legend.) Oddly, for Morganville, the professor wasn't skipping the parts about vampire-killing methods, but Claire guessed that she was one of the few in the class who'd ever know the score about the town, anyway. The rest would bumble cluelessly through their one or two years, transfer out to bigger schools, and never know they'd rubbed elbows at parties with real monsters.

She kept her mouth shut about anything that might get her in trouble, because the professor had a bracelet, too. She was trying to match up glyphs with vampires, and she thought he probably belonged to a female vamp named Susan, who seemed to be into finance. Susan owned a lot of property, anyway, and was some kind of bigwig at the Morganville Bank and Trust.

Claire began keeping notes in a special book about glyphs, vampires, who owned what. Not because she had any agenda, but just because it was interesting, and could be useful someday. She supposed if she'd asked, Amelie would have told her all about it, but it was more challenging to figure it out herself and this way, Amelie couldn't be really sure how much Claire knew, which couldn't be a bad thing. *She's nice when it suits her. That doesn't mean she's nice.*

And on Friday, Eve left a note stuck to the bathroom mirror for Claire to find when she got up.

CB – Don't forget tonight is the party. Objective: look hotter than Monica and make everybody totally forget who threw the party in the first place. Outfit on back of door. Pay me back. – E.

The outfit was nothing Claire would ever, ever, ever have bought for herself. For one thing, the black leather skirt was...short. Like, really short. There were some kind of patterned panty hose and a sheer red shirt with big red roses woven into the fabric in flocked material. And a black cami to go under it.

There was another sticky note attached to the skirt. *Shoes under the cabinet.* Claire looked. They were thick clunky platforms, in her size, in shiny patent leather.

She took it all back into her bedroom and put it down, backed off, and stared at it for a few seconds. *I can't wear that. It's not me.*

Eve would totally mock her if she wore her blue jeans

to the party. And she'd gone to a lot of trouble, because all of this stuff was Claire's size, not Eve's. Even the shoes.

And...it really *would* burn Monica if Claire looked hot. (She'd never be hotter than Monica; that was a fantasy, but still.) Imagining the expression on Monica's face, Claire slowly stroked her fingers down the soft leather of the skirt. *No. I can't.*

And then she imagined Shane's face when he saw her.

Well. Maybe she could, after all.

She hadn't got his expression quite right in her imagination, because the stunned, vacant expression on Shane's face when she started down the stairs was even better than fantasy. His mouth actually *dropped open*. Next to him, Michael turned around, and although she hadn't counted on it, there was a warm fuzzy feeling to making a hot golden-angel vampire blink and give her a quick, involuntary once-over.

Claire stopped on the steps above them and did a tentative hip shimmy. 'OK?' she asked. Shane's mouth shut with a snap, and Michael actually cleared his throat.

'Fine,' Michael said.

'*Fine?*' That was Eve, coming down the stairs behind Claire. She moved around the roadblock and punched Michael in the arm. 'She looks amazing. I'm not half-gay, and I think she's hot.'

Shane wasn't saying *anything*. Claire felt warm and a

little dizzy, the way he was looking at her. She resisted the urge to check to see if her skirt was straight – she'd done it a dozen times already – and forced herself to meet his gaze and smile.

'You sure this is smart?' Shane asked, which was not what she'd expected, not at all. 'You look fantastic.'

'Thanks—'

He interrupted her. '*Fantastic* in this town pops you to the top of the take-out menu.'

She held up her left hand and pointed to her wrist. The gold bracelet was clearly visible. 'I'll be OK,' she said. 'The vamps won't bother me.'

'Not even talking about the vamps. You're going to be drawing every guy there who's looking to get off.'

Eve rolled her eyes. 'Oh, *God*, Shane, buzz kill? She looks great, and you don't have to get all jealous and overprotective about it! She'll be with us; we'll all look out for her. And you've got to admit, girlfriend looks good all cleaned up. I did her hair, too. Smokin', right?' The hair, Claire felt, was just almost over the top. It was mostly gel and sprays and stuff, but it did have that carefully tousled look that models always seemed to wear.

Eve wasn't exactly wallflower quality tonight, either; she was wearing a dramatic, floor-sweeping black dress that left her pale arms bare, plunged a neckline halfway to China, and had a slit in the side that went all the way to her hip. Fishnet hose, even. It was outrageously sexy, and if Michael had noticed Claire's transformation, he was completely focused on Eve now.

Eve winked at him and spun around to show him the back. Of which there wasn't any. It was just her skin, and a crimson rose tattoo at the small of her back.

'Man,' Shane said. 'That's just...yeah.'

It wasn't until she'd got past their reactions – which were pretty fun – that Claire realised that Eve must have done a number on the boys, too...because they looked amazingly fine. Michael was wearing black pants and a black leather coat, and a dark blue silk shirt. It made him just...blaze, like white gold against velvet.

Shane looked good enough to drag back to her room. Eve must have forced him to get the worst of his shag evened up, which brought out his strong cheekbones and chin. He was wearing black, too, with a dark maroon knit shirt. Claire had never seen him in a jacket. She decided he needed to never take it off.

Michael shook his head and offered Eve his arm. She took it, smiling with her red, red lips, and winked at Claire. Claire winked back, suddenly feeling very wicked, and slid her arm through Shane's.

'I can't believe we're doing this,' Shane said.

This was going to be fun.

Claire hadn't forgot the address, even though she'd given away the invitation, and Michael knew Morganville like the back of – Eve's back, the way he kept looking at her exposed skin, especially the tattoo. And besides, if you were within a couple of blocks of the party, you couldn't possibly miss it. Between the glow of the lights and the low-pitched rumble of the music, there was no sleeping through it if you lived nearby.

Michael cruised around the block, looking for parking, and finally located a narrow few feet of kerb. As he pulled in, he said, 'Ground rules. We don't split up. Eve and Claire, you two especially. It's not just because of the vampires; it's because of Jason. Got it?'

They nodded.

'Besides,' Shane said, and playfully tugged at Claire's over-gelled hair, 'I want to see Monica's face when she catches sight of the two of you. Kodak moment.'

Eve fumbled in her tiny little coffin-shaped purse and held up a brand new cell phone, with camera.

'I'm ready.'

'Me too,' Claire said, and pulled out the fancy phone that Amelie had given her. She felt a blast of shame as Shane glanced at it, but controlled it. She couldn't be ashamed all the time, and besides, it wasn't so bad, right? What she was doing? It wasn't any worse than having a day job. Just...different.

'Be careful what you eat and drink,' Michael continued. 'Monica's party is probably roofie heaven. I can smell what they put in the drinks; you guys can't. And if you get into any trouble, step back; let me handle it. If you're going to have a freak vamp friend, you might as well get your money's worth out of it.'

Shane didn't answer, but Claire could see there was some smart-ass remark burning a hole in his tongue. She was glad he didn't let it loose. It was nice to feel like four friends again, instead of four people all about to spin apart in different directions.

'Anything else, Dad?' Eve asked. Michael kissed her, very lightly, sparing her lipstick.

'Yeah,' he said. 'You look good enough to eat. Promise me you'll remember that.'

Claire was caught between a smile and a shiver, and saw that Eve was, too.

The Morrell home looked like Tara from *Gone with the Wind*, post-Sherman's march. Claire watched, blinking, as a mob of drunken frat boys stumbled down the walk, roaring something she couldn't make out, and carrying a *couch*.

The couch they deposited in the giant European-style fountain in front of the house. Apparently they were relocating most of the living room out there. Some partyers were already sitting in chairs, soaking in the fountain's spray, and now three or four of them piled giggling onto the wet couch.

'Now this,' Shane said with respect, 'is out of bounds. I like it.'

It was totally out of control. The four of them stood together by Michael's shiny vampire-tinted car, watching in admiration. The house was blazing with lights, there were lit tiki torches tilting drunkenly all over the lawn, and partyers were *everywhere*. Making out under the trees, in full glare of the security lights. Doing shots on the big, white-columned front steps. A girl ran by, dressed in half a bikini. The top half.

'Damn,' Michael said. 'Monica does know how to throw it.'

No kidding. Claire watched as a big bobtail truck inched its way through a knot of people towards the back of the house. It had the logo of BOB'S FINE LIQUORS. Apparently, Monica had called in liquid reinforcements already, and the night was young.

'Well?' Eve said. 'Are we standing out here all night? Because I'm ready to knock somebody dead.'

The four of them strolled up the walkway, keeping an eye out for frat boys and wandering furniture. They went as a group up the front steps, where about ten people were playing some complicated game that involved drinking shots, spray cans of fluorescent paint, and giggling hysterically. Even the drunkest turned to look at the four of them and whistle.

The frat boys, the drunks in the fountain, and the even drunker people on the porch were all wearing standard college casual dress, mostly shorts and T-shirts. 'Um,' Claire said, 'Maybe we should have come a little less formal.'

'No way,' Eve replied. 'If you're going, go big.'

'Remind me to play poker with you later,' Michael said. 'I love a girl who'll go all in.'

She hip-bumped him. '*That's* what you want to do with me later? Dude. Respect the dress, at least.'

Michael trailed his pale fingers down her back, following the line of her spine, all the way to the red rose.

Eve shivered, and her eyes went half-closed. Whatever Michael whispered in her ear, Claire thought it was probably way too personal to hear.

Not that she could have, because right then the front door banged open and the noise flowed out in a syrup-thick wave of pounding techno and yelled conversations. Two people stumbled out of the door, arms around each other. Claire blinked and recognised two of the gamers whom she'd given Monica's invitation to that afternoon on campus.

'Freakin' awesome party!' one of them screamed, and fell flat on his face.

'Apparently.' Eve stepped over him and swept into the party, with Michael right behind her. Claire started to follow, but Shane's grip on her arm had tightened, and he was holding her back.

'What?' she asked, and turned to face him. God, he looked amazing. He needed to let Eve dress him all the time.

'Before we go in,' he said, and bent and kissed her. Claire distantly heard the whistles and catcalls of the shot drinkers – distantly, because the kiss was sweet and hot and wild, and there was something crazy in it that made her just quiver inside.

He pulled away way too soon. 'Stay with me,' he said, with his lips near her ear, and she nodded. *Like I'd let you out of my sight.*

And then they followed Michael and Eve into the party of the century.

It was the second big party of Claire's life – not counting birthday parties and ones where there were as many chaperones as kids. The first one, the Dead Girls' Dance thrown by the EEK fraternity, hadn't exactly come out well, what with Shane's dad going on a rampage through the place looking for vampires to stake. This one looked, if possible, even crazier.

She was grateful to be with her friends. She couldn't imagine how scary it would be if she'd stepped into this by herself. The main hall was wide and tall, but it was jam-packed with people talking, dancing, kissing, groping – it was like the hottest dance club with all the lights up full. Claire brushed up against a couple who were – what *were* they doing? She looked away before she could be sure, but the guy's hand was in places that she couldn't imagine a porn actress allowing in public.

Michael and Eve pushed through the crowd into the next room, and Claire and Shane followed, staying close. There were a few people in the big living area who were dressed fancy, but most had on standard-issue college wear, and somehow, Claire had the distinct impression the casual-dress crowd had *not* come invited.

Monica was standing at the top of the stairs, arms folded, looking right at them.

'Oooh, that *is* a Kodak moment,' Eve said, and held up her cell phone to snap a photo of Monica's scowl. 'Yep. We're good.'

She high-fived Shane, who seemed to be expecting it. Monica cleared the annoyance out of her expression with an effort and started down the steps. She was dressed in a pink, clinging sheath dress with huge lime-outlined flowers climbing the fabric, and her shoes were prissy-perfect in matching pink. Very fancy.

'Claire, you brought strays,' Monica said. 'How nice.' And then she looked strangely sorry. 'Michael, I didn't mean you. You're always welcome.'

He raised his pale eyebrows. 'I am?'

'Of course.'

Claire elbowed him. 'Because you're a VIP. Vampire Important Person.'

Two more of the gamers Claire had gifted with the invitation stumbled by; one grabbed Claire's arm and planted a sloppy, wet kiss on her cheek. 'We passed out copies,' he said, and giggled. 'Hope that was OK. Great party!'

Shane sighed and moved him off with one hand on his shoulder. 'Yeah, yeah, whatever. Naked Vulcan chick in the next room. Better hurry.'

The gamers sobered up fast, and moved on. Monica's glossy, perfect lips were open, her eyes wide.

'You?' she said. '*You* did this? These idiots made flyers! They put them all over campus! *This was supposed to be the best people!*'

'Don't worry,' Eve said sweetly. 'We're here.' She smiled, which in that lipstick was Wicked-Witch-of-the-West evil. 'Air kiss!' She *mwahed* the air somewhere near Monica's cheek. 'Lovely party. Shame about the furniture. Ta!' She sashayed on, Michael on her arm, as if she were the Queen of Everything, never mind Morganville. Claire got out her camera and captured a picture of the murderous fury on Monica's face as she watched her go.

'You treacherous little *bitch*!' Monica snarled.

Claire lowered the phone and met her eyes for a long second. She wasn't scared, not anymore. 'You got your friends to roofie me and told them I wanted it rough. All I did was recycle your invitation. Let's call it even.'

'Let's call it *not*!'

Shane leant forward, dropped his voice so that Monica had to work to hear it, and said, 'Calm down. You get blotchy when you're angry. And if you call my girlfriend a bitch one more time, I won't be so nice about it.'

Monica's eyes were fierce and fiery, but she didn't move, and after a second she turned and ran up the steps to the second floor, where her formally dressed friends were huddled together like the cast of Survivor: *Abercrombie & Fitch Island*.

'Score one for the little guys,' Shane said. He stared at a bunch of guys wearing football shirts who rumbled past, carrying a bed. Claire blinked. Yes, that was a bed. 'OK, I don't really think I want to know. So. Drinks?'

In the kitchen, a group was making punch in a trash can. Claire hoped it was a new trash can, but as blitzed as the guys were who were pouring stuff in, she really couldn't be sure of that.

'I'd avoid that,' Shane said, his mouth close to her ear. 'See anybody you know?'

She wasn't sure. There was barely room to move in here, with people crowding up to the counters, and streaming in and out with red plastic cups in their hands...

A shock zipped down her spine. 'Yeah,' she said. 'I see somebody.'

How the hell had Eve's brother got into the party? He was standing in a corner, slouching and sneering. Lank hair dripped towards his shoulders, and he wore the same filthy, dangerous-boy clothes that he'd had on when he'd threatened Claire at the UC. He had a drink, but he wasn't drunk; there was too much hot contempt in his eyes as he surveyed the crowd. Crazy eyes. *Oh God, that's how they look, those guys who shoot up rooms full of people.*

His eyes locked with Claire's, and he gave her a bent smile. Claire anxiously looked at Eve, but her back was to her brother and she was talking to Michael; she clearly hadn't seen the potential trouble at all.

'What?' Shane asked.

Claire turned back and pointed.

Jason was gone.

Shane shook his head when she told him, and moved away to talk to Michael. Michael nodded, then handed Eve off to Shane. Claire saw his lips move: *Watch her.*

And then Michael angled off through the crowd.

So much for staying together.

Shane draped his arms over both of their shoulders and said, 'Now this is the life. Want to get a room, girls?'

Eve rolled her thickly mascaraed eyes. 'Like you'd know what to do with one of us, never mind two. Where's he going?'

'Bathroom,' Shane said blandly. 'Even vamps gotta pee.'

Which, for all Claire knew, might be true, but she was sure that wasn't why Michael had cut out on them. Shane steered them up to the counter and snagged a sealed bottled water for Claire and two sealed beers, which he opened himself. *Not taking any chances*, Claire thought, and cracked the top on the bottle to take several gulps of the cool, sweet water. She hadn't realised how hot it was until then, but she could feel sweat sticking her flocked mesh shirt to her exposed skin.

Somebody grabbed her ass. Claire yelped and jumped, then turned and saw a drunk-off-his-butt frat boy leaning in next to her. 'Oh baby, me like!' he yelled in her ear. 'You, me, outside, OK?' He did a drunken pantomime of what he was thinking of doing outside, and she felt a hot roll of embarrassed shame.

'Get lost,' she said, and shoved him off. His buddies tossed him back towards her, and this time, he crashed into her off balance and pushed her up against the bar. He took advantage of it, too, hands all over her, hips grinding her right into the counter.

Shane grabbed him by the collar of his TPU golf shirt, spun him around, and punched him right in the face.

Great, Claire thought in shaken disgust. *That's always the answer around here. Punch somebody.* Then again, she didn't think reasoned discourse was going to be big tonight.

And of course, the guy's friends piled on. Eve grabbed Claire's hand and pulled her out of the way; a tight circle formed around the combat, with people whooping and clapping. 'We have to stop him!' Claire yelled. Eve patted her on the shoulder.

'This is Shane's idea of a good time,' she said. 'Trust me. You do *not* want to try to stop him right now. Let him do his thing. He'll be fine.'

Claire hated it. She hated seeing Shane get hit, and she didn't much like the way his eyes lit up when he was knee-deep in conflict, either. Stupid to be upset by it, she guessed, considering this was part of why she was so attracted to Shane in the first place the way he would unhesitatingly throw himself into things, especially when it came to protecting others.

Eve was practically reading her mind. 'Let him be who he is,' she said. 'I know it's hard, because in general, guys are clueless, and you just want to fix it, but just… let him be. You don't want him trying to change you, right?'

Right. She didn't, although he *was* changing her, whether he knew it or not. *Not in bad ways*, she thought.

Just...change. A year ago she'd have been paralysed with terror at the idea of coming to a party like this, and even more terrified to imagine being groped by a stranger like that.

Now, she was mostly just annoyed, and felt like she needed a shower.

Eve whirled. 'Hey! I know my ass is fine, but look, don't touch!' An eruption of drunken laughter. She took Claire's hand. 'We need a wall behind us. Less chance of getting the stealth feel-up.'

'But—' She gave up as somebody else patted her rear. 'Yeah. OK.'

That put them half a room away from Shane, who was now somehow at the centre of a knot of maybe ten guys, all whaling away at each other (mostly without connecting; they were all too drunk to really do damage). Claire leant gratefully against the wall and sipped water. Somehow, she'd ended up holding Shane's beer, and with a quick sideways glance at Eve, she took a sip of that, too. Ugh. Nasty.

'Acquired taste,' Eve said, laughing at her expression. 'Shane buys like a college boy. If it's cheap and the ad has a girl in a bikini, it must be great.'

'That's disgusting,' Claire said, and took another long drink of water to wash her tongue clean. Even the water tasted bitter, after that.

'Well, in fairness, beer is mostly about the buzz, not the taste,' Eve said. 'You want taste and buzz, you get something like rum and Coke, or White Russians.' She seemed to remember, suddenly, how old Claire was. 'Not that I'm going to let you have any of that, by the way. We promised your parents.' She managed to look almost righteous when she said it, and she took Shane's beer out of Claire's hand. 'I'll keep this.' Eve raised her normally soft voice to a parade-ground bellow. 'Yo, Shane! Quit screwing around or I'm drinking this!'

A ripple of laughter through the room. The fight was mostly over, anyway, and Shane shoved away the last stumbling frat boy who'd tried to take a swing at him, wiped blood from his mouth with the back of his hand, and left the field of battle. He looked rumpled and flushed and a little bit savage, and Claire felt something in her just *growl* in response.

She stared at him, wide-eyed. *I'm not ready for this.*

Parts of her clearly were.

'Have a drink, Galahad,' Eve said, and handed him his bottle. They clinked glass. 'Our hero. Here. Fix your hair.' She picked at it with her black-manicured nails, twitching it this way and that, until it had that glamour-boy, carefully careless look again. 'God, you're hot. Get felt up yet?'

'Couple of times,' he said, and smiled at Claire. 'Don't hurt them. They just couldn't help themselves.'

Eve snorted and looked around. 'Where's Michael?'

'Probably in line at the bathroom.' Shane shrugged. It was probably true, but Claire didn't think that was the reason. Shane did that thing where he looked at Eve too long and didn't blink. She thought she could tell when he was lying, and that definitely was a flashing neon sign. 'Ladies? Let's wander.'

It wasn't so much *wander* as *wriggle*, like salmon heading upstream. What Claire could see of the house was amazing fine art on the walls, gorgeous old furniture (mostly being splashed with drinks or shoved against the walls to make room for dancing), big, expensive Turkish rugs (Claire hoped they were dry-cleanable), and huge plasma TVs that were all playing the same music channel, blasting at ear-piercing volume. Nine Inch Nails' 'Closer' was on now, and despite her best intentions Claire found herself moving to the rhythm. Eve was dancing, too, and then they were dancing together, which should have seemed weird but didn't, really. Shane formed the third point on their triangle, but Claire could see that he wasn't really giving in to the festive atmosphere; he was scanning the crowd, looking for trouble. Or Michael.

Somebody tried to pass her something – a shot glass with a hit of something clear. She shook her head and passed it right back. Not that she wasn't tempted, but after what had almost happened to her at the last party, she wasn't going to be stupid.

Well, not any stupider than she already was to come here in the first place.

The drinks and drugs kept coming. Liquid E, poppers, shots, even something that she was almost sure was a crack pipe. Morganville liked its drugs, but she guessed that made sense. There was a hell of a lot to escape from around here.

She kept on dancing. Shane and Eve didn't take anything, either – not that Claire saw, anyway. Shane was looking less into the party and more worried all the time.

Michael didn't come back. Two songs later – two long songs – Eve finally got Shane to look for him, and the three of them moved out through the bottom floor, checking out the rooms (all packed) and not finding Michael anywhere. In the hall bathroom a line of people was waiting for the toilet, but no sign of a tall, blond vampire.

When they went up the big, sweeping steps towards the second floor, Claire couldn't help but think about *Gone With the Wind*, and Rhett Butler carrying Scarlett. Her mom loved that movie. She'd always thought it was boring, but that scene stayed with her, and she could almost see it in this house. But instead of Scarlett, Monica Morrell was still standing at the top of the steps, surrounded by her protective circle of toadies. Gina and Jennifer were back, each wearing a dress that was plainer than what Monica had on, but in complementary colours. Her very own back-up group. There were a couple of other girls in the crowd, but mostly it was guys – good-looking, polished types. The entitled of Morganville, and every one of them was wearing a bracelet.

'Well,' Monica said. 'Look who's coming up in the world.' Her crowd laughed. Monica's eyes were vicious. If she'd been sort of human when they'd been alone in the coffee shop, she'd got over it. 'Scrubs stay downstairs.

We're going to have to have the place gutted and rebuilt anyway, after this.'

'Yeah, I'll bet Daddy's going to be furious when he gets home,' Eve said. 'I meant to ask, is that dress vintage? Because I could swear I saw it on my mother once.' She swept up, heading straight for one of Monica's big strong linebacker types; he looked confused, and edged out of her way. Shane and Claire followed. Monica was dangerously silent, probably realising that any comeback she could try would sound cheap.

'We're going to have trouble getting out of here,' Shane said. It was quieter upstairs, although the continuing clamour downstairs throbbed through the floor and walls. The hallway was deserted, and all the doors were closed. It was lined with expensive portraits and framed formal photographs of the Morrell family. Not surprisingly, Monica took a lovely picture. Claire had never seen Mrs Mayor, but there she was in the family photos – a wispy, half-ethereal woman always looking somewhere other than her family. Unhappy, somehow. Richard Morrell seemed grounded and adapted to this town, and of course, so did the mayor; Monica might not be stable, but she was definitely Morganville material.

Her mom, maybe not so much.

'Wonder where her parents are?' Claire said aloud.

'Out of town,' Eve said. 'So I heard, anyway. Bet they'll just love getting back to find somebody did an *Extreme Home Makeover: Crackhead Edition.*' She tested the doorknob of the first room on the left. Locked. Shane tried the one on the right, opened it, and leant in. He leant out again, eyebrows arched.

'Well, that's new,' he said. Claire tried to look. He put his big hand over her eyes. 'Trust me, you're not old enough. *I'm* not old enough.' He carefully shut the door. 'Moving on.'

Claire opened the next room, and for a second she couldn't figure out what she was seeing. Once she did, she couldn't speak. She backed up and touched Shane wordlessly on the shoulder and pointed.

There were three guys in the room, and a girl on the bed, and she was passed out. They were taking off her panty hose.

'Shit,' Shane said, and moved Claire back. 'Eve, call the cops. Now. Time to shut this crap down before somebody gets really hurt.'

Eve got out her cell phone and dialled, and Shane went into the room and closed the door. He came back after about a minute with the unconscious girl in his arms. 'Anybody know who she is?'

Claire shook her head. 'What about those guys?'

'They're sorry,' Shane said. 'Eve? You recognise her?'

'Um...maybe. I think I've seen her around the UC... couldn't swear to a name or anything. But she's definitely gown, not town. No bracelet.'

'Yeah, I figured.' Shane adjusted her to a more comfortable angle in his arms. The girl – petite, brunette, pretty – snuggled into his embrace with a sleepy moan. 'Damn it. I can't just leave her.'

'What about Michael? We need to find him!'

'Yeah, I know. Look, I'll carry her. Check the other rooms.'

Claire was having trouble controlling her breathing. She'd almost been that girl, not so long ago. Only she'd been a little more alert, a little more able to take care of herself...

Get it together, she told herself, and opened the next door. She gasped and covered her mouth with both hands, because there was a vampire in the room, and he was bending over a girl lying limp on the floor.

He looked up, and she saw the hard gleam of fangs before his face came into focus and became shockingly familiar.

Michael.

There were two raw holes in the girl's neck, and her open, dry eyes had gone grey. Her skin was the colour of old, wet paper, more blue than white.

'Oh,' Claire whispered, and stumbled backward out of the room. 'Oh no, no, no—'

Michael shot to his feet. 'Claire, *wait*! I didn't—'

Eve was in the doorway now, and Shane. Eve took one look at the dead girl, one at Michael, and turned and ran. Shane just stood there, staring at him, then said quietly, 'Claire. Go after her. Now. The two of you, stay together. I'll come find you.'

Michael took a step towards them. 'Shane, I know you're looking for reasons to hate me, but you know I wouldn't—'

Shane backed up, fast, keeping distance between them. His eyes had gone very dark, his face flushed and set with anger. 'Claire,' he said again. 'Get the hell away from him. *Now.*'

'Shit!' Michael looked furious, but he also looked scared and hurt. 'You *know me,* Shane. You know I wouldn't do this. Think!'

'You come near me or the girls, I will kill you,' Shane said flatly, and then turned and yelled at Claire, full volume. '*Go!*'

She backed out of the room and ran after Eve. Her heavy platform shoes felt awkward, and her cool outfit was nothing but a cheap dress-up costume. She wasn't cool. She wasn't sexy. She was a stupid jerk to be here, and now Michael...God, he couldn't have, could he? But there was a flush to his skin, as though he'd fed...

Eve was heading down a set of back stairs. Claire caught sight of the sweep of her long black dress around the spiral. She followed as fast as she dared, with the treacherous shoes. As she neared ground level, the volume of the party swelled and broke into a roar.

When she got to the bottom of the steps, there was no sign of Eve anywhere. It was a sea of moving, swaying bodies, a drunken orgy of dancing (and maybe, in the corners, just an orgy), but she didn't see anybody in formal wear.

'Eve!' She yelled, but even she couldn't hear it. She looked back up the stairs but she didn't see Shane, either.

She was alone.

When she craned her neck, she caught a flash of black velvet heading out of a door, and threw herself into the crowd to follow. If drunks groped on her way by, she barely noticed; she wanted out of here, badly, and she couldn't let anything happen to Eve. Her dignity was the least of her worries.

A hand slipped under her skirt. She turned, instinctively furious, and slapped the guy, hard. Didn't even register his face, or anything about him. He held up his hands in surrender, and she turned and plunged on.

The next room was nearly empty for some reason that Claire didn't understand, until she saw (and smelt) some guy throwing up in the corner. She hurried faster. *Was* that Eve she was following? She couldn't be sure. It looked like her, but the glimpses were too short, the angles all wrong. Claire had to move quicker.

She wasn't sure how it happened, but she ended up in the vast, gleaming kitchen. A bunch of burly guys were carrying in boxes of liquor. Claire pushed past two frat guys who were high-fiving each other. 'Liquid panty remover's here!' one of them yelled, and there was a cheer in the other room.

Claire made it outside and gulped the cool, clear night air. She was shaking, sweating, and she felt utterly filthy, inside and out. That was *fun*? Yeah, she supposed if she were drinking and didn't care, it'd be fun, but then again, this was Morganville. Fun like that, you could end up passed out on a bed with strangers...or in a morgue drawer.

Eve was leaning against a tree in the glare of a security light, gasping for breath. She looked glamorous, like some lost Hollywood starlet from the days of black and white, except for the red blaze of her lipstick.

'Oh God,' she moaned, and as Claire came towards her she realised she was crying. 'Oh God, he's done it; he's really done it—'

'We don't know that,' Claire heard herself say. 'Maybe he just found her. Was trying to help her.'

Eve glared at her. 'He's a *vampire*! There's a *dead girl with holes in her neck*! I'm not stupid!'

'I can't believe he'd do it,' Claire said. 'Come on, Eve, do you? Really? You know him. Is he a killer? Especially when he doesn't have to be?'

Eve shook her head, but that wasn't really an answer. She was shaking off the question.

Shane came out of the kitchen door with the brunette still held in his arms. 'Let's go.'

'We came in Michael's car,' Eve said numbly. 'He has the keys. I could—'

'No. Nobody goes up there, and you guys stay the hell away from Michael until we know what's going on.' Shane thought for a second, then pulled in a breath. 'We walk.'

'Walk!' Claire and Eve both blurted. Eve improved it by squeaking, 'Are you freaking *mental*?'

'Claire's got Protection, and I'm in the mood to beat

the hell out of the first vamp to look at me sideways, and it's safer than getting the three' – he glanced down at the nameless girl in his arms – 'four of us in the car with Michael right now. I want room to run if I have to. And fight.'

'Shane—'

'We walk,' he interrupted. 'University first, we can drop this one off with the campus cops.'

Claire cleared her throat. 'Can't we wait for the police here?'

'Trust me, no,' Eve said. 'They're going to roust everybody that isn't tagged, and that includes me and Shane. And once they find a drained dead girl, it'll be a free-for-all. We can't take the chance. We need to go. Now.'

Claire was half hoping that Michael would show up, but he didn't come out after them. She wondered why. She wondered where he'd been, while they'd been searching the house for him.

Shane started walking towards the street, with the drugged girl murmuring and giggling in his arms. He'd saved one victim, but lost another. And he was taking that second part very personally.

Claire looked at Eve, put her arm around her, and hurried the both of them after Shane.

It was a quiet walk to the university campus. They didn't see anybody. The few cars that passed didn't stop, and although they heard sirens converging on the party, none of the police cars cruised their way.

The night was just cool enough to be pleasant, and the air felt dry and crisp. No clouds. It would have been pretty and romantic, except for the general crappiness of the evening. Eve had stopped crying, but that was almost worse; she'd been so happy before, and now she'd sunk into a gloom so deep she really did seem like a true Goth.

Claire's feet hurt. She was glad when they turned the corner and caught sight of the big, well-lit campus behind the wrought-iron fencing. They'd have to go to one of the four entrances to get through. She'd never really thought about it before, but the place looked unnatural, like a wildlife park.

Or a zoo.

Shane was getting tired, and put the girl down on the first bench they came to once they were inside the fence, while Eve flagged down a passing campus cop car. The Q&A went pretty well, but then, the campus cops weren't especially sharp. It took about half an hour, and then the girl was whisked off to the clinic for detox and check-ups, and the three of them looked at each other in the glow of the cop car's headlights as it backed up and pulled away.

'Right,' Shane said. 'Probably ought to get moving.'

Eve got out her phone.

'What are you doing?' he asked.

'Calling a cab.'

He snorted. 'In Morganville? At night? Right. Eddie doesn't even like picking people up during the daytime.

No way is he risking his ass out here for us at night. He probably took his phone off the hook, anyway. He hates frat parties.'

'What about Detective Hess?' Claire offered. 'I'm sure he'd give us a ride.'

'Light it up.'

Claire tried. The number rang, but nobody picked up. Same thing with Travis Lowe. She looked at Shane with a sinking feeling and shrugged helplessly. Eve stood up, shivered, and crossed her bare arms for warmth. Shane took his black jacket off and draped it around her shoulders.

'Guess we're on foot,' he said, and took Claire's hand, then Eve's. 'Don't slow down, and don't stop for anything. If I tell you guys run, you run. Got it?'

He didn't give them a chance to argue. They walked down the path to the exit from the university grounds. Outside, the street lights were few and far between, and Claire could just feel eyes on her in the shadows. Whether that was real or not, she didn't know, but it made her shake all over with fear. *Come on, Claire, get it together. There are three of us, and Shane can kick enough ass for all of us.*

They crossed the street and headed over a couple of blocks, then down. It was the straightest shot to the house, and the best lit, but it also was going to take them right by Common Grounds. Somehow, Claire felt even more uncomfortable at the idea that Oliver was going to see them trailing by, in all their not-too-smart glory. They'd had a rough enough night without that.

Although, it was a cheering thought that Monica almost certainly was having a worse one, trying to explain to the cops about why there were more drugs in her house than the Rite Aid Pharmacy, not to mention the underage drunken orgies and the dead girl in the bedroom.

By contrast, walking home in darkness in Vampire USA seemed a little bit mild.

At least until Eve whispered, 'Somebody's following.'

Claire almost faltered, but kept walking when Shane's hand tightened around hers. 'Who?' he asked. Eve didn't turn her head.

'Don't know; I just caught a glimpse. Somebody in dark clothes.'

Since only Amelie seemed to like colours in the pale winter hues, Claire figured that didn't narrow it down much. She walked faster, tripped over a crack in the sidewalk and nearly went down, if it hadn't been for Shane's steadying grip. But it slowed them all down, and they couldn't afford for it to happen again.

'Crap,' Shane breathed. They were still at least a block from the next burning street light, and now Claire could hear slow, steady footsteps behind them. Up ahead, a single open storefront spilt warm yellow light onto the street. Common Grounds. Neutral territory, at least theoretically. 'Right. We're not going to make it all the way home. We go into Common Grounds, and—'

'No way, I'm not going in there!' Eve blurted. 'I can't!'

'Yes you can; you have to. Neutral ground. Nobody

will hurt you there. We can make some kind of deal with Oliver if we have to, temporary protection or something. Promise me—'

Shane didn't have time for anything else, because all hell broke loose. The footsteps behind them suddenly accelerated to a run, Shane swung around and pushed the two girls behind him, and there was a flash of movement Claire couldn't really see. Something hit Shane in the head. Hard. He stumbled and went down to one knee.

Claire screamed and reached for him, but Eve grabbed her and hauled her by force towards the glow of Common Grounds.

'Get up!'

Claire twisted out of Eve's grip and whirled to see that the yell had come from the jerk from the party, the one who'd felt her up and then got his ass kicked by Shane. He'd followed them, and he had a baseball bat. He'd hit Shane in the head *with the baseball bat* and he was getting ready to do it again.

'No!' Claire cried, and lunged back towards them, but Eve grabbed her tightly and swung her around towards the coffee shop again.

'Get inside!' she screamed.

'Let go—'

They stopped fighting each other as a shadow stepped out of the alley, right in front of them, blocking the way.

A long silver line glinted in the starlight. A knife.

It was Eve's brother Jason, looking as greasy and starved and fevered as he had at the party.

'Hey, sis,' he said, and the knife turned, and turned, and turned. 'I knew you'd be coming this way. Soon as I heard you left the party without your blood-sucking bodyguard, I knew the time was right.'

'Jason' – Eve let go of Claire and stepped in between the two of them – 'this isn't her problem. Let her go.'

Claire was torn – watch Jason, who was terrifying, or pay attention to what was happening behind her, because Shane was fighting now, fighting for his life, and he was already hurt. She risked a glance back and saw Shane grab the baseball bat from his attacker, hit a home run to the guy's shoulder, and send him spinning into the brick wall. The frat guy went down, screaming, but Shane was clearly not doing well, either – he lurched, off balance, and went down to his hands and knees. The bat rolled away.

'Oh God,' Claire whispered. There was blood running down his face, dripping in a wet thread to the pavement. '*Shane!*'

Shane shook his head, and the blood flew in a spray, splattering the concrete around him. He looked up, saw her, and blinked.

Then he saw Eve, and behind her, with the knife, Jason.

Shane fumbled for the bat, found it, and climbed to his feet. He stumbled forward, grabbed Claire and pushed her behind him, then yanked Eve away from Jason, as well. He set his feet wide apart and took up a batting stance.

He looked pale and shaken and half-dead, but Claire knew he wasn't backing down.

'Leave them alone,' he said. Not a yell, not a threat, just a low, quiet voice with absolute control. 'Walk away, Jason.'

Jason lost his smile. He put the knife in his pocket and held up his hands. 'Sure. Sorry, man. Don't go all Sammy Sosa on me.' He lowered his hands again and stuffed them in his coat pockets, looking casual, but there was an avid glitter to his eyes, and a cruel twist to his thin lips. 'I heard you found a present in your basement. Something girl-shaped.'

Eve groaned, and Claire reached out to steady her when she swayed. 'Jason,' Eve whispered, and she looked awful, as though she was going to throw up. 'Oh God, *why*?'

Shane took a step forward, bat raised and ready, and Jason backed up again. 'Doing it there, that was just fun,' he said. 'But it's not about the girls. I had to show them I was ready.'

'Ready?' Eve echoed. 'Oh *God*, Jase, is that what this is about? You're just some pathetic wannabe vampire making his bones?' Eve sounded so freaked it made Claire's guts knot up. 'You're trying to *impress* them? By killing?'

'Sure.' Jason shrugged. He looked thin and weedy, almost lost inside that black leather jacket. 'How else do you get attention around here? And I'm going to get *lots* of attention. Starting with you, Claire.'

Shane yelled – it wasn't even words, just a yell of pure

fury – and swung at him. Jason jumped back, faster than Claire would have expected, and the bat missed him. Then he lunged forward. Shane was off balance, not really steady on his feet, but that wouldn't matter; if Jason was crazy enough to want to go hand-to-hand with Shane, it was all over.

Wasn't it?

Jason punched Shane low in the stomach, and Shane made a surprised sound and took a step back from him.

Shane was *backing away*...

And then Claire saw the knife in Jason's hand, glittering silver and red, and for a second she didn't understand, she didn't understand at all.

It wasn't until Shane's hand opened and the baseball bat hit the pavement with a noisy rattle, and Shane collapsed to his knees, that she realised that he'd been stabbed.

Shane didn't seem to understand it, either. He was panting, trying to say something, but he couldn't get the words out. His eyes were wide and confused. He tried to get up, but couldn't.

Jason pointed the knife at him, slung it in an arc that spattered them all with blood drops, and turned and walked away. He put the blade back in his pocket. People were coming out of Common Grounds, looking puzzled and alarmed, and at the forefront was Oliver. Oliver's head turned quickly to stare at Jason's departing form, and then he focused on them.

Claire dropped to her knees next to Shane. He looked

desperately into her face, and slowly collapsed to his side.

His hands were clutching his stomach, and there was so much blood…

Eve hadn't moved. She was just – standing there, in her lovely black dress, staring blindly after her brother.

Oliver grabbed her and shook her. Her black hair flew wildly, and when he let go, Eve sank down in a defeated slump against the building's brick wall. Oliver shook his head impatiently and turned to Claire, and Shane.

Claire looked up, mute with misery, and saw Oliver staring down at them.

For just a second, she thought she saw something in him. Maybe just a tiny glimmer of empathy.

'Someone is calling the ambulance,' he said. 'You should put pressure on the wound. He's losing a lot of blood. It's a waste.' The blood, he meant. Not Shane.

'Help me,' Claire said. Oliver shook his head. '*Help me!*'

'You'll find that vampires aren't particularly good with the wounded,' he said. 'I'm doing you a favour by staying away. And don't try to order me, little girl. That gold bracelet of yours means almost nothing to me, except that I shouldn't leave witnesses behind.'

Shane coughed, wet and hard, and blood trickled out of his mouth. He looked as pale as Michael. Vampire pale.

Claire cradled him in her arms. Oliver glanced at Eve, frowned, and went away. People were coming closer, murmuring, asking questions, but Claire couldn't make any sense out of it. She pressed down on the wet bloody mess of Shane's shirt, felt him tense and try to squirm away, and didn't let him. *Pressure on the wound.* It seemed to take for ever until she heard the distant sound of sirens approaching.

Shane was still breathing when they loaded him inside the ambulance, but he wasn't moving, and he wasn't talking.

Claire went to Eve, got her on her feet, and put an arm around her shoulders. 'Come on,' she said. 'We should ride with Shane.'

Oliver was staring at the wet, dark smears of blood on the concrete, and as Claire helped Eve up into the back of the ambulance, he looked at one of his coffee shop employees and nodded towards the mess.

'Clean it up,' he said. 'Use bleach. I don't want to smell it all night.'

Chapter Eleven

Shane survived the trip, and they rushed him right into surgery. Eve sat silent in her black velvet dress, looking more Goth than ever, and wildly out of place in the soothing neutral waiting room. Claire kept getting up and washing her hands, because she kept finding more of Shane's blood on her clothes and skin.

Eve was crying quietly, almost hopelessly. For some reason Claire didn't cry at all. Not at all. She wasn't even sure she could. Did that make her sick? Screwed up? She wasn't sure whom she could ask. She couldn't seem to feel anything right now except a vague sense of dread.

Richard Morrell came to take their statements. It was simple enough, and Claire had no hesitation in turning in Jason for the stabbing. 'And he confessed,' Claire added. 'To killing those girls.'

'Confessed how?' Richard asked. He sat down in the

chair across from her in the lounge area, and Claire thought he looked tired. Older, too. She guessed it wasn't easy being the semi-sane one in the family. 'What exactly did he tell you?'

'That he left one for us,' she said, and glanced at Eve, who hadn't said a word. Hadn't, as far as Claire could tell, actually blinked. 'He called them presents.'

'Did he mention any of them by name?'

'No,' she whispered. She felt very, very tired all of a sudden, as if she could sleep for a week. Cold, too. She was shivering. Richard noticed, got up, and came back with a big grey fleece blanket that he tucked around her. He'd brought a second one for Eve, who was still wrapped in Shane's black coat.

'Is it possible that Jason just said that because he knew about the bodies being found near your house?' Richard asked. 'Did he talk about anything more specific that wasn't in the papers?'

Claire almost said yes to that, but she stopped in time. The police didn't know about the girl being found in their basement. They thought she'd been taken to the church by her killer.

She had no choice. She just shook her head.

'It's possible Jason's all talk, then,' Richard said. 'We've been watching him. We haven't seen anything to prove that he's got any involvement with these dead girls.' He hesitated, then said, very gently, 'Look. I don't want to make this about Shane, but he did have a bat, right?'

Eve raised her head, very slowly. 'What?'

'Shane had a bat.'

'He took it from another guy,' Claire said, nearly tripping over the words in her hurry to get them out. 'A guy from Monica's party. Shane got jumped; he was just defending himself! And he was trying to get Jason to back off—'

'We have witnesses who say that Shane swung the bat at Jason after Jason had put away his knife.'

Claire couldn't find the words. She just sat there, lips parted, staring into Richard's weary, hard eyes.

'So that's it,' Eve said. Her voice started out soft, but hardened quickly. 'It's all going to be Shane's fault, because he's Shane. Never mind that some frat ass tried to knock his head off, or that Jason *stabbed him*. It's still Shane's fault!' She stood up, stripped away the blanket, and threw it at him. Richard grabbed it before it hit his face, but just barely. 'Here, you'll need it for your cover-up!' She stalked away, slender and pale as a lily in all that black.

'Eve—' Richard sighed. 'Dammit. Look, Claire, I have to have the facts, OK? And the facts are that during the confrontation, Jason put his knife away, Shane had a bat, and Shane threatened him. Then Jason stabbed him in self-defence. Is that right?'

She didn't answer. She sat for a few seconds, just staring at him, and then stood up, stripped off the blanket, and handed it to him.

'You're going to need a bigger cover-up,' she said.

'See if there's a circus in town. Maybe you can borrow a tent.'

She walked down the hall to see if Shane was out of surgery.

He wasn't.

Eve was pacing the hallway, stiff with rage, hands clenched into fists barely visible as knots in the too-long sleeves of the coat. 'Those sons of bitches,' she said. 'Those *bastards*! They're going to put Shane down; I can feel it.'

'Put him down?' Claire repeated. 'What do you mean, put him down? Like, a dog?'

Eve glared at her. Her eyes were rimmed with red, and wet with tears. 'I mean even if he makes it through the surgery, they're not going to let him get out of this. Richard practically told us; don't you get it? It's the perfect frame. Shane took the swing, Jason acted in self-defence, and nobody's even going to look at Jason for these murders. They'll just bury it, like they bury the bodies.'

She stopped talking, and her eyes refocused over Claire's shoulder. Claire turned.

Michael was striding towards them, lean and powerful and tall, and he headed straight for Eve. No hesitation, as if nothing had happened. As if they hadn't seen him bending over a dead girl at the party.

He stopped just inches away from Eve, and held out his hands.

'I went looking for you guys. I finally tracked you to

Common Grounds. How is he?' he asked. His voice was hoarse.

'Not so good,' Eve whispered, and flowed into his arms like water through a broken dam. 'Oh God. Oh God, Michael, it all went wrong, it's all wrong—'

He sighed and wrapped his arms around her, and rested his golden head next to her dark one. 'I should have come with you. I should have made you get in the damn car. I was going to, but...things happened; I had to take care of it at the party. I never thought you'd try to walk home.' He paused, and when he finally went on, his voice was thick with pain. 'It's my fault.'

'It's nobody's fault,' Claire said. 'You know you can't make Shane do something he doesn't want to do. Or Eve, for that matter. Or me.' She put a hand hesitantly on Michael's arm. 'You didn't kill that girl, did you?'

'No,' he said. 'I found her when I was searching for Jason. I was trying to find him and get him out of the party. He was probably already gone by then.'

'Then who –'

Michael looked up, and his blue eyes were fiercely bright. 'That's what I had to take care of. There were vampires there, hunting. I had to stop it.'

One of the nurses passing by slowed, watching Michael and Eve. Her eyes narrowed, and she stopped to stare. She muttered something, then walked on.

Michael turned to the nurse, who was already halfway down the hall. 'Excuse me,' he said. 'What did you say?'

The nurse stopped dead in her tracks and turned

to face him. 'I didn't say anything. *Sir.*' That last word sounded sharp enough to cut.

'I think you did,' Michael said. 'You called her a fang-banger.'

The nurse smiled coldly. 'If I muttered something under my breath, *sir*, that shouldn't concern you. You and your...*girlfriend*...ought to do your business in the waiting room. Or the blood bank.'

Michael's hands curled into fists, and his face went tight with rage. 'It's not like that.'

The nurse – her name tag said her name was Christine Fenton, RN – outright sneered at him. 'Yeah, it never is. It's always different, right? You're just *misunderstood.* You want to hurt me, go ahead and try. I'm not afraid of you. Any of you.'

'Good,' Michael said. 'You shouldn't be afraid of me because I'm a vampire. You ought to be scared because you just trash-talked my girlfriend *to her face.*'

Nurse Fenton flipped him off and kept walking.

'Wow,' Eve said. She almost sounded like herself again, as if having somebody diss her had helped, like a slap in the face. 'And people treated me bad when I dated Bobby Fee. At least he was breathing. Mouth-breathing, yeah, but—'

Michael put his arm around her, still staring after the nurse. He had a frown on his face, but he forced it off to smile at Eve and plant a kiss on her forehead.

'You need some rest. Let's go back to the waiting room,' he said. 'I promise not to embarrass you anymore.'

He guided her in that direction, and threw a look back. 'Claire? You coming?'

She nodded absently, but her mind was somewhere else, trying to sort through data. *Fenton.* She'd seen that name before, hadn't she? Not the nurse, though; she'd never met her before and now really didn't look forward to ever seeing her again.

Claire realised she was standing alone in the hallway, and shivered. While this was a modern building, not nearly as nasty as the old, falling-to-ruins abandoned hospital where she and Shane had been chased for their lives, it still gave her the creeps. She threw one last, aching glance at the frosted-glass doors that read SURGICAL AREA – ADMITTANCE TO AUTHORISED PERSONNEL ONLY. She couldn't see anything beyond except vague moving shadows.

She followed Michael back to the waiting room. Richard Morrell was gone, which was good, and Claire sat in silence, rubbing her hands together, still feeling the phantom slickness of Shane's blood on her skin.

'Hey,' Michael said. She didn't know how much time had passed, just that she was stiff and sore and tense. She looked up into his crystal blue eyes, and saw strength and kindness, but also just a little bit of a glitter that didn't seem...natural. 'Rest. I can almost hear the gears grinding in your head.' Eve was asleep in his lap, curled up like a cat. He was stroking her dark hair. 'Here,' he said. 'Lean in.' And he put his arm around Claire, and she leant, and despite everything that had happened, she felt warm and safe.

It all fell in on her then, all the fear and the pain and the fact that Shane had been stabbed, right in front of her, and she didn't know how to deal with that, didn't know how to feel or what to say or do, and it was all just...

She turned her face into Michael's blue silk shirt and cried, silent heaving sobs that tore up out of her guts in painful jerks. Michael's hand cradled her head, and he let her cry.

She felt him press his cool lips to her temple when she finally relaxed against him, and then she just slid away, into the dark.

Claire fought her way, panicked, out of a nightmare, and into another one. *Hospital. Shane. Surgery.*

Eve was shaking her with both hands on her shoulders, babbling at her, and she couldn't follow the words, but the words didn't matter at first.

Eve was smiling.

'He's OK,' Claire said in a whisper, then louder. 'He's OK!'

'Yeah,' Eve said, the words tumbling out in a confusing bright flood, way too fast. 'He's out of surgery. It was touch and go. He had a lot of internal bleeding. He's going to be in ICU for a few days before they let him come home, and he'll have a temporary bracelet, you know, the plastic kind?'

Claire tried to literally shake the sleepy fog out of her

head. 'Plastic...wait, don't you always get one of those in the hospital? Like an ID tag?'

'Do you? Really? How weird. Oh. Well, in Morganville you leave it on when you leave, and it protects you for up to a month after surgery. Kind of like a temporary vampire restraining order.' Eve actually bounced up and down. 'He's going to be OK, oh my God, he's going to be OK!'

Claire scrambled out of her seat, grabbed Eve's arms, and the two of them bounced together up and down, then fell into a hug and squealed.

'I'll just...let you guys do that,' Michael said. He was sitting in the chairs watching, but he was smiling. He looked tired.

'What time is it?' Claire asked.

'Late. Early.' Eve checked her skull watch. 'About six in the morning. Michael, you should get home; it'll be dawn soon. I'll stay here with Claire.'

'We should all go home,' Michael said. 'He's not going to wake up for hours yet. You could change clothes.'

Claire looked down at herself, and grimaced tiredly. 'Yeah, I could,' she admitted. Shane's blood had soaked into her patterned tights, and she thought Michael could probably smell it. She could even smell it, a musty, rotten odour that made her gag. 'Eve? You want to go, too?'

Eve nodded. The three of them walked out of the waiting room and down the long, empty hallway towards the elevators. They passed the front desk, where Nurse Fenton glared at them. When Claire looked back, as they waited for the elevator, Nurse Fenton was dialling the phone.

'Why do I know that name?' she asked, and then realised, *duh*, she was with two Morganville natives. 'Fenton? You guys know anything about her?'

The elevator arrived. Eve stepped in and pushed the button for the lobby, and she and Michael looked at each other for a second.

'The family's been here for generations,' Michael said. 'Nurse Charming out there's a new arrival. She came to TPU for school, married into the family.'

'You met her husband,' Eve said. 'Officer Fenton, Brad Fenton. He's the one who—'

'The one who showed up when Sam was attacked,' Claire blurted. 'Of course! I forgot his name.' Why did that still leave her vaguely uneasy? She couldn't remember anything that Officer Fenton had done that had made her think he was anti-vamp; he'd acted quickly enough when Sam was in trouble. Not like his wife, who clearly wasn't as open-minded.

She worried about it for a while, but couldn't see any real connection, and there were other things to think about. After all, Shane was OK, and that was all that mattered.

A shower helped, but it didn't banish the dull ache between Claire's eyes, or the strange grey cast the world had taken on. Exhaustion, she guessed, and stress. Nothing looked quite right. She changed clothes, grabbed her backpack, and went back to the hospital – this time, taking a cab, despite it being broad daylight – to wait for visiting hours to start in ICU. No sign of Jason, but then, she hadn't expected him to be that obvious. Or that stupid. He'd managed to get away with it this long.

But then again...He really hadn't struck her as all that far-thinking, either. More of a want-take-have kind of guy. So what did that mean? Was Eve right? Was this a giant official cover-up, and Jason had been given free rein to run around town raping and killing and stabbing as the mood moved him? She shuddered just thinking of it.

Nurse Fenton was, mercifully, off duty when Claire arrived. She checked in with the younger, nicer lady at the desk, whose name was Helen Porter, and went to find the least uncomfortable chair in the waiting area. The building wasn't completely lame; there were laptop connections and desks, and she set herself up there. The wireless was crap, but there was a LAN connection, and that worked fine.

Of course, the filters restricted where she could go on the Internet, and she quickly grew frustrated trying to find out what was happening in the world outside of Morganville...more of the same, she guessed. War, crime, death, atrocity. Sometimes it hardly seemed that vampires were the bad guys, given the things people did to each other without the excuse of needing a pint of O neg to get through the day.

She wondered if the vampires had made any headway

tracking down who could have staked Sam. Surely they'd found out something. Then again, they hadn't had a lot of luck cornering Shane's dad, either...

Her laptop connection stopped working, right in the middle of an email to her parents. She'd been avoiding making the call, because there was this dangerous temptation to start spilling out her hurt and fear and look for comfort – after all, wasn't that what parents were for? – but if she did, they'd either come running to town, which would be bad, or they'd try to pull her out of school again, which would definitely be worse. Worse in every way.

Still, she knew she was overdue to talk to her mom, and the longer she put it off, the more stress it was going to be for both of them.

Claire logged off the laptop, packed it, and opened up her new cool phone. It glowed with a pale blue light when she dialled the number, and she heard faint clicking. That probably meant the call was being recorded, or at least monitored. More reason to be careful about what she said...

Mom answered the phone on the third ring. 'Hello?'

'Hi!' Claire winced at the artificial cheeriness of her tone. Why couldn't she sound natural? 'Mom, it's Claire.'

'Claire! Honey, I've been worried. You should have called days ago.'

'I know, Mom, I'm sorry. I got busy. I got transferred into some advanced classes; they're really great, but there's been a lot of homework and reading. I just forgot.'

'Well,' her mother said, 'I'm glad to hear those teachers are recognising that you need special attention. I was a little worried when you told me the classes were so easy. You like challenges, I know that.'

Oh, I'm challenged now, Claire thought. Between the classes and Myrnin, being stalked by Jason, and being terrified for Shane...'Yeah, I do,' she said. 'So I guess this is all good.'

'What else? How are your friends? That nice Michael, is he still playing his guitar?' Mom asked it as if it was a silly little hobby that he'd give up eventually.

'Yes, Mom, he's a musician. He's still playing. In fact, he was playing in the University Centre the other day. He got quite a crowd.'

'Well, fine. I hope he's not playing in some of those clubs, though. That gets dangerous.'

There was more of that, the danger talk, and Claire worried that her mother was, if not remembering exactly, at least remembering *something*. Why would she be so fixated on how dangerous things could be?

'Mom, you're overreacting,' Claire finally said. 'Honest, everything's fine here.'

'Well, you started out this semester in the emergency room, Claire; you can't really blame me for worrying. You're very young to be out on your own, and not even in the dorm...'

'I told you about the problems with the dorm,' Claire said.

'Yes, I know; the girls weren't very nice—'

'Not very nice? Mom! They threw me down the stairs!'

'I'm sure that was an accident.'

It hadn't been, but there was something about her mother that wasn't going to accept that, not really.

For all her fluttering and worrying, she didn't want to believe that something really could be badly wrong.

'Yeah,' Claire sighed. 'Probably. Anyway, the house is great. I really like it there.'

'And Michael has our numbers? In case there's any problem?'

'Yes, Mom, everybody's got the numbers. Oh, speaking of that, here's my new cell phone—' She rattled off the digits, twice, and made her mother read them back. 'It's got better reception than the old one, so you can get me a lot more easily, OK?'

'Claire,' her mother said, 'are you sure you're all right?'

'Yes. I'm fine.'

'I don't want to pry, but that boy, the one in the house…not Michael, but—'

'Shane.'

'Yes, Shane. I think you should keep your distance from him, honey. He's old for you, and he seems pretty sure of himself.'

She did *not* want to get into the subject of Shane. She'd nearly stumbled over saying his name, it hurt so bad. She wanted to talk to her mother the way she'd used to. They'd talked about everything, once, but there was no way she could really talk about Morganville with her family.

And that meant that there was no way she could talk about anything at all.

'I'll be careful,' she managed to say, and her attention was caught by the young nurse standing in the doorway of the waiting area, waving for her attention.

'Oh...Mom, I have to go. Sorry. Somebody's waiting for me.'

'All right, honey. We love you.'

'Love you, too.' She hung up, slid the phone into her pocket, and grabbed her backpack.

The nurse led her through another set of glass double doors into an area labelled ICU. 'He's awake,' she said. 'You can't stay long; we want him to rest as much as possible, and I can already tell he's going to be a difficult patient.' She smiled at Claire, and winked. 'See if you can sweeten him up a little for me. Make my life easier.'

Claire nodded. She felt nervous and a little sick with the forcc of her need to see him, touch him...and at the same time, she dreaded it. She hated the thought of seeing him like this, and she didn't know what she was going to say. What did people say when they were this scared of losing someone?

He looked worse than she'd imagined, and she must have let it show. Shane grunted and closed his eyes for a few seconds. 'Yeah, well, I'm not dead; that's something. One of those in the house is enough.' He looked awful – pale as, well, Michael. The baseball bat had left him with technicolour bruising, and he seemed fragile in ways Claire hadn't even thought about. There were so many tubes and things. She sat down in the chair next to his raised bed and reached over the railing to touch him lightly on his scraped, bruised hand.

He turned it to twine their fingers together. 'You're all right?'

'Yeah,' she said. 'Jason ran away, after.' Walked, really, but she wasn't going to say that. 'Eve's OK, too. She was here while you were in surgery; she just went home to change clothes. She'll be back.'

'Yeah, I guess the diva dress might have been a little much around here.' He opened his eyes and looked at her directly. 'Claire. Really. You're OK?'

'I'm fine,' she said. 'Except that I'm scared for you.'

'I'm OK.'

'Except for the stab wound and all the internal bleeding? Yeah, sure, tough guy.' She heard her voice quiver, and knew she was about to cry. She didn't want to. He wanted to laugh it off, wanted to be tough, and she ought to let him, right?

He tried to shrug, but it must have hurt, from the spasm that went across his face. One of the machines near Claire beeped, and he let out a slow sigh. 'That's better. Man, they give you the good stuff in ICU. Remind me to always get seriously wounded from now on. That minor injury stuff isn't as much fun.'

It was wearing him out to talk. Claire got up and leant over to stroke her fingertips lightly over his lips.

'Shhhh,' she said. 'Rest, OK? Save it for somebody who isn't me. It's OK to be scared. It's OK to be hurt, Shane. With me, it's OK.'

For a second his eyes glittered with tears, and then the tears spilt over, threading wet trails into his hair. 'Damn,' he whispered. 'Sorry. I just...I felt it all going away, I felt you going away, I tried...I thought he was going to hurt you and there was nothing I could do about it—'

'I know.' She leant forward and kissed him very lightly, careful of the bruises. 'I know.'

He cried a little, and she stayed right where she was, his shield against the world, until it was over. Finally, he fell into a light sleep, and she felt a tap on her shoulder. The nurse motioned for her to step out, and Claire carefully pulled her hand free of Shane's and followed.

'Sorry,' Helen said. 'I'd like for him to sleep a while before we start with the poking and prodding. You can come back this afternoon, all right?'

'Sure. What time?'

Four o'clock. That left her the entire day to kill, and not the slightest idea what she ought to be doing with it. She didn't have to see Myrnin; Amelie hadn't given her any other instructions to follow. It was Saturday, so she wasn't cutting any classes, and she didn't want to go back to the Glass House and just...worry.

Claire was still trying to decide what to do when she spotted a familiar, well-groomed figure standing outside the hospital doors.

What was Jennifer, one of Monica's regular clique, doing hanging around here?

Waiting for Claire, apparently, because she hurried to catch up as Claire strode by, heading for the taxi stand. 'Hey,' she said, and tucked her glossy hair behind her ear. 'So. How's Shane doing?'

'Like you care,' Claire said.

'Well, yeah. I don't. But Monica wants to know.'

'He's alive.' That was no more than Monica could learn without her help, so it didn't really matter, and Claire didn't like having Jennifer this close. Monica was creepy, but at least she was Alpha Creepy. There was something pathetic and extra-weird about her two groupies.

Jennifer kept pace with her. Claire stopped and turned to face her. They were halfway down the sidewalk, in the full glare of early-fall sunlight, which at least meant it wasn't too likely some vampire would be sneaking up on her while Jennifer kept her distracted. 'Look,' Claire said, 'I don't want anything to do with you, or Monica, OK? I don't want to be friends. I don't want you sucking up to me just because I'm...somebody, or something.'

Jennifer didn't look like she wanted to be sucking up, either. In fact, she looked as bitter and resentful as a glossy, entitled rich girl could look – which was a lot. 'Dream on, loser. I don't care who your Patron is; you're never going to be anything more than jumped-up trailer trash with delusions. Friends? I wouldn't be friends with you if you were the last person breathing in this town.'

'Unless Monica said so,' Claire said spitefully. 'Fine,

you don't want to exchange friendship rings. So why are you bothering me?'

Jennifer glared at her for a few seconds, stubborn and angry, and then looked away. 'You're smart, right? Like, freak smart?'

'What does that have to do with anything?'

'You placed out of the two classes we were in together. You must have aced the tests.'

Claire nearly laughed out loud. 'You want *tutoring*?'

'No, idiot. I want test answers. Look, I can't bring home anything under a C; that's the rule, or my Patron cuts off my college. And I *want* my full four years, even if I never do anything with it in this lame-ass town.' A muscle fluttered in Jennifer's jawline. 'I don't get this economics crap. It's all maths, Adam Smith, blah blah blah. What am I ever going to use it for, anyway?'

She was asking for help. Not in so many words, maybe, but that was what it was, and Claire was off balance for a few heartbeats. First Monica, now Jennifer? What next, a cookie bouquet from Oliver?

'I can't give you test answers,' she said. 'I wouldn't even if I could.' Claire took in a deep breath. 'Look, I'm going to regret this, but if you really want help, I'll go over the notes with you. *Once.* And you pay me, too. Fifty dollars.' Which was wildly out of line, but she didn't really care if Jennifer said no.

Which Jennifer clearly thought about, hard, before giving her a single, abrupt nod.

'Common Grounds,' she said. 'Tomorrow, two o'clock.'

Which was pretty much the safest time to be out and about, providing they didn't stay too long. Claire wasn't wild about visiting Oliver's shop again, but she didn't suppose there were too many places in town that Jennifer would agree to go. Besides, it wasn't far from Claire's house.

'Two o'clock,' Claire echoed, and wondered if they were supposed to shake hands or something. Not, obviously, because Jennifer flipped her hair and walked away, clearly glad to have it over with. She jumped into a black convertible and pulled away from the kerb with a screech of tyres.

Leaving Claire to contemplate the afternoon sunlight and the odds of walking home through a Morganville where Jason was still on the loose.

She took out her cell phone and called the town's lone taxi driver, who told her he was off duty, and hung up on her.

So she called Travis Lowe.

Detective Lowe wasn't really happy to be the Claire Taxi Service. She could tell because he wasn't his usual self, not at all – he'd always been kind to her, and a little bit funny, but there wasn't any of that in the way he pulled his blue Ford to the kerb and snapped, 'Get in.' He was accelerating away even before she got strapped in. 'You do know I've got a real job, right?'

'Sorry, sir,' she said. The *sir* was automatic, a habit she couldn't seem to break no matter how hard she tried. 'I just didn't think I should be walking home, with Jason—'

'Right thought, just wrong timing,' he said, and his tone softened some. He looked tired and sallow, and there were dark bags under his eyes as though he hadn't slept in days. He needed a shave and a shower. Probably the shower more than the shave. 'How's Shane?'

'Better,' she said. 'The nurse told me he was going to be OK; it's just going to take some time.'

'Good news. Could've gone the other way. Why'd you try to walk home like that?'

She fidgeted a little in the seat. In contrast to the vampire cars, with their dark tinting, the glare inside Lowe's car seemed way too bright. 'Well, we tried getting a ride,' she said. In retrospect, none of the explanations seemed all that good, really. She didn't mention that she'd tried both Lowe's phone and Joe Hess's. No point in making him feel guilty. Guiltier. 'We thought with the three of us together...'

'Yeah, good plan, if it had been any other kids. You guys, you're just trouble to the power of three. And I'm no maths whiz, but I'm betting that's a lot.' His eyes were cold and distant, and she had the distinct feeling he wasn't really thinking about her at all. 'Listen, I've got to make a stop. I'm running late as it is. You stay in the car, OK? Just stay in the car. Do *not* get out.'

She nodded. He turned some corners, into a residential area of Morganville she didn't recognise. It was run-down and faded, with leaning fences that were marked with sun-bleached gang signs. The houses weren't much better. Most of them just had sheets tacked up in the windows instead of real curtains.

He parked in front of one, got out, and said, 'Windows up. Lock the doors.'

She followed his orders and watched him go up the narrow, cracked sidewalk to the front door. It opened on the second knock, but she couldn't see who was inside, and Lowe closed the door behind him.

Claire frowned and waited, wondering what he was doing – cop stuff, she guessed, but in Morganville that could be anything, from running errands for vampires to dog-catching.

He didn't come back. She checked her watch and found that more than ten minutes had passed. He'd ordered her to stay put, but for how long? She could have been home already if she'd been able to get the taxi, or even if she'd walked.

And it was getting hot in the car.

Ten more minutes, and she started to feel anxious. The neighbourhood seemed deserted – no people on the street, even in the bright sunlight. Even for Morganville, that didn't seem...normal. She didn't know this area, hadn't been through it before, and she wondered what went on around here.

Before Claire could decide to do something really stupid, like investigating on her own, Detective Lowe came out of the house and, after rapping on the window for her to unlock the door, got back in the car. He looked, if possible, even more tired. Depressed, almost.

'What's wrong?' she asked. The sheets tacked up as curtains twitched in the window of the house, as if somebody was peering out at them. 'Sir?'

'Quit calling me sir,' Lowe snapped, and put the car in gear. 'And it's none of your affair. Stay out of it.'

There was blood on his hand. His knuckles were scraped. Claire pulled in a fast breath, her eyes widening as she noticed, and he sent her a narrow glance as the car accelerated away down the deserted street.

'Were you in a fight?' she asked.

'What did I just tell you?' Detective Lowe had never been angry before, not with her, but she could tell he was being pushed pretty far. She nodded and turned face forward, trying to keep herself still. It wasn't easy. She wanted to ask questions, a dozen of them. She wanted to ask him where Detective Hess had gone. She wanted to find out who lived in that house, and why Lowe had gone there. And whom he'd hit, to scrape up his knuckles like that.

And why he was so desperately angry that he'd snap at her.

Lowe didn't enlighten her about any of it. He pulled the car to a stop with an abrupt jerk of brakes, and Claire blinked and realised that she was home. 'You need another ride, call a taxi,' Lowe said. 'I'm on police business the rest of the day.'

She climbed out and tried to thank him, but he wasn't listening. He was already flipping open his cell phone and dialling one-handed as he put the car in gear with the other. She barely got the door shut before he pulled away from the kerb.

'Bye,' she said softly, to the empty air, and then shrugged and went inside.

Michael was sitting in the living room, playing guitar. He looked up and nodded at her when she came in. 'Eve went to the hospital,' he said. 'She must have just missed you.'

Claire sighed and slumped down on the couch. 'They won't let her in. Visiting hours are over.' She yawned and curled up, tucking her feet under her. She ached all over, and everything seemed too bright, and not quite right. 'Michael?'

'Yeah?' He was working out a chord progression and was focused on the music; his response didn't mean he was listening, really.

'Shouldn't you be asleep? I mean, don't vampires—?'

He was listening after all. 'Sleep during the day? Yeah, mostly. But I...couldn't. I keep thinking...' The chord progression turned minor, then wrong, and he grimaced. 'I keep thinking that I should have fixed this crap with Shane by now. I don't know if he's going to get over it, not really. Not in the ways that count. And I hate it. I can't stop thinking... I don't want him doing this stuff. Not without me watching his back.'

Claire leant her head against the battered black pillow on the corner of the couch. It smelt like spilt Coke, a little, but mostly it smelt like Shane, and she gladly turned her face into it and took a deep breath. It made it seem like he was here, at least for a second.

'He wouldn't hate you so bad if he didn't love you, at least a little bit,' she said. 'We'll be OK. We're going to stay together, right? The four of us?'

Michael looked up, and for a second she wasn't sure what he was going to say; but then he said, 'Yeah. We'll stay together. No matter what.'

It felt like a lie, and she wished he hadn't said it.

She fell asleep, listening to him compose a new song, and dreamt about vibrating strings and doorways that led nowhere, and everywhere. Someone was watching her; she could feel it, and it wasn't Michael. It wasn't warm and kind; it wasn't safe. She wasn't safe, and there was something wrong, wrong, *wrong*...

She nearly fell off the couch, she jerked so hard. Michael wasn't there, and his guitar was in the case on the table. Claire squinted at the clock. It was nearly two o'clock, and she'd slept through lunch, but it wasn't hunger that had woken her up. She'd heard something.

It came again, a thumping knock on the front door. She yawned and pushed back the blanket that Michael had draped over her, and, still trying to rub the sleep out of her eyes, padded to the door.

She had to stand on tiptoes at the peephole to see out. Some guy, nobody that clicked any immediate recognition – not Jason, at least. That was good. Claire looked over her shoulder, but there was no sign Michael had heard. She had no idea where he'd gone.

She opened the door. The guy standing outside looked up and held out a padded mailer with stickers on it; she took it and read her own name on it. 'Oh,' she said, preoccupied. 'Thanks.'

'No problem, Claire,' he said. 'Be seeing you.'

There was something way too familiar about the way he said it. She jerked her head up, staring at him, but she still didn't know him. He was just...normal. Average height, average weight, average everything. There was a silver bracelet on his wrist, so he was human, not vampire.

'Do I know you?' she asked. He tilted his head a little, but didn't answer. He just turned and walked away down the sidewalk, towards the street. 'Hey, wait! Who are you?'

He waved and kept walking. She went a couple of steps outside into the early-afternoon heat, frowning, but she'd left her shoes off, and the concrete was blazing hot. No way could she run after him in bare feet; she'd fry like bacon.

She retreated back into the cool darkness of the house and sighed in relief at the feeling of cool wood under her soles. She looked down at the envelope in her hand and suddenly wanted to drop it and step away. She didn't know who this guy was, and it was really strange that he wouldn't answer her. And strange, in Morganville, was rarely going to be a good thing.

She closed and locked the door, took a deep breath, and tore open the top of the envelope. No smell of blood or disgusting rotting things, which was a plus. She carefully squeezed the sides to open it up, and saw nothing in it but a note. She shook it out into her hand, and recognised the paper immediately – heavy, expensive paper, cream-coloured, embossed with the same logo that was on her gold bracelet.

It was a note from Amelie. Which meant the guy who'd dropped it off had to be somebody she trusted, at least that far.

'Everything OK?' Michael's voice came from the end of the hall. Claire gasped, stuffed the paper back into the envelope, and turned to face him.

'Sure,' she said. 'Just mail.'

'Good stuff?'

'Don't know yet; I haven't read it. Probably junk.'

'Enjoy the fact that you don't have electricity, water, cable, Internet, and garbage to pay for,' he said. 'Look, I'm going upstairs. Yell if you need anything. There's stuff in the fridge if you're hungry.' A brief pause. 'Don't open the pitcher in the back on the top shelf.'

'Michael, *tell* me you're not putting blood in our refrigerator.'

'I told you not to open it. So you'll never know.'

'You *suck*!' Of course he did; he was a vampire. 'I mean, not in a good way, either!'

'Eat something! I'm sleeping.' And she heard his door shut, so she was effectively alone.

Claire fumbled out the letter and unfolded it. A smell of faint, dusty roses came from the paper, as though it had been stored in a trunk with dried flowers. She wondered how old it was.

It was a short, simple note, but it made her whole body turn cold.

It read:

I am displeased with your progress in your advanced studies. I suggest you spend additional time learning all you can. Time is growing short. I do not care how you arrange this, but you will be expected to demonstrate within the next two days at least a journeyman understanding of what you are being taught. You cannot involve Michael. He is not to be risked.

Nothing else. Claire stared at the perfect handwriting for a few seconds, then folded the note up and put it back in the envelope. She still felt tired and hungry, but more than anything else, now she felt scared.

Amelie wasn't happy.

That wasn't good.

Two days. And Michael could go with her only in the evenings…

She couldn't wait.

Claire checked in her backpack. The red crystal shaker was still inside, safely zipped into a pocket.

If she took Michael's car – no, she couldn't. She'd never be able to see through the tinting, even if she felt confident in her ability to drive it. And Detective Lowe wasn't going to give her a ride. She could try Detective Hess, but Lowe's attitude had made her gun-shy.

Still, she couldn't just go out alone.

With a sigh, she called Eddie, the taxi driver.

'What?' he snapped. 'Don't I get a day off? What is it with you?'

'Eddie, I'm sorry, I'm really sorry. I need a favour.' Claire hastily checked her wallet. 'Um, it's a short trip, I'll pay you double, OK? Please?'

'Double? I don't take cheques.'

'I know that. Cash.'

'I don't wait. I pick up, I drop off, I leave.'

'Eddie! Double! Do you want it or not?'

'Keep your panties on. What's the address?'

'Michael Glass's house.'

Eddie heaved a sigh so heavy it sounded like a temporary hurricane. 'You again. OK, I come. But I swear, last time. No more Saturdays, yes?'

'Yes! Yes, OK. Just this time.'

Eddie hung up on her. Claire bit her lip, slipped the note from Amelie into her bag, and hoped Michael had been serious about going to bed. Because if he'd eavesdropped on her, even by accident, she was going to have a lot of explaining to do.

It took five minutes for Eddie to arrive. She waited on the sidewalk, and jumped in the back of the battered old cab – barely yellow, after so much sun exposure – and handed Eddie all the cash she had. He counted it. Twice.

Then he grunted and flipped the handle on the taxi meter. 'Address?'

'Katherine Day's house.' One thing Claire had learnt

about riding with Eddie – you didn't need numbers, only names. He knew everybody, and he knew where everybody lived. All the natives, anyway. The students, he just dropped on campus and forgot.

Eddie threw an arm over the back of his seat and frowned at her. He was a big guy, with a lot of wild dark hair, including a beard. She could barely see his eyes when he frowned, which was pretty much always. 'The Day House. You're sure?'

'I'm sure.'

'Told you I'm not staying, right?'

'Eddie, *please*!'

'Your funeral,' he said, and hit the gas hard enough to press her back into the cushions.

CHAPTER TWELVE

Myrnin's shack was easy enough to get into – the trick, after all, wasn't getting in. It was getting out. Light slashed in thin ribbons through the darkness where the boards didn't quite meet, but it wasn't exactly easy to see, and she didn't much like roaming around in Myrnin's lair in the dark. Or even half dark. She found a flashlight on the shelf near the door and thumbed it on. A pure white circle of light brushed across the dusty floor and showed her the narrow steps at the back that led down.

She went very slowly. Very carefully. 'Myrnin?' She said it quietly, because he'd hear her; he'd told her that his ears were sensitive because of the silence and his lack of company.

He didn't answer.

'Myrnin?' Claire could see the hard edge of light at the bottom of the steps. He had everything on, it looked like

– the light had a funny colour, a mixture of fluorescent bulbs and oil lamps, candles and incandescents. 'Myrnin, it's Claire. Where are you?'

She almost missed him, because he was so still. Myrnin was usually in motion of some kind – moving fast, like a hummingbird, from one bright attraction to the next. But what was standing in the centre of the room looked like Myrnin – only completely still. Vampires did breathe, a little; the blood they took from humans needed oxygen, Claire had figured out, although a lot less than in a normal person. But his chest was still, his eyes were open and staring, and he wasn't moving at all. Not even to look at her. His attention was focused somewhere off to the side.

'Myrnin?' She put her bag down slowly. 'It's Claire. Can you hear me?'

His chest rose just a fraction, and he whispered, 'Get out. Go.'

And tears slid out of his wide, staring eyes to run down his pale cheeks.

'What is it? What's wrong?' She forgot about caution, and moved towards him. 'Myrnin, please tell me what's wrong!'

'You,' he said. 'This is wrong.'

And then he just – collapsed. Dropped like his knees had given out, and the rest of him followed. It wasn't a graceful fall, and it would have hurt a normal human, maybe badly. Myrnin's head hit the floor with a solid crack, and Claire crouched down next to him and put her hand on his chest – not sure what she was doing, what she was supposed to be feeling for. Not his pulse – vampires didn't have one, at least not that humans could detect. She knew that from leaning against Michael.

'I can't do this,' Myrnin said. His cold hand flashed out and grabbed hold of her arm, hard enough to bruise. 'Why are you here? You weren't supposed to come!'

'What are you talking about?' Claire tried to pull free, but she might as well have been pulling against a bridge cable. Myrnin could snap her bones, if he wanted. Or even if he got careless. 'Myrnin, you're hurting me. Please—'

'*Why?*' He shook her, and she could see the panic in his eyes. That made her take a deep breath and forget the ache where he was holding her. 'You weren't supposed to come back!'

'Amelie sent me a note. She said I had only two days to learn—'

Myrnin groaned and let her go. He covered his eyes with his hands, dry-scrubbed his face, and said, 'Help me up.' Claire put a hand under his arm and managed to get him upright, leaning against a solid lab cabinet that seemed like it was bolted to the floor. 'Let me see the note.'

She went back to the stairs, grabbed her backpack, and produced the note. Myrnin unfolded it in shaking hands and looked at it intently.

'What? Is it a fake?'

'No,' he said slowly. 'She sent you to me.' He dropped

the note in his lap, as if it had got unbearably heavy, and rested his head against the hard surface of the lab cabinet. 'She's lost hope, then. She's acting out of fear and panic. That isn't like her.'

'I don't understand!'

'That's exactly the problem,' Myrnin said. 'You don't. And you won't, child. I explained this to her before – even the brightest human can't learn this quickly. And you are so very young.' He sounded tired and very sad. 'Now we come to the last of it, Claire. Think it through: Amelie sent you to me, knowing that I do not believe you are the solution to my problems. *Why would she do that?* You know what I am, what I do, what I crave. Why would she put you in front of me if she didn't want me to...to—' He seemed to be begging her to understand, but he wasn't making any sense. 'You don't know what she is capable of doing, child. *You don't know!*'

There was so much fear in his voice, and in his face, that she felt a real sense of dread. 'If she didn't want you to teach me, why did she send me?'

'The question is, why – after being so careful to provide you with escorts – would she send you to me *alone*?'

'I—' She stopped, remembering. 'Sam said to ask you about the others. The other apprentices. He said I wasn't the first—'

'Samuel is quite intelligent,' Myrnin said, and squeezed his eyes tightly shut. 'You glow, you glow like the finest lamp. So much possibility in you. Yes, there have been others Amelie sent to learn. Vampires and humans. I killed the first one almost by accident, you must understand, but the effect... You see, the more intelligent the mind, the longer my clarity lasts, or so we thought at first. The first bought me almost a year without attacks. The second...mere months, and so on, in ever-decreasing cycles as my disease grew worse.'

'She sent me here to die,' Claire said. 'She wants you to kill me.'

'Yes,' Myrnin said. 'Clever, isn't she? She understands my desperation so well. And you do glow so brightly, Claire. The temptation is almost—' He shook his head violently, as if trying to throw something out of his mind. 'Listen to me. She seeks to fend off the inevitable, but I can't accept this trade. Your life is so fragile, just beginning; I can't steal it away for half a day, or an hour. It's no use.'

'But... I thought you said I could learn—'

He sighed. 'I wanted to believe, but it isn't possible. Yes, I could teach you...but you'd be nothing more than a gifted mimic, a mechanic, not an engineer. There are things you cannot do, Claire, not for years at best. I'm sorry.'

Myrnin was saying that she was stupid, and Claire felt a hot, strange spark of anger. 'Let go of my arm!' she snapped, and he was surprised enough that some of the blankness in his dark eyes went away, replaced with concern. He slowly relaxed his fingers. 'Explain it to me. You're not all-knowing; maybe you forgot something.'

Myrnin smiled, but it was a shadow of his usual manic grin. 'I assure you, I probably have,' he agreed. 'But Claire, attend: already, my muscles disobey me. Soon I won't be able to walk, and then my voice will lock in my throat. And then blindness, and madness, and I will end my days locked in a black, dark place, screaming silently as I starve. If there were any shred of hope that I could avoid that fate, don't you think I would seize it?'

He said it so...calmly. As if it had already happened. 'No,' Claire said. She couldn't help it. 'No, that isn't going to happen.' She'd somehow thought that he'd just...fade away. Without pain. But this kind of torture – he didn't deserve it. Not even Oliver deserved to have this creeping up on him. 'How... Do you know what causes it?'

Myrnin smiled, but the smile looked bitter. 'I thought I did, once. Amelie knows much of what I've forgot, but you may find your clues in the notebooks. I was cautious, of course, but if you look closely, you may find my theories. In any case, it no longer matters. I can feel myself slipping into the black. There's no return.'

'How do you *know*?'

'I've seen it happen. It's always the same. Amelie will lock me away because she'll have no choice; she must try to keep the secret, and it will take me a very long time to die, because I am so very old.' He shook his head. 'Doesn't matter. Not now. All that matters is that you go home, child, and never come back. I can't imagine I would have the unexpected strength of will to refuse such a lovely warm gift twice.'

It was stupid. She didn't like Myrnin, she *couldn't*. He was scary and strange and he'd tried to kill her not just once, but at least twice.

So why did she feel like she wanted to cry?

'What if we use the crystals?' she blurted. Myrnin's eyes narrowed. 'I learnt, when you had me take them. What if we use them now? Both of us? Would that help?'

He was already shaking his head. 'Claire, it's a fool's quest. Even if we continue research on the cure, there's not enough time—'

'The cure to your disease!' She felt a sudden surge of hope as she dug through her backpack and came up with the shaker of crystals. 'Isn't this what you've done so far?'

'It is. Clever of you to discover that. But the point is, it's taken years to develop it, and it's at best only a temporary measure. Even a large dose will wear off in a few hours for either one of us, and the consequences for you...'

'But if we can come up with a cure, a real cure?'

'It's naive to think that we could perfect such a thing in mere hours. No, I think you had better go. I have been quite noble today. You really should let me enjoy it while I can.' He looked at the shaker in her hands, and for a second she thought she saw a spark of that quick interest that had driven him so hard in earlier meetings. 'Perhaps...if I show you the research, you could carry that part of it onward. For the others.'

'Sam said you were all sick. Even Amelie.'

Myrnin nodded. 'As I am, so shall they all be. Every vampire who lives will suffer this in the next ten years, unless it is stopped.'

Ten years! No. Not Michael.

She couldn't stand by without trying to stop it, at least for him.

'Amelie brought us to Morganville to buy us time, to find a way to ensure our survival. She believed... she believed that humans might hold the keys to this plague, and she also believed that we could no longer afford to live as we had, preying in the night or hiding. She thought that humans and vampires could live in cooperation, and find the solution to our illness together. That quickly became impossible, of course; she realised, after telling the first few vampires, that they would go mad knowing what was to come, that they would kill indiscriminately. So it became a secret, a terrible secret. She told them part of the truth, that she was seeking a cure to what makes us sterile. Never the rest.'

'So...Morganville's a kind of lab. She's trying to find a cure, and protect all of you at the same time.'

'Exactly so.' Myrnin rubbed his hands over his face again. 'I'm getting tired, Claire. Best give me the crystals.'

She poured out a few in his hand. He met her eyes. 'More,' he said. 'The disease has advanced. I will need a large dose to stay with you, even for a while.'

She poured about a teaspoon out. Myrnin popped it into his mouth, made a face at the bitterness, and swallowed. A shudder went through him, and she actually saw the weariness and confusion fade. 'Excellent. That really was an amazing discovery. Too bad about the doctor; really, he was very bright.' Oh dear. Myrnin was swinging towards the manic now, thanks to the drugs. That was dangerous. 'You're very bright. Perhaps you could read through the notes.'

'I...I'm just *now* starting advanced biochemistry—'

'Nonsense, your native ability is clear.' He pointed towards the shaker of crystals in her hand. 'Take it.'

'No. It's your medicine, not mine.'

'And it will help you keep up with me, because we have very little time, Claire, very little.' His eyes were bright and clear, like a bird's, and with about as much affection. 'There are two ways you can assist me. You can take the crystals, or you can help me extend this period of clarity in other ways.'

She sat back on her heels. 'You said you wouldn't.'

'Indeed. But you see, the disease makes me a sentimental fool. If I am to find an heir to my knowledge, *and* find a cure for my people, then I can't be burdened with such considerations.' His gaze brushed over her, abstract and hungry. 'You burn so very brightly, you know.'

'Yeah,' she muttered. 'You said.' She hated this. She hated that Myrnin could change like this, go from friend to enemy in the space of a minute. Which one was real?

Or was any of it? Claire shook half a teaspoon of the crystals into her palm.

'More,' Myrnin said. She added a couple, and he reached out, took the shaker, and poured a heaping mound of it into her hand. 'You have a great deal to learn, and you are operating from such a disadvantage. Better safe than sorry.'

She didn't want to take it – well, she did, a little, because the strawberry smell of the crystals brought back flashes of the way the world had looked: diamond clear, uncomplicated, *simple.*

Hard not to want that.

Myrnin said, 'Take it, or I will have to take you, Claire. We have no more moves on our chessboard.'

She poured the crystals onto her tongue and almost gagged from the bitterness. The strawberry flavour was overwhelmed by it, and the aftertaste was rotten and cold on her tongue, and she thought for a second she might throw up...

And then everything snapped into hot, sharp, *perfect* focus.

Myrnin no longer looked strange and pathetic; he was a burning pillar of energy barely contained by skin. She could see that he was sick, somehow; there was a darkness in him, like rot at the heart of a tree. The room took on a fey glitter. *Neurotransmitters*, she thought. Her brain was rushing a million miles an hour, making her giddy and breathless. *My reaction time must be ten times faster.*

Myrnin bounded up to his feet, grabbed her hand, and dragged her to the shelves, where he began frantically pulling down books. Notebooks, textbooks, scraps of handwritten paper. Two black-bound composition books, the same kind Claire used in lab class. Even a couple of the cheap blue books she used for essay tests. Everything was crammed with fine, perfect handwriting.

'Read,' he said. 'Hurry.'

All she had to do was flip pages. Her eyes captured things, like cameras, and her brain was so fast and efficient that she translated and comprehended the text almost instantly. Nearly two hundred pages, and she paged through as fast as her fingers could go.

'Well?' Myrnin demanded.

'This is wrong,' she said, and flipped back to the first third of the notebook. 'Right here. See? The formula's wrong. The variable doesn't match up with the prior version, and the error gets replicated going forward—'

Myrnin gave out a fierce, sharp cry, like a hunting hawk, and snatched the book away from her. 'Yes! Yes, I see it! That fool. No wonder he sustained me only for a few days. But you, Claire, oh, you are different.'

She knew she ought to be afraid of the slow, predatory smile he gave her, but she couldn't help it.

She smiled back.

'Give me the next one,' she said. 'And let's start making crystals.'

* * *

When it wore off, it hit Myrnin first. He took more, but she could see it wasn't really working this time. Diminishing returns. That was why he'd only taken a few crystals last time, to prolong the effects even if the change hadn't been as dramatic.

This crash was like hitting a brick wall at ninety miles an hour.

It started when he lost his balance, caught himself, and knocked a tray off the lab table; he tried to catch it in mid-air, a feat he'd been more than capable of an hour before, and missed it completely. He stared at his hands in frustration and viciously kicked the tray. It sailed across the room and hit the far wall with a spectacular clatter.

Claire straightened up from spreading the crystals out on the drying tray. She could feel the effects, too – her brain was slowing down, her body aching. It had to be worse for Myrnin, because of the disease. *It was wrong to do this*, she thought. Wrong, because his manic phase always led to dementia, and he'd wanted so badly to be himself again.

But the crystals drying on the tray could change that, or at least, she hoped they could. It wasn't that Myrnin had been wrong, but that his last assistant had made mistakes; whether deliberate or not, Claire couldn't tell. But the crystals in the tray would be more effective, and longer lasting.

Myrnin could stabilise again.

'It isn't a cure,' Myrnin said, as if he were reading her thoughts.

'No, but it buys you time,' Claire said. 'Look, I can come tomorrow. Promise me you'll leave these here, all right? Don't try to take them yet; they're not ready. And they're more powerful, so you'll have to start with a small dose and work up.'

'Don't tell me what to do!' Myrnin barked. 'Who is the master here? Who is the student?'

This was familiar, and dangerous. She lowered her head. 'You're the master,' she said. 'I have to go now. I'm sorry. I'll come back tomorrow, OK?'

He didn't answer. His dark eyes were fixed on her, and she couldn't tell what he was thinking. Or even *if* he was thinking. He was right on the edge.

Claire took the shaker of the less effective crystals and stuffed it in her backpack – there wasn't that much left, but enough for one more dose for them both, and if he did something to the crystals during his manic phase, they might need it. She needed to ask Amelie for some kind of strongbox where she could store things...

'Why?' Myrnin asked. She looked up at him, frowning. 'Why are you helping us? Isn't it better for humans if we waste away and die? By helping me, you help all vampires.'

Claire knew what Shane would have done. He'd have walked away, considered it a win all around. Eve might have done the same thing, except for Michael.

And she...she was helping. *Helping.* She couldn't even really explain why, except that it seemed wrong to turn away. They weren't all bad, and she couldn't sacrifice people like Sam and Michael for the greater good.

'I know,' Claire said. 'Believe me, I'm not happy about it.'

'You do it because you're afraid,' he said.

'No. I do it because you need it.'

He just stared at her, as if he couldn't figure out what she was saying. Time to go. She shivered, shouldered her backpack, and hurried for the stairs. She kept looking behind, but she never saw Myrnin move... Even so, he was in a different place, closer, every time she looked. It was like a child's game, only deadly serious. He wouldn't move while she was looking at him.

Claire turned and walked backward, staring at him. Myrnin chuckled, and the sound echoed through the room like the rustle of bat wings.

When her heels hit the steps, she turned and ran.

He could have caught her, but he didn't. She burst through the doors of the shack into the alley, breathing hard, sweating, shaking.

He didn't follow. She didn't think he could, past the steps. She wasn't sure why – maybe the same way that Morganville itself kept people in town, or wiped their memories, kept Myrnin confined in his bottle.

She felt the hair on the back of her neck stir, and then she heard a voice. Whispering and indistinct. Shane? What was Shane doing here?

He was inside. He was inside and he was in trouble; she had to go to him...

Claire found herself reaching for the door to the

shack before she knew what she was doing.

'Myrnin, stop it!' she gasped and pulled away. She turned and ran down the alley towards the relative safety of the street.

It was only when she got there that she saw it was already nightfall.

Eddie wouldn't come for her after dark, and she was a long way from home. Too far to walk.

Claire was about to dial Michael at home when she spotted a police car cruising slowly down the cul-de-sac. Not a vampire squad car – this one had only light tinting on the front windows, although the back was blacked out. Claire squinted against the harsh brightness and waved. The effects of the crystals were ebbing fast, and she felt clumsy, strange, and exhausted. All she wanted to do was sleep. She'd have taken a ride with Satan in his big red handbasket if it had helped her get off her feet for a few minutes.

The cruiser pulled to a stop, and the passenger-side window rolled down. Claire bent over to look inside.

Officer Fenton. 'You shouldn't be out by yourself,' he said. 'You know better. Everybody's looking for you. Your friends called you in as missing.'

'Oh,' she said. That hadn't even occurred to her. She hadn't realised how long she'd been away. 'I just... Can I get a ride home? Please?'

He shrugged. 'Hop in.' She did, gratefully, and buckled herself in. Everything ached now – her head, her eyes, every muscle in her body. And she had the feeling it was going to get worse before it got better. 'Speaking of your friends, how are they? Heard about that thing with Shane. Damn shame.'

'He'll be OK,' she said.

'And the other one? Michael?'

'Yeah, he's fine,' she said. 'Why?'

'Just checking. Probably good to keep an eye on him, since he was the target of the hit in the first place,' Fenton said. He turned the patrol car in a slow, crunching circle and headed back out, away from the alley. 'Since the guy was looking for him, specifically.'

Claire's head hurt too much for conversation. 'I guess,' she agreed faintly. And then some last flash of cognitive clarity put together strings of chemicals, and she felt her heartbeat jump and hammer harder.

'How did you know that?'

'What?'

'I mean, about Sam not being the real target? He was unconscious when you found him. He couldn't have said anything.'

'Unconscious, crap. He was dead.'

'But anyway, he couldn't have said—' Things clicked into place, and the pattern looked bad. Very bad. 'You were there before the sirens.'

'What are you talking about?'

'When we first looked out, we saw you parked behind Sam's car and we just thought you'd found him there. But you didn't just find him lying in the street—'

Officer Fenton pressed the gas pedal, and the cruiser

shot forward at a high rate of speed. He turned on the lights. She heard the harsh clicking sound they made, and the night was flooded with flashes of blue and red strobes.

'Where are you taking me?'

'Shut up.'

Claire put her hand on the door handle, but they were going so fast she knew she couldn't jump. She'd be badly hurt, at the very least. 'If you hurt me, the Founder—'

'That's what we're counting on,' Fenton sneered. 'Shut up.'

Shane would have totally got off on the whole vampire-killer-secret-society thing. Claire just wanted to go home. Badly.

In addition to Officer Fenton, the group that gathered in the shed behind the photo processing store included Fenton's wife, the unpleasant nurse who treated Claire as though she were carrying some totally disgusting disease. She even wore latex gloves to tie Claire to the chair.

Claire barely recognised the others. One was a maintenance worker from the university; she'd seen him a few times. One was a bank teller. One was the smooth-faced, unremarkable guy who'd delivered Amelie's note to her that afternoon. He'd killed her courier, Claire found out. He spent a lot of time tracking down who worked for Amelie and trying to find out where she stayed.

He was the one who leant over into her space, hands

braced on the arms of the chair, and said, 'We don't much care for collaborators. Even little underage ones.'

Claire's mouth felt foul and dry, and she was shaking now with the after-effects of the crystals. Myrnin had been right: the consequences weren't going to be pleasant. 'Captain Obvious, I presume,' she said.

He laughed. He had nice, white teeth, no sign of vampire fangs. 'Aren't you the clever one. Living up to your reputation, I see.' He tapped a finger on her gold bracelet. 'Not too many breathers have ever seen the Founder, much less become her pet. Sam Glass was the last one, before you. Did you know that? This is his bracelet you're wearing. Probably sized down a little, though.'

She squirmed a little, but the ropes were too tight. 'What do you want with me?'

'Leverage,' said Officer Fenton. 'Vamps seem to like you.'

'Not all of them,' Claire said. If they asked Oliver to come running to her rescue, it wasn't too likely he'd so much as yawn. 'And if you think Amelie's going to sacrifice herself for me, you're crazy.' Amelie had already sold her down the river, by sending her to Myrnin with the clear expectation that Myrnin would...eat her. The fact that he hadn't was just Claire's good luck. 'In fact, I don't think any of them would raise a finger—'

'Michael Glass would,' Captain Obvious said. 'And he's the one we want. She knows that, of course. She's done everything she could to keep him away from us.' He flipped open the phone and pressed something on speed dial. 'Tell him where you are.'

Claire glared. 'No.' She clamped her lips shut as she heard Michael's distant hello on the other end. *I'm not going to talk; I'm not going to make a sound…*

The door at the back of the shed opened, and someone came in. Thin, greasy, dressed in a black leather jacket with a hole in the pocket. Crazy eyes. Fang marks on his neck.

Jason.

He took the phone from Captain Obvious. 'Hey, Mikey, it's Jason. Just shut up and listen. I've got Claire, and I'm thinking about all the things I can do with her until you get here. Better hurry.'

'No!' Claire blurted, and realised it was a mistake. She'd just confirmed that she was there, and now Michael wouldn't have any choice, would he? 'Michael, *don't*!'

She could hear the sound of Michael's voice, but not what he was saying. Jason put the phone back to his ear and listened. 'Yeah, that's right. You've got half an hour to show, or I'll bring her home in pieces. Oh, and it's not a trap; it's a business proposition. You walk in alone, you both walk out alive.' Pause. 'Where? Oh, come on, man. You know where. The captain's waiting.'

He snapped the phone shut, tossed it in the air, and caught it, smiling. His eyes never left Claire.

Michael wouldn't do it. He just wouldn't be that stupid, right? But Shane was in the hospital. He didn't have anybody he could turn to for help except the other vampires, and they wouldn't lift a finger to save Claire. She wasn't sure anymore that Amelie would bother, unless she was just saving her as Myrnin's midnight snack.

The door to the shed opened again, and both Captain Obvious and Jason turned to look.

Detective Travis Lowe stepped inside and closed the door, and for a second Claire felt a wild jolt of relief and satisfaction, but it faded just as quickly. Lowe looked at Jason and Captain Obvious as though he was expecting to find them there, and when his gaze moved to Claire, he didn't react except to seem angry and harassed.

Oh God. He was one of them. Whoever *them* might be.

'Could you screw this up any more?' he asked, low and vicious. 'I told you, Glass isn't important. We don't need to do this.'

'He's the youngest. He's a symbol, man,' Captain Obvious said. 'And he was one of us. He's a traitor.'

One of us? Did he mean – no, he couldn't mean that. He couldn't mean that Michael *knew* these people, that he'd been part of this skanky little conspiracy...but Jason had acted as though Michael knew where they were.

Nurse Fenton destroyed that hope by saying, 'We've already been over this. Michael knows too much. If he decides to talk, we're all dead. We can't take the risk. Not anymore.' She shot her husband a dark look. 'If you hadn't screwed up—'

'Don't blame me! Vampire car pulling out of the

vampire's house, how was I supposed to know it wasn't him?'

Of course. No wonder that had bothered her all along – the house had woken all of them up not because of the threat to Sam, but the threat to Michael, its owner. Even though Michael wasn't there, it was reacting to intent.

Officer Fenton hadn't been the first man on the scene; he'd been the one who staked Sam and left him to die, then pretended to be Johnny-on-the-spot. If Richard Morrell hadn't shown up to scoop and run, he would have succeeded.

Claire swallowed hard and focused on Detective Lowe. 'I thought you were a good guy.'

Something weary and painful passed across his face. 'Claire—' He shook his head. 'It's not as simple as that. Not in Morganville. You don't just get to be one thing around here.'

'It's not his fault,' Jason said, and grinned like a wolf. 'If he wants his partner back, he's not going to do anything stupid.'

Detective Hess. They had him. No wonder she hadn't seen him for days – and no wonder Lowe had been acting weird. She looked more closely at Officer Fenton, and found he had a dark bruise on his left cheek that matched the scrapes on Detective Lowe's knuckles. He'd been in the house, maybe with Detective Hess, and Lowe had taken a swing at him.

Lowe's eyes were dark and full of misery, and he

looked away from Claire. 'The kid has nothing to do with this,' he said.

'The *kid* hangs with the top-shelf vampires,' Nurse Fenton shot back. 'How many humans do you know with access to the Founder? She doesn't even let her own kind get close! Of *course* she's got something to do with this. Probably a lot more than you know.'

Truer than Nurse Fenton knew. Claire thought about what she'd learnt from Myrnin – the vampire sickness, the wormhole doorways through town, the network of Founder Houses – and realised that she knew enough to destroy Morganville.

She did her best to look scared and clueless. The first part, at least, wasn't much of a stretch.

When Jason sauntered over and put his hand on Claire's shoulder, she flinched. He smelt like a garbage heap in the summer, and she caught a lingering hint of blood from his coat. *He stabbed Shane.* And he'd smiled about it, too.

'Get your hands off me,' she said, and turned to stare right at him. 'I'm not afraid of you.'

Lowe grabbed Jason by the arm, swung him around, and slammed him face-first into the rough wooden wall of the shed. 'Me neither,' he growled. 'And I'm not tied to a chair. Leave her alone.'

'Big hero,' Nurse Fenton said bitterly. 'You and Hess, you're both pathetic.'

'Am I?' Lowe twisted Jason's arm painfully high. 'I'm not the one raping and killing girls for fun.'

'Jason's not the one doing it, either,' Fenton said. 'He just likes to talk about it.'

Claire said, 'Then how'd he know about the one in our basement?'

They all looked at her. 'I never saw a report about any body in your house,' Lowe said. 'Just the one in the alley.'

Jason laughed, a dry crack of sound. 'They moved it. Hey, Claire, you ever think that maybe it wasn't me? Maybe it was one of your two boyfriends *inside* the house. Shane, he ain't too stable, you know. And who knows about Michael these days?'

She wanted to scream at him, but she saved her strength. She had thin wrists, and Captain Obvious hadn't done a very good job of tying her; she could feel a little give in the ropes, and she wouldn't need much slack to slip at least one hand free. The rough surface of the rope sawed at her skin, but she kept pulling, trying not to make it too obvious, and felt a sudden sharp pain in her wrist as the cut Jason had given her broke open again, sending a slow trickle of blood down her wrist.

It helped, along with the sweat running down her arms. She coughed, and at the same time pulled, and her right hand slipped free of the ropes with a fiery scrape. She kept it behind her back and started working on the knot holding her left hand to the crossbar of the chair.

'So what are you?' she asked, to fill the silence and keep them from noticing what she was doing. 'Vampire hunters?'

'Something like that,' Officer Fenton said.

'Not that I've noticed,' Claire sniffed. 'Shane's dad

blew into town and killed all the vampires that I know about. What have *you* done?'

'Shut up,' Nurse Fenton said flatly. 'You've been here months, if that. You have no idea what this town is like to live in. When we're ready, we'll act. Frank Collins had the right idea, but he wasn't much of a planner.'

'So you're planning a revolution,' Claire said. 'Not just random attacks.'

'Would you *stop* telling the prisoner our plans?' Captain Obvious snapped. 'Jesus, don't you watch movies? Just shut up!'

'She's not going to tell anybody,' Officer Fenton said, in such an offhand way that Claire's heart sank.

They didn't intend to keep any promises to Michael. No way were they letting Michael, or her, walk out of here alive.

Don't do it, Michael. Don't come for me.

But fifteen minutes later, the door burst open and a vampire rushed in, wrapped in a heavy blanket. The greasy smell of cooking flesh filled the shed, and then the vampire kicked the door closed and collapsed against it, gasping. Smoke rose up from him in a thick, choking cloud. In a few places, Claire could see blackened skin beneath the covering.

'About time,' Fenton growled. Then he picked up a black stick from a crate next to him and drove it into the vampire's chest. For a second Claire thought that it was a stake, but then she saw sparks, and the vampire went down in a tangle of blankets and smoke.

He'd been Tasered.

Captain Obvious brought out a wooden stake and rolled the vampire over. Claire screamed. Somehow, she'd been avoiding thinking of him as Michael, but the flash of golden hair and the pale shape of his face were unmistakable.

His blue eyes were open, but he couldn't move. There were burnt patches on his hands and arms, but he was alive…

Captain Obvious positioned the stake.

Claire lurched to her feet and spun to her right. Her left hand was still tied to the crossbar of the chair, but the momentum helped her swing it with bone-breaking force right into Captain Obvious's back. He crumpled against the wall. Claire grabbed the chair in both hands and used it as a shield as Officer Fenton jabbed the Taser at her, knocking it aside, and managed to hit him in the gut with at least one of the chair's legs as she screamed for help. He stumbled backward.

Travis Lowe cursed and flicked handcuffs onto Jason's wrists. 'Sit,' he ordered, and pulled his gun. He looked strained and grim, but determined. 'Back up, Fenton. You too, Christine. Turn and face the wall.'

'You can't do this,' Officer Fenton said. 'Trav, if you cross us—'

'I know. You'll get me. I'll try not to pee all over myself in terror.' Lowe nodded to Claire, who was undoing the last of the knots holding the chair to her left hand. 'Put the cuffs on them. I'll cover you.' He tossed her an extra two sets, and she fumbled the unfamiliar weight in her numbed fingers. As she bent to pick them up, Captain Obvious – down, not out – reached over Michael's still body, grabbed her foot, and yanked. Claire cried out and fell, and Captain Obvious dragged her backward.

Lowe spun, aiming his gun, but it was too late. Captain Obvious had a knife, a big, wicked thing, and he put it to Claire's throat, right under her chin. It felt cold, then hot as it pressed into the tender skin. 'Put it down, Jeff,' Lowe barked. He took a threatening step forward. 'I mean it; I will put you down.'

He got Tasered in the back. Claire watched him convulse and fall, and felt panic well up inside. *They'll kill us now. All three of us.* Four, counting Joe Hess, who was being held prisoner somewhere else.

She heard a sharp, loud crack, and a pale strong hand exploded through the boards beside Captain Obvious's head, grabbed him, and pulled. The entire section of boards broke away, and Captain Obvious was yanked backward. Claire felt the knife slide along her neck, but it didn't have any force behind it. He dropped it, flailing for balance, and then he was outside in the bright, dusty sunlight, and there was a dry snapping sound.

Dressed in a black leather trench coat, a black broad-brimmed hat, and black gloves, Oliver stepped into the shed. He gave them all a vampire smile.

'Well, that was refreshing,' he said. He reached down and pulled Michael up to a sitting position next to Claire, then stepped in front of them.

'Could've come sooner,' Michael whispered. He was

shaking all over, but he was coming out of his paralysis. Claire hugged him. He fumbled in his pocket, came up with a handkerchief, and pressed it to Claire's neck. She hadn't even realised she was bleeding.

Oliver ignored them and walked towards the Fentons, who tried to get to the door. He flashed ahead of them with that easy snakelike speed vampires could display when they wanted, and Claire shuddered at the looks on their faces.

They knew what was going to happen to them.

'Don't worry,' Oliver said. 'There'll be a fair trial. Since Samuel didn't die, and you didn't succeed today, you won't burn for what you've done.' He reached for Christine Fenton's wrist, ripped her sleeve, and exposed her silver bracelet. It fit tightly around her wrist, but he slid a finger underneath the metal and it split along an invisible seam. He dropped the bracelet in his pocket, then did the same to Officer Fenton.

The places where their bracelets had been were sickly pale, and Christine kept rubbing hers, as if the shock of open air on the skin was painful.

'Congratulations,' Oliver said. 'I release you from your contracts.'

And then he grabbed Christine. Claire had a glimpse of his fangs flashing down, silvery and sharp, and then he slammed the woman against the wall of the shed and bit.

Claire hid her face against Michael's chest. He put his hand on her hair and held her there, turned away from the sight of Christine Fenton dying.

She heard the woman's body hit the floor and then Oliver, his voice thick and dark, say, 'Your turn now.'

A sharp, snapping sound, and another body hit the floor.

When Michael let her go, Claire didn't look at the bodies. She couldn't.

She looked at Oliver, who was staring down at Travis Lowe. The detective was just starting to stir. 'What about this one?' he asked. 'Friend or foe?'

He wasn't waiting for an answer. He grabbed Lowe by the collar and lifted him off the ground.

'Friend! Friend!' Claire blurted frantically, and saw Lowe's eyes close in relief. 'His partner's missing. I think they were holding him somewhere.'

Oliver shrugged, clearly not interested. He dropped Lowe back to the ground and turned a slow circle. 'There was another one,' he said. 'Where is he?' He pulled in a deep breath, then let it out with a disgusted cough. 'Jason. Well, well.'

Sometime while Oliver had been busy killing the Fentons, Jason had escaped out the door, and Michael hadn't stopped him. Maybe too weak, maybe just worried for Claire. But anyway, Jason was long gone.

'I'll find him,' Oliver said. 'I've been tolerant, so long as he didn't threaten our interests, but enough.' He glanced down at Michael and Claire. 'Go home.'

He stalked away, out into the sun, without a backward glance. Three dead bodies, and he didn't even pause.

Travis Lowe managed to pull himself to a sitting position, groaning, and rested his head in his hands. 'I hate Tasers.' He looked up and fixed his bloodshot gaze on Claire. 'You're OK? Let me see your throat.'

She moved the handkerchief. There was just a thin smear on the cloth. Her wrist was worse; she tied the cloth around it as a makeshift bandage and thought, *I'm going to have to buy Michael some new ones.* Though why she thought of that now, she had no idea. Maybe she just wanted to imagine normal life.

Because this definitely wasn't normal.

Michael stood up and helped Claire to her feet, then Lowe. He pulled keys from his pocket and tossed them to Lowe. 'Pull the car in with the trunk facing the door,' he said. 'Open it and honk when you're ready.'

Lowe nodded and went outside, into the blinding sun. Michael put both hands on Claire's shoulders and looked down at her, then cupped her cheeks in his palms.

'Don't do that again,' he said.

'I didn't do *anything*. I got a ride from a cop, that was all.'

'Not that,' he said. 'Myrnin. Don't do it again. You can't go back. He'll kill you next time.'

He knew where she'd been. Well, she supposed it hadn't been hard to figure out.

'You shouldn't have come,' she said. 'You knew it was a trap; what are you, crazy?'

'I called Oliver,' Michael said.

'You didn't!'

'It worked, didn't it?'

She looked around at the dead people in the shed. 'Yeah.'

He looked ill for a second and started to say something, but then the horn honked outside, and he changed it to, 'Ride's here.'

She nodded, and walked out into the dazzling glare. Something brushed by her, moving fast, and then the trunk of the sedan slammed closed before she'd taken more than two steps.

Claire trudged to the passenger side of the car. Exhausted and aching, and feeling a stupid need to cry, she said nothing at all on the ride home.

Chapter Thirteen

Joe Hess was in the run-down house on Spring Street, locked in a closet, filthy, with a broken arm and two broken ribs – Lowe had called with the news of his rescue two hours later. Claire tried to be happy, but the crash that had started for her before she left Myrnin's just kept driving her down. She felt sick and weak and hollow, and she couldn't even summon the energy to go to the hospital to see Shane. Michael told Eve that she was sick, which wasn't much of a lie; Claire stayed in bed, shivering, wrapped in layers of blankets even though the room was warm. Everything kept shifting in her head, from dull grey fog to glittering icy clarity, and she didn't know how long it was going to last. She developed a knife-sharp headache sometime during the night, and by the time she finally slept, it was nearly morning.

Her cell phone rang at two p.m. on Sunday. She'd got up to visit the bathroom and grab a bottle of water, but no food, and her whole body felt weak and abused. 'Where are you?' the voice on the other end demanded. Claire squinted at the clock and scrubbed a hand through her matted, oily hair.

'Who is it?'

A sigh rattled the speaker. 'It's Jennifer, idiot. I'm waiting at Common Grounds. Are you going to show or what?'

'No,' she said, and then tried again. 'I'm sick.'

'Look, I don't care if you're dying; I've got a mid-term tomorrow for half my grade! Get your ass down here *now*!'

Jennifer hung up. Claire threw the phone down on the nightstand with a clatter and sat – or fell – onto the bed. *I can't. I just want to sleep, that's all.*

Someone rapped gently on the door, and then it creaked open. Eve was standing there, with a cracked, much-abused plastic tray in her hands. On it was a frosty glass of Coke, still fizzing, a sandwich, and a cookie.

And a red rose.

'Eat,' she said, and slid the tray onto Claire's lap. 'Man, that's one hell of a hangover.'

'Hangover?' Claire looked at her oddly, and sipped the Coke. It went down sweet and cool, and that helped. 'I'm not hung-over.'

Eve just shook her head. 'Been there, CB. Trust me on this. Eat, shower, you'll feel better.'

Claire nodded. She did feel a spark of hunger, distant as it was, and managed to take two bites of the sandwich before weariness overtook her again. She tried the cookie in between.

The shower felt like heaven, and Eve was right about that, too; when she finally got dressed and finished half the sandwich she felt almost alive.

Her cell phone rang again. Jennifer. Claire didn't even let her get started yelling and threatening. 'Ten minutes,' she said, and hung up. She didn't want to go, but staying in bed didn't seem to be doing much for her. She took the tray downstairs, washed up, and grabbed her backpack on the way out.

'Where the *hell* do you think you're going?'

Michael. He was standing in the hallway, blocking the door, looking like he was guarding the gates of heaven itself. His hands looked raw and pink still healing from the burns. She thought about that, about how important his hands were to him, because of the music, and felt a sharp stab of guilt.

'I'm meeting Jennifer at Common Grounds,' she said. 'Tutoring. For money.'

'Well, you're not walking, and I can't take you until dark.'

'I can,' Eve offered. She joined Claire in the hall. 'I need to go into work, anyway. Kim didn't show again; they called a little while ago. Hey, overtime pay. Gotta love it. Maybe we can afford tacos.'

Michael looked exasperated, but it wasn't as though there were a lot of choices. He nodded and stepped out of the way. Eve stretched up on her toes to kiss him, and that went on for a while before Claire cleared her throat, checked her watch, and got her moving to the car.

It was a short ride to Common Grounds, but not exactly a comfortable one, because the first thing Eve said was, 'Is it true? Oliver killed the Fentons and Captain Obvious?'

Claire didn't want to talk about it, but she nodded.

'And Michael? Michael was there?'

Again, the nod. Claire looked out the window.

'He got hurt. I saw the burns.' This time she didn't even try to answer. Eve let the silence stretch for a few seconds, then said, 'Don't shut me out, Claire. The four of us, we're all we've got.'

Except that what Claire had couldn't be shared. Not with Michael, not with Eve, and certainly not with Shane.

She was alone, carrying an ugly weight of knowledge she didn't want and couldn't use. And every time she thought about Oliver's icy smile, about him ripping out Christine Fenton's throat, she felt sick. *I'm helping him, if I keep working for Myrnin and Amelie.* But she was also helping Michael. Sam. Myrnin.

Eve seemed to sense it wasn't time to push; she pulled to a stop in front of the coffee shop and said, 'Stay inside until dark; Michael will come get you.'

'I'm going to see Shane,' Claire said. 'But I'll get a ride home.'

'Claire, dammit—' Eve sighed. 'I can't stop you. But if you wait, you and Michael can go together. I'll see you guys tonight. Tacos for dinner, right?'

Nothing sounded very exciting to her right now, but Claire nodded. She got out and walked into Common Grounds, which was a sea of noise and conversation – packed, as always, with college students and a few locals. She was getting used to picking out the gleam of ID bracelets.

Jennifer was sitting at the same table Monica favoured, sipping a drink that Claire bet was the same thing Monica always had, wearing an outfit that was probably Monica's hand-me-downs, or at least copied from the same designers. She looked angry and scowled at Claire as Claire dropped her backpack on the floor and slid into her chair. 'You look like crap,' Jennifer said. 'Sick sick, or hung-over?'

'Does it matter?'

'Hung-over,' Jennifer said, and grinned. 'And here I thought you were all underage Goody Two-shoes.'

The smell of coffee was making her feel queasy, but Claire went to the counter and ordered a mocha anyway. Oliver wasn't on duty, and she didn't know the two working as baristas.

When she turned around, somebody else was sitting at Jennifer's table in the previously empty third chair.

Monica.

Crap. I can't deal with her. Not now. She felt horrible, and the last thing she wanted to do was match wits with the witch queen.

Monica gave her the X-ray scan, looked at Jennifer,

and did an over-the-top hand to the forehead. 'I thought the homeless look died in the nineties.'

'Shut up.' Claire slid into her chair, mocha in hand. 'I'm tutoring Jennifer, not you.'

'Bitch, I wouldn't *let* you tutor me. You'd probably give me all the wrong answers.'

Which was a totally good idea, and Claire saw the fear flash into Jennifer's expression. She sighed. 'I wouldn't,' she said.

'Why not?'

'Because...because this matters. School.' They both looked at Claire as though she were a lunatic.

'Never mind. I just wouldn't. You want my help or not?'

Jennifer nodded. Claire reached for her notebook and flipped to the notes she'd taken in Economics, and started explaining. Jennifer was trying, at least; Monica kept sighing and fidgeting, but Jennifer seemed to be kind of following along. She even got a couple of the formulas right, when Claire pop-quizzed her. It took about an hour to get her to the level of a solid B, but that was good enough. Jennifer wasn't interested in As, and Monica couldn't have cared less.

Claire's mocha was making her nauseated. She tossed the half-full cup and went to the bathroom. She picked up her backpack and brought it along; half out of an entirely reasonable expectation that Monica and/or Jennifer would do something mean if she left it at their mercy.

She was standing at the mirror staring at her sallow

face with its raccoon-bruise eyes and pale lips when the second of clarity hit again, a flicker of unforgiving beauty in a world that seemed drowning in grey.

Maybe a little. Just to get through the day. There wasn't that much left, anyway.

She didn't let herself think. Her head was pounding, her mouth dry, her muscles aching, and she needed to feel better. Because right now, she didn't know if she could make it through the day.

She shook about ten measly crystals out into her palm. The strawberry scent teased her, and she shifted them around, watching the light glint on the sharp edges. It looked like candy.

It's a drug. She was finally admitting it to herself. *It's not even for you. It's for Myrnin. What are you doing? It's making you sick.*

But it would also make her well.

She was in the process of dumping the crystals in her mouth when Monica shoved open the bathroom door.

Claire swallowed and choked and quickly wiped her hand on her pants. She knew she looked guilty. Monica, who'd been heading for the stall, stopped and looked at her.

'What was that?' Monica asked.

'What was what?' Wrong answer, Claire knew it as soon as she said it. Why not, *aspirin for my hangover? Or, breath mints?* She was a terrible liar.

She couldn't help but drag in a shocked breath as the crystals raced their chemical message through her nerve endings, ice in every vein, and the whole world turned sharp and bright and – for the moment – painless.

And Monica was way too savvy. She looked at the hand Claire was convulsively rubbing against her blue jeans, then gave her the X-ray stare again, and slowly smiled. 'Man, that must be good stuff. Your pupils just dilated like crazy.' Monica edged up next to her and checked her make-up. 'Where'd you get it?'

Claire said nothing. She reached for the shaker, which was sitting on the edge of the sink, but Monica got there first. She looked it over and shook a crystal out in her hand. 'Cool. What is it?'

'Nothing. It's not for you.'

Monica pulled the shaker back when she reached for it. 'Oh, I think it is. Especially if you want it so bad.'

Claire didn't think; she just acted. Her brain worked so fast that she moved in a blur, slamming Monica back against the wall, then twisting the silver can out of her hand. Monica didn't even have time to yell.

Monica straightened her clothes and tossed back her hair. There was a crazy light in her eyes, and a glow in her cheeks. She *liked* this.

'Oh, you stupid bitch,' Monica breathed. 'That was such a bad idea. So, it makes you faster. And I'm betting it's something from the vamps. That makes it *mine*.'

'No,' Claire said. She'd screwed up, she knew that, but talking was only going to make it worse. She put the shaker in her backpack and zipped it up, shouldered the load, and turned to go.

Her hand was on the doorknob when Monica said, 'Shane's still in ICU.' There was something about the way she said it...Claire turned slowly to face her. 'That means he's not out of the woods yet. Funny thing, people can have all kinds of setbacks. Maybe he gets the wrong meds or something. That can kill you. They did a story about it on the news.' Monica's smile was vicious. 'I'd hate to see that happen.'

Claire felt the wildest, coldest impulse that had ever come over her – she wanted to lunge for Monica, knock her head into the wall, rip her apart. She could *visualise* it. That was terrifying, and she pulled herself back with a snap into sanity.

'What do you want?' she said. Her voice wasn't quite steady.

Monica just held out her finely manicured hand, raised an eyebrow, and waited.

Claire put down her backpack, pulled out the shaker, and handed it over. 'When that's gone, I don't have any more,' she said. 'I hope you choke on it.'

Monica poured some of the red crystals into her palm. 'How much? And don't be stupid. You OD me, and it's your neck, not mine.'

'Don't do more than half of that,' Claire said. Monica scraped half of the crystals off her palm, back into the container. It looked about right. Claire nodded.

Monica dumped it into her mouth, licked the residue

from her palm, and Claire could tell the exact second that the chemicals hit her – her eyes went wide, and her pupils began to grow. And grow. It was eerie, and Claire felt her skin crawl as Monica began to shake. *This is what it looks like*. It looked awful.

'You're pretty.' Monica sounded surprised. 'It's all so clear now—'

And then her eyes rolled back in her head, and she fell down and started to convulse.

Claire screamed for help, jammed her backpack under Monica's head to keep her from knocking it against the tile floor, and tried to hold her down. Jennifer ran in and screamed, too, then came at Claire, swinging. Claire moved out of the way of the punch – it seemed slow to her – and shoved Jennifer out of the way. 'I didn't do it!' she yelled. 'She took something!'

Jennifer called 911.

This wasn't how Claire had intended to end up at the hospital. Worse, by the time they got there, Monica had stopped breathing, and the paramedics had to put a tube down her throat. They were hooking her up to machines now, and the mayor was coming, and half the cops in town were converging on it.

'I need to know what she took,' the doctor was saying. Claire tried to look over his shoulder; she saw Richard Morrell coming through the parking lot doors. The doctor snapped his fingers in front of her face to get her attention. 'Your pupils are dilated. You took something, too. What is it?'

Claire silently handed over the shaker. The doctor looked at the red crystals, frowned, and said, 'Where did you get these?' He was wearing a bracelet, silver, with a symbol she didn't recognise. 'Look, I'm not kidding. That girl is dying, and I need to know—'

'I can't tell you,' she said. 'Ask Amelie.' She held up the bracelet. She felt numb. Even though she'd wanted to kill Monica, she hadn't really meant to *kill* her. Why had this happened? It was the same dose Claire had taken, and she knew the crystals weren't contaminated...

The doctor gave her a look of cold contempt, and handed it to an orderly. 'Lab,' he said. 'I need to know what this stuff is, right now. Tell them it's priority one.'

The orderly left at a run.

'I want you in the lab, too,' the doctor said, and grabbed a passing nurse. He rattled off tests, talking faster than even Claire's heightened brain could process, though the nurse just nodded. *Blood tests,* she thought. Claire went without complaint. It was better than waiting for Richard Morrell to hear that she'd poisoned his sister.

As soon as the nurse was finished drawing her blood, Claire went to ICU. Shane was awake, reading a book. He looked better, and his smile was warm and relieved. 'Eve said you were sick,' he said. 'I figured maybe you were just sick of seeing me here.'

Claire wanted to cry. She wanted to crawl into the

bed with him and be wrapped in his arms and not have all this guilt and horror bearing down on her shoulders, just for a minute.

'What's wrong?' he asked. 'Your eyes—'

'I made a mistake,' she blurted. 'I made a terrible mistake, and I don't know how to fix it. She's dying and I don't know how—'

'Dying?' Shane struggled to sit up. 'Who? God, not Eve—'

'Monica. I gave her something, and she took it and she's dying.' There were tears sliding cold down her cheeks, and she could feel every icy pinprick. 'I have to do something. But I don't know what I can do.'

Shane's eyes narrowed. 'Claire, are you talking about drugs? You gave her drugs? Christ, what are you thinking?' He grabbed her hand. 'Did you take something, too?'

She nodded miserably. 'It doesn't hurt me, but it's killing her.'

'You have to tell them. Tell them what you took. Do it now.'

'I can't... It's—' She knew what it would mean, saying this. She already knew how it would change things between them. 'I can't tell because it's something to do with Amelie. I can't, Shane.'

His hand tightened, then released. He let go and looked away. 'You're going to let a human die because Amelie told you not to say anything. Not even Monica ranks that low. If you don't do something—' He paused and took in a long, slow breath. His voice wasn't quite steady when he went on. 'If you don't do something, that means that you put the vampires first, and I can't deal with that, Claire. I'm sorry, but I can't.'

She knew that. Tears continued to burn in her eyes, but she didn't try to talk him out of it. He was right, she was wrong, and she had to find a way out of this; she had to. Enough people were dying in Morganville, and some of them had died because of her.

The notes. The notes I left at Myrnin's. Those could tell the doctor exactly what the crystals were, and how to counteract them. She could start reconstructing them now, since her brain was still working at high speed, but she could already feel things starting to fade at the edges.

'Shane,' she said. He didn't look at her. 'I love you.' She wasn't going to say it, but she knew that she might not come back. Ever. And as if he knew that, he grabbed her hand and squeezed it. When he did finally look at her she said, 'I can't tell them anything, but I think I can help her. And I'm going to.'

His brown eyes were tired and anxious and understood way too much. 'You're going to do something crazy.'

'Well,' she said, 'not as crazy as what you'd do, but... yeah.' She kissed him, and it felt terrifyingly good, the perfect way his lips fit to hers, the way time seemed to stop when they touched. 'I'll see you,' she whispered, and stroked her fingers down his cheek.

And then she escaped before he could try to talk her out of it.

'Wait!' he called after her. She didn't.

Claire left the hospital at a run, moving faster than anyone could react to stop her, and headed for the last place on earth she wanted to go.

It was deathly silent inside Myrnin's lab. Claire came down the steps very slowly, very carefully, listening for any hint of his presence. All the lights were burning, oil lamps flickering, and a couple of Bunsen burners hissed under bubbling flasks. The whole place smelt of strawberry and rot, and it felt strangely cold.

*If I hurry...*Myrnin had a bedroom somewhere down here, right? Maybe he was asleep. Or reading. Or doing something normal.

And maybe he's not.

Claire picked her way across the room, moving very slowly and taking care not to tip over any of the leaning books, or crunch on any broken glass. At the back of the lab she saw that the tray where she'd put out the red crystals for drying was empty. There was no sign of the crystals themselves, but the notebooks were stacked neatly on one corner.

As she picked them up, Myrnin's voice came from right behind her shoulder. She felt his breath cool on the back of her neck. 'Those don't belong to you.'

She whirled, backed up, and overturned a stack of

books that slithered into another, like stacks of dominoes crashing.

'Now look what you've done,' Myrnin said. He seemed very quiet, but there was something wrong in his eyes.

Badly wrong.

Claire backed up, glancing behind her to be sure the way was clear; in that instant, Myrnin was on her. She shoved the notebooks between them, and his claws tore into them, shredding them. 'No! Myrnin, *no*!'

She threw him off, mainly because his knees slipped on fallen books, and she scrambled away, panting. Somehow, she remembered to hold on to the damaged notebooks. Myrnin snarled and tried to follow, but the debris made for uncertain footing, and his jump went wrong. He crashed into a bookcase, and it toppled over on him, raining volumes.

Claire tried to get to the stairs, but there was no way she was going to make it. He was already flanking her, angling to cut her off from any hope of rescue or escape.

She was going to die, and Monica would die, too. And so would Myrnin, because he was too far gone now. She hadn't seen any flicker of recognition left, not even for an instant.

She backed up, and her shoulders hit the hard stone wall. She slid, trying to put herself in a corner, but there was a leaning bookcase in the way. When she fell against it, it slid sideways, revealing the door that Myrnin had shown her before.

The heart-shaped lock was hanging open.

Unlocked.

Claire gasped and grabbed it, ripped it away, and swung open the door.

She felt Myrnin's claws catch in her hair, but she pulled free and fell forward…into the dark.

No, no, this showed me my house; it led to the living room…

It didn't now. Myrnin had changed the destination, and this was no place she recognised at all. It was dark, damp, and it smelt like a combination of sewer and garbage dump. She blinked, and her eyes adjusted much more quickly to the darkness than they should have – the crystals, still doing their job. She was feeling an ache in her extremities now, working its way in. Once it reached her core, she'd be into withdrawal again.

She had no idea how bad it would be this time, but she couldn't afford to wait.

Claire whirled, and the doorway was still there, right where it had been.

Myrnin was framed in it, staring at her.

She couldn't go that way. She had to find another path.

Claire ran into the dark. There was just enough light filtering in from very narrow, very tall windows, that as her eyes adjusted, she realised she was inside a prison – a filthy, horrible prison, with very little light.

And some of the cells were full.

It took her a while to realise it, because they were all so *quiet* – pale, quiet things, one to a cell, that flashed to the bars like ghosts as she ran past. That changed, the farther she went. A sound went up – a whisper at first, rising to a howl. She heard metal rattling.

They were trying to get out.

Claire was gasping, and she was getting tired, and Myrnin was behind her.

This is where she keeps them. The ones who can't be fixed.

It was where all the vampires would end up, one after another. Left to die in the dark, alone, trapped, and starving.

Amelie let that happen.

It got quiet suddenly, and that was worse than the howling and rattling. Claire glanced over her shoulder and saw that Myrnin was slowing down, then stopping.

There was only the sound of her feet hitting the stone floor, until she skidded to a stop, too.

'Claire,' Myrnin whispered. 'What are you doing here?' He sounded confused, but at least he knew her name. He fumbled at his pockets, found some kind of small silver box, and opened it. Red crystals spilt out into his palm, mounded up, and, choking and retching, he forced them into his mouth.

The effects sent him staggering. He braced himself with one shoulder against the wall of the hallway and moaned. It sounded like it hurt. A lot.

'Not much time,' he said. His voice was barely there at all, but in the cold silence, she heard every word. 'The notebooks. You need them?'

'I...I made a mistake. Somebody else took the crystals. I need to give them to the doctors.'

'Someone else took the crystals?'

'Yes.'

'Most die,' he said, as if it didn't matter. 'Maybe you can find a way from what you wrote; I don't know. I never tried.'

That meant that when he'd given her the crystals that first time, he hadn't even known if they would kill her.

God. And she'd thought he actually cared.

He sounded very tired. 'You understand how to use the doors now?'

'No.'

'All you have to do is find a doorway, then concentrate on your destination. Mind you, it's the rare human who has the mind to manage it even once, never mind on a regular basis...and the doors have a subtle go-away to anyone not invited to use them. You can go to any Founder House, or to seven other doorways in town, but you must have a mental picture of where you are going first. If you fail to do so, you end up' – he raised a hand with effort, and gestured feebly – 'here. Where she keeps the monsters.' Myrnin smiled faintly, but his smile looked broken. 'After all, I ended up here, didn't I?'

Claire fought to still her heartbeat. 'How do I get back? Back to your lab?'

'That way.' Myrnin looked down at his hand, as if it seemed odd to him. He turned it this way and that, examining it, and then pointed. 'Stay to the right; you'll find it. Don't go near the bars. If they grab you, you must not let them pull you close enough to bite. And Claire...'

She clutched the notebooks tight to her chest as he met her eyes. He still seemed rational, but even that massive dose of crystals hadn't driven the beast completely back.

'I need you to do me two services,' he said. 'First, promise me that you'll continue to work to find the cure. I'm no longer able to carry it forward.' She swallowed hard, and nodded. She'd have tried, anyway.

'I can't do it alone,' she said. 'I'll need help. Doctors. I'm going to give them the notes and see if we can find something.'

Myrnin nodded. 'Just don't explain what it does.' He looked around. On the far side of the wall was an empty cell, with its door standing open. There was a decaying bunk, but nothing else.

He took a breath, let it out, and walked into the cell. Then he turned and firmly closed the door behind him. Claire heard the lock engage with a thick, metallic *clank*.

'Second thing,' Myrnin said, 'do bring me some books, when you visit. And perhaps more crystals, if you're able to produce more. It's so nice to think clearly again, even for a few moments.'

She felt as though he'd punched into her chest and ripped out her heart. She felt hollow, light, and empty.

And very, very sad.

'I will,' she said. 'I'll be back.'

When she looked back, Myrnin had settled himself on the edge of the bunk, staring at the floor.

He didn't look up when she said, 'I won't just leave you here. I promise. I'll come see you.'

She hesitated, and thought she heard something whispering to her. A voice.

Her mother's voice.

'You should go,' Myrnin said tonelessly. 'Before we both have cause to regret it.'

She ran.

Nothing got her on the way back to the door, although a lot of the sick vampires reached out mutely to her, or screamed; she covered her ears and ran, heart pounding, feeling sicker and more terrified all the time. The relief of seeing the open door ahead was like a warm blanket after the cold. The doorway was black, just black; she couldn't see Myrnin's lab on the other side. Couldn't see anything.

Think! Myrnin had said she had to focus, visualise where she wanted to go. Of course, he'd also said that she probably wouldn't be able to do it. *No, don't think about that. If you want out of here, you have to focus. Hard!*

Nothing. Nothing at all.

She closed her eyes, even though it was terrifying to do it here, in this place, and slowed her breathing. She thought about the lab, about the confusion of clutter, the books, the bottles, the new and the old. She *smelt* it, like a breath of home, and when she opened her eyes she could see it on the other side of the door.

Claire took a deep breath, stepped over the threshold through a slight tug of resistance, and turned to close the door as soon as she was through.

When she turned back, Amelie was waiting.

She stood in the centre of the room, hands folded. Her ancient, smooth face was untroubled by any kind of expression, but there was something bitter in her eyes.

'He's gone,' Amelie said. 'Where is he?'

'I... The prison.'

'You took him below.' Amelie frowned slightly. '*You* took him below.'

'I think he wanted to go there. He...put himself in a cage.' Claire struggled to keep her voice steady. 'How... how can you leave them like that?'

'I have no choice.' It would never occur to Amelie to explain, of course, and it would probably get Claire nowhere to demand it. 'If he is truly lost, then it's over. The experiment is ended, and there is no cure. No way to savo my people.' She sat down in one of the threadbare armchairs, shoving books out of the way as she did. It was the first ungraceful thing Claire had ever seen her do. 'I thought...I never thought we would fail.'

Claire came a step or two closer. 'I have the notebooks,' she said. 'And...Myrnin must have left more stuff here I can read. You haven't failed yet.'

Amelie shook her head, and a wisp of hair broke free from the coronet. It made her look young and very fragile. 'I must have someone trusted to maintain the machines, or it will all fail, anyway. And only Myrnin could do that. I had hoped that you…but he told me only a vampire could. And there is no one else.'

'Sam?'

'Not old enough, and nowhere near powerful enough. It would have to be someone near my own age, and that would mean—' Amelie looked at her sharply. 'I can't give such power to my enemy.'

Claire didn't like the thought, either. 'What else can you do?'

'End it.' Amelie's voice was so soft Claire barely understood the words. 'Let it all go. Destroy it.'

'You mean…let everybody go?'

Amelie's gaze locked with hers, and held. 'No,' she said. 'That is not what I mean at all.'

Claire shuddered. 'Then…why not let Oliver in? You've been fighting so hard to keep him out. Why not try this first? What do you really have to lose?'

Amelie's pale eyebrows slowly rose. 'Nothing. And everything, of course. But you should fear that we would succeed, Claire. Because if we do, if the vampire race is not doomed to die, where does that leave you? An interesting question, for another day, perhaps.' She nodded at the notebooks in Claire's hands. 'If you intend to save the Morrell girl, you should hurry,' she said. 'Use the portal. I will send you directly to the hospital.'

There was a portal to the hospital? Claire blinked and looked back at the closed and locked door. 'Um…are you sure it won't open to—'

'To below?' Amelie shook her head. 'I have no intention

it should. If you do not, then it will do as we say. Myrnin could only make the doorway work to below, never back here. So only you and I have such abilities, for now.'

Claire thought about something, with a sickening wrench. 'Are you sure?'

'What do you mean?' Amelie looked up, slowly, her eyes fierce and bright.

A rush of images flitted through Claire's mind: Oliver, grabbing her in her own house. The dead girl in the basement. Jason appearing and disappearing from Monica's party, and reappearing near Common Grounds.

Oh no.

'Can you tell?' Claire asked. 'If somebody's using the portal?'

'Myrnin could, I suspect, but I cannot. Why?' Amelie stood up, and this time the frown was definite. 'What do you know?'

'I think you've got a traitor,' Claire said. 'Somebody showed Oliver, and Oliver showed Jason. And Captain Obvious and his friends probably knew, too. Jason must have shown them—'

'Impossible,' Amelie interrupted with a flash of impatience. 'My people are beyond suspicion.'

'Then how did Jason bring a dead girl into Michael's house without permission? Because you said he'd have to be invited in. And he wasn't.'

Amelie froze, and her eyes went cold and flat. 'I see,' she said, and then whirled towards the small door that led into the narrow, overstuffed library, and the door that Claire had once used to come in from the university. 'You seem to be proven right. Someone's coming in. Go, take the doorway. *Hurry*.'

Claire opened the door. Beyond it, air rippled, and shifted...her living room. A stranger's house. A quiet white room with a stained-glass window.

'Now!' Amelie said sharply. 'That's the hospital.'

Claire stepped through. As she looked back, she saw Oliver walk into Myrnin's lab, look around, and focus on Amelie. Jason was right behind him, grinning, clearly Oliver's new pet. Or maybe, Oliver's pet all along.

'Interesting,' Oliver said, and then turned his head to look at the open doorway, and Claire. 'And unexpected.'

She slammed the door between them, heart pounding, and it vanished on her side. That didn't mean it couldn't reappear, but at least she was safe for the moment. She didn't think Amelie would let Oliver follow her.

She hoped.

She flipped pages in the notebooks. Myrnin had clawed them, but only the last one, and only at the back. The rest were intact.

She left the white room and found that she was standing in the hospital's nondenominational chapel – more of a meditation room than anything else. It was empty, except for one person kneeling near the front.

Jennifer. She scrambled to her feet when she saw Claire, and blurted, 'What are you doing here?' Her eyes were red, and she sniffled and swiped angrily at her eyes, smearing mascara and ruining what was left of her make-up. She had freckles. Claire had never known that.

'Saving your friend,' Claire said. 'I hope.'

It took three days for the lab to work out a counteragent, but once they did, Monica came off the ventilator within hours. Or so Claire heard from Richard Morrell, who dropped by on Wednesday night, as the four of them – Shane being finally released from the hospital – were sitting down to dinner.

'I'm glad she's going to be OK,' Claire said. 'Richard... I'm sorry. If I'd known—'

'You're lucky that stuff didn't fry you, too,' he said, but without any real heat. 'Look, my sister isn't the best person I've ever met, but I love her. Thanks for helping.'

Claire nodded. Michael was nearby, seeming to be just lounging but, she knew, ready to step in if Richard went postal. Not that Richard would. So far, he was the best-adjusted Morrell she'd met.

'Don't come by the hospital,' Richard continued. 'I'm trying to convince her you weren't out to kill her. If you show up, I may not be able to keep a lid on things. As it is—' He shifted uncomfortably and looked away. 'Just watch your back, Claire.'

'She doesn't need to,' Eve said, and put her arm around Claire's shoulders. 'Tell your sister, if she messes with Claire, she messes with all of us.'

Richard's expression went deliberately bland. 'I'm sure that'll terrify her,' he said. 'Night, Claire. Eve.' He nodded to Michael. Shane hadn't got up from the table, partly because hey, gut wound, but also he wasn't about to put himself out for any Morrell, even Richard. Claire had the impression Richard was just as happy not to have to make nice.

Claire saw Richard out the door, locked it, and came back to fight over who would get the last taco. Which, of course, turned out to be Shane. 'Wounded!' was his new comeback, and it was one they couldn't really argue with, at least for a couple of weeks. He happily loaded up his plate, and Claire sat back and felt, for the first time in days, a little of the tension relax. Shane was even being civil to Michael again, especially after she'd explained to him how Michael had raced to her rescue. That mattered to Shane, in ways that other things didn't.

When the knock came on the front door, the four of them froze, and Michael sighed. 'Right. My turn to play doorman, I guess.'

Claire nabbed some meat off Shane's plate. He pretend-stabbed her hand, and ended up licking Claire's fingers for her, one at a time.

'OK, that's either gross or hot, but I'm thinking gross, so quit it,' Eve said. 'If you're going to be licking each other, get a room.'

'Good idea,' Shane whispered.

'Wounded!' Claire shot back mockingly. 'And

anyway, I thought you wanted to play it safe.'

'Dude, I live in Morganville. How exactly is that playing it safe?'

Michael came back down the hall with a very odd expression. 'Claire,' he said. 'I think you should come.'

She pushed away from the table and went after him. He opened the door and stepped aside.

Her parents were standing on the step.

'Mom! Dad!' Claire threw herself into their arms. It was stupid to be so cheered by the sight of them, but for a second she enjoyed being stupid, through and through.

And then the dread hit her, and she backed up and said, 'What are you doing here?' *Please say you're dropping something off. Please.*

Her mother – dressed in pressed blue jeans and a starched blue work shirt and a Coldwater Creek jacket, even in the heat of summer – looked taken aback. 'We wanted to surprise you,' she said. 'Isn't that all right? Claire, you *are* only sixteen—'

'Nearly seventeen,' Claire sighed, under her breath.

'And really, we ought to be able to come see you when we want to, to be sure you're safe and happy.' Claire's mom gave Michael a distracted, nervous smile. 'All right, then, I'll tell you the truth. We've been very worried about you, honey. First you had that trouble in the dorm; then you were attacked and ended up in the hospital... and someone told us about that party.'

'What?' She sent Michael a look, but he looked just as surprised as she felt. 'Who told you?'

'I don't know. An email. You know I can never figure those things out; anyway, it was some friend of yours.'

'Oh,' Claire breathed, 'I really don't think it was. Mom, look, it was—'

'Don't tell us it was nothing, honey,' her dad cut in. 'I read all about it. Drinking, drugs, fighting, destruction of property. Kids having sex. And you were at this party, weren't you?'

'I... No, Dad, not like—' She couldn't lie about it. 'I was there. We were all there. But Shane wasn't stabbed at the party; it was after, on the way home.' She realised as soon as she said it that neither one of them had mentioned anything about Shane. And it was too late to take it back.

'Stabbed?' her mother echoed blankly, and covered her mouth with her hand. 'Oh, that is just *it*. That's the last straw!'

'Let's talk about all this inside,' her father said. He looked so grim now. 'We've decided we had to make a change.'

'A change?' Claire echoed.

'We're moving,' he said. 'We bought a nice house on the other side of town. Looks kind of like this one, maybe a little smaller. Even has the same layout to the place, I think. Good thing we did. Clearly, things are much worse than we thought.'

'You're—' She could *not* have heard that right. 'Moving *here*? To *this* town? You can't! You can't move here!'

'Oh, Claire, I was so hoping you'd be happy,' her mom said, in that tone that Claire dreaded. The *I'm-so-disappointed-in-you* tone. 'We've already sold our old house. The truck with the furniture should get here tomorrow. Oh' – she turned to Claire's father – 'did we remember to—'

'Oh, for heaven's sake...yes,' he rumbled. 'Whatever it is, yes, we remembered.'

'Well, you don't have to be—'

'Mom!' Claire interrupted desperately. '*You can't move here!*'

Michael put his hand on her shoulder. 'Just a second,' he said to her parents, and pulled Claire a few feet back. 'Claire, don't. It's already too late. If the Council hadn't wanted them here, they wouldn't be here, and they wouldn't have a Founder House. If it looks like this house and has the same layout, that's what it is, a Founder House. That means Amelie wants it to happen. She probably made it happen.'

That didn't exactly make her feel any better. She was shaking all over now. 'But they're my *parents*!' she whispered fiercely. 'Can't you do something?'

He looked grim and shook his head. 'I don't know. I'll try. But for now we'd better just make nice, OK?'

She didn't want to. She wanted to drag her parents out to their car and *make* them go.

How could Amelie do this to her? No, that was obvious: it was easy. Her parents were just another way to force Claire to do whatever the vampires needed. And now that she knew so much, now that she was their only hope of working with Myrnin on a cure, they'd never let her go.

'Hello?' Claire's mom called. 'Can we come in?'

Michael kept his expression blank and friendly. 'Sure. Everybody inside.' Because it was getting dark.

Claire's mom and dad stepped over the threshold.

As Michael started to swing the door shut, a third person stopped the door from closing with an open hand and stepped through. Claire had no idea who he was. She'd never seen him before, and she was sure she'd have remembered. He had thick grey hair, a big grey moustache, and huge green eyes behind thick, fifties-style eyeglasses.

Michael froze, and Claire knew instantly that something was very, very wrong.

'Oh,' Claire's mother said, as if she'd forgot all about him. 'This is Mr Bishop. We met him on our way into town; his car was broken down.'

Mr Bishop smiled and tipped an invisible hat. 'Thank you for the kind invitation to enter your home,' he said. His voice was incredibly deep and smooth, with an inflection that sounded like Russian. 'Although I really didn't require one.'

Because he was a vampire.

Claire backed slowly away. Michael looked like he couldn't move at all as Bishop walked into the house.

'I don't want to upset your nice family,' Bishop said in a lower tone, focusing on Claire, 'but if Amelie isn't here to talk to me in half an hour, I'll kill everyone breathing in this house.'

Claire involuntarily looked after her parents, but they were already moving down the hall. They hadn't heard.

'No,' Michael said. 'You won't touch anyone. This is my house. Get out now, or I'll have to hurt you.'

Bishop looked him up and down. 'Nice bark, puppy, but you don't have the teeth. Get Amelie.'

'Who are you?' Claire whispered. There was menace boiling off this old man like fog. She could almost see it.

'Tell her that her father's come to visit,' he said, and smiled. 'Aren't family reunions nice?'

ACKNOWLEDGEMENTS

Fast turnaround reading and commenting from a select group of people, including (but probably not limited to) Jackie, Sharon, Donna, and Lisa. Especially Donna, who reminded me that if you put a knife on the table in the first act, you'd better not switch it to a gun in the third...thanks, Donna!

Just don't stay out after dark.